TRILOGY OF EVE BOOK TWO

BLOOD OF EVE

PAM GODWIN

Editor: Lesa Godwin, Godwin Proofing
Interior Designer: Pam Godwin
Cover Artist: Okay Creations

Visit my website at pamgodwin.com

The Trilogy of Eve must be read in order.

Dead of Eve #1
Blood of Eve #2
Dawn of Eve #3

PART 1

There's one difference between reality and the spirit world.
In reality, I think there is a spirit world.
In the spirit world, I know it exists, for it becomes my reality.

~ Jesse Beckett

PROLOGUE

Jesse
Three months post-apocalypse

I chased the unthinkable, running mindless in my pursuit. Dry leaves crunched beneath my leather boots, and branches tore at my arms. My bow and quiver swung against my back. The tomahawk's handle warmed my palm. My legs heated with exertion, propelling me forward with urgency, following the invisible tracks of a dead child.

Fear of failure spurred me faster, harder. I couldn't fail. Couldn't fail *her*. Drawing in a silent breath, I squinted through the dark hush of the forest.

The silhouettes of skeletal trunks haunted the landscape, threatening trespassers from going deeper. Vines crawled all over the damned place, covered in a thick mist. Where did she go? I couldn't see shit.

Hell, why had she approached *me* in the first place? Why did I believe her…believe in her? Things like ghosts and human-turned-insects belonged in folklore. Fucking bedtime stories. The outbreak had really fucked the boundaries between reality and nightmares.

As I slid down a mossy embankment, her melodious giggle tiptoed across my skin, pebbling goosebumps in its wake. The echo retreated to the black sky and the dense foliage, awakening an unexplainable yet familiar feeling in my chest. I held that feeling responsible for why I was there, deep in the Allegheny Mountains of West Virginia, my entire being aching in anticipation of our next conversation.

I couldn't abandon her. Not now. I needed this untarnished, mystical connection with another being. Loss and love, purpose and potential, all concentrated in an ethereal realm of *what if?* She was the only connection I had to a promise beyond this miserable life.

Twenty yards away, an unnatural gathering of vapor shifted the fog, dissipating and solidifying into the moonlit shape of the little girl I'd pursued for three long months. Golden hair levitated around her tiny shoulders, every inch of her transparent…yet not.

"Jesse!" She waved, smiling and swinging the hem of her dress, as if she weren't haunting a world where children no longer existed.

Now that I captured her attention, I locked down the urge to run toward her, afraid she'd vanish like so many times before. "Annie, can we talk for a minute?"

She shook her head, smile faltering, and dug the toe of her red-buckled shoe in the soil. The dirt didn't move. The silence was deafening. I'd cleared the woods of snarling threats. It was just her and me and this game she played, the rules created by her. The power to end it lay in her unearthly hands. *Please, don't end it.*

She was the first ghost I'd ever seen. The elders told stories of such things, but I never believed. Then she appeared.

The first time was the day after the outbreak. The day she died. Her diaphanous form had hovered on the balcony of my Paris hotel room. Once I'd finally recovered from the shock, she told me her name was Annie, speaking in a soundless voice, words I could feel but didn't understand. *Find your people. Follow my brother. Protect my mother.*

During the first few weeks of the outbreak, a shocking ninety percent of humanity, billions, perished or mutated. No children survived. No women. But there was something about her that made me believe. Not just her unearthliness. Something about her determination dialed me in, filling my chest with purpose. What that purpose was I didn't know. It was powerful enough, however, to guide me across the Atlantic Ocean, around the husks of U.S. cities, and now through the dangerous shadows of the forest.

My heart raced for answers as my mind tried to link her intentions to the death and misery that closed in around me, day after day. The imminent extinction of mankind. Concepts she seemed oblivious to.

Movement stirred in the nearby bramble, only feet from Annie. Leaf litter rustled, cautiously, quietly, then silenced with frozen steps. Too smart to be a forest critter. Too controlled to be a mutated monster. Human?

My heart rate elevated, every muscle in my body on high alert as I tightened my fingers around the handle of the tomahawk. The only humans in these mountains were my three Lakota brethren, and they knew better than to sneak up on me.

Annie's silhouette flickered, her hands waving around her grinning face, not a hint of surprise in her eyes as they locked on the location of the unknown intruder. She didn't appear worried. Were she and the stranger linked in some way?

Soundlessly, I evened my breathing and lowered in a crouch, waiting, despite the urgent thump in my chest.

The thing was, I'd found my people, the last of the Lakota, *just like she foretold.* I led them from North Dakota to West Virginia, following another ghost—her brother, Aaron—*just like she foretold.* But her final prediction was my greatest ache.

Protect my mother.

I hadn't seen a woman since the virus exterminated every last one of them three months earlier. Annie's entreaty to protect her mother made no sense. How could I protect a woman when none survived? She had led me to the States, to these mountains, yet not once had she taken me to meet a female survivor or a female spirit.

Her head turned, and her gaze found my hiding place. Lifting her finger, she pointed to the movement beyond the thicket. "Mama."

I flinched, hoping—always hoping—but definitely not prepared. My focus swung toward the approaching footsteps, breath stuck in my throat, my eyes straining to make out the blurry shape emerging from the shadows.

Moonlight washed over the slender form of a woman, and the startling sight of her skittered electricity through my body. I clutched my stomach, shocked, elated, goddamned fucking beside myself, even if it was for selfish reasons.

Her. Not a ghost but a living, noisily-breathing woman, *in the flesh.* My purpose. What I was looking for, what I needed. I felt it behind my ribs, fuzzy and restless and alive, more now than ever before. Fuck me, but I clung to that feeling, something to fight for, hope in a world full of nothing.

For a moment, the woman stood there, staring in my direction. She couldn't see me hidden in the sedge, but I stared right back. It had been months since I'd seen a woman, left with only my memories of the female form to fuel my fantasies. She could've been butt ugly and my dick would've woken at the sight of her. But she wasn't.

Her arms were toned, strong, the profile of her ass round and tight in denim. Glowing skin, graceful neck, and her tank top struggled to contain her full, perky tits. Very much alive and not just a woman. A fucking breathtaking woman. My reaction was violent, hardening my cock and laboring my breaths, my muscles heating and tightening with the primal impulse to overpower and fuck her.

"Annie?" She approached the giggling ghost, her lips curling up despite the sadness straining her face.

What was missing was shock. The woman could see dead people and didn't seem surprised by it. Was it an all-the-time thing? Or was this a special connection?

Her huge eyes, the blond in her hair, and her bone structure were mirror images of Annie. *Her daughter.*

Annie danced toward me, singing something about ladybirds. But I couldn't look away from the woman, devouring her beauty with greedy eyes and forgetting to breathe as more blood surged to my dick.

Then it hit me. A woman survived. One woman and God knew how many men. My shoulders tensed, and my thoughts turned wild, vicious.

Protective.

As surely as nature would reclaim paved roads and metal structures, man would return to his most primal instincts. She would be prized, hunted, fought over, claimed…and destroyed.

Protect my mother.

Annie skipped through the brush, stopping a foot before me. The woman trampled after her, too far behind, losing the trail.

Annie gestured at me to bend down, and as I did, she quickly spoke of places and events, guardians and demons, and things that didn't make sense. I concentrated on the details, committing them to memory, but it was her final words, about the future, her mother's future, and my part in it, that stole the oxygen from my lungs.

I stumbled back, my teeth clamped to the point of breaking. "No."

She cocked her head. "You must."

I dragged my hand through my hair, ripping at the ends. *Don't believe her.* I could change it, goddammit. Nothing was absolute.

But as she darted away, leading her mother toward my camp, I knew that no matter how hard I tried, everything she'd told me would come to pass. The prophecy she'd spoken in my ear flooded me with strength and terrible pain and everything in between.

I cannot put my faith in one divinity.
Nor can one sun light my way.
I need three.

~ *Evie Delina*

ONE

Evie
Two years post-apocalypse

Death surrounded me, infecting the mountain air, soaking my shirt and jeans, and snarling in the ravine beneath my dangling feet. I had a helluva lot of fight left, but bone-aching fatigue clawed at the edges of my will power. Sweat slicked my grip on the rope, the only thing preventing a fatal plunge.

The rope attached to the top of the cliff. A daring climb away. Too daring. Too fucking far. What a miserable thought to have as I twisted fifty feet above the ground. Above *them*. Gathered below, they hissed in drooling sibilants, spraying globs of aggression through insectile mouths.

Dozens of hard-shelled bodies filled the bottom of the ravine. Some had already begun the menacing crawl upwards, their sharp claws digging into the rock face and closing the distance. Worse was my internal connection with them, some kind of biological weirdness evolving inside me. I could feel them before I saw or heard them, like a thousand snapping rubber bands in my gut.

I pinched the end of the rope between my boots and stretched upward, the nylon fibers creaking with the sway of my weight. The sun's glare pushed through the gap in the trees, blinding and unbearable. I licked cracked lips and wiped my forehead on my shoulder, realizing too late I'd just smeared my face in rotten blood.

What I wouldn't give for an ice-cold beer and a clean

shower, back in my boarded-up home in Missouri. My family…

All gone. Dead.

An ache splintered behind my eyes, spread through my jaw, and tightened my throat. Grief was the worst enemy, sneaky in its assault, smothering and crippling.

Shut it down, Evie.

I anchored my hands, curling them tighter around the rope. But the bugs on the wall below were gaining speed, aided by talons and driven by hunger. Only ten feet away now. I wouldn't be able to out-climb them. Switching my weight to one hand, I reached for the rifle with the other, adjusting how it hung across my chest on the sling and hoping for an accurate aim.

With the barrel trained on the closest bug, I squeezed the trigger. The bullet plinked off the rock, a foot from the snapping creature. Shit. I squeezed again and again. Missed. Missed. Missed! My blood pressure skyrocketed.

I fucking survived the fall of civilization, the mutations, the anarchy, and the monster who started it all. Deep breath. I could do this.

"Evie." Jesse's voice rode in on the humid breeze. "Forget the gun and climb the way I taught you. Brake and squat."

Easy for him to say. The bastard wasn't hanging over a gorge crammed with mutated humans. Diseased slobber hung from misshaped jaws. Strings of the oily gunk flung side-to-side, striping bloated chests. And the smell… Rancid and decomposing, I could taste that shit in the back of my throat.

Bile simmered, choking my words. "Go to hell, Jesse."

He crouched on the ledge a few yards above. "Already there, darlin'."

His copper gaze caught me, punching me with a challenge that had nothing to do with my climbing technique. He wasn't a man who showed affection easily. Instead, he watched me from afar, prowling like a hungry predator. A predator with bed-ruffled hair, kissable lips…and a pissed-off scowl.

Oh, he wanted to help me. Bow and arrow in hand, eyes sharp, and muscles flexed, he vibrated with the need to swoop in and save. All I had to do was say the word, and he'd yank me to safety. But that would defeat the purpose of this training session.

With the rope wrapped around one leg, I clamped a boot down on the other, trapping the knotted end. Brake and squat? Right. The effort shifted more weight to my hand and shoulder, straining and popping the joints. God, that burned.

I didn't consider myself scrawny. More like the strong side of petite. Still, it hurt like a motherfucker to hang a hundred and ten pounds from one arm. But not enough to let the M4 carbine hang on its sling. The short-barreled rifle saved my hide countless times since the virus hit two years prior. Locked and cocked, it would save me again.

A crustaceous body moved into the carbine's cross hairs and grappled the ridge below. Viridescent skin. Pincers for hands. Pinpricked pupils in eyes shadowed by traces of humanity. Hard to imagine this thing was once someone's son, mother, or lover. One toxic bite changed that.

"The bugs are climbing." Jesse's drawl, honeyed with a cadence once affiliated with cattle ranchers and oil barons, suffocated my senses, irritating and arousing.

I gritted my teeth. "They need a distraction. How 'bout you throw your ass down there?"

Six feet below my swinging boots, the aphid's jaw flowered open in a macabre bloom of mouthparts. I tightened my grip around what was left of the rope bridge we'd constructed across the ravine. A rope bridge I'd secured my arm through moments before I cut the supports and followed its fall.

"Find the focus you had when you cut the bridge." He was holding a black and red feathered arrow and pointed the sharp end at me, as if his glare wasn't piercing enough. "This is the part you struggle with."

Yeah, because the drop always left my stomach in my throat. And no matter when or where I practiced the stunt, aphids always came. Too many. Too fast.

Despite the tremble in my arms and the maddening beat of my pulse, I kept my tone even. "Jesse?"

He leaned down and arched a dark eyebrow. "Hmm?"

"Shut the fuck up."

He bared his teeth, not a hint of humor in that gorgeous almost-smile.

The aphid on the wall crept close enough to throw a rock at. I steadied the carbine and squeezed the trigger, but my fingers slipped on the rope, wobbling the aim. Shit!

A spiny forearm ripped away. Missed the kill shot, the one that would pulverize the brain. The aphid leveraged its shredded stump on a handhold and gained another yard. Heart rate spiking, I adjusted my grip. Exhaled. Squeezed.

Meaty chunks exploded from the back of its head. The aphid fell, but relief was fleeting. Two more scaled the cliff and took its place.

Fuck this. I dropped the rifle on its sling and climbed with both hands, going nowhere fast. "Get me out of here."

Pebbles rained on my head, and the rope jerked. Each hitch in the line tore at my fingers. With a final heave, Jesse pulled me over the edge.

Shaking with adrenaline, I scrambled from the cliff and ran through the dense brush, far away from that damned ravine. I must've run a half-mile. My insides burned with frustration. I didn't want help, didn't want to be reliant on others, so asking Jesse to pull me up was a big blow to the ego. Not that I nurtured an inflated sense of pride. I just didn't want to be a burden.

Already hours beyond exhaustion, my legs weighed a thousand pounds, and when they finally gave out, I fell to my back with a thunder of exhales.

I didn't hear Jesse's footfalls, but he told me once he'd never be farther than a heartbeat. My ever-loyal stalker. A moment later, his shadow fell across my chest. His knees landed beside my hip, and his head dipped, the short waves of his reddish-brown hair ablaze in the sunlight.

"If you let go of the damned gun..." He feathered

calloused fingers over the gashes on my palm. "You'd have both hands to pull up."

The rare tenderness in his touch didn't match his reprimanding tone. He bent closer, fanning warm breaths on my face, eyes focused on the heave of my chest. His woodsy scent reminded me of camping trips, s'mores around the fire, embers popping, and children laughing. A time when it was safe to look away from the shadows and gaze forever at the stars.

I closed my eyes, breathing him in, and opened them to find him inches away, staring back. Christ, he was intense in beauty and stature. Blade-sharp cheekbones, youthful skin bronzed by the sun, and a powerful body sculpted with rugged exercise and a high-protein diet. But he had a caginess about him that exceeded his thirty-one years. Something in his life—maybe even before the virus—had hardened his eyes into guarded copper shields.

I reached up and trailed fingers across his scruffy cheek. "There's a soft guy in there somewhere."

His jaw twitched beneath my caress, and he knocked my arm away. "You need a lot more training—"

Running footsteps approached, stopping on my other side. The intruder knelt, mirroring Jesse's position, and a halo of blond dreadlocks moved in. Ahhh, those jade eyes, softer than Jesse's but no less potent. So easy to get lost in them, to forget the world had become such a horrific place.

Jesse sat back on his heels, his scowl directed at the other man. "You're supposed to be guarding the perimeter, Father Molony."

Ignoring him, Roark scanned me for injuries, hands roaming my exposed skin with familiarity.

I swatted at him. "Stop it." When he moved to lift my shirt, I shifted to a crouch. "C'mon, Roark. I'm fine."

His nostrils flared, and he gripped my jaw. "This is reckless, love." His accent, as rough as the streets he grew up on in Northern Ireland, never failed to curl my toes. "Why do ye keep attempting it?"

Jesse grabbed his bow and stood. "You know why, Priest." He stalked up the embankment, in the direction of our temporary cabin.

Roark glared after him. "I den' give a shite about your visions."

But he did. As a priest, he not only held a great deal of interest in Jesse's visions, he might've even believed in them. His objection to this training was simply one of worry. For me.

Jesse's retreat didn't slow, and I missed his glare instantly. He stirred up my insides, left them fluttering and buzzing with electric vibrations. Like now.

I stared at his back. "Roark just doesn't want you putting me at risk." I lowered my voice. "For something I don't even know will happen."

He glanced over his shoulder. "My visions are never wrong."

So he claimed. His visions also kept our relationship nonsexual. Rooted in his Lakota beliefs, Jesse alleged he and I were spirit walkers, seers of visions and dead people. According to his visions, one of two things would result in my death. Falling off a cliff or falling into bed with him. Despite his reluctance to elaborate on either, I practiced cliff diving, and he slept alone. Not that I needed another body on my bedroll. I slept snugly between the doctor and the priest.

Didn't stop me from watching Jesse's muscular ass disappear in the brush. Damn, that man could work a pair of jeans.

The flutter in my belly buzzed all over again. Wait, what? This wasn't arousal. My head jerked up, my gaze wildly scanning the depths of the trees.

Roark shot to his feet, followed by the flash of steel and the swing of his arm. Shit, shit, shit. Hand on my arm sheath, I freed the blade, reared back to throw it, too slow. Black blood sprayed the surrounding foliage, accompanied by an inhuman squeal.

The sword lowered, and a mutated body slumped from behind a tree. I spun the blade at the severed head, nailed the eye, certain I saw it blink.

Fuck, what was I thinking? I'd felt that damned bug before it arrived and mistook the sensation for *arousal*? Stupid, stupid, stupid.

I drew in a calming breath and with it came a fume of raw decay. Coughing, I breathed through my mouth, my pulse a heavy beat in my ears.

Roark retrieved the dagger from the stinking thing and nudged the carnage with a steel-toed boot. Then he looked down his freckled Irish nose at me. "Distracted, love?"

A few feet away, Jesse lowered a nocked arrow and vanished into the thick growth of trees.

I didn't encourage Roark with a response. Though he grinned, sexy and smug standing there in the afterglow of saving my ass, we both knew dropping my guard was a serious fuck up.

He wiped his sword and my blade on the hem of his cassock. "While ye were goggling the Lakota's arse, ye missed one of me best moves."

"I doubt it. You're much better with your fists."

Watching him pound an aphid in the British pub the night we met had done things to my girly bits. Things a Catholic priest had no business doing. But times had changed with the virus, if my unorthodox, complicated relationships were anything to go by.

He reached for my hand, returned the dagger to the arm sheath, and pulled me up. "It's worth noting..." That sexy grin grew. "The Lakota throws ye a' the beasties, and I save ye from them."

I turned toward the trail. "This isn't a competition, Roark."

He muttered something about a wanker and followed me through the thicket. Spindly branches crowded the trail, no evidence of Jesse's pass through.

A long one-hour later, the brush thinned and gave way to a clearing. There stood the sagging cabin, sheltered by Appalachia pines. Jesse emerged from the tree line beside us.

The shock of being here again still hadn't released its claws from my heart. I was a different person the first time I came to West Virginia, broken and alone. Wandering into these mountains lush with life and mystery, I'd met Jesse Beckett and his Lakota brethren. Not long after, I followed some strange intuition to this cabin and found the nymph within.

The hellacious trip that followed had taken me across the Atlantic and back. I'd come full circle to stand here again, with a cure, facing yet another journey.

I adjusted the carbine on its sling and studied the crumbling cabin, the blooming life in the surrounding woods, and the rocky ridge beyond. "I'm ready to leave the mountains."

Jesse gazed down at me. "There's a lot of cliffs out there."

I blew out a breath. "Yeah. And a lot of worse things than cliffs."

"Like priests?"

"That was uncalled for." I pinched the bridge of my nose. How old were they? Five?

Roark glared at Jesse, his stance all tall, broad, and fierce with a hand on the pommel of his sheathed sword.

His eyes softened as he looked down at me. "Ye won't be alone, love."

As long as I lived, I would be protected and cherished. I vowed to do the same in return, even if my guardians tried to strangle one another behind my back.

We approached the cabin's porch, and a harvest of orioles took flight from the roof. The door opened, and Michio stepped out, followed by Elaine, our living proof of the cure.

Michio leaned against the railing, the rustic wood at odds with his exotic looks. Striking brown eyes clinically roamed my body as my doctor, then they affectionately lingered on my face as my lover. We shared a suspended moment of eye-contact, a sweet kind of torture, that begged to be reinforced with a passionate kiss, a shredding of clothes, and a rough fuck on the creaky porch. But privacy was a rare luxury.

Elaine placed a hand on his forearm. With the other, she twirled a dark lock of hair. Color bloomed in her cheeks. No hint of the gray complexion she suffered only a month earlier when I'd found her again, still holed up in this cabin. I shivered at the memory of her matted hair, all-white eyes, and skeletal limbs crouched over the corpses of her children.

No child survived the airborne virus. The madman who created it bragged about its success while he imprisoned me on Malta. He was delighted when every woman on the planet contracted the infection and transformed into a nymph. Every woman except me.

Nymphs appeared more human than aphid, but they didn't escape the insectile mouth. And it was the nymph's bite that initially spread the infection to men. The bite that turned both victim and nymph into aphids. Two years later, aphids outnumbered humans.

As for the unusual nymphs that remained nymphs—those that never bit—no one could explain it. Elaine remembered nothing from her life as one. Just as no one knew why I was the only woman with the evolving DNA to evade the virus. But it was my DNA that carried the cure. The cure for nymphs, if we could find them. I'd found Elaine.

Her palm slid up Michio's arm, fingers stroking his bicep. A tingle of tension pricked across my jaw.

When he shifted his arm away, she bumped his thigh with her hip and licked her lips. Creepy as hell, considering we'd seen her with claws and squirming mouthparts. Wasn't hard to imagine her with fangs, stabbing his neck. Or me with a knife, stabbing *her* neck.

Though she was cured, she still had a lot to learn.

I removed a blade from my arm sheath. "How many humans are left on this planet?"

She knew enough to guess. We spent many nights calculating our survival rate.

She shifted her weight, rocking that curvy hip against Michio. "A hundred million?"

Ten percent of the human population survived the initial outbreak. We guessed a quarter of that remained human.

I tilted my head. "And how many are men?"

She glared, her brown eyes sparking. "All of them."

Except her and me. I rolled the dagger's hilt between my fingers. "Then I'm not being unreasonable when I tell you to keep your hands"—and those fucking hips—"off *three* of the hundred million."

Michio's lips twitched. Oh, this was just making his day. Two women fighting over him? Every man's dream, right?

Elaine's mouth pinched in a straight line. "Your three *guardians.*"

Who else? Her sarcasm sat heavy in my chest as my husband's dying words floated to the surface. *Trust mind, body, and soul. Your guardians.*

I turned my head and met three sets of eyes—Jesse, Roark, Michio—and returned to Elaine. "Yes, my guardians."

Her delicate fingers flexed on Michio's arm, and she waved her free hand in Jesse's direction. "But you're not even sleeping with him."

Heat surged through my blood. Seriously, this woman had no clue.

"Careful, Elaine." Jesse's gaze fixed on me as he leaned against a tree, whetting an arrow.

I aimed the blade at the porch post an inch from her shoulder and nailed it with a *thunk.*

She screeched, stumbling back. Good grief, it was just a warning. But if she touched him again, she'd need more than my doctor to reattach her fingers.

Michio collected the blade and closed the distance between us in three strides. His expression was unreadable, but his dark eyes didn't waver from mine as he kissed my lips then the soreness on my palm. My doctor, guardian of body. Our trust in each other was the anchor for our plan.

As soon as we set foot outside our little isolated refuge in the mountains, we would become outnumbered by men and aphids. Some of us would get hurt. Or worse. But I couldn't spend the rest of my life sitting here while there were women out there trapped in mutated bodies. Not when I could cure them. And I had Michio, a medical doctor with a lethal skill in martial arts, at my back.

I gave him another kiss on the lips. "Since Elaine's at full health, we can head out soon."

She gasped. "For good?"

I softened my voice. "For now."

She crossed her arms, lowered them, and crossed them again. "I'm coming with you."

Michio rubbed his head. "No, you're not."

She hadn't been off this mountain since the virus hit. She couldn't fight, refused to learn how to use a blade or a bow. Hell, she couldn't even shoot a gun. She wouldn't last a week out there. Hauling around a woman in a lawless world full of men was dangerous, and protecting her would risk all of us.

Her face paled. "What if I need a doctor?"

I bit my tongue, fighting the need to tell her to find her own fucking doctor. I relaxed my hands and met her eyes. "You'll stay with the Lakota Indians."

Jesse's brethren scouted the lower hills. They healed me after my husband died. They would take care of Elaine.

She fidgeted with the tie on her breeches. "While you're off hunting and curing nymphs, what will I do?"

"You'll bloody stay alive." Roark walked toward the tree line, apparently done with this conversation.

"And make babies," I added, cringing inwardly.

Michio stroked his jaw, eyebrows gathering. "Humanity's future."

God help us. Two women were not enough to repopulate the world, especially since I refused to take on that particular role. We were doomed to extinction or at the very least, a fucked-up gene pool.

But if we found and healed hundreds of nymphs? Thousands? If we hurried, if we left the cured women protected by good men, the future of humanity had a fighting chance.

And I intended to fight to the wretched, bloody end.

TWO

That night, I woke to the crackle of wood in the fireplace. Toasty and inviting, the amber glow warmed my skin and tempted me back to sleep. I let my forehead fall forward against Roark's shoulder, senses dimming, until Michio's soft lips grazed the top of my spine.

Alertness tingled through my veins and aroused every point of contact. We lay on our sides on a blanket covering the hard floor, all three of us in cotton shorts, chests bare, with me in the middle. My breasts pressed against Roark's back. The hard ridges of Michio's chest pinned me from behind. My fingers rested on the deep cuts of Roark's abs, and Michio's legs hooked around mine. Roark's feet angled away—heaven forbid, the guys accidentally touch.

Through skin-on-skin, their masculine force of Yang somehow protected me, a theory that stretched the limits of my agnostic beliefs. But I couldn't argue with the evidence. Swaddled by strength and satiny flesh, I escaped the nightmares that had terrorized me since the outbreak.

Warm breaths glided across my shoulder. The nearby flames flickered shadows over our cuddle, the waft of hickory smoke smothering the mildew that clung to the cabin walls.

Michio's hand curled around my hip and flattened over my stomach, his knuckles so close to Roark's ass he had to have bumped it. His caress dipped beneath the elastic of my shorts, and all the heat in my body descended, throbbing beneath his fingers, as he rubbed and teased and spread me open.

I held still, certain I shouldn't encourage him while sharing the makeshift bed with another man. But those fingers persisted, his intention blatant in the hard jab against my thigh. My inner muscles clenched, and I lifted a knee to part my legs, even as my stomach tightened with guilt.

A glance around the room confirmed Jesse was outside, either sleeping on the porch or guarding the edge of the woods. The single interior door closed off the room where Elaine slept. When we cured her a month earlier, we burned her bed and the three bodies decomposing atop it. Thankfully, she only remembered her children alive and healthy, her nymph fever saving her from the gruesome details of their deaths.

The hand between my legs pulled me back, mentally, then physically, stroking with the intoxicating skill of a doctor. He scissored his fingers, sliding deep, in and out to the pace of his quickening exhales.

Goosebumps prickled my spine, and wet heat eased the entry of his fingers. Of my three guardians, he knew my body best thanks to months in his care during my captivity on Malta. In the span of a few panting heartbeats, he took my arousal from a low burn to a frenzied boil.

I flexed my fingers, brushing the short hairs below Roark's naval. His blond dreads tickled my nose, the strands knotted with leather ties and braids, yet soft against my face and clean with his oaky scent, like his skin. If he were awake, his hips would've rocked to urge the path of my hand. So responsive, my priest.

He was celibate in the most literal way. Other than our one time, he didn't fuck me. At least, not my pussy. He found relief in my mouth, my hand, and most often, grinding against my leg. The man had mastered the art of dry-humping.

Technically, his vow was long past violated. Blow jobs, hand jobs, all of our stolen moments forbidden by the Church. The Vatican was gone, the Pope likely hunting the streets of Rome with a serrated mouth. Laws and doctrines no longer existed, but Roark's integrity and faith remained intact, practiced through his own rules. Foreplay without shagging gave him some whacked-out balance between his god and the woman he loved.

My feelings about that wrestled in constant battle. Relief. Frustration. It made a mess of my emotions. I wanted him. That much, I knew. I also wanted Michio and Jesse, and if asked to choose between them, I couldn't. I wouldn't. I shared something different and special with each of them. Did that make me selfish? Would it be kinder if I ignored their reciprocated desire? God, their heated looks. I would have to avoid eye contact. It would make things weird.

And empty.

It was already uncomfortable, my nipples pressed against Roark, as Michio fingered me with long strokes. The diabolical rhythm of his thrusts produced a quiver in my thighs and a sheen on my skin. His erection nudged my ass, and his free hand shoved down his underwear just enough to free his cock.

I turned my head and found his eyes. Black as the night and too deep to measure, they sucked me in and swallowed me whole. Hints of his Japanese heritage delineated their large shape, as well as his olive skin and the inky shine of his cropped hair. But his Caucasian father must have given him the square chin, thick neck, and long legs.

His powerful frame flexed into a tight curve around my back as his fingers thrust deeper, harder. He kissed my mouth, neck, and shoulder, and slid his cock against his strumming fingers, prodding my flesh, seeking entry.

Firelight outlined his body, his thickly muscled arm around my waist, the bunching of his shorts below his ass, the bulging calves of his legs where they entangled with mine…and Roark's.

Michio removed his hand to wrap it around my throat, his breath tumbling against my temple. "Let's go."

Okay, yeah. Good idea. To the shadowed corner of the room? The creaky porch? The dusky recesses of the forest? Nowhere was private enough. Not with two *other* overprotective men breathing down my neck.

I pulled away from Roark, but he caught my hand and pressed it against his erection. His eyes raised to my face, the emerald depths rotating like a windy forest. "Stay."

My chest hitched, and I yanked against the shackle of his fingers. Michio understood the nature of my relationship with Roark, perhaps better than I did, but that didn't mean he liked it. The sudden stillness behind me confirmed it.

I yanked again, no give. "Roark? What are you doing?"

The fingers around my neck vanished, as did the heat at my back. In the next breath, Michio stood over us, shorts in place and expression as forthcoming as a rock. Ever the strong, silent type, Michio simply looked at my hand where Roark held it against his hard cock. Michio's stance was unreadable, but the man who simmered beneath it did *not* like to share.

I will kill any man who tries to own ye like a thing to possess.

Roark's words, and I'd learned not to take anything he said lightly. But he'd never been so bold as to interfere while I was in Michio's arms. If my suspicion was correct, Roark was asking—no, demanding—he join me and Michio.

Problem was, Michio was seconds from a throw down.

I twisted and jerked my wrist, and when Roark finally released it with a shove, I grabbed the t-shirt beside the bedroll and climbed to my feet. Hurrying to cover myself—*neck hole, arm hole, inside-out, fuck it*—I shoved the hem down and backed away from the approaching storm. I should say something, but what exactly?

"Ye den' own her." Roark's brogue rumbled low and deep.

I dropped my head back and stared at the rotting rafters. "He knows that."

Roark sat up and dangled his arms over bent knees. "Den' think he does, love."

The only thing Michio moved was his eyes, tracking the flex of Roark's hands and probably the change in his breaths. Michio never attacked, never threw the first strike. No, he waited for it, his impossible stillness baiting it, and whenever it came, he annihilated.

So when Roark rose and rolled back his shoulders, I stepped between them, facing Roark. "Talk to me."

A head taller, he lowered his chin, eyes on mine. "This isn't going to work."

"What?" I knew what but needed specifics.

"Him"—he jabbed a finger over my shoulder—"stealing off with ye in the middle of the night." His hand lowered, fisting at his side. "Scuppering me chances with ye."

"He's not—" *Scuppering?* "We're just trying to be respectful."

"He can fuck the arse off ye right here." His expression hardened, not a flicker of conflict in his eyes. "I can handle it."

Oh my fuck, he wanted to watch? My greedy cunt spasmed just thinking about it. I didn't just want him to watch. I wanted him to participate. Two men? At the same time? What hot-blooded, woman in her sexual prime wouldn't want that?

Michio wrapped a hand around my elbow, his body heat suddenly against my side. "You took a vow, Father Molony."

Roark's nostrils flared. "Convenient, eh?"

"Can you shut up out there?" Elaine called from the bedroom.

I rubbed my temples and whispered, "Michio, listen. Roark's not trying to..." I waved my hand around as if it would summon the right words. "Get with me. He just wants...affection."

"You're wrong," Michio said, eyes on Roark. "The priest very much wants to fuck you."

The veins in Roark's forearm bulged, the knuckles on his fists blanching.

Michio cocked his head. "His vow is unraveling as we speak."

Shit. I tried to meet Roark's gaze, but he refused to look at me. Man, these two knew how to dump cold water on a woman's libido. Pop. Fizzle. Done.

I stepped back and pointed a finger, first at Michio, then Roark. "If you fight, I'm outta here."

He swung, and Michio swerved, releasing my arm. Roark threw another punch, but I was already moving, grabbing the carbine on the way out the door.

As I closed it behind me, the far wall shook, followed by a muffled grunt. Probably Roark's fist. Hopefully, not his head.

The midday's humidity had cooled off, and the moon cast a dim glow over the porch and surrounding woods. I scanned the tree line and spotted Darwin at the boundary. My vigilant German Shepherd lifted his head, twitched his ears, and returned to his slumber.

And there, in the corner of the porch, waited another complication, another confusing relationship, the guardian of my mind.

Jesse sat against the cabin wall, one leg bent, the other stretched out, and flicked something into the vines that crept around the railing. His bow lay over his leg, and his tomahawk rested beside his hip. He carried handguns and blades as well, but none were visible beneath his fatigues.

I plonked down beside him and settled the carbine over my lap. "This might be their worst fight yet."

The corner of his mouth kicked up, but his eyes remained fixed on whatever he cupped in his palm. *Crumbled leaves?* He picked through the brown pieces, flicking some away. *Tobacco.*

I leaned back and tried to tune out the whisper-shouting inside. If they raised their voices, the aphids would come.

I glanced over at Jesse, my shoulder brushing his. "You heard all of it."

Of course, he did, but I wanted his thoughts on it.

"Every creature on the mountain heard."

Something thumped on the cabin floor, and the whispers died down. Maybe they knocked each other out.

Jesse reached for a broad leaf from the pile before him, his boot scraping along the floorboards. "Some things are worth fighting for."

His deep voice reverberated through my chest, his words layered with meaning. He fought in his own way. Following me to Europe. Freeing me from Malta. And lounging on the porch now so monsters wouldn't break through that door while I slept.

"I owe you my life."

He shifted, glanced at the trees and back at his hands. "Don't say that."

I would never stop saying it.

There was something so unique and earthly about him. Raw. Feral. With his unkempt hair, disregard for social pleasantry, and preference for crude weaponry, he was an extension of the soil and the woods and the wild beauty that was now reclaiming the earth. But the intelligence in his eyes was staggering.

I looked away, studying my hands, as his gaze heated my face. After a silent moment, the movement of his fingers drew my attention. He was rolling the tobacco in leaves. He didn't smoke. He rolled them for me.

He tied off the end, lit it with a match, and passed it to me.

I accepted it and raised it to my mouth. "Trying to give me lung cancer?"

He turned his head, eyes on the star-speckled sky. "That's not how you die."

Oh right. "The cliff or your cock." I pulled a drag from the cigarette, relishing the burn in my throat. "Let's talk about that."

"We have."

"No. I talk and you sit there all closed-up and glare-y."

He glared.

"Yeah, just like that."

His glare lowered to the fingers I rested on the carbine, staring at my hand like he wanted to hold it.

I reached for him, and he jerked back, hissing through his teeth. Jesus. I was really making a mess of everything tonight.

Closing my eyes, I spoke into the dark. "I'm trying to understand why you're so distant with me." I peeked at him.

"If romantic involvement with you is supposed to kill me, it must have something to do with sex. Like you transferring the virus to me?"

His jaw set.

My heart raced. "But I'm immune."

"Don't get ahead of yourself." He nodded at the cabin door. "You have enough going on in there."

As if on cue, the door opened. Roark stepped out, swiping blood from his lip, and turned toward the man inside. "I found her first."

Wow, I really needed to lay down the law. "You know—"

"Actually." Jesse raised a finger. "I found her first."

I gave him a narrowed look. "You're making it worse."

He shrugged, slouched lower to the floor, and shut his eyes, evidently tucking in for the night.

As Roark sat on the top step, Michio emerged. I scanned him for injuries, found none, and met his eyes. He offered me a smile, which loosened some of the tension in my shoulders, but instead of joining me, he strode to the steps and sat beside Roark.

Huh. "So we're all sorted then?"

Roark grunted. Michio leaned his elbows on his knees. Somewhere in the distance, a bird chirruped.

Jesse lay beside me, eyes closed and arms crossed over his chest. No help there.

I tapped my fingers on the carbine. "You could at least tell me who won."

Roark rubbed a hand over his stubble. "We were just communicating, love."

"With your fists."

His big shoulder lifted, flexing the muscles in his back.

There were no manuals for these guys. Just a murky collection of stubbornness to wade through.

"I don't appreciate all the grunting and shrugging and breathing." I sucked on the cigarette and snuffed it out. I knew what I wanted. *All three of them.* And what I didn't want was them fighting it out and making decisions for me.

"Will you be *communicating* again tomorrow?"

Michio turned, bracing his back against the post. He was the depiction of survival—the strength in his hands, the black abyss of his eyes, the threadbare cotton of his shorts, and God knew what churned in that brain. But his body was his weapon, quick as a bullet and sharp as a blade. "Tomorrow, we leave."

To go out there, where we had to stick together, work together, and move together seamlessly. Because if we didn't, there would be no more tomorrows.

THREE

I struggled to keep Jesse's pace, tripping over a tangle of roots, as he led our little group down the mountain terrain. The sun beat down, and a layer of dust worked its way beneath my tank top and jeans. Just behind Jesse, Roark and Elaine trudged through the undergrowth, and though I couldn't hear Michio, I could sense his heat behind me.

Our group had enough eyes and ears to perceive oncoming danger—a black bear, a rogue aphid, or an ambush of armed men—but the constant caution was exhausting. Humidity saturated my lungs, and blood pumped into my overworked muscles. All of this made worse by the weight of our food supplies, bedrolls, and weapons. We carried everything we owned on our backs.

I shifted the strap of my pack away from a raw spot on my shoulder and rolled my sore neck. In the past, back in my suburban life, a hike like this would've been impossible. But I'd broken in my body over the last two years. Long lean muscles replaced my old, puny physique, and with that honed strength came stamina. I had hours left before fatigue really set in.

The hills below stretched to the horizon, bathed in the emerald glow of spruce-firs. What lay beyond wouldn't be peaceful though. In a few days, we would be neck deep in twisted metal, weathered skeletons, and the stench of despair.

We would reach the Lakota camp soon to drop off Elaine and pick up Tallis and Georges. Pre-virus, the two men worked for Jesse. A hired gun. An aircraft pilot. And after?

The same, but without laws, currency, or contracts. They remained in Jesse's employ for one reason: loyalty. I totally got that. Jesse was a leader, fierce and strong in every way. He would put our lives before his to protect us.

While Michio spent the last month nursing Elaine back to health, Tallis and Georges gathered medical supplies—syringes, blood collection tubes, whatever was on Michio's list—for our journey ahead. I didn't know how far they traveled or how much they collected. I only hoped they had returned to the Lakota camp unharmed.

From out of nowhere, a streak of black and tan fur bolted by.

I patted my thigh. "Darwin. *Hier.*"

My German Shepherd slowed but didn't obey. He tiptoed wide paws through a stream as quiet as the man he pursued. Damn Jesse. He'd even secured Darwin's loyalty.

"Traitor," I whispered.

A bushy tail waved back.

Michio's gait picked up, bringing him to my side. He matched my stride, the granite lines of his profile cut by shards of sunlight. "How many nymphs are left do you think?"

"Thousands." Hopefully more.

"My assessment as well." He bent a branch from our path. "We're too small a team to find them all."

Leave it to a doctor to point out the shitty odds.

I drew a weary breath. "I know."

"The world's a big place."

Knew that too. The miles I covered since the outbreak had hardened the soles of my feet. From Missouri to England, Malta to Iceland, I could count my nymph encounters on two hands. "We'll find who we can." Wherever they were, holed up in empty buildings, haunting alleyways and sewers, or hiding in the shadows. "Free as many as possible. That's all we can do."

He ducked beneath a low-hanging tree, his attention on the sloping hillside below. "And what about you?"

I raised the hem of my tank top to wipe the sweat from my

lip. "What about me?"

He clasped my hand, gave it a squeeze. "Who will set *you* free?"

Free from what? From carrying the only known cure and giving it to the world?

I laced our fingers, savoring the contact. "I *am* free, Michio."

"It's your blood that's needed." He tugged my hand, stopping my forward motion. "Doesn't mean *you* have to do the hunting."

"I don't know about that. I can sort of sense nymphs like I can with aphids."

But it was odd, somewhat confusing. I just didn't have a good handle on differentiating the sensations.

"Yeah." His eyes flicked away, and his lips tightened. "Your unique biology could expedite the search."

Or complicate it.

There was a valid concern behind his reluctance to bring me along. If I died, the cure would die, too. *Unless* I'd passed it to Elaine when I healed her. Wouldn't that be cool? If I cured a hundred women and each of them cured a hundred, it would certainly make this world-saving business more feasible. We just needed to find another nymph to test the theory.

If I had that kind of help, maybe I wouldn't have to spend the remainder of my days searching for creatures that didn't want to be found. I'd never endeavored to be a missionary. The role didn't fit. Before the virus, I'd spent most of my time behind a desk, crunching numbers for Christ's sake.

I looked up into the dark eyes that stared back, breathing in his aura of sandalwood and patience. "Let's say we assembled some scouting parties and sent them off. What about the refrigeration issue? We can't back up my blood or store it anywhere, which means they can't carry around vials of the cure. When they found a nymph, they'd have to come back and retrieve me." I'd just sit around, waiting. "Sounds like a waste of time."

"Time you could use to build your own life. Your own

family."

Flashes of Annie and Aaron, their tiny sallow bodies entwined in death, roiled my gut. My mouth went dry, and the backs of my eyes burned. I tried to pull my hand from his.

His hold tightened, his gaze a heavy sea of black. "A new family would never replace the one you had."

"No?" My voice snapped low and harsh through the woods.

Was he *trying* to provoke me? Damn him, I needed detachment from those memories, and I sure as fuck didn't want new ones. Losing my children and husband had twisted me into a killing, fucking, fighting shell of the person I'd been before the aphid plague. Soft-heartedness made me weak, and I refused to be a liability.

A few paces ahead, Roark paused and met my eyes over his shoulder. His eyebrows dug together, questioning. Could he hear the conversation?

I shook my head. *Stay out of this.*

Michio lowered his chin, lips inches from mine, his tone deep and unyielding. "Repopulation is the priority."

Why was he hitting so hard on this? I was just one woman, and *one* was not enough to repopulate the planet with a viable genetic distribution. My focus was on reviving the female population. So they could do the reproducing. So I wouldn't have to birth children and risk losing them.

I couldn't go through that again.

"I'm not getting pregnant." I twisted my wrist in his grip. "I still have the IUD and—"

"Your implant is nearing expiration."

"It lasts five years. I've had it for four."

"Its effectiveness will start to decrease soon. Not to mention infections and other complications that could happen without regular checkups." He released my hand. "I need to remove it, Evie."

"The hell you do." I stepped back, stumbling over a fallen branch.

He moved to close the distance, and I slashed a hand

between us, halting his approach.

I needed him to understand so we could move forward and never have this conversation again. "This is not the same world that invented candy sprinkles and merry-go-rounds." I pointed a shaky finger at the horizon, my whisper seething with vehemence. "I'm going to go out there and cure women so *they* have the choice to conceive, but *I* will not bring a little girl into this raping, stinking hell we now live in." I couldn't fail another child.

His nostrils flared. "Your attitude is disappointing."

"Fuck you, Michio." Blood and death boiled through my veins. I'd watched Annie and Aaron grow for seven years. Watched them die for ten hours. This wasn't *attitude*. It was fucking heartbreak. "You've never had a child, never had one ripped away. You have no right to judge me."

"I have the right to want my own child," he said quietly, hauntingly.

My face heated. He'd never voiced it, but I'd glimpsed the longing in his eyes when I talked about my children. I pressed a hand against my aching chest, hating myself for being so selfish, hating him for asking this of me. I couldn't do it. "Not with me."

Roark leaned against a tree twenty yards away, but the bounce of his Adam's apple and his hard-staring eyes, purposefully directed away from mine, meant he'd heard the exchange. Did he want children, too? But he was celibate!

Beside him, Elaine's doll-like face held way too much interest.

Michio loved me, but I wasn't so arrogant to believe that was enough. That *I* was enough.

I turned back to him with lead in my stomach. "Will you turn to another to bear your children?"

Shifting his gaze to Elaine, he didn't answer. Which was the answer I didn't want. I waited for him to look away from her, silently pleading him to give *me* his eyes. Every second stabbed like a sword through the heart until the hurt roared into burning rage.

My elbow connected with his windpipe. He shuffled back, gasping. Elaine shrieked, and the approach of Roark's boots landed behind me.

I lunged at Michio again. A prickly bush caught our fall, and my thighs caged his ribs. I freed a dagger from my arm sheath and angled the blade across his throat, the hilt burning in my palm. "You don't need my permission to fuck her."

The woman who—just that morning—announced she wanted babies and smiled gleefully when Jesse told her the Lakota would gather more men while we were gone. Men to protect her and father her children.

Good for her. The lucky bitch didn't carry memories of the cruelty the virus inflicted on children. The butterfly-printed sheets soaked in bloody vomit, tiny hands contorted in pain, their struggling, heart-wrenching, final gasps of air…

My grip tightened, aching to punish Michio for bringing this shit to the surface. The memories, jealousy, resentment, none of it would keep us alive.

Roark's broad shadow hovered, his mouth uncharacteristically silent. Maybe he was disappointed in me, too. I released a staggering breath. I was a fighter, but I didn't want to fight *them*.

Truth was, I knew why Michio had picked this moment to rile me. He was no longer distracted with healing Elaine, and in a few days, we would be out of the quiet mountains, our full attentions zeroed in on new dangers. This was the lull before the storm, and he was taking advantage of it.

Or maybe he was second-guessing his future, with me.

Cold sweat licked my palms. I relaxed my fingers and forced the words. "Stay with Elaine and share her bed with countless others. Or come with us and try your luck with the women we save. Either way, you *will* be sharing the mother of your children."

The days of monogamy were gone, the ratio of men to women fucked to hell. *Stand in line. Take a number.* How would that work for a man who refused to share? And with others rutting before and after him, what were his chances for fatherhood?

The answers didn't soothe and instead thickened in my throat. I ached for his happiness, and denying him filled my gut with loathing and shame.

My hand shook, and he reached for it, holding the blade against his neck and clamping down on my fingers as if to stop the trembling. His arms were free, yet he wasn't fighting me. Hell, he was a master martial artist. I only bested him because he allowed it.

Pulling from his grip, I moved the blade from his throat and stabbed it into the dirt beside his head. I'd chosen three men, the three I trusted with my life, but maybe I hadn't made that clear. "My body *and my heart* belong to my guardians. There will be no others for me."

"Evie." My name floated off his tongue like a prayer. His dark eyes searched my face, the compassion there as soft as the finger he now brushed across my lips. "I have no interest in Elaine or anyone else. I want *you.* Only you. With or without a child."

I wanted to believe him, to forget this conversation ever happened. Would he still love me years from now, despite my refusal to give him children? As I pushed up from his chest and returned the knife to its sheath, doubt chewed at the edges of my mind.

His lips flattened and his face tightened as if he could read my thoughts. He touched the lock of hair that had fallen from my ponytail and brushed it away from my eyes. The sharpness in his gaze missed nothing, but it was the flex of severely-honed muscles beneath me that reminded me exactly how determined he could be.

I shifted to stand, but he gripped my thigh, holding me in place.

"Don't run." His voice was stiff, commanding.

"Running isn't my thing."

"Shutting us out is your *thing.*" His hand clenched on my leg. "Don't."

Us. Interesting word choice. I looked up at Roark and

found him scratching the stubble beneath his jaw, his scowl directed at me.

And here came Jesse, gliding on silent feet despite the fury in his eyes. Great.

He dropped a knee beside mine, his low voice a thin edge. "Do I need to remind you what is prowling in these woods? Only takes one aphid to smell a cut, hear a branch snap"—he glanced at the broken bush beneath us—"and we'll be fighting off dozens." He leaned toward Michio, forearm on a bent knee. "Next time you decide to piss her off, wait till our perimeter's in place." He rose. "Stay here. And be quiet." Then he was gone.

The arrogant ass was right. I'd lost my cool and put the entire group at risk.

I climbed to my feet and adjusted the carbine sling on my shoulder. "Go ahead, Roark. Say what you're thinking."

"Ye both need a good kick up the arse."

Michio brushed off his pants and stepped beside Roark. "Some more than others."

I scanned the trees for Jesse, waiting for whatever bizarre Irish insult would tumble out next. "And?"

Roark lifted his chin, his eyes as green as the glowing landscape. "Ye love us."

More than they knew. "I never said that."

He tapped my lips. "Your heart belongs to your guardians."

Well, he had me there.

Darwin jumped out of the brush, tongue flapping and ears twitching. Seeing him so carefree replaced the lingering burn for a fight with a gentle kind of warmth. The virus only mutated humans, but aphids fed on all mammals. Darwin had escaped every aphid that ever came at him, but he couldn't dodge a bullet. I hated it, but it was safer for him to stay behind with the Lakota.

Jesse emerged next, glancing at each of us before turning toward the trail. "Found tracks. The camp is near."

By nightfall, we united with the only survivors of the North Dakota reservation Jesse grew up on. The Lakota elder,

Akicita, and the brothers Naalnish and Badger, all three of them were there. When they tackled me in hearty hugs and wide smiles, the knots in my shoulders began to loosen.

I received the same warm welcome from Tallis and Georges. The three duffel bags they'd filled with medical supplies energized all of us. I felt the excitement in the air, despite the long day of hiking.

As roasted rabbit wafted from the campfire, Elaine retired to one of the nearby tents. I stood by the warm blaze, my clothes soaked with sweat, and itchy grit crept into crevices I didn't want to think about.

Two years ago, my hair had been a shimmery blonde. The clumpy strands that now clung to my chest… Ugh. Still shiny, in a greasy, brown-with-dirt way. But there were no rivers or ponds to scrub in.

Jesse squatted over his maps, his reddish-brown hair just as filthy as mine. But man, he pulled it off like a rugged savage warrior. I bet he smelled manly, too.

The others walked the perimeter. Except Tallis. He perched beside Jesse, as if waiting for whatever orders a hired gun waited for. His short hair spiked in tufts on his head, bronze, like his complexion. I wanted to touch his face to see if I could feel the Australian sun there, evidence of his life on the reef. Instead, I plucked the leaf-wrapped cigarillo from his lips and took a drag. He lit another.

I waved the smoky treat at the map. "So, where we headed?"

Tallis' eyes glinted. Then he screwed them shut, cocked his head and belted the chorus from *U2*'s "Where The Streets Have No Name."

I grabbed his imaginary microphone and switched the song to "I Still Haven't Found What I'm Looking For." Thankfully, he joined in because...good God, I was tone-deaf.

We stumbled through some verses until we were choking on laughter and smoke.

I cleared my throat. "Think Bono survived?"

Tallis shook his head. "Nah. I heard the mate led an aphid

relief campaign. Bet the bities got him." A quirk pulled his lips. "Think he can sing 'Wake Up Dead Man' with mutated vocal cords?"

Jesse closed his eyes and swiped a hand over his face. Then he looked at me. "We're going south. Gives us the most coastline and a milder winter."

Made sense. Water repelled aphids. Since the August heat didn't grant us much rain, we could stick close to the gulf shores and run for the water if we were ambushed.

"Okay, what's left to do?" We still had to find transport, fuel, say our good-byes. I puffed on the cigarillo, paced, puffed again.

A hand on my shoulder stilled my movements, as did the soft baritone of Jesse's voice. "Get some sleep."

He quickly pulled away, as if the contact had burned him, and shoved stiff fingers through his brown hair. But his eyes stayed on me, rich and coppery, flickering in the firelight. "Doc and Father Molony are due in from patrol. We're heading out before sunrise."

"I'll take a shift tonight."

"We're covered, and you'll need your strength." The fullness of his pouty mouth didn't soften the tension there. "With any luck, you'll be donating blood soon."

Yeah, with luck indeed. The amount of blood needed to cure a nymph was nominal. A blood-tipped arrow would do, but injuring them defeated the purpose. So Michio used a tranquilizer gun filled with my blood.

Movement rustled behind me. I turned to find Elaine standing at the entrance of her tent, wearing only an overlarge shirt. The hem hit her thighs, and the neckline hung off her slender shoulder. Evidently, she'd rifled through Michio's backpack again.

Tallis and Jesse stood, both facing her, and Jesse asked, "What's wrong?"

The peaks of her nipples pebbled beneath the thin cotton. She laced her fingers in front of her chest. "I don't have to sleep alone tonight. If you guys want to…umm…" She gestured at her tent.

My vision clouded in red, and my hand twitched to punch her face. But the sudden and unequivocal attention she'd wrangled from Tallis and Jesse gave me pause. They stood side-by-side, bodies frozen, jaws rigid, and eyes bright and firmly fixed on her.

Neither man had been with a woman since before the outbreak. *Two years* without sex. And we were leaving in the morning to travel however many weeks, months—*years?*—before encountering another woman.

If Tallis' cock wanted at her, he should jump on the opportunity. But Jesse—

A tremor took hold of my legs, and my stomach caved in. I walked to the far-side of the campfire, grabbing a stick along the way, and sat beside the hearth. The position would require me to turn around to see Jesse's face, which I would *not* do.

"Just to be clear, you're offering us sex?" Jesse asked, slowly, with way too much interest. "Both of us?"

I jabbed the stick into the fire and tried to keep my expression blank, despite the godawful burn in my throat. Jesse abstained from *me.* Didn't mean he had to abstain from sex.

"I just thought..." She stared at her hands, shyly, awkwardly. "You're leaving tomorrow, and it's been...a long time since a woman...umm...held you." Her voice danced softly around the words, her chin tucking as she spoke.

I sank my teeth into my lip, fighting the urge to tell her to go fuck herself. But she was right.

Her black hair rippled around her pretty face, her long legs pale in the moonlight. She shifted from foot-to-foot, peering at them from beneath her lashes. Christ, she seemed so young.

Because she is *young.* Only twenty-three. Twelve years my junior.

Where her hands were soft with youth, mine were calloused from throwing blades and climbing cliffs. While I spent my days fighting aphids and cleaning weapons, she used that time to keep her hair clean and her body groomed. She depended on men to care for her, and I argued with them every step of the way. Her tits were perky, and mine were scarred. She was gentle and docile. I was jaded and difficult.

She wanted children, and I didn't.

Tallis approached her and raised her chin with his hand. "Are you sure?"

She nodded, smiling, that smile growing wider, shakier, as Jesse walked toward them. His gait was slow, his eyes on her and nothing else, as if floating like a bug to a bug zapper.

I jerked my gaze away, toward the ground, and pulled my knees to my chest. I couldn't watch him follow her into that tent. And I wouldn't tell him not to. He deserved the pleasure of a woman, something I was already giving two other men.

But goddammit, what was this pain inside me? It seared my chest and burrowed into my bones, building a horrible pressure in my sinuses. I felt helpless, rejected. So fucking betrayed.

And hypocritical.

What would his touch feel like? Would he fuck as passionately as he kissed? Would he groan as he slid his cock inside her? My fingernails dug into my jeans, and my teeth sawed together. I couldn't accept this, couldn't just sit here and pretend I didn't care.

I jumped up and slammed into the brick wall of Jesse's chest. My heart raced. Did he turn her down?

He stepped back, hands on his hips, and just stared at me. Always with the staring and glaring and watching.

God, I loved that about him.

He canted his head. "Gonna tell me the same thing you told Doc?"

Oh. My chest tightened, and I closed my eyes, whispered, "You don't need my permission to fuck her."

I kept my eyes squeezed shut as his woodsy scent slipped away with his presence. Wrestling through a silent moment, I measured my breathing and relaxed my hands, but nothing could calm the firestorm inside me.

When I opened my eyes, he was sitting on the ground a

few feet away. Legs bent, forearms resting on his knees, he watched the flames spit sparks into the black sky.

Elaine's tent was zipped closed, whispers drifting from within.

A torrent of relief washed over me. Why walk over there if he didn't intend to bang her? Did he change his mind? Sometimes I wondered if he did this shit just to fuck with me. Every time I got all self-righteous and worked up, he was right there to mock it.

I sat beside him, close enough to feel his warmth without touching. Maybe his head games were payback for having to coexist with me and my relationships with Michio and Roark?

Swallowing a few times, I found my voice. "It makes me sick imagining you with her."

"She's not my type."

Some of the pressure in my head and muscles released. I tried to let it drop, tried to just enjoy the heat from the fire and the company of the man who didn't choose Elaine.

But I had to ask. "What's your type?"

Please say thirty-something, stubborn, and fierce with a blade.

If our impending mission was successful, there would be other women. How was I going to deal with that? Everyone would be competition.

He watched the fire, not a single hint of his thoughts in the sharp lines of his cheek bones, the relaxed part in his lips, or the soft blinking of his eyes. One would think he was so lost in his head he hadn't heard the question. But he was always listening, always watching. He simply chose not to answer.

Without looking in my direction, he finally said, "You're staring, Evie."

Oh, now that was funny. I might've called him out on his own staring problem if I didn't love it so much.

As I sat there beside him, my skin felt alive, electric, thrumming with heat. Before I could stop myself, I leaned toward him and placed my lips on the bare skin of his bicep. He didn't jerk away, so I held the contact long enough to relish the goosebumps skating across his flesh.

He'd told me once that he desired me, yet he couldn't tolerate my touch. But what he gave me tonight was better than a touch or a kiss or sex. Maybe there would be another woman along the way who was his *type.* But tonight, he chose me by not choosing her. In return, I accepted his abstinence. Truth be told, I was happier than I'd been in a long damned time, sitting beside the fire, not quite touching Jesse at my side.

FOUR

It took a week to hike out of the mountains and three days to find a set of wheels large enough to fit Tallis and Georges, me, my guardians, and our weapons. I leaned against a truck, which held some promise for quicker, safer travel. Parked on an abandoned highway in some small town, it wasn't smashed up like the others we'd encountered, but the damned thing wouldn't start.

I squinted through the sunlight that reflected off the windshield. Would our six person team return to West Virginia someday? Would we bring back victorious stories to share with the three Lakota we left behind? Or would we come back with our heads hanging and fewer in number?

If Georges managed to resurrect the truck's motor, we'd be underway. He'd been cursing the hood for hours, dicking around with injectors and system pressure and who the hell knew? Half the shit he said was in French.

What did an airline pilot even know about trucks? A delivery truck, to be specific, plastered with decals of a woman pulling steaming loaves of bread from an oven.

My stomach grumbled. What I would've given for a can of spray paint to cover the taunting smile on the bitch's face.

Metal gleamed on the four lane road. Roll-overs. Abandoned cars. A few vans we passed up because we didn't want to scrape out the mummified occupants. In those final days, no one knew where to go. No safe destination. After the virus killed the children and elderly and transformed the women into nymphs, the surviving men fought, killed, hid, and stole what they needed to stay alive.

Men who once obeyed laws became vicious predators, wandering traumatized, pissed-off, and completely ungoverned to spread their septic misery. Unpredictable, with nothing to lose, they posed the biggest threat.

I could only hope there were still men out there as decent as the one jogging up the highway.

Tallis slowed as he reached me, gas can in hand. "This is the last of it until the next town."

"Thank—" A pinching sensation ripped through my stomach. I wrapped an arm around my waist and breathed through it.

After two years, I should've been used to the ripples of discomfort, but I was still figuring out my evolving DNA and my predatory link to the mutated. The sensations were a sort of communication with them, a language I didn't understand. When they got stirred up, so did my insides.

Which meant more lurked nearby. We'd already cleared the area and killed dozens. I held the carbine to my chest and scanned the landscape, shielding my eyes from the sun, as my gut vibrated with chaotic signals.

Georges grumbled beneath the hood. Suitcases and rifled supplies had long ago exploded from hatchbacks and scattered the blacktop in both directions. Jesse and Roark squatted on this side of the road, studying a map.

Where was Michio? I clutched my abdomen and concentrated. A single pulsing thread, a sound wave, whatever it was, strummed inside me. Straining. Rabid. Howling without sound.

The surrounding wreckage, my companions, the distant tree line, nothing moved.

I looked at Tallis, who was still standing at my side. "There's another aphid...somewhere. Where's Michio?"

He turned and pointed down the road, toward the last of the abandoned vehicles. Michio jumped from the bed of a single-cab pickup truck, too far away to yell, but I could make out his arm waving me over. As I cautiously walked to him, tremors coiled low in my belly, growing stronger, the silent warning of a single aphid.

I slowed a few feet away from the truck, and an ear-grating screech rattled inside the cab. Michio stopped me with a hand on my chest. The look on his face said, *It's okay.* Then he glanced at the truck.

A human-sized figure blurred within the cab and slammed against the window. Pincers scraped across the glass, and spittle flung from the snapping mandible.

The internal sensor in my stomach reverberated in sync with its screams, sending shock waves to my teeth. Why hadn't Michio killed it? I sidled around his arm and raised the carbine.

Tight black curls covered its head, its flannel shirt bloody but not worn with dirt, and its brown skin had yet to turn green.

I moved my finger off the trigger. "It's newly mutated."

"Yes." Michio pressed down on the carbine's barrel, lowering it to my side. "I want to show you something."

With a hand on my waist, he turned me toward the bed of the truck. A small deer bled from a fresh wound in its flank, its lifeless body surrounded by a bundle of arrows, a bow, canned goods, and bags of clothes. Michio shoved a hand in one of the bags and held up a flower-printed dress. And another woman-sized dress. And another.

I opened a second bag and found more frilly garments, hair ties, earrings, and...fingernail polish? I shared a look with him and stepped back to the window.

The aphid's bulbous head swung side to side, the sharp tip of its humanoid mouth ripping the hell out of the dashboard and seat. A scruff of hair dusted its distorted jawline, and a large silver belt buckle flashed beneath its mutating abdominals, the skin there hardening with scales as I watched.

Distress wasn't just apparent in its wide eyes. I felt its confusion and pain shuddering through the link between us. "He was man not too long ago." It only took a couple hours to mutate after a bite. "He must've been overrun by the aphids we'd just killed."

Michio braced an arm against the truck beside me. "A man gathering food and *women's* clothing."

Tiny pupils flickered as it opened its mouth and bared the insectile mouthparts in its throat. The man might've escaped to his truck, but not without a puncture wound in his neck. The bloody hole no longer leaked, and it would solder completely closed by nightfall thanks to its new healing abilities.

"Take a look at the photo." Michio pointed at the picture taped beside the gauges on the dash.

Unable to see it from this angle, I jogged around to the driver's side. Jesse strode toward us, his bow gripped in the hand at his side, but I kept my attention on the aphid as it skittered to the other side on double-jointed legs and arms. When I reached the window, it smashed its head against the glass, splintering a crack through the pane.

I flinched, and my fingers tightened on the carbine. Another good whack, and it would break through. But there was a reason Michio hadn't killed it yet.

The photo on the dash showed a man and woman, arms around each other, her head tilted up and her smile pressed against his whiskered jaw. Both had dark skin and black hair, but it was the silver belt buckle at his waist that confirmed the aphid in the truck was the man in the photo.

If she was still alive, caged somewhere as a nymph, he must've been protecting her, feeding her, and *collecting pretty things for her.* It was kind of sad. *And hopeful.*

"What are we looking at?" Jesse mirrored my lean, his face inches from mine as he took in the aphid and the photo.

"He was either a cross-dresser or he was gathering supplies for a woman." As I gestured toward the bed of the truck, I had a panicky thought. "All the aphids we killed on this road were fully-mutated, naked, and hairless, right?" A freshly-turned female in clothes would've stood out amongst the monstrous faces we'd slaughtered our way through. Fuck, if we'd killed her by mistake—

"None were recently turned." He glared at the aphid and cocked his head. "Let's say he's holding a nymph somewhere. How do you propose we find her?"

Michio tapped on the side of the truck, where a logo was airbrushed in faded paint. PINE MOUNTAIN ANIMAL SAFARI.

Okay, but the man could've stolen the truck. If he hadn't, we didn't know the area, didn't have the luxury of Googling the addresses of local safaris. Besides that, he might've traveled half the country looking for supplies.

Michio gripped my hand. "Command the aphid to take us to the nymph."

Uh huh. I could control the aphids with simple orders and a lot of concentration, but I didn't know how to direct them beyond *Stay, Come, Go.* And did new aphids even understand commands? This one seemed torn between its humanity and its mutation.

He pulled my carbine from my grip, leaned it against the truck, and nodded at Jesse, who smirked and nodded back. What was this? Some kind of silent bro code? I'd spent enough time with them to know when they were ganging up on me. As Jesse nocked an arrow and trained it on the aphid, Michio stepped behind me.

His bare arms wrapped around my mid-section, sliding beneath my tank top, his skin warm and soft against my belly. "Try."

My stomach clenched, the dread of failure taking hold. But it was worth a shot. I relaxed my back against Michio's chest, pressed my cheek against his, and closed my eyes. His heat, his breaths, his exotic essence flooded my senses. I opened my mind to it, to the bright light I could feel but not see, to the weightless energy creeping down my spine with purpose. He called it Yang. It felt like fire and blood, electrifying every point of contact between us.

The energy coiled through my belly, wrapping around the invisible thread to the aphid. I mentally latched onto it, following it out of my body like a breath of air, and pushed my soundless transmission. *Home.*

A bang crashed against the door, and I opened my eyes. A spider-web of cracks spread over the window. The aphids eyes grew impossibly whiter, its pupils shrinking to nonexistence as its deformed face focused on me. A foot away, Jesse didn't move, his arrow aimed and his stance stiff.

I reached under my shirt and rested my forearms against Michio's. "I don't know what command to give."

His lips brushed against my cheek. "Ask about its girlfriend, wife. Try to get a reaction."

I wrapped my thoughts around the ethereal connection, holding tight with imaginary fingers as I focused on the woman in the photo. *Female. Nymph. Wife. Where?*

A powerful hum slammed into my stomach, pulsing and stretching my insides. I buckled over Michio's arms, gasping for air and losing strength in my legs. Tremors ricocheted through my body, and the connection strained, pulling with painful vibrations. Then it snapped.

Glass exploded from the window with the ram of the aphid's head. Jesse let the arrow fly, and the aphid slumped against the car door with the feathered shaft protruding from its skull. The pulsing in my stomach instantly vanished with a whoosh.

"Shit." I straightened and wiped the sweat from my forehead. "Well, we got a reaction."

Michio untangled his arms from around me and kissed my temple. "With more practice, you'll get better."

I couldn't argue against the possibility of it. The Drone, the monster who created and spread the virus, had commanded armies of aphids and sent messenger bugs on missions. If I could harness that kind of power, we would be unstoppable.

Jesse pulled the aphid to the pavement, collected the arrow, and rifled through its pockets. "No wallet."

Which meant no address, no confirmation this man…aphid was even from around here.

Jesse gathered the bow and arrows from the truck bed and dropped them in my arms. "'Bout time you learned how to use a real weapon."

Oh no, he didn't. I carried a carbine on my back, four throwing knives on my arms, and a USP .40 handgun on my thigh. If I added any more weapons, I wouldn't be able to walk. "I'll stick with the guns—"

"The noise endangers us and ammo is difficult to find," he snapped, dragging the deer to the tailgate.

It wasn't what he said—arrows were easier to make than bullets—but *how* he said it. His pretentious tone made me want to fire an arsenal of middle fingers at his face.

"I use the knives—"

He put his palm up and closed his eyes. "Can you just"—he turned back to the deer—"*not* fight me one goddamned time?"

Was he peeved because I couldn't control the aphid? Or was this really about my guns? I hadn't fired a shot since we left the mountains.

I looked at Michio, who crossed his arms and shrugged. This, from a guy who fought with his bare hands?

Jesse hauled the carcass over his shoulders and strode toward the delivery truck. "I'll check the maps, see if I can find that animal reserve."

For the next three hours, we cut what we could eat from the deer, roasted the steaks on the side of the road, and filled our bellies. And Georges still didn't have the motor running.

I sat on the hood of a smashed up Ferrari GTO, keeping guard as Roark rummaged through the glove box. My fingers drummed on the carbine, my patience thinning. "We're going to have to keep walking and find another truck."

Or several cars to fit us all. Which would delay our search for the nymph. How long could she go without food?

He shut the car door and stood by the front tire. Ropes of muscle outlined his shoulders and biceps, his bare chest hairless and broad, tapering to the carved *V* that vanished beneath the waistband of his black fatigues. He'd shed the cassock that morning, and though the sun had dipped below the horizon, I could still cut the humidity with a knife.

"Georges will get it running." He loosened the belt and unzipped his pants, his eyes focused on his hands.

My pulse picked up. The others milled around the delivery truck in earshot, but no one was looking in our direction.

I grabbed his forearm. "What are you doing?"

"Having a piss."

Yep. His cock was out, spraying a yellow stream at the tire below my dangling boots.

I spun my legs toward the front bumper, but my eyes remained glued on the thick, gorgeous girth in his hand. "Why do you do that?"

He looked at me, at his cock, back to me, and grinned. "It's just piss—"

"You're a fucking tease." I looked away and skimmed the shadowed tree line for movement.

Loose pebbles crunched beneath his boots as he rounded the car and wedged his hips between my knees. "So I have to be modest around ye now?" His accent clipped with aggravation, reflecting my frustration.

"Civilized people don't just pull it out and piss where they're standing."

"Oh, we're civilized? I didn't realize."

Was his dick still out? I rubbed my head. "I know what you're doing, troublemaker."

He dropped his brow on my shoulder, sliding one hand around my back, the other trying to right his pants and fighting with the weight of his scabbard and sword.

"You're not just torturing yourself." I reached for his belt and knocked his hand away. "You're torturing me, too."

Damn, he was still hanging out, his warm length overfilling my hand. I tucked him back in the pants but let my fingers linger, tracing the soft skin. How could I not? He was a beautiful temptation, and I wasn't the one with the damned vow.

His mouth found my neck, and his hands clenched on my hips. But when he hardened against my palm, I released him.

He buried a groan in my shoulder. "Evie."

"I need to keep watch—"

"Tallis is on it." He nodded his head behind me.

Craning my neck, I found Tallis standing down the road with his back to us.

I zipped up Roark's pants and buckled his belt, fully aware the action contradicted my words. "Doesn't have to be like this, you know. Don't you think, after all the suffering you've been through, God would be forgiving of this? Us?"

He closed his eyes and made a stubborn expression.

I struggled to understand his idea of *God*, but if I were I believer, I'd be questioning the hell out of my faith. "You made your vow to God in the old world. In a world where God made promises back. Promises he didn't keep. I mean, he told Noah he'd never destroy the world again, right? But the Drone did, and God didn't stop it. Instead, he let us suffer and perish, and here we are, trying our damnedest to start again."

His thumbs stroked the indentations in my hips. "Genesis 9:11 states 'And I will establish my covenant with you; neither shall all flesh be cut off anymore by the waters of a flood; neither shall there any more be a flood to destroy the earth.'" He drew a long breath. "The earth is not destroyed. Humanity is. And it wasn't because of a flood."

Note to self. Never use biblical references when arguing with a priest.

"I'm afraid..." He cupped my face, his throat bouncing with a swallow, as he lowered his brow to mine. "Our first shag was massive and brilliant. We do that again and...I'll lose myself inside ye. I'll lose me love for Him."

Wow. Okay. Unsure what to say to that, I fell back on one of our favorite jokes. "Voodoo vagina?"

He grinned, but it faded quickly. His palm warmed my cheek, guiding my face to the hard bricks that defined his chest. "Do ye know wha' I would do if something happened to ye?"

"Yes."

"No." A fierce rejection. "Ye den' know. Wha' I went through when the Drone took ye from me, ripped ye from me arms…" Steel bands wrapped around me and stole my breath. "In that moment, I lost me faith. Why would God send ye to me only to rip ye away?"

"Why would God send the only woman on the planet to a virile, celibate man?"

"To tempt me. I would've sold me soul to get ye back."

Not a comforting thought considering he was the guardian of *my* soul. I wiggled my arms free and hugged his neck. "But I *am* back. You freed me." In more ways than one.

He made a noise low in his throat. "Ah sure. But when the Drone had ye, I was off me nut imagining brutal, desperate things." His brogue thickened, the whole accent coming from the front of his mouth. "I couldn't get to ye. Didn't know wha' that sick tosser was doing to ye—"

I silenced him with my lips on his, and he bathed me with a shuddering exhale. Maybe his dwelling on bad memories was an indication we'd been idle on this road too long.

I leaned away and he followed, chasing my mouth and catching it. His tongue dragged against mine, and his hands curled around my neck, tilting my head to deepen the kiss. The way he ate at my mouth, the sheer and intense focus as he licked and sucked, showed exactly how much my captivity on Malta had tormented him.

When his brow touched mine, I moved my lips along his whiskers and paused at his ear. "I'm here. We're fine. And we're going to stay that way." Unless Michio strangled us over this display of affection.

I risked a glance over Roark's shoulder, and sure enough, Michio stood across the street, jaw hard as stone and eyes full of fire. Seeing him like that both turned me on and filled me with guilt.

Roark kissed my cheek and nuzzled my neck. "Is Doc cheesed off?"

"You could say that." I gave Michio *Are you okay?* eyes with a lift of my brows.

He nodded once, but his jaw remained rigid.

Blocking my view, Roark kissed my lips, opening my

mouth with his.

I pulled back. "Don't taunt him."

"He needs to learn, love. Ye both do."

"I don't—"

"Ye love three men." He lifted my chin and stared into my eyes. "That's a big deal, considering when I first met ye, ye didn't even love yourself."

He'd saved me the night I stumbled into that bar, my belly and soul empty, my chest ripped open from an attempted mastectomy. I'd come a long way since then. With his help. But he was right. "Loving three men is…" Foolish. Selfish. Impossible to balance.

And certain.

"Love us equally." He placed a hand over my left breast. "And I vow to guard every portion of your heart with the whole of my own."

This…*this* was why I loved him. Maybe it was because he struggled with the dichotomy between me and his god, but when he looked at me, he *saw* me. And what he saw, he accepted.

"Thank you." *For believing in me. For protecting and understanding me.* "For being such an amazing man."

As his thumb brushed over my lip, the delivery truck roared to life, filling the street with a hearty, hopeful echo. I bit my cheek, waiting for it to sputter and die.

But the purr of the engine grew stronger, revving every cell in my body and tingeing my inhales with exhaust.

Georges dropped the hood and whooped. "*C'est bon.* She's ready, *Monseigneur.*"

Standing from the curb, Jesse rolled up his maps. "Never doubted you, Georges." He caught my eye and jogged over, grinning.

Roark stepped from between my legs and propped a boot on the bumper. "Your Lakota looks unfashionably happy."

It was a good look on him, too. He still exuded his usual fierceness, with the bow and arrows on his back, the wild mess of fuck off hair, and the aggressive square of his shoulders. But that smile… yeah, that smile made me think of cozy campfires and tangled blankets.

Jesse perched beside me on the hood and lowered his mouth to my shoulder. For a maddening second, I thought he might kiss me there, but he paused just before making contact. "Still pissed at me?"

What was he up to? I narrowed my eyes, our breaths mingling. "I'm suspicious."

"What if I told you I found the animal safari on one of my maps?"

"No shit?" I jumped off the hood and landed on feet that felt sturdier than they had three seconds ago.

Roark joined me, his jade eyes darkened by the ink of night. "Where?"

"Four-hundred miles south of here." Jesse leaned back on his arms, his smile glimmering.

We could be there by morning and cure the nymph by lunchtime. Hope burst through me, tingling my skin and energizing my blood.

"Jesse Beckett…" I started toward the truck and turned, walking backwards, unable to contain my grin. "You get us there, and I'll let you teach me how to use that bow."

He slid off the hood, following me with a smirk on his face. "I'll remind you of that after we find the nymph, when you're kneeling at my feet and yielding to my better judgment."

Roark threw his head back and laughed. "She's not the kneeling, yielding type, lad."

Maybe I wasn't. But I could be. I would do almost anything for their happiness. The more they laughed and smiled and worked together, the more optimistic I was about the journey ahead and our future beyond that.

The future I wanted…God, I didn't have a word for it. But it looked like my guardians, smelled like them, felt like them. The future was theirs. That was what I wanted.

FIVE

The four-hundred mile drive ended up being a gruelingly slow trip through the night. We took turns sleeping and driving, and stopped twice to refuel with the gas we carried. And we weren't alone. Through Virginia and North and South Carolina, the hissing snarls and scraping of feet and nails joined the static that traveled through my insides.

Despite our attempts to avoid infested urban towns, aphids skittered out of the darkness, cluttering the lonely roads and chasing the rumble of our truck. Several times, we had to angle out of the windows to shoot, stab, and smash them off the hood.

The constant attacks, the lack of human life, the mystery surrounding what we'd find at the animal safari, all of it had me on edge. The short naps I managed to grab in the back of the truck didn't ease the burning in my eyes or the tightness in my shoulders.

About fifty miles outside Atlanta, the sun peeked above the horizon. Warm air flowed in with the light and caressed my face. I shifted to my other hip in the *V* of Roark's thighs and resettled my head against his chest. With his cassock back on, the row of buttons dented my cheek. Beside us, Georges and Tallis snored softly, their necks crooked at awkward angles.

Roark's fingers lazily combed through my hair, and just as I began to drift off, a rustle of papers drew my attention to the front of the cab.

Jesse bent over his maps on the dash and squinted in the glare of dawn. "Doc, slow down." He pointed at something on the left. "Pull off there."

I crawled away from Roark and knelt between the front seats, my sleepy voice cracking. "What do you see?"

Dark circles smudged the rims of Jesse's eyes but didn't dim their intense focus. "According to the map, it should be here." He leaned forward, staring at a dirt road that led into a thick clump of woods. "Fresh tire tracks."

A flutter skipped through me as I took in the various widths of ruts in the mud. Multiple vehicles? Survivors? "So we follow them."

"It's a risk." Michio stopped the truck and rested his forearm on the steering wheel. "If there's a nymph, she could be guarded."

Because the man in the safari truck, presumably her boyfriend or husband, might've left her in the care of others.

His brows lowered, and a frown line etched between them. "Are we prepared to confront armed men who might not be happy to see us? Maybe a couple of us should scout ahead?"

"We stay together." I gripped his thigh. "We don't have a way to communicate if we're separated, and we're safer in this truck."

"Men have fought for centuries without radios," Michio countered.

"But they haven't been fighting aphids."

Their horrendous talons could break the truck windows, but it would slow them down and give us time to kill them.

A flex rippled in Jesse's jaw. "I agree with her. Just be ready to turn us around, Doc."

Michio nodded and drove up the path. Several miles carved through the woods and surrendered to a wide pasture. A gate lay discarded, its sign still attached.

PINE MOUNTAIN ANIMAL SAFARI. STAFF ONLY.

Excitement and fear bubbled through my stomach. "Wild animals without caretakers." I scanned the barren landscape. One could assume all the animals had been eaten by aphids, but just in case… "Can a hungry lion break through the windshield?"

Roark leaned over my shoulder, his stubble scraping my face as he planted a kiss on my cheek. "Not if we kill it first."

It would be a shame to kill one. Who knew how many species the aphids had eaten to extinction?

Michio followed the tracks across the plain. Halfway through the stretch of tall grass, he stopped the truck and rested on the steering wheel, his eyes searching the area before us.

Single story concrete buildings squatted on the horizon. Peeling paint. Broken windows. Cages separated a few of those lonely structures. But no beasts. At least, not the kind one would expect on a wild animal reserve. The cages crawled with aphids, all of them locked within, clinging to the bars, wanting out.

A stripe of blue moved between two chain-wire fences, there and gone before I could blink.

"Did you see that?" I pointed.

Roark handed a pair of binoculars over my shoulder. Jesse adjusted them and scanned the compound. "Blue shirt. Dark skin. He looks human." A hiss pushed through his teeth. "Shit, he ran."

I blew out a breath. "He saw us? Do we chase him?"

Jesse passed the binoculars to Michio. "He could be getting reinforcements. We don't want to scare him. Let them come to us."

Outside the truck, grasshoppers sprung through the feathery grass. Beside me, Jesse's thumb slid back and forth on his bow string. The musk of anxious men saturated the cab.

A moment later, a tremor sparked in my chest, pulling and expanding to my stomach. "There's...there's something."

Jesse pivoted, the scruff on his jaw glowing red in the sunlight. "Be more specific."

Michio raised the binoculars, angled at the cages. "The aphids, Evie?"

I closed my eyes and mentally searched my body's responses, focusing on the weird sensations. Invisible pulses stitched across my skin and folded inward, colliding and forming a knot of hostility in my stomach. Magnetic feelers stretched from the coiling energy, reaching outward and strengthening.

I opened my eyes. "Aphids at one o'clock. They're coming."

Boots scuffed the metal floor behind me, and leather creaked as weapons were removed from holsters. I grabbed my carbine from the floor and checked the magazine.

Jesse strapped his quiver on his back, eyes on me. "How many?"

I followed the threads of vibrations. Ten…twenty…thirty came from the cages, growing closer. Lighter strands tingled from farther away. "At least thirty are out of the cages. More are coming."

"The fucker released them to scare us away." Jesse nodded to Michio. "Get us out of here."

Shit. I didn't want to leave without talking to the guy or searching for the nymph. "He wouldn't release them unless he had a safe place to hide. We could find him, flush him out."

Michio ignored me and threw the gear shift in reverse. The tires spun.

Then I felt it. A keener pitch amid the vibrations. A twinge beyond the basic hunger. A spark of something...more. "Wait. I think…" The magnetic current didn't feel like communication. Not like the aphids. The electricity knitting into and through me was neither attraction nor repulsion. It was simply a shared sense of each other. "She's here. I can feel her."

Jesse twisted to look at me, the skin around his copper eyes tight with impatience. "I thought you couldn't communicate with them?"

"The nymphs on Malta...their pain leaked to me. And Elaine, I called her out of that cabin." I rubbed my chest. "No wait, that's not right. I shared her sadness and somehow controlled her with warm feelings."

Jesus, that even sounded crazy to my own ears.

Jesse spoke through clenched teeth. "And now?"

"Same, I think."

The truck stopped, and Jesse gripped the back of my neck, his glare hard and pressing against me. "Be sure, Evie."

The tiny spasm in my chest pulsed amid the frenzy of vibrations. Then it faded.

I jerked out of his grip. "Fuck if I know. I'm still trying to get a grip on this—" I waved a hand over my gut. "Whatever this is."

Heavy breaths in the close quarters marked the passing seconds. Metal gear and weapons clinked, and clothing rustled. The prickling feeling in my core spread to my limbs and seemed to intensify the anxiety bouncing between the six of us.

"Okay." Jesse glanced at the buildings, his gaze darting over the sparsely-treed landscape and the woods beyond. "Tallis, Georges to the tree line. Your gunfire will draw the bugs away from Evie. The priest's sword and my bow will cover the truck." He looked at Michio. "Doc?"

Michio's head dipped. "I'll stay with her."

I was the best aim in the group. And my weird genetics gave me a predator's speed and reflexes. The genetics of the aphid's natural predator. But my guardians wouldn't risk it, not in situations like this when they didn't have a perimeter in place or a full handle on what we were facing.

The truck's metal walls screeched. The sound of talons scratched the rear door, and the vibrations inside me went ballistic.

My throat closed, and my finger jumped to the trigger on the carbine. The field of grass lay motionless around us. They'd sneaked up from behind.

A skitter scraped across the roof.

My pulse spiked, and Tallis' whisper crept through the tension. "Oh fuck."

SIX

A hard-shelled body dropped on the hood, its limbs folding into an aggressive crouch. Double-jointed legs propelled it to the windshield, and claws hammered the glass, cracking spider webs across the center. My muscles locked up as two more climbed onto the hood, the metal groaning beneath the weight.

Their eyes bulged like eggs, searching for a way in. I traced the psychic links, tapping into each jumbled brain. Their thoughts were uniform, simple. *Catch. Feed.*

The rear door rattled open, and sunlight rushed in behind me. The aphids on the hood cocked their heads and scrambled off, toward the noise. Shuffling boots signaled Roark's, Tallis', and Georges' exit from the delivery truck. I tried to swallow down my fear for them, but it shook through my body with an almighty chill.

When the metal door slammed shut and a dark quiet settled over my back, the hairs on my nape stood on end. That unnerving feeling magnified as I watched Roark in the side mirror, his powerful frame sprinting around the truck and slicing his way through a throng of aphids.

Jesse clasped the door handle. "Evie?"

I nodded, my gaze glued to Roark, as I hissed through my teeth, "Stay behind like a good girl."

Jesse jumped out, arrow nocked at his cheek. A scaly arm swiped from behind him. He spun. The arrow flew, and the door shut on a shriek. In a blur of muscle and flinging arrows, Jesse ran into the fray.

My guardians were so different from one another, but they shared a common skill in crude weaponry. Roark wielded a sword like Viking King. Jesse not only crafted arrows but flung them with mind-boggling accuracy. And while Michio's agile body was his deadliest weapon, he carried a *shinobi-zue.* It was… well, I wasn't exactly sure, but it looked like a thin, harmless wooden tube. Hidden inside, however, were retractable blades, chains, and deadly hooks. It was elusive, unpredictable, and he swung it with supernatural force.

Michio's hand covered my white knuckles. "Still feel the nymph?"

The vibrations in my chest made my heart pound for two reasons. The aphids' hunger was multiplying, and the nymph's spark was gone.

I shook my head, focused on Roark's cassock billowing around him. The sword's pommel arced up in his two-handed grasp. Steel streaked, and death fell in its wake. He dodged a speared mouth, tackled the back of another.

I couldn't stop shaking. If he made one misplaced step… "I need to get out there and help them."

Michio's fingers shot to my wrist, forming a shackle. His glower underscored his unspoken *no.*

A stabbing mouth lashed toward Jesse's chest. He ducked, freed his tomahawk, and severed the head.

Stinging sensations lit my neck, the aphids' hostile unrest overwhelming my own. Gunfire thundered from the tree line, and it seemed to be drawing the aphids. Would it be enough?

I spat a chewed fingernail. "I'll try to command them."

"They can handle this, and we need you coherent."

How many aphids did I control in Iceland? A whole damned army. But I had skin-to-skin contact with all three guardians. I had their energy source, their Yang, to fuel my command. If I tried to harness more than one with just Michio, I'd pass out in seconds.

"Evie." Michio pulled my finger from my gnawing teeth. "They've fought off more than this countless times. Relax."

To say I was incapable of relaxing was an understatement.

The bugs slowed their march toward the woods, and one by one, they turned back to Roark. A crimson smudge glistened amid the black splatter on his face.

No, no, no. I couldn't breathe as I yanked against Michio's hold on my arm. "Roark's bleeding. They smell him. It'll draw their hunger."

Michio's attention flicked from Roark to Jesse, the tree line, back to Roark. Muscles bounced in his jaw. His squeeze on my arm punctuated every syllable. "If we go out there…" He pulled in a deep breath. "If the aphids don't kill us, your Lakota will."

Roark stumbled backwards, outnumbered. A single arrow danced in Jesse's quiver. Maybe fifteen…twenty aphids remained. Some were dragging themselves back up.

I flashed Michio a fearful smile. "I'd rather deal with a pissed-off Jesse than a dead one."

"Shit." He released my arm. "I'll be right behind you."

My fingers grazed the magazines on my belt. Sidearm on my thigh. Carbine on its sling. The brace of knives on my forearm. Michio's door opened with mine.

I slammed into the foul stench of aphid blood and raised the carbine. My strides tangled in the overgrown grass. I ducked, missed a lunging body, and squeezed the trigger.

A green shoulder exploded in bone bits. Beside me, Michio released the spike from his *shinobi-zue* and pierced the aphid's orb. Without looking back, I ran toward the center of the battle, making every bullet count.

Screeches haunted the air. The report of rifles boomed. And Jesse's shouts. "Goddammit Evie. Back in the truck! Fuck no. Evie—"

The carbine reverberated against my ear drums, spitting brass and paring Roark's attackers. I leapt over a tree stump, spun away from the thrust of stabby mouthparts, firing at the bugs as they blurred around me. Their speed was supernatural, their limbs twitching with energy. Just like mine.

I fought like them, blurred like them. Good ol' benefits of my creepy DNA. Only way I was going down was if *all* the creatures swarmed me at once.

One shouldered into my stomach, snarling and snapping. I kicked it away, but its taloned foot snatched my leg, stabbing my shin with five daggers. Its spiny hairs were like razors, shredding my jeans. I tried to swing a leg up to wipe my bloody scratches against its skin, hoping the contact would cause its insides to explode.

The damned thing evaded my kicks, but not my hand. I swiped the knife, and the hissing mouth tore away under the slice of high-carbon steel. I finished it with a stab in its gutted maw and shoved it off.

Another jumped toward me, and I spun the blade. Shit, I missed and quickly rolled out of its way. It fell on me, and I caught its shoulders, holding it away. Its jowls chomped toward my neck, slapping strings of warm, fetid slobber on my face. Son of a bitch, it was pissed.

My arms grew weak, its weight pressing down. I couldn't hold it off much longer, couldn't fucking push it away.

I met Michio's fierce eyes across the field. He dodged a swinging pincer, his expression feral as he sprinted toward me, skidding and slamming into the aphid on top of me.

In a blur, he twisted its head halfway around. Bones cracked and ripped through green skin, but that wouldn't kill it. I released my last blade and stabbed it in the face. As it dropped, I yanked the knife from its sightless eye and fell upon my stomach. Fuck. My pulse whooshed loudly in my head, and my body thrummed with adrenaline.

"Stay down," Michio said through labored breaths.

Yeah. No problem. I dragged the carbine into position and sneezed against the swirled up pollen and dust. With shaking hands, I adjusted the scope, trained it down field, and picked off the ones bounding after Jesse.

Brain matter spurted and ribboned from punctured skulls. Those I missed dragged their bodies and crawled on stubs to continue their hunt.

Exhale. Squeeze. The carbine's telescoping stock tapped my shoulder. I rocked with it, settled in a zone, wrapped in the caress of gun powder. When the bugs moved toward me, Michio fought them. With his hands, his spiked cane, his musculature and speed impossible to follow. Goddamn. He was as fast and strong as the aphids. Was he injecting steroids?

Sweat dripped into my eyes, and I backed my finger off the trigger, afraid I'd pop him. He thrust a thumb, plucked an eye out of one. Then he tumbled away, his arms just smears through space as he fell on the next. The bulbous head canted, hung by sinews with a glazed stare.

He leapt again, twisted mid-air. Another blur. He'd always been limber. But that fast?

Soon, Michio stood alone among the fallen creatures, chin tucked against the rise of his chest. Black blood splattered around his flickering eyes. Christ, he was the deadliest creature of them all.

Maybe he'd somehow imbued some of my speed? A side-effect of being intimate?

The ricochet of weapons ceased. Moments passed, strained and breathy. Did we kill them all? I didn't feel them.

I squinted, blinking through the gunk on my face and the glare of the sun.

Movement near the woods drew my focus. Tallis and Georges jogged toward us, seemingly unharmed. I released a breath, and the air awoke with the buzz of grasshoppers and the drift of loam. A turkey vulture flew low, perched on a severed head. Several bodies away, Roark stooped on his sword.

I stumbled to my feet and half-sprinted, half-limped to his side. A river of blood painted his temple, and my heart rate slammed into overdrive.

"A bite, Roark? No!" I grabbed a fist full of his hair and pulled his head closer.

He swatted at me, a sword-sharp glint in his eye. "Bollocks, love. 'Twas the wanker's claws."

My muscles loosened, and my pulse slowed down. I shook out my hands and surveyed the carnage.

Jesse bent over a mound of bodies, collecting his arrows,

electricity sparking in his gaze. That gaze was aimed at me, or more specifically my body, likely inspecting it for injury.

"I'm still alive." I raised my chin. "And so are you. A *thank you* will do."

Jesse straightened and barked a mirthless laugh. "Hardly. Where my head's at, darlin', throwing you over my knee and welting your ass doesn't begin to cover it."

My breath caught. That was…unexpected. And tantalizing. His tone might've been teasing, but there was a claim there. He wanted to deliver that punishment, and the reason had nothing to do with me getting out of that truck.

Okay, maybe that was just hopeful imagination, but I couldn't stop the twitch in my lips. "Promise?"

His eyes flared, consuming me in molten copper. Then he looked at Michio, the moment gone. "And you. You were supposed to keep her—"

"Go back where you came from," a shaky voice bellowed across the field. "There's nothing here for you."

I sucked in a sharp breath, but all I got was a fume of rotten blood. Coughing, I turned toward the direction of the voice, a crumbling building.

A man and his rifle peeked over the ledge of the roof. "I…me and my friends don't have anything you want. Get on outta here."

More men? I doubted it. This motherfucker released a swarm of aphids on us. Why? Because he was alone.

My feet moved forward, my lips parting to speak, but Jesse's hand clamped over my mouth. Then he shoved me behind him.

Standing in front of me, he eclipsed my view. "We have something you want, Mr…"

A pause, then "Amos. Just Amos."

Jesse inclined his head. "Amos, we can help your nymph."

"No, sir," he yelled. "Ain't seen one o' dem since the virus. Go on now."

I poked Jesse's tailbone. "He's lying."

He lowered his chin, lips peeled back. "Shh." He hooked

his arm behind him, pressing the back of a hand against my spine and holding me against him. "We found your friend. He was collecting clothes and food for her."

"You found Jackson?" Amos' voice pitched with worry.

Shit. This wouldn't go over well.

Jesse raised a hand to shade his eyes. "Did Jackson drive a white Chevy? With the safari logo on the side?"

"Where is he? Whaddya do to him?"

Roark leaned around Michio and whispered to Jesse, "If he doesn't stop arsing around with all the questions, I'll climb up there and fuck him off the roof myself."

Jesse ignored him. "We found your guy in West Virginia." His knuckles pressed against my lower back, his thumb rubbing restlessly over the skin beneath my tank top. "He was turned, Amos. I'm sorry. But he would've wanted us to help his girl."

A heavy quiet drifted over the field. When Amos finally spoke, it was choked. "You can't do nothing for the girl."

Relief rushed over me. We found the nymph. I buried my smile in Jesse's t-shirt, the wet cotton clinging to his spine. Strange how much I liked the feel of his sweat melding with mine. But that didn't stop me from digging my nails into his hips to remind him not to screw this up.

He uncurled my fingers and pulled my arms around his waist, holding my hands against the stone slabs of his abs. "We have a cure for nymphs."

"Bullshit. Ain't no cure."

"You're outnumbered, Amos. And your guard dogs are dead." Jesse gestured at the battlefield and thickened his drawl. "Come on down from there, and we'll talk like civilized folk."

Silence. I peered around Jesse's arm just as Amos and his rifle disappeared from view. A few moments later, he walked, barrel raised, from behind the building. A blue flannel shirt and grimy work pants hung from his wiry frame. His mocha complexion was wrinkle-free, but silver peppered his unkempt hair.

"Lemme see what ya hiding." He jerked his gun toward Jesse from ten feet away. "I wanna see its face."

Jesse tensed, his arms holding mine against his stomach. My cheek rested against his back, and I had an errant thought about how well our bodies fit together. The curve of his spine cradled my breasts. His muscular ass fit perfectly against the dip of my pelvis. He was hard where I was soft, and if I stood on tip-toes, I could— *Focus, Evie.*

I tried to untangle my arms from his hold. "He's not going to shoot me. I'll go slowly." I waited for him to release me and stepped around, hands up.

Amos wet his gaping lips. "What is this?"

"See? We have our own girl." Jesse's voice was calm, charming even, but his fingers wrapped around my wrist in a death grip. "We're not here to steal yours. We just want to help her."

Amos wobbled the rifle's aim at my face. "This…this is a trick."

It was in moments like this when I desperately missed Darwin, his loyal protection, and his ability to sense a person's intentions. I would've looked to him now for signs of distrust or indifference toward this man.

"She carries the cure." Michio clutched my other hand, his frame moving in to block half of mine. "She can cure your nymph."

"No." Amos shook his head and angled his neck to look at me. "Ain't no woman survived. It's one o' dem sex-changers."

Wow. I'd been called everything from Satan's whore to an undeveloped nymph, but sex-changer was a new one.

A few feet away, Roark's hand moved to the pommel of his sword. Evidently, he was as offended as I was.

"A transvestite?" Michio's jaw tightened, and the cords in his neck strained. "Not possible. They lacked the testosterone needed to survive the virus."

"So did women." Amos pointed at me, and spit flew from his mouth. "It's a nymph then. Explains how it moved like those damned bugs."

My molars ground together. "Call me an *it* one more time and you'll find out just how well I move like the damned bugs."

Michio's arm slipped around my shoulders, his voice low. "You're not helping."

Like I cared. What did Amos need to see? Anatomic proof? No way was I stripping.

"Where are your *friends*?" Michio nodded at the buildings.

"It's just me." Amos seemed distracted, his eyes wild and locked on me.

Curling my finger, I gave him a come-hither gesture. "Look for yourself." I opened my mouth and stuck out my tongue. It felt childish, and I wanted to retract it immediately. But how else could I prove I wasn't a nymph?

Michio held up his hand at the other man. "Not another step until you get that gun out of her face."

Amos lowered the rifle, the stock rattling in his clutch as he crept forward like an injured aphid. When he stopped an arm's length away, I fought a squirm under his scrutiny and kept my tongue out. Around me, my guardians shifted with the same unease.

Finally, he stepped back and rubbed his head. "I don't know. Can't see nothing, but I ain't no doctor."

"C'mere, Evie." Michio gripped the back of my thighs, lifting me up his body until our lips were the same height.

I glimpsed a mischievous spark in his eyes right before his mouth fell over mine. I tilted my head and opened for him, giving him what he wanted. My fingers dug into his shoulders as our tongues slid together, licking and swirling. He was proving a point, but his kiss wasn't softened or moderated. He attacked my mouth, grazing my lips with some really sharp teeth.

Ow. Was that a bite? Jesus, I tasted blood.

He jerked back, eyes widening, but his shock didn't last long. His hands clenched on my thighs, and he dove back for my mouth, his breaths quickening and his tongue plunging deeper, hungrier, tingling every cell in my body.

When he broke the kiss, my head reeled. Sweet mother. I licked my wet, throbbing lips.

He set me down, holding me upright against his side. "You kiss your nymph like that?"

"No, sir." Amos gaped, his voice awe-struck. "How's this possible?"

I touched my mouth and pulled my hand away to find a smear of red on my finger. Crazy.

Michio tightened his hold. "She's special, Amos. You won't harm her."

Amos shook his head and continued his cagey perusal over my thighs, my chest, my face, back to my chest.

I cleared my throat. "The nymph?"

"Yes"—he swallowed—"ma'am."

The pause on *ma'am* bristled. Distrust noted.

His bushy eyebrows crawled together as he turned. "This way."

SEVEN

Long fingernails, jagged and yellow, dragged over the rungs of the cage, stripping what was left of the paint. Swaths of pink satin hung from a cadaverous body, and dark skin stretched like translucent paper over the joints of the skeletal arms. And the moans. The disturbing lament penetrated my bones and made them ache.

What was that guy in the safari truck thinking with the nail polish and the hair ties? Seriously, was he going to sit here and paint its talons? It would thank him by opening its mouthparts and stabbing him into an aphid. Maybe, he was just being hopeful. Hopeful for a cure.

I leaned against Roark, who hadn't moved from the entrance of what appeared to be an animal clinic. Dented steel tables, dust-covered sinks, empty refrigerators, and a wall of cages crammed the space. If there had once been an antiseptic smell, it was now smothered in mildew and neglect.

Michio and Jesse checked the closet and cabinets—*For dead bodies? Bogeymen? A stash of weapons?* I didn't blame them for being cautious.

The nymph rolled its head back and stretched its jaw. Thin tubular appendages squirmed past its lips, sliding around a longer, spear-like tentacle. The fleshy mouthparts grasped at the air, reaching with urgency.

It was a ghastly sight, but I could still make out remnants of the human woman. Long eyelashes fluttered as it screamed. It swatted at the tangle of black hair in its face. And it seemed to recognize Amos, its tiny pupils tracking his movements as he entered the room.

But the creature's chemical resonance was what rooted me in the doorway. Whether it was the physical nearness or some emotional association through our shared link, the strange frequency waving from it twisted my stomach to the point of pain.

I turned to poke my head outside and fill my lungs with fresh air. Tallis and Georges patrolled opposite ends of the reserve, which spread over the grassy plain, encircled by scrubby woodland. I didn't sense aphids and felt confident we were safe. For now anyway.

The din of winged insects and chattering birds drifted in from the sprawling valley. The landscape was scenic under the blaze of the sun, blooming in a hundred shades of overgrown. Rustic wood fences corralled the property, but huge sections had collapsed beneath the creeping, flowering arms of Mother Nature.

If we succeeded in saving the human race, what would the world look like in several hundred years? Would the land mammals be gone, eaten? What about the birds and the insects and the critters that were too small for the aphids to care about? Would they flourish? Or perish because of a ripple in the food chain?

I swallowed those thoughts and shifted back toward the room.

Amos assumed a chin-up, chest-out pose in front of the nymph's cage. "This is Shea, Jackson's wife." Legs spread, he angled the rifle at the concrete floor in a tight grip. "I worked the grounds here with them...you know, before..." He glared at each of us and settled on me. "You sure Jackson is turned?"

I stepped away from the doorway. "We found a newly-mutated aphid in his truck."

Roark's arm hooked around my waist, stopping me. Thank God, because the sonority of the nymph's fear and confusion barreled through me, wobbling my knees.

"Your friend, Jackson?" Michio picked through the cluttered drawers, tossing back empty pill bottles and setting aside gauze and bandages. "He wore a silver belt buckle?"

Amos nodded, his brown eyes closing for a moment then flicking open. "Two years we been feeding her blood from deer, vermin, pig when we have it. As long as we kept her fed, she ain't got worse." He peeked at the nymph and returned to us. "She ain't got better either."

Smart that they knew to cage it before it bit one of them.

Michio dropped the duffel bag he'd retrieved from our truck. "When I inject the nymph with Evie's blood, it'll reverse the mutation."

The nymph swayed side to side, crouched behind Amos. Its clawed hand swiped at him through the bars, missing his backside. Amos knew exactly how far away to safely stand, and his distance seemed to infuriate the creature as it curled back its lips in a spit-soaked screech.

My insides flinched, the connection between us crushing my airway. It felt like a pair of hands gripping my organs and smashing them together. They shook me until the nymph's screams bled through my veins and became my own.

"Enough!"

The nymph fell silent, its head whipping in my direction, followed by every other head in the room.

Roark wrapped both arms around me, his mouth at my ear. "Breathe."

He inhaled, exhaled, slowly, evenly, setting the pace.

As I matched his breaths, my pulse returned to normal and my insides contracted and loosened. After a few minutes, the nymph slouched against the back wall, its chest rising and falling in sync with ours. Could it sense my emotions the way I sensed its desperation? Really fucking eerie.

Amos glanced between the nymph and me, his expression perplexed, but he didn't budge from his protective stance. "Show me how it works on one o' dem bugs first." He jerked his chin toward the doorway. "Bring back a live one, prove your cure, and I'll consider it."

Seriously? We didn't have time for this. Would it always be this tedious, having to explain, negotiate, and plead for a nymph's life? Too bad we couldn't record the healing of one and let the footage do the explaining. But that would require a charged battery. Maybe we could raid a Best Buy.

Michio squatted, removed a dart gun from the bag, and passed it to Jesse. "The cure doesn't work on aphids, Amos."

I rested against Roark's chest. "My blood is poisonous to an aphid. One drop and their heart explodes." I spread out my fingers, imitating fireworks.

Michio's brow arched.

"What?" I said too much?

Maybe he didn't want Amos to know I could explode hearts.

I wished I could use blood-dipped bullets in fights. Not that I wanted to be blooded before battle, but exploding aphids would be wicked. I'd tested the idea on Jesse's spears. It worked while the blood was fresh and wet. But bullets were a no go, because the blood burned off when the gun was fired.

Michio tossed Jesse a plastic-wrapped syringe and a hypodermic. Evidently, Jesse would be drawing my blood while Michio dealt with Amos.

Michio held out his hand to the cagey man. "You don't need the rifle."

Amos stared down at his gun, his eyes burning holes into it. Lines grooved his forehead, and his finger tapped on the trigger guard. Then he looked at Michio and handed it over.

Releasing a breath, I followed Roark into the room and sat on the edge of a steel table. Michio explained his medical degree and qualifications in molecular biology and genetics. He quickly brushed over what we knew of the Drone, the monster's religious motivation for creating the virus, and how we killed him in Iceland.

Amos set his lips in a straight line, determined to distrust everything he said. "You've been overseas?" His tone was dry, mocking.

Michio dug through his bag, nodding. "None of us are from here. I was in Japan when the virus hit. Jesse and Georges were in France, though Jesse's from the States. Tallis' was in Australia. Father Molony's from Ireland." He gave me a sad smile. "Evie lived in Missouri."

Amos narrowed his eyes. "I don't believe you."

Geez, weren't our diverse accents proof enough? I glanced at Roark beside me, who simply shrugged.

"You don't have to believe me." Michio rested a forearm on one knee. "In fact, it's good that you're questioning us. Suspicion will keep your guard up. After we cure your nymph, it'll be your responsibility to look after her, and part of that role is protecting her from men who might be hiding their intent."

Maybe it was a bit highhanded of Michio to expect Amos to care for her. But we couldn't bring the women with us. They wouldn't just slow us down. We didn't know what we'd face down the road. What if we were attacked and every woman we'd saved was killed? Separating them and tucking them away with good men was best way to ensure future generations.

Amos stared at his dusty loafers. Either he still didn't believe we could cure the nymph or he was considering the ramifications of what Michio suggested.

Jesse twisted the needle onto the syringe barrel, his mouth sliding into a lazy grin as he stepped beside me.

I didn't trust that grin, not when he was seconds away from sticking me. "Is this payback for saving your hide out there?"

Roark perched at my side, his attention darting between Amos, the now docile nymph, and the low hills beyond the doorway. His soft eyes and relaxed shoulders radiated calmness, but since he wasn't talking—or swearing—I knew he was on high-alert. My guardians worked efficiently like that, one of them always on the lookout when the others were distracted. Made it easier to relax sometimes, knowing we had each other's backs.

Jesse swiped the inside of my elbow with iodine, cleaning away the aphid guts. "You disobey me because you think it gives you control. But the only thing your hardheadedness will accomplish is getting yourself killed."

Oh, we were back to that again? "Maybe I don't listen because you use words like *disobey*."

He tied a rubber hose around my bicep, tighter than necessary, and touched the hypodermic point against the crease of my arm.

Blood didn't bother me, but I'd rather not see it drain from my body. So I closed my eyes. "I thought I was supposed to die on a cliff or at the end of your—"

He shoved the needle into my vein.

"—prick." I flexed my hand against the sting and opened my eyes to find him steadily watching me.

There were so many facets of that watchful gaze. Sometimes it was creepy and invasive and judgmental. Other times it was so damned sexy, I felt it in places he never physically touched. But it was always steady, as if the only thing that mattered to him was reading my thoughts and predicting my actions.

Jesse Beckett was a strange one, mercurial in his moods, precarious in his affection for me. If I didn't share his belief in his visions, I'd question his mental health. Maybe I *should* question it. I mean, I used to see visions too, but it had been months, and now I wondered if it was all just a coping mechanism for the loss of my children.

How was Jesse coping with this fucked up world?

As he filled the vial with my blood, his eyes didn't waver from mine. His strong cheekbones formed a dramatic ledge for that deep-set glare. The vivid copper of his irises churned with gold flecks, sucking me in. He was so damned hypnotic.

I sat taller and blinked to break the trance. "Have your visions changed? Did you really think I would die out there?"

He looked down and removed the syringe, lips pinched, eyes hidden by his lashes.

"Awesome." I jerked my arm from his grip and pressed a finger against the tiny well of crimson. "Great talk. We should do this more often."

On the other side of the room, Amos answered Michio's questions. No, he hadn't encountered other nymphs. Yes, this was a remote area. No, he hadn't left the reserve in two years. Evidently, it was Jackson who captured all the aphids, luring them into the cages to unleash on trespassers. And Jackson made all the supply runs, which didn't give me a lot of hope for Amos' ability to protect and care for a cured woman.

Jesse loaded the vial of blood in the gun and stepped toward Michio. Halfway there, he stopped and walked back. Without pausing to catch his breath—to let *me* catch my breath—he leaned over my lap and braced his arms on either side of mine.

Holy shit, he was close. His legs pressed against mine, his full lips a kiss away. My lungs, my muscles, everything froze up.

"Just because I know how you're *supposed* to die," he whispered against my gaping mouth, "doesn't mean I know how often or badly you'll be injured between now and then."

My heart thumped wildly at his words, his proximity, and the shock of it all coming at me at once. He glanced at Roark, who glared at the doorway as if it were filled with aphids. It wasn't. That was Roark pretending not to listen.

Jesse bent closer, drugging my inhales with his woodsy scent and shoving his sexual energy, frustration, whatever this was in my face as his lips brushed my ear. "I'm not going to let you die, Evie. *We* won't let you die. It's time you start depending on us."

I understood what he was saying, but maybe he didn't realize just how vital *his* safety was to my peace of mind? "I get it, but—"

"I want more." He lifted his hand to cup my cheek but drew it back before he made contact.

"More?" Dependency? Touching? Mixed signals and sexual frustration bounced all over the damned place, spinning my head into a fog of *What the fuck?*

"You're not the only one affected by this." He gestured between us and strode off, holding the dart gun out to Michio.

I growled low in my throat. Typical Jesse, making cryptic

declarations and leaving too many questions at the most inopportune time and place to ask them.

Michio accepted the dart gun and held it up for Amos' inspection. "This is blood, not a bullet. It won't hurt your nymph."

He went on, explaining how the healing process worked as my mind replayed the last few minutes.

Jesse made me feel like a fool. My hand clenched. I did depend on them. *Like an equal.* I pulled my weight, dammit. We all did.

Roark remained silent beside me. He might've been listening to Michio's conversation with Amos, but I felt the weight of his eyes urging me to talk.

I kept my voice hushed beneath the medical chit-chat across the room. "I was married to an overprotective man for fifteen years."

His hand settled on my thigh and squeezed. "I know, love."

Yeah, they all knew. I'd spoken of Joel often. "Living with Joel, I had two choices: become a pushover or push back."

"A pushover wouldn't have survived out there alone as long as ye did."

Agreed. Marriage to Joel made me stubborn, but it also toughened me enough to survive. "Dependency is dangerous, Roark." Truth was, I was scared. *Reliance* scared me. Didn't matter how strong and brave my guardians were. "You're not bulletproof either. Or aphid-proof or fall-off-a-cliff-proof." Considering how people had died trying to protect me, I had every right to continue training in battle and protecting myself. And every opportunity I got to protect my guardians was a chance I'd take. "Too many dangers could take you away and leave me alone again."

Roark nodded, his eyes on Jesse. "He knows that. He's just…frustrated."

Fucking understatement. Jesse stood against the far wall, hand resting on the tomahawk at his hip and his glare shooting laser beams of frustration across the room.

Roark lowered his head and whispered, "He needs a release."

A release?

"A blow job, hand job, something…"

Umm, was he suggesting I step up and take care of it? Roark wasn't possessive like Michio, but his open-mindedness had my head shaking and my stomach flip-flopping. "How they ever let you in the seminary is beyond me."

Michio drew my attention as he took a slow step toward Amos and the cage. "The genetic code that makes us human is dormant in the nymph. Evie's blood will unlock it." He raised the dart gun. "Move out of the way, Amos."

Show time. I hopped down from the table. "We've done this twice, and we're batting two for two."

Didn't need to mention the first nymph was murdered after we cured her.

Amos rubbed a hand on his pants, and his gaze bounced between us. With a trembling exhale, he shuffled to the side.

Michio's finger stretched toward the trigger. The nymph's head tilted back, and a wet scream ripped from its mutated gullet.

The ear-piercing squeal rattled through the room, and the invisible vibrations smacked me directly in the stomach. But the attack didn't just come from the nymph. Its link grafted onto multiple telepathic streams coming from outside. My insides lit up with at least a dozen aphid signals, the familiar feeling waving over me and causing the hairs on my arms to stand up.

"Aphids." My gaze flew to the doorway. "Twelve or more. Down the hill, I think."

As Jesse ran out the door, the boom of rifles echoed in the distance. Georges and Tallis could handle them. In fact, the pulsing links were disintegrating with the blast of gunfire.

Amos stared at me like my skin had turned green. "Your eyes…they're black."

Shit. That was an annoying side-effect of my aphid communication. Good thing he couldn't see the black spots on my back.

Michio used Amos' distraction and raised the dart gun at the nymph.

It dragged its jaw along the bars, the fleshy parts in its throat worming, stringing snot from the stabbing spear. As it threw back its head, Michio let the dart fly. The tranquilizer casing hung from the nymph's neck, and the creature slumped to the floor.

Relief washed through me. It was done. Finally, Amos would see—

He fell against the cage door and reached for the unconscious nymph through the bars, his cry strangled and angry. "What have you done?"

I ground my teeth. I'd only been half-listening, but I knew Michio had explained this part.

Outside, the fire of rifles ceased, as did the pinching vibrations in my gut.

I met Michio's eyes. "The aphids are dead."

"What?" Amos turned wide eyes on me. "You can feel them?"

Crap. He was already suspicious.

I nodded, slowly. "It's complicated."

His expression distorted into oh-shit-you're-a-monster terror, the only warning I got before he withdrew a small pistol from his waistband and aimed it at me.

My heart slammed into my throat, and my hand went to the sidearm on my thigh. Then everything happened at once. Jesse appeared in the doorway, Roark's boots squeaked behind me, and Michio flung himself across the room to reach me.

I raised the handgun. "Wait! I'm not—"

Michio plowed into me as the explosive bang of Amos' gun reverberated the walls. I squeezed the trigger.

So many things went through my mind in that slow-moving second that hurdled me to the floor beneath the impact of Michio's lunge.

I hadn't checked Amos for concealed weapons, hadn't questioned how he would react to my bizarre biology. I'd seen the change in his expression. I could've stopped him.

Next came the realization that I felt nothing but the hard floor at my back and Michio's weight on my chest. The bullet hadn't hit me.

I refused to accept that and gave my insides a thorough once over, searching for the burn of lead lodged beneath my skin.

No bullet wounds. Which meant…

Michio convulsed on top of me, and fear rose up, paralyzing my muscles in cold shock. Wet warmth seeped from his shirt to mine, and the bitter scent of blood saturated the air.

He'd blocked the bullet. With his fucking chest! Every cell in my body screamed in denial. I couldn't breathe. Couldn't move. He was going to die.

EIGHT

"Michio?" Blood drained from my face as I tried to shift him off me to the floor.

His bulk suddenly lightened and rolled with the help of Jesse and Roark.

Amos lay sprawled a few feet away, a red stain spreading from a hole in his shirt and his head hanging to the side. Passed out. Or dead. I didn't give a shit.

Michio's chest heaved in time with the noisy breaths wheezing past his lips. The crimson blot over his heart doubled in size with each rise and fall.

Ohmygodohmygod, this couldn't be happening. I bent over him, wrestling with the harrowing seconds between terror and responsibility. *Do something!*

My pulse pounded past my ears as I spread my hands over the wound, unsure, helpless. *He* was the doctor, the only one here who could fix this.

Blood seeped between my fingers, and his face grew paler with each shallow breath. *Please, open your eyes.*

"Michio? Michio, talk to me." My teeth sank into my lip, and I put my weight into my hands until I couldn't compress any harder.

But the blood kept coming. It soaked his clothes, pooled on the concrete, and stained his neck. My hands were gloved in shiny red. My arms, my tank top, my lap, I was covered in it. I hadn't seen this much human blood since that asshole sailor tried to saw off my boob in Dover.

A terrified noise rattled in my throat, and my entire body

shook with tremors. I couldn't stop the blood flow, didn't know how to save him.

Jesse sat back on his heels and ripped off his shirt. Then he shoved the wadded fabric beneath my hands and pressed. "Doc? Doc?"

Michio's eyes fluttered. Scared eyes, peering from red-rimmed sockets. "Roll me."

Jesus, okay, still conscious and talking. That was good, right? My walloping pulse didn't agree.

Roark rolled him, and I helped Jesse hold the shirt to the wound. A smaller circle of blood wet his shoulder blade.

Michio drew a shallow inhale. "Did it go through?"

"Yeah." I found a tiny breath of relief in not having to remove a bullet. But his cheek was so fucking clammy under my hand. I swallowed past the helplessness wedged in my throat. "What now? How do we control the bleeding?"

"Doc?" Roark gripped Michio's chin. "Tell us what to do."

Michio's eyes rolled back in his head, and his body slackened against the floor.

No, no, no! Determination seared up my spine. I ran fingers along the side of his windpipe, seeking and finding his heart beat. "His pulse is rapid, weak…God, it's barely there."

Jesse ripped away Michio's shirt and used the scraps to stanch the exit point. I strained to hear each of Michio's inhales as they teetered in, each breath as uncertain and fragile as I felt.

My guardians remained silent. Like the nymph, who lay on her back, dart in her neck. Like Amos, unconscious or dead.

Roark kicked the gun away from Amos and knelt beside Michio's duffel bag. "Does he have QuickClot or Celox?" His accent strained with worry. "Surely he has something in here to seal it with?"

"I don't know." I should've paid attention to his supplies, should've been better prepared.

I swallowed hard and turned my attention to Jesse, his glare intense and blistering. I wanted to scream at him. *See? This is what happens when you rely on others.* I depended on Michio for all things related to first-aid. I didn't even know if we had bandages or pain-killers.

Minutes passed. It felt like hours. I laid my hand on Jesse's to take over the compress. But he left his there, twining his fingers through mine.

I cleared my throat and looked to Roark. "I can't go through this again." I reached out to touch Michio's closed eyes and hesitated, my fingers caked in blood. I lowered my hand. "Michio let me grieve your death for days."

At the time, I didn't know he'd lied about Roark's death to protect me. He was my captor, and I'd hated him vehemently. I wanted to die in that prison.

Roark met my eyes over his shoulder. "He might've caused ye that pain, love, but he didn't give up on ye."

No, he'd pulled me through those dark days on Malta. My lips touched Michio's cold ones, his heart a faint beat against mine. I wasn't about to give up on him now.

"You're not escaping hell without me, Michio." I hovered there, a breath away, until Roark gripped my arm, drawing my attention to the pouch of QuickClot in his hand.

He squatted on my other side, closer to Michio's head, and pushed Jesse's hand away to lift the sopping-wet compress.

Beneath the slick of blood, the injury seemed to…distort. My head swam. Not just from waves of panic and adrenaline. My brain wobbled and lagged with hallucination, like I was submerged in a dream. But it wasn't a dream. His wound was transforming. Shrinking? No, that couldn't be right. Had it stopped bleeding?

I blinked and leaned closer. "Water. Does someone have water?"

Jesse's shadow moved away and returned a moment later. He twisted the lid off a plastic bottle and emptied it on the wound. The hole shriveled, paled.

"What the…" I shook my head and licked cracked lips. "Do you see this?"

Jesse reached across Michio's torso, pushing me out of the

way, as he bent down for a closer look.

Crouched beside me, Roark wasn't looking at Michio's chest. I followed his gaze to the tiny white points protruding from between Michio's lips.

Nausea turned my stomach as my mind flitted in and out of memory. The Drone's superhuman speed, his wings, his fangs…

Beside me, Roark lowered to his knees and put his face in Michio's, a breath away.

Michio's eyes shot open. "What are you"—he sucked in wet breath—"doing, Priest?"

Hope and disbelief collided inside me then poured out in a rush of exhales.

With a sudden jerk, Roark straightened and pulled me with him. "Bloody hell, Doc. Wanna explain wha's poking outta your trap?"

A groan gurgled in his throat. "Not…at the moment."

"Michio, something's happening." I swatted away Roark's attempt to pull me back and touched the pockmark on Michio's chest with a tentative finger. "I don't…understand…it's…"

No longer a well of blood, the thin bubble of skin stretched and expanded over the hole. Holy Mother. I jerked my hand back.

I'd seen that before. Right after my husband died, I took my grief out on an aphid. I dissected it…while it was alive. It couldn't regrow limbs, but the efficiency in which it repaired injuries was inhuman. Just like this.

My ears rang, and my pulse whooshed loudly in my head. Had Michio contracted the infection? But when…how… Oh fuck, no.

"The Drone," I whispered, as if saying the name aloud would conjure his ghost. The hairs on my nape rose, and I shivered. "He bit you in Iceland." I scooted back, apprehension scratching up my throat. "He passed along his mutation?"

He gave me a pained look beneath heavy brows. "Evie."

I covered my mouth. "Did you get his spider shit, too?"

He closed his eyes.

I jumped to my feet and paced, swirling up the tension in the room. The Drone's own creations had turned on him, infecting him. But he'd stunted his mutation with his homemade strands of spider DNA. Hence, the fangs.

"Son of a bitch." I stopped, swinging around to face him. "Why didn't you tell us?"

"I..." His breath shuddered, and he reached up to touch a tooth. A fucking *fang*. "Studying...wanted proof..."

Always with the damned proof. Distrust plowed through me in full force. He'd pulled that shit when he was studying my blood, refusing to disclose his conclusions until he could authenticate them.

I knelt beside him and touched the fading scar on his chest with a shaking hand. "Did you know you could heal like this?"

He nodded then shook his head. "I didn't know the extent...until now."

His breathing was returning to normal, his face regaining its olive glow.

"You lied to me. Again." I tried to swallow my distrust, hawking it back and choking on it.

I couldn't trust him, and that realization simmered bile through my stomach and swelled an ache behind my eyes.

Jesse and Roark watched me carefully, probably worried about an impending explosion. They were right about that, but I managed to keep the detonation inside, gritting my teeth against the nausea surging through my insides.

"So ye have the aphid's healing abilities?" Roark crouched over him and cast him a drawn-out look.

"And their speed." I mentally replayed his supernatural movements on the battlefield, his bite from the kiss, all the pieces linking together in a dizzying mix of emotions. "What about bloodlust?"

The Drone had struggled to keep his greedy fangs away from me. Something to do with my evolving biological characteristics of the ladybird and the spider being my natural predator.

What did it mean for Michio and his attraction to me? Would the bloodlust turn him on? Would it affect me the same way? Or could it make him lose control and hurt me?

Images flashed through my mind. His mouth covering my neck, sharp teeth biting and drawing blood. Our naked bodies sliding together. His fingers bruising my skin. The richness of his voice deepening into an animalistic growl.

The sudden heat low in my belly warred with the itch to bury a dagger in his heart. "There better not be any negative side effects."

His Adam's apple bobbed.

My hands curled into fists in my lap. Blood coated the nail beds and splattered up my arm.

I'd almost lost him. Whatever changes were happening to his DNA, it had saved his life. *Focus on that.*

Jesse moved to Amos' side and checked the man's pulse. Amos hadn't twitched in his silent sprawl, and I knew what Jesse would find.

He met my eyes and shook his head. *Dead.* Amid all the emotions rioting through me, guilt rose to the top. Yeah, I had been defending myself, but so had Amos. He thought I was a monster, and could I blame him? I should've checked him for weapons. Stupid fucking hindsight.

I managed a small smile. "Looks like Shea will be joining our road trip."

Michio looked at me, his eyes fried with taut lines of exhaustion and tension. "We won't be able to bring along every woman we cure. We need to find a safe place for her."

We really did need a plan for keeping the cured women safe. The best bet would be to ship them back to the Lakota in West Virginia. But how would we do that? At the end of the day, it would be up to each woman to decide where she wanted to live.

"Let's get her healthy first." Roark shifted his gaze from Michio to the still nymph-like, unconscious woman. "Then we'll worry about traveling."

Jesse strode toward the door and scanned the hillside. Beyond his broad frame, the horizon swallowed the final haze of daylight.

Despite the gun shots, Georges and Tallis would've known not to give up their positions on guard to come investigate.

Jesse hadn't said a word about the situation. Was he plotting Michio's death? Or thinking about ways to use the doctor's abilities as a weapon? I wished I could read his locked-down mind.

When he looked back at me, I tried to decipher his eyes. Coppery, paradoxical, and contemplative, sometimes they gave a glimpse into his stormy emotions. But not now. They were as guarded and secretive as his thoughts.

Back on my feet, I holstered my sidearm on my thigh and adjusted the carbine's sling on my shoulder. The mark on Michio's chest had vanished, along with the fangs. How had I not noticed his teeth before? Could he retract them at will?

I opened my mouth to ask but caught myself. His eyes were closed, and I had more important questions bucking inside my skull. Like would he continue to evolve? Would he turn into the monster the Drone became? I chewed the inside of my cheek, my fingers restlessly tapping the carbine. No, the Drone had been a monster long before the virus.

Roark stood and pulled my hand from the carbine. Was he trying to separate me from the gun? Worried I'd shoot Michio on principle?

He massaged my fingers, tenderly, lovingly. My nerves were so overloaded I shook against the sensation.

"Why den' ye go clean up?" He glanced at my tattered jeans and blood-soaked tank top. "I'll watch over Doc and Shea."

The nymph-woman breathed in a deep, steady rhythm, but even in sleep her face began to narrow. The sickly hue of her complexion receded, her muscles filling with blood beneath her skin, her cells growing and changing from *my* blood. And the sounds. Ugh, the sucking sounds of her throat breaking down and reforming saturated the room. Indentations climbed up and down her neck, like fingertips pressing from the inside. I could almost feel her mandible cracking apart, the inhuman pieces disintegrating, the gruesome snap and grind of bones.

As horrific as the transformation was to watch, it was the reason we were here. Despite whatever we now faced with Michio, we'd succeeded in freeing another woman from the creature she had been trapped in.

I flexed my fingers, my steps a little lighter as I joined Jesse at the door. "I need a smoke."

Maybe I could burn away the rest of the tension with a couple or twenty cancer sticks.

Jesse untied a tiny leather pouch from his belt and passed it over. "There's a water hole round back. I'll guard while you bathe."

He strode out the door, not bothering to wait for me. Damn the confidence in his gait, the imposing bow at his back, and the way his jeans cupped his ass. He could've modeled for the Playgirl edition of Outdoor Life magazine. But it was a good distraction as I left the drama behind me, if only for a short while.

The brawn in his shoulders and biceps moved sensually beneath his sun-soaked skin. Messy spikes of hair paired perfectly with the dirty, glistening sweat on his nape and back. Worn denim accentuated his battle-toned thighs. Even the mud-caked boots looked intimidating. He really was a savage. If I pressed my nose to his neck, I'd smell the wildness wafting from his pores.

He made me feel safe, despite the vulnerability wheezing from my lungs.

But his feral appearance wasn't half as reassuring as the intelligence working behind those fierce eyes. He harbored opinions about Michio, even if his casual indifference said otherwise. I needed to hear his thoughts, wanted him to tell me our team of four still had each other's backs, that we'd survive this. Together.

Smokes in hand, I followed on his heels with every

intention of prying the hulking, reluctant conversation from his clamped lips.

NINE

Hues of deep purple streaked the sky, casting an unnerving gloom over the clearing behind the animal clinic. Without a breeze, the stifling air didn't stir. Neither did the shadows between the skeletal trees that surrounded the field and small pond. The area was eerily still, too quiet, like a fog from the water hole was suffocating the environment.

Except there was no fog.

A few steps ahead, Jesse's long-legged strides slowed. When I reached his side, he said, "Stay here."

"Do you feel it, too?"

He squinted at the trees, his eyebrows burrowing together. "What? Are there aphids?"

"No." I pressed a hand against my stomach, feeling strangely calm yet not calm at all.

His nostrils flared as his attention darted around us, his body posed, as if ready to attack the shadows.

"Tell me what you're feeling." Impatience clipped through his Texan drawl.

"Nothing. That's just it. Nothing is always *something*." I stood halfway between the building and pond, giving serious thought to abandoning the bath. "I don't know. This place creeps me out."

He scanned the mirrored surface of the water, the border of woodland, and returned to me. "Do not move from this spot." He looked directly in my eyes, and a shimmer of anxiety reflected back in his, straining the inches between us. "I'll be extremely unhappy if you do."

When I nodded, he jogged off toward the copse, keeping to the edge and remaining in sight. But the shade strewn by dead trees closed in around him. Dried-up husks splintered with broken branches, their dark silhouettes hunched over like spiny bones, like aphids crouched on double-jointed limbs, waiting to attack. I shuddered and rubbed my arms.

As Jesse moved in and out of the shadows, my nerves rattled around in my stomach. What was up with me? I wasn't usually this strung out.

I pulled out a cigarillo, struck a match, and tied the pouch at my belt. A few seconds later, the burn of tobacco and smoke curled through the dark and relaxed my lungs.

Smoking grounded me, each pull and puff connecting me to an easier life, when stress was brought on by a traffic jam on the way to work or an argument with Joel about hanging up his clothes. Nicotine had a way of mellowing my mind and dousing my nerves.

But not now. A strange sensation nipped at my nape and tingled my scalp. I twisted to look behind me.

Nothing moved. Not the shadowy grassland around the animal clinic or the dense spaces between the clusters of buildings a few acres to the south.

As I exhaled the final drag, Jesse strode back to my spot, blasting me with those copper eyes. "There's nothing out there. What do you feel now?"

I touched a hand to my cheek. Cold fingers on a warm night? I stomped out the cigarette, feeling light-headed, out of sorts, but… "Still nothing. Overactive imagination, I guess."

A foot away, he bent his knees and put his face in mine, his eyes softening. "Or lingering shock from Doc's revelation?"

I couldn't have asked for a better opening. "Yeah, about that—"

"I don't…" His jaw set, and his back straightened, as he scrubbed a hand through his hair. "Listen, I don't want you fucking him."

My eyes must've bulged out of my head. I was shocked speechless and completely unnerved on so many levels. I mean, Jesse didn't acknowledge my sexual relationships. He made himself scarce when I was with Michio and Roark intimately. He never showed signs of jealousy. One would think he didn't give a shit, or for that matter, didn't even notice. I knew better, but for him to voice an opinion about it was huge.

He loomed over me, hands on his hips. "You need to replace your IUD as soon as possible."

Wait. "What?" I knew he noticed more than he let on, but the IUD? "How do you know about that?"

He gave me a pointed look. "I make it my business to know everything about you."

My pulse kicked up, and my chest thrummed with warmth. Why did I like hearing that so much?

I stared up at him and hoped my expression didn't look overexcited. "Why?" When he started to shake his head, I rushed forward. "You have to give me something. Your secrets aren't helping either of us."

Shifting his weight from one boot to the other, he pinched his lips together and glanced away. I didn't want to surrender to his silent treatment, to the closed-mouthed Jesse Beckett, who seemed to know everything about me but offered nothing in return. Something had to give.

"Do you want me to replace the IUD because you're afraid of what kind of child Michio and I would conceive? Or do you have some premonition about what will happen if I became pregnant?"

Would my baby be something other than human?

He stared at the horizon for long seconds then slid that pensive gaze to me. His eyes roamed my face so intensely I wanted to shrink into my shoulders. But he seemed to be considering something. Talking? Sharing? *Open your stubborn mouth.*

I held still, examining his features as diligently as he searched mine. Stubborn jaw covered in reddish-brown whiskers. Strong cheekbones from his Native American heritage. Full lips that separated, just enough to reveal a restless tongue. And his eyes... Even when squinting in the dark, they had the power to heat my skin and pin me in place. Like now.

The current that ran through our shared look was staggering. He must've felt it, because he gripped the back of my head and pressed my cheek against his chest, breaking the spell. Holy hell, every inch of his body was solid rock, the ridges of his muscles so very warm and hard against my face.

But it was his words that sent my pulse into overdrive.

"If you get pregnant..." He inhaled deeply, the pause ratcheting my heart rate. His hand clenched in my hair. "You'll die, Evie. A child will kill you."

My stomach dropped, and I jerked back to meet his eyes. "What? How? You mean, childbirth? Or after?"

I flinched against the sudden image of a spider-baby skittering from its bed and sucking my blood while I slept.

He tightened his hand around my nape, his gaze stark and unblinking in the moonlight as he rasped, "I don't know."

The mere thought of pregnancy made my blood run cold. "Find me another IUD, and I'll let Michio replace it. What else are you not telling me?"

He licked his lips, his attention bouncing between me and our surroundings. "The night I met you, Annie said..."

My entire body froze in remembrance of that night. Chasing her ghostly manifestation through the woods. Falling into the fire. Meeting the Lakota. My daughter's spirit had been so vivid and real in the mountains, her toothy smile so full of life.

A tremor shook my fingers. I curled them against my thighs. "Annie said?"

He closed his eyes, and his mouth tightened.

No, he couldn't shut down. Not yet. I placed my hand over his, holding it against my face. "Please?"

His eyes opened, locking on mine, and his expression sharpened with severe lines. "She told me all the ways I would save you from death. The hunting trip in the mountains. The sailor in Dover. The Drone's dungeon on Malta. The volcano in Iceland. The cliff in America."

The air shriveled, sucking all the moisture. My mouth dried, and my throat sealed up. I would've died in those places? How was I supposed to wrap my mind around that? "You were there. Every time. God, you've saved me over and over..."

"Except the cliff," we said in unison.

I dropped my hand, and his followed. Straightening my stance, I lifted my chin. "So we avoid cliffs in America."

"We can't—" He snapped his teeth together, and his body stiffened with frustration. "She said if I change your path, an unpredicted death would take you."

"That's why you didn't tell me the details of the visions?" Or Roark and Michio. So we wouldn't make decisions based on prophecy, decisions that would alter those premonitions and send me on a path he couldn't see. "That's why Annie didn't tell me."

He nodded and leaned closer, a hint of hickory dancing on his breath. "I let you lead the way for two years, didn't sway your course, and intervened only as her predictions happened."

Oh, Jesse. My God, the burden he carried all this time. I rewound every event since I met him, playing and replaying those near-death encounters. Then I drifted back to our conversation in Italy. He'd told me then about the spirit world and his interactions with Annie and Aaron's ghosts. *The veil between our realm and theirs shows me other things, darker things. Things I must keep from you.*

He'd claimed he could prevent those *things* if he kept distance between us. So damned vague. But he always had this uncanny ability to show up at the right time, when I was bleeding, cornered, fighting for my last breath. Now it made sense...in a bizarre, fucked-up, out-of-this-world kind of way.

I didn't like it. It made me feel like an unwanted tether, a noose around his neck. "You've been shackled to my ass for too long. I'm not your responsibility." I lowered my voice, vulnerability trickling in. "I don't want to be this...this obligation to you."

"I've told you this, Evie, and I'll tell you again." He framed my face with his huge hands, tipping back my head to peer into my eyes. "I want this. Fuck, the moment I saw you in the mountains, *before* Annie shared her visions, I knew I would live to protect you. But…"

I stared into the fiery abyss of his eyes, soaking in the rawness in his voice and the strength of his words. His honesty was as mesmerizing as his beauty. I gripped his wrists, a silent plea to continue.

"I just hoped…" He slid his hands from my face, pulling out of my hold, and stepped back.

"Jesse."

A private smirk twitched his lips. I knew that smirk. If it had a voice, it would say, "Fuck off. We're done here."

The pause that followed grew dark and steep, erecting a cliff between us. A *fuck-off* cliff, reverberating with *fuck-off* echoes.

He turned away and inspected the trees.

I wasn't ready to fuck off, dammit. "You hoped…"

"Doesn't matter." He strode toward the water hole.

I ran after him and jumped into his path, facing his foot-taller frame. "What did you hope?"

He stared over my head, focused on nothing…and everything.

"Come on, Jesse." I placed a hand on the brick wall of his chest. "We're making progress."

He shook his head, his eyes hardening with anger. "We *can't* make progress. Don't you get it?"

"No." I lowered my hand before I choked him with it. "I don't, because you won't explain it to me."

A hiss pushed through his teeth, more like a snarl, and he pierced me with razor-sharp eyes. "I hoped you would be mine, that I could have you the way he does." He slashed an arm behind him, in the direction of the animal clinic.

God, this man twisted me up, jangling my insides with both hope and confusion. I wanted to touch him, kiss him, hold him.

"I *am* yours. You *do* have me." I reached for his face.

"The fuck I do!" He stepped back, out of arm's length, his gaze blinding and fierce and so incredibly pissed. "You know what I really hoped, Evie? I hoped I could fuck you every night, that I would have *that* to look forward to. I hoped a few hard thrusts in your cunt would make this miserable, goddamned lonely existence a lot less miserable and goddamned lonely."

He swiped a hand over his mouth and resumed his trek toward the pond.

White heat exploded through my head and seared my sinuses. I drew deep breaths and tried to calm my pounding heart. His words were deliberately insensitive, meant to push me away. Yeah, there was truth there. Roark was right. But Jesse needed more than a release. He needed affection, love, companionship, and whatever else he was too afraid to admit.

But I was done chasing him. Done begging for peeks behind the *fuck-off* cliff.

My hands shook, balling at my sides. "Stop running, you fucking coward."

His gait faltered but didn't stop.

No matter what happened, whether we embraced our bond or remained separated by his visions forever, I had to confront his fears. Because they were mine, too.

I spoke into the dark expanse between us. "What did Annie say about my child? *Your* child."

He stopped dead in his tracks, maybe twenty steps away. His head angled down, his back a rigid mountain of tension. "Can't tell you that, Evie."

"Because it will change my fate?"

A slow nod.

Christ, I wished he would look at me. "I don't want a child. Didn't you hear my argument with Michio?"

Another nod.

I still didn't understand why he wanted me to stop sleeping with Michio.

"No matter what you're holding back, *that* path won't

change. Losing Annie and Aaron…" I sucked in a breath. "I won't go through that again. If I can't replace the IUD, I'll find other birth control. I'll abstain if I have to."

Fuck me, what a wretched thought.

He slowly turned and walked back to me, refusing to meet my eyes. When he stepped into my space, he stared at my mouth, didn't blink, didn't move for an eternal moment.

Something stirred at the back of my mind. Or was it a shift in the air? Whatever it was roused my skin in a ripple of chills.

The pond stretched before us, the surface a sheet of black glass. There were no chirping crickets, no trilling birds, not a whisper of rustling leaves. My discomfort about this place heightened.

Or maybe it was just Jesse and his ominous secret.

With agonizing hesitancy, he dragged his gaze to mine. As we stared at each other, the atmosphere rotated, soundless and shifty. It was a breeze. It had to be. So why was I struggling to breathe?

The air shuddered as he touched my chin, lifted it. "Annie said I must give her a sister, that it was my *purpose*. And in doing so, you would finally join her in her world."

I tried to fill my lungs and failed. My lip trembled. What he said, the ache in his voice… I wanted to cry. Pressure built in my head and tightened my chest, but it wouldn't release.

I blinked dry eyes, unable to let it go. "She said *you* must do it?"

Not Michio or Roark? Or the last thing I wanted to consider…What if I was raped again?

"Me." He released my chin, his tone grim. Too grim. He was still holding something back.

"Annie's spirit"—*my sweet, little girl, who didn't know how babies were conceived*—"told you how to keep me alive long enough to get me pregnant?"

"And long enough to spread the cure." He glanced up at the moon, its gleam partially smudged by gray clouds. Then he looked down at me. "She said the creatures would evolve."

Like it or not, that rang true. The first time I noticed their evolving behavior was the night I met Roark, when they invaded the pub, steady and deliberate, working together like a goddamned SWAT team. Were they growing smarter? Faster? Modifying and adapting to their environments? They were certainly growing in number.

I squinted at him through the dim light. "What does their evolution have to do with me?"

'She said *you* won't be able to save future generations from them..."

An unspoken *but* hung between us.

I whispered on a ragged exhale, "But our child can?"

"Our daughter." He closed his eyes. "Without her, there will be no human race."

TEN

A child, our daughter, could save the future.

Waves of skepticism dripped off my exhale and clung to the dark and humid air. "What about the nymphs we'll be saving? Those women's children wouldn't save the human race? What will all those offspring do exactly?"

Jesse glanced at the ground then back to me, his eyes shining like copper tin. "They'll replenish mankind *if* they're not wiped out by our biggest predator."

Emotions bubbled up inside me and spilled out in a surge of tremors. Denial, anger… raw fucking fear. I teetered to remain upright, wrestling with the conviction of Jesse's words. "You're saying if I had this child, I wouldn't live long enough to raise her?"

A muscle bounced in his jaw. "Which is why I won't touch you." So much pain in his voice. "Do you understand now?"

Would I die from childbirth or from something else related to having a child? I supposed if someone discovered I was the mother of a superbaby, they might kill me in spite. Jesse said he didn't know the details, only that he had to have sex with me to save mankind, and in doing so guaranteed my death, which meant he would spend his life without me.

Talk about a mood killer. No wonder he was so grouchy.

Well, I refused to accept his all-or-nothing reasoning. "I can't get pregnant from touching or kissing."

Or anal sex. Would he freak if I said that out loud? See, this was the kind of shit I didn't know about him.

My greedy sexuality demanded a deeper connection, and yeah, I ached for all three of the men who protected me. "There are so many other things we can—"

"No." He sucked a seething hiss through his teeth, and his eyes flashed away. "I can't…" He rubbed a palm on his jeans. "Christ, I only have so much control."

My heart slammed against my ribs. He wasn't giving himself enough credit. Roark and I fooled around without having sex. Sure, the priest had a lifetime of practiced celibacy, and he *did* slip up once. And what a colossal backslide that had been. The night he lost his virginity had led to an exorbitant amount of resentment.

But the likelihood of Jesse taking it too far was slim. Wasn't it?

Arghhh. I didn't know because he'd given me very few hints of his sexual nature. "I'm still on birth control."

"I don't trust it."

Double Arghhh! My thoughts circled round and round, and my feet twitched to move. "I need to walk."

I strode the distance to the shoreline and slogged along the edge. He matched my strides, my persistent and vigilant shadow.

Our boots squished in the marshy soil as I pondered aloud. "Keeping your…*hands* to yourself to prevent a…a fatal pregnancy alters my path, something you claimed we couldn't do." I rubbed my temples. "But I'm preventing it already with the IUD and my refusal to have children." I pivoted, colliding with his rigid chest. "Are you sure she said *your* daughter?"

"Yes, dammit."

Okay, fine, only Jesse could father a superbaby. But I was sleeping with Michio. If left to my own devices, which is what Jesse had determined to do, I'd never have another child. Except by accident. Even knowing about Jesse's visions, that could still happen. What if the IUD was failing for some godforsaken reason?

I dared to meet his eyes. "Does that mean no one else can impregnate me?"

His hands clenched. "I don't fucking know."

Was that jealousy? *From Jesse?*

I scratched at the crusted blood on my arm, unsure how far I could push before he shut down this conversation. "Why did you tell me to not fuck Michio?"

He gripped the back of his neck. "Annie said there would be two other guardians, but she never mentioned Doc's changing DNA. That's a huge omission."

What did that mean? Goosebumps skated up my arms. "You believe my path has already changed? That Michio could be a danger to me?"

His gaze skirted across the pond. "I wish I knew."

He seemed upset with himself, his voice missing its usual bite. Crazy how quickly we'd gone from awkward distance to ripping open our chests and exposing our sorry, fearful hearts. To be honest, I couldn't have been happier with the progress, regardless of how badly this conversation fucked with my head.

All because of an irreconcilable vision. Maybe we were both losing our minds.

I bumped his bicep with my shoulder, the simple contact comforting. "The little ghost of Annie is quite the meddler. It's strange… I mean, she was a very bright child, but how does she know so much in the afterlife?"

"Guess we won't know that answer until we join her." The corner of his mouth bounced, prompting the same sad smile from mine.

I kept the gruesome memories of Annie and Aaron buried, but their animated spirits would forever live inside me. Sometimes I felt them so keenly it was as if they were still here, awakening the air with their laughter and crushing my chest with their hugs. "I miss her. I miss them both so damned much."

"Me too."

He'd only met the ghostly footprints of their former lives, yet they'd still managed to leave an unforgettable impact. Would they ever appear to him again? Or me? I didn't think so. Their last visit felt painfully final.

A lifeless quiet settled around us. The pond seemed to absorb it, its depths muddied and dreary as if saddled with our impasse. We stood on the shore, breathing in unison, silent with our thoughts.

I could dispute the credibility of the visions. I could argue he fabricated all of it. Hell, I wanted to deny every hokey-ass premonition that had spewed from his mouth. I mean, come on. A divine child? From *me*? Would she be godlike in power? Were my fears about protecting a child not applicable to this hypothetical daughter? She'd have to be pretty damned mighty if she could save the future from evolving aphids.

It sounded ridiculous, far-fetched, and completely irrational.

But was it really?

In a few hours, there would no longer be a mutated creature in the animal clinic, and in its place a woman with *human* DNA. DNA that was unlocked by *my* blood. And I stood here now because I'd evaded multiple deaths. Miracles. Because Jesse had seen them, long before they happened.

I only had one life to give. What was it going to be? A cliff or a world-saving child? Jesse could physically catch me from a fall off a ledge, which was no doubt his plan. Just like all the times before. If I got pregnant, however, he wouldn't be able to fix that.

But he could prevent it.

Maybe I could put this to rest with logic and sane reasoning. But I trusted my gut. That spiritual sense deep in my core had led me to my guardians. The same instinct told me to trust Jesse's visions.

All I had to do was give birth to a savior and die in the process. Hell, might as well nail her to a cross and resurrect her three days later. How very biblical.

I touched Jesse's hand where it curled against his thigh. "I don't want to bring a baby into this world. Heaven knows, I'm no Virgin Mary."

He huffed out a laugh. "No, you're certainly not."

"And I don't want to die. But there's more at stake here than *me* and *my* wants."

He whirled on me. "What?" His brows slammed together. "What the fuck are you saying?"

"I'm scared, Jesse." Even admitting it aloud knotted my stomach. "But this isn't a decision we can make in a single conversation. We need to talk to Roark and Michio."

"No."

"Nothing good comes from circumventing group input. We're in this together."

"I shouldn't have told you." He shook his head, his jaw turning to steel. "I thought, after your confrontation with Michio, you would be sensible about this." He trudged along the shoreline, shoving a hand through his hair. "Fuck."

Moonlight reflected off his bow and quiver, which were strapped tightly to the sculpted contours of his back. With each stiff, decisive step he put between us, I could actually feel him rebuilding his emotional distance.

My breath slipped from my lungs, pausing at my lips, as I tried to find the right thing to say. He was angry, hurting, and I ached to console him.

"What do you want me to do?" I whispered across the ten or so yards between us.

"I want you to stay at my side." His feet paused, his back rigid with tension. "And that's the problem. The closer you are, the weaker I become."

His words enveloped me in a powerful embrace. Jesse was the epitome of strength and ferocity. Not just his physique but the air that surrounded him. The world seemed to move at his will, in sync with the motion of his muscles.

He shoved his hands in his pockets and looked to the side, giving me his profile. "Just…don't make decisions based on what I've told you."

"Then I'll continue to want you." Like I had a choice. "I'll keep pushing and kicking and pestering until I break down your damned walls."

The skin around his mouth tightened, but I swear there

was a ghost of a smile there, too.

"And what do I do when I encounter a cliff? Why did you tell me about that?"

"Because it's ambiguous as fuck." He angled his head back to look at me, his cheekbones casting dark shadows beneath his hard gaze. "A cliff isn't specific like, oh I don't know, *the dungeon in Malta.* There are cliffs everywhere." He jerked his arms out, indicating the landscape, as he turned to face me. His voice rose a few notches. "You could die on any one of the ridges, ravines, or embankments we come across. I told you so I could train you how to survive the fucking fall."

I melted a little. I wanted to hug him, kiss him, thank him the best way I knew how. But he'd never allow it, so I just nodded in understanding, though I wasn't sure I understood at all. "When is this supposed to happen? The cliff? The pregnancy? Is there an order of things?"

"The predictions have happened in the order she recited them. The cliff is next." He stalked toward me. "It'll happen anytime."

That was comforting.

His eyes fixed on the strap of my carbine, his mouth clamped and determined. When he reached me, he jerked the sling off my shoulder. Evidently, he was ready to move on with the bath.

Fingers curled around the strap, he waited for me to relinquish the weapon.

I glanced at the motionless water, the murky shapes of the surrounding trees, and the weak beam of moonlight pushing through the clouds. Swear to God, there was something in the air, a leeching kind of stagnancy. It was gathering, concentrating, somewhere out there. In the pond? Across the shore? Above the trees? Was it moving?

I couldn't pinpoint it, which strung my nerves on tenterhooks. I strained to feel the familiar vibrations of aphids, waiting for a crunch of a twig or a splash in the water.

Nothing.

Jesse watched me, his sharp eyes so damned perceptive.

"There are other ponds nearby, but this one's the cleanest."

The heat from his body tingled across my skin as he pulled the carbine from my grip and unbuckled the holster on my thigh.

I didn't want to hand over my weapons, but fighting him would only delay the inevitable. What was my problem anyway? I'd needed a bath since we left the mountains. We all did.

With a resolved exhale, I began to remove the arm sheathes, my attention on the water hole. Unarmed, on edge, in this abysmal place?

On second thought, I tightened the straps on my arms. "I'm keeping the knives."

"Good. I'll be..." He gestured at the woods. "On guard."

"You can watch the perimeter from here." I hated the pleading pitch in my voice.

He glanced at the woods and shook his head. "Not easily." Then he took off with my guns, running away like he always did when my clothes were about to come off.

Talk about feeling vulnerable. But leaving guns on the shore for someone to use against me was out of the question. Besides, Jesse was there... Well, I couldn't see him now, but he was near, ever protective and watchful, tormenting himself. And me.

Stripping quickly, I lit another cigarette and waded into the pond. My feet slipped over moss-covered pebbles, and the water lapped around me, warm and soothing.

Halfway across, the inky surface reached my hips. Far enough. I drew a slow drag from the cigarillo and held it in my lungs, unable to shake off the creeping dread. My first encounter with an aphid had really made me anxious about swimming. Water killed them quickly, but I would never forget the claw pulling me under. Its body bubbling with fungus-like tumors. Its eyes open and staring as it sunk to its death.

I ran a hand over my legs and ass and washed away the grime, all while making careful sweeps of the surroundings.

Blackness stretched from the shore to the trees. Not a trace of Jesse's tall frame. If he was watching, I couldn't sense him.

"Jesse?" My voice ricocheted through the dark, louder than I intended. I might as well have screamed, *I'm here. Come kill me!*

The longer I waited for a response, the more I was convinced something was off. A menacing *wrong-wrong-wrong* coiled around me, itching my skin. My legs burned to haul ass out of the water, but it wasn't the pond that spooked me. Whatever it was…was out there.

Stop it. I was making myself crazy. I didn't sense aphids, couldn't see or hear a goddamned thing. I was just impaired by tweaked-out emotions and lack of sleep.

"Eveline."

I jumped at the frighteningly familiar whisper, and the cigarillo hit the water with a hiss. My sharp exhales rose in the air, my muscles locked in shock.

That voice… *He's dead. He's dead. He's dead.*

Wasn't he?

I never saw a body.

Because the lava would've disintegrated it.

I listened hard, my gaze jumping from shadow to shadow. I was just hearing things. Crazy, overactive nerves.

The surface of the pond rippled away from the far shore as if something had slipped in.

My chest hitched. But nothing was there.

The breeze again.

I focused on the wind but couldn't feel it. Not a damned thing moved. But I sensed something. Something slick and oily slithering behind me.

My heart bolted in fear. Paralyzing fear, the kind that freezes the lungs and shivers breaths along the spine. I was stuck in an unblinking, wheezing, high-alert stance.

The air was deadly still, yet the sound of flapping fabric drifted over my shoulder.

The hairs on my neck stiffened, begging me not to turn around. If it was an aphid, the water protected me. But I'd heard that accented whisper, the unforgettable flap of a cape. *I could feel his oily presence.*

My pulse raced as I slowly turned my head and looked over my shoulder.

ELEVEN

The muscles in my neck strained and stiffened as I stared over my shoulder, my fingers tensing in the water around my hips.

The silhouette on the shore stole my breath, every ounce of it. The dark outline of a man was cut out of the black backdrop, his features cloaked by the hood of the cape. But I didn't need to see the face to identify the source of my two-year nightmare.

My body went cold, and my stomach caved in. I spun to face him, my panic escaping in a piercing shout. "Jesse!"

This wasn't real. It wasn't, it wasn't, it wasn't, it wasn't, it wasn't, it wasn't. The Drone was dead. Which meant I'd been pulled into the spirit world. Jesse should've heard me. He'd promised to guard my mind, to make sure I'd always find a way back to the living.

The looming shadow reached up and slid back the hood. My backbone began to buckle. One by one, the bones of my vertebrae crumbled as a mutilated face came into view. I hurdled into nightmares, reliving the threat of fangs. The snap of demonic wings. The pungency of sulfur. The lava river engulfing the Drone's fall. Bend, bulge, collapse. My spine melted, and water washed over my shoulders.

I wasn't dreaming. My body pulsed with wakefulness, shivering beneath the warm water. But that didn't mean I wasn't stuck in the spirit world.

With a monster.

I couldn't pull my gaze from the disfigurement. From

hairline to collar, his cheeks and jaw drooped with loose, melted flesh, the skin beneath his black eyes sagging hideously.

He prowled closer, the sable ringlets of his hair snaking around his cloak-covered chest. "You look healthy, Eveline. I'm very pleased."

Unable to move, unable to come to terms with what I was seeing, I shouted again. "Jesse!"

The Drone's laughter erupted around me just as the visceral hum of aphids annihilated my insides. Oh fuck, oh fuck, oh fuck. Was Jesse fighting them off? A telepathic battle writhed in my stomach. With the pinch of each aphid death, more moved in.

But the tree line remained comatose. Where had Jesse run off to? Could all this be happening in my mind? Maybe he couldn't hear me screaming because I was stuck in some other dimension? My muscles trembled to find him, and my hand shot to my forearm, releasing a blade.

With a steely breath, I aimed it at the Drone's chest and sent it hurdling across the distance.

He blurred to the side. If I blinked, I would've missed the movement. But I hadn't blinked, and I still missed him by a fucking foot. Goddammit, I wanted to see him bleed, to see if he *could* bleed.

I went for another blade and threw again. It hit the loose folds of his cape, and I swear I heard a rip in the fabric before it vanished in the tall grass behind him.

I kept throwing. He kept dodging. My fingers flexed in frustration, my breath sharpening. I wasn't far from the shore. I should've hit him at least once.

Dead or alive, he still had more power than me, to outmaneuver my attacks, to laugh in my face with each failure. Which he did, his demented enjoyment crackling through the air.

I reached for the next blade and… Fuck!

I'd run out. My blades scattered the shore, kicked away by the Drone's boots. Could ghosts do that? His feet should've floated through the steel.

Where the hell was Jesse? The animal clinic was too far away to alert Roark, the cinder-block walls too thick to penetrate. But I tried anyway. "Roark!"

The area surrounding the building held still.

The Drone crossed his arms, and a terrifying smile morphed his mouth into fangs, melted skin, and insanity.

The thought of Jesse alone and in need of help flooded my blood with adrenaline. My heart rate blew up, and vicious energy surged through my body. Should I leave the protection of the water without weapons?

It wasn't just my life I risked. *The cure. The future child.*

Where were the others? Still guarding the perimeter?

"Georges! Tallis!" I bellowed their names until my throat burned, pausing every few breaths to listen for the boom of their rifles.

More silence. Where were the aphids? Their vibrations strummed from… I couldn't locate a position. The threads buzzed from everywhere and nowhere.

I concentrated hard and tried to reign them in, pushing my command along each insectile lifeline with urgency. *Leave. Leave. Leave.*

The effort sucked me dry in seconds. Without masculine energy from skin contact, I was powerless. Spots invaded my vision. Ice spread through my veins. And wet warmth trickled from my nose, followed by the scent of copper.

"You're wasting your time." The Drone's voice drew my attention, his mouth twisting against his mangled cheek. "You can't control them."

Because he could override my control, even when I was fueled by Yang. He could also scramble the signals. *He* had created the mutations after all.

My chest collapsed with helplessness, and the heave of my breaths shook my body. I ducked my face beneath the surface to wake the fuck up. But when I blinked at the shore, the monster was still there.

I swiped at the blood tickling my lip. "What do you want, Aiman?"

"The Drone." Fangs glistened, so much longer and pointier than I remembered. "Address me by my title."

He's a phantom. A harmless, residual puff of nothingness. I armored myself with that thought and stood to my full height.

Water rushed off my body, and the surface lapped at my hips. "I'll address you however I want. You're dead."

His eyes blackened, as dense and dark as his cloak. "Am I?"

A goddamned volcano had swallowed him. Apparently, ghosts couldn't grasp the fact that they were dead. My children's apparitions never seemed aware of it.

I gestured to the stagnant stillness around us. "We're in the spirit world, asshole. Which means you're just a fog of hateful energy and neurotic memories."

So why wasn't he transparent like Annie and Aaron? I inched forward until a few yards separated us.

His chest and shoulders were broad and solid, standing a few inches taller than six feet. The toe of his boot peeked from beneath the cape, firmly planted on the dirt, *indenting* it and leaving a footprint.

He didn't have to be floaty and airy, but it certainly would've eased my wildly beating heart. Could he have survived that fall? I never actually saw his body hit the lava.

"You look confused, Eveline, but I think you know what is real and what is...spirit." His Arabic inflection tumbled out with sophistication despite the mouthful of teeth. "Besides, you and I have a connection that defies all rules."

"There is no *you and I.*"

And *he* was an illusion.

Maybe Jesse was okay. Maybe the aphid sensations in my gut were illusions, too.

In the distance, a toad croaked. A toad? Couldn't be. Whenever I crossed over to never-never-land, the ripple of life vanished.

But that wasn't true, was it? Aaron told me once I could bring life with me.

My fingernails dug like knives in my palms as I willed myself back to reality. Silence cocooned the landscape, my heartbeat the only sound as it rushed past my ears. "Why am I here?"

"*I* am here because I've grown tired of waiting."

Though I stood as tall as possible in the pond, my insides shrunk with dread. "Waiting for what?"

"We want the same thing," he said, matter-of-factly.

My lungs constricted. "And what is that exactly?"

"We both want nymphs."

When the Drone was alive, he'd twisted his religious beliefs beyond sanity and massacred the human race in the name of Allah. He used nymphs to breed a *perfect*, Drone-serving species. Obviously, we didn't want nymphs for the same reason, and evidently, death hadn't cured his madness.

Sliding footsteps marked his approach, pausing when the hem of his cape touched the water.

Then it dawned on me. He'd never fully escaped his aphid mutation, which meant he couldn't enter the pond. I splashed, splaying my hands and directing waves of water as I rushed forward. He backed up, the hem of the cloak sloshing over the dirt.

Shadows swelled behind him, taking the form of hard, shell-like wings.

Oh shit. Not good. I stumbled backward, dipping lower in the water.

The black holes of his eyes impossibly darkened. "How is Dr. Nealy's health?" He dragged his tongue over one fang. "Any new cravings?"

Had he bitten Michio as part of some plan? Fury blasted through my body, inflaming my face.

I charged forward, splashing frantically. "It must suck knowing your life's work is so easily washed away with a drop of my blood."

And now I had a new weapon. Trustworthy or not, Michio was stronger, healthier, maybe even invincible. No one could stop us from reversing the nymph mutation. That thought fueled my stupid courage as I continued to spray water at the retreating shadow.

His wings snapped out, shooting him skyward like a bullet in the night. His godawful roar followed him as he swooped back down, his melted face warping in rage.

I dropped to my ass, sinking into the water until the surface submerged my chin. *He can't hurt me. He can't hurt me.*

His claw swung out, and a cold painful smack slammed into my face, hurling me into blackness.

TWELVE

My body spiraled in a sea of black, and suffocating terror washed over my face. I wanted to draw air, but I was submerged beneath water. My legs and arms flailed, connecting with nothing, falling…

The Drone. His wings in the sky. The claw in my face. Was he hovering above the surface? Waiting for me to come up?

The pebbly bottom bumped against my back. I swallowed my breath, and sharp pains stabbed through my chest. *Need air.* But I was safe here. For now. How much longer could I stay underwater?

Not long. My lungs burned, reaching capacity, and panic squeezed my insides.

I kicked until my face breached the surface. Gulping for each inhale, I gasped and choked while scanning the sky and shore, blinking rapidly to clear my vision.

The Drone wasn't there.

Water splashed at my back. My heart stopped. I wasn't alone? The splashing grew dizzyingly closer. Before I could turn around, arms came around my waist from behind. I was seconds from swinging a punch, but the moment of fear gave way to the soothing warmth of a familiar body.

"Evie. Shhh." Jesse's voice wrapped around me in soft, raspy echoes. "You're okay."

I clutched the arms around my waist as a wave of questions rushed up my throat and poured out in waterlogged chokes.

He hugged me tighter and rubbed a hand over my spine.

"Cough it out. There you go."

After a few more wheezing spasms, I managed a quiet breath. "Did you see him?"

"Who?" He twisted me around and pulled me up against the wall of his bare chest, his hands clenching against my head and back. "I saw…" His chin tilted up, eyes on the sky. "I don't know. A huge fucking stork?"

Definitely not a stork. Did that mean the Drone was alive? Was he still here? I clung to Jesse's neck, shoving my arms beneath the bow and wrapping my legs around his thighs. I wasn't wearing clothes, but he didn't push me away. Instead, he moved a hand around my waist, holding my body against his, while the other cupped the side of my head.

His gaze landed on mine and widened. "Jesus, what happened to your face?" He swiped his thumb over my cheek.

I flinched. "The Drone. He was here."

His expression blanked. "You crossed over?"

"He fucking hit me. How can a dead guy do that?"

I'd tried to make physical contact with Annie and Aaron once, but my fingers just waved through their airy forms.

"He can't. Spirits are just lingering memories holding on. They can't hurt you." He padded around the swelling egg. "Not like this. You must have slipped, hit your face on a rock."

His words didn't match the horror creeping across his face.

"He flew at me, Jesse. *With swinging claws.*" I glared at him. "Claws he didn't have when he died. And I didn't mistake the punch across my face." I sucked in a breath, knowing he needed a few moments to work through his denial. "Do you think—?"

"We watched him die." His tone was low, his eyes hard as they darted up to the dusky expanse of sky.

"We watched him *fall.*"

I'd stabbed a knife in his chest as he stumbled backward into the canyon. Could he have flown out of sight and missed the lava? His face was burned, but his hair wasn't singed. How was that possible?

Jesse glanced around, chewing on his lip. "Think about it. If he was really here, why would he leave?"

Even more perplexing, this place didn't weird me out anymore. It was as if all the niggling feels had vanished with the Drone. But that was beside the point. Jesse still didn't believe me.

I pulled in a slow breath, which did little to calm my irritation. "I'm naked in a pond, coughing up water with a goose-egg on my cheek from my mortal enemy who's supposed to be dead." I jerked my arms out, wobbling in his hold. "And the guy who was supposed to be guarding me thinks I imagined the whole thing."

"Hey." He wrestled my arms back to my sides. "Stop. I believe you, okay?"

Hugging me closer, he rested his chin on my shoulder. I was spectacularly aware of every heated point of contact with him. His hands on my head and waist. My breasts pressed against his chest. My ankles hooked beneath the wet denim on his ass. My body hummed with sensory overload.

He had held me in similar bare-chested positions before but always with a purpose. To fuel my control over aphids. To ward off my nightmares. This though… This was different. I didn't want him to let me go, and evidently, neither did he.

His arms wrapped tighter around my back.

I rested my head on the hard flex of his shoulder. "I felt aphids when you disappeared. What happened?"

"They slipped past the perimeter Georges and Tallis had set up. Too many to count. I was trying to lead them away from you." He kneaded strong fingers along the crook of my neck. "They're getting smarter. More methodical."

Or the Drone was directing them, telling them how to move under our radar, to surprise Jesse. To kill him. I bit down on a shivering breath.

He lowered his brow, settling it against my shoulder. "I heard you screaming my name. I couldn't break away."

The guilt in his voice produced a pang in my chest. "I shouldn't have distracted you." A reminder that the buzzing inside me from earlier was gone. "You killed them all?"

The quiver on his back was half-empty, and the arrows he'd recovered dripped with black blood. And not once did I hear gunfire.

My eyes widened. "What about Georges and Tallis?"

"They're fine, patrolling nearby and making sure I didn't miss any." He sighed against my shoulder. "Thank you for not leaving the pond." His chuckle huffed out, short and strained. "I was convinced you were going to come crashing through the woods, naked and unarmed, and get yourself killed."

"I thought about it."

I ran my nose along the pulsing vein at his neck. The action felt…normal. Even our surroundings, the pond, the gloomy skyline, all of it felt normal.

After a period of silence, he trailed fingers over the swell on my cheek. "The Drone didn't enter the water?"

"No. He backtracked when I splashed him."

"Then we know his weakness."

"The safest place in the world is in the water," I mumbled, absently, eyes on the sky. "Fuck, Jesse. He's alive."

"We'll get him again, and this time we'll cut him up and burn the pieces." He dragged his whiskered jaw from my brow to my temple. Man, that felt nice. Even better was his warm breath on my face. "When we're done with this road trip, let's retire on a boat."

"Deal."

But could I even hope for such a thing? I just needed to cure every nymph on the planet. Survive a fall from a cliff. Gather enough supplies to live offshore. Evade pregnancy, possibly dooming the human race in the process. Oh, and kill the Drone. Again.

Heavy thoughts. I could tell by the sudden grooves in his forehead he was thinking the same things.

For now, I was content to stand in the protection of this pond, wrapped up in Jesse, for as long as he'd allow it. "You know that creepy feeling I had when we first came out here?"

"It's gone."

I leaned back for a better look at his face. "You felt it, too?"

"I feel *you.*" He shrugged. "You're easy to read."

It was more than that, like the man was attuned to my every thought. It made me feel naked, and not in the physical sense.

I glanced at the shore, searching for my weapons. "Uh huh. What am I feeling now?"

"Vulnerable. Unarmed." He lowered his chin, his gaze brushing over my chest as he stroked a finger down my back. Then he looked away and nodded at the tree line. "I hid your guns under the brush."

I shook my head, smiling. "Lucky guess."

When my eyes flicked back to his, he asked, "What did the Drone say?"

Prickles iced down my back. "He knew what his bite would do to Michio."

He inhaled through his nose and leaned in to— *Holy shit.* Was he going to kiss me?

I held still as his mouth lowered to mine, hesitantly, maddeningly erasing the inches. He paused, angled his chin up, and kissed my brow.

Well, it was something, and damn if I didn't memorize the brief brush of his lips, the heat of his exhale, and the tightening of his fingers against my waist and neck.

He lowered my body, steadying me until my feet touched the muddy bottom. Then he reached beneath the surface and tugged a beige bar from his pocket.

I raised an eyebrow. "You have…soap in your pocket?"

"You can thank Georges." He lathered it up. "He tossed it to me when I told him to guard while we bathed." He looked away, his eyes shuttering, and glanced back. "I shouldn't have left you alone."

I strained my vision to examine the surrounding woods, and off in the distance, the shadowy outline of Tallis' shoulders came into view. "But now we have soap." I attempted a smile, and it came easy because *Wow.* I hadn't seen soap since, hell, a lifetime ago. "Wonder what else Georges is keeping from us."

"He found some girly supplies in one of those buildings." He nodded to the structures off to the south.

What did Jesse consider *girly*?

"Like what?"

"You wanna highlight your hair?"

Ridiculous. I shook my head.

"Paint your nails?"

I crinkled my nose.

"How about some Midol for your crabby moods?"

Funny guy. I hadn't had a period in four years because of the IUD. "I'm not crabby."

"Lower your head."

I did, bracing my hands on my thighs beneath the water. He combed the bubbles through my hair, rubbing the bar over my scalp as he went. His fingers were attentive, distracting, magical. All I could do was breathe. So I breathed some more, sucking air as quietly as humanly possible.

"What else did the Drone say?"

He expected me to have a conversation right now? Sweet pissing hell, this was torture.

Bent slightly forward, my upper body was still unnervingly exposed above the waist-deep water as I scrubbed the edges of my fingernails. "He said we want the same thing. Nymphs."

The carved ridges of his abs flexed inches from my face as his fingers worked the bar through the ends of the ratty mess. "You can rinse."

Sweet hell, the hoarseness in his voice and the hooded glaze in his eyes produced a tingly throb between my legs.

Squatting, I dipped beneath the surface and shook out the bubbles. When I rose before him, his gaze lowered. The turquoise necklace he'd given me hung between my breasts, but his eyes were fixed on the *C*-shaped scar that curved from my collarbone to beneath my boob. His lips bowed down at the corners.

Not this again. He had stopped the mastectomy from being

completed, but he blamed himself for not killing my attacker before the dissection began. For that reason alone, I resented the ugly thing.

"If this scar wasn't here," I said softly, "where would your eyes be?"

His head snapped up, mouth set in a grim line. Suds floated along the waistband of his narrow hips, his white-knuckled grip around the soap creating more bubbles.

I grinned. "Taking off those jeans will be fun."

The soap bar plunged into the water between us.

I eyed him through my lashes, and man oh man, that scowl. He was so volatile, standoffish, very much the loner in the group. No wonder his Lakota name was Lone Eagle. But despite his coarse personality, his body was a work of art, every sculpted edge polished and honed with care. From the lean cut of his waist to the broad stretch of his shoulders, corded muscles sloped and flared over a canvas of strength. And those indentions that dipped low on his hips served as a teasing road map to the mystery he refused to expose.

My face heated. I'd never seen him without pants, never felt even a nudge of an erection, but I bet his cock was just as hard and intimidating as the rest of him.

Shit, I was staring. "I just meant… Wet jeans are, you know, heavy, sticky?" *Awkward.*

He cleared his throat and paddled the water for the runaway soap. "I'm multitasking. Laundry and bath. Two birds…" His hand rose, one soap secured.

My bloody clothes scattered the shore. Wish I'd thought of that.

He jerked his chin in the direction of his pack. "I brought you fresh clothes."

Of course he did, always looking after me. As he stood there with water beading on his flat stomach, I wanted to catch those drips with my tongue, follow the rivulets beneath the surface, and thank him intimately.

The hardness in his glare warned me off. Seriously, as an experienced stalker…err, tracker, he was as deadly with those looks as he was with the bow.

I snatched the soap from his hand. "Your turn."

To my surprise, he unstrapped his bow and quiver and sank to his knees. Holding the weapon to the side, he wet his hair then stared up at me expectantly. The way the moonlight glanced off the coppery pools of his eyes… Fuck, he was killing me.

He didn't look at my boobs, which were right there, inches from his face. But we were both aware of my nudity, pretending to ignore the heat stirring the small sliver of air between our bodies.

His distance had become so ingrained, I felt knocked off my axis. My hands actually shook as I pushed the sudsy soap through his hair. The strands fell around my fingers in thick, heavy, shockingly soft clumps.

I'd done this often for Roark and Michio. But Roark's hair was a tangle of dreads and braids, and Michio kept his short, leaving little to hold onto.

A hum rumbled from Jesse's chest. Or was that a moan?

I massaged his scalp, smoothed out the knots, and lost track of time, discovering, giving, and…closing the distance. When his forehead brushed the skin between my breasts, he jerked away, ducked his head, and rinsed.

I chewed my lip, wondering if it would always be this strained between us. The impact of his visions returned with a vengeance, pushing against my chest and weighing down my shoulders.

He stood to his full height, slipped the bow and arrows over his back, and plucked the soap from my grip. I expected him to haul me out of the pond and return to business as usual. We needed to check on Michio and the nymph and give the others a chance to bathe.

But he didn't move. His hair, which normally stuck up in finger-raked spikes, now hung in wet strands across his forehead. His nostrils flared with a deep breath, and his lips bounced between a grimace and a smirk. He seemed to be wrestling with something.

My hand reached up of its own accord and traced the ridges of his chest.

His muscles bunched beneath my fingers. Again, he didn't push me away. He wanted affection, *needed* it. What would he do if I demanded we pick up where we left off in France and move beyond that first and only kiss?

As I roamed his chest, a shudder went through him. There, battling across his expression, was something I recognized. His arousal was palpable, charging the air, shortening his breaths, and spiking my pulse. If I voiced it, would he bolt? Only one way to find out.

"We both want this. If it's your restraint you're worried about—"

"Evie—"

"—I'll stop you. I'll say *no* before it goes too far."

His knuckles blanched around the soap. "I wouldn't…"

"Wouldn't what? Stop?" I slid my hand down the hairless planks of his torso and traced the *V* of his abs. "You wouldn't force me. Trust me to say *no*."

Shadows deepened his dilated pupils. A heartbeat passed. Two. Thr—

Plunk went the soap.

He gripped my waist and yanked me against him, bringing his mouth to mine. The electric slide of lips shimmied through my whole body, the movement of his jaw restrained and slow but deliciously mouth-covering. Finally, he licked along the seam, requesting entry. I gave it up in the next breath and parted my lips.

THIRTEEN

The first touch of Jesse's tongue was a shock to my system. The next came like a tidal wave, ripping through every cell of my body and tingling my fingers and toes. Our mouths melded, our breaths collided, and our hands began to move.

His hands slid into my hair and gripped the back of my thigh. I stretched on tip-toes, climbing his towering frame and hooking my arms around his neck.

Tilting my head with his hand, he deepened the kiss, his restraint loosening with each diving reach of his tongue. "Say *no.*"

To a kiss? I laughed into his mouth and held him tighter. "Not yet."

He dug his fingers against my back, bringing me closer for a better angle against my mouth. I hugged his shoulders, reveling in the slide of our chests. The way he lifted me and the position of my groin against his belly, I knew he could feel the friction of my pubic hair against his skin. He'd never been this close and personal with my nudity.

We kissed for an eternity, making up for so many lost moments. He sucked and licked and ate at my mouth, the intensity and skill of his tongue expressing his thoughts before he spoke them.

"Fuck, Evie." Sultry tones infused his breath. "There was a spring-fed creek near the reservation." His hands roamed the rise of my ass, fingers sliding down the crease and squeezing a fleshy cheek. "The water was so pure and clean you could taste the minerals from the soil and the fallen sprigs of mountain mint." He nibbled, pulling my bottom lip with his teeth. "You taste like that." He sucked on my tongue, released it. "Natural." Another sip. "Vital." Then he kissed me like he was taking the flavor of his memories from my lips.

God have mercy. I was lost in his poetic honesty, the heat of his mouth, the velvety feel of his lips. I wanted to know all of him, feel him, and bite after bite, he fed me more.

The water lapped at our hips, and the humidity in the air enveloped us in a warm cocoon. So many sensations burst inside me, but one in particular concentrated below my waist and throbbed between my legs.

His breathing slowed, and his hands returned to my waist. I felt immediate loss when he tore his mouth away, panting.

"Jesse."

He put his frown on my uninjured cheekbone. "I shouldn't have—"

"Don't ruin it."

His frown became a scrape of teeth across my jaw and ended with a nibble on my lips. "Don't you know? You are my everything. My anguish. My heaven. There is nothing but you."

I hummed, unable to contain the conflicting rush of contentment and loss. "And your visions?"

His palms traveled up my arms, over my shoulders, down my back. He pulled me closer, chests aligned, our breaths in sync. "You are my visions."

I hated them, the omens that burdened him, but my feelings didn't make them go away. "We're not stopping at that kiss." His jaw set, but I kept talking. "Doesn't have to be tonight, but Jesse, we're not going to pretend this didn't happen. We'll work through it, figure it out." I tilted my head to catch his eyes. "Which means more talking. Okay?"

He dipped his chin in a nod, rubbing his cheek against mine. The scruffy hairs on his face tickled against my skin. Just another coarse, masculine attribute that deliciously defined him.

"I have another request."

He looked away, the muscles in his face tightening.

"Are you listening?"

His eyes flicked back to mine.

"Never ever shave that stubble."

He rubbed his jaw, the scratchy sound drifting around us as he returned my grin. "I lost the soap."

What a gorgeous fucking smile. It filled me with all kinds of hope. "I'll trade the last bar of soap on the planet for a kiss like that any day."

His smile dimmed to a smirk then faded completely. His eyes seemed to darken, deepening with purpose and responsibility.

I held his gaze, aware he was seconds from shutting down, and clutched the turquoise stone on my breast bone. "A wise man told me that turquoise strengthens one's ability to love and connect with others."

Though the stone was a gift from Jesse, Akicita had explained its value when he tied it around my neck the first time I left the Lakota in the mountains. It had been with me through some ugly shit, but it had done its job. I'd learned to accept love again, three times over.

Lifting the leather strap over my head, I held it up. When he lowered his head, I secured it around his neck. "Just a loaner. When it's done doing its thing, I want it back."

The corner of his mouth tugged up. "Indian giver."

"Since you gave it to me, I think that makes you the Indian giver."

His hand covered the rock on his chest, and the shadows on his face softened.

"Evie. Evie?" The voice called out behind me, drawled in an Irish accent.

I spun toward it, suddenly blinded by the beam of a flashlight. Jesse took two steps back, his movements rippling the water.

The stark light darted to the shore, and Roark's worried expression appeared through the lingering spots in my vision. "Doc did a legger."

"What the hell does that mean?" Jesse snapped, already on the move.

I rubbed my forehead, my attention on the trees. "Means he ran."

Jesse threw his arms up. "You're supposed to be watching him."

Roark jogged to the water's edge. "Have ye seen how fast the bugger moves? What was I supposed to do? Hack off his noggin?"

My heart gave a horrified thump. "No! If anyone—" My voice came out harsher than I intended. I softened my tone. "If anyone hurts him, I swear—"

"No swearing needed, love." Roark waved the light over the trees. "He wanted to see ye. Couldn't be arsed when I refused him, so—" The flashlight beam flicked back to my eyes. "Wha' the feck happened to your face?"

"We'll get into that *after* we find Michio." I waded to the shore and dressed on autopilot, with Jesse glued to my side.

"Jesus suffering fuck." Roark slammed his boot into a rock, sent it skittering along the shore. "Nothing worse than a standing prick."

Whatever that meant. I pulled on the t-shirt, buttoned the jeans, and gathered my blades from the shore. "It's not like we were keeping him prisoner, Roark."

Of the four of us, Michio had always been the fastest and smartest, trained in hand-to-hand combat and a genius IQ to match. And now? He was a force of nature. Roark wouldn't have been able to restrain him. And I didn't want him to.

If they made an enemy out of Michio, the outcome would be devastating. My heart felt like it was folding in on itself, as if protecting me from some unimaginable decisions on the horizon. But of all Michio's faults—his jealous possessiveness, his omissions of truth, his new *craving*—one thing was certain.

"He would never intentionally hurt me." I finished lacing my boots and strode to the tree line in search of my guns. "I just need to tread carefully."

"And always have backup," Roark bit back in warning, matching my strides.

Jesse jogged ahead and led us to a drooping bush. As he removed my guns from the ground cover, his voice dropped low and growly. "I trust you to say *no.*"

I strapped on my weapons. "I told you—"

His finger pressed against my lips. "I don't mean just me."

Michio. When I glanced at Roark, he had an eyebrow cocked, watching our interaction.

Was this the time to remind Jesse my nightmares were a living hell if I slept without a bed partner, and with Michio out of the rotation, he might have to take a turn in filling the empty spot on my bedroll?

Jesse's eyebrows slanted in a *V*, his gaze tapered with impatience.

Nope. "Fine." It was anything but fine.

Michio was out there somewhere, alone with whatever was happening to his body, and no doubt worrying about me and his place in our group. I'd hated him once, but that hate had been misguided and eventually developed into something selfless and joyous and *safe.*

I held onto that as I walked toward the animal clinic. "Which way did he go?"

FOURTEEN

Nervous energy coursed through my veins as Roark led Jesse and me to a man-made island on the north side of the animal reserve. Took us thirty minutes to hike there in the dark, and not a single trace of Michio. I wasn't sure what worried me more. Finding him mutated into a crazed monster. Or not finding him at all.

But how fast would mutation occur? It had been three months since he was bitten, and I'd noticed very little change, aside from the teeth and the inhuman reflexes, both of which he'd been hiding. What else was he keeping from me?

With Jesse's shadow hovering at my elbow, I walked the edge of a concrete moat of black water, squinting at the strange structure towering over the land at the center. Trees surrounded massive rock walls, which were hollowed out with crevices and caves. Way too many places for creatures to hide.

I couldn't stop my nerves from rattling my voice. "What is this place?"

Roark paused in front of me, his hand resting on the hilt of his sword. "Relax the cacks, love." His gaze roamed the ring of water, snagging on the rippling reflections of moonlight. "It was an island for monkeys. See the vines?"

He pointed to the canopy, and sure enough, braids of thick rope snaked between the trees. But not a monkey in sight. A closer look at the field surrounding the moat confirmed that Georges stood some thirty yards off, rifle in hand. And we left Tallis with Shea, who was still safely caged and sleeping.

I drew a deep breath. "Are you sure Michio headed this way?"

What if he left? Would he do that? Leave me? Panic spiraled through me, but I paced my breathing, shoulders squared, chin up.

"Georges caught movement in his long-range rifle scope." Roark rubbed the back of his neck. "Lost sight of him when he jumped over the water."

Could Michio jump that? The moat was at least fifteen feet across. An aphid couldn't cross it. I spied a bridge on the far shore, but it lay on its side in pieces. And given the pungent smell of algae, I wasn't keen on swimming through fetid black waters to search for him.

"Michio?" My voice echoed through the stale hush, bouncing against the walls of the cavernous habitat. "Are you there?"

"I don't like this," Jesse said, fitting an arrow to his bowstring.

I glanced at the tense pull of his face. "I hope you don't intend to use that on him."

He pressed his lips into a stubborn line then inhaled a long breath. "Doc! Get your ass out here."

Without warning, a surge of energy spasmed through my insides. Restless and disoriented, it spun around my bones with nowhere to go. My knees buckled as I turned, stumbling backward against Roark's chest.

"There's an aphid." I scanned the island, tracing the magnetic hum across the moat. Why hadn't I felt it sooner? I could usually pick up their vibrations within fifty yards. My emotions must've been wreaking havoc on my senses. "It's on the island."

As the words left my mouth, a green glow skittered from the shadows on the other side of the trench. Its hunger hammered my belly from the inside out, wild and vicious, and more desperate than most.

Roark circled an arm around my waist, pulling my back closer to his chest. His other hand raised the sword before us.

"Where?"

Unlike my guardians, my evolved eyesight enabled me to see aphids in the dark, illuminating them like radioactive glowworms. "Ten o'clock. It can't jump the water, right?"

"We're not chancing it." Jesse trained the bow and let an arrow fly, but his aim was off by several yards. "Can't fucking see it. Where, Evie?"

I slid a blade from my arm sheath. "To the left—"

Roark clicked on his flashlight, and the beam caught something stirring behind the iridescent bug. The movement drew my eyes, but that wasn't all. I sensed it, a strange yet familiar presence, like a warm trickle through my veins.

"Wait." I touched Jesse's arm. "Don't shoot."

A man-shaped shadow launched from the rocks and tackled the aphid to the ground. The struggle ended as quickly as it began, and in the next breath, the humanoid head was wrenched halfway around with a fatal crack.

My chest collapsed in a relieved exhale. The attacker was too far away to make out his features, but I knew with certainty who he was. "Michio."

He dropped the limp body, its glow extinguishing with its life. As he rose and stepped into the glare of Roark's flashlight, he seemed bigger, more muscled, and seething with ferocity. It sharpened his cheekbones, set his brown eyes on fire, and graveled through his voice as he shouted across the moat. "Who did that to your face?"

The beam of light illuminated his features, but how the hell could he see mine?

Roark tucked the flashlight under his arm, cupped my jaw, and angled my cheek for a closer look. "The black and blue swelling is fecking pony, love. We need an explanation."

This wasn't the place or time I'd had in mind to tell him about the Drone, but the hard squint of his eyes meant I wouldn't be able to put it off any longer.

I shifted out of his grasp, glanced at Michio, and slid my gaze away. Amid the milieu of looming shadows, the stench of blood, and the chilling glare of my fanged lover, no wonder my skin crawled with icy prickles. I didn't feel the strange nothingness I'd sensed at the water hole, but that didn't mean the Drone wasn't watching us, his evil presence blanketed in darkness. Because evidently, dead or alive, he was hell-bent on haunting me.

Michio prowled to the water's edge, a powerful mass of shirtless brawn. The gleam of Roark's light followed Michio's upper body, which stretched wider, tauter than normal, his posture radiating barely-leashed animosity. Maybe he looked more murderous because of the kill he'd just made with his bare hands. Or maybe it was a result of his changing DNA.

Regardless, he was still Michio, the territorial man I adored, and when his eyes imprisoned mine, the intense devotion reflecting there burned as bright as ever.

I returned my knife to its sheath, holding his gaze. "I had a run-in with Aiman Jabara."

Michio's fists locked at his sides, and sinews corded in his neck.

Roark shifted beside me. "The fuck face is dead." He leaned around me, eyes on Jesse. "Tell me I'm right."

Jesse kept his attention—and his arrow—aimed on Michio. "Can't do that, Priest."

Given the rigidness in Jesse's posture, it was on the tip of my tongue to demand he point the weapon somewhere else. But could I guarantee Michio wouldn't hurt them?

When it came to their safety, failure could not be accommodated or bargained with.

"As I live and breathe." Roark dropped his head back and glared at the black arch of sky. "This day just keeps getting better and better." Then he narrowed tired eyes at me. "Wha' happened?"

Standing at the edge of the moat, three of us on one side, Michio on the other, I tried to ignore the fifteen-foot divide between us. A divide that felt increasingly like an enemy line.

I gave Roark a shaky smile, met Michio's eyes, and told them about my encounter with Aiman.

Aiman and Michio had grown up together in Okinawa,

their fathers stationed there in the U.S. Air Force. I could only imagine how hard this was for Michio. A childhood friend had turned into a genocidal monster, died at my hands, or fucking hell, maybe he didn't, which meant we'd have to hunt him down and kill him again.

As I talked through the confrontation, the muscles in Michio's face tightened in the glow of the flashlight, his chest twitching and stretching, the gunshot wound no longer visible. I lowered my eyes to his feet, which were planted shoulder-width apart, as if ready to fight.

I detailed the Drone's fangs, the wings, and the words exchanged, my voice floating over the moat as I moved my gaze back up Michio's body. Black pants hung loosely over long legs, the waistband dipping beneath the indented *V* of his hips. Carved abs rippled into defined pecs, the thick column of his neck powerfully still as he listened.

I dared to return to his eyes, which didn't blink or waver from mine. "He came to me in dreams when he was alive. Maybe he can do the same in death?"

A hand gripped my arm, and Roark turned me to face him. "Hold on, love, for fuck's sake. You're saying he had a face like a melted wheelie bin? And he couldn't touch the water?" He removed his hand and swiped it roughly over his mouth. "Sounds like the knob licker survived."

I pointed to the bump on my face. "Kinda felt that way."

The stillness around us grew darker, deeper, and I wanted to leave all discussions of the Drone with the creepy shadows and whatever lurked within them.

I nodded at the dead bug behind Michio. "Your eyesight is evolving? You see their glow, don't you?"

"Yes." Michio crouched at the edge of the moat and splashed water over his forearms.

I flexed my fingers, unable to release the tension. "The water doesn't hurt you?"

His head whipped to the side, as if to hide the snarl hissing past his clamped teeth. Then he nailed me with a furious look. "I'm not a mutant, Evie."

With a long forced blink, I broke the intensity of his gaze. "You're evolving."

"We're *both* evolving. I'm offended you think my changes are more repulsive than yours."

Ouch. I gritted my teeth. "You've been infected by the Drone, Michio."

"I'm not him!" he shouted, eyes blazing. Then he rose slowly, jaw set, his fingers scraping over his cropped hair. "I'm the same man you made love to four nights ago."

Jesse flinched beside me, his raised arrow following Michio's head. I glanced at Roark and found him watching me with a squinty glare, the point of his sword digging against the concrete decking.

Why did I suddenly feel like I needed to defend myself? Michio and I had sneaked in a private moment on our last night in the mountains. They had to know, right? Michio was my lover. Didn't mean he sucked my blood and turned me into…whatever he was.

Releasing a tight breath, I returned my attention to Michio's disarming gaze. "What happens if you bite someone? Is the infection transferred through saliva? That's how the Drone gave it to you, right?"

"It's multifaceted." His eyes hardened into brassy shards, swirling with too much goddamned intelligence. "I need time to validate my conclusions."

It fucked with me how little I understood him, the way a nightmare fucked with me—from his unreadable expressions and elusive fighting techniques, to his exotic looks and naturally-toned physique. When I met him, he was dangerous and untrustworthy, but now…now that dangerous distrust was all wrapped up in messy feelings.

"What about sex? What if you transferred your infection when we—?"

"It's not an infection!" His eyes flicked between Jesse and Roark. "Sheath your weapons."

That wasn't going to happen. And his reluctance to answer my questions only infuriated me. Just because he was stronger and faster and smarter, didn't mean I was a pushover.

I couldn't outfight him, but I could affect him with words. "You know why Jesse hasn't slept with me?"

The arrow beside me wobbled as Jesse said in a growly tone, "Now is *not* the time."

Roark rubbed his bare chest. "Nah, I think ye should keep going. Though I might need a garden full of Bushmills for this conversation."

I had no idea how they would react to Annie's warning. And maybe this wasn't the right moment to disclose it, but I sensed something mounting in Michio. Not the same kind of sensation that connects me to aphids, but rather something dark and bitter slithering through the air around him, threatening to steal away the man I loved, the man who desperately wanted a child.

My chest felt like it was wrapped in rubber bands. "The night Jesse and I met, Annie told him how I would die."

A noise rumbled in Roark's throat, and Michio's complexion paled in the ray of the flashlight. I kept talking, explaining each near-death encounter over the past two years, and how Jesse foresaw the order of events and where to intervene.

"That's why you've been throwing her off a cliff?" Roark aimed a pointed look at Jesse.

Jesse nodded, stiffly. "The cliff is next."

In a fluidity of swift movements, he swung the bow over his back, snatched the handgun from my thigh holster, and trained it on Michio. His arm must've grown tired from holding the stretched bow, but neither a bullet nor an arrow would stop Michio if it came to that.

Unless it hit his head? I shoved that painful image past my subconscious.

"Wha' ye haven't explained," Roark said, his glare still locked on Jesse, "is why you're pricking around, your pissflaps clearly itching with desire, when ye could be throwing it into her."

I rubbed my forehead, exasperated. "Thank you, Roark,

for phrasing that so gently."

"We're a bloody apocalypse past gentle, love." He pressed a kiss on my temple and resumed glaring at Jesse.

"If she survives the cliff..." Jesse glanced at my stomach, his eyes shutting briefly and flicking back to Roark. "She'll die from a pregnancy."

Roark laughed, but it was strained and cut short. "Then we'll glue our dicks to our fecking legs."

This, coming from the celibate one. Guess that made him an expert on glued dicks.

"There's more." A muscle jerked in Jesse's jaw, the gun in his hand resolutely aimed on Michio. "The aphids are evolving. Isn't that right, Dr. Nealy?"

We were back to proper names? Not that Jesse and Michio had become best buds, but this was Jesse drawing a clear line of separation.

Michio cocked his head. His blank expression gave me nothing to go on, but his stance was tenser than I'd ever seen. If I had to guess, I'd say he was as scared as I was about his status in our group.

He cleared his throat. "The older mutations are adapting. I've been monitoring their progress since day one. Based on empirical evidence, the aphids are evolving in intelligence, physiology, and behavior." He nodded over his shoulder at the dead bug. "When you were taking Evie's blood, Amos told me he hadn't fed this aphid since he trapped it on the island."

My breath caught. "When did he trap it?"

"Two years ago."

Two years without eating.

"Wha' a fucking fuckhole." Roark swung his bulky body into a furious pace along the moat. "An actual national fucking fuckhole. Bet they'd survive a nuclear blast, and do ye know why?" He pivoted back toward me, his eyes ten shades of frustrated. "Because they're cockroaches. Clatty, freckly, sloppy-cunt cockroaches. It's not even funny."

Were there even enough bullets left in the world to wipe

them all out?

I looked at Michio. “But nymphs can starve? Amos said he had to feed Shea to keep her from getting worse.”

Michio nodded.

“Evolving creatures,” Jesse said, “are why this prophesied pregnancy is troublesome.” In a monotone voice, he explained the final prediction, the child that could save the human race, *his* child, and the price of bringing her into the world. “This pregnancy would destroy the very reason we fight day after day, the only reason we continue to live.”

I closed my eyes against the severity of their gazes pressing against me. “I’m not the only reason—”

“You are,” Jesse said, simply.

A calloused finger traced the skin around my eyes until I opened them.

Roark stared back from inches away, worry lines spreading across his raw expression. "You really are, love."

A sharp twinge pinched my chest and stuttered my breath. “And you are mine.”

If the roles were reversed, I couldn’t fathom letting one of them die to save the faceless humans of future generations. The integrity and goodness in the men I loved was certain. I couldn’t say the same about the men this cruel world would breed going forward.

No one said a word as Jesse rehashed the validity of the prediction and the looming what-ifs he and I had already discussed.

When he finished, the silence dragged out for an eternity. It was more uncomfortable than I’d imagined it would be. Neither Roark nor Michio commented on Jesse’s conviction about the child being his. And they didn’t ask for my thoughts on the vision, which hovered somewhere between horror, confusion, and overwhelming indecision. In turn, I didn’t prod them to voice theirs. I wanted each of them to come to terms with this on his own.

Eventually, Roark broke the silence. “Not that it matters, seeing how I’ve only been sexually ravaged once in me life.”

He slid me a smirk that quickly flattened into a sober line. "I'm infertile."

"What? How?" I studied his pensive eyes and followed his gaze across the moat.

Michio stood tall and foreboding, like the rock structure behind him. "When he was imprisoned on Malta, I ran some tests on his sperm."

My breath left me. "What the flipping fuck?"

"With my permission." Roark squeezed my hip. "The good doctor made some valid points about ye being the only surviving woman amid the dwindling human race." He shrugged. "So I splooged in a cup and let him poke around me clackers."

"His sperm ducts are damaged," Michio said. "Whether it's genetic or a problem during development, his tubes cannot transport sperm."

Was the flutter in my chest from relief? Or apprehension? Roark never expressed desire for kids, so this was an advantage for him, really. He could have me without worrying I'd get pregnant and die. That was, if he gave up the whole celibacy thing.

I shared a look with Jesse and knew he was thinking the same thing.

Michio shoved his hands in his pockets and stared at the murky water between us. "I don't have the proper equipment to validate if my fertility has changed after the bite, but Tallis and Georges were able to find a home sperm test."

The pharmacies might've been picked over, but it made sense that fertility products were left behind. But where was he going with this?

He looked up and met my eyes. "I used it on myself the last night we were in the mountains."

"Why? Until now, you didn't know about the prediction. Yet you checked this a week ago?"

"I'm going through so many changes, I had to know." He looked away, scanning the field at my back, then returned to me. "I had to know if I could still father a child."

His guarded tone produced a cold sweat on my spine. He did this test *after* our argument about children.

I wasn't sure what to make of that. "And?"

"My sperm count is zero." His voice dropped, low and pained. "An apparent effect of the bite."

My heart constricted. Knowing how badly he wanted a child, a heavy pang swelled inside me, made worse by the physical distance between us. I ached to wrap my arms around him. "I'm so sorry."

His chin dipped. "The home test is ninety-five percent accurate, but sperm count is only one factor in a man's fertility. I need to run more tests."

"Fertile or not," Jesse said, switching the gun to his other hand without lowering it, "you are not fucking her."

Michio's head snapped up, and two white points glimmered menacingly between his lips. "That's Evie's decision, not yours."

"Some massive set of teeth ye got there." Roark rolled back a shoulder, casual as can be, but I didn't miss the tightening of his fingers as he dangled the sword. "Ye could eat a face through a fecking letterbox."

"I would *never* harm her." Michio remained as still as a statue.

My lungs burned as I breathed in the stifling atmosphere, the air thickening with the gravity of Roark's and Michio's infertility. It meant Jesse didn't necessarily have supernatural baby-making genes. No, the startling revelation was, of my three guardians, he was the only one who *could* impregnate me. Just as Annie prophesied.

A pregnancy I wouldn't survive. We were all thinking it, and the moat dividing our group grew tenuous. I knew, could feel it brewing deep in my core, that Michio was a desperate breath away from jumping the water to get to me. Then what? I wasn't sure.

He stared at me for a long moment, long enough to signal a tinge of fear to my brain. *Run.*

I jerked to backup, *to run*, but didn't finish the step before

Michio bolted into a dark streak, leaping over the moat and straight toward me. He was so damned fast I thought he'd sprouted wings.

Jesse fired the gun, over and over, each ear-splitting burst stopping and restarting my heart. But I knew the bullets hadn't hit him. His approach was too swift, his movements indistinct to the eye.

I didn't have time to run or fight or draw a breath. One moment I was standing there, and the next I was pinned against Michio's chest. Then we were moving at an inhuman speed, his legs blurring beneath me as he carried me into the night.

FIFTEEN

My hair whipped in my face, and my pulse pounded past my ears. At the rate of speed Michio was running, it felt like I was hurling through a tornado on a sportbike.

As much as I wanted to let go of his shoulders and reach for the carbine strapped to my back, it wasn't the best plan. Maybe I'd survive a fall at this velocity, but goddamn, it would hurt. I'd definitely break a bone.

There was also the little issue involving my aching need to help him, not hurt him.

Leveling my mouth at his ear, I screamed, "Slow the fuck down."

The wind caught my voice and tossed it behind us. Cradled in the unbending cage of his arms, my body barely jostled with his fluid sprint.

I flattened a hand on the bare skin of his shoulder blades, half-expecting to find wings, but instead my fingers slid over ridges of muscles bunching beneath smooth, hot flesh.

The field he just bolted through lay silent and unruffled, a trail-less expanse of grassy ground stretching to the moonlit backdrop. Somewhere back there, Jesse and Roark would be tracking us, at a much slower clip.

"Michio, stop." I dug my fingernails into the hard flesh of his back.

The son of a bitch picked up his pace.

"Where are you taking me?"

"Not far." His voice feathered out, easy and measured.

How was he not winded? It wasn't human. *He* wasn't

human.

My skin shivered where it pressed against his, and my head spun with dizziness. "This is unnecessary. Put me down, and we'll walk there together."

He laughed, more like an incredulous huff, as his legs surged in a haze through the tall grass, taking me farther and farther away from Jesse and Roark.

Blasts of air chased my pulse into a faster rhythm, cleaving sharp pains in my chest. I shoved my hair from my face. "You're scaring me."

He sliced his eyes to me, his expression startled, maybe even heartbroken. I didn't trust him, but with his face so close, I did the only thing I could think of to slow him down.

I kissed him. First, on his cheek, then I slid my lips to the spot beneath his ear, my breathing ragged and desperate.

"Evie."

His growl chilled my blood, but I didn't back off.

I kissed along his hairless jawline, and his steps faltered. When I leaned closer to kiss the corner of his mouth, he angled his head away.

"I know what you're doing."

Wish I could say the same about him. I shoved at his chest, going nowhere. "Let me go!"

A breathless moment later, he slowed to a walk. "We're here."

I turned my head to find the animal clinic twenty yards away. The broad outline of Tallis' back filled the doorway, illuminated by the interior glow of a kerosene lamp.

As I opened my mouth to shout, Michio muffled it with his hand, his other restricting my thrashing body in a painful arm lock. "Not a peep, or I'll knock him out."

He'd lost his goddamned mind. My eyes widened with a mixture of terror and venom as I nodded reluctantly.

He released my mouth and arm, soundlessly darted around the building, and holy shit, we were going up. As he scaled the ladder on the stony backside, I reared back a fist to smash his face. But the plan was as fleeting as the ascent. Before I connected with his jaw, my feet touched the flat roof, and the warmth of his body was gone.

Heart racing, I released the carbine from its sling on my back and aimed it at his twisted fucking brain.

He stood a few feet away, arms at his sides, and cocked his head. "You're not going to shoot me."

A swallow lodged in my throat. Could I paint the shingles with his brain matter? I didn't want to. Heaven help me, it would destroy me, but adrenaline and fear made people do desperate things.

"Right now, anything's possible." I stretched a shaky finger over the trigger. "Why did you bring me here?"

He slid a hand in his pocket and walked a slow circle around me, his posture relaxed, his eyes on the pitch-black horizon. "We don't have much time before they catch up."

Pivoting on the balls of my feet, I followed him with the barrel of the carbine. I didn't even consider fleeing. He'd stop me before I made one step toward the ladder. How long would it take Jesse and Roark to find me? Thirty minutes?

I refused to fear this man and straightened my spine. "Good thing Jesse's an excellent tracker. What do you want?"

He stepped an arm's length away and inclined his head. "Put the gun down."

"Fuck y—"

Air brushed against me, and my arms suddenly lightened. The gun…

It sailed off the front side of the roof. Dazed, I stared at my empty hands then at his casual stance a foot away. What the unholy fuck? I hadn't even seen him move.

A tremor shook my body. I didn't stand a chance.

"Evie?" Tallis' Australian accent floated up from the front lawn.

My breath hitched.

"Let him see you. Then make him go away."

Michio's whisper lacked any hint of emotion, but his dark eyes promised Tallis would wake with a busted skull—or maybe not wake at all—if I set off alarms.

With cautious steps, I moved to the edge. If Michio intended to harm me, he would've taken me off the property, far out of reach of the others. But how much of the Drone's evil was circulating in his blood? How much control did Michio have over himself?

Waffling on a plan of action, I plastered on a lazy smile and peered over the low wall. "Hey."

"You dropped your gun, mate." Twelve feet below, Tallis held up my carbine and pursed his lips.

One look at his adorable face decided it. I couldn't put him at risk. "Yeah, I'm…uh, having a little tiff with Michio. You know how we like to work things out with our hands." No truer words. The first time Michio fucked me was during a no-holds-barred scuffle of bruising punches and kicks. "We need some privacy, okay?"

"The doctor's with you?" Tallis didn't move, boots planted a foot apart, shoulders squaring with tension. "Where's Jesse?"

"He's on his way back. Didn't he say Shea was your number one priority? We really need your focus on her until he gets here."

He glanced at the valley behind him, at the doorway of the animal clinic, then lifted his eyes to me, his voice lowering. "If you call for me, I'll hear you."

With that promise, he strode into the building below.

A gust of air vacated my lungs. Jesse had my handgun, but I still wore four knives on my arms.

Without turning around, I asked quietly, "What do you want with me?"

"Sex."

No emotion. No elaboration. The man who had surreptitiously and cleverly seduced his way into my heart was nowhere to be found.

Stabbing six inches of high-carbon steel between his eyes sounded more appealing by the second.

With the speed of a single heartbeat, I plucked a blade from its sheath, spun on my feet, and flung it toward his face. It whistled across the distance and clanked somewhere behind his dodging head.

The musculature of his bare torso looked menacing in the dim moonlight as a smile slanted his mouth, his voice deep and husky. "Do it again."

He was toying with me, knowing full well there wasn't a chance in hell I'd hit him. And deep in my soul, I knew I didn't want to. Still, I refused to go down easy.

I released another knife, sucked in a breath, and ran toward him, swinging the blade at his face.

He sunk on flexed knees, snapped his hands up, and drove a palm against the outside of my striking arm. The action smacked the knife from my grip and sent my forward motion whirling sideways.

I stumbled to right myself, too slow. His chest collided with my back, his weight an inescapable force barreling down on me, aided by the sweep of his leg.

My feet lost purchase, flailing out behind me, and I slammed chest-down against the roof. The strength of his body pinned my chest to the hot shingles.

Motherfucker never held back when he fought me, and now… "Arrgh! You fucking asshole." I was so fucked.

He wrenched my arms behind my back and restrained them with one hand against my backbone. I bucked against him, twisting my wrists, unable to break the hold. To my horror, he removed his belt and coiled it around my arms.

I redoubled my efforts, kicking for leverage and scratching at the skin on his stomach as the shingles seared my face. "Don't do this."

Unsure of what *this* was, I was damned certain I didn't want to find out.

Given the unforgiving cinch of the belt, the set of his jaw, and the strength of his legs trapping mine, he was operating on pure instinct.

"Michio." I writhed and spat and wore myself out. "You're hurting me. You don't want to do this."

"Just listen." His snarl seared my neck in wet heat. "Don't speak until I'm done. Then you can fling your knives anywhere you want."

Pinpricks tingled my fingers, and my hands numbed from lack of circulation. But I stopped fighting, my muscles heavy with exhaustion.

He straddled my thighs, his chest a lead weight against my restrained arms and back, and his forearms caged my head. "Take a deep breath."

Seriously? The bastard was crushing my lungs.

He didn't move, simply waited until he had my undivided, bound-by-a-fucking-belt attention. "If Shea's recovery follows Elaine's, she'll experience flu-like symptoms for a week. Force fluids. Broth if you can find it. After a couple days, make her eat."

What? I turned my neck to look at him, the grit from the shingles tearing into my cheek. "Why are you telling me this?"

His expression, threatening with its ruthless, sharp lines, was enough to shut my mouth. "I knew something was wrong within days after Aiman bit me."

I thought back to that day in Iceland, when Michio lay on the edge of the lava canyon with the Drone's fangs buried in his shoulder. I'd been so desperate to help him, I offered myself in his place, to be the Drone's snack. What would've happened if the Drone had bitten me? How would it have affected my already changing biology?

Michio continued, "While you were training and hunting with Jesse and Roark, I tested my blood on the aphids I found in the mountains."

And here I thought the sneaky jerk had stayed behind to take care of Elaine.

"My blood has the same lethal properties as yours. Explodes the aphid's heart within seconds. I also concluded we are *both* immune. Neither of us carry the infection nor would we mutate from a bite."

We'd already suspected my immunity. But his?

"You tested this?" Sweat gathered on my neck. "You let an aphid bite you?"

He nodded.

I balled my hands into fists. What a reckless fucking decision, one he'd made with the hope his science wouldn't be proved wrong. And those harrowing minutes afterward, waiting to mutate or not. What if he had? Did he even consider what that would've done to me?

"I hate you for taking such a selfish chance with your life."

"You don't hate me." His palm swept down my arm, his voice soft and coaxing. "And now we know."

"How is it possible? Aiman was infected. He would've transferred—"

"Before he bit me, he consumed Frida's blood, remember?"

Frida. The nymph I'd cured in Iceland. The woman Aiman killed shortly after.

"Whatever you passed along to her cured Aiman of the aphid infection, because *I* don't have any of the aphid traits."

Then it clicked. "You have *my* traits. My speed, my night vision, my—"

"Sex drive," he said.

I clenched my teeth. Once upon a time, I'd been diagnosed as a sex addict, but I thought the apocalypse had cured me of that. The whole fighting-everyday-for-my-life thing didn't leave a lot of room for addictions.

Also, now knowing what I did about my high testosterone and its effect on libido, I wondered if I'd been misdiagnosed. "If what you're saying is true, wouldn't I be passing my traits to the nymphs I cure? Elaine might be a horny little man-stealer, but she didn't show signs of evolving strength and speed."

"Elaine is…" His eyebrows pulled together.

"Useless?"

"A weak sample," he corrected, in his professional tone. "Time will tell with Shea."

"Why did you tell me how to care for her? Where are you—?"

"Let me finish," he snapped. "Have I made it clear enough

that I have *not* contracted the aphid infection?"

I nodded, but it didn't dismiss the fangy-spider shit poisoning his veins.

"And since a cured woman reversed Aiman's aphid infection, it suggests that the *cured* can cure other nymphs."

Hallefuckinlujah. I could actually feel some of the tension in my chest loosening and falling away. But with all good things, there was always a downside. Like how I could telepathically command aphids but needed physical contact with a man to power the energy. What was Michio's handicap?

His body crowded closer around mine. He must've read the question in my eyes, and I suddenly feared the answer.

"When I take your blood for regular testing..." His hands gripped my head roughly, one on my nape, the other wrapped around my jaw. "I've been ingesting what I don't use."

Ingesting? Horror crashed over me. "You drink my blood?" My face ground against the rooftop as I tried to jerk free. "Oh my God, why would you do that?"

"Your blood doesn't reverse my changes, but it makes me stronger." Something nebulous and foreboding darkened his expression. "It satisfies the cravings."

Ice enveloped my spine. "Blood?"

"Yes. The hunger is prominent during extreme emotion or pain." He held my head in an iron grip, forcing my eyes to his. "And arousal." He lowered his razor-sharp gaze to my neck, to the pulsing artery right there, an inch from his mouth. "And when I've lost a lot of blood. Like tonight."

I curled my fingers, trying and failing to reach the belt that imprisoned me. "If you fucking bite me, I won't think twice about testing the various ways your new genetics can heal you."

He stared at me blankly, then a goddamned smile twitched his lips. "There was enough left in the blood dart to take the edge off."

The one he'd used on Shea. I felt sick, so fucking horrified my voice choked with it. "Does it have to be my blood?"

"Yes."

"How do you know?" *Oh God.* "You sampled Elaine's?"

"Yes, from a syringe. Her blood is ineffective. Impotent." He rested his forehead against my temple, his grip on my head stopping my attempt to turn away from him. "Just as your adapted genetics drive you to hunt the aphid, the arachnid strand in me seeks the coccinellidae."

The ladybird. When my DNA evolved, it took on the characteristics of the aphid's predator. Even if I didn't believe Michio's research, I had a dozen spots on my back to prove it. And since spiders preyed on ladybirds… "I have a predator for a guardian. Are you hearing yourself? What am I supposed to do with that?"

Something shifted in the way he restrained me. He didn't relax his grip on my head or lighten his weight against my back, but it felt more…purposeful. More intimate. With my ass flush with his groin and our lips so close together, his aggressive imprisonment of my body suddenly felt aggressively sexual.

He lifted his head, and his hypnotic eyes became my focal point, a view that could seduce me, consume me…infect me. No biting needed.

My breathing sped up, and my face burned in the possession of his gaze. "Why didn't you tell me about the cravings? About all of it?"

"The last thing you needed was the burden of another person dependent on your blood." His hot breath fanned over my cheek. "Because I need it, Evie. Desperately. I've never felt anything like this…this need to devour you." His body grew heavier on top of me, his hips pressing against my ass. "*While* I'm deep inside you."

A shudder raced down my spine, but rather than tensing to fight, my body melted beneath the grind of his pelvis, the unmoving confinement of his arms, and the hard swell his erection trapped against the seam of my jeans. How could he disgust me and turn me on at the same time?

This was bad, so fucking wrong. I sensed it in the tingle of my skin against his, in the booming tempo of my heart, and in the ache gathering between my legs in anticipation of being stretched and filled. Had he cast some kind of spell over me?

Somewhere amid the debilitating lust, I found the strength to recoil from his hips. "Don't do this. You'll infect me."

Even as I said it, I knew he wouldn't. We'd had sex numerous times since he'd been bitten, and on several occasions, his teeth had drawn blood. So why was I trembling with fear now?

He grabbed my throat in a bruising grip and yanked my face toward him. "The arachnid pathogen can only be transferred through the venom glands."

He parted his mouth, and his canines stretched before my eyes. Two ivory blades, whiter than the moon, protruded between his full lips.

My heart slammed against my ribs, and my mind screamed *vampire*. Of course, vampires didn't exist, but given this world I was in now—with insectile creatures and winged men who came back from the dead—would vampires really be that strange?

"The glands are located in the hollowed grooves." His tongue glided over a fang, and his voice reverberated in smooth, heated tones, a mesmerizing melody of sensuality and power. "I can extend and retract the teeth at will."

"Put them away," I said hoarsely.

He wrenched my head back with a hard jerk and exposed my throat, his breath dragging over my skin. His chest crushed my back, his lips moved to the curve of my neck, and as his face moved closer to mine, his eyes…fuck. They lured me in, and it was so very, very dark in there. I couldn't speak, couldn't breathe.

His entire being transformed into a seductive command. One look controlled the tightening of my gut. A single touch gripped my spine. And the curl of his lips opened the vast, hungry reaches of my sexuality.

SIXTEEN

"Michio." I twisted my arms in the binds and scraped my boots over the roof shingles, panic rising with my voice. "This is *not* okay."

With his chest pressed against my back, he replaced his lips with his teeth and dragged the sharp points down the side of my neck. "I can bite without releasing the spider pathogen."

He could draw blood without injecting me with the toxins? I shuddered against the stinging scrape, my muscles locked with fear and an unnerving amount of arousal. He terrified me, and I still wanted him, which scared me even more. He was so beautifully and intellectually compelling I felt hooked by a wire. A wire of unbreakable energy, pulling me to him.

"Are you bewitching me? This…this"—*Magnetism. Allure. Possession*—"whatever this is. Are you doing this?"

He leaned back and studied my face, his eyes cutting through me like amber glass. Then he shoved a hand around the curve of my hips, finding the button at my waist, releasing it. The zipper followed, and his finger found my center, slipping through the slick evidence of my desire.

"Oh, Evie," he breathed against my neck. "This is all you."

I had a millisecond to squeak an incoherent objection before he breached my opening, sinking two fingers to the knuckles.

Sharp, tingling pleasure electrified my inner muscles. "Ahhhh, fuck."

His touch, this connection…I wanted it, needed more.

I trust you to say no.

I bore down against the diabolical curl of his fingers and clenched my legs. "Stop it." My voice was breathy, unconvincing. "Remove your hand." Still fucking breathy.

In a blur of urgency, he yanked my jeans to my boots and released the belt from my arms. Suddenly free of his weight and restraints, I flipped over and snapped up my hands to punch him.

He caught my wrists an inch from his face and slammed them against the shingles above my head. But it was the pained look on his face that knocked the wind from my lungs. "I'm leaving, Evie. This is our last night."

My head swam through the fog of arousal, trying to catch up yet still stuck on the fact I was naked from the waist down, vulnerable against his will.

With one hand, he held my arms above my head. The other fumbled with the fly on his pants.

He was going to give me what I needed, and that realization heated my skin with equal measures of relief and alarm. "You can't leave."

He shoved his hips between my legs, which were restrained by the fabric around my ankles, and the head of his cock pressed against my opening.

What was I doing? There would be consequences, *something*.

I grabbed hold of the first repulsive image that popped in my head. "Are there venom glands in your cock?"

"What?" His eyes widened. "Fuck no." He pressed his erection closer, perfect alignment. "Now shut up."

"We shouldn't—"

He thrust.

The invasion sparked a cascade of bliss through every cell in my body. He didn't give me time to adjust, seating himself to the hilt, pulling out, and pounding inch after vicious inch of his length inside me. Hard as steel, he fucked me with vigor, endless stamina, and dominating skill.

Was it better than all the previous times because his body was stronger, more potent? Or because the danger and risk felt so insanely right? Or maybe it was because he'd threatened this would be our last night together?

The reason didn't matter. I loved it, needed it, and never wanted it to end.

Then my thoughts hurdled to Jesse, his hands around my throat, strangling me with his rage. Maybe I didn't tell Michio *no* because he'd explained how the venom was transferred. Maybe I let him in my body because I thought it would make him want to stay. Or maybe it was simply because I loved this man and would do anything to hold onto him.

His pace picked up, centering my attention fully on him. Frantic and powerful, his body flexed above me in a massive ripple of strength, grinding my tailbone painfully yet ravishingly against the roof, the hot shingles burning my skin. I rocked with him, arching my back and widening my knees, proving I was still with him. He didn't have to leave.

Our hands laced above my head, and his mouth slammed onto mine, his kiss feverish yet lacking the sharpness of oversized teeth. Had he sheathed them? I didn't care, kissing him back with greedy licks, tongues lashing and rubbing, our breaths melding.

He united our bodies in a fury of thrusts, his sweaty, hairless chest moving over me, and his growly moans in my ear. It was carnal, wild, free of barriers and scientific studies and harrowing premonitions.

I felt his need as if it were my own. His breaths, his heartbeat, his urgency, it was all mine. Like a molecular fusion, a binding of energy.

It didn't take long for the ecstasy to build and peak. My legs shook, my ass burned against the shingles, and my nipples tightened into painful points against my shirt. "I'm there. Oh fuck, oh fuck, don't stop."

Groaning, he thrust harder, more frenzied and frantic than ever, his hands shifting to grip my waist and his brow dropping to mine. As I tumbled into that glorious place between the rise and fall of heaven, the drive of his hips lost rhythm, the noises in his throat deepened, and his body trembled violently.

He slammed to a stop, his cock buried as deeply as possible, and met my eyes. "Evieeeee."

I watched him as he watched me, captivated, lost. *Happy.* His climax was the most beautifully human thing I'd ever witnessed.

As we came down, a sultry hush enveloped us, stirring with the heave of our breaths. Disoriented by the aftershocks of orgasm, my body deliciously crushed by the weight of his, I rested my gaze on his sweat-slicked face, half-mast eyes, and satisfied smile.

"You're so exquisite and fierce. Raw perfection." He looked me dead in the eyes, and I knew he meant it. It was there in the gentle stroke of his finger over my bruised cheek and in the worshiping kiss of his fang-less mouth. *He* was there, my doctor, the guardian of my body, the man I fell in love with.

"So are you." But with those words, reality settled in. "Don't leave. We'll work this out."

He pushed himself up, his lips flattened into an expression of resignation. He yanked my jeans into place with determination, tugging and pulling as he shoved them up my hips.

He adjusted his own pants, his face blanking, and his tone hollow. "I have to go after Aiman."

I zipped and buttoned my jeans, my heart rate jumping back to hysteria. "He'll kill you."

He knelt between my legs and pulled me to him, chest-to-chest, my body mirroring his. "I can sense him. Not now but earlier tonight."

Did that mean Michio could sense *me*? Because the connection I'd just felt during sex had gone beyond physical. Of course, we'd always connected on a deeper level, but this time left me profoundly shaken.

He brushed the hair from my face and tucked it behind my ear. "I can't explain it, but I..." He closed his eyes, opened them. "I have to go to him." His head snapped up, his gaze narrowing on the ladder on the backside of the roof. "They're coming."

Jesse and Roark? I focused, listening, hearing nothing. How did Michio hear them? Some weird spidey sense? I moved to put some distance between us, but he grabbed my hips and held me in place.

My palm rested on his face, my thumb moving over his soft upper lip. No fangs. "Let me talk to them first. I'll explain—"

Footsteps landed on the roof, then Jesse's arrow was there, bow stretched, the sharp point touching Michio's temple. From the other side, Roark's sword appeared beneath Michio's chin, pressing against his throat. Both Jesse and Roark were still naked above the waist, a reminder that they'd stripped their shirts in their urgency to stanch Michio's gunshot wound.

Given the stiffness of his scruffy, blond jawline and the give-me-a-reason-to-throw-down creases around his eyes, Roark wanted to finish this with his fists. "Let her go, Doc."

I caught Michio's eyes, silently begging him to release his grip on my hips, but my words were for Jesse and Roark. "You don't need the weapons. If he was a threat, he would've attacked you before you made it to the roof. But you can see, he's here, on his knees, making himself vulnerable."

Calm and composed, Michio held my gaze. "I'm a possessive man, Evie." His hands tightened, fingers digging into my waist. "But I trust them with your life. Enough to leave you with them, to do whatever makes you happy."

There was unspoken meaning there. A willingness to compromise, to share me with them. Which really meant jack shit, considering he meant to leave me with a celibate priest and spirit walker bound by a vision.

My hands curled into fists. "Don't you dare leave."

"What's he talking about?" Jesse said, his eyes tapering into slits.

Michio turned his head toward Jesse, as much as the nocked arrow would allow. "I owe you my life. Both of you." He glanced at Roark and back at Jesse.

Roark leaned down and clamped a hand on Michio's shoulder. The gesture might've been touching if he'd lowered the sword. But it remained lethally angled at Michio's jugular. "Ye referring to the dungeon? I den' think Evie would've let us leave ye there."

Jesse shifted his weight, confusion etching his face.

Michio looked at Jesse with something akin to compassion softening his eyes. "I owe you my gratitude and my respect. You carried the burden of Annie's predictions quietly and alone, saved Evie's life time and time again. And the hardest tribulation of all, you love her as deeply as Roark and I do, yet you selflessly prevent yourself from bedding her."

My chest tightened against the truth of his words and the sadness in his tone. "Michio—"

A brush of lips warmed mine, there and gone like a breath. Like the man himself. With a whisper of displaced air, Michio vanished from the spot before me, from the roof, and several anguished heart beats later, I *felt* him leave the property.

I ran to the edge of the roof, willing him to appear in the dark field, to see him running back to me. But the landscape held still. Lifeless. Empty. He'd left, to go who knew where and how far, on foot, *without me.*

Intense, helpless grief ruptured behind my ribs, and my chest collapsed in agony. With the pain, came the events of the night, crashing into me, each one punching that painful spot, over and over. The bullet in Michio's chest, the intimate moment with Jesse, Annie's premonition, the Drone's survival, the evolving aphids. And the final punch…I might never see Michio again. Never feel his arms around me again. Never taste his lips. Hear his voice.

I buckled at the waist and gripped the concrete ledge, my mind shutting down as if trying to evade the painful reality. He'd left to kill Aiman. To protect me. *Because* he loved me. Everything else blurred into one giant *Fuck*.

Jesse and Roark stood on either side of me, their eyes gentle and watchful, and their weapons now sheathed. They remained quiet, giving me time to compose myself. But worry radiated from their taut postures. They needed answers.

I sucked in a few breaths, pulled myself together, and shared what Michio had told me. As I spoke, Roark offered me his hand, and I twined my fingers with his. Then I braced myself as I finished the recitation with, "We had sex."

Jesse grew deadly still beside me, as if everything from his chin down had been forgotten in lieu of whatever was crashing and burning inside his head. He just stood there, expressionless, his eyes on me but not really looking at me. He didn't blink. Didn't speak.

I wasn't sure he was breathing. "Say something."

That got me a blink. His eyes cleared, focusing on mine, his voice in a state of suspended feeling. "I'm processing."

I shot Roark a look. "Then you say something."

His eyelids half-shuttered, framed by a tangle of blond dreads, and his mouth crooked up as if he were on the verge of a colorful insult. But the jade of his eyes became harder, unsmiling, consumed by some internal decision and darkened by a ruminating brow.

Then a somber line replaced the sarcastic smirk. "He didn't bite ye. Didn't take ye off the property. And didn't *force* ye to have sex." He rolled a broad shoulder. "Fair play."

Roark was the epitome of agreeable. He was the wisecracker, the counselor, the roll-with-the-punches guy. So it was easy to forget that when he did strike, it was with lethal decapitation. And beneath that happy-go-lucky exterior, he nurtured some serious passions, one of them being a fierce protection of my heart.

Which was why I wasn't surprised when he shifted into my space, his muscled chest flexing and pushing around me. "But if he tells another spoof, I'll smash his bloody testicles until they turn square and fester."

Spoof? "He didn't really lie, per se."

"He omitted. Same difference."

My hackles went up, and I bit my bottom lip to keep from lashing out. Michio had kept his secrets to protect me.

"There was never any ill-intent," I said.

"Hey, I get your need to defend him." He looked down at me, his brogue warm and thick. "But he's a risk."

"It's not about the risk. It's about persevering, and shattering the boundaries we're facing, and learning from it. Becoming better people for it." I stared across the hush gloom of the valley, my skin dripping from the humidity. "Michio's secrecy wasn't acceptable. But he wasn't the only one keeping secrets." I glanced at the silent man at my side.

Jesse strode away, stopping at the far-side of the roof to collect my knives, his expression concealed by shadows.

Roark nodded at Jesse. "That one's a risk, too. If he puts a child in ye, and that child takes your life, to hell with persevering. I wouldn't want to."

My womb tightened against his words. "I still have the IUD, and he's..." I peeked at Jesse's dark silhouette. "Determinedly abstinent."

"And pissed." Jesse marched back to us and handed me the knives. "I told you not to fuck him."

The disgust in his voice made me feel dirty, cheap, and yeah, really fucking defensive.

I turned to face him, straightening to meet his furious gaze. "If it had been you instead of him, with your fertility taken away and a protective need to leave me, I would've done the same thing. I would've shown you I love you the best way I know how."

Fire burned in his eyes as he said slowly and harshly, "I would never ask that of you."

"You wouldn't have to!"

"He's afraid, love." Roark locked eyes with Jesse. Something unspoken passed between them, something I didn't understand, then Roark continued. "A little rivalry and jealousy is healthy. Jesse's jealousy isn't from greed but from love, and it's nursed with worry." His gaze lowered to mine. "Worry that he'll lose you to a man who can offer you intimacy without killing you."

Jesse glared at Roark like he wanted to throttle him but didn't move a muscle. Nor did he deny what the priest had said.

The turquoise stone lay against his bare chest, serving as a reminder that, not long ago, I was afraid to accept love or any kind of tenderness. I had needed time to learn how to trust again, and apparently, so did Jesse.

With a loss of what to say, I stepped into his space and wrapped my arms around his rigid torso. His hands remained stiffly at his sides, but his chest gave a gentle sigh against my cheek.

I didn't know what I was doing trying to juggle the physical and emotional needs of three men. I had the experience of a fifteen-year marriage, but that was hardly the same thing. If Joel were here, he'd tell me to *listen to the song*, my tactile interpretation of love, like the tingles across the skin, the bounce in a step, and the involuntary pull of a smile.

Jesse remained stubbornly tense in my embrace, and I had a sudden urge to change that. I grabbed his waist, didn't exactly dig my fingers in his sides, but I put some wriggling pressure there, right along his ribs.

He jumped around like crazy, trying to wrestle free of my tickling fingers. And there, shining on his face, was a shocked—but no less gorgeous—smile. "Why did you do that?"

I shrugged, smiling with him.

He brushed away the hair that had fallen across his forehead and stared at me like I'd lost my mind.

Roark's hand found mine, drawing my focus to him and the memory of when I'd found *his* tickle spot. I smiled up at him. "Remember when we were in the bunker—"

"When ye dug your bloody toe in me ribs?"

We'd shared our first kiss that night. Not even a year had passed since then. It felt like an eternity ago.

His thumb stroked my knuckles. "Jaysus, ye were a temptress."

"And you're still a prude."

He chuckled, though we both knew he'd been the one

doing all the tempting.

As silence settled in, the three of us stood at the concrete ledge, watching the dark horizon. No one made a move to climb off the roof, each of us rooted in our thoughts.

Mine centered on Michio, agonizing over his lonely nights, his confrontation with Aiman, and his craving for blood. *My* blood. How long could he go without it? What were the ramifications?

But despite the ache in my chest, logic told me if anyone could defeat Aiman, that person was Michio. Aiman had made a fatal mistake biting one of my guardians. He'd created a powerful enemy, one who would risk his life to save mine.

I swallowed around the mass of emotions in my throat. "What are you guys thinking about?"

"The bug on the island," Roark said. "No sustenance for two years, and the whole time, just a shallow moat away from freedom."

Jesse picked a brittle chunk of concrete off the ledge and flung it into the field below. "A small obstacle for a creature so hard to kill."

"There's power in water," Roark said thoughtfully.

Yeah, but unless his god decided to flood the planet again, or the fertile man at my side put a fatalistic baby in me, the future was fucked. Didn't matter if we found and cured every nymph out there. Since the aphids couldn't starve to death, their numbers would evolve while ours faded away.

Forever outnumbered, scraping by and counting our every breath. What kind of life were we fighting for?

PART 2

SEVENTEEN

I woke alone on a musty mattress, wearing one of Michio's t-shirts that no longer carried his scent. That exotic scent, filled with memories and anguish, punched me right in the gut.

Sucking in a breath, I squinted through the glare of the morning sun that penetrated the open door of the animal clinic. A week had passed since we'd moved the mattress in there. A week since Michio had vanished from the roof.

Given his speed, he could be on the other side of the country by now. But maybe, just maybe, he never left Georgia.

I focused inwardly, searching for a warmth of electricity, the low hum in my veins I'd never noticed until it was gone, until Michio was gone. Was it some kind of supernatural connection? A sixth sense to help me locate him? I didn't know how to explain it, only that I couldn't feel it now. I couldn't feel *him*.

He could be dead.

The hollowness in my chest constricted painfully as I imagined him sleeping alone and unprotected. Then I pictured him fighting the Drone, clenched in a bared-teeth lock of bodies, choking, punching, and spinning through the air like an out-of-control bullet against the force of the Drone's wings.

Michio was a badass, but the Drone was so much more. Michio wasn't using his overeducated brain, running off into the night, thinking he could smite the Drone's brand of evil.

Dumb, arrogant man. Didn't he know he couldn't face the Drone without me by his side?

With Michio's ability to heal, I wasn't sure what he could survive. Could the Drone drain him of blood? Tear off his head? Rip out his heart? An ache swelled behind my eyes and weighed down my limbs. What would I do if I never saw him again?

I imagined him treating his injuries alone, suffering from his cravings, my inability to help him, and his memory of our last night together. The thought gripped my insides and wouldn't let go. I blew out a breath.

Time to stop the unproductive wallowing. Michio didn't have to leave, didn't have to become some lone cowboy to prove himself. So fuck him. My resentment burrowed as deep as my fear for him, like a poisonous fuel burning up my blood. I let it fester and build, because anger was a steadier, more vicious companion than fear. It made me feel in control and resolute. Two things I needed for the road ahead.

I rolled over and found Roark kneeling on the other side of the room. He faced the wall, his broad shoulders straining the seams of his tattered cassock. Head bowed, his breaths rose and fell rhythmically. I didn't need to see his hands to know they were moving methodically over a rosary.

Pushing to sit, my back pinched in pain from the broken mattress springs, but I was used to sleeping on much worse. My attention drifted to the cage across the room, where Shea recovered the past six nights. She was now fully human but still weak. Keeping her behind bars had been the safest solution against an aphid attack.

Only this morning, the cage stood empty. Was she finally strong enough to go for a walk?

Excitement sifted through me. As much as I wanted to stay in Georgia and await Michio's return, I couldn't hold onto that hope. Michio never promised he'd come back. In fact, the night he left, he told me it was our last.

I couldn't let those thoughts cripple me. I had to look forward, get back on the road, and find more women to save.

I rose quietly and tiptoed toward Roark. He looked so chaste and peaceful when he prayed. An untouchable man of the cloth. But that never stopped me.

He didn't look up as I circled his position and crouched before him. His lips moved silently through his prayer, his finger and thumb gliding along each black bead in the strand. He must've been feeling extra guilty for burying his face between my legs last night. And for shoving his fingers in my ass. Oh, and for jerking off on my belly.

I reached out and toyed with a chipped button on his cassock. "God forgives you."

"Ah sure." He didn't look up, his expression creased with concentration. "You're the one who was after suckin' the pipe off me in the focking woods, ye little harpy."

That wasn't true, and he knew it. I'd joined him on his perimeter walk, but it had been him doing the attacking. I didn't deny it though, because I'd damned well enjoyed it.

I flattened my hands on his chest, gliding them over the heavy, black fabric, which was soaked in sweat. I really should just leave him to his penance, but I hated his guilt. Besides, the clerical collar had squeezed his neck into a blistering shade of red. Fucking ridiculous choice of clothes in this heat.

"You're going to give yourself heat stroke." I reached behind his nape, released the snaps and tugged off the white collar, setting it—and the piece of black material attached to it—aside.

His muted prayer hurdled into a vocalization of accented syllables. "Pray for us sinners, now and a' the hour of our death…"

As he continued aloud, I tuned him out and went to work on the buttons along his sternum, popping them free and exposing his hard chest and sexy stomach. His skin felt like fire beneath the brush of my fingers.

"Ach. Stop it." He scooted back on his knees but didn't relinquish his hold on the beads.

"You're burning up, Roark."

He stared at the rosary, his thumb rubbing along the strand.

"So?"

"You sound like a child." I finished the rest of the buttons.

He raised his eyes to the peeling paint on the ceiling and said, "See wha' I'm dealing with? She never listens to me, that one."

With a sigh, I started to stand, but he grabbed my arm and held me in place. "Ye do it."

"Undress you?"

"Aye." He grinned then launched back into his prayer, chanting it out loud.

Moody pain in the ass. I pushed the garment off his shoulders, dragging it to his elbows. Wow. So much better. The deep ridges of his pecs bunched and played beneath my scrutiny.

I traced a finger down the cut lines to the indentions of his hips, which framed bars of muscle on his stomach. All that smooth, tight skin glistened with sweat and channeled into black briefs that sat low on his waist and cupped his groin. So perfectly packaged and ready for handling.

I inched closer and pushed a knotty braid away from his face. Letting my fingers linger on his stubbly cheek, I relished how his prayer cut off with an exhale against my lips.

In the next breath, his hands found my bare ass beneath the shirt, pulling me to straddle his thighs where he knelt. The rosary beads, still tangled in one hand, dug into my butt cheek.

He looked down at me with glittering jade eyes and an indulgent smile. "Mornin', love."

"Good morning, Father Molony." I returned his smile then leaned in to whisper seductively in his ear. "If you move those beads up and a little to the right, you'll find another use for them."

He buried his laughter in the curve of my neck then proceeded to nibble and kiss the skin while he was there. "I should just shag ye and get it over with."

That might've made me breathless, except I'd heard it before. Like every time he got worked up.

With his hands on my ass, he ground his quickly-swelling cock between my legs, separated only by his cotton briefs. If I sat there long enough, he'd dry hump me to exhaustion. Then he'd have to change his underwear. And pray for his sins again. And well, we had shit to do.

But God in heaven, it was hard to deny those hooded eyes and pouty lips.

I cupped his scruffy jaw and kissed him long and hard. "You're a sexy…" I kissed him again. "Wickedly tempting." Another kiss. "Celibate man." I rubbed his tongue with mine until a moan vibrated in my throat. "And I need coffee."

It was his turn to moan. As I stood, he lifted the hem of my thigh-length shirt, the intensity of his eyes heating my already-simmering parts. When he reached out to slide his hand between my legs, I knocked his arm away and went in search of some pants.

He huffed. "Isn't she the bitch?"

Impossible to take offense to that when there was a smile straining behind his lips.

I grabbed the first pair of pants I found on the floor. "Sucks to be teased, doesn't it?"

"I think it's fair to say I'm the only one suffering from a serious chub." He pulled the waistband of his briefs from his stomach and peered down. "Look a' the color of it!"

"I'll pass, drama queen." I gave him my back and dragged on a pair of denim cut-offs. "Where's Shea?"

His arms came around me from behind, his skin warm and bare of the cassock, his hands pushing mine aside to zip and button my fly. "She wanted to go explore. Jesse's with her."

I leaned my head back against Roark's chest, my jaw clamped against unwanted thoughts of Jesse and Shea walking together…bonding. "That's great. She's recovering faster than Elaine."

Like Elaine, Shea remembered nothing of the aphid plague. It would be a kind of bliss, sleeping through the past two years. But her shock over what she'd missed had been painful to watch. Hearing how much the world had changed. Losing her husband and everyone she cared about.

She'd taken it better than Elaine had, but she'd yet to experience the scariest by-product of the virus. She'd yet to see an aphid. I hoped we hadn't kept her *too* isolated in this tiny building.

Roark threw on some cargo pants, strapped on his sword, and strode to the door. Man, he looked good without a shirt. All that golden skin showed off his muscle definition. And the pants barely clung to his narrow hips under the weight of the sword.

I snapped out of my hungry trance, gathered my weapons, and shoved my feet into boots. "Where are you going?"

He paused outside the door and glanced back at me with smiling eyes. "Figured ye wanted to find Shea before she molested your Lakota."

I walked past him and stopped. "What's that smell? Do you smell it?" I looked around and met his eyes. "Oh. Never mind. It's just you. The shit stirrer."

The field swallowed his laughter, but his words…yeah, those stuck with me. Shea seemed like a nice lady. Quiet. Unassuming. And sick with fever. What was she like at full health? What if she was Jesse's *type*?

I paced my steps, trying not to hurry. This was reality, just another obstacle on an endless road. I would confront my competition like I confronted everything else. Armed with possessiveness and high-carbon steel.

EIGHTEEN

Ten minutes later, Roark and I emerged from the field and found Jesse leaning in the doorway of the only residential house on the animal reserve. The home Shea used to share with her husband.

I stepped beside Jesse, a little taken back by the fatigue reddening his eyes. I shouldn't have been surprised. With Michio gone and Roark sleeping at my side, he was running a skeleton crew on the night shift. But I was willing to bet Tallis and Georges were getting more sleep than my overprotective guardian.

His faded jeans encased his ass and hips too well for my wandering eyes, but they were covered in rips and dirt, and who knew what those black stains were? The sleeves had been torn off his button-down shirt, and it looked like a rat had nibbled through the collar. Somehow, the homeless look made him even more tempting.

I glanced at the floor, feeling like a thoughtless, fickle bitch after the breathless moment I'd just shared with Roark. They made it hard to *not* be attracted to them. Impossible to *not* entertain fantasies. But it wasn't their fault. I needed to spend less time ogling them and more time considering their feelings.

Jesse turned his head, drawing my eyes back to him, and gave me a head-to-toe once-over. "Sleep well?"

I nodded. "When was the last time *you* slept?"

His gaze darted back to the front room of the two-room house. A stained couch, recliner with tattered arms, and small kitchen table with mismatched folding chairs lined one wall of the living and kitchen area. The windows were barred and closed, so the musty scent of damp dirt must've been seeping from the carpet.

He glanced back at me, ignoring my question. "Shea's in the bedroom."

He pointed at a door in the back, which was half-open, revealing a bed piled with clothes.

The house didn't look lived in. Spider webs and dust clung to everything, and I tried not to stir it up as I entered the front room, the linoleum-covered subfloor creaking with each step. Evidently, Shea's husband had chosen to stay with her in the animal clinic over the comfort of his home.

"I'm taking over your watch rotation tonight," Roark said to Jesse, his trailing footfalls turning the creaky floor into loud groans of wood.

I looked over my shoulder to catch Jesse's expression.

He emanated casualness, leaning against the door frame, bow strapped to his back and arms crossed over his chest. But the way he watched me was anything but casual.

He lifted a hand to chew on the edge of his thumb, eyes locked on mine. "Someone needs to sleep with Evie."

It bothered me that he wouldn't volunteer for the job, but I understood. Kind of.

"Some of my nightmares can be enlightening." I shrugged. "Maybe I should let them in, you know, to see what the Drone is up to." The idea made the hairs on my arms stand on end, but I suggested it because… "Maybe Michio could reach me the same way?"

"No." Jesse straightened, his tired eyes awakening with ferocity. "End of conversation."

An argument for another time then. I held Jesse's gaze. "Sounds like you're snuggling with me tonight."

I turned away to avoid what I assumed was a deeply-lined scowl. Roark patted my ass as he passed, and I followed his floor-groaning strides to the bedroom door.

"Shea?" I knocked and waited as her soft footsteps grew

closer.

The door opened all the way, and the sight of her healthy smile pulled my mouth into a relieved grin.

She was at least five years younger than me, barely thirty, with a broad forehead, wide mouth, slender nose, and huge brown eyes. Her long, black hair frizzed a bit at the edges, but holy hell, she looked nothing like the nymph I'd found a week ago.

I shrugged off the carbine and set it by the door. "You look amazing. Even better than yesterday."

"Oh, shut up." She waved my words away and strode to the bed full of clothes. "I look like I crawled out of a half-eaten carcass."

"Load of bollix." Roark lounged across the messy bed, his bare chest rippling with the movement, and tucked an arm behind his head. "If ye keep walking around in those hot pants, every lad in Georgia will be knocking down the door to rasher the arse off ye." He grinned. "I can't fecking concentrate."

Shea's jaw dropped as she shared a look with me. Then she burst out in laughter. "You keep saying he's a priest, but girl, I think you're bullshitting me."

"I know, right?"

Strange how, if he'd flirted with Elaine like this, my hackles would've been all sorts of unhappy. And though Shea flirted back, it was neither sneaky nor serious. Something about her genuine smile and confident nature put me at ease.

"And that accent." She picked through a pile of clothes, her dark skin glowing against her tight, white shorts. She was absolutely beautiful, her eyes warm and soft like molasses as they roamed Roark's muscular chest. "Say something else."

His fingers tapped the sword's hilt where it lay at his hip. "Eh, now ye got me ripping me knickers and scundered for a hundred."

She rolled her full lips between her teeth then glanced at me. "What did he say?"

"I have no idea." I sat on the edge of the bed beside him,

biting back a smile. "I don't speak potato head."

"Den' be talking shite, ye bleedin' woman." He gave me a blinding grin, evidently enjoying the attention. "Me accent turns ye into a dirty slapper."

Shea arched a thin, dark brow at me.

I shook my head. "I think he just called me an easy lay."

His guffaw confirmed it, prompting me to go after his nipple with pinching fingers, which he blocked with a pumped-up bicep, the showoff.

"Okay, absurdly sexy priest man…" She put her hands on her hips and cocked her head. "Say thirty-three and a third."

His smile fell. "No."

Oh, this was good. I nudged his knee with mine. "Say it."

Casting me a dirty look, he rubbed his whiskers and grumbled something under his breath.

I nudged him again. "What was that?"

"Thirty-three and a third," he said, which sounded like *turty tree and a turd.*

Shea doubled over with laughter, and I couldn't help but join her. Her contentment was contagious. Even Roark's scowl eventually gave in to a grin.

With the teasing out of the way, I helped her parse through her pre-apocalypse clothes. She urged me, more than once, to try on some of her dresses. I'd never been a girly-girl. And now, well, I considered clothes about as practical as cell phones. I didn't even own a pair of panties.

As the conversation switched to fake nails and high-heels, Shea sat on the floor, surrounded by frilly stuff I couldn't identify. She talked, and I nodded. I couldn't relate to her fashion interests, but damn if I hadn't missed the company of another female. Of course, I'd spent a month with Elaine, but she'd rather spit on me than talk to me. Not that I'd made any amicable efforts, either.

"Jackson loved these shoes." She ran a hand over a strappy red stiletto, her lips trembling, unable to hold her smile.

"I lost my husband, too."

I had no words of solace, no comfort to share. After Joel

died, I'd found some semblance of peace in silence, so that was what I gave her now.

In the quiet moment that followed, I sensed a welcome sort of bond pulling us together. Her gaze drifted to mine, her stricken expression cleared, and her gentle smile returned.

Roark grew quiet beside me, and I realized he'd fallen asleep.

"Hey." I tugged on his dreadlocks until he opened his eyes. "Go switch places with Jesse. He needs a nap more than you do."

Arguing that we didn't need a guard in here *and* one at the front door would've been a waste of time, so I didn't bother.

Roark left with a kiss on my nose, and a few moments later, Jesse walked in holding a mug.

Shea looked up from her elaborate makeup kit and watched him out of the corner of her eye. She seemed suddenly more guarded, her fingers moving slowly, distractedly, through her supplies. Surely, he hadn't scared her on their walk over here? Or was there something else going on?

I nodded in his direction. "He doesn't bite."

Her eyes flicked to me and back to him. "He doesn't talk either. Is he mute?"

He scanned the room, his body stiffening as he took in the flowered wallpaper, the spread of makeup on the floor around Shea, and the lingerie strung on hangers around the room. He looked really uncomfortable and out of place, with his frayed clothes and fuck-off expression. Was he allergic to girly crap?

I thought back to the first time I saw him. His gorgeous looks aside, I had *not* been impressed. How many times had I watched him walk away, mumbling to myself, *What a dick*?

"He's not mute," I said. "He'll grow on you." *Then he'll steal your heart.*

Hopefully not Shea's heart. I didn't want her to discover how big of a possessive bitch I could be. I really liked this girl.

Glancing down at the mug in his hand, Jesse approached me and held it out.

I accepted it with a smile and moaned as I sipped, the

robustness of dark coffee warming my throat. "Ahhh, that's heaven. Thank you."

Chin lowered and shoulders back, he stared at me with his silent watchfulness, the kind of stare that used to make me insanely uneasy. Now I expected it. Loved it, even.

With nothing else to do but look at each other, I joined Shea on the floor. Jesse propped his bow against the mattress and sat on the bed, his unwavering gaze caressing my face.

Shea chattered on, lamenting the end of fashion magazines and celebrity styles and the manufacturing of push-up bras and tampons and well, everything. My thoughts drifted to weapons training, building her strength and endurance, and transforming her into an aphid-slaying machine. Yeah, okay, she was very feminine, and the nymph fever had eaten away her body weight. But her frame was sturdy and solid, and with enough cardio and strength training, I bet she could wield a fierce amount of muscle.

My fingers twitched with restlessness, anxious to get started. But this was her first day out of the animal clinic. She needed time to go through her things, to mourn her husband, and to accept this miserable world she'd woken in.

I glanced back at Jesse, and just as I'd hoped, his dark lashes lay over his cheeks, his upper body slumped, still and comatose, in its upright position. My heart gave a heavy thump. For him to let his guard down enough to fall asleep while *guarding* was a testament to his level of exhaustion.

No need to worry, though. My carbine sat a few feet away, and I knew Roark stood on look out at the front door. So I silently crawled across the floor and joined Jesse on the bed.

His eyes fluttered then snapped open in shock, locking on his bow beside him.

"Shhh." I pressed against his chest and shoulder, coaxing him to lay down.

He pushed back at first then let me guide him to rest on our sides. Across the room, Shea ducked her head and picked through her makeup kit.

With my chest against Jesse's back, I ran my fingers through his soft hair, trailing them over his face and smoothing out the creases in his forehead and around his eyes. Soon, his breathing evened out and his muscles grew heavy against me.

Shea watched us from the floor, picking at the skin around her fingernail, her voice quiet. "Is that how you tame him?"

I traced the outline of his short beard, marveling at the hues of brown and red. "This one can't be tamed," I whispered. "I wouldn't want to anyway."

"You said you have three guardians?"

With that question, our conversation took a somber turn, flowing back and forth in hushed tones. We talked about Michio. We shared stories about her husband, my husband, Annie and Aaron. Then we talked about the Drone.

I considered sliding to the floor with her, but Jesse hadn't stirred and I was reluctant to give up such a rare moment of unguarded nearness with him. He looked so at ease and beautiful in my embrace with his jaw relaxed and lips slightly parted.

For the next couple hours, I combed my fingers through his hair and caught her up on everything I knew and some of the things I speculated. She was a natural listener, asked smart questions, and took it all in with astounding bravery. Not a tear in sight. Not even a tremble. She had just been told that ghosts existed and mutated bloodsuckers prowled the perimeter by the hundreds and the future was dependent on an unborn child.

Maybe she thought I was full of shit.

Still sitting on the floor, her legs stretched out in front of her, she stared across the room, her focus narrowing on the sleeping man wrapped in my arms. "I'm a believer. Practicing Baptist, actually. But the religious institution doesn't really matter anymore, does it?" She smiled to herself. "Point is, I'm a woman of faith, Evie. If God has a plan, not you or anyone will be able to stand in His way."

"Noted." I gave her a half-smile and lowered my mouth to Jesse's bare shoulder, relishing the heat of his back against my chest. "But I'm *not* a woman of faith, and I don't think *God* has anything to do with who I have sex with and if I get pregnant. We don't even know if women can carry to term. Or if a child can survive its first breath." I swallowed, suddenly anxious to change the topic. "How are you feeling? No more nausea and headaches?"

She chewed on her lip. "I feel weak. Too damned skinny. I mean, look at these puny arms." She tried to flex her bicep and sighed. "But I'm ready to get out there and help y'all however I can."

Yeah, she and I were going to get along just fine.

"But there's one thing." She lowered her voice. "I don't know if it's because I haven't had sex in two years, or if it's from all the man meat you've got walking around up in here." She glanced at Jesse. "But I'm itching to get laid. Like, for real. I've never been this horny."

If Elaine experienced a heightened libido, she never mentioned it. But she did *show* it, with her hands and hips all over Michio. I wished more than ever he was here to answer Shea's questions.

She squeezed her eyes shut. "Jackson, I'm so sorry, baby. I miss you terrible, and if you were here, I'd fuck you senseless. But you're not, and I'm going to have to deal with this little problem without you. I love you. You know I do. Always will, baby." Her lashes fluttered up, her eyes watery. She pulled in a deep breath and smiled at me. "I'm good." She sniffed. "I'll be fine."

What exactly was she planning to do about her problem? I felt a tug of possessiveness over my guys, but that faded quickly in light of the overwhelming awe I had for her. She confronted her grief with inspiring determination. I'd been a barely-functioning zombie for weeks after Joel died, wandering alone and longing for death.

And to think, Shea's husband died the day before we found her. Such bittersweet irony that he survived and cared for her to the end and inadvertently led us to her, yet he never got to see her healed.

Beneath her watery smile, her grief strained, tightening the skin around her mouth.

I started to move away from Jesse to—*I don't know*—hug her? Did she need that? I was out of my element here.

She held up a hand. "Stay with your man." She cleared her throat. "So what's up with my urge to hump anything that moves? Cuz, honey, that ain't normal."

I rubbed a lock of Jesse's hair between my fingers. "Remember I said I might've passed on some of my…traits?"

Her brow furrowed. "You're horny, too?"

I pulled my fingers from his hair and shifted to the edge of the bed. "Something like that. It has to do with high testosterone."

"Ah." She stood and stretched her arms over her head, exposing the skeletal outline of her ribs through the thin shirt. "You said your missing guardian is a doctor?"

I closed my eyes, my chest clenching. "Yeah."

Her footsteps approached, and her soft hand on my cheek drew my gaze to hers.

"I'm a veterinarian," she whispered. "Now don't ask me to do brain surgery, but I know my way around organs and bones. Maybe that'll relieve some of the worry you're carrying on your shoulders, yeah?"

"Yeah." Seriously, I loved this woman. "Would you be able to check my IUD?"

She chuckled, lowering her hand. After our little heart-to-heart, she knew about Roark and Michio's infertility and Jesse's stance on intimacy.

"Only one reason you need an IUD, and he's sexy as sin." She pursed her lips, eyes on Jesse. "You're optimistic, girl. I like that."

A hand squeezed my hip, accompanied by Jesse's groggy voice. "She's delusional."

I squinted at him over my shoulder. "How long have you been awake?"

"Long enough." He jack-knifed into a sitting position beside me, hooked an arm around my waist, and tugged me against him. Then he brushed his mouth over the shell of my ear. "Thank you for the nap." He inhaled deeply. Was he smelling my hair? He was definitely stealing my air. "Really needed that, darlin'."

"Sweet Jesus." Shea fanned her face. "I feel like a voyeur."

I laughed, meeting Jesse's eyes inches away. "She's awesome, right?"

"Yeah," he said, without breaking our eye-contact.

"Pfft. You ain't seen nothing." She strode to the door. "Let me show you where we keep the generators and other cool toys. Like my ultrasound machine." She winked at me. "You know, to check the position and effectiveness of your IUD."

NINETEEN

The fume of machinery oil and corroded sheet metal choked the air. Sweat trickled between my breasts in the stifling heat. I stood in a shed the size of a basketball court with Roark, Jesse, and Shea, the four of us gathered around the only section not piled with clutter. The vacant spot had clearly been occupied at one time, given the square outlines of dirt on the concrete and the amount of stuff filling every other inch of the space.

A stripe of sunlight filtered through the smudges on a single window, illuminating trucks, tractors, weed eaters, rusted skeletons of chain-link cages, and veterinary machines I couldn't name. An old vending machine lay on its side, and long feeding troughs stacked against the far wall. But no generators.

"We kept them here." Shea glared at the bare spot on the floor, fisting her hands on her hips. "Jackson must've…" She slapped a palm on her brow. "Of course, he used them. Duh. No electricity."

Jesse turned in a circle, eyeing the space. "We've rummaged through every building on the reserve. There're no generators."

"Maybe he traded them?" I stepped through the clutter, searching for an ultrasound machine, though I didn't know what one looked like and was fully aware we wouldn't be able to use it. "You know, for food or weapons?"

We'd found her husband four-hundred miles away. Maybe he'd been desperate for supplies? Generators were among the first things looted when the lights flickered off. Two years later, locating one abandoned and still working was no easy feat.

Shea jutted her chin. "The fool better not have traded them for bling or dresses. That man loved to dote on me." She lowered her voice, mumbling, "Even when I looked like a parasitic swamp donkey. God love him."

I bit down on my cheek. Given the amount of feminine shit we'd found in his truck, my suspicions ran along the same lines. What a damned shame. A generator would've given us some comforting luxuries, like light at night, refrigeration for blood, and power for a sonogram.

Jesse reached into a plastic container and removed a football. He palmed it, testing its weight in his big hand, a small smile playing on his lips. How strange to imagine a life of football games, universities, young men competing against each other for something other than survival, and Jesse smack at the center of all of it. But that had been his life in Texas, attending college on football scholarship.

I watched him put the football back and caught his eyes. "You miss it?"

He shrugged. "Yeah."

Shea broke the nostalgic moment as she pulled a roundish, laptop-looking thing off a nearby shelf. "Well, here's my portable ultrasound. Not that we can use it without electricity." Her face fell. "I'm sorry, Evie."

Maybe we could use one of the cars to power it. If we found one of those AC/DC power adapters that plugged into the lighter and turned it into a normal plug, we could pull electricity from a car battery.

I shrugged, my armpits sticking with the motion. "I still think you're awesome."

She flashed me a smile and started to put the machine back.

"Hang on." Jesse pushed a hand through his hair. "We'll take it with us."

I stared at him, stunned. He stared right back, daring me to question him. He'd followed us in here without a word, and

I'd assumed he was interested in the generators, not the ultrasound. If we found a power supply down the road and the ultrasound validated the effectiveness of my birth control, would he trust it enough to let me love him the way we both wanted?

The intensity of his gaze told me he would. The tight clench of his fingers at his sides promised he would not be gentle.

Heat flooded my skin, and the hot flash had little to do with the Georgia climate. Mental images of his naked body, his urgent hands, and his hard, needy cock moving over my skin and between my legs did nothing to cool my rising temperature.

My chest tingled, and my breath lodged in my throat. I thought I'd done a bang-up job reigning in my libido since Michio left, but evidently, I was powerless against Jesse's lusty glares.

He turned away, as if uninspired by whatever he saw on my face, and nodded at the machine in Shea's hand. "We'll put that in the truck."

Then he strode out the door and into the blinding sunshine, leaving me flushed and unbalanced. Shea glanced at me, raised her brows, and followed after him.

I shared a look with Roark. His forehead wrinkled beneath the sheen of sweat. Not with jealousy. No, he was immune to that weakness.

"What?" I asked, following his gaze to my upper arm.

There, clinging to the curve of my shoulder, was a ladybird. Inches from my face, it stretched blood-red wings, dotted with tiny replicas of the black spots on my back. Its triangular head canted, twitching twin antennas, as if tasting my breaths.

Was it looking at me? I sensed a…a…I didn't know what it was. A soft hum? A dribble of energy? Like the beetle was telling me something, maybe telling me I was an idiot because I didn't understand. My skin tightened against the sensation, every conscious thought narrowing on the fact that it was here, and I was here, and that was supposed to make sense. Perhaps that explained everything in some transcendental world where spiritual forces made plans beyond my comprehension.

The ladybird whirred its wings and took off, spiraling above my head and out the door. The trickle of energy went with it, as if drawing an invisible path to Jesse, one I felt a strong urge to follow. But why?

I rubbed my head, berating myself for being so goddamned spiritually constipated.

Roark stared at the doorway long after the ladybird disappeared. His shoulder-length dreadlocks gathered into a knot at the back of his head, giving me a clear view of his jaw, which sawed side to side.

"I can hear your brain chugging over there." I adjusted the carbine on its sling and wiped the sweat from my forehead. "It was just a beetle. Doesn't mean Jesus is calling."

He closed the distance in three long strides and planted his bulky frame in front of me. "Do ye know the *lady* in ladybird refers to the Virgin Mary?"

I dragged my eyes to his, wary about where this was going. The first time he'd witnessed the crazy beetles swarming my body, he told me it was a sign. That was the night we had sex. The night that wrenched us apart.

"The term originated in the Middle Ages." He brushed the rough pads of his fingers over my shoulder, his brogue thickening. "Pests were plaguing the crops, destroying the food source. Famine was inevitable. So the farmers prayed to the Blessed Lady, the Virgin Mary, and soon after, the red and black beetles came."

I took in his thoughtful expression, strong nose, and the rugged outline of stubble. His eyes radiated every shade of vivid green, like a dewy meadow at dawn. He was achingly beautiful, physically, soulfully.

I touched his full lips, because I could, because he didn't just belong to his god. He was mine, too, and he craved the affection as much as I did. "Let me guess. The ladybirds ate the pests, and the crops were miraculously saved? Famine averted?"

"Aye." He smiled against my fingers. "The farmers owed their prosperity to the beetles and divinity who'd sent them, so they named them lady beetles. Mary beetles. The red wings represent her cloak, the black spots her sorrows."

I lowered my hand, my limbs suddenly too heavy for my body. Something inside me pulled and pulled hard, toward the door, toward the man who'd exited through it moments ago. Where was this coming from, this impulse to follow Jesse right this minute? My mind? My heart?

My womb.

It contracted in response, and vertigo spun over me as the meaning of Roark's story took hold. I had enough spots on my back to account for my sorrows, but I was no *Blessed Lady*. I wanted to fuck three men, not to become pregnant and save the world from its pests. I wanted to have sex with them for the carnal pleasure, the intimacy, and the possession. Because I loved them, greedy sinner that I was.

My legs felt weak, wobbly. I hardened my stance. "Ladybirds also bleed from their knees when they're scared." Startle one, and a foul-smelling fluid might drip from its joints. Something I'd read in the insect book I pilfered in the U.K. "What's your point?"

He held my face in his hands, his jaw hardening into steel. "Part of me believes ye are meant to give the world this miracle, to bear a child that would be reared and trained by three men of three faiths and three weapons."

I shook my head in his hands, working my throat to swallow the shock. "What?"

"That part of me heart belongs to God." He pressed my cheek against his bare chest and wrapped his arms around my back.

Of course, he would apply his own theological beliefs to Annie's forewarnings.

"But the other part..." He rested his lips against the top of my head. "The half of me heart that belongs to *you* wants an ultrasound to guaran-fecking-tee that no one can get ye with child. Because, prophecies aside, pregnancy will slow ye down, make ye weak and vulnerable. And we den' know the effects of the virus on a babe. It could become sick in your womb. It could kill ye."

A sharp pang stabbed in my chest. Like Jesse, he was torn between spiritual purpose and his need to protect me.

My exhale stuttered out. "Jesse won't go there, and I'll stop him—"

"He will, and you're incapable of saying *no* to your guardians." He pulled the strap off my shoulder and set my carbine on the ground. "I saw the chubbed-up look in his eye before he left."

True, Jesse needed to get laid, and perhaps any woman would do at this point. It was a miserable thing to accept. He gave me his life, following my crusade and providing me unconditional protection. Yet he wouldn't allow me to give him the simplest, most human thing. My body. I couldn't take away his pain.

Roark circled his arms around me. "He's fighting a battle he won't win, love." His accent dropped a few notches. "And so am I."

I sucked in a sharp breath and pulled back to see his face. "You? What do you mean?"

His eyes lowered, hooding into emerald slivers. "I'm a man, first and foremost. And you're..." Calloused fingers slid over my tailbone, crept under the hem of my shirt, and splayed across my spine. "The greatest words in the English language can't begin to describe ye, but..."

As he studied me, I savored the oaky scent of his breath, waiting for some vulgar colloquialism I had no chance of decoding.

"When I look into your eyes, I den' see yellow or green or... Is there even a name for that color? All I see is liquid sunshine."

Wow. Okay. "That's..." *Decipherable.* I kissed his lips. "Thank you."

His hands moved over my hips, across my belly, and cupped my breasts beneath the shirt. "These are… bloody hell. Ye could breastfeed the baby Christ and all the animals around the manger."

"Ew!" I knocked his hands away. "What's wrong with you?"

Laughing, he gripped my butt and yanked my hips against his, grinding the hard evidence of his wrongness against my pubic bone.

"Ye have an arse on ye made for slapping." He demonstrated, ripping a startled yelp from me. Then his big hands cupped and squeezed both cheeks. "I bet these steely muscles would break me knob on the way in."

The fantasy of him fucking my ass suspended me somewhere between resentment and need. Resentment of his vow and a thrilling need for him to break it. I was torn. Should I shut this down? Or molest him until his rosary burned a hole through his pocket?

"Roark—"

"I want that." He buried his face in the curve of my neck and groaned. "I want to feel wha' it's like to fill ye there."

Oh, my dirty, dirty priest. His religious beliefs gave him precepts to follow, a sense of structure to live a moral life during a time of terrible violence. But the precepts he'd made for himself forbid anal sex. Which baffled my mind since he regularly, albeit guiltily, fucked my mouth.

I slid a hand over the tangle of dreads and braids and stroked the skin on his temple. "You fill me in other ways. Important ways. Like my heart."

"It's not enough. Not for me. I lay beside ye every night, connected to your body, aching. A *man's* ache. Doc is gone. And Jesse…" He paused, considering, then moved his mouth to my ear. "I wish that I had Jesse's girl."

"What? I'm not—" *Oh my Rick Springfield.* I narrowed my eyes, unable to hold back my grin. "How long have you been waiting to use that line?"

"Too long." He smiled. "Seriously though, I have ye all to

myself now." Leaning down, he pulled my lip between his teeth and released it. "I'll have ye again, love. I'm not as obedient as ye might believe."

My lungs stuck together, laboring against the thickness of the humid air and the strain in his voice. I'd grown used to the constant tension between us, accepted his self-imposed rules, and presumed sex-without-intercourse was the forever future of our relationship.

But since Michio had left, there wasn't a night I slept without Roark, held tight in his big arms, his erection trapped between our bodies. He was a torment and a refuge. A tempter and a protector. A solid, defined boundary between right and wrong. I was so grateful for every moment I had with him, but I didn't want to be the reason for his fall from God.

I unraveled my body from his and took a couple steps back. "You ever get the feeling that no matter what our intent is, no matter how hard we try to follow our own convictions, it's all pointless? Like all the plans in the universe have already been determined, and the decisions we make mean nothing? Like we can't stop what's coming because the very energy that forms the molecules in the air, in the ground, in *us*, are already set on an unwavering path that ends in devastation?"

Okay, maybe I was feeling a little defeated lately. Or maybe it was just the wretched heat getting to me.

"It's called the Great Tribulation, love." He reached out, hooked a thumb in my belt loop, and yanked me against him. "The Gospels of Matthew, Mark, and Luke predicted the abomination of desolation and fleeing to the mountains during a time of terror, famines, and deadly disease. 'Tis written that the scourge will affect pregnancies and children and spread throughout the flesh, save for the elect."

Ugh. He was talking about the End Times, the return of Christ. I didn't like what that implied.

I took a deep breath, chasing away the cringe in my shoulders. "The elect are the chosen, right? The believers? We both know I'm not a member."

All this biblical talk was putting me on edge.

"Doesn't matter what ye believe." He placed his lips against the juncture of my neck and shoulder. "Ye survived, untouched by disease, an example of God's grace. You're the Mother of the living."

I could argue Shea and Elaine were candidates for that role, but my voice escaped me as his hand freed the button of my jean shorts, slipped beneath the zipper, and cupped the sensitive skin between my legs. A shiver surged through me, and my inner muscles squeezed, empty, hungry.

"God portioned your heart like water," he breathed against my neck, "so your guardians may share the chalice."

"Pretty words for such a filthy mouth." I gripped his huge shoulders and crashed my lips onto his, tasting salt and sweat and the delicious familiarity of Irish whiskey.

His fingers plunged exactly where I wanted him, and the tingling invasion rippled through my entire body. He shifted us, pressing my back against a metal cage, and rocked his fingers inside me, softly, more gently than the greedy thrust of his tongue.

There was something so honest and crude in the way he kissed, such a contrast to the delicate motion between my legs. The disciplined priest would forsake his own pleasure and finger me until I came. But the man would be needy and selfish like his kiss. He would hold me down with powerful arms, yank out his cock, and own me the way his tongue did. Ravenously. Convincingly. Unrestrained.

Priests were supposed to be trustworthy, yet I placed my body and my heart in the care of the man beneath the cassock. Because I trusted his openness, related to it, found comfort in it. Because there was no shame in his kiss. Only raw desire and love.

The unbearable heat clung to my skin. Sweat and arousal slicked my inner thighs. And my breaths coalesced with his, forming a swelter of gasps against our faces.

I lifted my hips, encouraging the thrust of his fingers. "Harder. I won't break."

He dragged his lips over my jaw, his whiskers scratchy and damp. "No, but *I* will."

My chest collapsed, twisting with lust and hope and the pang of resentment that refused to let go.

His fingers eased from inside me, trembling as he buttoned my cutoffs. Guess that meant we were done.

As I debated the selfishness in pushing for more, the tease that was Roark moved in, so close his lips brushed my face. "We'll finish this later. Our visitor looks as pained as the back of me bollix."

Visitor? I spun around and peered through the holes of a tall cage.

Jesse stood inside the doorway, fingers clenched around the bow strap that crossed his chest. His discomfort was palpable in the hunch of his shoulders, the hollows of his cheeks, the shadow of his furrowed brow, and the taut slash of his mouth.

But I also recognized arousal. It hooded his eyes as he watched me move around the cage. It staggered his inhale as I approached, holding his gaze. It made me feel bolder, more decisive, as I raised a hand and placed my palm over his rigid jaw.

My insides throbbed, pooling heat to my center, left unsatisfied by Roark and now focused on the man before me.

His nostrils flared, his eyes burning me from the inside out. "Shea's ready to see an aphid. I need you." He turned and walked out, tossing over his shoulder, "Southeast tree line."

I sighed. Yeah, he needed me. To beckon an aphid, to control it so Shea could get a good look, to prepare her for weapons training, or whatever the task list might be. But to demand he needed me for himself? That went against his martyrdom. If he did lose the battle, he would survive, but how badly would he get hurt in the process? He was strong enough to endure my death, if it came to that. But was he strong enough to withstand the guilt?

Roark's hand rested against my spine, his body a furnace beside mine.

I turned my neck and kissed his shoulder. "How long was

he here?"

"The entire time. He's a perv, that one."

"Says the priest with pussy juice on his fingers."

He popped two in his mouth and licked them clean, grinning.

What a troublemaker. He'd shoved those fingers inside me, knowing Jesse was watching.

I grabbed the carbine from the floor and walked to the door. "You need to stop taunting him. He's struggling enough as it is."

Matching my strides, he squinted against the sun's glare and laced his fingers with mine. "His struggle is headed toward a desperate end, Evie. I want to be there when it happens."

I pushed sweat-soaked hair from my face. "Why?"

Was he afraid Jesse would take me forcefully?

He shrugged. "I like to watch."

TWENTY

A snarl sounded deep in the woods, punctuating the waspy buzz soughing through my insides.

I'd walked here to summon an aphid, and my heightened senses instantly latched onto one without effort, tracing a direct line to its location. "Five o'clock. About forty yards in, headed our way."

Jesse strode from Shea's side and paced toward me with determined steps, his hand already on his bow, sliding it off his perfect shoulders. "How many?"

Despite his nap earlier, dark bruises smudged his eyes. He carried himself with a high degree of intensity and strength, but the stiffness in his face and arms marked his fatigue. He was going to get some sleep tonight, even if I had to knock him out to make that happen.

"One aphid." I reached out with my mind, probing the vicinity for more. "I'll try to isolate it if others show up."

I glanced at Shea, taking in her restless hands and tense shoulders. I'd killed hundreds if not thousands of these nasty things, but watching someone lay their eyes on one for the first time was like experiencing *my* first all over again. The bulbous head, cricket-like legs, sucking mouthparts, and the putrid stink of lizard skin were unnerving enough. But the twitchy, inhuman way they moved could make a grown man—as Roark would say—*pass a motion in his knickers.*

So yeah, my heart pounded and my palms slicked with sweat in anticipation of reliving that day in my backyard, when my first aphid encounter ended in a terrifying struggle at the bottom of my pool.

Jesse reached for the handgun on my thigh, and I gripped his arm, stopping him.

"Shea should shoot with the carbine." I offered mine from my back. "It'll give her confidence."

Elaine had refused to touch a gun or a knife, but as Jesse held the carbine out to Shea, she snatched it from his hand and turned it over, studying it. There wasn't a hint of alarm in her thoughtful expression. No fear. No reluctance. I fucking loved that.

"Ever shot a gun?" I brushed a hand over the knives on my arm, already missing the weight of the carbine.

She shook her head and swatted at a fly on her skinny thigh. "Jackson always shot the tranquilizer guns."

Jesse spent a few seconds instructing her how to use it. Basic weapons safety to ensure she didn't shoot herself or us, but nothing so detailed as to prepare her for a gunfight. That would come later, *if* the next few moments didn't scare the bajeezus out of her.

The lone aphid in the forest emitted a burst of ghastly signals, vibrating a hunger cry through my gut, seemingly as aware of me as I was of it.

I nodded to Roark, assuming he would be my energy source. "Two minutes tops before it breaches the clearing."

Roark stepped into position, then stopped at the bark of Jesse's voice. "I have Evie."

A blond brow inched up Roark's forehead. "Do ye now?"

Surprisingly, Roark backed away and even waved a hand at me in invitation.

Jesse yanked off his shirt and slid in behind me, his bow hovering across my chest as if he was unsure what to do with it. His body tensed around my back, and he dropped the weapon, his hands falling to my hips. "Your shirt."

Taking it off would leave me nude from the waist up, but Jesse and Roark had seen it all before. Tallis and Georges were out of eyeshot, keeping watch somewhere on the reserve and holding the perimeter in place, which was impressive by any standards. They'd set up crude booby traps and audible alarms—like rattling aluminum cans—and monitored the vast property through scopes. In the week we'd been there, only a handful of mutants had slipped through, and they'd been taken down before they sneaked up on us.

I pulled my shirt over my head and leaned back against Jesse's chest. The humid air thickened the sheen of sweat on my skin and trickled between my breasts. "Shea, I'll have complete control over the bug."

That morning in her bedroom, I had explained how this worked, including the skin-to-skin contact.

A swallow bobbed in her throat.

"The gun is to help you feel safe, but you don't have to use it, okay?" My stomach clenched against the telepathic drone of the aphid. "It's coming. Just on the other side of that forked tree."

Her eyes darted to Roark's sword as he slowly unsheathed it and stepped behind her.

Jesse's hands slid across my belly, hot and slick, inching upward until his thumb rested against my breastbone. His fingers curved beneath the underside of my scarred breast.

"Do you have control of it, darlin'?" he asked in that southern twang of his.

I licked my lips. "You're distracting me."

His chest pressed closer against my back, his breaths becoming louder, shorter. "You better get un-distracted real quick."

Grrr. I wanted to hip-check him, but the bushes at the edge of the woods rustled with movement, startling a flock of birds in the canopy.

Twenty feet before us, a low growl rumbled over the ground, followed by the blur of a mutated body erupting from the overgrowth. All-white eyes scanned our group and locked on me.

Focusing on my contact points—my back against Jesse's chest, his hands and arms on my ribs, and his mouth resting against my neck—I tapped his masculinity. A trickle of heat seeped from his skin to mine and crashed into hot waves through my body. A bright light flashed behind my eyes, dizzying, intoxicating, tingling across my jaw and gathering in my chest.

I coiled my mind around the energy, wove it through the aphid connection, and silently pushed the command. *Closer. Slowly.*

A soundless hum rippled between me and the growling creature. The tiny bristles on its translucent skin stiffened, sensing my transmission. Snot dribbled over its oblong jaw, and segmented feet dragged forward, scraping yellow talons through the dirt.

I peeked at Shea, and her muscles were frozen in shock. The only thing that moved was the carbine, trembling in her hand.

Roark leaned over her shoulder, whispering something that made her chin bob tightly. Then he stepped to her side with the sword in a two-fisted grip. If I lost my focus, he would take the creature's head without a moment's hesitation.

I continued to guide the bug forward, siphoning Jesse's vitality and mentally reciting directions. Ten feet away, *Stop* bloomed in my chest and tumbled along the invisible leash.

The aphid paused, lowering on double-jointed legs, and a tremor shook its hands, which weren't hands at all. Its fingers were fused together, curled into hooks, like misshapen pincers.

Shea pulled in a sharp breath. Her body swayed, as if the wind was rocking her, but there was no disturbance in the air, nothing blowing the hair from my face.

Would she pass out? Elaine's first encounter resulted in a convulsion of spasms, eyes rolling back in her head, and a dramatic collapse on the ground.

I held the aphid immobile, thoroughly pissing it off, given the hissing snarls and clawing buzz in my stomach. Shea watched it, locked in a stunned, unblinking stance, the carbine forgotten in her grip as the barrel dipped toward the ground.

Her gaze shifted toward mine, and her eyes bugged out.

"Your…your…"

"Black eyes?" I gave her a small smile. "My pupils dilate when I'm controlling them. It's normal."

"That can't be your pupils." Her chest heaved. "There's no whites in your eyes. That's…that's not normal, girl."

I had to give her credit. She didn't put a bullet in my head and run away. Instead, she lifted the carbine and retrained it on the aphid.

Something tickled my arm and the back of my leg. Fucking flies. I slapped at them, too slow to squash them.

"Jesus, you described what they looked like." Her voice lowered to a whisper, rattled and reedy. "But nothing could've prepared me for this, you know?" Her finger trembled on the trigger. "And what in the name of God is that smell?"

"Some bang of odour off the buggie." Roark grinned, but the vigilant way he watched the aphid over her shoulder was anything but amused. "The smelly cunt doesn't shower. It feasts on blood and death. And I bet the dirty growler between her legs is leaking some rotten fanny farts."

"Roark." I gave him a disgusted glare.

"That thing is female?" Shea's chocolate complexion took on a grayish hue. "How can you tell?"

Good question. Not a scrap of clothes on the aphid's dome-shaped body. No distinguishing characteristics either, like remnants of hair, tattoos, or ear piercings. Genitalia were among the first things to recede in mutation, followed by lips and fingers. But there was a small trace of her human life.

I pointed to the bulging chest. "See the two hanging lumps of flesh?"

Shea cocked her head and wrinkled her nose. "Tits?"

I shrugged. "Silicone implants."

"An insect with a boob job." She let out a strained laugh. "Now I've seen it all." Her teeth sank into her bottom lip. "Can they reproduce?"

"No." Jesse shifted behind me, his fingers tightening beneath my breast. "Dr. Nealy studied their physiology. They don't have working reproductive organs."

In two years, I'd never seen aphids mating. Never encountered a baby bug. They were driven to do one thing: Feed. And if they devoured every mammal on the planet, what then? If their adaptable bodies couldn't starve, would they just wander the earth in an eternal stupor, unable to feed, unable to die?

The aphid pulled on our connection, testing its strength. As long as Jesse stayed put, I had an inexhaustible energy supply to hold it.

I turned my chin toward Jesse. "Do you feel an energy drain?"

"No, darlin'. I feel *you.* Like a subtle vibration beneath my hands, but nothing threatening."

Roark and Michio had said similar things before. Evidently, they didn't run out of power the way I did.

The bug seemed to realize my control over it was endless, throwing back its head and releasing a thunderous buzz that resonated through the clearing like a million wasp wings. Tubular parts writhed in its throat, flinging strings of black snot as its hooked hands clawed at the ground.

Shea watched in open-mouthed horror. "Do they feed on each other?"

Oh, how I wished they did. "Mutated blood is poisonous to aphids and nymphs. It kills them, and I guess they instinctively know this, because I've never seen them turn on each other."

"But if I had bitten a human, I would've turned into that," she mumbled to herself.

If she'd turned into that, she would've been beyond saving. Nymphs could only bite once, the bite instantly turning them into aphids.

I sent a silent thanks to her dead husband for keeping her locked up for two years. We needed her. Mankind needed her.

She confronted this creature remarkably well and would make a hell of a fighter. Shoulders now squared, chin up, she planted her sneakers stubbornly in the dirt. It was hard to believe only a week ago her body had undergone a drastic transformation, reforming bones into human ribs and dissolving tubular mouthparts designed for piercing and sucking blood.

The ashen tint of her brown skin and the bags under her eyes were the only hints that she wasn't at full health.

I nodded to Roark. "It's time."

Shea glanced between me and the agitated aphid and tucked the butt of the carbine tight against her shoulder. "I want to kill it."

Roark moved to her side, scrutinizing the way she held the gun, the pull of his brows drawing worried lines around his eyes. I knew his concern. The boom of the carbine could draw attention, and he could kill the bug quietly.

"Let her do it," Jesse said from behind me. "Who knows when we'll have another controlled environment like this?"

A stretch of silence passed between Jesse and Roark, some kind of wordless communication that involved glaring and swatting at flies, and ended with Roark turning away to touch Shea's arm. "Bit of advice. Ye can blow a hole in its nappy arse and it'll keep on walking like John fecking Wayne. Gotta hit the brain, eh?"

She nodded, chin quivering. "Got it."

Jesse moved his mouth to my ear, his breath sending shivers down my neck. "Doing okay?"

I couldn't sense other aphids and didn't feel any wavering strain from the commands I was pushing. "Super."

He traced a finger over my shoulder blade. "Some of your spots are fading. But here—" He touched the top of my spine. "And here." His finger circled an area beneath my shoulder. "These are new."

The canvas on my back morphed every time I communicated with aphids. Freaky as hell, but I should be thankful I hadn't grown antennas and an exoskeleton shell.

Shea slowly inhaled, exhaled, and squeezed the trigger. The bullet zipped off into the forest, missing its mark by several feet. She adjusted her stance and missed three more times, taking raspy breaths between each trigger pull. "Son of a bitch."

I held the aphid's body as stiffly as possible, preventing it from dodging or moving. It was damned disgruntled about that, its screeches pitching into ear-splitting war cries.

Shea's nervousness was expected. She'd never shot a gun, and her target was far more intimidating than the paper outlines I'd practiced on with Joel.

Roark tightened his hand around the sword. "Put some bitch in it." His voice was teasing despite the tick in his jaw.

"I'm trying, alright?" She blew out a stream of air, stirring the black curls around her face.

I recognized the determination in her eyes. The same kind of ferocity I felt every time I slayed a monster. It wasn't hard to reach that level of brutality. All I needed was a flash of memory, of aphids gathered around Joel's body, the tendons in his neck taut with pain, his lips pulled away from his gums, his eyes bulging like porcelain orbs, mutating.

"Shea," I said, quietly. "One of these things killed your husband." Pain flashed across her face, but I kept going. "Jackson traveled a long ass way to gather clothes and food for you, and a mutation just like this one stabbed its suckers into his neck and drained his life."

A noise gurgled in her throat, and her lips disappeared between her teeth. Her transformation happened in seconds. Her chest rose, her shoulders rolled back, and her arms locked in place, steadying the gun.

Then the bullets flew. She hit trees, riddled the ground, and grazed the aphid's limbs. Lead found its torso, ripping a squeal from its gaped jaw. She squeezed the trigger over and over, and finally, a bullet pierced through its skull.

The body jerked then dropped to the ground, unmoving. The vibrations inside me snapped, disintegrating with its life.

She didn't let up, spraying bullets at limbs and guts as it lay in a pile of peppered flesh.

"Whoa, whoa, whoa!" Roark grabbed her elbow. "Stall

the balls, Annie Oakley. You'll use up all the ammo."

She stopped, but the report of booms continued. Multiple shots fired, off in the distance, echoed across the field.

Georges and Tallis. Oh fuck, no. I bit my lip hard, hard enough to jerk me into action. Contracting my stomach, I choked all the energy there and sent it out, across the field, in the direction of the noise.

I was met with…nothing. "I don't feel aphids. They must be out of range."

Jesse's heat vanished from my back. In the next breath, he sprinted away, bow in hand, shoulder muscles flexing in the glare of the sun.

My heart raced, as did my mind, imploding with concern for Georges and Tallis. I yanked on my shirt and spun toward Roark.

His body was poised to bolt after Jesse, but his teeth were clamped in frustration. "Can't leave ye two alone."

"Stay with Shea." I caught Shea's eye, and she tossed me the carbine.

The muscles in his chest flexed. "Evie—"

"Not arguing this." I exchanged the magazine in the carbine with a full one on my belt and took off after Jesse, sprinting through tall grass, the exposed skin on my arms baking in the unforgiving heat.

Halfway across the field, I felt them. Dozens of pulsing beacons, wild and menacing. The pauses between the rifle booms stretched longer and longer, until silence weighted the air.

The closer I got, the faster I ran. Maybe it was my super speed kicking in. Maybe it was the fear building in my gut. I passed Jesse's sprint, his shout chasing me into the valley, where I skidded to a stop, lungs burning, and adrenaline surging through my blood.

At the bottom of a shallow hill, a throng of aphids corralled Tallis and Georges. They swung their rifles like swords, evidently out of bullets. Out of time.

Jesse slammed into my back, ripping my shirt to my neck.

"Stop them."

They were what…a thousand yards away? It would take another sixty seconds to cover the distance, and the bugs were out of range of bullets and arrows. Could I even telepathically reach that far?

I gave Jesse a weak nod and broadcasted *Leave* with every ounce of energy I could suck from him.

Standing outside of the cluster was one massive bug. It towered over the others, its scaly green back shimmering in the sunlight as it watched the swarm close in, shrinking the circle around Tallis and Georges. It produced a sound so foreign, so spine-tinglingly potent I felt it in my bones. My first thought was that it was left out, rejected from the group. Then it swung its pupil-less glare at me and cocked its head.

I couldn't see it so much as *feel* it. Intelligence. Control. *Authority.*

I shivered. "Jesse." My voice wavered, my stomach twisting with dread. "That's their leader." The commander of their army.

He pressed his chest against my back, our flesh sliding with sweat, his arms wrapping me in a skin cocoon.

White-hot energy jolted through me, and I frantically pulled on it, casting my order over and over, until it ripped from my throat. "Leave. Go. Run!"

A wave rippled through the swarm, and green bodies scattered in all directions. But not without their meal. Tallis and Georges went down, their arms flailing in wild panic. I watched, helpless and terrified, as mouthparts speared through their chests.

"Noooo!" Jesse shouted.

Instinctively, I broke away from his embrace, my heart pounding as fast as my feet. I bolted toward the hill, scrambling to get to them, stumbling and throwing myself forward again.

A hand grabbed the back of my shirt, and Jesse yanked me against him with a strength I couldn't match.

"You can't save them. You can't…" His breaths labored,

his voice low and pained. "It's too late."

I buckled at the waist, consumed with denial and horror, as Georges and Tallis' bodies were dragged away.

"No," I screamed, jerking against his arms. "We can still reach them."

But we couldn't. Two aphids slammed into each other, hissing and smacking claws as if fighting over Georges' limp body. Tallis was already gone, carried into the woods in a frenzied feeding.

Bile burned through my chest, and my hands went to my mouth. I swallowed it back, drowning in helplessness. I failed them. I knew the distance was too far to command the mob. I should've run down there immediately, shooting and killing the old-fashioned way, the goddamned reliable way, instead of relying on my bullshit superpower.

"Jesse. I…I'm sorry. I'm so sorry."

"Shhh." His arms tightened around me, his mouth pressing hard against my neck, letting me know he was there. When his breaths slowed, he said blankly, "The bugs know we're here. They'll be back."

And Georges and Tallis would be with them. Mutated. Hungry. No longer human. They had been Jesse's friends. Companions long before the virus. I knew what that loss felt like. It changed something in the brain, gnawing at hope and injecting a sickly kind of indifference. It made a person abandon her heart, trading it for apathy, to avoid future pain.

But Jesse still had connections to his prior life. He still had the Lakota, if and when we ever made it back to the mountains.

I pulled in a shuddering breath and turned in his arms. "Jesse, I'm… God, I'm so sorry. I'm here…whatever you need." My throat closed up, my voice reedy and choked as I touched the taut lines of his face. "I… Just tell me what to do."

His shoulders lifted in a barely noticeable shrug, his complexion pale, and his eyes a dull shade of copper as he stared at the macabre scene behind me. "We leave tonight."

TWENTY-ONE

We didn't leave that night. Shea had put up a brave front with her first aphid, but the walk there and the stress from seeing it resulted in fever, chills, and a headache so blinding she couldn't open her eyes. As daylight faded into the horizon, Roark carried her to the animal clinic and tucked her into a swathe of blankets.

My heart did a little flip. The downturn in her health wasn't something my heart should be flipping over, but it gave us a reason to stay. Jesse needed a full night's rest, and I needed one more night of hope.

Hope that Michio would return.

After some persistence on my part and a few impatient glares from Roark, Shea reluctantly choked down three Vienna sausages.

Desperate times called for canned meats. It was an easy meal, already cooked and packed with protein, and Shea's husband had collected a pantry full of dented, peeling cans of sausages, oysters, corned beef, tuna, and the ones missing labels? Canned surprise.

Jesse slipped outside with the remaining sausages and a stale bag of peanuts while Roark and I shared a can of deviled ham and a bottle of Irish whiskey. As I swallowed down the last bite, I thought of Darwin. If he were here, he would've planted himself in front of me, staring at the can of shit and licking his chops. God, I missed him.

After dinner, I changed into the yoga pants and tank top I'd borrowed from Shea. Then I moved to the mattress to check on her, relieved to find her face cool to the touch and her breathing relaxed in sleep.

Another relief was the sound of thunder rattling through the walls. Rain would keep the aphids away, and maybe, just maybe we would all be able to sleep tonight.

I stepped over Roark's massive body, where he stretched out on the floor beside Shea's mattress, his eyes closed. Quietly, I grabbed the carbine and tiptoed outside to look for Jesse.

Lightning crackled across the black sky, illuminating Jesse's slumped form and watchful eyes beneath the eave of the animal clinic. The downpour pelted the cracked soil that surrounded the concrete patio, and the wind splattered drops against my face.

Shutting the door behind me, I filled my lungs with the musty-earth scent of damp ground, content to stand there all night and soak in the safety of moisture.

Until a sting pricked my arm. I smacked it, smearing blood on my bicep. "Ugh. How the hell do mosquitoes fly in the rain?"

Tucked in a dry area against the building, Jesse stared out into the blackness of the storm. "They ride the raindrops for a fraction of a second then their water-resistant bodies shake off the moisture. Barely disturbs their flight path."

Thank fuck aphids couldn't do that. Rainwater was toxic to them, shriveling their bodies into a deathly fungus. But where did aphids find shelter? Did some perish and dissolve into the ground? Or did they have an instinctual sense of approaching storms and burrow like other rain-fearing species?

I held my face skyward, letting the droplets pepper my cheeks. "This is one of the few times I really feel safe, you know?"

He bent his legs, draping his arms over his knees, and rested his head against the building. "We should be traveling right now."

"Maybe it'll still be raining when we leave tomorrow." I studied his expression, and my heart sank.

Defeat slouched his body, and pain etched his eyes. He needed sleep, but if his mind was as crammed with as many worries as mine, rest would not come easy.

Did he want to be alone with his thoughts? He seemed to prefer isolation, but then again, he was a tough one to read.

I gestured to the dry patch of concrete beside him. "Mind if I join you?"

He scooted over a couple inches and pulled a cigarette from the pouch at his hip. I set the carbine by the door and dropped beside him.

Huddled together, we shared the smoke and a few moments of wordless solitude, listening to the steady patter of rain. He drew puffs off the cigarette with the ease of a practiced addict, though I could count on one hand the number of times I'd seen him smoke.

I finished the rest and flicked it into the rain. "Where do we go now?"

His shrug rubbed his shoulder against mine, and I savored the warmth of his skin. But the physical contact made me want things. Things he wouldn't give.

Leaning down, I rolled up the cuffs of the yoga pants to keep them dry. "You always have a plan. Let's hear it."

He picked at the frayed hole on the knee of his jeans. "Now that we're down two men, it'll be tough to keep Shea safe."

Hard to swallow, but true nonetheless. Holing up in a barren building was one way to stay safe, but we couldn't do that and expect to find nymphs. We needed to go to populated areas, large cities where there would be lots of inhabitants…aphids, men, and a panoply of danger. That was where the nymphs would be.

His restless fingers stilled. "We should take her back to the Lakota."

I liked that idea. Loved it actually. "It's only a day's drive back. A week to hike up the mountain."

We already knew the roads and shouldn't encounter too many unexpected obstacles. We would see those three friendly

Lakota faces, and that alone would do wonders for morale.

I gnawed on the edge of a brittle fingernail. "After we drop her off, would we return to this area and continue on our original path along the gulf?" I waited for his nod. "Then we'd only be delayed by two weeks."

Two weeks we would've spent on the reserve anyway, giving Shea time to heal and train.

"I'll talk to Roark," he said, quietly.

"We need to talk to Shea, too. We can heal these women, but it's up to them what they want to do with their lives. We can't force them into hiding."

He nodded again, his lids low, his eyes glazed with exhaustion. Or was that sorrow?

I instinctively turned to face him. "Do you want to talk about Tallis and Georges?"

"No. Do you?"

Had one of my guardians mutated, I would've needed the outlet he was offering, a supportive shoulder, an ear to sob to, or more likely, a knife to bury in my heart. I was angry over the loss of our friends and my failure to protect them. But I had no tears. No grief-stricken stomach pangs. I'd never allowed myself to become attached to Tallis and Georges.

It was an awful thing to admit, even to myself, but the price of attachment in this world was too high. People died, abruptly and often. This was our life. Death was our life.

He was waiting for an answer, and I gave him an honest one. "I don't like to talk about my regrets. I like to shove them into a numb corner and let them inflame and grow revengeful until they make me crazy."

"You're already crazy." The smile in his voice evaporated some of the heaviness in the air.

At the risk of ending an open exchange before it even started, I placed my hand on his forearm. "Then let's talk about the shed. What you walked in on..."

The muscles beneath my fingers hardened, and his eyes cut to mine. "There's nothing to talk about."

"There's *a lot* to talk about."

His chest rose, and his lips surrendered a sigh. "Such as?"

"Intimacy. Relationships. Sex." I drew out the last word and watched him squirm. "You and me. Roark and me."

He closed his eyes, shutting me out. The distant rumble of thunder marked the passing seconds.

I leaned closer to his ear, deepening my voice to feign total seriousness. "And butt sex. You know, between you and Roark?"

His eyes snapped open. "What?"

Smiling, I traced the tight skin beneath his lashes. "Just trying to get a reaction."

He dropped his head back to the wall. "What do you want me to say, Evie?"

"I want you to tell me how you feel and what you think about when you see me with another man." My fingers pressed against his arm, anchoring me. "Because if I saw you with Shea, or with another woman, I'd have a helluva lot to say."

Motionless and stubborn, he slipped into a stiff quiet place. Maybe it wasn't so quiet in his head, but the longer he refused to talk, the more deafening his silence became.

Just when I thought he'd pull away and run off into the rain, he surprised me.

"It's unfair."

I hung on his words, which were made more poignant when he gifted me with his doleful gaze. He was making an effort, using his voice, letting me see him, and I loved him for it.

He didn't look away as he untangled his thoughts. "Of the hundred million men left in the world, it's hard to comprehend that *I* was the one who found you. *Me.*" He chewed on the inside of his cheek. "Annie's ghost, or whatever powers are at play, could've chosen anyone for this job."

Chosen? *Burdened* was the word I would've used. There should've been resentment in his voice, but I didn't sense it. On the contrary, his shoulders relaxed and his mouth curled up at the corner.

"I was charged to protect the only surviving woman." He swiped a hand over his face and met my eyes. "A sexually-charged, embodiment-of-every-man's-fantasy, gorgeous fucking woman."

The intensity of his compliment sizzled through my veins and sent my stomach into somersaults.

I didn't deserve all that. "I'm not—"

"You radiate sex, darlin'. I could watch you gut a rabbit and get an erection."

I could watch his gorgeous mouth move for hours. My breathing picked up, and I tried to calm the sudden heave of my chest.

"But that's not what makes you beautiful." He licked his lips. "It's not about the perfect shape of your body, or the way your little shirts accentuate your tits, or the natural roll of your hips when you walk."

Unbidden, a grin grabbed hold of my mouth. "I don't roll my—"

"It's your smile…fuck. I feel like I might die when I see your face soften with happiness. Or when you challenge me with that mischievous gleam in your eye. Or use witty jabs of humor when you're frustrated. You're sexy, but that's a lazy man's adjective. Your beauty is so much more."

My skin flushed and heated, aching to erase the inches between us. My need for him came so suddenly, so viciously, I was afraid to move, to speak, to do anything. I wasn't outside anymore. I was in. He'd let me in with his feelings, his candor, and his vulnerability. One wrong move, and he'd shove me out.

So I chose my words carefully. "How do you define beauty?"

He lifted my hand from his arm and traced the skin between my fingers. "It's a carefree laugh, the rain, people coming together in survival." He swallowed. "Falling in love. It's when you're enraptured by a distant mountain range and it looks so far away you'll never reach it. It's impossible to possess. *You* are beauty. Strong and independent. Intimidating as fuck. Brave to the point of stupidity—"

"Hey!"

"—and damn if I can't explain why, but you want me. You want me, and I can't have you." His eyes blanked on the dark landscape. "It's unfair."

I felt the apology in his voice as painfully as the inches separating us. "Jesse—"

"Yeah, yeah, I know. Life isn't fair. But why couldn't you be asexual and bitchy and not so goddamned beautiful?"

"Give me a few more hard years of malnutrition, harmful UV rays, and life on the battlefield. You'll be stuck with a shriveled old lady covered in scars."

Without warning, he yanked me into his lap, circled his arms around my hip, and cradled me against the beat of his heart.

His mouth brushed my ear, the protective affection emphasizing his words. "No more scars."

The richness of his voice wrapped around me. I hugged his neck and softened against the hard ridges of his shoulders. His embrace felt surreal. Safe. Perfect.

I didn't want to lose it, lose *him*. "We could look for condoms during our next supply run."

"Condoms that have been sitting in a hundred degree heat for two years?" He made a noise in his throat. "I trust that about as much as I trust the pull-out method."

"A generator then." Seated on his groin, I wanted to wriggle my hips, seeking his arousal, to *feel* him for the first time. "If we could power the ultrasound, we could check the IUD."

His palm slid over my thigh and squeezed my leg through the yoga pants. "Maybe."

That wasn't a *no*. My fingers dug into his shoulders, and for a moment, I almost believed if I didn't let go, he wouldn't either.

But his hands dropped away, falling to his sides. "You've explained how the IUD works, but I need to learn more about it, understand its weaknesses. Seeing it on a sonogram would go a long way in helping me trust it."

I brought my face to his, watching his dark eyes. They were hypnotic, the way they snagged mine, bold and arresting. And they calmed me, the way they waited, patient and discerning.

The layers between us thinned, replaced with a hopeful kind of electricity. My lips tingled with it. "So it's an option. We have *options*. I'm not giving up."

"We can't... *I* can't ignore this feeling." He slipped his hand between our chests and rubbed his sternum. "It's a foreboding feeling, telling me there's a very real, inescapable finality attached to us. Like the little piece of plastic in your cervix is a trivial precaution against fate. Because fate always wins." He let his weight sink into the wall, reclining lower to the ground and taking me with him. "This is going to sound nuts..."

Curled against the warm skin of his chest, I played with the hair on his nape. "Tell me anyway."

"I don't jerk off." He laughed, mirthlessly. "Because I'm fucking paranoid the powers-that-be are going to somehow transfer my sperm to you. Like a trace of it will land somewhere, and you'll inadvertently sit on it or some shit."

Seriously? I stroked the hair around his ear, watching the strands curl around my fingers. "Come on, Jesse. You know I can't get pregnant that way."

"Humans don't grow fangs and run at the speed of light, either."

He had me there.

Distant lightning flashed behind a wall of clouds, and the sky pulsed in bursts of electricity. The storm was too far away now to hear thunder, which left the peaceful rhythm of tapping rain.

I adjusted my weight in his lap to better see his face. "Will you tell me about the last time you had sex?"

One sexy eyebrow lifted, shadowed beneath the protection of the eave. "You don't want to hear about that."

No, I didn't. But as long as he was talking, I'd listen to every painful detail. "Please?"

TWENTY-TWO

Cradled in Jesse's arms, I raised my eyes and cleared my expression. This was it. A glimpse into his mysterious past.

"She was a French woman." He stared off into the rain. "A couple nights before the outbreak, I picked her up in a bar and took her back to my hotel room." He let out a self-depreciating laugh. "She smelled like mothballs and fruitcake. Big ol' nasty bush. And her moans…Good God, they were horrendous."

That was his last sexual experience? The memory he carried with him into the apocalypse? He was so damned attractive he could've had his pick of women.

"She fucked like a wildcat." His timbre rasped, grating across my skin. "I'm pretty sure I lost consciousness."

"Oh." My mouth dried, and my stomach twisted. The urge to crawl off his lap and cuddle my jealous heart was jabbing, but I'd asked for it.

He shifted, and his hand rested on my jaw, tilting my head upward. "She wasn't you."

I closed my eyes. "You don't have to say that."

"Love your jealousy, darlin'." He brushed a kiss over my eyelid, stuttering my breath. "Shows me you care."

"Of course, I care."

But could I fuck like a wildcat? I'd never caused a man to lose consciousness. No, that wasn't true. When Roark lost his virginity, he passed out on top of me.

I squared my shoulders. If Jesse and I crossed that path, I would give him my all and make damned sure our first time wiped that whore's memory right out of his mind. I would claim him, love him, and erase all other women in his life.

Jesse kissed my other eyelid, and I melted against the touch of his mouth. When he leaned back and removed his hand from my face, I immediately missed his heat.

I peered up at him through my lashes. "What about long-term relationships?"

"The longest I spent with a woman was three nights. I didn't do relationships. Or names. Or attachments."

Really? I'd always thought he'd lost a girlfriend during the outbreak. Especially after his uncomfortable reaction to Shea's girly bedroom.

He read the question in my eyes. "The job didn't allow it."

Another topic he'd never allowed me to breach. I devoured the information, greedily. "You were military? Secret service? Some kind of underground international humanitarian? What?"

"Humanitarian?" He huffed. "Not quite. I worked for an American-sponsored terrorist association. We didn't look at people as human beings. They were just a means to an end." Remorse thickened his voice.

"I don't understand. Tallis told stories about you digging through blown-up Afghani sidewalks and having tea with the Dalai Lama."

Hooking an arm around my back, he rested his other hand against my neck, his fingers floating across my skin.

After a long pause, he looked away. "I was CIA."

I let that settle over me. His knowledge of weapons and stratagem, his cryptic demeanor and lack of relationships, it made sense. But he grew up on a Lakota reservation and won a football scholarship to some big school in Texas. What happened?

"How did you get involved?"

"I was an attractive, physically fit male, a Texas A&M football star, the shooting champion at the local gun club, and I filled up Facebook news feeds with my support for the country and its interests. I checked a lot of boxes."

"A young patriot." I smiled with thoughts of the youthful man he described. "So the CIA recruited you?"

"And brainwashed me." His eyebrows dug together. "Doesn't matter. I survived the aphid plague with a lethal set of skills."

His clipped tone put a full stop on that discussion, which was fine. I was still fixated on the sexual proclivities of the man pressed against me. "*Only* one-night stands then? Ever?"

"I went through a lot of women, Evie."

Which blew my mind. He didn't strike me as a casual-fuck kind of guy. At least, not with me. I mean, he believed he couldn't have me, so he put a thousand emotional miles between us. He was all or nothing.

Though sitting in his lap, wrapped in his arms, and *talking*, I felt suspended in limbo. This was the most he'd ever shared. I worried an ill-timed question would break the spell and erect his impenetrable wall.

But the questions piled up. "What are you like in bed?"

"I liked to be adventurous. Liked it rough and raw and spontaneous. No restrictions. No barriers."

Simple words. Direct and artless. In fact, he spoke so stiffly and with such finality his voice scattered into the rain as if he were shedding his *likes* like dead skin.

Yet the images they produced sparked a sharp throb between my legs. I wanted more. More talking. More touching. More Jesse.

I brushed my fingers across his stubble. "What's the kinkiest thing you've ever done?"

Silent, tight-lipped breathing was all he gave me. It lasted so long I didn't think he'd answer. When he finally spoke, his quiet voice sounded like an explosion in my ear. "A threesome."

Two women? Two women touching him in places I'd never even laid my eyes on?

Fuck, I hated that, and I felt that hate in every tensed-up muscle in my body. "Who?"

He rubbed a hand across my tight shoulders. "Just a man

and some woman. Does it matter?"

"What?" My eyes must've bugged out of my head. "You shared a woman with another man?"

"I shared a whore with a colleague. And before you get all excited, I didn't touch him. I'm not into dudes."

I pressed my smile against his warm neck. Jesse and another man? What would it have been like to be the woman between them? Not between *them*, but between Jesse and Roark? Jesse and Michio? Hell, between, over, and under all three of them?

Jesse's words came back to me. *Rough and raw and spontaneous.* My nipples hardened beneath my tank top, and a quiver gripped my inner thighs. What a lucky fucking woman, whore, whoever she was.

His breath fluttered along my neck. "What are *you* like in bed?"

Oh. Well, I certainly wasn't having threesomes. "Um…my uh, sexual experience is limited. Joel was my first and only until…"

I was raped. In front of him. The night he died… God, I didn't want to think about that. I cleared my throat to loosen the sudden lump of emotion.

Jesse didn't press. He knew the circumstances surrounding Joel's death.

"And the priest?" He laughed. "What was *that* like?"

"Sweet." I smiled through a soft sigh. "A sweet disaster."

My thoughts drifted to the third man I'd had sex with. Michio's model-perfect physique. His logical mind. The way he put me before himself, helping me escape Malta, and now, going after the Drone. My chest ached.

"I miss the doctor, too, you know." Jesse stroked fingers down my arm, making my skin shiver. "I genuinely like the guy. Trust him even, against my better judgment."

"You trust him?" I wasn't sure *I* trusted him.

"I trust he left to protect you from the Drone, and maybe even to protect you from himself."

I agreed with the first part, but whether or not Michio was a danger to me sat heavy in my stomach. He would never *try* to hurt me. The amount of control he still had over his actions, however, was another story.

Jesse's fingers lingered on the inside of my elbow, tracing the crease there. "Tell me your favorite fantasy."

I glanced up at his strange expression as images tumbled through my mind in vivid detail. How would he react to my unconventional thoughts? I feared his judgment, and that strained look on his face made me hesitate.

"I don't know, Jesse. You have that I'm-gonna-run-far-and-fast look in your eyes."

"I promise I'm not going anywhere." He pulled me closer to his chest. "I answered your questions. You owe me."

"You're right. It's just…" I didn't want this to change the way he looked at my other guardians. "It's just a fantasy. It doesn't mean—"

"Spill it."

Ugh. So bossy. I cuddled closer to his chest, resting my cheek on his shoulder and avoiding eye contact like a coward. "I think about being with all three of you. At the same time. A willing union. You know, with no fighting. No angry glares. No shame. All of us coming together."

He seemed to process that, taking his time in a thoughtful trance, his fingers roaming up and down my arm. "That's not very graphic, darlin'."

Not the response I expected. "I wasn't sure how much imagery you wanted."

"So when you say coming together, do you mean *cumming* together?"

I chewed on my lip. "Both."

"Like three dicks in one hole?" He smirked.

"No." I laughed, comforted by his lighthearted tone. "I have three holes."

"Which one would I get?"

Wow. He was humoring me. And torturing me. I squeezed my thighs together to dull the damnable ache. An ache that could be soothed with so many possibilities. And risks. "Which hole? Um… Any? All?"

His hand dropped to the seam formed between my pressed thighs, his finger following the line from my knees to the crotch of the yoga pants. "The one I want I can't have."

I swallowed, hard. "Which is why it's a fantasy."

"I want to be inside you." The gentle cadence of his voice drifted around us, melding with the rain and licking my skin. "I want to make you come and see the look on your face."

I lifted my head and peered into his hooded eyes, my heart thrashing with hope and wonderment and a whole lot of nervous energy. "Now?"

His jaw set, and he jerked his hand back, looking away.

"Have you ever seen me? Come?"

"No." He lowered his head, focused on my lap, his muscles hardening beneath me. "Christ, I've been tempted to watch, but I won't. The first time I see you come, I want it to be with me, by me, and my eyes you're connected with."

My pulse sped into a wild gallop, and my clothes suddenly felt too heavy, too confining.

He pulled his hips back and nudged my ass away from his groin, but not before I felt it. Stiff and jerking beneath the denim of his jeans, his erection formed a long stark outline beside his zipper.

My breath caught, my tongue went numb, and my fingers curled against his shoulders.

"Evie."

His voice cracked, snapping my attention to his beautiful face. Despite the dark surroundings, his eyes glowed like molten copper. His lips separated, revealing the tip of his tongue, and his body was so still, his chest and arms frozen with so much tension, I wasn't sure he was breathing.

I wanted to drag down his zipper and release his cock. I wanted to look at it for the first time, hold it in my hands, and stroke it until his control exploded into frantic limbs, panting breaths, and slick skin. Fuck, I would've given anything to see *him* come. But if I voiced it, begged for it, would he run?

I pressed my lips together to trap the plea and uncurled from his lap, rising on wobbly legs. His arms fell to his sides, his eyes locked on mine.

Walking backwards, I stepped into the steady rain, beneath the cover of nightfall, holding his unwavering gaze.

His eyes followed me as I toyed with the hem of the tank top. As I bit my lip, pulled the material over my head, and bared my chest. As I trailed fingers over my collarbone, around the outer curve of my breast, and teased the waistband of my pants.

He didn't look away as I drew a trembling breath and slid down one side of the pants, then the other, the sodden fabric sticking to my thighs.

His gaze darted between my hands, my breasts, the *V* of my legs as I guided the pants downward, exposing inch by soaking-wet inch of my body. I kicked the pants away and stood before him, nude, vulnerable, trembling head-to-toe in the warm drizzle.

I stood in the rain to remind him we were safe from aphids. I removed my clothes to prove I was safe with him. I held his gaze to assure him he was safe with *me*.

His eyes didn't jerk away. He didn't run. Didn't speak. Instead, he slowly rose to his feet and stepped into the rain, his unhurried strides gnawing away the distance until he towered over me.

My heart slammed against my ribs, and my fingers twitched to reach out, to grab him, to pull his mouth to mine. But I was too wet to move. Too wet to blame it on the rain.

Standing a foot apart, neither of us spoke. But his eyes said everything as he drank in my nudity, his gaze touching every curve, every shadow and goosebump, openly devouring me. I shivered and burned all at once, watching him the way he watched me.

His soaked jeans clung to his powerful thighs and hung low on his hips, exposing the cuts of his abs and the rivulets of rainwater following the ridges. Shadows cast over his face, streaked by wet strands of hair that plastered his forehead and temples. And his eyes… They blazed with a look I'd never seen on him before. He looked consumed. Possessed. *Starved.*

Closing the final foot between us, he leaned down and pressed a kiss to my hairline, to each of my eyebrows, and the bridge of my nose. With a hand on my chin, he tilted my face upward and brushed his lips over my cheeks, across my jaw, and the tip of my nose.

I held my breath, afraid I'd miss the sound of his, afraid one wrong movement would shatter the moment.

The rain immersed us, washing away the day's regrets, oblivious of the night's impossible choices. There was a limit to how far this could go. I closed my eyes and accepted whatever Jesse was willing to give.

His hands curled around my neck, and his mouth moved across my cheek, slow and teasing, lingering on the corner of my lips. It was too much.

I sank my fingernails into his biceps and centered my stance, fully aware that I, Evie Delina of Hornyville, was about to use a Kung Fu move with the intent to molest him. "If you don't kiss me—"

He crashed his mouth against mine, his hands locking my head at an angle as his tongue plunged past my lips. I fell against him, adrift in the hard grip of his fingers, in his earthy taste, and in the ferocity of his aggression.

I returned the kiss with fervor, holding onto his arms with shaking hands, my feet braced in the wet grass, determined to stay upright. Though I knew, heaven help me, I'd already fallen.

My need for him burst into an insatiable hunger, jolting through my body and tightening between my thighs. Mouths locked in a frenzy, our lips mashed together, hot and wet and bruising. I hooked a leg around his ass and ground against him, wantonly, wildly, unable to relieve the demanding pressure.

Kissing was the ultimate sexual seduction, a man's tongue an extension of his arousal. It mimicked the thrust of his cock like a warning, a promise of pleasure so intense it could stroke away all thought and leave a woman quivering and breathless and completely under his power.

Jesse had conquered the exquisite skill and made it his own. Each whip of his tongue sent electricity to my toes. Every bite of his teeth rang a tinkling note of pleasure in my ears. His full lips were everywhere, his gasps pushing me harder, higher, elevating me to a state of intoxication.

As the rain ebbed into a sprinkling shower and my lips smarted with delicious prickles, his hands closed around my shoulders. He sucked and nuzzled my bottom lip, his tongue sliding over the swollen skin. I could feel him preparing to pull away.

I dug my fingernails into his biceps, holding him to me.

He broke the kiss, breathing heavy and fast against my mouth. "This is a first for me."

I stared at his hands as they glided down my chest, cupping and squeezing my breasts. I was lost, trembling, aroused to the point of insanity. "What?"

His caress became rough like his breaths, his fingers pinching and rolling my nipples then molding around my breasts and testing their weight. "I've never kissed in the rain."

A first with Jesse? This thrilled me to no end.

I stared at his lips. Swollen, perfectly-shaped, and beaded with moisture. Good lord, his mouth thrilled me, too.

"I've never done *this* in the rain either." He dropped to his knees, bringing his hungry eyes inches from my pussy.

My hands sank into his sopping hair. My legs trembled so viciously I wasn't sure how long I'd be able to stand.

He'd never been this intimate with my body, and as his palms traveled down my sides, over my hips, and curved inward to part my legs, I hoped for a long night of firsts.

He ducked his head, pressed his nose against my clit, and stilled.

Oh God. Was he smelling me? When was the last time I bathed? I'd had laser-hair removal years ago, but I needed to shave the stragglers and—

"Heaven." Arousal thickened his voice. He ran a finger up and down my slit, sliding deeper with each pass. "You're wet." His tongue darted out, teasing my folds. "For me."

"For you." My head dropped back, and the precipitation quickly formed a sheen on my face.

Like his kiss, his tongue dove between my legs without apology. He licked and sucked savagely, his groans vibrating against my soaking skin.

His hand clamped my ass, holding me immobile as he drove his fingers inside me. A cry burst from my mouth, but he didn't relent. My inner muscles clenched around his maddening thrusts, and my clit pulsated against the assault of his tongue.

"Look at me when you come, darlin'. His southern twang was dipped in sex, his eyes like twin flames in the dark.

I gripped his hair and melted around his fingers. Pleasure coiled in my core as he strummed my sensitive nerve-endings, his head leaning back to look up at me.

Tingles scattered through my body, the intensity pulling down on my eyelids. But I concentrated on his beautiful face, his fierce expression, and the eyes that wouldn't let me go.

That was all it took. I fell over the cliff as my release powered violently around his fingers and spread through every greedy cell in my body. And through the blinding ecstasy, I looked in his eyes and whispered his name.

He stared up at me with a staggering, all-American-rough-around-the-edges smile. "Wow," he mouthed. He cleared his throat, making a low, rasping sound. "Perhaps I've laid it on a little too thick tonight, but Evie, you really are beautiful."

I held his gaze, completely and totally gobsmacked. I felt him beneath my skin, torching his way inside me, lighting me up with his smile, his husky words, and his diabolical touch.

He pressed his forehead against my belly, his fingers slowing inside me but not pulling out. "Is this...?"

I was overstimulated and sated down there, but I could feel the dull prod of his fingers against my cervix. "You feel the string?"

"Yeah." He pushed deeper. "That's the IUD?"

I ran a hand through his thick hair and held his head against my stomach. "Yeah. I check it regularly."

He held his fingers inside me for a long moment. Was he playing with the string? Trying to figure it out? When he finally removed his hand, I squatted down before him, my attention zeroing in on the hard bulge behind his zipper.

"Jesse. I want to…" I reached for him, making a beeline for his cock, anxious to return the pleasure.

He gripped my wrist and used it to shove me out of the way.

I stumbled and fell on my ass. What the hell? I glared up at him, hurt, confused, but he wasn't looking at me.

Crouched and motionless, he stared out across the field. The intensity etching his profile and locking his muscles made my scalp itch.

I followed his line of sight, but all I saw was pitch-black nothingness. "Jesse?"

"Do you feel aphids?" he whispered.

"No. Nothing." Not a hint of vibrations. No neon-green silhouettes either.

The flicker of the distant storm pulsed the horizon like a strobe light, illuminating two glowing yellow orbs about fifty yards away.

The sky went black, as did the landscape. I waited for more lightning, waited in the dark, without breath, straining my gaze over the nebulous shapes on the foggy horizon. Smudges of trees, buildings, hills…nothing moved.

I focused on the vicinity of where I had seen the pair of reflective eyes. Had they belonged to a wild animal? A man? Were they moving closer? Fuck, where was the lightning when I needed it?

Digging deep, I searched my internal radar for some indication of aphids, the Drone…or Michio, but my nerves got the best of me, muddling my senses. Was I feeling things that weren't there, seeing things that didn't exist?

I was seconds from crawling out of my skin. "Jesse, what was it?"

"Don't know." He snapped out of his frozen crouch and

gathered my clothes. Then he grabbed my hand and dragged me back to the porch, to our weapons. "Get dressed."

The sound of rustling grass crept over my back. The squishy slap of wet footfalls drummed in my ears. I spun, facing the wall of rain and inky gloom and the undeniable pound of feet.

Something was running straight for us, and running fast.

TWENTY-THREE

Whatever was hurtling toward Jesse and me wasn't going to wait for me to dress. Spurred by a rush of adrenaline and panic, I darted for the carbine on the porch. Fingers clenched around the familiar weight of the stock, I aimed into the inky darkness.

Behind me, Jesse pounded a fist against the door of the animal clinic and shouted, "Roark!"

Without waiting, he nocked a black and red feathered arrow and stepped beside my barrel, slightly in front of me. His expression transformed into a fearless mask.

The door opened and snicked closed at my back. Roark appeared on my other side, sword raised, his musculature flexed and exposed, encased in a flimsy pair of workout shorts. "Aphids?"

I shook my head, too afraid to make a sound. Could it be Michio? That hope rose and died in my chest. There was no electric hum in my veins. No shouts to warn us he was advancing. Unless…unless the Michio I knew no longer existed, and in his place was…whatever this was.

The footsteps in the distance softened, closer now, maybe twenty yards, almost stalkery in their approach. A reverberating, animalistic growl rumbled from its shadowy location, penetrating my chest like a slow, rattling bass beat.

Roark lifted the sword higher. "What the feck?"

Flashes of lightning forked through the sky, spotlighting not one, but two pairs of eyes. Two four-legged bodies, low to the ground and wolf-like in their shape, but the closest one was three times the size of the one trailing it.

That was all I could make out, before an interval of lightning flashed again. Ten yards away, I glimpsed one creature. Huge powerful muscles illuminated with the landscape. A thick, wet mane encircled a feline face. Huge shoulders seesawed atop a sleek golden back as it glided gracefully through the rain.

I frantically scanned the field behind it, searching for the other animal. But I wasn't fast enough. The sky darkened, cloaking everything in shadows.

Dread and amazement gripped my insides. Where had a fucking lion been hiding all this time? I fingered the trigger, flinching like a tiny, cornered rabbit, and at the same time loathing the idea of killing such a majestic beast.

"Hold your fire," Jesse whispered, his elbows locked with the stretch of the bow. "We'll do this quietly."

No doubt it was starving, and now that it scented us, there was no chance it would leave without a meal. Better to kill it now than to be trapped in the building while it waited us out.

I felt sick. How many lions were left in the world? What if this was the last one I ever saw? "There's two... *things* out there."

The massive cat bellowed a spectacular roar and charged. My heart stopped, and Roark's arm slammed against my chest, shoving me backward.

I stumbled, trying to remain upright, and caught a glimpse of movement behind the lion's sprinting silhouette.

Jesse released the arrow, and the beast jerked sideways, spinning through the rain with a guttural howl. It recovered quickly, its shadow lurching into the air, in our direction, just as the smaller animal slammed into it.

Whatever had been chasing it—*A hyena? A bobcat?*—clung to the lion's flank by its jowls, growling and shaking its head. The snarling figures tumbled to the ground in a blur of feral biting, claws, and snapping jaws.

What the fuck kind of animal would attack a lion? I trained the carbine on the wrestling bodies, unsure whether to shoot blindly in the dark or run into the building. Shit! I didn't want to kill a lion, and I definitely didn't want to shoot the other animal until I knew what it was. But if Jesse and Roark weren't running, neither was I.

Jesse didn't waver, flinging arrow after arrow. He seemed to be hitting them, one or both. It was too damned dark to tell, but eventually, the thrashing slowed and the pained howls silenced.

Jesse glanced at Roark. "Get her inside." Then he seated another arrow and cautiously stepped into the rain.

"Go down on yourself," Roark huffed and followed Jesse into the dark, but not before giving me a once over.

I looked down and felt ridiculous, standing there nude and aiming an assault rifle I hadn't had the balls to use. With my eyes on the black landscape, I snagged my clothes off the porch and dressed in record time.

The door opened behind me, and Shea poked her head out. "Evie? What happened?"

"I'll explain in a minute. Go back inside."

I waited for the click of the door then tiptoed into the rain with the carbine at high-ready.

Thirty paces into the dark, I froze. Up ahead, Roark's silhouette bent over a huge lump, his hand moving along the dark outline. The lion lay motionless on its side, its flank and neck bristled with arrows.

My heart twisted then collapsed inward as Jesse carefully gathered something from the ground. Several feet from Roark, he rose, turning toward me with a bundle of black fur draped over his arms.

"Jesse?" Confusion spun through me. Why was he cradling a wild animal? "What is that?"

He bolted forward, and the urgency in his approach kicked up my pulse. As he ran closer, my eyes adjusted on his taut expression, then lowered, taking in the thing he carried so gingerly. Black hair. Long bushy tail. The triangular point of an ear.

Leather collar.

No. *No no no no no.* I dropped the carbine on its sling, my hands covering my mouth. "Jesse? That's not..."

It couldn't be. Darwin was safe in the mountains. With the Lakota. Hundreds of miles away.

"Evie! The door!" The strained catch in his voice launched me into motion.

I couldn't swallow, couldn't breathe, as I sprinted toward the animal clinic, slamming a shoulder into the door and fumbling with the handle. "Shea!"

The door flew open, and I stumbled in, my toe catching on the metal lip. Shea had lit a kerosene lamp, the dim light guiding my way.

I grabbed it, darting for the nearest metal counter and wiping it clear with a sweep of my arm. "Shea. My dog. He's hurt. He's—"

My throat closed up, my attention on the wall of cabinets, the doors hanging from their hinges. I scanned for medical supplies, bandages...fuck. What the hell was I looking for?

Shea ran to a lower cabinet and dug through its shelves. "You have a dog?"

Jesse burst into the room and skidded to a stop beside me, shouting something at Shea. His voice garbled through my head, his profile blurring in my periphery. He faded away as all of my senses narrowed on the limp, skeletal German Shepherd he laid on the counter.

The black and tan fur was thin and spotty, balding around crusty green sores from head to tail. Blood caked around his toenails and muzzle, and trickled from a fresh gash along his ribs. His chest heaved, his jaw a rictus of pain, tongue lolling against the counter, as he whined and wheezed.

I buckled over him, my hands clenching around his hackles, my fingers brushing the engraved *Darwin* in his collar. His eyes rolled up, dull and cloudy as they locked on mine, and he whined louder, his head lifting weakly as if to lick my face. He yelped, and his head dropped back to the counter, his tongue slavering anxiously over his jowls.

We should have brought him with us. I could've protected

him from making this journey alone. What if he hadn't reached us? What if he—?

Pain swelled in my throat, robbing my air. My fingers tightened in his fur. What have I done?

I sensed Roark entering the room behind me, but I was too frozen, my chest hurting so fucking badly, to pull my eyes from Darwin.

Shea pushed me toward the direction of Darwin's head as she lined up plastic packages and metal instruments beside his bloody body. Her movements were focused, calm and clinical, like her voice. "Roark, there's a black case on the floor in my bedroom at the house. I need that, as well as some supplies from the shed."

She listed off the labels on the boxes she needed, and Roark's footfalls faded quickly beyond the doorway.

"Pulse is weak," she said softly beside me. "Dehydration. Blood loss. Infection. It's going to be a long night."

I dragged my gaze away from Darwin's big brown eyes and placed a hand on her face. "How are you feeling?" *Can you do this? Can you save him?*

"Honey, I'm fine." Her skin felt normal, her expression alert, but her mocha complexion still lacked its warm color from this morning.

She prodded the chewed up flesh around Darwin's gash with gauze. "Let's just focus on your boy. What happened?"

I slid my hands over his bony cheeks, cupping his head in my hands. When my fingers reached his ear, I bumped into scabbed skin and torn cartilage around the ear against the counter.

My pulse hammered in my throat as I angled for a closer look. Oh my God. Where his left ear used to be was now just a twisted hole of severed flesh and dried blood. I gasped, and a mass of emotion clogged my voice.

"Evie." Shea glanced at me. "Looks like he lost that ear a couple weeks ago. I need to know how he got the laceration on his side."

I nodded, my fingers pushing through the fur on his neck

as I tried to calm his heavy panting. I swallowed, and swallowed again, unable to croak out a coherent sentence.

"He attacked a lion tonight," Jesse said, his quiet voice floating from the doorway. "We left him in the Allegheny Mountains over three weeks ago." His eyes, stark and bloodshot, found mine. "He must've followed us."

Shea's head shot up, her neck craning to look over her shoulder at Jesse. "That's…"

"Four-hundred and thirty-six miles away." He glanced outside and rubbed a thumb over his eyebrow, his other hand tightly gripping the bow. "This dog…" He looked back at Shea, his voice thick and raspy. "We *cannot* lose him."

My stomach caved in, and a sharp burn lit behind my eyes. So much death. Too much goddamned death… A fierce spasm gripped my muscles and squeezed my lungs. Oh God, he couldn't die.

"Okay." Shea turned back to Darwin and injected him with a shot of something. His whining quieted, and his eyelids grew heavy and closed.

A jolt of panic crashed through me, and I hugged his slackened neck. "What did you do?"

She touched my shoulder. "A heavy duty painkiller. He's just dreaming." She went back to work, cleaning the wounds and setting up a makeshift IV drip. "We only had one lion on the reserve. Goliath was his name." She smiled, sadly. "I'm surprised he lived this long. He was a big baby."

My chest clenched, and I breathed through it. Big baby or not, Goliath wanted to eat us.

The sound of Jesse's pacing steps saturated the silence. I knew what he was thinking. We had been on the lookout for wild animals, but after losing Tallis and Georges today, our perimeter was down, our defenses gone.

I looked back at the door, and my muscles locked up. Roark was out there, alone. "What other predators were on the reserve?"

"A cheetah." Shea dug through another cabinet. "She was old. Pretty harmless. I doubt she survived a week. A few alligators. Snakes. That's it."

I shivered, thinking about the waterhole I'd been bathing in.

Thirty minutes later, Roark returned with an armload of boxes and bags. Darwin slept through Shea's prodding, pricking, and stitching. I sensed my hovering annoyed her, and she refused to give me a definitive answer on his chance of survival.

My body buzzed with worry and dread, and my hands twitched with restlessness. I reached out and gripped Shea's fingers, where they softly stroked the fur on Darwin's hindquarters. "Thank you. For everything."

She smiled. "He's a fighter." Her eyes flashed. "And so am I. Now give me some space."

Space? I wanted to be right here, breathing down her neck and putting the pressure on. I pulled a shuddery breath through my nostrils, which only made me feel more jittery and amped up.

Fuck, I was unraveling, fucking eyes burning and throat swelling. If I stood here another second, watching Darwin heave through his pain, I might blow a gasket.

Shea was right. She needed space, away from me and my impending breakdown. And I needed space, away from Darwin to pull my shit back together.

I turned away, thanking my lucky stars for Shea's veterinary skills, and zeroed in on Jesse. *There's my distraction.*

The rims of his eyelids glowed pink with exhaustion, the skin around them sagging and bruised. I suspected the wall was the only thing holding him up.

Planting myself before him, I stared up into his eyes. "You need to sleep."

He harrumphed and leaned away from the door frame. "Not gonna happen."

I grabbed the carbine and a bedroll and pushed past him to step outside, confident he would follow. *Heaven forbid I step out of his sight.*

The soles of my feet ached as I spread the bedroll on the

porch and collapsed onto it, settling on my back, emotionally drained and mentally wired.

The rain had stopped, leaving a cloud of moisture hanging beneath the black sky. The aphids wouldn't venture out until the ground dried. We had a few hours to sleep.

The door opened and shut as Jesse slipped out. He set his bow beside me then did something I would've never expected.

Lowering to his knees, he crawled between my legs and slumped against me. His chest lay heavy on my stomach, and his cheek rested between my breasts.

My hands went to his hair, pushing the strands away from his face. I adjusted my hips, relaxing into a comfortable position beneath his weight. He felt so good against me I could almost forget about the struggle Darwin was enduring inside. Almost.

Jesse lifted a finger and pointed at the darkness. "Look."

I followed his gaze, my eyesight adapting to the shadows. Flickering over the landscape were hundreds of fireflies. Their glowing yellow beacons danced over the field, a synchronicity of nature, pulsing to a song I couldn't hear.

I'd never seen so many in one place, and I felt like I was witnessing a magic trick, Mother Earth's serendipitous balance in such a violent world.

I leaned down and kissed the top of his head. "Beautiful."

"Even in death." He nodded at the spider web that stretched between the beams of the building's canopy above us.

A spider bounced at the center of the silken strands, legs spinning threads around a trapped firefly, its meal still pulsing light from within its gossamer cocoon.

I shivered, my mind flicking to the Drone and Michio and the genomes they carried from the spider. "Did you believe Michio when he said his transformation might've made him infertile?"

Jesse rested his arms beneath mine, his head growing heavier against my chest, as if snuggling against my heart. "He had no reason to lie about that."

True. No matter how badly Michio wanted a child, he wouldn't resort to tricking me.

"Have you thought about…if Michio returns, if he bit you…" My thoughts circled around this idea, my mind rebelling at the mere mention of it. "He could make you infertile."

Assuming Michio could mutate others to be like him, he could create an army of men to fight the Drone and kill aphids. That sounded pretty badass, but there was always a downside. Could those men transform other men? Would the bite be sought after, traded, and spread like a coveted superpower?

A planet filled with infertile men would not fare well for the longevity of the human race.

"I've considered the ramifications." Jesse traced a thumb along my arm. "If I were him, I'd bite me to eliminate the threat of fatal pregnancy. But I'm not him. Nor am I inclined to play God and fuck with my genetics."

His response both relieved and disappointed me. An infertile Jesse would un-complicate our relationship, but the last thing I needed was another fangy guardian with a craving for blood.

For the umpteenth time that day, I mentally reached out for Michio, searching my senses for some sign of him. Was he still alive? Was he biting men and gathering an army? Did he miss me as much as I missed him?

Oh Michio, where are you?

A long period of silence hung over us, neither of us brave enough to talk about Darwin. Neither of us willing to vocalize the scariest questions: Why did he leave the Lakota? Did he miss me? Or was the answer more harrowing? Had something chased him away?

Jesse's breathing slowed, and his body relaxed heavily against mine. Finally.

I didn't move from the porch, didn't move a muscle. I spent the remainder of the night clinging to the peacefulness of Jesse's slumber and holding his powerful body close to mine.

Hours passed, and I watched the night sky ebb into the golden blush of dawn, keeping a vigilant eye on the hillside, agonizing over Darwin, dreading the moment that door might open to deliver the kind of news that would destroy my heart.

TWENTY-FOUR

The sun climbed the sky, bringing with it a blanket of heat so stifling my back stuck to the bedroll in a puddle of sweat. And to think, it was probably only eight or nine in the morning.

Didn't help that Jesse was smothering my body with nearly two-hundred pounds of hard muscle. He hadn't moved since he passed out. I might've thought he was dead, but his heart beat solidly against my stomach, and his breaths whispered across my breast.

A couple feet away, the door to the animal clinic stood tall and disheartening in its silence. Neither Shea nor Roark had emerged since we shut it. No sounds from within. Not a voice or a footstep.

The mental pep talk I'd given myself through the sleepless night waned in the daylight. Dread coiled inside me, eating a hole through my stomach and nagging me to open that door.

Which meant waking Jesse. Checking on Darwin wasn't the only reason we needed to move. In another hour or so, the ground would be completely dried up, and the aphids would come out of hiding.

My bones ached beneath his weight, my back cramping, my legs tingling with loss of circulation. And my bladder…holy hell, the pressure was unbearable.

Just one more moment. A moment to absorb the tranquility breathing from the man in my arms.

His hair stuck up in haphazard strands, reflecting the sunlight in reddish-brown hues. His facial features, while slack with sleep, were sharp and pronounced in the most masculine way. From this angle, I could see a slight bend in the bridge of his nose. His eyelashes, thick and coppery like his hair, lay against his cheeks, hiding the intense glare I'd fallen in love with.

Asleep, he almost looked gentle. I chuckled, soundlessly, but the heave of my chest bounced his head.

His breath stuttered, and his fingers curled against my ribs. Slowly, he lifted his cheek from my chest, blinked against the sunlight, and turned his neck to find my eyes.

Oh my. His eyelids hooded, heavy with grogginess, his full lips parted and pouty. Sleepy Jesse looked positively mouth-watering.

"Hey," he rasped.

"Hi." I reached up and traced the lines between his furrowed brows. "Feel rested?"

He inched up my body and buried his face against my neck, drawing a deep breath. "Never felt better."

Perfect answer. Except the adjustment in his weight caused two problems. One, the thick press of his morning wood against my clit produced a sudden and tingling surge of arousal through my body. And two… "Ugh, my bladder."

He dropped a kiss to my lips so quickly I almost missed it and rolled to his feet with way too much grace for a man his size.

Scratching at his stubble, his bicep flexed with the movement. All that sweaty skin on his torso stretched tight over chiseled packs of muscle, each dip and ridge guiding my gaze downward, over his flat stomach and narrowing on the dusting of hair that trailed into the waistband of his jeans.

He stared at the door, his bottom lip rolling between his teeth, causing the whiskers beneath his mouth to stand on end. "Any news?"

I shook my head, unable to stop my gaze from lowering again and latching onto the stark outline of his erection.

Rising to my knees on the mat, I nodded at his pants. "You…uh…need help with that?"

He glanced down at the distracting bulge and disregarded it to look out over the tall grass in the field.

His eyes lingered on the dead lion ten yards away and returned to the door. "We need to get going."

Pivoting, he grabbed his bow and quiver, strapped it over his back, and stepped to the corner of the porch. His zipper sounded, and damn if that didn't fill my head with all kinds of dirty thoughts.

With his back to me, his shoulder leaned against the building, and one hand in the vicinity of that zipper, he stood motionless.

I chewed on my lip. Was he really doing what I thought he was doing?

The discernible sound of urine splattering dirt knocked my brain into gear. I scrambled off the bedroll and ran toward him. *Jesse had his cock out.*

I skidded around him and stepped into the grass just as he tucked himself away. I twisted my lips into a pout. "What are you hiding? A little dick? Warts? Scales?"

With the exception of last night, Jesse used glares in lieu of words. This morning was business as usual, his opinion about my questions hardening his eyes and tightening his face.

The bastard thought he could return to the way things had been?

I fisted my hands on my hips. "Don't point that glare at me."

His expression blanked a millisecond before he launched. Grabbing me around the waist, he lifted me off the ground, twisting my body in his arms and pressing a hand against my belly. Hard. "Thought you had to pee?"

Bent over his arm, I folded at the waist, the pressure testing the strength of my bladder. Fuck, I might've peed a little in the struggle. "Put me down."

He dropped me to my feet, and I staggered, yanking my pants down and squatting right there in the open. I spread my bare feet as much as the stretchy pants allowed and angled my ass away as my bladder released. *Ahhh, relief.*

His footsteps circled around me, the golden skin of his muscled torso shimmering with sweat. It was daunting the way he watched me so intensely—while I was peeing no less—but something had definitely shifted between us.

Walls had fallen last night, and a comfortable, intimate kind of closeness had nuzzled its way in. No more awkwardness. No more hiding.

He crouched before me, his eyes glimmering like crystals of copper. "I loved watching you come."

"No sexy talk while I'm peeing, Jesse." But I couldn't stop a happy smile from spreading across my face.

The corner of his mouth twitched.

Bladder empty, I stood, yanking my sweat-soaked pants into place. "I *will* be returning the favor."

He rose with me, his gaze on the horizon, furrowed brows firmly in place.

I looked at the door of the animal clinic, sobering instantly. Seducing Jesse would have to wait.

His hand slid into mine and squeezed tight. "No news is good news, right?"

"Unless they didn't want to wake us."

We stood there, hand in hand, staring at the door, the air growing heavier by the second. I willed it to open, to see Darwin bounding out with his tongue flapping and tail wagging.

Jesse didn't seem inclined to move from the spot. So I took the first step, then the next, gaining speed and ironing out my nerves as I dragged him behind me.

At the door, I grabbed the carbine, pulled in a deep breath, and turned the knob.

Sunlight streaked past us, and my eyes adjusted beyond the glowing stripe, searching the dark corners of the room for movement.

Shea lay face down on the mattress, her head lifting, her eyes weighted with sleep.

I let go of Jesse's hand and scanned the shadowed cages lining the wall. The door stood open on the last one, a cage large enough to hold a lion.

Roark was stretched out on the floor inside it, his arm hooked around a curled-up ball of fur and gauze.

"Darwin?" I breathed, my heartbeat ricocheting through my chest.

A shaggy head rose from beneath Roark's arm, one ear flicking, and large dark eyes twinkling in the dim light.

I sucked in a series of ragged breaths, my fingers shaking as I set the carbine on the nearest counter. Jesse rested a hand on my lower back, his smile pressing against my shoulder.

Darwin pulled his legs beneath his body and clumsily pushed against Roark's arm, trying to stand.

Roark jerked to his knees, grabbing Darwin's neck. "Whoa whoa whoa, boy."

There was something to be said about loyalty, adaptability, and sheer determination. I'd named him Darwin, after all, because he was the purest example of survival against nature.

I'd witnessed his survival when I met him in Missouri's Ozark Mountains, when he pulled me from my solitude and made me his. And I witnessed it now as his nails scratched across the concrete floor, driven by one thing. *Devotion.*

Covered in bandages and stitches, he wrestled away from Roark and scrambled through the doorway of the cage. His legs gave out around the corner, sliding his rear across the floor.

My heart lurched, and I ran toward him. "Darwin. *Nein. Nein.*"

Ignoring my command, he wobbled, regaining his footing, and scrabbled toward me in a frantic slide of claws and shaky legs.

I skidded across the floor to reach him and slammed to my knees. My arms flew around his neck, fingers stroking through his patchy coat, careful not to disturb the dressings. "Oh Darwin, what happened to you, huh? Why did you follow us?"

His eyes found mine, communicating in a language I wished I understood. Then he pushed himself against me, flattening my back against cool concrete as he licked my face and rubbed his wet muzzle around my ears.

"Did you need a hug? Is that it?" I gripped his head, my attention falling on the maimed hole where his ear used to be, the cartilage red and ugly and covered in black stitches.

How had he lost the ear? A bear in the mountains? An aphid along his trek to find me? The thought made me want to hurt something. I slammed my molars together against the sudden rage, surprised my teeth didn't break in half.

Jesse knelt beside me, his hands following mine. My chest clenched as our fingers encountered more stitches, bumps, and protruding ribs.

Shea yanked the quilt from the window, and the light flooding the room illuminated Darwin's sunken cheeks, mangy skin, and emaciated hip bones.

Crouched beside us, she cocked her head and smiled at Darwin, her voice a whisper. "You made it."

So it had been touch and go then? My stomach sank. Good thing I hadn't stayed the night in here. I would've been a fucking mess.

Overwhelmed and so fucking grateful, I pulled away from Darwin and tackled Shea in a hug. "Thank you. You have no idea what this dog means to me."

She leaned back and flashed me a smile. "Oh, I think I do. Roark filled me in, and he might've threatened my life a few times during the night." She narrowed her eyes at Roark. "Or more specifically, he threatened my...what was it? Oh yeah. My big filthy bum."

"Roark," I said in a scolding tone, matching Shea's narrowed glare.

He really needed to do something about that mouth.

He sat with his back against the wall, one leg bent at the knee, his hands laced behind his head, and eyes fixed on me. "Ah sure. All judgey and faultfindy, like. But while ye were on the porch snogging this guy"—he thrust his chin at Jesse—"who do ye think spooned your pup all night? That's right. Muggins here."

My face softened, and I climbed to my feet, leaving Darwin in Jesse's embrace. I stepped into the cage and straddled the thigh of Roark's outstretched leg.

With my hands on his whiskery cheeks, I looked into his emerald peepers. "Does Muggins need a snog?"

"Always, ye bleedin' harpy." He wrapped a hand in my hair, his other dragging my hips closer, as his mouth covered mine.

His tongue was absent of its usual whiskey flavor, his taste raw and male and all Roark. He kissed me slowly, exploring my mouth with lazy caresses, his breaths dragging across my lips.

It wasn't a kiss fueled with urgency or arousal. With his tongue trailing along the inner side of my bottom lip and his thumb stroking gentle circles against my scalp, he was simply saying, *Good Morning. I missed you. I love you.*

Did he wonder what happened between Jesse and me last night? Was he concerned we'd had sex and tempted the prophecy? Or was he afraid a change in my relationship with Jesse would leave him out in the cold?

He was the most laid-back of my guardians and probably wasn't thinking about any of those things. But I reassured him anyway, with my hands tangled in his braids, my tongue rubbing lovingly against his, and my smile curving against his mouth.

Behind me, Shea updated Jesse on Darwin's injuries. At the edges of my concentration, beyond the sweeping bliss of Roark's tongue, I listened to her concerns about blood loss and malnutrition. She didn't have fresh blood to administer a transfusion, but her supply of antibiotics would fight the infection.

I nuzzled Roark's lips, relieved, almost happy. I'd feel better once we arrived in the mountains with Shea and Darwin safely in tow.

"No broken bones?" Jesse's timbre rose over the sound of Darwin's heavy panting. "Damaged organs?"

Shea hummed a sigh. "No. A fight with a lion, and he

damned near walked away. Pretty amazing, if you ask me."

I sucked on Roark's tongue, kissed each corner of his mouth, and leaned back, taking in the sight of his swollen lips. "Better?"

"Me plums could use some love." He pointed a look at the crotch of his workout shorts. "Your sinful mouth can have a go a' the whole lot."

Insatiable as ever. I adored how unapologetic he was about his sexuality, such a paradox with his vow, even when he was teasing. Which he was doing now. He wasn't even hard.

The conversation behind me quieted, so I sat back and spoke loud enough for Shea to hear. "Without Tallis and Georges…" I breathed deeply and continued. "What do you think about taking Shea to the mountains before we continue west?"

Roark's brows pulled down, and his eyes flicked to Jesse. Calloused fingers absently caressed the skin above my waistband, and a moment of silence passed between the two men.

Then Roark slid those jade eyes back to me. "I'm up for that. It's the safest place for her."

I looked over my shoulder and met Shea's eyes.

She glanced at Roark, then Jesse, and stared down at her hands. "You need a doctor with you. I can feed and take care of myself now. And treat your injuries if needed. I won't be a burden…"

"Hey," Jesse said softly, his fingers scratching behind Darwin's good ear as he waited for her to look at him. "We need you *alive* more than we need a doctor."

She was a smart woman. I didn't need to read her expression to know she was mulling over her lack of weapons training and inexperience with aphids, and more than that, her role in the future of mankind.

She stood, hands on her hips. Her curves looked remarkably fuller this morning, her ribs less pronounced beneath her thin shirt.

Black hair framed her round face in frizzy curls. Her lips

pursed, dark and sensual, as she looked at us with intelligent brown eyes. "Okay. I'll go wherever you send me. When do we leave?"

Beautiful. Fierce. *Amazing woman.* If I were a guy, I'd hit that hard and often. Which was a huge fucking reason why we needed to hide her away. Naalnish and Badger would help her find men who deserved her. Hell, she wouldn't have to look further than my handsome Lakota friends.

Jesse gently scooped up Darwin and turned toward the door. "We leave within the hour, and until we reach the mountains, we stay within eyeshot of each other. No exceptions."

As instructed, the four of us ate canned chicken, fed Darwin, shit in the woods, and packed the truck side by side. We worked efficiently, and thankfully, there wasn't a flicker of aphids.

Without Georges to work his magic on the motor, I waited beside the bumper with sweaty palms as Roark put the key in the ignition.

After a few rattling groans of gears, the engine purred blissfully to life.

One less problem to worry about.

Shea climbed in the rear of the truck with Darwin, her eyes hidden behind a pair of sunglasses. If she was remorseful about leaving her home, she didn't show it. The three of us had hovered over her as she packed practical clothes, enough for her and me, and abandoned her makeup, hair products, and other girly things without a backward look.

But there was one thing I couldn't leave without doing.

With a heavy heart and a can of spray paint I'd found in the shed, I scrawled a message across the door of the animal clinic.

Michio

We stayed 7 days

Returned to Lakota

Evie

I even drew a heart beneath my name.

Because love made people soft and squishy, crazy and

weak.

Which scared the ever-loving shit out of me.

I tossed the can of paint and pushed my boots forward, toward the two men waiting in the truck, their eyes on the landscape, watching, always protecting.

Because love made people vigilant and selfless, crazy and *strong.*

Like my guardians, I fought and killed viciously and without hesitancy to defend those I loved. But when Darwin lay on that counter, bleeding and whining with pain, I went from tough to weak in a blink of an eye. I did the only thing I could. I put his life in more capable hands and hid on the porch with my grief.

Love softened the heart when it needed to be weak and hardened it when it needed to be strong.

Which was why mankind would endure. The human race was capable of so much love, and that love *would not end* with us.

I felt that conviction in every step to the truck, in every mile toward West Virginia, and in every aching muscle cramp as we climbed the mountains in search of the Lakota camp.

TWENTY-FIVE

Twenty-six days passed. If I went by weather patterns, I figured it was July or August. But to circle a day on a calendar was anyone's guess.

The morning we left the animal reserve, I started tracking the days with grains of rice from a box none of us had the energy to cook. Every morning, I added a new grain to the outer pocket of my backpack.

This morning there were twenty-six grains in the pocket, some sticking together from the goddamned humidity. And I might've dropped a few along the way.

We'd been traveling about a month, and it had only rained once, leaving behind a sweltering haze of misery. The truck ran out of gas fifteen miles before we reached the mountains, forcing us to walk the barren interstate in search of fuel with no luck. So we walked, snatching an hour of sleep here and there, holing up in broken-down cars, barns, and gas stations.

Darwin couldn't tread long distances, let alone repel the mountainous inclines. Shea was no better, given the lingering affliction of her mutation.

We lost time while Jesse made a simple litter to carry Darwin, crafted from branches and blankets. We were further delayed as Jesse and I carried that stretcher over the rough terrain.

And Roark carried Shea. It injured her pride to allow it, but she didn't have the muscle strength or endurance to keep our pace.

We'd spent fourteen of those twenty-six days in the

Allegheny Mountains. As I crested another peak, my lips cracked from the heat, and my shoulders jerked against the stinging bites of a gazillon flies. And still no sign of the Lakota.

I juggled Darwin's stretcher between my arm and thigh to free a hand. "Hold up."

Jesse stopped, breathing heavily, as he glanced back at me. A sunburn reddened his nose and cheeks, and his eyes creased with fatigue.

I swiped the itchy sweat from my upper lip, somehow managing to smear more dirt and salt into my pores. Flies swarmed my face, maddening in their assault. I waved a hand around my head, useless in my attempt to scatter them. Fucking irritating bastards. Fuck!

"How bloody long have we been hiking in this heat?" Roark griped behind me. "Good thing me last bath was with a baby wipe, because I'm about to finish this walk through the valley of the shadow of death in me fecking birthday suit."

Jesse hissed through his teeth. "Shut the fuck up, Roark. And for the love of God, keep your damned clothes on."

Twenty-six days, the toiling uphill hike, the heat, *the fucking flies*, all of it was more than I'd bargained for.

This was a mistake. We could've delayed the hike, waited until Shea and Darwin were at full health. Only we didn't have a home, didn't have a hideout that could be safeguarded for more than a day or two by our exhausted group of four.

And forget about sleeping. Jesse and Roark talked, walked, and breathed on a tripwire of edginess. It was the two of them against a brutal world of men who still believed women were extinct.

None of us wanted to find out what would happen if Shea and I were discovered. Jesse and Roark weren't prepared to take on a gang of hard dicks.

So we hid every time we smelled, heard, and saw human life. And barbarous men were out there, everywhere, the trappings of their existence in the bullet holes covering fresh human corpses, in the scent of nearby fires, and in the distant shouts and booms of gunshots.

And the aphids… The numbers we'd fought off to reach this far had beat us into spiritless shells. Those ugly green fuckers came at us at all hours of the day and night.

I was down to my last two magazines of ammo.

And that was before we began the hike up the mountain.

The safety of the Lakota camp was the only thing that kept us going. Safety in the isolation of backwoods mountain country. Safety with men we trusted.

Exhaustion burned through my muscles and burrowed deep into my bones. Slopes and branches tripped my feet. And the unrelenting heat turned my body into a thermal current, breaking me down, step after grueling step.

Shea was more vocal in her discomfort. For the last hour, she lagged behind with Roark on her heels, opting to walk to give him a reprieve.

"I've changed my mind. I can't live here." She piled her sopping hair on her head, her armpits dripping rings of sweat to her waistband. "Let's go to Alaska. Or the Antarctic. I bet aphids hate glaciers."

Roark scooped her up and threw her over his shoulder, his cassock tossed off and left on the trail behind us. Cotton shorts clung to his narrow hips, the brawn of his chest flexing beneath a sheen of moisture.

Had he lost weight? I guessed we all had.

He tramped past us, muttering, "Mouthy woman is mad out of it."

Darwin wagged his tail weakly, curled on his side and confined by the wooden sides of the litter, as flies circled his head and crawled around his eyes.

Jesse balanced the stretcher, wobbling the opposite end in my hands. He angled his profile in my direction, droplets trickling over his stubble and clinging to the tip of his nose.

"I should've seen tracks by now. I would've thought…" He made a hocking noise in his throat and spit a loogie in the cracked dirt. "The Lakota haven't hunted in this area since the last rain."

I dragged my sandpaper tongue against the roof of my

mouth, feeling the sudden urge to spit, too. Instead, I wriggled a water bottle from my pocket and finished it off.

We used our canned foods sparingly, and our water filter and nearby streams kept us hydrated, but… "How long since it's rained here?"

He stared at the ground, the surrounding trees, and the canopy above. "Two weeks. Maybe three. Their camp has to be close."

I dropped the empty bottle beside Darwin's sleeping body and adjusted my hands on the branches that supported his stretcher. "How close?"

"I don't know."

"What do you mean, you don't know?"

His jaw locked down tight, and a thundercloud rolled across his face. "I follow the tracks. And there aren't any fucking tracks!"

Geesh, he was crabby. Maybe exhaustion had impaired his tracking skills. But in the back of my mind slithered a horrendous thought, one that would explain why Darwin left the mountains and why the Lakota hadn't followed him.

At the top of the hill, Roark's lumbering steps froze. Turning slowly, he lowered Shea to her feet, steadying her with a hand on her arm as his other hand lifted the sword. Then his eyes found Jesse.

Roark didn't speak, and his stone-cold silence shivered across my overheated skin, raising hairs in its path. It was the kind of silence that rang alarms in my head. Every muscle in my body snapped into maximum readiness.

"What?" Jesse mouthed at Roark.

Roark covered his nose and shook his head. Shea did the same, her face twisted in disgust.

I sniffed the air, filling my lungs with loam and vegetation and the ripe odor of my own funk. Whatever they scented hadn't reached my nose.

Jesse crouched, bringing Darwin's stretcher to the ground, and I followed his lead. Wordlessly, he pulled his bow off his back, and I lifted the carbine from mine.

Darwin scrambled off the stretcher and stalked toward Roark, his muzzle to the ground. He'd recovered enough to walk short distances, but he was in no shape to protect himself.

"*Hier*," I whispered.

Darwin paused, his scraggly face looking back at me, his body poised to turn around and obey.

"No." Jesse said, quietly, shooing him with a hand. "Go on."

Shit. I clenched my hands against a rising tide of fear. I didn't like this, not one bit, but Jesse was right. Darwin knew these woods better than any of us, and the twitch of his ear and rise of his hackles were invaluable gauges of the dangers that lurked here.

Jesse gave me a stern look and stabbed a finger at the space behind him. He wanted me glued to his back? Fine. *For now.*

I trailed him up the hill, sticking close. My sweaty finger pressed tightly against the trigger guard of the carbine as I studied Darwin's slinking jog.

About forty paces in, I smelled it.

Death and decay hung in the air. My gag reflex kicked in, and I instinctively breathed through my mouth, dragging the vile taste of rot across my tongue.

Jesse staggered, his hand reaching back to grab my arm, his eyes frantically searching the depths of the woods.

Panic spread through my limbs and crushed my lungs. *Please don't let that smell be the Lakota. Please, oh fucking God, please.*

Darwin zipped past Roark and Shea, his steps picking up speed. His nose lifted from the ground, pointed left, and he took off through the brush.

We followed him, the godawful stink growing stronger, more potent, with every step.

Up ahead, Darwin stood in a small clearing, his head cocked to the side. His hackles weren't up and his fangs weren't out. No, he was waiting for us. *And whining.*

It was at that moment *I knew*. I knew what we'd find, and

Jesse did, too. His hands trembled his outstretched bow, and a guttural noise sounded in his throat.

We ran toward the clearing where Darwin waited, passing shriveled, dead trees, our boots crunching yellow and brown leaves. It looked—*felt*—like the life had been sucked from the landscape.

"Jesse." I grabbed his arm, trying to slow him. "The Drone…"

He ran faster, burst into the clearing, and smacked into a maze of spider webs. Right on his tail, Roark, Shea, and I didn't see it until we were tangled amid the sticky strands.

I swung my arms, wiping at my face and clothes in a frantic attempt to shake free, but the strands clung to me like double-sided tape. The creepy-crawling sensation itched over my skin, and I continued to paw at it as I peeled my eyes for spiders.

The webs were normal-looking, but my association with them was tainted by memories of the Drone in Iceland, his naked body pulsating beneath thousands of squirming spots. The abscesses bubbling over his abdomen, festering and erupting with gossamer strings. The sticky threads clutching my shoulders and jerking me backward.

I shivered, relaxing a little when I didn't spot any spiders. Didn't sense the Drone or any sign of life for that matter. This place felt like an abandoned graveyard.

"Sweet fecking hell," Roark choked beside me, the sound of his gagging almost as bad as the smell itself.

I searched for the source of the stench, my gaze landing on funnels of silk, which burrowed off in multiple directions, creating holes large enough for a man to walk through.

A ring of stones sat at the center of the clearing, filled with ashes and dust. An old campfire? A network of silk draped over it, as well as the ground, the surrounding trees, and…

"No," Jesse croaked. "Oh God, no."

He sprinted after Darwin, toward an embankment on the far side. Dropping his bow on the ground, he shoved his hands through his hair and stared at three human-sized, silk-wrapped sacs hanging between the trees.

My stomach twisted, taking my heart with it as I ran to his side. Together, we ripped away layers of gossamer, starting at the top and working downward until…

Three bloodless faces stared back at us, frozen in death. Paper-thin skin stuck to pronounced cheekbones. Long hair matted human skulls, the strands hanging over hollowed-out eye sockets and jaws stretched in horror. Black hair. Gray hair.

Naalnish. Badger. Akicita.

No Elaine.

A low, pained cry ripped from Jesse's throat. Or maybe it was me. I inwardly prodded myself, unable to feel my legs, my fingertips, or my heart.

Jesse stumbled backward, his expression tightening, his hands curling into fists. I watched numbly, coldly, as he plowed into the nearest tree, punching it, over and over.

Roark tackled him from behind and slammed him into the ground, speaking into his ear. I looked away, unable to swallow, finding it goddamned difficult to breathe.

A gentle hand rested on my shoulder. "These were your friends?" Shea whispered. "The Lakota?"

I nodded. At least I think I did.

"And the woman who was with them?" Shea's touch slid down my arm. "Where's she?"

My hand went to my mouth to hide my trembling chin. How did the Drone find Elaine? Was Michio involved? Maybe he rescued Elaine from the Drone? Or maybe he'd led the Drone to Elaine?

No. I gritted my teeth. Michio wouldn't do that. He wouldn't betray me. I was the one who could communicate with the Drone through shared dreams. I must've accidentally given away the Lakota's location. Or perhaps the Drone had known it all along.

I waited for my eyes to burn and well with tears, but they never did. Instead, an icy self-hatred trickled in. It snarled things through my mind like *I led the Drone to them* and *It's my fault they're dead* and *They died because they loved me.*

The self-hatred wanted me to curl up and close my eyes and never open them again.

The Lakota had represented so many things for us. They were our friends, our refuge waiting in the mountains, and the final connection Jesse had to his past. With the entire world dead and dying, Jesse had clung to something few could claim. He'd had family, and they'd been ripped away from him.

Shea's hand fell away, and my gaze followed her retreating form. She sat beside Darwin and moved his head to her lap. They were both listless, unwell, and likely seconds from passing out.

A few feet away, Roark knelt over Jesse's slumped body, his hands cupping Jesse's head, speaking at a volume too low for my ears. Hopefully, Roark knew what to say to take that stricken look off Jesse's face, because I was at a complete and total loss.

I was prayerless.

Hopeless.

Numb.

TWENTY-SIX

Leaves and twigs swirled around my legs, the water sun-warmed yet refreshingly cool against my calves as it rippled by. The stream was wide enough to offer protection against aphids but shallow and calm enough to stand in. Though it was probably too late to wonder if the boots I'd borrowed from Shea were waterproof.

I blew a clump of sticky hair from my face and concentrated on the angle of my elbows and the placement of the arrow. My biceps burned and my fingers cramped around the bow, but I'd grown used to the discomfort over the past couple weeks.

Distraction. That's what this was. Something to occupy our minds, something other than the three bodies we'd cremated and scattered to ash ten days ago and however many miles up the mountain. And maybe, just maybe, I'd shoot an accurate arrow before Shea and Darwin were strong enough to make the rest of the hike down.

"Wider," Jesse breathed against my nape, his tone a darker shade of annoyed.

His fingers dug into my hips from behind as he kicked the insteps of my boots, knocking my feet farther apart in the stream.

Beside me, the water lapped against Shea's knees as she adjusted her stance to mirror mine, her pretty face creased in concentration. When it came to archery, she and I were closely matched in skill, though she looked a helluva lot more comfortable holding the bow.

How was I supposed to angle my chest again? I copied her position, pointing my shoulders toward the target, only to have Jesse twist my hips where he wanted them.

Ugh. Would I ever master this? And why wasn't he giving Shea the same hell he was giving me?

I pulled the arrow back, squinting at the wide base of the tree on the shore. I was going to hit the motherfucking target this time.

"Evie." Jesse grabbed my hand and pushed the arrow forward, loosening the tension in the string. "Look at your fingers. You're ten yards from the target." He gritted his teeth, his face inches from mine, his full lips and strong jaw irritatingly attractive. "What have I said?"

"The closer I am," I grumbled, adjusting my hand, "the lower my fingers should be on the string."

Roark sat on the shore, stroking the top of Darwin's head, his emerald gaze on the surrounding woods.

I nodded my chin at him. "Why isn't that guy training?"

"*His* weapon isn't out of ammo. Bend your elbow sideways." Jesse smacked my outstretched arm and waded behind me to take more frustration out on my other arm. "Lift this one higher. See? Puts the proper back muscles in-line."

To think, the archery lessons had been my idea. Jesse hadn't been interested at first, despite the fact he'd told me months ago I needed to learn how to use the bow and arrow. I still wore my knives, and frankly, there might've been a part of him that liked me depending on his protection. But beyond that, he hadn't shown interest in anything. He'd shut down that first week following the deaths of our friends, his grief running so deeply and inwardly, I thought I'd lost him.

He'd gone back to sleeping alone in the forest, giving me vacant glares every time I approached him. I didn't have the energy or desire to be pissy about it. I was grieving, too.

My mind was plagued with memories of fishing with Badger, sleeping in the warmth of Naalish's platonic arms, and listening to Akicita's vivid stories while drinking his hickory coffee. Akicita had led me out of a very dark place after Joel died, his palliative humming and patient words saving me from myself, right here in these mountains. The scent of evergreen, the beady eyes of a rabbit, the gurgling of the stream, every breath of woodland life was a painful reminder of the men I'd lost, and those reminders threatened to crash down the wall I so carefully held my emotions behind.

The same wall that kept me from falling apart every time I thought of Annie and Aaron.

Strangely though, Jesse didn't seem to have a problem sharing his grief with Roark. Over the last couple weeks, the two of them spent every daylight hour together, talking quietly, hunting for food, or simply sharing silence.

Even weirder, Roark touched him. A lot. A hand on his shoulder, a nudge of his knee, even a hug here and there. Such a foreign thing to witness. I felt as though I was standing outside of some inner bro circle, uninvited and warded off by the disgusted twist of Jesse's lips whenever he looked at me.

As a priest, Roark was well-equipped to be an effective counselor. If Jesse was in need of a friend with faith, someone who could offer hope and prayers and wings, that person wasn't me.

But I wanted those wings, the kind of strength that could be found in the blind belief that there was something greater than this sweltering, soulless hell. I wanted that faith so I could be there for Jesse as Roark had been.

Instead, the best thing I could offer was distraction.

I pulled the arrow back, moving to anchor position, and rested my top finger at the corner of my mouth. Looking down the shaft of the arrow, I aimed at the center of the tree trunk, released the shot, and held the stance.

The arrow flew past the target and wobbled through the woods. Well, shit.

Jesse strode away, kicking through the stream, head down, and his hands pulling at his hair. "What the fuck is wrong with you?"

I lowered the bow, my spine straightening. "Excuse me?"

He spun back, his eyes flashing, vicious and angry. "You can't even hit a target at ten yards. An *unmoving* target. You're a goddamned waste of time."

My breath caught. He didn't say *this* was a waste of time. He said *me. I* was a waste of time.

Shea hugged her bow to her chest and stepped upstream, her expression pale with shock.

I felt something a whole lot more venomous than shock. I plowed forward, my heart punching against my ribs, the heat in my cheeks rising to an inferno.

"Fuck you and your arrogant fucking face." I held the bow out to him. When he refused to take it, I slapped his chest with it. "Maybe the weapon is out of alignment. Did you think of that? Or maybe it's fucking cursed."

I regretted that as soon as I said it. The bows he'd given Shea and me had belonged to the Lakota, the ash wood softly worn by their gentle hands, the arrows crafted with skill and love.

The same bows we'd pulled from their dead fingers. The same arrows that *hadn't* saved their lives.

Jesse yanked it from my hand and strapped it on his back. "No such thing as an inaccurate bow. The person is inaccurate." His tone scathed with rage. "*You* are inaccurate."

Splashing sounded Roark's approach and in the next breath, he sidled in front of me, his hand tightly gripped on Jesse's shoulder. A warning grip.

"Well done." Two words Roark said when he didn't mean it. His fingers squeezed, shoving Jesse backward. "If ye talk to her like that again, I'll break your face and send ye off seeing triple with your sphincter leaking ass juice. Feel me?"

Jesse jerked out of Roark's grip, his glare stark red and aimed at me.

This had nothing to do with my archery skills and everything to do with the deaths of our friends. Jesse hadn't verbally blamed me, but I could see the censure that put shadows in his eyes and grooved angry lines across his face.

But I'd rather him blame me than Michio. If Michio had

led the Drone to the Lakota camp…

I shut the door on that thought. We couldn't determine the timing of the Lakota's deaths given the mummified state of their bodies, but if Darwin had left the mountains *because* of the Drone, his travel time to the animal reserve didn't add up to the timing of Michio's departure.

Jesse was smart enough to work that out, which made my telepathic link to the Drone the most obvious point of blame.

As Jesse trampled downstream, all I could do was stare after him, my pulse pounding in my throat. How would we move on from this? What could I do or say to return to the way things were between us?

Walking away wasn't the answer. I released a blade from my forearm sheath, aimed it at the tree branch he was about to duck beneath, and flung it with the same numbness I'd hidden behind for two long weeks.

It landed with a thunk, inches above his head.

He stopped, glanced up at the buried blade, and turned his neck. His glare found me, tunneled into my chest, and bit a chunk out of my heart.

I swallowed the unbearable hurt and raised my chin. "How's that for *inaccurate*? Maybe I should've aimed a few inches lower?"

His brows dipped over red-rimmed eyes. Then he turned away and continued downstream.

"Bastard." I hated watching his retreating form. *Hated* it.

"Evie." Roark sighed, turning to face me. "He's—"

"Grieving? Well, so am I." I just chose not to take it out on other people.

"Give him time, love."

I'd given him two weeks, and the coldness was shattering me from the inside out.

I pushed past Roark, gave Shea a strained smile, and waded after Jesse. As I trudged beneath the overhanging branch, I collected my knife and returned it to the arm sheath, my attention on the muscled form of stubbornness incarnate. "Stop walking away from me, Jesse Beckett!"

He continued his slogging pace, not even acknowledging me with one of his condemning glares.

I charged down the middle of the stream, fuming and clumsy, lifting my heavy boots out of the water to gain speed. No more running away. The bastard was going down.

A few splashing stomps later, I spun around him, grabbed his wrist, and pulled it across the front of my body. As intended, the momentum fucked with his balance and forced him to take a step.

Surprise rounded his eyes as I ducked down and gripped the back of his denim-clad thighs, hooking in and dropping to my knees. The rocky bottom jarred pain through my knee caps as I locked a leg around his forward-stepping ankle.

Sure, he was bigger and stronger, but he hadn't spent years learning Jiu Jitsu under my husband's ruthless tutelage.

He saw the confidence in my eyes, and he knew it, too. "Evie…"

With his ankle trapped, I drove into his chest, laying him flat on his back with a colossal splash.

He crashed beneath the water, the stream washing over his face. He thrashed and bucked under me until my thighs straddled his waist.

His hands broke the surface first, wrapping around my throat. His head followed as he sat up and gasped for air. "The fuck?"

"Fucking say it, Jesse." My throat worked against the press of his fingers as my miserable damned emotions chewed away the edges of my voice. "If you're going to blame me for their deaths, use your fucking words."

"Blame you?" His face fell, as did his hands, dropping to my lap. "What are you talking about?"

I stabbed a finger at his chest. "You look at me with contempt. With *hatred*."

My chin wobbled as an aching jolt of sadness punched through my anger. I covered my mouth with shaking fingers, attempting to hide the vulnerability plastered there.

Gathering my composure, I lowered my hands and curled

them against my thighs beneath the water. "You're breaking my heart with your…your goddamned silent treatment. What do you want me to say, Jesse? I'm sorry. I'm so fucking sorry." My voice broke, and I swallowed to strengthen it. "I've said it a million times, but dammit, I can't express how sorry I truly am."

Leaning back in the stream with water splashing over his shoulders, he held his head up to see me, to search my eyes, his own growing wider, glassier. "Evie, you…I'm not…fuck!" He swiped a hand over his face. "You couldn't be more wrong. If I look at you with anything, it's with…"

His raspy voice trailed off as he stared past me. When his eyes returned to mine, they were soft and full of regret.

I really needed him to finish that sentence, but I wouldn't force him. Instead, I slowly, cautiously, traced the corner of his mouth, trying to tease the words from it.

He sat there, his body rigid beneath mine, forming an imposing cliff in the stream. Flexed biceps, strong neck, bunched pecs, the power in his thighs invisible beneath the water, but they tensed against my ass as he leaned forward, pushing the hair from my face, his gaze following the movement.

"I look at you with fear, darlin'." His voice rumbled in that vibrating twang of his.

I leaned back. "Fear?"

"Panic. Dread. Afraid-of-the-dark-and-crying-for-my-momma *terror*."

I shook my head, scrunching my brows. No way was he afraid of *me*. Hell, this man wasn't afraid of anything.

He toyed with the ends of my hair where it lay across my chest. "When I look at you, I see you trapped in a spider sac, your blood sucked dry, your life…" His fingers squeezed around the wet strands, his voice hollow. "Gone. Then I see you pregnant, the child in your womb clawing its way out, and you're bleeding and limp and…"

"Okay. It's okay." I wrapped my arms around his neck and pulled his head to my chest, my fingers lost in his hair.

So the deaths of our friends had made the prophecy more real for him? Fuck, why hadn't he just told me that?

"Did you think ignoring me or treating me like shit would make me go away? That it would make your fears go away?"

Footsteps splashed behind me with all the gracefulness of Roark's heavy-booted approach.

Jesse dragged in a breath and exhaled thickly against my chest, his arms hugging my back. "No, Jesus. I'd never want you to go away. I just…I don't know. It's easier to harden a hurting heart, to force it back into its vault."

Easier for him, but fucking hell on me. "You have to talk to me, Jesse. You can't shut me out or throw me away."

"He's working on that." Roark crouched beside us, positioning his body to keep an eye on Shea and Darwin upstream.

"He's working on it with *you*." I leaned back so I could peer into Jesse's eyes. "Why him and not me?"

A look of confusion drew across Jesse's expression. "Maybe because he doesn't fling knives at my head."

I huffed. "No, he just threatens to beat you until diarrhea leaks from your ass."

Jesse's mouth lifted with a small smile as he traced the lines of my lips with a wet finger. I didn't know it until that moment how much I *needed* that affection. The gesture in his touch filled my chest with warmth, expanding it, healing the hurt inside it.

"He needed some distance," Roark said, "to set things straight in his head." His eyes cut to Jesse. "Though ye made a right balls of it, lad."

Jesse's lips flattened, twitched. "Let's leave my balls out of it."

Roark scratched his jaw and arched an eyebrow. "Want a go a' mine then, do ye?"

"No." Jesse pinched the bridge of his nose. "Definitely not."

"Ye should, because you're gonna need a whole fecking bag of balls."

Seriously with the balls talk? I was straddled on Jesse's lap, surrounded by a rippling landscape of bare-chested muscles. *Show a girl some mercy.* "Why does Jesse need a bag of balls?"

Roark cocked his head. "To work himself up to a man-sized apology for being such a squirrel-faced cunt."

"Squirrel-faced?" That was a new one. I searched the brutal angles of Jesse's very un-squirrel-like features.

"Aye." Roark rolled a shoulder. "His nuts are currently lodged in the vicinity of his cheeks."

I couldn't stifle my grin as I glanced between Jesse's scowl and Roark's wide smile. "Jesse doesn't do apologies."

It was a Lakota thing. If a mistake was made, they simply said *Wanunhecun.* Loosely translated: Oops.

But Jesse didn't utter that word. Instead, he studied me with a strikingly raw expression, his lips parted, and his copper eyes burning bright, communicating so much in that single look. Then he punctuated it with his hands in my hair, his mouth locked onto mine, and his tongue pushing past my lips.

I grabbed his shoulders and clenched my thighs around his waist, knocked off balance and instantly aroused. He apologized with the roll of his tongue and the slide of his lips, his kiss so thorough and intense I felt it in every inch of my body, breaking me apart and making me whole again.

His skin slipped hot and smooth beneath my fingers, his body hard as stone between my legs. I was fully aware Roark was right there, watching, but the urge to rock against Jesse's pelvis, to forgive him completely and passionately, outweighed my inhibition. Besides, Roark said he liked to watch, and knowing that only turned me on more.

Roark climbed to his feet. "When you're done apologizing to her tonsils, help me catch some fish, will ye? I'm about to gnaw me own fecking arm off here."

Jesse smiled against my mouth, breaking the kiss. "That guy…" He shook his head.

Yeah. That guy. Roark towered over us, regarding our embrace with something like contentment glimmering in his eyes. I wasn't sure I'd ever figure out his role in my relationships, but one thing was certain. He wanted us to be happy. The three of us, if there were such a thing. Or the four of us, if I were willing to stab myself with the slowly deteriorating, rusted prong of hope.

I unfolded my limbs and stood, making my way back to Shea. Halfway there, a sudden charge of energy slammed into my stomach. I buckled over, breathing through it, and angled my head to make sure Shea and Darwin were still in the stream.

"Don't leave the water," I shouted, my mind coiling around the invisible threads, counting them. "Fifteen aphids. East side."

Without hesitation, Shea raised the bow, seated an arrow, and moved into anchor position.

I watched her carefully for a moment, studying her expression for discomfort. "Do you feel them? The aphids?"

She shook her head, her attention on the treed shoreline. It was unfortunate she hadn't picked up the internal aphid sensory from me. It would've been an extraordinary defense mechanism to pass along to cured women.

Jesse handed me my bow and pecked a kiss on my temple. "You can do this, darlin'."

He waded upstream to stand beside Shea. Darwin was already on point, his ear pinned back against his head, his back and shoulders barely breaching the rolling water.

Our packs lined the shore on the west side, my carbine and handgun there, just a useless pile of metal without ammo. If we needed to run, at least we could grab our food.

Roark arched a brow at me, and I raised mine in challenge. Oh sure, I could do this without bullets. Ha! Worst case, I could hug the closest guy and telepathically command the aphids into the stream and let the water kill them.

A few minutes later, the four of us stood in a line, three anchored arrows and one raised sword.

The breeze brushed past my nose, carrying with it the scent of rot. Beside me, Darwin raised his hackles, his body silent and still in the water. Not even a growl. He'd learned over the years not to announce his location.

Now if only he would stay put when the aphids arrived.

I delivered my command for him to stay with a stern whisper. "*Bleib.*"

Then we waited. It felt like an eternity as we watched for movement in the trees, listening for the rustle of foliage and the hissing snarls of wet mouths. I could sense their approach like claws scraping the lining of my stomach, but when they finally emerged, it wasn't with a monstrous explosion from the forest.

Fifteen aphids slipped silently and lightning fast along the shoreline. A terrifying sight if we had been standing anywhere else but in the water.

"They're getting smarter." Jesse wrinkled his forehead. "But they're still allergic to water."

Thank fuck for that. We held our positions and released our arrows into the horde. Roark swept to the edge, taking down the braver bugs that swung their bulbous heads close to the shore.

My aim with the bow was still shit, and as I reached for each arrow from the quiver on my back, I wondered if I'd run out before the last aphid fell. I wondered how many aphids prowled the planet, and how many arrows it would take to even make a dent in their numbers.

There were about seven billion people when the aphid plague hit, spread across seven continents. How many mutated? How many men were still mutating, perishing beneath the aphids' evolving intelligence? How many humans were we losing every day?

As far as battles went, this one ended quicker than most, thanks to the protection of the stream and the bugs' hungry drive to get to us but *not* hungry enough to dive into the water to collect their food. The skin on my index finger burned from the friction of the arrows as I nocked another one and scanned the shore.

Fifteen scaly green bodies covered the ground, a few

missing heads, the rest prickling with arrows.

I lowered the bow and ran my hand through Darwin's dense fur. He licked my fingers then bounded out of the stream, circling and sniffing through the carnage.

"Hot damn." Shea bumped a shoulder against mine. "Bona-fide warrior princesses for the win. I'm ready to do that again."

I laughed, delighted with the excitement brightening her face, and dared a peek at Jesse. The quiver on his back was completely full. What on Earth?

He caught my eyes and grinned. "I didn't want to dirty my arrows unless I had to. That was all you, ladies." He glanced at the few detached heads. "And Roark."

I reassessed the gory shoreline. The majority of the arrows hung from some part of a mutated body.

"Most of those are yours, Shea." I was certain I'd only hit a couple bugs.

And so it went. As the days and nights slipped by, we slowly made our way down the mountain, sticking to the stream, practicing with our bows, and testing our new skill on the dozens of aphids we encountered.

Jesse taught us how to make arrows, and I stayed on his ass about using his words. It wasn't a walk in the park by any stretch of the imagination. The days were blistering and long, the aphids persistent, and the hike perilously steep. I was forced to shed the weight of my carbine and handgun. Jesse and Roark left bulky supplies along the trail as well. Canned foods, extra water, and the ultrasound machine. The latter was the most difficult to let go.

But the evenings were the hardest. The four of us huddled together, in the shadows, next to the stream, relying on Darwin's nose and my internal sensor to alert us of aphids.

Beyond the usual dangers and the torment of insomnia, nightfall brought another kind of torture. The proximity of our bodies pressed together, mine sandwiched between Jesse and Roark, produced an agonizing tension. Tension in the form of not one but two erections prodding at my body.

Sexual frustration smothered our bedrolls. If Shea had inherited even a fraction of my libido, she would've been miserable too, sleeping at Roark's back night after night. But she was smart enough to never try anything with my guardians, and I thanked her by not messing around in front of her. Without privacy, there was no fooling around, no self-pleasure, and definitely no sex. Not while guarding Shea. And honoring a vow. And avoiding pregnancy.

Yeah, I dreaded the evenings. We all did.

But a month later, we walked out of the mountains, physically healed and emotionally on our way to *better*.

As we footed south along Route 220, the days shortened and the nights grew cooler. Shea and I had gained confidence with our bows, but we were only four people strong. We needed more guards. We needed to find nymphs. We needed transportation and food and shelter.

We needed to ensure we didn't lose another woman the way we'd lost Elaine.

On the third night on Route 220, we bedded down in an abandoned house.

The night that changed everything.

TWENTY-SEVEN

The sound of scratching came to me in a dream. It wanted in, pushing at the edges of my mind and clawing along the exterior of the house. Sharp and menacing. Insistent and desperate. In that hazy stasis between slumber and awareness, I answered instinctively.

Come in.

Vibrations coiled around my spine and whipped through my stomach like live wires, wild and raging and singeing my insides with electrical sparks. I wrapped phantom arms around the sensation, the impulse to soothe it as natural as drawing air. This was what I was born to do.

This? What the hell was *this?*

My eyes snapped open, and my senses powered up as I peered into the darkness of the room. But my internal sensor was quiet, and deafening silence rang in my ears.

The hairs on my arms stood on end as I waited, muscles locked, everything narrowing to the sound of...*nothing.*

There were three bedrooms upstairs, but after we'd nailed pieces of furniture to the ground floor entry points, we opted to sleep in the living room near the front door. I lay half-on, half-off Roark's chest on a musty couch. Jesse and Darwin shared the rug on the floor. Shea took the recliner.

I couldn't make out their forms in the dark, but the steady pacing of their breaths told me they hadn't woken. Even Darwin was snoring lightly.

Weird. Maybe the scratching was all in my head? I focused inwardly, searching for the magnetic charge I felt moments ago.

A ruthless quake shivered through me, cutting off my air, accompanied by the faint sound of clawing against the rear of the house. The front window rattled. The wind? The house settling? Or was there more than one *thing* out there?

What kind of *thing*? I couldn't trace any links to aphids. Couldn't hear their distant growls. If it were the Drone, wouldn't I have felt a deathly sort of warning? Could it be Michio?

Maybe Michio, but my recognition of his presence would've been automatic, right? Unless he'd changed even more than he had when he left?

Something sharp rubbed along the outside walls and scraped over a window in the rear. It circled both sides of the house, everywhere all at once, patient and deliberate, as if searching for a way in.

I listened hard to identify the timing and placement of the scratches. Whatever was out there was either circling with inhuman speed or there was more than one of them. I swallowed around my hammering pulse, my stomach twisting in on itself.

The scratching ceased and took my breath with it.

Abrupt silence was the worst. It was worse than the reverberations of hungry snarls chasing me in the woods. Worse than the gurgling screams of humans amid mutation. Worse than the rip of clothing and the creak of rope when men took my body without permission.

It was silence. Which could be nothing. Or *something*. A trap. A deceptive relief.

I breathed quietly, my muscles stiff against Roark's. Then I felt it. The soundless echo of pain, creeping over me like a frigid whisper. A summons without words. *A conjuring.*

My bones turned to ice, and my nails dug into my palms. Could it—*they*—break in?

A voice in my head said, *Let them.*

My voice. Against all logic, the compulsion to open the front door sent me scrambling to my knees. One hand landed on the back of a couch, the other on the warm skin of Roark's chest, grounding me. But my attention locked on the vicinity of the door, its location blackened by shadows.

The cushions bounced under my legs. Roark sat up, and his arms encircled my hips, every muscle in his body taut and alert beneath me. "Wha' is it?"

My fingers found his mouth in the dark and covered his parted lips. I concentrated on the energy circulating through my insides, trying to make sense of the chaotic sparks. Each stinging transmission felt like liquid ice piercing my veins, spreading to my limbs and producing a cold ache in my joints.

Whatever this was wasn't aphid. It was too shivery, too pleading, too emotional. It was ice-cold sadness.

My heart skipped. Was it Michio? A nymph? One of the Drone's tricks?

I released Roark's mouth and reached for the floor, my fingers finding and gripping a muscled shoulder.

Shaking it harshly, I whispered, "Jesse, wake up."

In an instant, he stood, flashlight in hand, and aimed a beam of light at the circular tabletop we'd nailed to the front door's frame. Table legs and cabinet doors barred the windows on either side.

He swung the beam to the recliner, spotlighting Shea's fuzzy head. She shielded her eyes against the glow and bunched her shoulders up around her ears. Darwin stood beside her, head cocked, his body low to the floor and frozen in readiness. They knew the drill. *Don't make a noise. Wait for orders.*

A thump rattled the front door, followed by the sound of a keen edge scoring wood. It dragged over the handle, wobbling it, then continued on, creaking across the wood siding and pausing at the window barred with table legs. My blood ran cold, and a shiver gripped my body.

It stood at the window. Glass, wooden bars, and a handful of nails wouldn't stop the blast of a shotgun, or a hungry aphid, or a monster with wings. But whatever waited on the other side seemed content with a psychological attack as it *tap-tap-tapped* on the pane.

Jesse flicked off the flashlight, and the rasps of our breaths clotted the sudden darkness. My eyes adjusted, squinting at the window and whatever stood on the other side.

Dimly backlit by the moon, a human form took shape on the porch. Bony shoulders, stringy hair, and cavernous stare of vacancy peered back through the crisscross of table legs.

Unless Michio had lost a foot of height, it wasn't him. The icy tremors inside me agreed. My entire body throbbed with gnawing prickles, growing colder by the second in my aching need to reach this creature.

Because *it* wasn't just any creature. It was exactly what I'd been searching for, and it was here, not because *I* found it. *It* found *me*.

My heart kicked up. "It's a nymph."

Were there more? I'd heard multiple scratching sounds, hadn't I?

I wrestled free of Roark's hold and leapt from the couch, headed for the window. "There's a nymph on our fucking doorstep."

I couldn't believe it, even though every twitch and pinch inside me said it was true.

Jesse grabbed my arm and yanked me backward. "Where the hell are you going?"

The tapping against glass grew louder, more urgent. Blood barreled through my veins, rushing toward my heart and chilling my extremities. *Go to it. Go to it. Go to it.*

Why was I panicking? Or was the nymph projecting its panic onto me?

What if it ran before I could remove all the boards? It needed my blood, and my body knew this, every inch of me attuned to its movements, heartbeat, and sentience.

I could feel the glass beneath its talons, hear the stirring in the woods behind its body, and smell *my* blood through its nostrils. The scent rolling into the nymph's lungs was so heady and intoxicating I let out a cry of anguish.

It cried with me, and the charge of its wail punched me in

the chest. I *needed* to help the poor creature.

There was no holding back. Urgency heated my muscles as I twisted my arm from Jesse's grasp and ran toward the window. "Go upstairs. Wait there."

They would be safe upstairs. I'd be able to focus.

I slammed into a massive chest and bit my lip from the impact, tasting blood.

"You're out your fecking mind." Roark lifted me, his arms like metal bars at my back.

My feet lost purchase on the floor as he hauled me against his chest. I pushed and writhed, availing zero wiggle room in the iron cage of his arms.

"Goddammit, let go." I kicked at his legs and twisted my arms, the balls-out effort producing a massive ache in my head.

He dragged me to the rear of the house, and with each step away from the window, my struggle become more crazed, desperate, and fucking painful. I gouged skin with my fingernails, lifted my knees to hit and slow him down, and my teeth found the fleshy part of his shoulder.

"Jesus suffering fuck!" Roark pinned my hands at my back, his size and strength overpowering me. "I'll give ye a clatter in the hole if ye bite me again, ye disagreeable woman."

"You don't understand." I strained my neck, trying and failing to see the face in the window. Was the nymph still there? It was too dark, and the agonizing imperative to let the creature in was fucking with my head.

But I could sense it. Not just the nymph. My insides caught fire, thrashing with electrical impulses. More nymphs? Aphids?

"I have to help it." My stomach roiled, activating my gag reflex with the sudden urge to throw up my guts.

I swallowed repeatedly, breathing through it, and managed to hold down the stomach acid, all while trying to free my hands and reach my toes to the floor.

Trapped. Confined. My pulse went ballistic, and my breaths wheezed in my chest. "Put me down. Put me down. Please, Roark. Fucking let go!"

A hand gripped my chin, and the dark outline of Jesse's messy hair filled my view.

"What's wrong with her?" His voice chafed across my face, pissing me off.

Somewhere around Jesse's feet, Darwin was circling, scratching his nails across the floor as he shuffled, trying to get to me.

"There's nothing wrong with me." I bucked my hips, going nowhere, pinned between two walls of muscle. "I just need…I need to—"

"To do what?" Jesse released my chin, only to grab my hair and yank my head back. "You gonna run out there and what? Let the nymph bite you? Is that your plan?"

I didn't have a plan, but that was a great idea. It would take too long to draw my blood and load the tranquilizer gun. If it bit me, it would consume the cure, and the godawful ache bludgeoning my organs would stop.

Fuck, the pressure inside me was more than I could bear. Endless, stabbing, unbearable torture.

"It can bite me. I'm immune." I kicked out a bare foot and collided with Roark's shin, causing both of us to grunt. "You're *not* immune. Take your asses upstairs."

A low growl rumbled deep in Roark's throat. "Ye gonna tell her to fuck off or should I?"

Jesse released his grip on my hair. "You might be immune, Evie, but you're not immortal. Can you survive the bloody hole it will leave in your chest?"

Good point, but amid the agony, I felt this…this strange intuition, this certainty. "The nymph won't hurt me."

Except it was hurting me now, piercing me with telepathic shrapnel and shredding my insides.

"You guys? Shea called from the recliner. "What's going on?"

"Keep your arse in that chair, Shea." Roark jostled me, adjusting his hands to more securely lock my arms at my back.

Jesse squeezed Roark's arm. "Just hold her there while I get the kit to draw her blood."

But before he took a step, a battle of white-hot vibrations exploded in my gut, coming from everywhere and nowhere. An ungodly scream tore from my chest.

Roark hugged me tightly, his hand stroking my back and his mouth pressed to my temple. "Bloody hell, love. What's happening?"

"Evie?" Jesse pushed the hair from my face. "What is it?"

Everything ached, from the roots of my hair to the tips of my toes. I panted, certain the next anguished breath would be my last. "Aphids? Don't know. Doesn't feel…right."

Each burning pinch resonated like the familiar hunger of bugs, but it was indirect. I couldn't separate the threads. Couldn't trace them. It was as if I were sensing the aphids secondhand.

I clenched my stomach against the cramps. "Feeling aphids…through the nymph? Could be too far away?"

Roark shushed me with his lips on my forehead. "Aphids den' harm nymphs. If one bit the other, they both perish."

In theory. A theory we'd never tested.

Jesse stood beside us, invisible in the dark, and silent except for the scrape of his breaths. He must've been torn between staying at my side and going to get the supplies to draw my blood. We were wasting precious time.

As I opened my mouth to hurry him, another jolt of pain iced through me. My back bowed in Roark's arms, and the scent of blood tickled my nose. That smell…it was more of an out-of-body perception, arousing my stomach, but not *my* stomach. The nymph's stomach. And it wasn't *my* blood I smelled this time. The intoxicating scent was coming from…

No. I twisted my neck to see the window, squinting through the pitch-black. "Wait!"

Glass shattered across the room.

TWENTY-EIGHT

Something or someone broke the window. The dark room wrapped around me as I sucked in a breath. Then everything happened at once.

The incapacitating pain in my stomach burst a blinding light behind my eyes, wrenching a scream from my throat. Roark's arms tightened around me, lifting me into a cradle hold. And Jesse's feet pounded across the floor as he ran toward the broken window.

Before I took the next breath, an implosion of warmth released in my chest. I gasped, trembling all over, as the worst of the pain vanished. Darwin whimpered somewhere beneath me, and electric currents flickered at the edge of my senses. But all of it faded the moment Jesse turned on the flashlight.

Shea stood at the window, blinking against the stark light with a hammer dangling from one hand. Her other arm was poked between the nailed table legs and through a foot-wide hole in the glass, hanging out of sight on the other side. *With the nymph.*

She stared at the jagged hole without moving a muscle to pull her arm back, her dark complexion paling with…shock? Unthinkable pain? Was the nymph eating her arm off?

"Shit!" Jesse tucked the flashlight under his arm and grabbed her shoulder, slowly easing her free of the broken shards.

Would she pull back a bloody stump? Would the nymph try to crawl through and attack Jesse? Why couldn't I feel the nymph anymore?

The moment her arm was free, Jesse dragged her away from the window.

I pushed against Roark's chest, my body shaking in terror. "Put me down."

Instead of releasing me, he carried me to them with the clickity-clack of Darwin's claws at his heels and took the flashlight from Jesse. Then he redirected the beam on the mocha-skinned arm held in Jesse's hands.

Cuts from the glass left bloody grooves across her skin, but none of the gashes looked deep. What curdled my stomach was the puncture on the inside of her wrist.

It was the size of a nail-head, perfectly round, and welling with dark red blood. The kind of puncture made by the tip of a speared mouth.

Shea's eyebrows dug together, the whites of her eyes stark in the light still illuminated on her arm.

Jesse moved the beam to the empty window and returned it to her arm. "What the fuck were you thinking?"

A grunt rumbled in Roark's chest. "Were ye dipping into me whiskey, woman, and blowing out your mental capacities?"

"No! I had to..." She shook her head, confusion drawing down the corners of her mouth. "I don't know. I didn't think. I...I just had to go to the nymph."

The same confusion twisted through me, seeking answers I didn't have. "I felt that pull, too." I met her eyes. "Did it hurt? Are you in pain?"

She shook her head, her lips pinched in a line.

The room held its breath. This was uncharted territory. Were cured women immune to a nymph's bite?

If she mutated, the signs would appear immediately. Her eyes would glass over. Her throat would convulse with bubbling noises. Her face would contort as bones shifted and pressed against the underside of her skin.

I couldn't sense the nymph anymore and assumed it had passed out, but we moved as one farther away from the window. No one spoke. No one breathed.

A minute was more than enough time to be certain. As that minute ticked by, I clung to Roark's shoulders and divided my attention between the window and Shea. Darwin sniffed around the crack under the door then sat on his haunches, his tongue flopping out of the side of his panting mouth.

Neither the nymph nor the signs of mutation appeared. When Roark's chest relaxed against me and Darwin lowered to the floor to rest on his belly, I finally released a ragged exhale.

The nymph *hadn't* maimed or eaten Shea.

It *hadn't* given her the infection.

I might've shouted with joy if I thought the night was over. But it wasn't. I felt it…something…pacing around the perimeter of my senses.

If the nymph was still out there, we needed to capture it, cure it, and protect it.

I wriggled to get out of Roark's arms, and he finally let me down.

When my feet hit the floor, I dove toward the window. But Roark beat me to it, holding me back with a stiff arm. He shined the flashlight through the toothy frame, tipping the light down, down, down, and paused.

"Well?" I put my hand over his on my chest, seconds from bending his fingers back and skating around him.

He aimed the light on the door, releasing me as he strode toward it on bare feet. "It's on the ground."

I followed him and began working my fingers beneath the tabletop barrier. "It's on the ground because they pass out as soon as the cure hits their bloodstream."

Shea was still staring at her arm when her voice came out on a gasp. "Do you know what this means?"

It meant Michio had been right. I could feel myself standing taller, lighter, because Shea's crazy fucking stunt proved that cured women could cure nymphs and the survival of the human race no longer rested on my shoulders.

I yanked on the wooden edge, my hands straining to free a nail. "You can heal them."

Not only that, the nymph had sensed us. How far away had it traveled? Could other nymphs locate us as well? Would they seek us out, searching for us as we searched for them?

My insides fizzed with excitement at the thought of how many more women this would allow us to save.

Roark helped me tear off the tabletop and shoved on his boots. "I den' care if nymphs are coming down two by fecking two, holding hands and singing Kumbaya." He grabbed his sword and looked between Shea and me. "The pair of ye will *not* be throwing yourselves a' them like a bloody free-for-all buffet."

I hadn't exactly envisioned a buffet, but maybe the nymphs weren't as vicious as I'd always thought. Maybe the ones that had lived this long were innately passive, and only bit when the cure was hanging within arm's reach. Maybe we didn't need to bother with the tranquilizer gun anymore.

"We continue as usual." Boots on and bow in hand, Jesse reached for the doorknob, hip-checking me out of the way. "Taking as few risks as humanly possible."

For Jesse, that meant putting my survival before his own.

I wrapped my fingers around his wrist and looked up at the shadows cast across his face. "If the cure didn't take, if there's a nymph lying in wait on that porch..."

Horrifying images played behind my eyes, of Jesse's hands curling into claws, of Roark's jaw elongating to accommodate suckers, of Jesse's gorgeous copper irises receding beneath pools of all-white. My chest squeezed painfully.

I needed to convince them to hang back while I checked the nymph's vitals. "If it bites you, how are you going to protect me?"

Jesse raked a hand through his hair and stared at the doorknob.

I shoved on my boots, grabbed the flashlight from Roark, and reached for the door.

Faint buzzing fluttered through my stomach. It was so subtle I had to concentrate to feel it. Was something else on the property? Aphids? Another nymph? My imagination?

We were about a half mile off Route 220 on an isolated lot of treed land. There were no tracks, no human or animal remains, no indication of life whatsoever when we found this house the prior day. No one had lived here or in the vicinity for a long time, possibly not since the outbreak.

I dragged in a steady breath. "Shea?"

"I'll be right here, girl," she whispered from the couch. "Just get it in here, and I'll take care of its health." The springs creaked beneath her shifting weight. "There're more out there, aren't there?"

Goosebumps shimmied down my spine. "You feel it, too?"

She couldn't feel aphids like I could, but nymphs?

"Pinpricks woke me," she whispered. "In my gut, you know? I'm still feeling that a little."

Pinpricks? She must've experienced a watered-down version of what I'd felt. Lucky her.

Jesse shoved his face in mine. "What are you not telling me?"

"Um, so there might be more nymphs, or I don't know, aphids out there? But they're not close enough to trace." I turned the knob. "We're losing time talking about it."

I didn't wait for a response and threw open the door, armed with a flashlight. As expected, Jesse and Roark flanked me. When I gave them a narrowed glare, they let me lead but held their weapons out and raised around me like a cage.

I wasn't a doctor, and the only time I'd encountered a sleeping nymph was in the minutes and hours following an injection of the cure. Did nymphs need normal sleep like humans?

This one lay on its back, eyes closed, breaths even, its ghastly pale face slack with unconsciousness. I shone the light over the skeletal body. Not a stitch of clothing. Hair fell in clumps around its head. *Her* head. She looked as if she'd been living in the wild for two years. Probably not far from the truth.

I nudged her head a few times with my toes. When she didn't respond, I handed the flashlight to Roark, hooked my fingers under her armpits, and dragged her hundred-pound body inside.

Roark locked the door and joined us on the rug, moving the light over her corpse-like frame. Her complexion glowed as white as the moon, and under all that dirt and grime, I bet her shoulder-length hair was blond. Blue and red veins forked beneath paper-thin skin, her organs and bones grotesquely visible where her body wasn't caked with mud and blood.

No matter how many times I encountered a nymph, it was always horrifying. Her femininity was there, in the roundness of her small breasts, in the delicacy of her face, and in the dark patch of hair between her legs, which made the gruesome effects of the infection all the more apparent.

She just lay there, neglected and sick, withered away to bone and skin. Did she have a husband? Children? What were her dreams? Her hobbies? Where did she grow up? What was her name?

I wanted to cover her, to protect her modesty from our eyes. She was a woman, or would be again soon. A woman waking up in a nightmare.

Shea read my mind and pulled a blanket from the couch, tossing it over her and tucking the frayed edges beneath her chin. "I looked like that when you found me?"

I laced my fingers through hers and squeezed. "Without the pasty skin." I shared a smile with her. "And way more attitude."

She sighed. "Now what?"

"She won't wake for hours. Maybe a day." Roark paced to the broken window and peered outside, his brogue thickening. "When she does, we'll fill in the gaps and make her whole again."

The memory loss, the flu-like symptoms, the survival training, all while protecting her from aphids and men. A mountain of work for the four of us. My bones ached just thinking about the road ahead.

But tonight, we needed to focus on boarding up the window and door. And preparing, waiting, for whatever was still out there.

We didn't have to wait long. As Jesse pounded the last nail into the cabinet door on the window, I dropped to my knees against an onslaught of tremors.

I could sense them clearly now, dozens of writhing links, the threads reaching from across the property, each one connecting to a charging aphid. Hungry, rabid, and heading this way.

"Aphids are coming." Scrambling to my feet, I grabbed my bow and two quivers—mine and Shea's, leaving a few arrows on the floor beside her bow.

Some of the vibrations were fading, but for each one that slipped away, more flickered into place.

Darwin brushed against my leg, nudging me with his nose. I gripped the fur around his neck and wrapped an arm around my middle. "Shit, there's a lot of them, but I think some are dying."

Jesse met me at the door, and the sound of his arrow sliding into place whispered past my ear. "Something is killing them?"

"Yeah. Maybe?" Could it be Michio? Human men? I couldn't feel him or hear the boom of gunfire, but beneath the frenzy of aphid transmissions, I sensed something non-aphid. Like a cold breath. A hush of something human but not. "There might be another nymph out there, so watch what you're aiming at."

Roark gripped my arm and pulled me back. If I could see his face in the dark, I'd recognize the intent firing in his eyes. He wanted me to stay here.

I yanked my arm away. "Here's a thought. I know this will eat at your overprotective soul, but how about you have a little confidence in me?" I stabbed a finger at the door even though he couldn't see it. "Against them, I'm faster than you. Stronger than you."

"And more stubborn than me." A smile teased through his brogue.

"Count on it."

I could command the aphids to run away, but how long before they returned? And if there was a nymph out there, would she run away with them?

I let Jesse and Roark sidle in front of me as I spoke into the dark. "Shea, you'll stay here with Darwin, right? And watch over the nymph?"

We could've used her skill with the bow, but it wasn't worth the risk. She survived a bite from a nymph, but we still didn't know if she was immune to an aphid's bite.

"Be careful."

Her voice followed us into the temperate darkness. With two quivers on my back, I carried about forty arrows. Would I use them all? I'd have to remember to collect them as I went.

The property stretched several acres, dotted with thick groves of trees at every turn. Jesse led, his bow up and ready, and his shirtless muscles flexing in the moonlight.

Each time he glanced back at me, I pointed in the direction of the vibrations. My arteries felt near to bursting with adrenaline, my skin chilling in the cool breeze.

Roark stayed on my heels, his finger hooking in the belt loop on the back of my shorts whenever I ran too far ahead. I didn't fight him. Poor guy needed some semblance of control.

A few minutes later, Jesse held up a fist and gestured at the low-lying brush on the left. Roark ushered me into the bushes and squatted behind me, pulling me down to crouch between his thighs.

Jesse sat on his heels beside us, his hand hot and heavy on my knee. "I thought I saw movement in there." He nodded at the small clump of trees thirty yards to the right.

I traced the dozens of threads squirming inside me, each trajectory leading to the left. "They're still gathered at ten o'clock." I reached out my senses, scanning the circumference of my telepathic limits. "No stragglers. But I still sense some winking out."

Roark grazed a thumb over my elbow. "Are they stepping out of your reach?"

"No. They're too close." And too quiet. My heart pounded, and my palms grew clammy. "Only twenty or so yards away. We should've heard their growls or their movement through the brush by now."

"They're stealthier." Jesse's profile cut a severe outline in the moonlight. "Especially if they're being hunted."

I followed his gaze to the clump of trees on the right. *Men.* It had to be. Men with quiet weapons.

The vibrations on the left shifted, the aphids moving with inhuman speed toward those trees. In the next heartbeat, their glowing neon bodies flickered into view, scattering over the open landscape.

I held my breath as the silhouette of a man stepped from the shadowed area Jesse had been watching. He stopped within eyeshot of the aphids, then another man joined him, and another, until five men stood beneath the moonlight, holding crossbows, huge hunting knives, and axes.

For a desperate moment, I thought Michio might've been with them. That he'd built an army of men and had come here to find me. I mentally reached out, searching for his warm presence. But I couldn't feel him amid the riot of sensations.

Roark's arm hooked around my waist, and Jesse moved to crouch with his back against my chest, effectively pinning me. Or *shielding* me.

With one hand on my bow, I gripped the other against Jesse's waist as the aphids charged toward the men. I couldn't hear the bugs, but I sensed them moving in a line, slinking through the overgrown brush, their hearts drumming, drumming, drumming for blood.

I wanted to warn those men, but Roark's hand slammed over my mouth. Didn't matter. When the first bulbous form blurred into view, the arrows flew and the men bolted. Not away. No, those crazy fuckers ran *toward* the horde.

Without the report of gunfire, I could hear every grunt, footstep, and whooshing arrow.

Jesse and Roark tensed against me, the sweat on their skin

seeping into my shirt. They wanted to help them, but not with me here, their precious liability.

The connective strands in my stomach pulsed wildly. Some cut off, dying, dead, but not enough. There were too many. The bugs were too fast. I needed to command them.

I reached for the hem of my shirt and stopped. Feral quakes raged inside me, but stabbing through the network of noise was something steadier, saner, colder.

Not something. *Somethings.*

"Nymphs," I whispered.

Jesse turned his neck, giving me his strained profile. "Where?"

I lifted the bottom of my shirt to my neck and hugged his naked back. "Smack in the middle of that battle."

Would the aphids attack or protect the nymphs? Could the nymphs command the aphids?

Pulling in a deep breath, I projected the visceral order to the aphids. *Go.*

Roark pressed his chest against my back and rested his whiskered cheek along mine. I soaked in his masculine energy with each inhale and repeated the command with each release of my lungs. *Go. Go. Go.*

The aphid links bristled in response, then one by one, they began to retreat.

But so did the icy beacons of the nymphs. If I was identifying the varying sensations correctly, holy fucking shit, there were at least ten of them.

"The nymphs are leaving." I struggled to breathe in my excitement. "*Ten* fucking nymphs, you guys."

"Bloody hell." Roark's whisper shuddered around me. "Den' lose them, love."

I squeezed my eyes shut, trying to separate them from the aphids as I broadcasted my command. "I don't know how to isolate them. They're following my order. *All* of them are retreating."

Jesse pivoted on his heels to face me. "Let's go collect the nymphs." He gripped my neck. "But don't—"

"Don't fall off a cliff? Don't get pregnant? Don't die? Got it." I tugged my shirt back in place.

I got a flash of teeth right before he slammed a hard kiss against my lips. As far as kisses went, it was glorious in its absence of elegance. He broke away, jumping to his feet and pulling me with him.

The house stood somewhere behind us and out of sight as we ran forward, away from Shea, away from the nymph in her care, our feet flying with the wild hope of saving more.

If we cured them all, Jesse and Roark would have thirteen women to protect. How would we travel? How would we train and feed them all?

I was getting ahead of myself, but I couldn't help it. My body buzzed with energy, fueled by the aphids' thundering hunger, the nymphs' whispers, and my own anxiety.

Ahead of me, Jesse and Roark sprinted side by side, the sheer size of their upper bodies blocking my view. By the time we reached the melee, I'd clamped down my jaw so tightly my molars ached.

We skirted around the outermost boundary of a field. Keeping to the shadows and out of view, I fell in line beside Roark and stared down the shaft of my anchored arrow.

The full moon illuminated the expanse of golden grass, trammeled and crushed beneath a brutal battle.

Men flung knives, fired arrows, and swung axes at the aphids. Not five men. Ten? Twenty? Where had they come from? Had they led the aphids here? Were they herding the nymphs?

They zipped in and out of the nearby grove, making it impossible to count their numbers. There were twice as many aphids blurring around the men, swiping claws, and stabbing with mouthparts.

At the center of it all, stood two, four, six…holy shit, I was right. *Ten* nymphs. The chaotic brawl clashed around them, but they didn't engage, didn't flinch when aphids bumped up against them.

This went against any assumption that aphids attacked

nymphs. Why would they? They couldn't bite one another and survive. But the aphids didn't go out of their way to protect them either. Some just plowed right over the nymphs to chase the men.

The men were definitely the reason the aphids were here.

A bald man trained a crossbow on an aphid that was barreling down on another man. He reached for the trigger, but a nymph stood in his line of fire. I sucked in a breath, preparing to scream.

He moved around her and fired, missing her and hitting the aphid between the eyes. I released a huge fucking sigh.

Neither the aphids nor the men noticed our arrival. But the nymphs did. The only thing they moved was their heads, turning in my direction and fixing ten pairs of milky eyes on me.

The clawing pain in my stomach returned with a vengeance. I bit down on my tongue to hold back a cry, my fingers struggling to keep the nocked arrow in place.

Roark rested his hand on my back, stroking a calming path up and down my spine. "Okay?"

I gave a jerky nod, my body shaking in agony.

The nymphs turned as one, eerily synchronized, and started walking. All paths led to me as their gaits quickened, walking, then running, then heaven help me, charging.

"Run," I said to Jesse and Roark. Then louder, "Run now!"

"Shut up." Roark raised his sword.

"You gonna take off their heads? If they bite you—"

"Not leaving ye, love."

I looked at Jesse. His jaw tightened beside his nocked arrow as he shook his head.

Pain in the fucking asses. I lowered the bow and took off, making a beeline toward the approaching nymphs.

An aphid skittered close to a dark-skinned nymph. She hissed at it, hunching her knobby shoulders and throwing talon-tipped hands over her head to ward it off.

My heart leapt to my throat. If the nymph bit the aphid or

got bitten, they would both die.

The aphid leapt away, its sights on a man with shaggy hair and a scary-looking blade.

Jesse's arrows fired into the fray as I ran. I knew the guys would follow me, but I ran faster than them. If I could beat them there…fuck, I didn't know. As usual, I didn't have a goddamned plan.

Those final ten yards to impact lasted an eternity. I'd never seen so many arrows and blood flying through the air. There were so many men…strangers. Why were they here? What if they killed the nymphs before I reached them?

But they weren't targeting them. In fact, they took cautious steps to *avoid* hitting them. From what I could tell, they weren't shoot-em-up, rebel-flag-waving, living-the-apocalyptic-dream roughnecks. These guys were sophisticated. They knew how to fight, predicted each other's movements, and flowed together like a highly-skilled army.

They would either join us. Or kill us.

As those last ten yards shortened to one, I found myself in the middle of the field, on the edge of the battlefield, surrounded by ten white-eyed nymphs. Roark's chest pressed against my back. Jesse's arm hooked across my stomach. Their weapons moved in my periphery, but the nymphs weren't interested in them.

Ten pupil-less, slack-jawed expressions locked on me. I felt their purpose in the pit of my marrow. They'd come for me.

Taking in their assortment of dresses and adornments in their hair, my first assumption was that they hadn't been traveling with the naked nymph back at the house. My next thought wandered to the multiple scratches I'd heard on the windows and door. Had they walked around the cabin on their way here?

But every conscious thought flickered out as a burst of agony wrung my insides, the pain so harrowing I wanted to vomit. *Make it stop.*

Instinctively, I dropped the bow and raised my arms in supplication, palms up and eyes closed.

BLOOD OF EVE

TWENTY-NINE

The closest nymph wrapped jagged-sharp fingernails around my wrist. My eyes shot open, and my insides splintered into a thousand shards of agony. Its telepathic pain pushed those shards deeper, harder, slicing the air from my windpipe.

Roark pressed against my back, his breathing ragged. "This is your most idiotic idea yet." There were a lot of *i*'s in that sentence, and the worry in his accent made them all sound like *oi*.

Jesse clenched his fingers against my hip, his arm barred across my belly. "Just keep your eyes open, Roark."

Their anxiety was making me anxious, but I expected the same treatment from the nymphs that Shea had received. Just a quick bite on *my* arm. *Not* on Jesse's or Roark's.

The nymph watched me with overlarge eggshell eyes, its cheeks sunken beneath protruding cheekbones. Its complexion took on a grayish hue in the moonlight, but I knew it would look just as bruised in the glare of the sun.

Talons dragged over the delicate skin on my wrist, and the jaw stretched open.

It wasn't until that insanely vulnerable moment that I realized I'd run out of the house without my arm sheathes. In two years, I'd never mindlessly shown up to a battle without my blades, carbine, and USP handgun.

But I had the bow. Which currently lay somewhere at my feet. Lot of good that did me with so many aphids engaged in battle just yards away.

The nymph's weapon stretched toward me from the back

of its throat in an intimidating display of squirming, tubelike mouthparts. One thrust of the vicious-looking spear at the center of those tentacles, and it would carve a huge ass hole in my chest. I'd never witnessed a nymph feeding, but I'd heard all about their gruesome attacks in the early days following the plague.

The tentacles curled around my arm, and I held my breath. Then, with the striking speed of a snake, it tapped the tip of the spear against my wrist. I hissed in surprise. It was just a pinch, hardly painful, as if the nymph knew how to be gentle with its prey. Then its body promptly dropped to the ground.

One after another, the vacant-eyed creatures stepped forward and poked their spears into the veins in my arms. Each pricked a new hole, sipping the smallest drop of blood. It was so orderly and civilized. Like the puff and pass of a joint. Or a wet kiss from grandma. So very fucking…friendly.

The tiny stabs felt like a flu shot, there and gone in the span of a heartbeat. Even better, with every poke, the harrowing pain inside me lessened.

Jesse and Roark didn't move from their protective stances against me, but each time a new nymph moved in, their bodies turned to steel. When a speared mouth darted out, they flinched.

The nymphs went out of their way to avoid contact with Jesse and Roark, like they knew if they bit a man, they would die.

Five of the ten nymphs lay comatose at my feet. The rest bumped into one another and stepped on the fallen to get to me. I shifted my huddle with Jesse and Roark backward, leaving a trail of bodies as the remaining nymphs followed.

The fighting had moved closer, the men now distracted as their eyes followed the nymphs, widening as each one fell to the ground. Some of the men stumbled. Others completely stopped fighting to watch us in horror. The distraction was going to get them killed.

I might've sucked at strategic planning, but I could multi-task. "Roark, rip my shirt."

Pressed against my back with the quivers of arrows pushed to the side, he angled the sword between us and sliced. The cool breeze lasted a second before the hot skin of his chest slid against my spine. "Talk to me, love."

He wasn't asking why I wanted the shirt ripped. That, he could figure out. He wanted to know how I was doing.

"The bites are painless, and each one is making it a whole lot easier to breathe again."

Jesse hadn't moved his chest from my side, hadn't unlocked his rigid arm from around my waist, his posture on high-alert as he vigilantly watched the encroaching battle. "Make them lie down."

I glanced at the sharp lines etching his profile. "The aphids?"

"Yeah."

I didn't question him. It was brilliant, really. As the last five nymphs fell around my feet, I exhaled a command that forced thirty-three aphids to lay like cockroaches, on their backs, with double-jointed legs pointing to the heavens.

The men on the field faltered and tripped at the bizarre sight, shouting at one another in confusion. But it didn't take long before the arrows and blades flew.

The final aphid vibration snapped from my insides within thirty-seconds of me giving the order. And I hadn't fired a single arrow.

Scattered around my feet lay ten sleeping nymphs. Ten *cured* women. My stomach relaxed, my lungs expanded, and my heart soared, every inch of me free of pain. And happy. So damned happy I couldn't keep the smile off my face.

Until I met the angry black eyes of the bald man racing across the field. He sprinted toward us, crossbow aimed, those deep dark eyes pinned on me.

Jesse jumped in front of me, arrow anchored. "Stay back."

I dropped my head against his shoulder blade as footsteps circled around us. The man was still approaching, and so were his friends.

"I said stay back!" Jesse tensed, his breathing picking up.

I peered around his torso and locked eyes with the bald man. In that shared look, the pull of his eyebrows asked, *What are you?*

He looked down, scanning the nymphs as anguish creased his rugged features. "What have you done?"

Jesse and Roark crowded in front of me, always blocking my damned view.

I spoke at their backs. "I cured them."

"Cured?" The man's gravelly voice boomed.

I poked my head around Roark's arm. The crowd of men circled behind the bald man with arrows and knives raised, all eyes on their leader, as if waiting for his command. Were some of these men related to the nymphs? Such as husbands, brothers, fathers? Probably not fathers. There wasn't a gray hair or wrinkled face in the group.

The bald man held a nymph to his chest. "Liliana?" He patted her cheek. "Wake up."

I was experiencing a nasty case of déjà vu, only this time it was with an army of men instead of Amos and his concealed gun.

He glanced up and found my eyes. "She's breathing. Why isn't she waking up?"

I pushed on Roark's back until he shifted an inch to the side. I spoke carefully and clearly. "She'll sleep through the transformation. They all will."

"Call off your men." Jesse aimed his bow at the armed gathering of blood-drenched faces. "Do it now!"

The bald man glanced over his shoulder and returned to the nymph. "Stand down."

It was a trivial request with twenty-some-odd soldiers against the three of us. We didn't stand a chance if it came down to a fight.

I wedged my body between Jesse and Roark. "What's your name?"

"Lincoln. They call me Link." His black eyes took me in from head to toe. Not in a pervy way. It was more of a *Yep, she looks like a woman.* "You're cured."

It wasn't a question, and I didn't bother correcting him. This wasn't the time to give lessons on new-world genetics. First, I needed to convince him not to kill us.

"Link, my name is Evie. This is Jesse and Roark. And in a few hours, your nymphs will begin the physical transformation back to human. My blood is working in their bodies right now, erasing the nymph genome from their DNA."

Wow, didn't I sound all smart and calm? Beneath my plastered smile, I was chomping the hell out of my tongue.

He stared at the limp bodies around him, deep grooves rutting across his bald head.

Roark shifted beside me. "We need to move them to a safe environment. If more aphids come…" His accent faded in his bid to make Link understand. "The aphids won't bite a nymph, but they are no longer nymphs. They den' look human, but the aphids will scent their human blood."

"How did you do it?" Link whispered.

I looked around the field, standing in the spotlight of the moon and surrounded by shadows. "We need to move."

Link nodded at the field of dead bugs. "How did you do *that*? They don't just lay down and wait to be killed."

We had a long night of talking ahead of us. Could we trust them enough to bring them to the house? To have a sit-down with bottled lake-water and cans of beans?

I took in the hungry faces of the men who corralled us, counting each one in turn.

Twenty-one.

Twenty-one strong, fierce men. They didn't look starved for food. Ages ranging from early twenties to late forties, their physiques rippled with muscle and health, their hair clean and combed. They looked as though they didn't miss a meal, or a shower, or a work-out. But they did look hungry.

A hunger of another flavor.

They hadn't seen a woman in over two years, and I felt their starvation in the way their eyes scoured my body, lingering on my most private places. Jesse and Roark pressed closer at my sides, trying to squeeze me backward. I crossed my arms over my chest and held my ground, painfully aware that my shirt gaped open at my back.

No, they couldn't be trusted.

But when I scanned the cadaverous, helpless bodies at my feet, I knew we didn't have a choice. What was I going to do? Fight them, kill them, and walk back to the house with ten nymphs on our backs? Right.

The other option was to run. Away from the scary men. *Away from the women.*

I couldn't leave them. "We're squatting in a house a few minutes away. We should talk there."

Jesse still hadn't lowered his bow, his expression harsh in the moonlight. "Evie is *ours*. Do I need to explain what that means?"

Roark leaned forward. "If one of ye touches her without her permission, I'll kick in your stinkers bridge until ye can't tell your cunt from your arsehole." He held out his hand. "Hi. I'm Father Molony."

Nice one, Roark. Nothing said *priest* like kicking in a man's taint.

Link reached up and shook Roark's hand, his teeth biting down on his lip.

Then he stood with the nymph he called Liliana cradled in his arms. "You understand this is the first time I've touched this woman—or *any* woman—in two years? My men are looking at your girl because they're, well, *men*."

Roark made a noise in his throat. "That's wha' we're afraid of, lad."

"They're *good* men, and these nymphs were our women long before the plague." Link shifted his weight, his jaw flexing. "We already lost two of them while chasing their crazy asses across five states."

My breath caught. "Did you say *five* states?"

How had they kept so many nymphs from changing? Man, I hoped they weren't part of some fucked-up cult that kept nymphs tied up for sexual rituals.

Link looked around. "We're in West Virginia, right? We

were on the Mississippi Queen in Baton Rouge when the plague hit. Been there ever since." He read the question on my face. "The nymphs never tried to leave the steamboat. We kept them confined to the upper deck. Fed them. Took care of them." He sighed. "We didn't know they could swim."

My jaw dropped. "Water doesn't hurt them?"

He glanced at the nymph in his arms, shaking his head. "Nine weeks ago…I don't know, something prompted them to jump overboard. All twelve of them, all at once. They ran east. Never stopping. Never sleeping. Always running east."

Nine weeks. I'd been traveling so long, I'd run out of grains of rice. How long ago did we leave Elaine in the mountains? How long had it been since I'd seen Michio? Smelled his breath on my face? Kissed his lips?

"Nine weeks," Jesse mumbled. "We arrived at the animal safari about that time."

My chest clenched painfully. I hadn't seen Michio in two months. Not that he had anything to do with the Mississippi Queen. The nymphs must've sensed me when I reached Georgia and come running.

Roark tied my shirt together at my back. Then, after some awkward shuffling, the strangers carried the nymphs back to the house. Jesse and Link bandied glares, each trying to outpace the other for the lead, as the rest of us fell in line behind them.

Ten nymphs and twenty-one men. Boy, did we have a surprise for Shea.

As it turned out, she had a surprise of her own.

THIRTY

I entered the house to find not one but two nymphs in Shea's care. Steadying my breaths, I crouched at the edge of the rug where we'd left the first one and rubbed my eyes. Then I blinked again at the bodies on the floor. Nope, there were still two.

Two comatose nymphs.

The second one was younger, definitely more rebellious than the first, given the sleeves of ink on her arms and the amount of piercings in her face.

"Are you mad at me?" Shea perched on the couch, twisting the flashlight between her hands.

Jesse and Roark waited outside with the new arrivals, giving me a couple minutes to update Shea. I knew they were using that time to explain Shea's background to the men, as well as spelling out rules about not touching her without her verbal consent.

Darwin plopped beside me, nudging my hand with his head. A world of chaos was about to walk through that door—men with nymphs and weapons and carnal desires—and Darwin was all like *Scratch behind my ears!*

I grinned, running my fingers through his dense coat and rubbing the place on his head that made his back leg kick. "I'm not mad. Just..." Why were nymphs popping up everywhere *now*? I stood and paced the room. "What happened?"

"She rattled the door. I let her in." Shea shined the flashlight on her arm, revealing a new puncture mark beside the first, both of which were sealing quickly.

I glanced at my own arms, dotted with ten tiny holes, the marks already closing. Maybe the nymphs had some kind of healing agent in their bite?

I needed Michio. To make sense of all this. To share the excitement with me. To hold me. And if I were being honest, after two months without an orgasm, I desperately needed him to fuck me.

Where did this sudden arousal come from?

The scent of twenty-plus hungry men outside. Alpha males. Men with the kind of presence a woman couldn't ignore. Men who oozed ferocity and confidence and the promise of protection. Men who knew how to take care of their bodies, which meant they would know how to take care of mine.

Stop it. None of those men could hold a candle to my guardians.

I gave Shea a brief run-down on everything she'd missed and reminded her these men hadn't seen a woman in a very long time. Her smile was contagious when I told her about the ten nymphs waiting outside.

I followed her gaze to the two on the floor. Two nymphs explained the multiple scratching sounds I'd heard. And the second one had come to the door *after* I left, which meant they weren't just drawn to me. They were drawn to Shea as well.

Which also meant when these twelve nymphs were fully healed, *they* could beckon other nymphs and those nymphs could beckon more nymphs and so on. If we traveled in opposite directions, our reach across the continent would be endless. We could cross oceans, our small numbers building, becoming larger, more effective. We could potentially spread the cure to every corner of the world.

My hopeful thoughts shifted to the door as the men marched in with the women. The room filled with footsteps, deep voices, and a fuckton of testosterone. Within seconds, the small three-bedroom house grew exponentially smaller.

A tiny, closed-in boudoir of testosterone. I could smell it, like the sweetest cologne, sifting through me and lathering my inner thighs.

As Roark and Shea led the ten men with women upstairs, I treaded to the far wall and watched the parade of muscle move in. Darwin circled around their boots, sniffing their crotches and wagging his tail. If his hackles rose, mine would, too. When it came to men, I trusted his instincts more than my own.

And the men poured in, carrying packs, barbaric weaponry, flashlights, candles, and kerosene lamps. Soon the house was flooded with light.

More than enough light to illuminate sculpted faces, tight jeans, and even tighter asses. Black men, white men, a few Hispanic, there wasn't an ugly man in the group. Each one blood-splattered and dangerous-looking, they redefined sexy with a ruthless edge. Most were covered in tattoos, all of them carved to brawny perfection.

I squeezed my thighs together and tried not to make eye-contact, because they were most definitely looking. Every man that strutted through the door set their eyes on me. It shouldn't have turned me on. I should've been watching them for suspicious activity, but evidently my libido overruled my self-preservation.

Jesse gave me a narrowed look from across the room.

"What?" I mouthed.

It wasn't like he could smell the arousal pooling between my legs. And so what if I was horny? Weirder things have happened.

Oh shit, he was coming over here.

I rested against the wall, all cool and collected, but damn, if his confident fucking swagger didn't get my pussy excited. My inner muscles quivered in anticipation.

His eyes never left mine as he wove through the crowded room, casually avoiding the brush of his body against the gatherings of men here and there. His bow strapped over his back, his tomahawk hung from his waist, and his hair stuck up in messy ruts from his raking fingers.

When he reached me, he braced a forearm on the wall beside my head and put his mouth at my ear. "You want to fuck these guys?"

His muscular chest heaved against me. It had been so long since I'd seen a shirt on him or Roark, I wasn't sure either man owned one anymore. Two months of sleeping against all that skin had reduced me to a one-second-from-exploding bundle of aching need.

I closed my eyes and whispered, "I want to fuck *you*."

His breath rushed out, fanning across my neck.

"She'll settle for your fingers." Roark's brogue shivered through me, flooding more warmth between my legs.

I opened my eyes, locking on his beside me. "You left Shea upstairs alone?"

"She kicked me out." Roark leaned against the wall, facing us, his eyes glimmering like polished emeralds. "Where can we find some privacy around here?"

Fuck privacy. I was soaking wet. Fucking throbbing. Fingers would finish it. Just a quick fondle, round and round my opening. Then slide those circular strokes around my clit, and sweet mother…

I hummed and it sounded like a moan.

"We'll find a place, darlin'." Jesse breathed, his southern twang caressing the words.

I almost came. "Now? Or two months from now?"

The gap between Jesse's chest and mine gave Roark just enough space to reach up and pinch my nipple. A golden dreadlock fell across his eyes, that heated gaze fixed on me. "Go upstairs and check on Shea."

They were torturing me, and they knew it. I needed an escape from this testosterone-choked room, so I slipped around Jesse and walked a direct path to the stairs.

The upper floor had become an infirmary, every bed and inch of floor space piled with blankets and pillows and bedrolls to hold recovering women. The sight of so many skeletal bodies was a cold wash of reality, instantly blasting away my arousal.

Shea bustled around her sleeping patients, tucking them in and checking their vitals. As she hopped from room to room, she shooed the men out. When the last guy descended the stairs, I followed her into one of the bedrooms.

"I'm going to stay up here with them, okay?" She smiled at me, her fingers gently combing the tangled hair of the tattooed woman.

She was a natural care-taker, evident in the way she moved from woman to woman, fussing over their bedding, cleaning their bodies, and humming as she went along. She practically glowed with the need to nurture. I envied that.

I'd survived by shedding the warmer, softer parts of myself and rebuilding something colder, harsher. I was no longer the gentle, loving mother of two beautiful children. I was the acid that filled my stomach whenever I thought of them. I was the colorless ash left beneath their cremated bodies. I was a shadow that carried the excruciating memories of the day they died.

I felt uncomfortable and useless up here with Shea, surrounded by soft bedding and tender touches. I could cure the women. I could kill their enemies. But I didn't know how to *comfort* them.

I shoved my hands in my back pockets. "Do you need my help?"

"Nope." She blew out a content breath, her eyes shining in the dim glow of a candle. "We're going to be okay, Evie."

She wasn't just talking about the women. She meant me and her and the whole damned world.

Given everything we'd endured the last two months, this was the first time I'd seen hope on her face. It softened her brown eyes, lifted her bowed lips, and colored her cheeks. She wore it beautifully and powerfully, emitting it from her pores and lifting the very air I drew into my lungs.

I inhaled another breath of her hope and let that invigorating feeling settle through me. "I love you, you know."

I hadn't intended to say it. I wasn't even sure I'd said those words to my guardians, but once they were out of my mouth, I heard the truth in them. It terrified me, knowing I could lose her in so many horrific ways, but it also strengthened me. I loved this woman, who exemplified all the good that still existed in the world.

She studied me with perceptive eyes. “You’re having a moment, aren’t you?”

I shrugged awkwardly, unsure what to do with myself. “It was bound to happen.”

“I love you, too.” She blinked rapidly, her chin quivering. “Now go on. Get outta here.” She shooed me with a hand. “Go tell those men downstairs your badass story.”

And so I did. Back in the living room and squished between Jesse and Roark on the couch, I talked until the candles dripped to shallow stubs and my voice rasped with overuse.

Link sprawled in the recliner with a flask of bourbon, volleying questions like an eager reporter. His men moved quietly around us, cleaning weapons, repairing shoes, and scraping forks in various cans of food. Some slept. Some kept watch outside. Others sat with us, listening to me ramble.

I detailed every event that affected my life over the past two years, and Jesse and Roark filled in their own experiences. The Drone, the Lakota, the men who raped me, the scar on my chest, our journey to Europe and back, Michio’s biological changes, my inhuman ladybird abilities, the prophecy. There were no stones left unturned when I twisted around and showed the room the spots on my back.

Link took a slug of bourbon and lit a cigarette, holding the smoke in his lungs as he studied Jesse and Roark with razored black eyes.

He exhaled slowly, his gaze landing on Roark. “You’re a celibate priest, but you won’t turn down a blow job.”

I’d just told him there was a monster with wings flying around out there, and *this* was what he wanted to talk about?

Roark’s hand tightened on my knee, his thumb tracing the crease between my pinched legs.

Link waved the cigarette in Jesse's direction. "And you're a spirit-walker, following the advice of a dead child."

My hackles shot up, and I jerked forward. Jesse's arm across my waist pinned me on the couch.

Link reached toward his ankle and stubbed out the cigarette in the folded cuff of his jeans. "I mean no disrespect, Evie. Didn't have kids of my own. Don't want to think about what it feels like to lose one." He looked back at Jesse. "So you follow a prophecy that says your seed will kill your woman."

Jesse, Roark, and I were pressed together so tightly I felt our collective tension running back and forth between us.

Leaning back in the recliner, Link lit another cigarette, his eyes on Jesse. "It's been two years since I've laid eyes on a woman, but I recognize beauty when I see it. Evie's a fucking wet dream, and neither one of you are boning her? Fuck, man. That's some fucked-up shit right there."

Roark sprung from the couch and slammed into Link with fists flying. His heavy punches connected with flesh, over and over, pummeling Link's face, ribs, and arms. They rolled off the recliner, Roark punching and Link grunting, as they thrashed across the floor.

Jesse didn't move, his face relaxed, his eyes following the scuffle.

"Aren't you going to stop him?" I tried to stand, but his arm held me down.

Ten or so of Link's men stood around the room, smoking cigarettes and palming flasks, all casual like, watching the fight. Not a single weapon raised.

What the hell was this? Some kind of men-establishing-dominance bullshit?

Bent over Link, Roark continued his attack, his fists raining down, viciously, brutally, with no end in sight. Link raised his arms to block, but he didn't fight back.

Was this Link testing how sexually repressed Roark was? Or was this his way of proving he and his men were not a threat to me?

Please tell me that sound wasn't the crunch of bone.

Link's gurgling manic laugh erupted from beneath Roark's relentless hits.

Roark jumped up and put his hands on his hips, breathing heavy as he stared down at Link. "All bleeding and having a laugh like. Maybe ye need another come-to-Jesus meeting with me fists?"

Link sat up, knees bent, blood dripping from his nose and the cuts around his mouth and eyes. He flashed a red-stained smile and raised his cigarette, still pinched between his fingers. It was bent to hell but still smoldering.

A heavy exhale hissed past Roark's clamped teeth. "Bloody hell, your face looks like me dead uncle's ball sac."

With his elbows on his knees, Link straightened the cigarette and perched the end between his bloody lips. "Saw the scars on your knuckles, Father Molony. Wanted to see if they were what I thought they were."

Seriously? He couldn't have just asked?

Roark flexed a hand, eyeing his knuckles. "I was a street boxer in Northern Ireland, ye fecking muckshit fuck."

Link choked on a drag of his cigarette, nodding and grinning. "Got some dirty fucking power in those fists, my friend. And the sword? They teach you how to use that in the seminary?"

Roark's sword leaned against the couch beside me. He told me once he preferred it because there weren't many guns in Ireland.

He closed his eyes, opened them. "I dragged the church youth group to SCA armored combat activities, before…" He pushed a loose dreadlock out of his face. "The sword fighting was all for sport. Gave the young lads something to do." He shrugged. "I took a liking to medieval weapons and made a hobby out of it."

Link watched him for a long moment, puffing on his cigarette and bleeding all over the place. "You're the strangest priest I've ever met."

"And you're a clatty prick. Now clean the floor there, will ye? Your ugly focking head is leaking all over it."

Bursting with laughter, Link pulled his shirt over his head and wiped his face with it. The swollen, broken bridge of his nose was painful to look at, but he didn't show a hint of discomfort. He climbed to his feet, his musculature playing and bunching beneath darkly-tanned skin as he dropped the shirt and used his boot to wipe the fabric over the blood.

Flicking the finished cigarette onto the shirt, he kicked it to one of his guys and strode toward Jesse. "So you're the quiet one."

Jesse perused all six-foot-and-imposing-inches of Link's frame with a disinterested expression. A thin patch of dark hair dusted Link's chest and abs, and a few faint scars drew lines over his ribs. He looked like a younger, meaner, broken-nosed version of Vin Diesel.

"I've met guys like you." Link cocked his bald head, his nostrils ringed with crimson. "You're the kind that slices throats in dark alleys and slips away into the night before the first drop of blood hits the pavement."

Jesse stared back, the bored look on his face giving nothing away. When we'd shared our stories, we hadn't touched on our lives before the plague. Link didn't know about Jesse's CIA background, yet his assessment was uncannily accurate.

"What about you?" I raised my chin. "What's your *kind*?"

He hooked his thumbs in the pockets of his jeans. "I headed the security detail on the Mississippi Queen."

"Why would a steamboat need security?" I arched a brow. "Saw a lot of action, did you?"

"Liliana"—he nodded at the ceiling, indicating the nymph upstairs—"is my boss. She *is* the Mississippi Queen. Or was. She was a celebrity in our parts. Had a voice on her that hardened every cock on that cruise ship, and a body that men would sell their souls just to touch. You get me?"

Loud and clear. "You were a bodyguard, a bouncer…"

"All of it, and not just for her. The nymphs upstairs were singers, dancers, entertainers on the boat. Not *those* kinds of entertainers. Get your minds out of the gutter." He grinned and licked the cut on his lip. "They were stunning women.

Men wanted them. Creepy, obsessive men. So I protected them, and some of these guys…" He glanced around the room. "They worked for me then in the same capacity they do now."

A team of bodyguards? We'd landed the fucking lottery. That was, if they kept their hands and their cocks to themselves.

The men loitering in the room were still sneaking glances at me when they thought I wasn't looking. I could handle a heated look, liked it even, but I didn't know them. Didn't know what they were capable of.

I tried to keep my face blank, but my efforts felt debilitated by the pound of my heart. "Were there only twelve nymphs all along? Or did you lose some?"

The rugged planes of his face softened. "Thirty women in the beginning. We lost more than half in those first days and months. And just as many crew members. Took us awhile to figure out how to contain them without getting bit."

"What about before? Did you and your security guys have sex with your *stunning* women?"

"Yes. Some of us had relations." Link crouched before me. "I'm aware of your concerns. We're a risk to keep around. Twenty-one *hard* risks, right?" He pointed a look at his groin. "But I can offer you something in exchange for that risk."

The couch groaned as Roark sat beside me and rested a hand on my lap, his knuckles scratched and glowing red but cleaned of blood.

Link glanced at Roark's hand and returned to my eyes. "I need your special aphid-controlling skills to keep the bugs away and your experience with the nymph transformations to help me through it. You mentioned the memory gaps and healing process. I don't have the emotional know-how or energy to deal with that hormonal shit. I fuck, and I fight."

He was a straight-shooter, a trait I greatly appreciated. And frankly, he didn't have to offer me shit. We were outnumbered. If he wanted my help, he could take it by force. The thing was, I intended to see the women through their recovery. That was always the plan.

If there was a catch, it was hidden in the details.

I chewed the inside of my cheek. "You want us to help them heal, then you'll take it from there?" *To do the fucking and the fighting.*

He nodded. "I just want my girls whole and healthy again. We've got a species to save, am I right?"

I envisioned a lot of baby Link's in the future.

He sniffed, a wet bloody sound. "In return, you'll have my protection and *services.*"

Services? Was he seriously offering to fuck me right here in front of the man who just broke his nose?

He flashed me a wolfish smile full of straight, white teeth. "I'd love nothing more than to offer you *those* services, sweetheart, but if his angry looks don't kill me…" He glanced at Jesse, then pointed at Roark. "His fists will."

"Jesus fuck." Roark braced an elbow on his knee, leaning forward. "Explain the services, ye long-winded cunt."

Link laughed and rose to his feet, rubbing his knuckles beneath his nose. "You need ammo? I got a guy who makes shells, arrows, and blades." He pointed at a dark-haired man across the room.

I'd left my guns in the mountains, along with the ultrasound and other cumbersome supplies, like spare boots and clothes. At the time, nothing had been more important than shedding the weight of my load and getting the hell out of those mountains.

"You have a toothache? He's a dentist." Link's finger moved through the crowd of men as he spoke. "You want another ultrasound machine? Need a generator? Batteries? Fuel? Fucking hemorrhoid cream? I've got a gatherer. This guy right here can find anything. Need a hunter, a farmer, a mechanic, a cook? I've got those guys, too. Sewing, soap and candle making, masonry, alternative medicine, you name it, every man on this property has a skill. You know why?"

I stared at him in stunned disbelief.

He paced through the room, eying each man he passed

with a critical expression. "I spent the last two years hand-selecting my crew. I required three things. First and foremost, he had to be a damned-good soldier. Two, he needed to bring a specialized skill. And three, his moral compass couldn't, under no circumstances, deviate from mine. Why, do you think, would I go through all this trouble? Why would I care?"

As he walked a circuit around his men, they looked at him with reverence and respect. I felt a little of that awe, too, though the skeptic in me wondered if he was blowing smoke up my ass.

Darwin lay in a curled-up ball by the door, his head on his leg, his hackles at rest. Not a care in the world.

Then it dawned on me. Link was interviewing us. He'd goaded Roark to see how well the priest could fight. And he'd called Jesse a dark-alley killer to test our reactions. What did he do to the men who didn't pass his tests?

I leaned back and wrapped my hand around Roark's on my lap. He and Jesse sat so silently and motionless I couldn't read them. If their hearts were racing as fast as mine, they were keeping that shit locked down.

Link painted a fantastical picture. His crew was small but highly valuable. Sharing those resources with us in exchange for something I would've done anyway was hardly a fair trade. I didn't want to be indebted to anyone, especially someone I didn't know.

"Farmers, trackers, cooks, and soldiers." Link strode toward me, his eyes hard with conviction. "All twenty-one of us and our nymphs lived on a steamboat large enough to accommodate a hundred people, but I knew…I *knew* one day there would be something more. I didn't know that something would have blond hair, yellow eyes, and perky tits, but the moment our nymphs jumped ship, I knew they'd found that *something*. You."

Shit, that was heavy. I was just a woman, surviving like everyone else, who got the luck of the genetic draw. Or the unlucky draw, depending on how I looked at it. And Link was just a man, taking a colossal risk.

I met his eyes. "I get that the women upstairs were *your women* before it all went down and you feel protective of them. But you're saying they weren't your wives or girlfriends or sisters."

He watched me wordlessly, giving me time to frame my thoughts.

"I mean, nymphs look like women, but they're dangerously *not.* So why keep them on the boat? In your company? It seems an enormous risk to take."

"Because nymphs are rare," Link said. "Because if I set them loose, they might've died. And because I believed there was cure. I just had to be patient."

Patient or crazy.

I let out a slow breath. "What happened to the two nymphs you lost?"

Link stared at the floor, his eyes frozen and unblinking. "They stumbled upon a camp of aggressive men in Alabama. We tried to corral them away, but Cora and Penny bit the men in self-defense."

Fatal bites. My chest squeezed.

Jesse shifted beside me. "You didn't lose any men out there tonight, did you?

Hands in his pockets, Link rocked on his heels. "Nope."

I followed Jesse's train of thought, which hurtled into the future, beyond the recovery of the women and establishing a safe place for them to live, whether it be in a fortified mansion or on a steamboat.

He was thinking about the protection we needed. Protection against threats that still awaited us. The cliff I'd yet to fall from. The pregnancy. The continual evolution of the aphids. *The Drone.*

Despite Link's prolific speech about me being the answer to his *something more*, it was possible he thought I was helpless, that he could manipulate me with words and cut me while I slept. He didn't know that behind my blond hair, yellow eyes, and perky tits, I held the greatest power in the world. The kind of power that drove me to fight just as viciously as every man left on this hateful planet.

I held the love of three men.

One of which needed my help. I could feel it like a stabbing blade in my soul.

For Michio, I would gladly put myself in debt.

I grabbed Jesse's hand and pulled it into my lap beside Roark's. Squeezing their fingers, I looked at Link. "We need to move the women to a safer, bigger place. When you're satisfied with their recovery—and you *will* be satisfied—you'll give me a mechanic, a hunter, a tracker, whatever I need to find the Drone."

Link crossed his arms over his barrel chest and narrowed his swollen eyes. "You're going after your missing guardian."

Of course I fucking was. "Will you do it?"

His mouth slanted in a lop-sided smile. "I thought you'd never ask."

THIRTY-ONE

Daylight spilled through the window of the upstairs bathroom, illuminating the thick surface of grime and dust that clung to the non-working toilet, vanity, and tiled walls. I dropped my bow, quiver, and backpack in the tub as Roark checked the locks on the window.

My muscles and joints ached, a cramp spasmed in my back, and I couldn't stop rubbing my gritty eyes. It must've been eight or nine in the morning, and the only sleep we'd gotten in two days had been the hour or so before the nymphs began scratching.

Jesse strode in, taking up too much room in the small space, and closed the door behind him. He carried multiple packs, bedrolls, and a hammer, all of which bumped and scraped the walls as he turned to face me.

"Shea wants to sleep beside her patients," he said. "Darwin's with her."

Maybe it wasn't the safest decision, but I reminded myself that we'd cured her and trained her and she was more than ready for us to set her free. And if Link and his crew hid a sinister agenda, they wouldn't act on it right now, not while Shea was caring for their women.

Besides, Shea would be more comfortable sleeping out there. I took in the bathroom's floor space, its width barely wide enough for three bodies. Would the length of the room even accommodate Roark's six-foot-four height?

Jesse dropped the packs, the bow, and his tomahawk in the tub. Then, with a handful of nails from his pocket, he hammered the door shut.

When the pounding racket quieted, I rubbed my aching head. "Guess that means you don't trust our houseguests?"

He tossed the hammer on top of our supplies and rested his tired gaze on mine. "The only people I trust are standing in this room."

I gave him a confused look. I knew he trusted Roark, and Michio was a big *if.* But… "What about Shea?"

He lifted a shoulder.

Roark leaned against the window sill, grinning. "Oh, Jesse, ye make me clackers feel all tingly."

His smile was as arresting as always, though fatigue drew it a little flat, pulling at the edges of his mouth and eyes.

"Speaking of tingles…" Jesse looked around the bathroom, his voice so low it hummed through my blood. "I told you I'd find a place."

I looked around the room. The space was small and uncomfortable and the opposite of sexy, yet his promise from earlier rolled over me with enough heat to make me dizzy.

He toed off his boots and unfastened his jeans, dragging them down his muscular legs. My pulse swished through my veins, quickening and heating as I openly stared at six feet of sun-soaked brawn.

Standing there in his tight black boxer briefs was a sight that would make any woman tingle. All that taut skin, stretched over ridges of muscles on his abs and chest, begged for my fingers, my lips… Hell, I'd straddle his chest and grind against it if he let me.

I jerked my gaze upward, colliding with his. Caught. Yep, I was checking him out, which didn't help with the tingly feeling. I drew a slow breath through my nose and sucked on my tongue. I really wanted to suck on his. Not just his tongue. His lips. His fingers. His cock. I wanted… Fuck, I wanted to eat him.

No. I rubbed my palms on my shorts, wiping away the building heat with urgent strokes. Jesse had locked the three of us in here to sleep in privacy, right?

So why was he just standing there and not rolling out the bedrolls?

The turquoise stone I'd loaned him lay against his chest, its purpose realized. He'd let me in, accepted my love, and returned it a thousand times over. We hadn't had sex, but our bond transcended the limits of physical connection. We didn't need to fuck to solidify what we meant to one another.

Just keep telling yourself that.

The rasp of Roark's clothes falling to the floor sounded behind me, and I turned, backing up until my ass hit the vanity.

Roark sat on the edge of the tub, elbows on his knees, wearing a thin pair of white boxers that were frayed and unraveling at the seams. His eyes glowed in the sunny glare of the window as he watched me through his lashes. Watching me as a man, not as a priest.

Ugh, these guys…these hot-blooded, fiercely loyal, overprotective men, with their brutally-honed physiques and flirtatiously attentive eyes, had already stolen my heart. Now they were just playing with it, along with every nerve-ending and pleasure zone attached to it. I could only endure so much teasing before I internally combusted.

I pulled at the frayed hem of my jean shorts, fingers sweating, and voice quiet. "What are we doing?"

I couldn't let myself hope. I was too damned tired to deal with the disappointment.

Roark laced his hands between his knees, his thumbs rolling together. "Ye ready to sleep, Jesse?"

Crossing his arms over his chest, Jesse leaned against the door and shook his head. The heat in his eyes sent a wave of shivers sprinting around my body and landing with a jolt between my legs.

"I'm just gonna say what everyone's thinking." Roark didn't move, his head tilted down, his eyes up and fastened on mine. "We haven't had privacy in months. Long, *chubbed-up* months."

My heart jumped, sparking quivers down my legs. I swear

on all that was holy, I had to dig my fingers against the counter behind me to stop myself from coming at the implication of his words.

He hissed through his teeth. “Me knob’s wanting out, love. If I den’ get it *in* ye soon, it could well fall off.”

In me? He meant in my mouth, right? My chest hitched, my toes curled, and my clit flared with throbbing need. Maybe instead of puddling into a quivery mess, I should’ve been worrying about what they would think of me, themselves, and each other in the morning?

Jesse regarded me, his eyes hot and smoldering, fire on fire, stoked with intensity.

Fuck. I stood on the corner of Gravelly Brogue Street and Burning Glare Boulevard. It was a dangerous place for a woman to venture, alone and unarmed. Yet I’d never felt safer or more excited.

I wanted to be smothered by them until the only thing I smelled was the musk of their arousal. Until all I felt was the slide of hot, tight, sweat-soaked skin. My pussy clenched painfully, aching to be filled by their tongues, their fingers, their cocks.

Not their cocks. They wouldn’t give me that, but I’d come…I’d most definitely, assuredly come just thinking about it.

Jesse pushed off the door. My lungs didn’t contract once during the long second it took for him to close the distance. His eyes never wavered from mine, a dark and devious intent sparking in the copper depths.

Would he let me touch his cock? Wrap my lips around it? Sweet holy fuck, I wanted to see him tremble with release, taste it on my tongue, and feel his relief slide down my throat.

“Take off your clothes.” He crowded my space, arms braced on the counter on either side of my hips.

I’d never stripped so fast, especially in such a confined area. My elbows banged against the vanity. My knees bumped into Jesse’s legs. As I tore at the laces on my boots and wrenched them off, he didn’t back up, didn’t give me an inch of wriggle room.

Roark watched me wrestle with the button on my shorts, his expression tightening as if he were seconds from launching off the edge of the tub to help me along.

Socks and shorts off, shirt next, I stood naked and breathing heavily in the rigid prison of Jesse's arms and chest.

In those lust-filled seconds as he watched me, drawing out the anticipation, I reached for the waistband of his briefs.

My fingers dipped beneath the elastic and brushed against a patch of thick hair. My eyes begged, *Please let me touch you,* as I said, "I still owe you for last time."

"No." He grabbed my wrists, pulled my arms behind my back, and held them there with one hand.

Was he afraid his seed would get on my fingers and I'd inadvertently touch myself and become pregnant?

His free hand traced my collarbone, fingers dragging over and around one breast. He caressed my ribs, my hip, the crease between my thigh and pelvis, and dipped between my legs. He lingered there, cupping, the pads of his fingers lightly dancing over my folds.

Tremors rippled down my legs, and I widened my stance, unabashedly pleading for more.

Roark hadn't moved, elbows still resting on his knees, his head tipped down, and hooded eyes locked on mine.

"Come here," I mouthed at him.

He shook his head, the corner of his mouth lifting.

He likes to watch.

I sucked my bottom lip into my mouth, playfully pouting, even though I trembled at the idea of Jesse bringing me to orgasm while he watched.

The hand between my legs slid along my seam, fingers teasing without entering. I moaned against the diabolical sensation, jerking my hips toward him, struggling to keep my arms still in the manacle of Jesse's hand. The desperation constricting my pussy demanded to be stroked harder, rubbed deeper, and pounded into ecstasy.

All three of us had desires to fulfill, but beyond that, I

sensed another need from Jesse and Roark. A need to erase any interest I might've had toward the Link's men. Sharing me among three men was hard enough. It would've been harder to share me with a fourth or a fifth or more, especially since neither Jesse nor Roark would have *actual* sex with me.

They were staking me as theirs.

When I released another moan, Jesse's mouth caught it, our lips sealing our breaths, his tongue rolling against mine. My body stilled, all thought and feeling zooming in on the warm, wet seduction of his mouth.

His breathing, frenzied and hot against my lips, had the most intoxicating effect. He was as turned on as I was, and dammit, I was leaking all over his curling fingers.

I twisted my arms against his hold at my back and spread my legs wider, rocking my hips. "Inside." I rubbed my tongue against his, the kiss intensifying, growing faster, wetter, harder. "Please, Jesse."

He tore his mouth away and buried a groan against my neck, his fingers working deeper with each pass, spreading me open and slipping around my drenched opening.

Roark still hadn't shifted. His hands, folded between his knees, didn't budge to stroke the hard length of his cock, which lay trapped against his leg beneath the tight stretch of his boxers. His lips parted to accommodate his labored breaths and the heat in his eyes melted my insides.

Footsteps passed outside the door every few minutes, and muffled voices penetrated the walls. But all distractions disappeared when Jesse's fingers burrowed inside me, fucking me *hard*, harder, so jarringly rough my legs gave out.

He lifted me, planting my ass on the counter, and swallowed my scream with his mouth. His fingers thrust mercilessly, working me into a panting, back-bowing creature in heat. I didn't even recognize the noises garbling from my mouth.

Without breaking the kiss, I bent my knees and dug my heels against the edge of the counter. The position tilted my pussy upward, giving him easier access as he fingered me harder, pounding his knuckles against my swollen flesh, and hurtling me closer toward the bliss of release.

If he had any reservations about Roark's presence, he didn't show it. Maybe he'd completely forgotten about our voyeur in his crazed fever. I'd never seen him like this, the wild look in his eyes, the out-of-control breathing, and the frantic thrusting of his erection against my inner thigh. He was two-hundred-pounds of desperate, starving insistence, and I was spread wide open for him, slick, aching, and ready.

He released my arms, shoving his hand between us to join the other. Then I felt it, the wet head of his cock, free from the confines of his briefs, nudging against my center and blocked only by his fingers. Holy fuck, he was stroking himself, his fist jerking along his shaft, his breaths hot against my mouth.

A roaring fire exploded inside me, stealing the oxygen from my lungs as it spread through my body, building, shooting me toward the scorching horizon. I pushed my hands through his hair, his face pressed against my neck, and leaned back to look at him between my legs.

His hand wrapped around the base of his cock. Yes, it was just a cock, but it was more beautiful than anything I'd envisioned, the length hard as steel, throbbing with veins, and angry red.

At the edge of my vision, Roark stood, towering over us. But I was too far gone. Too much pressure, unraveling, tearing apart. I couldn't stop it. I didn't want to.

My inner muscles pulsed around his fingers, and I felt like I was ripped open with spectacular force, coming, coming… Holy fucking motherfuck, I was screaming, every cell in my body catching fire and blowing up, over and over and over.

His fingers continued to slam into me, the shaft of his cock rubbing against my folds. The tip rubbed across my clit, the base ground against my center, and his mouth…fuck, his mouth consumed me, sucking my air, drinking my cries, and drawing out my orgasm with a sinfully talented tongue.

He choked, a pained sound at the back of his throat, but he

wasn't done. His chest collided with mine, his fingers shaking as they swirled through my wetness. The head of his cock replaced his hand, growing more urgent, sliding, pressing, and punching aggressive spasms through the aftershocks of my climax.

"I want in." He rubbed himself against my clit and slid back to my center, nudging, demanding, his breaths rushing out in wild pants.

I shivered, dazed from the magnificent force of the orgasm and so damned turned on I couldn't see straight. "Jesse—"

"Just the tip." He clutched my hips and lined himself up. "I won't come."

"Ye will." Roark launched to my side, his breathing erratic as he looked at Jesse, at me, back to Jesse. "Did ye feel the string? The IUD?"

Jesse stabbed two fingers inside me, curling and searching, the heel of his hand grinding against my clit and sending unholy shivers through my body.

"I— I can't…I don't know." He yanked his fingers away and gripped his cock.

Shit. I flattened my hands on their chests, trying to catch my breath. "Sometimes it shifts deeper in my cervix. Even if you can't feel it, it's still there."

Was I certain? Was it worth the risk?

Fuck yes! warred with visions of carrying a life to my uncertain death.

Roark grabbed Jesse's forearm, his eyes hard shards of green glass. "If she gets pregnant…"

The rest of his sentence hung in the air. The world-saving child, my grim fate, the harrowing fucking mystery of it all.

I could tell from Jesse's labored breathing and the insistent thrusts of his erection against my opening that he was beyond listening. Would he turn on Roark, spitting and throwing punches? He had a delirious look in his eyes. But maybe he'd wanted Roark in here all along to stop him from going too far?

He began to sink deeper, breaching my entrance, and I

shoved my hands between us. He swung his hand, and despite the force with which he knocked my arms away, the pressure of his cock eased, cautious, uncertain.

His chest heaved, and his desperate breaths hissed out. But so did mine and Roark's. There wasn't enough air in the room to accommodate our sexual tension.

Roark pressed against my side, crowded around me, his arm at my back, his other hand now flat against the clench of Jesse's abs, his hard glare on the precarious location of Jesse's cock.

For a dense moment, I thought Jesse might cringe away, but when he looked into my eyes and an agonized sound burst from the back of his throat, all hell broke loose.

The stoic, untouchable guardian I'd known for two years attacked me like a man possessed.

THIRTY-TWO

Every ounce of tension in the tiny bathroom exploded all at once. In a blink, Jesse was all over me, his chest barreling into mine, the momentum banging my tailbone painfully against the faucet. His hands were everywhere, darting back and forth between pushing at Roark, restraining my arms, squeezing my breast, and grabbing his cock to shove it inside me.

Oh fuck, that beautiful cock. I wanted it, invading and stretching and pounding, until all I could feel was the brutal impact of his possession.

I ached for it to thrust us right out of the realm of reality. "Roark, please. Just wait a—"

Jesse's lips slammed against my mouth, his tongue lashing, only to pull away every other breath to argue with Roark. "Get the fuck off me." He turned back to me, leaning his forehead against mine, panting, as he tried to line up his cock. Then he was gone again, shoving at Roark. "I won't hurt her."

His mouth returned to mine, hot, heavy, and wild with need. I shouldn't have been kissing him back. Shouldn't have threaded my hands through his hair. He deserved a knee in the balls. But I couldn't…I couldn't push him away. I wanted him as furiously as he wanted me. Somewhere in my fog of lust, however, I had enough common sense to squeeze my thighs together, even as Jesse wrenched them apart.

Roark slammed a fist against his jaw. "For fuck's sake, I'll give ye a scrotum of a headache if ye den' cop on to yourself."

"Roark!" I untangled my hands from Jesse's hair and

grabbed Roark's arm. *Damn his Irish temper!*

Jesse clenched his teeth, spun away from me, and launched at him, fingers curling around his throat. They flew backward, the force of their bodies cracking against the tiles, and the next few moments blurred by in a heart-pounding scuffle of grunting, punching, and choking.

"Stop." I jumped off the counter, my hands balling into fists. "Fucking stop it!"

I fought to keep my vocal chords from waking the entire house, but if I saw a single drop of blood, I was going to leap into that brawl and do a helluva lot more than scream.

Roark swung toward Jesse's face but didn't seem to be using the full power of his fists. It was just a graze, enough to momentarily distract Jesse's hungry eyes away from me. No blood or swelling lips. *Yet.*

They staggered and twisted through the tiny room, arms clamped around each other, falling and banging against the walls, their biceps contracting with the effort to restrain one another.

Jesse's briefs hung halfway down his ass, his cock still hard and angry, trapped beneath the elastic band. Even as Roark dug bruising fingers into his jaw, Jesse couldn't stop looking at me, his eyes clinging to mine as if I could free him, not from two-hundred-and-thirty pounds of cursing Irish anger, but from the pent-up torment I'd unleashed in him.

I stood in a state of suspension, my back against the wall beside the window, my palms pressed flat on the tiles. Could I help him? Should I interfere? Maybe I could talk them down?

No, they were beyond reasoning, their eyes wild with the need to fight and fuck. There weren't any serious injuries that I could tell, but if I stepped in and accidentally got a hit to the face, oh man, they would both lose their ever-loving minds. As small as the bathroom was, I might get hit in the face anyway.

They crashed to the floor at my feet. Jesse ended up on his back, his thighs trapped beneath Roark's leg, and his head pinned to the tiles by the shackle of Roark's fingers around his throat. With their feet by the door, their heads lay directly beneath me, thrashing around, Jesse head-butting, and Roark dodging every strike.

My fingers ached to push Roark off of him, but I couldn't take sides, and as crazed as Jesse looked, he really did need restraining. His hair stood up in every direction as if he'd just fucked me raw. Which he hadn't, but my God, he wanted to.

My chest squeezed tightly, choking my breaths as Jesse scraped his heels across the floor, trying and failing to find leverage. His hands shoved at Roark's face, not even close to unbalancing the man. Roark had thirty pounds and four inches on Jesse, and I'd taught Roark how to fight on the ground. Jesse didn't stand a chance.

Jesse bucked, gritting his teeth, his eyes locked on mine, and his cock straining against the band of his briefs. "Evie, goddammit. Please?"

I didn't understand the question, but I knew the answer. He needed relief, and he needed it…not yesterday. Not two months ago. He'd needed it for two fucking *years.*

I climbed around Roark and dropped to my knees behind him, my hand resting on the powerful leg he pinned against Jesse's thighs.

Roark looked back at me, his eyes narrowing. Then he did the last thing Jesse would've ever expected.

In one sweeping movement, he slid off Jesse's legs. Wrapped a hand around the base of Jesse's erection. Leaned over those startled copper eyes. Then, with his other hand around Jesse's throat, he planted a full-on, open-mouth kiss on Jesse's lips.

I froze, locked in a terrible, *beautiful,* mind-blowing fantasy. *My* fantasy.

Jesse punched his hips toward the ceiling, as if to knock away Roark's hand, but his thrusts only managed to stroke his cock within the clench of Roark's grip.

He shouted against Roark's mouth, his words garbled and biting with fury. "Get…off me! Motherfu— Arrrgh! I…killlll you."

Roark needed affection, needed to give and receive love, regardless of gender. Affection was his vice in a way, the reason he'd adjusted his vows when he found himself alone in a bunker, without the love of his friends and family. When all he had was me.

Threesomes had been around longer than the Bible. It had nothing to do with gender preference. In some cultures, it was an art, a way to wind down and escape the hardships of life. Or in our case, an expression of something much more.

But some men couldn't bend their minds around omnisexuality. Would Jesse be able to see past another man touching his cock, kissing his mouth, *violating* him? Was that what this was? A violation?

I would've stopped Roark, except Jesse appeared to be kissing him back, his tongue clashing and whipping against Roark's, desperately, begrudgingly. *Consensual* wasn't the word I would've used. Not with the way Jesse held onto Roark's shoulders, pushing, no, pulling…wait, definitely pushing. But his mouth worked beneath Roark's kiss, lips meeting lips, his muffled voice anguished, despite the frantic drive of his cock within the tight curl of Roark's fingers.

The scent rolling off them ripened the air with sweat, the musk of testosterone, and the raw exquisiteness of male desire. The smacking of their lips and the deeply-growled grunts in their throats was so arousing and potent I had to press my fingers deep inside myself to ease the painful clenching.

With Roark bent over Jesse's upper body and out of my way, my gaze locked on his hand and the blood-filled erection gripped between his fingers. It was right there, aching, *ready*.

I reacted on impulse. Sliding beneath Roark's arm with my feet toward their heads, I aligned my body along the length of Jesse's in a sideways sixty-nine. I bent a leg over Jesse's chest and wrapped my wet fingers around Roark's fist. A silent request. *Let me have it.*

Roark broke the kiss and let go of Jesse's cock, both hands pressing on his chest, holding him against the floor. With Roark arched above us, I had a direct line of sight to Jesse's shocked face.

Whatever this was, between Jesse and Roark, between me and Jesse, I wouldn't take anything without asking.

I hugged Jesse's side, my breasts against his hip, my bent leg clenched across his abs as my pussy slid along the side of his ribs.

With a tight grip on his cock, I strained toward it, my mouth an inch from the tip, and met his wide-eyed gaze, waiting for him to move.

His body trembled beneath me, his eyes flickering with fire and pinning me in place. Even as he was restrained beneath Roark's hands and shaking with mindless need, he still held the ability to overpower me with a look.

He lifted his hips, rocking toward me and shoving at his briefs as though he couldn't get close enough, naked enough. "Suck me, Evie. Fucking do it."

I yanked the last of his clothes down his legs and off. Then, angling over his cock and opening my mouth wide enough to accommodate his girth, I drew him inside.

He shouted something indiscernible, kicking his head back, as violent tremors spasmed along his legs. I sucked harder, stroking my hand along his length in time with the suction of my mouth.

His fingers stabbed through my hair, holding me to him as he drove his cock in and out of my mouth. The flared tip brushed the back of my throat, triggering my gag reflex. I breathed through it, shivering at the sound of his labored breaths and choked groans.

Roark shifted at the edge of my periphery, sitting back on his heels. His hand found the juncture of my legs, his fingers slipping easily through my wet folds.

I ground against Roark's hand, my mouth working harder, more frantically along the ridges of Jesse's shaft. With my knee over his abs, I was spread wide open for their eyes. It would be so easy for Roark to pull his cock out, climb over me, and fuck me from behind while Jesse watched.

A gush of liquid heat saturated my cunt, soaking Roark's

fingers. I whimpered, frustrated, shaking with need.

"Jaysus, love." Roark plunged a thumb inside me, his fingers rolling over my clit and teasing me open. "Ye like gagging on his cock, do ye?" A noise rumbled in his chest. "With me hand between your milky thighs?"

I made a wretched noise in my throat. *More. Please. Please, fuck me.*

Roark's free hand gripped my thigh, wrenching it upward and opening me further as he fingered me toward another orgasm. "Look a' her creaming all over us." He lowered his voice, deep and gravelly, his accent thick with command. "Come in her mouth. Now."

Jesse's body turned to stone beneath me, and a hum ran beneath the hard surface of his muscles, vibrating, trembling. Suddenly, this fiercely-strong iron will of a man crumbled, his voice howling, his legs quaking, and his cock spurting, erupting, fucking shooting down my throat with so much force I choked on the insane amount of come he released.

I swallowed repeatedly, savoring the salty taste of him, and my heart soaring at the blissful, hooded look in his eyes. He regarded me with something like worship, and yes, *love*. I knew he loved me, but to see it shine so openly in his gaze snapped something in place behind my breast.

Roark's hand tangled in my hair, but before he could drag me toward him, I spun, my hands cupping his whiskered jaw and my mouth falling over his waiting lips. I nuzzled and licked and sucked, our tongues sliding together with warmth and affection and delicious familiarity.

I trailed my fingers down his thick throat, over his wide shoulders, across the hard bricks of his pecs and the grooves of his abs.

Inching around his hips, I slipped beneath his boxers and gripped the hard muscles of his ass. "You're a beautiful man, you know that?"

"Fecking apt." He grinned. "Definitely more attractive than him."

"Maybe." Jesse lay on the floor beside us, sprawled like a

lazy cat, his eyes half-mast. "But neither of us can compete with Doc's trendy *Abercrombie & Fitch* boy looks."

I snorted. It was kind of true.

Roark raised his eyebrows at me and passed Jesse a sideways look. "I can mess up his face when we find him."

When we find him, not *if.* I appreciated the hopeful sentiment, at least, without the messing-up-his-face part. I also recognized the fact that I'd decided to go after Michio without consulting either of them. "You're okay with that? Searching for Michio?"

"We go where you go," Jesse said, his eyes feasting on my body as if he hadn't just ejaculated enough sperm to repopulate the human race.

Roark dragged his boxers over his erection and shoved them to the floor where he knelt. He let me grip him, stroke him, and tug on his balls, the sac hot and heavy in my hand.

I faced him on my knees, the hard tiles grinding against bone, my head tilted back to gaze up at him. "So you and Jesse are buddies again?"

"We just had a talk, love."

Talking with fists? And kisses? Because there hadn't been many words exchanged. Men were so weird.

Jesse hadn't moved, collapsed on his back, chest still heaving and eyes tracing my breasts, my hips, pausing on my wet and very much aroused pussy.

I slid my thumb over the wetness leaking from the tip of Roark's cock. "How do you want me?"

Depending on how guilty he was feeling about his vow, he might not want me at all. Sometimes he just wanted to jack off while he watched me masturbate. Other times, he held me against a sturdy surface and dry humped my ass.

He put his hands on my shoulders, adding slight pressure to guide me lower, lower still, until my mouth was level with his cock. "Lick me with that brilliant tongue, love."

My inner muscles clenched, shooting electric pulses through my body. I lowered to my hands and knees and greedily took him into my mouth. He groaned and pulsed against my lips, his hands pulling my hair as I brought him to the edge of climax and back, teasing and licking and sucking like my life depended on it.

I felt strong, powerful, despite the submissive position. I'd damned well earned an equal ranking among my guardians, and they knew it. Which made them not only value me in this position but also respect me, evidenced in the way Jesse reached up and lovingly traced the lines of my body. His touch made my pulse sing through my veins as my tongue worked Roark's cock with maddening licks.

As Roark's breathing quickened and his thighs flexed around me, I delighted in the way the tiles ground against my knees. The pain was worth it. Because *I* was the one rocking his fucking world.

Beside me, Jesse's hand moved, lowering to his cock and squeezing.

Roark clenched his fingers in my hair, yanked me off of him, and used his grip to pull me up, dragging my mouth to his.

He teased his tongue around mine, hungrily, lovingly tasting me. I knew he wanted to fuck me. I heard it in the rush of his breaths and felt it in the hard jab of his arousal against my belly.

But he broke the kiss, panting heavily, and looked away. I followed his gaze down the length of Jesse's body.

Jesse apparently had an impressive recovery rate, because he held a very hard erection in his fist, his fingers clenching like he was trying to strangle it.

I glanced at the tension straining his face and asked in dumb disbelief, "Again?"

He squeezed his eyes shut and said in a pained voice, "Again."

I looked back at Roark, breathless, and maybe even a little worried that Jesse couldn't be sated with a blow job.

With his hands on my hips, Roark spun me, pushed my head toward Jesse's cock, and slapped my butt with a stinging swat. "I love to watch, Evie."

As the sun rose higher behind the window, I knelt along the side of Jesse's body, my pussy angled toward his head, and sucked him off for the second time that morning. My muscles burned with fatigue, my jaw ached from stretching, and my stomach grumbled with hunger. But I loved it. I loved hearing his tortured groans, seeing the sinews stretch in his neck, and feeling the tremors in his thighs beneath my hands.

Roark didn't do much watching. With his grip on my waist and my ass hovering above Jesse's face, my gorgeous priest licked and sucked at my pussy, flattening his tongue along the seam, biting my clit, and propelling me into a tunnel of blind need. I grew insane with it, moaning and grinding against his whiskers.

I was two seconds from telling him to piss on his goddamned vow and fuck me like a man, when Jesse did it for me.

"If you don't fuck her—"

Roark was already there, his chest covering my back, his breaths hot against my nape, and his cock…

I cried out when he thrust, burying his steel length to the hilt. He grunted, his lips pressed to my spine and his hands palming my breasts.

OhmyGodOhmyGod. Roark was fucking me. It felt like an out-of-body experience, one that would crash and burn with resentment and guilt and prayers. Sweet pissing hell, would there be enough prayers to put him back together after this?

But I'd wanted it. Still did. He felt incredible, stretching and filling me in a way nothing else could. I clenched around him, and he shuddered against me, picking up speed.

Jesse grabbed my head and shoved his cock back in my mouth. From his vantage, with me on hands and knees beside him and facing his feet, he could watch Roark moving in and out of me, and holy shit, did Roark move.

He hammered his hips like a piston, his balls slapping my clit, and his weight on my back growing heavier and heavier until I wasn't sure I could hold him much longer.

My legs wobbled, my tongue rolled and licked, and my jaw extended with delicious pain as Jesse pumped his hips, fucking my mouth.

As they took me at both ends, their thrusts fell in sync, and it felt as if a string of nerve-endings ran through my body, vibrating between them, connecting them, and tying us together.

Roark's hands moved all over me, caressing every dip and curve, covering my breasts, my waist, my thighs. His fingers sank between my legs, finding my clit, and circling. Right there… Right there…

I screamed around Jesse's cock as I let go, allowing them to hear the orgasm rolling over me. Their hips jerked, both of them gasping and shaking, then they fell with me.

The hot stream of Jesse's release hit my throat as Roark collapsed against my back, sucking in staggered breaths.

I wanted to stay lost in my fantasy, dancing and fucking in the realm of possibilities, but Roark's weight pulled me back to the ground. Literally.

I crumbled beneath him, my cheek landing on Jesse's thigh and Roark's big body spooned around my back.

Jesse reached down and tucked a strand of hair behind my ear. "I came so hard you're probably pregnant."

I grinned, tiredly. "That's not even funny."

As his breathing returned to normal, he seemed to be gathering his thoughts, his expression sobering. "I won't apologize for earlier, but I owe you an explanation."

I held his gaze, my face open, waiting.

He trailed his fingers over my arm, where it lay across his abs. "I let myself believe, for one rosy fucking moment, that I could have you. *All of you.* But once I tasted that belief, I didn't want to give it up. I couldn't."

"Just promise me we'll find another ultrasound on our way to find Michio."

"Promise," he mouthed, and my heart gave a thump.

Roark pressed a kiss to my spine, lingering there for a long moment. This was the dreaded part. How would he compartmentalize his broken vow? How much damage had I caused?

I rolled toward him, but he'd already pulled away, climbing to his feet, his face closed off, shadowed in conflict.

"Roark." I stood and grabbed his hand. "Please don't do this."

His thumb caressed my knuckles, his gaze on the floor, looking for something. He narrowed his eyes on his boxers and released my hand to pull them on with shaking fingers.

Fuck.

He stepped over Jesse, who watched him with an unreadable expression, and removed his rosary from his pack in the tub.

Double fuck.

I knew he'd pull out his cassock next. With a tight chest and a resolved breath, I joined him, rooting through the packs to help him find it. Wait, where was it?

"Roark, don't you have a spare cassock?"

"Tossed the last one out in the mountains." He stared at his pack, and the lost look on his face broke my heart.

I pressed a fist against my mouth. *Stupid selfish woman.* I stood there, naked, with his come dripping down my thighs, and I couldn't bring myself to regret a single second with him. He must hate me.

Golden dreadlocks and braids hung in his devastating eyes, his whiskered jaw taut with emotion. Maybe he wanted to say something to me? Maybe he wanted me to go the fuck away?

I reached up and untied the leather strap in his hair. He closed his eyes as I gathered all the twisted strands away from his face and retied them into a knot at the back of his head. Then I stepped back and let him do what he had to do.

He knelt in front of the door, in his boxers, rosary draped over his hands, and bowed his head.

I wrapped my arms around my waist, aching to hold him and feeling for all the world like an evil-doer, a temptress, like a slithering snake that had just shit in his well-kept garden.

"Evie."

I turned toward Jesse's voice.

He pulled the bedrolls from the tub, spread them over the floor, and sprawled on his back. "Come on." He stretched out his arms, naked and waiting for me to climb into his embrace. "We haven't slept in two days."

"Almost three days."

The sky blazed through the window, another day half gone. Maybe we could sleep until nightfall.

I dropped beside Jesse, snuggling against his side with my cheek on the hard expanse of his chest, and watched Roark. I stared at the knotted bun on the back of his head, the little blond curls on his nape, the flex of his shoulders, and the strong, straight line of his spine until my eyes grew too heavy to hold open.

Just as I began to drift into unconsciousness, Jesse's whisper hummed through his chest. "Sex doesn't have to be shameful, Roark. It doesn't have to be sinful or controlled or feared. It can be something as honest and pure as love."

I held my eyes closed, my ears ringing in the silence, waiting for Roark's response.

When he spoke, his deep accent shivered through me. "I made a promise to God."

"Then make a new promise, dickhead." Jesse's arm flexed around me. "He sent you something rare and beautiful, a goddess in her own right. The only vow that matters is the promise to *love* her."

My pulse raced. I wanted to climb up Jesse's chest and kiss him senseless, but I held still, feigning sleep.

"I do—" Roark lowered his voice to a whisper, "I *do* love her, ye arrogant fuck."

"Bullshit," Jesse hissed, his heart banging against my ear. "You drop to your knees and turn to God every time you touch her. How the fuck do you think that makes her feel?"

The floor groaned as Roark rose to his feet and took a step toward us. He stood above me. I could hear the steady pace of his breaths and feel his eyes tracing the lines of my back, and the curves of my arms and legs where they wrapped around

Jesse.

The bedding rustled as he lowered behind me and scooted in. His chest slid against my back, his hand snaking quietly around my waist and following the path of my arm across Jesse's stomach. He stopped at my fingers, flattening and straightening each of my digits with his closed fist.

There was something in his hand, and when he opened it, a string of beads cascaded into my waiting palm. My breath caught as he closed my fingers around the rosary.

I turned my head and searched the calm features of his face. "Roark?"

Leaning over me, he kissed my lips, rested his forehead against mine, and stared at me with bright, clear eyes. "I know ye were listening, and he's right." Another kiss, this one delivered with a soft smile. "Ye are the incarnation of love. The only vow that matters."

THIRTY-THREE

I hoped we would sleep until nightfall, but instead we slept *through* it. I woke with the light of a new day glaring in my eyes and an impatient fist pounding on the bathroom door.

"Rise and shine, motherfuckers," Link sang from the hall.

Jesse cracked an eye open, his hand curled around the crease between my thigh and ass. "You hungry?"

I lay half-on, half-off his chest, my leg hooked over his thigh and my cheek on his shoulder. My body felt lovingly-used, yet recuperated and quenched, despite the gnawing hunger in my stomach. "I could eat."

"I'm fecking famished," Roark mumbled against my spine. He uncurled his body from around my back and shouted at the door, "If ye didn't bring us cheeseburgers, feck off!"

The doorknob rattled, and the wood frame groaned against the nails Jesse had hammered into it.

"Get your asses up," Link shouted, but I heard the smile in his rumbling voice. "I've got thirteen women out here, asking a million fucking questions and giving me a goddamned headache."

The doorknob stilled, and the scrape of his footsteps faded down the hall.

Grinning, I rolled to my back and stretched my arms and legs, the sunlight warm on my nude skin. "Did you hear that? The women are awake."

"God help us." Roark stood, retied his knot of dreadlocks, and slipped on a pair of cargo shorts over his boxers.

Standing there in the halo of the window, looking rested

and as gorgeous as ever, did he remember what he'd said last night? Did he really intend to surrender his vow?

I picked up the rosary where it lay beside my hip and threaded the beads around my fingers. "I can't accept this, Roark. I can't ask you to give up your vow."

Jesse sat up and bowed over my back, his lips resting at the juncture of my neck and shoulder. "That's just it, darlin'. You didn't ask him. You accepted him with or without his stuffy robes."

Roark cast Jesse a narrowed glare and crouched before me, his fingers beneath my chin, lifting my face. His expression softened, content, maybe even relieved. "Ye didn't ask me to give it up. Ye love me too much to ask that."

I released a shuddering breath. "I do. I love you both."

The risk in loving people I could lose combined with the gravity in admitting it out loud sank into my heart, pulling it down. But the strength in this moment—in their understanding smiles and mere presence—floated my heart right back up and held it firmly in place in my chest.

I leaned back against Jesse, my eyes on Roark, my fingers sliding over the rosary beads. "So you're done with celibacy? Just like that?"

"Just like that." Roark planted a kiss between my furrowed eyebrows.

With his face so close, I could smell myself on his whiskers, the tangy scent flooding me with images of his mouth between my legs.

But he'd clung to his vow for so long. Had he considered the ramifications? Turning away from his promise to God and running toward me, right foot, left foot, until the nights sprinted away beneath our blankets? Until he'd ran so far from his beliefs that the man who remained was no longer the bleeding heart I fell in love with? Until all that was left was a hollowed-out renegade consumed with angry regret?

"Sex has clouded your brain." I rested my forehead against his. "Think about the reality of what you're giving up."

"I have. Every single day since I met ye." His exhale

caressed my lips. "God sent ye to me, not to make me choose ye or Him. He sent ye so I could love ye *through* Him."

I wanted to understand what that meant, and maybe I would have if I was a believer. "But—"

"Are we going to sit around and recite vagina monologues all day?" He kissed my lips and climbed to his feet. "Or are we going to scrounge up some grub and check on the bettys?"

I gave him an exasperated look, which he laughed at and turned away to tackle the nails on the door.

An hour later and our bellies stuffed with cinnamon Brioche French toast—*Brioche!* Seriously, the blond-haired cook with the missing finger knew his way around dough, a skillet, and a fire—we made our rounds with the women.

There wasn't a room large enough to hold twelve dazed and thoroughly terrified patients. So Jesse, Roark, and I spread out between the three bedrooms, updating them on the years they'd missed.

Link's presence at my side eased some of the fear, since all of the women but two had known him before. By midday, I'd recounted the details of the plague's origin and the expectations of the healing process so many times Link and his men were able to take over and answer questions from the women who were still trying to wrap their foggy heads around their new world.

As I watched them interact, it became apparent that none of the men belonged to a specific woman. No brothers or husbands or boyfriends. Just as Link had said. Some might've been sexual partners before, but there weren't defined couples. It was still too soon to imagine how territories would be established. The women could barely hold their heads up, let alone begin picking their mates.

Shea tended to their physical recovery with the grace of Mother Teresa. She darted from bed to bed, sometimes singing, always smiling, with a trail of male volunteers on her heels. Her muscle-boys listened to her instructions and jumped on her orders to fetch water, wash blankets, and empty vomit buckets. But their motives snaked a wary amount of suspicion through my gut.

After lunch, I caught her arm in the doorway of one of the bedrooms. "Can we talk privately for a sec?"

"Uh…" Her black curls smoothed into a ponytail high on her head, the hair tie pulling so tightly it stretched the skin on her face, making her eyes appear larger as they darted over the five women filling the beds and sleeping bags in the room. "Liliana needs aspirin. Brooke is demanding a vibrator, and—"

"Wait." My head jerked back. "Did you say *vibrator*?"

She lowered her voice and nodded at the brunette writhing on the mattress across the room. "If I don't strap that girl to the bed, she's going to be pregnant by nightfall."

Did that mean I'd passed on my overactive libido, not only to Shea, but to the whole damned house of women? Shit.

Shea squeezed my hand, her focus locked on the women, her mind likely racing through a list of things she wanted to get done. "Just tell me what you need to tell me."

I glanced around the small bedroom, meeting the eyes of her three male *nurses,* who were feeding the women from cans of applesauce. There was—shit, I really struggled to remember everyone's names—African American Beefcake with a trim goatee and two white guys, Sexpot with a tongue ring and Hottie with sleeved tattoos. As illogical as it sounded in my head, they were way too attractive to be trustworthy.

With my hand on her spine, I angled our backs to them and whispered, "I don't trust them."

She stuck her chin out, tilting her head slightly and giving me a *huh?* look.

I kept my voice quiet. "They're following you around, you're in here without protection, and—"

"Okay, stop." She grabbed my arm and turned us to face them. "You." She pointed at the black guy. "What did I tell you when you got all up in my personal space?"

He rubbed a hand over his neatly-cropped black hair. "That I smell…muscular?"

"No. Well, yeah, you do." She put her fists on her hips.

"But I'm referring to the part about touching me without asking?"

He held his hands up. "I didn't touch you!"

"But if you did?"

"Oh." He lowered his arms and lifted his chin. "That I won't believe what you can do with a scalpel, not even while it's happening." He flashed her a gorgeous, panty-dropping smile.

"Breathtaking," she whispered in my ear then straightened, giving him her own wide smile. "You, sir, are a breath of stolen air."

Oh, brother. She was flirting with him? I couldn't stop my grin.

"See? I've got this." She gripped my shoulders and pushed me into the hallway. "Out."

I let her boot me, but as I fed, clothed, and talked with the women in the other bedrooms, I asked Jesse and Roark to keep their eyes on Shea's *volunteers*.

The afternoon limped by, every minute of it dedicated to the women and what they needed. When they tucked in for the night, peacefully asleep beneath Shea's attentive gaze and guarded by two armed men posted on the stairs, I shuffled outside to acquaint myself with some of the crew.

Jesse and Roark followed me out, and it wasn't long before we were reclining on the wide porch, passing around flasks of gut-burning whiskey, and sharing stories with three of Link's men.

Stars lit up the sky in a maze of distant universes, and not so far away, beyond the shadowed landscape of clustered trees and fields, prowled countless herds of aphids.

Their vibrations pulsed inside me, the network of threads spreading out through the cool night air and connecting to hungry beacons in every direction. I would've been lying if I said I wasn't on edge, but the aphids never came closer than fifty yards, their pulsing signals blinking out before I felt the urge to grab the bow that lay at my feet.

Sitting on the wood decking at the far end of the porch, I

draped my arm over Roark's lap beside me. "How many guards are out there tonight?"

Paul, the black man with the goatee from upstairs, leaned against the railing. "Eight. They wear night vision and sit high in the trees, picking off the bugs before they reach the perimeter of the property."

My shoulders hunched around my ears, tightening with the chorus of insectile humming in my gut. "No one in your group uses guns?"

"Too loud." The Hispanic man said. Could I even call him a man? He barely looked twenty.

He'd introduced himself as Hunter, his fingers constantly shoving his long black hair out of his boyish face. Like he was doing now. "We all carry crossbows."

"Among other silent weapons." The blond cook, Eddie, passed me a grin. "Knives are my specialty."

I shared a look with Jesse, who sat on the stairs, the only one not drinking…or talking.

I accepted the flask from Roark, took a fiery gulp, and passed it to Eddie. "Is that how you lost a finger?"

"Yeah." Eddie flexed his left hand, his ice-blue eyes on the knuckle where his index finger used to be. "Chopping a grisly hunk of deer meat."

"While he was completely inebriated, mind you." Hunter laughed then looked at the front door as sudden scratching from inside began to rattle it.

Jesse jumped up and opened it enough to let Darwin slip out.

In a flash of black fur and blurring legs, he scampered off the porch and into the dark.

Hunter stared after him with wide brown eyes. "Did your dog really walk four-hundred miles to track you down *and* go after a lion?"

A heavy medley of pride and regret tightened my chest. I would *never* leave that dog behind again.

"Yep." Jesse returned to his spot on the stairs and stretched his legs along the top step, leaning his back against the post, his eyes roaming over Hunter's Hispanic features. "How did you become the gatherer on this crew?"

Hunter picked at the cuticle on his thumb, his hair hanging around his face and neck. "Link caught me stealing weapons off the Mississippi Queen. Said I was the only guy who'd been able to breach his security and make it on board without getting caught."

I pursed my lips. "But you said you got caught?"

He nodded. "On my way back to the shore. There were a lot of aphids waiting, and I only carried guns at the time."

His gunfire must've alerted Link's crew.

"I grew up on the streets." Hunter dropped his head back against the wall behind him, staring at the porch canopy. "Stealing was survival. Link calls it *gathering,* but the mechanics are the same. I go out there, find what we need, and snatch it without dying in the process."

I sized him up, taking in his youth, his thin yet muscular frame, and his long legs. A runner's build. I bet the kid could squeeze into small places and sprint like a motherfucker.

I shifted my attention to the black man beside him, his hands huge and calloused, and his biceps stretching the sleeves of his t-shirt.

Paul watched me studying him, the intelligence in his dark eyes a little unnerving. "I'm the mechanic. My daddy taught me, and his daddy taught him. We also dabbled in alternative fuel. You know the gunk that got left in fat fryers? There's still a ton of it out there. I know how to filter it and use it as diesel fuel."

Damn. That would've been useful when we couldn't find gas on our way to the mountains.

Roark leaned forward, his fingers absently tapping my leg. "When we go after Michio and the Drone, we'll need a mechanic with us. All that fecking walking…" He rubbed his stubbly jaw. "It's wheels only from here on out."

I couldn't agree more.

Paul rested his elbows on the railing and looked at Roark. "Already talked to Link about it." His eyes hardened. "After losing my wife and kids, I would love a chance to gut the monster who created the plague."

I bit down on my bottom lip, waiting for my overzealous hoots of joy to break free.

"He desecrated the religion of Islam." Paul's brows pulled down, forming a harsh line. "I'm Muslim, and we're a peace-loving people. I hate that he wiped out the planet in the name of Allah."

"Me too." I offered him a soft smile. "But you realize he's mentally deranged, right?"

"Yeah." Paul nodded. "I'm not sure Allah would forgive him at this point. I don't, which is why I want to help take him down."

"You need a cook?" Eddie held up a hand, waving it. "Count me in."

"Me, too," Hunter said, his knees bouncing. "I want to go."

That did it. I laughed loudly and shook my head. I didn't get it, though. I mean, why would they want to leave all these women and join us?

There it was, my poisonous suspicion.

Jesse sat quietly, chin tilted down, seemingly lost in his head until his eyes drifted up, scanning the three men. "A thief, a cook, and a mechanic. None of you were on Link's security team before the outbreak." He nodded at the house. "Why are you here? What do you get out of this?"

Paul straightened and met Jesse's eyes.

"Twenty…fifty…hell, hundreds of years from now, people will tell stories about the brave men and women who ended the suffering and gave hope to the new world. They'll write children's songs about us, name cities after us, and erect bronze statues of our naked bodies." He made a face. "They better give me a full-sized penis. None of those little shriveled-up Roman peckers."

He wanted a statue of himself with his dick hanging out?

Hunter and Eddie nodded their heads in agreement.

I scrubbed a hand over my face. "Sounds a little narcissistic, don't you think?"

Eddie cocked his blond head. "Would you rather us be motivated by something more cliché, like raping and killing?"

I dropped my hand. "Of course not."

Hunter frowned at the dark landscape. Maybe he was older than twenty, but the twin dimples denting his hairless cheeks made him appear permanently boyish. "We want a better life, Evie, and we want to be a part of its creation. We'll sweat and bleed for it. Some of us will die in the process. So why not be remembered for our efforts?"

Understandable. They wanted to be forefathers, legends, and maybe they would be. Not through gathering or cooking or killing the Drone, but through the most basic, most important responsibility of all: Reproduction. There were thirteen women upstairs, most of which would likely become pregnant within the next couple months.

Even now, I felt more women on the horizon. It was a subtle feeling, just a blip here and there, lost in the vibrations of aphids. But nymphs were coming, the flickering chill of their torment tapping like ice-cold fingers against the lining of my stomach.

I gripped Roark's hand. "There are nymphs out there. They're far away, farther than I thought I could sense them, but they're headed this way."

Five pairs of eyes locked onto me, the men's shoulders snapping to attention.

"How many?" Roark pulled me into his lap, moving my legs to straddle his. He was probably recalling the agony I'd suffered last time, his arms wrapping around my back as if to comfort me. "How far away?"

I smoothed a hand over the bumps of braids above his ear. "Miles. Days. I don't know. It's so faint, but it's an accumulated feeling. A gathering? There could be hundreds of them."

"Hundreds?" Jesse jumped up, grabbed his bow off the ground, and strode across the front lawn, searching the darkness. "We don't have the capacity to help hundreds. Why now? Why so many?"

I sighed. "I don't know."

He paced in front of the porch. "Are you evolving? Sending out signals? Or is it the combined potency of so many cured women together?"

"I don't know!" My teeth gnashed in frustration. I softened my voice. "But we have a little time before they show up."

"Okay." He shoved a hand through his hair and climbed the stairs to crouch beside me. "Okay. We'll figure it out. We have help now."

He looked at Hunter, Paul, and Eddie like he wanted to trust them, but I wasn't sure he did. I wasn't certain *I* trusted them. Reaching that level of confidence, believing a person was good, honest, and able to be depended on took time. It required consistent proof. Especially in this brutal world.

I swung around on Roark's lap in a half-straddle with my leg draped over his groin. Hooking an arm around his bare shoulders, I nuzzled his ear and trailed my fingers through his whiskers. I had an ulterior motive for my open display of affection, but the twitch of his cock beneath my leg was a nudging reminder that he was no longer celibate.

His breathing kicked up, and he shifted beneath me, probably wondering what the hell I was doing.

I set my gaze on the three men watching us. "You talked about the glory in children's songs and bronze statues, but none of you have uttered a word about the one thing I know you all want."

All three of them looked away, hands curling, jaws flexing.

"I don't trust people who don't curse or talk about sex." I watched their nostrils flare and shoulders tighten. "Everyone has at least a sliver of crudeness that slips out. If you don't show any vices, I have to wonder what you're really hiding. My mind immediately jumps to…oh, I don't know, whips and chains and locked doors in dark basements."

"Evie…" Jesse said in a scolding tone.

Yeah, I was baiting them, but I wanted to sleep tonight, knowing at least one dirty secret about the men we were rooming with.

"I heard you screaming yesterday." Hunter looked up at me. "We all did."

I wasn't ashamed, but I should've felt bad. Really fucking bad. Twenty-one men, men who hadn't had sex with a woman in over two years, had to listen to me bellow in all my orgasmic wonder.

It worked to my advantage though. If they'd harbored any doubts in my lovers' abilities to satisfy me, they didn't now. Maybe they wouldn't be as eager to step in and try to fulfill that role.

I cleared my throat. "And?"

"I wanted to be in that bathroom with you." Hunter tucked his hair behind his ear, his eyes on his sneakers. "I wanted to see you while you—" He coughed. "While you made those sounds. I want to know what you taste like, feel li—"

"Alright, that's enough." Jesse thrust a finger at him.

Roark put his hand on Jesse's arm, lowering it. "Let them talk."

Eddie crossed his arms over his chest. "If we're speaking candidly…" He arched a blond brow at Roark. "I don't want a broken nose."

Roark gave him a nod, but the air on the porch stretched with tension.

Eddie drew a deep breath. "Every man in this house is wondering what he has to do to become one of your— What do you call them? Your guardians? That's assuming you only let guardians into your bed."

Jesse's posture became so rigid he looked like he was seconds from exploding out of his skin. But Eddie and Hunter had given *normal* responses, the kind I would expect from normal, healthy men. Normal was good. I could deal with that. It made me sympathize with them. They had gone so long without the love of a woman. But they had options now, right upstairs. If they left with me, it was possible I'd be the only woman, so I needed to be very clear.

I reached over and flattened my hand on Jesse's stone chest. "I only let men I *love* into my bed, Eddie."

Eddie grinned. "I've got an apple pie recipe that's left a trail of broken hearts in my wake."

His teasing tone coaxed me into laughter.

A small smile twitched at the corner of Jesse's mouth. I moved my hand from his chest, and just as the tension faded from the air, a low growl sounded off the side of the deck.

Darwin sprinted from around the corner, hackles up, ear pinned close to his head, and slowed at the stairs. His body lowered to the ground, slinking forward, his lips drawn back in a snarl. He wasn't walking toward the surrounding field. No, he crept up the stairs, eyes on the door, tail straight out, his barrel-chested growl reverberating through my bones.

I was already moving, heart racing, bow in hand, but Jesse beat me to the door. I didn't know what spooked Darwin, and I didn't question it as the tornado of black fur whipped past us and into the house.

Several men in the front room gave us curious looks as we tumbled in and ran after my dog. Darwin darted straight, then left, his claws scrabbling across the floorboards and toward the interior stairs.

The stairs that were no longer guarded by armed men.

Dread crashed over me, shaking my limbs. Darwin bounded the steps, and my feet slapped against the wood floor to keep up with him and Jesse, and now Roark, who shoved past me.

The sudden scream of a woman rang in my ears and chilled my blood. My eyes darted up the stairs, toward the sound, my legs pumping harder. Then more horrified screams, the cries of several women, followed by footsteps pounding across the ceiling and Link's enraged shouting.

My breath stuttered. Fuck, fuck, fuck! What the fuck was happening up there?

Jesse and Roark gripped the railing as they took the stairs two at a time, their heads tilted back and eyes up.

I strained my ears, picking through the varying pitches of

cries, listening for Shea. I couldn't hear her, I couldn't hear her, I couldn't… Oh God, if anything happened to her…

At the top of the stairs, I threw myself forward, following Jesse and Roark and Darwin, and fucking hell, the cries grew louder. No, not cries. They were blood-curdling, oh-Jesus-save-me screams of fear.

My spine turned to ice, and the hairs on my neck stood on end. I picked up my pace, down the hall, into the third bedroom, and slammed into Jesse's back.

The screaming was so loud I stumbled back, my view blocked by Jesse and Roark. I pushed forward, my bare feet slipping on the wet carpet. *Wet?* I glanced down.

Blood.

It was everywhere.

THIRTY-FOUR

The unholy screams in the small bedroom shivered my skin with goosebumps. But it was the smell, the overwhelming scent of copper and iron, that sent my heart crashing into my ribs.

My hands shook and my toes squished through wet puddles as I pushed around Jesse and Roark. They didn't stop me from stepping in front of them, but I only had a millisecond to question that before my vision filled with blood.

Streaks on yellow walls. Splatters on brown work boots. Smears on pale skin. Pools around limp bodies. Torn pink pajamas, zippered flies spread open, lacerated flesh, stab wounds, and holy fuck, one of those bodies was castrated.

My limbs went numb, and my ears rang. Death pervaded the air so thickly I inhaled through my mouth and held my breath as I took in the rest of the room.

Link squatted over the bodies of a woman and a man, his hand wrapped around a red-stained blade. And Shea…oh God, her eyes were hard but *alive*, showing no signs of physical pain, no visible wounds. She stood beside Link and glared down at the third body. Another man.

A total of three dead.

Four women huddled on the bed in the corner, their shrieks muffling into heavy sobs, hands covering faces, arms hugging stomachs. No blood on their pajamas. The slaughter concentrated on the walls and floor near the door, spreading out around the three bodies.

The dead man at Shea's feet lay on his back, a metal

instrument—*Shea's scalpel?*—buried in his eye socket. His tattooed arms lay askew around his head, the zipper of his jeans gaped open.

I looked away and reminded myself to breathe, releasing a heavy exhale.

"Wha' happened, Shea?" Roark's brogue slipped out without censure. He abhorred murder, but it was obvious she'd killed this man in self-defense.

She closed her eyes and wiggled her jaw, as if struggling to unclench it.

Darwin skirted around her and rooted his head under the arms of the wailing women, licking their hands and faces.

Link watched them for a moment, rubbing the knuckles of his knife-wielding hand against his bald head. "When I noticed the guards missing from the stairs, I ran up here and—"

"I want to hear it from Shea." Only my lips moved, the rest of my body detached as I stared at the hunk of flesh in Link's other hand.

Blood dripped from his fingers, plopping on the mangled hole between the spread legs of the man beneath him.

I shouldn't have been shocked by all the gore. It wasn't the first time I'd seen a castration. When I'd killed the Drone's brother, I'd relieved him of his pathetic dick. And before that, I'd severed all of Steve's parts in my haste to split him sternum to groin in my father's basement after he'd raped me.

The clash of past horrors and present fears spun through my head, jerking me off balance and thrusting me into a fever of heaving breaths and hot skin. The room vanished as remembered pain ran riot through my body, stretching my limbs and cutting my flesh, locking me in a nightmare of memory, in a place where men couldn't be trusted.

My hand jerked to my forearm sheath and started to release one of the blades.

"Evie. Breathe." Roark's arms came around me from behind, hooking across my belly. "I'm here. You're safe."

His accent was calm and coaxing in my ear, a voice that

would never hurt me or rape me or lie to me.

I gripped his arms, holding him to me, letting him know how grateful I was for his constant protection.

Beside me, Jesse lowered his head, glancing at me then up at Roark out of the corner of his eye. He and Roark exchanged a look, then he turned his attention back to the room.

Link shot another glare at the sobbing women. "Fuck. Someone get them out of here before my head explodes."

I lurched forward to help them, adrenaline surging through my stupor, but Roark held me in place.

Shea's head snapped up. "I'll take them."

"No." I didn't want her out of my sight, and I needed her to tell me what happened, to assure me she was okay.

"I'll do it." Liliana pulled herself from the huddle of women. "Come on, ladies."

The queen of the Mississippi Queen really was stunning. Her chocolate skin glowed in the flickering light of the candles, her body tall and lean beneath the satin of her ivory slip. But the horror of what she'd just witnessed trembled her delicate hands and stained her cheeks with tears.

"Liliana." Link stared at her, his black eyes creased with warning. "Until I get this sorted, you should..."

A look passed between them, and she tilted her head. "Watch my back?" She gestured toward the women to follow her and stopped at Link's side, her focus on his face instead of the massacre soaking the carpet beneath him. "Sugar, I was fighting off men before you were a bullet in your daddy's gun."

The tanned skin around his eyes tightened. "What the fuck are you implying?"

I didn't understand what they were talking about, especially since I still didn't know what had happened here. But I could guess on the latter. Rape. Self-defense. Perhaps Link blamed himself for trusting the men who turned on these women?

The blond woman had died during the fight, her eyes staring blindly at the ceiling. I hoped her final thoughts reflected on a happy life rather than on the two brutish men who lay dead beside her.

My chest ached, and I forced a deep inhale, pushing past the tightness.

Liliana reached for Brooke, the brunette standing behind her, but her eyes remained on Link. "You're not on my payroll anymore. You have nothing to prove to me."

With that, she led the women out, tugging on Brooke's hand. I'd been introduced to all of the women throughout the course of the day and remembered Brooke as the girl who'd demanded the vibrator. But now that I saw the colorful cosmography of stars inked on her arms and the metal rings pierced through every feature in her delicate face, I knew she was the rebellious one Shea had cured after I left the house.

Angie, the blonde with shoulder-length hair, stumbled after Brooke. The rabid look in her hazel eyes wasn't just from all the bloodshed. Two days ago, she'd been the nymph tapping on the window, the one who looked like she'd lived in the wild for two years. She wouldn't remember those years, but they seemed to have left a savage kind of vibration humming across her skin.

Jillian trailed behind them, also blonde, her hair falling in sheets around her elbows. She quickened her bare feet to keep up with Angie, but her gaze strayed to Jesse. Even as she sniffled and blinked her swollen red eyes, the flushed look on her face was undeniable. She tripped, her fixation on Jesse never wavering until she was out of sight down the hall.

Jesse seemed oblivious to his admirer as he stepped beside Link, his attention on the bodies. "Shea?"

Darwin brushed against her leg, nuzzling her fingers. As she absently petted his head, he angled his neck to give her easier access, his little black eyebrows pulling against the golden fur on his forehead.

Shea wiped her other hand on her sleep shorts, streaking the yellow cotton with blood. "That one came in first." She pointed at the man with the metal handle protruding from his eye. "I woke with him on top of me." Her expression darkened. "He didn't know I slept with my scalpel."

That's my girl. My lungs expanded with a heady swell of pride. "Did he…?"

She shook her head. "I stabbed the son of a bitch in his brain before he got his dick out."

The man she'd knifed in the eye was the tattooed volunteer who had been following her around all day. The same man who'd been assigned to guard the stairs while the women slept.

"The other one…" Her chin trembled, and her hands balled into fists as she glared at the man beneath Link's bent knees. "He was the second guard on the stairs, right?"

Link nodded, his eyes tapered into dangerous slits.

Shea flexed her hand at her side. "He was over by the door, wrestling Jennifer to the floor. I…I think she attacked him first. She tried to protect us."

I pulled away from Roark's arms, stepped around Jennifer's body, and hugged Shea to my chest. She pushed away at first, but as I tightened my embrace, she deflated against me, hugging me back.

Self-defense was all well and good, but Shea was still new to this world. Deep down, she needed a certain level of normalcy, and standing over the body of the woman she'd been taking care of was a reality few could stomach. Even I struggled to maintain my composure, regret chewing painfully at my insides. The valuable and very rare life of a woman ended tonight because of the greedy, selfish needs of a man.

Footsteps shuffled around the doorway, drawing my gaze to the six men gathering on the threshold. I couldn't remember the names of three, but Paul, Eddie, and Hunter were among them, their expressions seething and growing hotter by the second.

A single tear skipped down Shea's cheek, the steadiness in her voice crumbling. "I couldn't get to her before his knife pierced her belly. Before he ra…" She covered her mouth with a shaky hand. "He stabbed her while he was raping her. He would've gone after the other women, but Link showed up."

"Too fucking late." Link stared at the bloody wound in Jennifer's stomach, his gaze igniting as he lowered her nightie over her hips, tugging it down her thighs. Then he pinned his blade-sharp eyes on the men at the door. "You know the rules. You touch a woman against her will, and what happens?"

Paul stepped forward, fury shadowing his dark complexion. "We lose our dicks. Then we lose our lives."

Link held up the sawed-off penis. Blood trickled down his forearm as he squeezed his fist. Then he bent over the corpse of the other man, swiped his knife, and removed those genitals, too.

The gush of blood and the sickening sound of squishy meat were enough to trigger my gag reflex. I fought back the bile, but Shea wasn't as lucky. She jerked away and turned her back to puke on the floor.

"That one got off easy." Link pointed his knife at the man Shea had stabbed. "I prefer them alive while I castrate them."

He stood and dropped the severed dicks on a discarded towel.

The sudden silence coiled around me, shuddering with adrenaline and testosterone and the hunger for revenge. Considering Link and his men hadn't been around women for the past two years, I suspected his no nonconsensual-touching rule was something he'd implemented on the steamboat prior to the aphid plague.

They glared at the dead men like they wanted to resurrect them and kill them all over again, their palpable need for violence shivering through me. The walls in the small room closed in, made excruciatingly more unbearable with the hot scent of Shea's vomit.

Saliva pooled in my mouth, and my stomach folded in on itself. These guys hadn't survived the past two years without killing or watching those they loved being killed. Yet beneath the anger storming across their faces were glazed eyes, parted lips, hunched shoulders. Shell-shocked. Had Link put enough fear in them to prevent another attack within the group? I wouldn't hold my breath.

Roark broke the awful hush as he knelt over Jennifer's body and touched her forehead. "*In nomine Patris.*" His thumb moved to her breastbone. "*Et Filii*". He brushed her left shoulder then right shoulder as his brogue vibrated through the room. "*Et Spiritus Sancti.* Eternal rest grant unto her, O Lord..."

As he continued to pray quietly, some of the men stepped into the room and joined him. Hunter knew a few verses, his lips moving along silently, his hair hanging in his face as his gaze rested on the bodies.

Link stood in the doorway with Jesse, his head bowed, nodding every few seconds as Jesse spoke in his ear. Then they both looked up at me.

"We have to move." Link's brows dug together. "We don't have the space to shelter ten more nymphs, let alone *hundreds.*"

Ah. So Jesse had just filled him in on the next problem.

Link strode toward the pile of genitals, gathered them in the towel, and carried them to the door. "I'm recruiting more men."

"*More* men?" I pushed my way out of the room, trailing after him and Jesse. "How?"

Link moved in quick, silent steps down the hall. "I sent out four guys the night we found you. Two are rounding up more soldiers. The other two are checking out Arkendale."

My head swam. "I didn't even know four men left the property."

He stopped at the top of the stairs. "I only sent out four. I've got eight guys on guard outside. Two dead. And six men just standing around." He pointed at the crowded bedroom we'd just left. "Put them to work."

Alrighty. As soon as I was done with this discussion, I'd tell them to drag all the mattresses downstairs. We would all sleep in the living room, whether we fit or not, because there was no way the women would feel safe upstairs, separated from each other and us.

"What's in Arkendale?" Jesse asked from behind me, his tone more curious than skeptical.

"Widewater Beach." Link glanced down the stairs. "It's a peninsula on the Potomac River, surrounded by water on the east, south, and west. The strip of land is heavily wooded. Lots of large homes. Would be easy to build a barricade, one huge fortified wall, across the north side where it connects to Virginia. Even with only a few guards, it would still be damned difficult for anyone to enter the peninsula without getting shot."

A place where the women could spread out and safely live? Maybe not safe from men, but at least aphids wouldn't be able to reach them without crossing a guarded barricade.

The tension in my spine loosened a little. "How far away?"

"A hundred and thirty miles east."

Jesse stepped beside me, his bow on his back and his arms crossed over his chest. "And if men already inhabit the area?"

"If they meet my requirements, they can stay." Link smiled, his eyes edged with a cruel glint. "If they don't…"

He left the rest of that sentence hovering on the upper floor like an ominous cloud as he stomped down the stairs with his terrycloth sac of dismembered flesh.

A few minutes later, the pounding of a hammer reverberated through the house. Somehow I knew what he'd done, but it didn't make me any less disgusted when I walked outside later that night to help the men bury the dead.

Yep, Link had nailed the dicks to the front door, one on each side. Every time I stepped in or out, the mutilated reminders swung in my face.

The shriveled meat hung on the door while we all slept crammed like sardines in the living room night after night. While we ate the meals Eddie prepared for us day after day. They blistered in the sun while Paul worked on the engine of an old school bus. While Hunter gathered food and medicine. While Link, Roark, and Jesse interviewed the arrivals of new men. And they attracted flies and made a nesting ground for maggots while the rest of us prepared to transport eleven recovering women one hundred and thirty miles east.

The stinking, rotting flesh sagged on the door for a week.

The week after that, the nymphs came.

THIRTY-FIVE

I knew it was coming, but I was powerless to stop the pressure of hundreds of anguished whispers. As the nymphs grew closer, my body crumbled into a ferocious fit of convulsions. My veins froze up, my muscles seized, and my bones turned to ice. For a panicked moment, I thought I would plummet to the floor and crack my head, but Roark's grip around me was as inflexible as a straitjacket.

Cradling me in his arms, he ran out the door and into the sunlight. I was aware enough to recognize the yellow paint on the bus and the heavy fume of exhaust. Then a dark fog surrounded us.

Amid the hellacious agony of the nymphs' pain, I remembered Paul had boarded up the windows of the bus. We must've been inside it. That was the plan anyway. When the nymphs were close enough for me to identify their numbers, we would load our women into the bus and drive them to Arkendale with the trail of nymphs behind us.

One-hundred-and-thirteen nymphs. That was how many I'd counted before I lost consciousness the first time.

Expecting so many to follow us was a Hail Mary shot in Hell, but at least the aphids wouldn't fuck with them along the journey.

I heard the whimpers of the women around me. Felt the kick of gravel beneath the spinning tires. But beyond that, I wasn't able to focus on anything other than the icy daggers skewering my insides.

Roark's mouth touched my brow. I could feel that,

concentrated all thought on it. The heat of his breaths, the softness of his lips, melting the pain, calming me. But not for long.

The trembling returned, shooting unbearable spasms through my entire body. An arctic wind slammed against my skin, and a metallic taste coated my tongue. I couldn't breathe, couldn't keep warm, couldn't open my eyes.

"Shea!" Roark's voice punched like a jolt of electricity on the top of my head. "She's having another seizure!"

It felt as though my organs froze solid, dead and splintering, too late to thaw out. I screamed at the agony, trying to shove free and unable to make my arms or legs work.

Everything went black.

The pain disappeared, and I floated in a vacuum, watching myself from above, circling around my distressed body as it writhed and tumbled into the emptiness.

A bright wash of light flooded my senses, illuminating my house in Missouri. Hundreds of cracks forked across the stone facing, each fissure in the foundation sprouting leafy tendrils that stretched upward, swallowing my beloved home. The driveway crumbled into broken slabs, the concrete pieces tilting, giving way to the soil pushing free beneath it. And there, in Annie's window on the top floor, waited the dark silhouette of a man, the outline of wings behind him, and the black unfathomable caverns of his soulless eyes.

The dream flickered, like a light bulb turning on, turning off, on, off, until all I saw was that pulsing globe.

Light bulbs didn't glow in the real world, but I was certain I was no longer dreaming.

"Where am I?" Ow, fuck. Had I swallowed razorblades?

The surface beneath me bounced. A bed?

I tortured my throat again. "Where—"

"Shhh." A voice hushed in my ear.

The cool lip of a glass rested against my lips. I swallowed, choked, and lifted my head for more, but the water moved out of reach.

"Evie."

I opened my eyes at the sound of Jesse's voice, blinded by the glare of an overhead light. I blinked rapidly, focusing on the bulb. A light bulb?

There it was, screwed into a socket in a ceiling I'd never seen before, surrounded by peeling paint and cracked plaster, its filaments burning with electricity.

"Where are we?" I tried to sit up but my arms wouldn't cooperate. I looked toward his face, and yellow halos blotted my vision. I'd stared at that damned bulb for too long. "Where's Roark?"

"Here, love."

I gasped at the nearness of his accent, so fucking relieved he was lying on my other side. I tried to move toward him, and my aching body clenched in pain. "What about Shea? Darwin?"

"Everyone's safe." Jesse's face filled my view, his stubble thicker but trimmed, the hair on his head clean and clipped short around his ears.

He smiled softly, his expression content despite the fatigue swelling his pink-tinged eyelids.

I turned my head to see Roark, and my breath caught. His dreadlocks were gone, his face completely shaved. I wouldn't have recognized him at first had it not been for the jade pools of his gorgeous eyes. My God, he looked young. Refined. Like a goddamned *gentleman*

I reached up, my arm wobbling in a haze of disorientation, and smoothed my palm over the soft skin on his jaw. I pushed my hand over his ear, his blond curls sifting through my fingers. He leaned closer, allowing me to feel the textured length around the back. Short, but long enough to curl at the ends.

My nostrils filled with the scent of soap and fresh linen. "You smell different."

It wasn't a bad smell. It just wasn't *his* smell. I played with the satiny curls around his ear and nape. His hair felt amazing, and I bet he didn't miss the itchy dreadlocks, but I mourned the loss, aching for the comfort of familiarity.

"A shave and a shower, love. It's feckin' cla, isn't it?"

A working shower? A glowing light bulb? My hand fell away. "How? Wait, how long have I been out?"

Jesse cupped my face, angling it toward his. "Two weeks."

I inhaled a deep breath, chasing off the shock enough to speak. "How? That's not possible. I mean, how did I eat? Why don't I feel hungry?"

He tucked my hair behind my ear. "You ate what we fed you. Your body did all the things it needed to survive, but your mind wasn't…" He glanced up at Roark and returned to me. "It wasn't here."

Awake but not aware? Was it a self-preservation mechanism? A cataleptic way to block out the pain?

Jesse gripped my hand and placed my palm against the coppery whiskers on his face. "I wanted to get rid of this, but you told me once to never *ever* shave."

My heart gave a heavy thump. Could I love this man any more than I already did?

He turned his head, pressing his mouth against my fingers. "We're in Charlottesville, Virginia. About eighty miles from Arkendale."

My pulse revved up, and my muscles tensed, triggering sudden pressure in my bladder. I clamped my hands over my lower belly. "What happened to the plan? The peninsula? Where are the women? All the nymphs?"

"Up ye go." Roark scooped my naked body into his arms. "Told ye the bettys are safe. Empty your bladder, then we'll tell ye the rest."

He carried me through the bedroom, passing heavy wooden furniture, ornate rugs, and framed pictures of unfamiliar faces peeking through a layer of dust and cobwebs. They'd found an extravagant house to hole up in, but it was quiet. Too quiet. The women weren't here.

I lay my heavy head against his shoulder, noticing he wore a shirt for the first time in months. Jesse trailed behind us, hands in the pockets of clean-looking jeans, his beautiful torso also hidden by a t-shirt, the red cotton unsoiled and free of holes and tears. Despite the new clothes, my savage man still had his scruff, his predatory gait, and his intense glare.

Inside the attached bathroom, Roark set me on a toilet. Marble spread out around us, and a single bulb burned over the vanity. Little flower-shaped soaps lay in a ceramic dish on the counter. Embroidered towels hung on brass hangers. A pair of men's slippers waited beside the glass shower. What the hell was this place?

"Toilet and shower works." Jesse perched on the tub across from me, his gaze glued to mine as if he was afraid I'd disappear. "There's a generator pumping the well water and powering the lights."

I'd woken in another dimension, in a land of marble and crazy filled with what-the-fuck shit, where everyone used toilets and wore clean shirts and shaved their beards beneath electric lights. Once upon a time, this was the only place that made sense, but now it was all so very odd. Fancy little things and ideas spun round and round. Or was the room spinning? Maybe it was just the weak state of my underused mind and body.

Roark squatted beside me and steadied my teetering shoulders as I released my bladder.

"Shea and Darwin are downstairs with Paul and Eddie." His thumb stroked over my arm. "We left everyone else in Arkendale this morning."

"What?" My head snapped up. Oh fuck, I felt dizzy.

"Back to bed." He tore off some toilet paper and made a move to wipe me, obviously accustomed to performing this task.

I swatted at his head and grabbed the wad, my fuzzy head muddling through this alternate universe of toilet paper and flushing water.

That done, I glimpsed a toothbrush on the counter, the sight of it prompting my tongue to drag over my teeth. The enamel felt smooth. No grit.

I licked my lips and tasted mint. "Did you guys brush my teeth?"

"Aye." Roark lifted me and carried me back to the bed. "And daily baths."

It was probably insignificant compared to all the things they did for me while I was out of it, but something about the simple gesture in cleaning my teeth and washing my body filled me with an insane amount of warmth.

I lay on my back, my gaze locked on the bulb in the ceiling. "Does Arkendale have electricity and running water?"

"Yes." Jesse climbed in bed beside me, pulling the sheet over my chilled skin. "The scouts Link had sent ahead negotiated a partnership with the existing residents."

"There were men there?"

"Forty or so." Roark sat on the edge of the mattress. "And a handful of nymphs. The men kept them confined on the peninsula to protect them. They'd already constructed a wall where the cape connects to Virginia."

I could guess the rest. "Link offered to cure their nymphs as he barged his way in and took over their sanctuary?"

"He's a brutal one right enough." Roark pushed his fingers through the curly waves of his hair, such an odd thing to witness having never seen him without knots. "Can't say I agree with his methods, but they're fecking effective. Over two-hundred cured women now reside on the peninsula, and there was a rake of nymphs still marching in when we left this morning. They'll run out of room soon, if they haven't already."

Holy fucking shit. My mind scrambled through all the issues that would come with that many people. Water, food, medicine, housing, sewage, protection… How could Link manage it?

"Why aren't we there?" As soon as the question left my mouth, I knew. "Because of me?"

Jesse placed his hand on my breastbone, his fingers curling against the thin sheet. "Evie, you struggled for every breath *for two weeks*. Seizures. Screaming. Vomiting blood. All those nymphs in one place was killing you."

Thank fuck I couldn't recall any of that, though the

rawness in my throat and aching weakness in my muscles whined in memory.

"We had to get ye out of there." Roark braced his elbows on his knees and stared at the carpet between his bare feet. "We drove until your breathing normalized."

"The other women didn't have the same reaction?"

Jesse watched me in that way he did, his eyes not just seeing me, but *assessing* me. Measuring the pace of my breaths. Gaging how much muscle I'd lost. Estimating my current pain levels. "Some of them complained about nausea and chills, but you took the full brunt of it, darlin'."

The women didn't suffer. I let my head sink into the pillow and breathed deeply. "I didn't lead any of the nymphs away from Arkendale? Those that still needed to be cured continued toward the larger congregation of women?"

In a way, every woman alive was *my* descendant. They would give off similar signals, like the scent trail ants left for their buddies. Assembled together in one place, they formed a boosted signal, a powerful beacon that no doubt muted mine.

Of course, Michio would call all this hypothetical, but he wasn't here, which left me to operate on instinct and guesswork.

"Yeah." Jesse picked up the blonde lock of my hair that lay across my chest, watching the strands fall around his fingers. "When we drove past a few nymphs on the road, their heads tracked you. They knew you were in the car. But they continued in the direction of the peninsula."

"A few stragglers came by today," Roark said, gently. "Shea healed them, and they've been taken to Arkendale."

Jesse closed his eyes. "Had we known not *all* the nymphs would follow you, we would've taken you away immediately. We just assumed..."

"Hey." I curled my hand around his. "It's okay. I'm fine."

I didn't remember the ride to Arkendale or the two weeks I'd spent there. I remembered nothing except the dream about my home and the Drone and the light bulb.

Jesse and Roark had taken care of me all that time. If I

really thought about what that meant, it was difficult to accept. I'd been vacant, helpless, and unable to defend myself. They'd hauled around my dead weight, feeding me, cleaning me, and searching for a way to ease my pain. But who took care of them?

I went with an easy question. "Who cut your hair?"

Jesse gestured between them, and Roark stared at the floor, a smile pulling at his lips.

Cutting hair involved touching, fingers trailing over scalps, showing one another attention. Maybe even affection. *They* had taken care of *each other*, and I'd missed the pleasure in witnessing that. "What other bonding moments did I miss? Any more kissing?"

Roark crawled up the bed, carrying a grin tucked in the corner of his mouth, and stretched out on my other side. "Why do ye think I shaved?" He rubbed his hairless chin over my cheek and pointed that grin at Jesse. "He prefers me smooth."

I expected a fist to come flying at his face, but Jesse simply reclined against the headboard and folded his hands on his chest, smiling and shaking his head. Roark might've been taunting him, but there was definitely an easy comfort between them. Fuck, I loved that.

And of course, I couldn't let it drop. "Two weeks together…" When Jesse met my eyes, I nudged his leg with mine. "You thought about that kiss."

He didn't move, didn't let go of his smile as he watched me from beneath heavy eyelids. "I thought about kissing *you,* and you weren't in a position to stop me."

Like I would ever stop him. "I really don't know how you resisted between all the seizures and bloody vomit."

His smile fell, and he rolled against me, burying his face in my neck. "Damn, it's fucking good to have you back, darlin'."

I held him to my chest, combing my fingers through his hair. Roark curled against my other side, and I wrapped my arm behind his shoulders, hugging both of them to me, as my mind drifted with the steady beats of their hearts. Here, in the complacency of fresh sheets and haircuts, without the aroma of body odor, the sight of weapons, or the hungry buzz of aphids gnawing at my stomach, it was easy to imagine the plague had never happened.

Outside the windows, the sky faded down into darkness, yet we easily saw one another beneath the light of a bulb. I wanted to believe that bulb meant something, that it symbolized a turning point in our struggle, that life would get easier, that a bright and shiny future was already in motion.

But we wouldn't have had electric light without the aid of a generator. And if I checked the mattress, the packs on the floor, and the clothes they wore, I'd find an arsenal of weapons. Shea, Paul, and Eddie weren't sitting downstairs watching reruns and eating ice cream. They were holding their blades and arrows close, tense in their vigilance, guarding the house.

"I'm glad I'm here, with both of you, but I wish *here* was ten years from now." I drew a breath, my chest rising beneath Jesse's weight. "I wish *here* included Michio."

Roark parted his lips to say something, but instead, he grabbed hold of my face, pulled me from Jesse's embrace, and buried his tongue in my mouth. My senses flooded with an incredible taste of oak, chocolate, and whiskey, the eclectic medley exuding a sharpness and vitality that worked so well together, combined with the comforting scent of his skin. *These* tastes and smells were the signatures of my priest.

As he stretched my mouth open with his, I expected urgency and heat and weeks of pent-up need to come barreling down on me, but he didn't give me that.

He slowed down, drawing his tongue over my lips, not to arouse but to soothe. The velvety skin of his hairless face slid against mine, warming my nerve-endings, and his hands on my jaw didn't force. They *supported.*

The gentle glide of his mouth told me he missed me, that he'd been worried, and the parting bite of his teeth punctuated his words. "I've died a million deaths since I've met ye, but all it takes is your kiss to remind me why I'm still breathing."

I reached for his face only to be guided away by the grip of Jesse's hand on my neck. He gave me a burning flash of copper eyes right before he kissed me, the press of his mouth rougher than Roark's, more intense in its message. His tongue lashed and whipped, scolding me for scaring him, warning me not to do it again.

He pushed my back against the mattress as he forced himself deeper inside my mouth, his groin grinding against my thigh, ensuring I felt the hard length of him as he sucked and ate at my mouth.

I wrestled with the sudden swell of arousal, the desperation inside me throbbing to be stroked and filled. But my body was weak, and their cocks wouldn't magically mend me.

Jesse knew this, too, but he was reluctant to pull away, his groan vibrating through me as he tore his mouth from mine. He leaned back, breathing heavily, his eyes on Roark. They exchanged a look, a shared mélange of misery and relief, and turned their gazes back to me.

They weren't looking at me for answers. They were waiting for me to catch up.

I pulled in a breath, drawing all of my thoughts together. "I can't go back to Arkendale, can I?"

Jesse stared at me silently, and Roark grabbed the glass of water from the nightstand and set it in my hands.

I sipped and handed it back as I said, "That's not where we were headed anyway."

Roark leaned forward, his knee bent against the mattress. "Hunter followed us this morning and returned to Arkendale after we settled."

My drowsiness was fading by the second, my body alight with excited energy. "So Link would know how to find us."

"He'll send more men in a few days to help us track down the Drone."

I wasn't sure we'd need to do much tracking. "I saw the Drone in a dream."

Was the Drone waiting for me in my motherfucking house? Desecrating my memories?

"What? How?" Jesse shot up, his eyes hard. "We didn't leave you alone for one second. One of us was always touching you."

Shea chose that moment to run into the room and launch herself at me in an emotional and fervent crush of toned limbs and black curls. Seemingly oblivious of the men in the bed, she wrapped her arms around my neck and peppered kisses across my face. "You scared the shit out of me."

I returned her embrace, grinning. "I missed you, too."

"Shea." The air buzzed with the impatient tone of Jesse's voice.

"Okay, okay. I'll come back." She slid off the bed, flashed me a huge smile, and darted out of the room.

When the door shut, Jesse and Roark turned their attentions to me. They were a stunning scenery of copper and jade eyes, each of them so uniquely different yet living in symbiosis, like now as they watched me with the mutual intensity, waiting for me to tell them about the Drone.

I put my hands on their thighs. "Maybe he didn't find me in my dreams. But I found him. In my home in Missouri."

Roark folded his hand around mine, his voice cautious. "And Michio?"

I closed my eyes and shook my head. Maybe Michio hadn't been able to track the Drone. Maybe he'd died trying.

My lungs hitched, stuttering my breath as I teased my eyes open. "We'll find him."

My belief in those words catapulted me through the next few days. I ate, slept, and regained my strength. Hiding out in an evacuated, high-end, gated neighborhood had its advantages. We acquired new clothing and shoes, found more generators secreted away in garages, and beneath the hum of a florescent light, mapped out our journey to Missouri.

Home. The house I'd shared with Joel and Annie and Aaron. A place of joyful memories and irreconcilable sadness. I never expected to return. Never *wanted* to.

Stay alive. Seek truth. And do not look back.

That was our agreement the day Joel and I fled our home. I'd held up my end, and would continue to do so with every ounce of fight left in me. My guardians were my future, and if the key to locating Michio waited in that house, I would find it, *without looking back.*

Four days after I'd woken in Charlottesville, Link arrived with three more men.

Roark met him at the door. "You're coming with us?"

"Yup." Link pushed his way inside, his frame thinner, and his bald head creased with more lines than the last time I saw him.

"This is Gary and Lee." He gestured at the attractive white guys behind him. Evidently, muscles were a requirement to work for Link. "You already know Hunter."

As Link and Roark spoke quietly, Hunter shuffled past, offering me a chin nod, his arms loaded with boxes. Wedged in the top of one was a bulky white laptop-like machine.

"Wait." I grabbed his arm, stopping him. "Is that—?"

"You found one!" Shea ran in from the kitchen and snatched the machine from the box. "Does it work?"

Hunter shrugged. "I found a few of them between here and the peninsula. You know that nurse you cured in Arkendale? She checked them out. Said they would do."

"An ultrasound machine," I said with disbelief, but my thoughts were already skipping to the generator and the knowledge that we wouldn't be leaving until the morning and…

I found Jesse's eyes across the room, searing into mine. He sat on the floor against the far wall, knees bent, and his thumb sliding over the string of the bow between his legs. Anyone else might've thought he was disinterested in the conversations around him, too bored to interact with or pay attention to his current company. But I knew better. He was listening, always watching, and right now, he was thinking about all the possibilities that machine might give us.

Shea ran up the stairs with it, hell-bent on her mission, her finger crooking at me to follow.

I turned back to Hunter. "Thank you."

Juggling the boxes, he twitched his head back, trying to jerk his long hair out of his face. "It was on Link's grocery list. He wanted the women of Arkendale to have some." He gave up on the hair, letting it fall over one eye. "Shea had mentioned you wanting one."

Made sense. Prenatal care would be crucial soon. That was, if the virus no longer infected the air and future babies survived.

Link strode toward him and clasped his shoulder. "Put those boxes in the kitchen." He passed his dark gaze to me. "Welcome back to the land of the living. I hear we're heading to Missouri."

I narrowed my eyes. "Who's running Arkendale?"

"At last count, seventy-eight men and two-hundred-forty-three women."

Fucking unreal. Arkendale could very well become the capital of the future world. As it stood, it was the only place on the planet where women outnumbered men.

He swiped a hand over his mouth, failing to muffle his amusement. "It's a goddamned democracy."

Really? Because it sounded like he left them high and dry.

My teeth slammed together. "A democracy has people in power. Elected officials."

"I left my best men *and women* in charge, sweetheart. If they kill each other, that's on them." He laughed at my wide eyes and strode toward the kitchen.

I held my arms at my sides and tried not to be morally affronted by his jackassery. I really tried, but fuck, I wanted to thrust both middle fingers in the air. "Why are you here?"

He stopped in the doorway, his big hand curling around the framework as he faced me. "I like to fuck as much as the next guy, but I *love* to fight. Doesn't exactly make me a candidate for Mayor of Utopia-dale, does it? Where you're headed, Little Ladybird, awaits a battle for the history books, and I just accepted the position as General of your army.

You're welcome."

Roark watched him from the other side of the room, hands in his pockets, his face unreadable. And Jesse, well, he was silent and glarey as usual.

Maybe for Link, it really was as simple as fighting the good fight and becoming a legendary hero, dead or alive.

I couldn't give a flying fuck if future generations knew my name. Whether or not I became the champion of my own life depended on the long and happy lives of three men. Period.

"Evie!" Shea shouted from upstairs. "Get your ass up here."

THIRTY-SIX

I jerked away from the steaming electric iron in Shea's hand. "I don't remember agreeing to this."

She gripped a hunk of my hair and used it to pull my head where she wanted it. "Sit still, or I'm going to burn you."

A ragged exhale pushed past my lips. Out of my comfort zone much? That didn't begin to describe the unease crawling over my skin. I came upstairs, expecting an ultrasound, but Shea refused to turn on the machine until she'd cleaned me up. Yeah, the shower had made me feel like a new person, but this was something else entirely.

No wonder we were in the hall bathroom and not the master en-suite, because she'd taken over it, transforming the small room into a kingdom of girlishness. Sparkly makeup, tweezers, razors, and lotions covered the counter. Dresses, tops, and lingerie hung from every nail and hook in a tapestry of sequins and lace. And the Duchess of Glitter World stood amid a pile of shoes of every color, wrapping my hair around a curling iron and staring at my chewed-up fingernails like they were a direct insult to her vagina.

I tucked my hands at my back, the movement threatening to loosen the towel knotted around me. "All this effort to make me look like a woman and—"

"You *are* a woman." She set down the iron and fluffed out my curls. "Hottest damned woman alive."

I smiled my thanks, though I disagreed. "Pretty sure I'm staring at *that* woman."

She was always gorgeous, but right now…heaven help the

men in this house. Her complexion was buffed and powdered into a silky sheen of chocolate. Smoky shadows enlarged her brown eyes, deep red gloss painted her pillowy lips, and her eyelashes went on for days. Evidently, she'd spent a lot of time rifling through the wealth of Charlottesville.

She smiled, flashing perfect white teeth, her hand wielding a makeup brush like a weapon. "Quit flirting with me, and close your eyes."

I glared at her. "I haven't felt the IUD string in weeks. If there's something wrong with it, all of this is just icing on a cake that won't get eaten."

She glared right back. "Oh, they're going to eat you, because you're going to strut your fine ass out there and gobsmack them into next week. They won't even care what shows up on that ultrasound."

I pulled at the blond curls falling around my arm, stretching one out and watching it spring back. "That's what I'm afraid of."

It had been two weeks since I had sex with Roark. He was infertile, so pregnancy wasn't a worry. *Yet.* How long could I restrain my sexual relationship with Jesse?

"Have a little faith, honey." She knocked my hand away. "Give them this one night of burning, yearning, instant-boner seduction. Tomorrow, you can return to your ponytails, shit-kickers, and leather holsters."

Seduction I could do. Worst case, the IUD was MIA and we'd repeat our night in the bathroom, which had been nothing short of mind-blowing. And other blowing.

I sighed at the invasion of tingles in my core, fantasizing about my guardians as Shea did her thing. As much as I wanted to graciously bow out of this little makeup party, it seemed to make her ecstatically happy. So I let her brush shit over my lids and cheeks and smear my lips and lashes in more shit. Then she moved to the clothes.

A fist knocked on the door, accompanied by the scratch of claws.

Shea peeked her head out. "Hey, handsome." She lifted her

knee against the cracked opening, blocking the shove of a shaggy head. "No, Darwin. No dog hair allowed."

"Hey." Paul's deep voice filtered through the door. "How much longer? Jesse's pacing around that machine, glaring at it like he's waiting for it to grow eight-legs or something."

Poor Jesse. Tonight would either be a night of colossal disappointment or one huge final step in intimacy.

"Ten minutes." Shea closed the door and slumped against it, wearing a floaty-heart smile, one that had nothing to do with me and everything to do with the man in the hall.

"Have you slept with him?"

"Maybe." She ducked her head, gathering the clothes from the edge of the tub.

"And Eddie?"

She smiled at me over her shoulder then sighed, her lips pinching. "They're not Jackson, you know?" She shook her head, her dark curls falling across her face.

I lifted her hair, tucking it behind her ears. "It gets easier."

"Yeah? I mean, the sex is good, really good, and who knows? Maybe it'll turn into something like you have someday?"

"I hope so." I leaned in to kiss her forehead.

"Lipstick!" She dodged my mouth and shoved the bundle of clothes against my chest. "Get dressed."

Ten minutes later, I flattened my palms on my thighs, smoothing out the fabric of the short, flirty black skirt. A shimmery blue strapless top clung to my boobs and the dips in my waist. I got away with going bra-less, but Shea won the fight about the white lace thong, claiming the tags were still attached because it was destined for my ass. She was right about that, considering I couldn't stop the strip of lace from crawling its way into my crack.

On my way out of the bathroom, I glanced at the mirror. Staring back was a woman from another time and a different place. She was the career woman who dressed for the office every day. The wife who dined at fancy restaurants with her husband. The mother who attended talent shows to watch her daughter dance and karate tournaments to see her son show off his kicks.

I missed that woman deeply, longingly. My chest ached at the knowledge that I was looking at an artificial layer and deep down that person was well and truly gone.

Behind the light makeup and clean hair was someone else entirely, a woman with eyes that had seen a thousand deaths, with ears that had heard the screams of unfathomable horror, and a heart that had slogged through bloodshed and found a way to love again.

In that moment, staring at my reflection beneath the warmth of a single light bulb, I realized I was proud of the woman I'd become. Maybe I'd lost the graceful ability to sashay in a pair of four-inch heels, but I could use the spikes to defend a life. Maybe I no longer dominated a boardroom, but I could hold my own on a battlefield. Maybe I'd forgotten how to comfort a child, but I had spread a cure that gave women a chance to love generations of children.

"You're beautiful." Shea stood behind me and rested her chin on my shoulder, meeting my eyes in the mirror. "I'll handle the ultrasound, and you just stand there and watch the zippers bust open, m'kay?"

I burst out laughing and followed her through the door and into the hallway.

THIRTY-SEVEN

My heart hammered, my palms slicked, and the high-heels pinched the circulation in my toes. But I held my head up as I stepped into the bedroom I'd been sharing with Jesse and Roark.

In the bright glow of the overhead light, Jesse saw me instantly, his eyes wide and frozen, like his stance. He blinked, blinked again, and his gaze lowered, lower still, then traveled back up, over my skirt, lingering on my chest, and locking on my face.

He licked his bottom lip, and I wasn't sure he was aware he did it. Then he went back for another scan, devouring my legs, my hips, back to my breasts, clinging there, heating me up with the intensity of his expression.

"Well?" I stalked toward him, checking the room for Roark and finding it empty.

Shea's footsteps moved toward the bed where the ultrasound waited.

Jesse dragged his eyes from my chest and stepped forward, meeting me halfway. His hand lifted toward my face and hovered as if he was unsure whether or not he'd smudge the makeup.

I caught his wrist and pressed his palm against my cheek. "Is it too much?"

"No," he said, breathless, his eyes roaming again, up, down, up. "Beauty has always defined you. I've just never seen you so…"

"Feminine?"

He swallowed. "Exquisite."

My damned cheeks flushed, the warmth spreading down my neck and kick-starting my pulse. "Thank you. You don't look too bad yourself."

He glanced down at his black button-up shirt, the sleeves rolled up to his elbows and exposing the strength in his forearms. He still had his stubble, and the hair on his head pointed in all directions, untamed and stubborn. Combine that with the deceptively quiet way he observed me, and I was sucked in, captivated, and insanely turned on.

Roark strode out of the attached bathroom, glanced up, and slammed to a stop. The look on his face was priceless. He gripped the back of his neck and gave me the same thorough perusal Jesse had, with his jaw hanging open. When he lowered his arm and closed his mouth, his smile was huge and mischievous.

I braced for it, could practically hear his brain searching for something ridiculous to say, and grinned in anticipation.

"Den' panic, love, but one of me balls has gone right up inside me." He wriggled a leg, looking down at his zipper then at my skirt. "Are ye wearing knickers under there? Feck it. I just need a screed of enthusiastic hand action. I'm in quite a lot of pain."

Jesse lowered his head, chuckling.

Roark strode toward us, pointing at him. "Wha' are ye laughing at? You're looking a' her like a cat eying a cream-flavored arsehole."

I smacked his chest. "You did not just call me an asshole."

He wrapped his big hands around my neck and pressed his forehead against mine. "Cream-flavored, love. A delectable, tight, creamy arsehole." His exhale brushed over my lips. "And I've worked up an appetite."

"Okay," Shea said from behind us. "It's ready."

I gave him a squeeze on his wrists and a nervous smile and pulled away to join Shea on the bed.

With my top tucked beneath my breasts and the waistband of the skirt rolled down, I lay on my back as she squeezed a dollop of cold gel on my lower belly and rubbed the wand through it.

All eyes moved to the machine beside my feet as the screen came to life.

Jesse sat beside my hip and leaned toward the black and white viewer. "What are we looking at?"

Shea pointed at a small white blob on the image. "That's an acoustic shadow, a void behind something with substance. We see this often with solid structures like bone or kidney stones. Or in this case, the shaft of the IUD."

My lungs heaved with an influx of air.

Jesse glanced at me and returned to the screen. "When I talked to the nurse in Arkendale, she said IUDs can move around, get dislodged, and become ineffective. Which could be harmful to Evie."

Jesse's attention to my wellbeing wasn't a surprise, but seeing the concern on his face tightened my throat.

"True." She jiggled the wand. "But see that? The string is tucked just inside her cervix. It's there. Everything's positioned correctly, even if you can't feel it vaginally."

He placed a hand on my knee, fingers trembling, his eyes a harsh and fiery landscape. A muscle bounced in his jaw as he slid his palm beneath the skirt, up my inner thigh, and stroked the edge of my panties.

A quiver shimmied down my legs and a rush of heat gathered between them. "Jesse, what are you doing?"

"I just want to see…" He stared at the screen, fingering the crotch of the thong as he inched it to the side.

"You can use the gel." Shea held out the bottle.

"She doesn't need it." He flashed me a wicked smile, his finger swirling around my wet opening.

Holy fuck. He intended to finger me right here in front of Shea and— Oh God, he just did. The invasion ignited a ripple of pleasure through my body. I couldn't stop my gasping breaths or the shameless rock of my hips.

His breathing staggered and his arm flexed as he bent over me, his finger reaching deeper, searching for…what? My cervix?

Roark sat beside Shea on my other side, his eyes staring intensely at the screen. “Stop squirming, Evie.”

He gripped my waist, holding me still.

Like Jesse, he had an invested interest in the validation of my IUD. As much as he’d seemed to enjoy wrestling Jesse into submission in the bathroom, I doubted he wanted to beat Jesse’s ass on a continual basis to keep me from becoming pregnant.

Pressure built inside me as Jesse’s finger pushed and curled. He stretched deeper, and a shadow bounced at the edge of the screen. He watched the image for a moment, making it jump with the thrust of his hand.

He slid his hand away and straightened my skirt. “Okay.”

“Okay what?” I arched a brow and closed my knees.

He sat back. “I wanted to see the screen interact.”

“What? You thought it was a recorded image or something?”

He crossed his arms and chewed on the edge of his thumb—same hand he fingered me with—as he studied my face. “You’ve had the IUD four years?”

Was he still doubting its effectiveness? I looked at him out of the corner of my eye. “Yeah, it’ll last—”

“They were only approved for five years, but they’re actually effective for seven years or longer.” His mouth crooked up behind his thumb. “I picked the nurse’s brain in Arkendale.”

My heart rate increased, and a sheen of moisture formed on my skin. Did that mean he trusted the IUD? Trusted it enough to give me that final part of himself?

Shea wiped the gel off my stomach with a tissue. Then she slid off the bed with the ultrasound machine tucked under her arm, singing, “Somebody’s getting laid tonight.”

Jesse didn’t take his eyes off me, ever calculating and patient, without acknowledging Shea at all.

“Okay then.” She walked backward. “I’m just going to…uh…” She wiggled her fingers at me and slipped out the door, shutting it behind her.

Jesse continued to stare at me, stringing along the tension. How long would he keep me waiting?

I rose on my knees and faced him head-on in a battle of glares.

The bed bounced behind me, followed by Roark's footsteps, his soft voice absent of all humor. "Since this is your first time together, I'll give ye some privacy."

"Stay," Jesse and I said at the same time, without breaking eye-contact.

I didn't know what prompted Jesse's desire for Roark's presence. I wanted him there because he loved to watch, because I hoped he would eventually join in, and because this wasn't just a relationship of two.

The chair beside the bed creaked, the sound of Roark settling in. I grinned at Jesse, trembling with a heady flush of arousal. There were endless ways to jump full-speed ahead. I could remove my clothes, play with my nipples, or finger myself until Jesse attacked me. But I didn't want to rush him or control this.

It was incredibly arousing the way he watched me, possessing me with a look, making me wait. I wanted his command, wanted to bend beneath the steady, imposing strength of his will.

The weight of his eyes held me in place for an eternal moment, then he looked away. But the spell wasn't broken.

My gaze followed him as he stood. As he pulled the heels from my feet and dropped them. As he gripped my skirt and yanked it, along with my panties, down my legs and off. As he lifted the shirt over my head and tossed it behind him.

I stared up at his face, magnetized by the raw sexuality of his gorgeous features, and held my breath.

"On your hands and knees. Face the headboard. Legs spread."

Holy hell, the sternness in his voice sent my inner muscles into a clenching frenzy. Spinning into position, with my ass in the air, breasts hanging beneath me, and pussy bared, I'd never felt more desired.

He prowled around the bed, viewing my body from every corner, his gaze tracing my mouth, the curve of my ass, the *V* between my legs, as if he didn't know which end to fuck first.

The fall of his steps glided steadily along the carpet. I held my lower body still, braced on hands and knees, and pulse thundering as I tracked his movements with my eyes, craning my neck, willing him to move closer, to touch me. Fuck, I needed him, needed his hands on me, the force of his hunger holding me down, his cock shoving inside me, dominating my pleasure with every breath in his body.

He stopped at the foot of the bed. "Eyes forward."

I moaned and sneaked a peek at Roark. A few feet away, he reclined in the chair, ankle propped on a knee, elbow on the armrest, and fingers curled beneath his chin. He wasn't looking at me. His eyes were on Jesse, lazy and hooded, watching the other man with curiosity, respect, and maybe even love.

"Eyes!" Jesse's hand smacked against my ass with a stinging *crack*.

I jerked my head forward, glaring at the filigree carvings that edged the king-sized headboard, even as my pussy heated and throbbed. "Bossy."

"Ye love it," Roark said, his brogue thick and husky.

"Only in the bedroom." I ground my hips in the air, the urge to glance back to see their faces overwhelming. But I fought it.

The loosening of Jesse's metal belt sounded behind me, followed by his zipper lowering and the whisper of his clothes falling to the floor.

My diaphragm heaved, my breaths rough and uneven. Liquid heat collected between my thighs, cooling in the air, my sensitive flesh swelling, opening, so fucking ready.

"You're leaking down your legs, darlin'. I don't even need to touch you. I could just slide right in."

"Come on, Jesse," I groaned, breathless. "Stop teasing me." I writhed on my hands and knees, my pussy clamping down, empty, needy, waiting. "Fuck me."

He grabbed my hips from behind, and the mattress dented beneath his knees. I bit down on my bottom lip, anticipating a warlike thrust, but it was his mouth…Oh, sweet fuck, his tongue that drove into me, quickly joined by his fingers, his lips, his teeth.

With a hand on my hip, he controlled my movements as he fucked me with his mouth. His whiskers burned against my folds. His fingers rolled over my pulsing clit, and his thumb hooked inside me.

I lost the strength in my arms and my shoulders fell against the mattress as he continued his assault. I thought I heard Roark's zipper, but couldn't track the sound amid the panting of my breaths and the wet smacking noises of Jesse's mouth.

Jesse pressed impossibly deeper, his tongue tracing the walls of my cunt, coaxing me closer, faster… *Ohfuckohfuckohfuck.*

A scream tore from my throat as the orgasm burst in vicious waves through my body, gripping my limbs, shaking, blinding, stealing all my oxygen.

His hands wrapped around my waist, holding my ass against his face as he nuzzled and bit, burying his stubble between my cheeks, his tongue sliding and flattening against my asshole.

"Oh my God." My eyes rolled back in my head, my breath trembling and fingers curling into the bedding.

He sought out every pleasure zone in reach as his mouth slid down the back of my thigh, up the other one, over my ass, and heated a breathy trail along my spine.

His hand flattened on my belly, caressing upward, cupping and squeezing my breasts. He stopped to trace the *C*-shaped scar around my boob, his touch tender yet heavy with memory. As my skin warmed and shivered and my cheek lay against the mattress, my thoughts chased all the miles we'd shared together, the places we'd been, and the destinations we'd yet to reach.

With his chest pressed to my back, his body flexed against me. His hand vanished behind his head, and before I could question him, the turquoise stone lowered to the mattress beside my face.

His mouth moved to my ear. "I love you."

My throat closed up, my choked response pushing past it. "Love you."

Instinctively, I turned toward Roark and mouthed the same words, my voice stolen by the raw desire flickering in his eyes and the hard erection lying bare and ignored against his abs.

The weight of Jesse's body lifted. He grabbed my leg, flipped me on my back, and settled his hips between my thighs, hands braced on either side of my shoulders.

There was a sliver of air between our heaving chests, but he was so close I could feel his muscles trembling, hear the hammer of his heart, and see the wetness of my arousal coating his stubble. The hot, hard press of his cock nudged my pussy, the tip gliding through the wetness, his hips shaking with the need to thrust.

I cupped his face with my hands, moving down the stretched cords of his neck, over his shoulders and around his biceps. I couldn't get enough of his bare skin. It made my own chill beneath a stampede of goosebumps. But I wasn't cold. I was burning up.

He lowered his chest, his hard body hovering in a push-up, his arms bunching under my hands as he held himself up. "I'm going to fuck you now."

THIRTY-EIGHT

I'm going to fuck you now.

My heart sang at the thick drawl of Jesse's words. This wasn't about fucking me or owning me or taking me. He was giving himself to me.

An oath without ceremony.

Till death do us part.

At the edge of my vision, Roark sat back in the chair, his jeans bunched around his thighs, the hard length of his cock jutting from his lap and gripped in his fist.

"Oh God." I gripped Jesse's ass. "Please."

Something snapped behind his eyes, and his restraint shattered with the drive of his hips. He shouted as he entered me, his head falling beside mine and his cock slamming with urgency.

The body-tingling stretch of his girth was unfathomable. I scratched at his back and ground my hips, meeting him thrust for thrust. He raised his head, his lips finding mine, his tongue lashing through my mouth. I opened for him, angling my neck for a deeper taste, wanting more, to devour, to be consumed.

He pulled his mouth away and buried it against my neck. His hand shoved between us and gripped the base of his cock while he continued to thrust.

"Evie. You need to come. I'm not—" He grunted, panting, his hips pounding ruthlessly. "I'm not gonna last. I can't...I can't—"

His arm jerked away, and his hands slammed against the

mattress as his spine bowed and his body locked up.

"Fuuuuuck!" His head fell back on his shoulders, and sinews stretched and pressed against his throat.

Holy hell, he was a glorious sight. His eyes squeezed shut, lips parted, pecs contracting, and thighs like steel against mine. Then he groaned, a vibrating guttural sound, as his cock pulsed inside me, hot and hard, spurting his release.

He collapsed on top of me, his forearms on either side of my head, supporting his weight. As we caught our breaths, we watched each other openly, happily. No words exchanged or needed. For a long moment, with his cock twitching inside me, we simply enjoyed the intimacy of the connection.

I could've drifted to sleep in that blissful dream-state, wrapped in the warmth of his skin, our legs intertwined, and hearts beating as one. But I hadn't forgotten Roark, and contrary to my assumption about a man's recovery rate, Jesse was still hard inside me.

He turned his head toward Roark, eyes narrowing on the erection Roark gripped in one hand. With a grunt, Jesse reached for the bottle of ultrasound gel on the nightstand and tossed it at him.

Was he telling Roark to jerk off? Or holy shit, was he planning on fulfilling my fantasy?

He rolled us, his arm cinched around my back and a hand on my thigh, keeping his cock firmly seated in the clutch of my body, the movement inside me flaring wonderful sensations through my body.

I ended up on top, with him on his back, staring up at me. Shit, he was so sexy it was no wonder I was in a perpetual state of arousal.

I stared back and rolled my hips. "Again?"

I'd asked this last time, but seriously, how was he still hard?

He pulled me down until I lay flat against his chest, my thighs straddling his waist, and his cock sliding ever-so slightly along my inner muscles.

"Evie, I haven't had sex in over two years. To say I'm a little excited right now is an understatement. Besides…" He grinned, and there was a whole lot of cocky in those shiny copper eyes. "I've got to prove I can last longer than three seconds."

Oh, well, who was I to come between a man and his ego?

Roark climbed on the bed behind me. Just thinking about the view laid out before him, with Jesse's knees bent and legs spread and my cunt stretched around a huge length of cock, surged a renewed quiver in my pussy.

Jesse palmed my ass, spreading my cheeks apart, and pressed a finger against the ring of muscle. "Have you ever been fucked here?"

He used his grip to move me up and down his shaft, teasing both of us.

I groaned in response, my breath catching. "Michio. A couple times."

Just thinking about it heated every cell in my body. I loved anal sex, fucking jilled off to fantasies of it.

I met Roark's eyes over my shoulder, and the need dilating his pupils had everything and nothing to do with fucking. He'd only had sex twice in his life, but this moment…this connection between the three of us was as meaningful for him as it was for me.

He knelt between Jesse's legs, gorgeously nude, his cock hard and long between his powerful thighs. Lowering to his elbows, he slid his hands under Jesse's thighs and along my calves where I straddled Jesse's torso. It was such an intimate position, his arms hugging us to him and his face inches from where we were joined.

Then I felt him, his lips dragging along my folds, tongue sliding upward, pressing against my puckered hole and returning to lave my pussy.

Jesse groaned beneath me and locked his arms around my back, hips thrusting. There was no way Roark could be tonguing my cunt without licking the shaft buried inside it.

I pushed Jesse's hair from his brow, framed his face with my hands, and stared into his eyes. He struggled to maintain eye-contact, his lids closing and jaw clenched. Roark's mouth moved lower, lower, then his breaths floated away from my pussy.

Jesse's eyes widened, and his hands clenched the back of my head, holding my face to his neck.

"Oh Jesus." His chest heaved. "Oh fuck."

Was Roark licking his balls? Teasing his asshole? Something was making Jesse punch his hips and shudder beneath me.

I pulled back and studied his expression, his shock contorting into confusion then tightening and straining into pure pleasure.

The sound of squirting gel filled the room, and cold wet fingers caressed my anus. The heat of Roark's body smothered my back, and his thighs pressed against the insides of Jesse's. His lips brushed my shoulder, and the head of his cock pushed against my tight ring.

As his mouth moved over my cheek, I turned my face toward his, giving him a long, deep, torturous kiss.

He leaned back, breathing heavily, and looked at Jesse. "Got her all oiled up like, but I've never kicked the back doors in before. I den' want to hurt her."

Jesse barked out a strained, husky laugh. It really was funny hearing Roark admit that, something we already knew, in such a serious tone.

"Okay." Jesse widened his legs and gripped my rear, pulling my cheeks apart. "Straddle my thigh, Roark."

He did, wrapping his hands around my ass, his fingers curling over Jesse's.

"Evie's going to push back against you." Jesse dug his fingers against the fleshy meat of my butt. "Go slow. Watch her body for cues."

I leaned down and kissed Jesse's lips. "You've done this before."

He kissed me back. "Anal? Yes." Another hungry kiss. "But not this."

He'd shared a woman with another man before, but he hadn't gone as far as double-penetration?

I grinned, licking his lips. "I'm getting another first with you."

"With both of us." He glanced at Roark then ducked his head to nuzzle and suck my breasts.

Roark ran a hand along my spine and slowly, cautiously, worked his way into my ass. I pushed back against him, trying to fit as much of him inside as I could, but my God, I was full, stretched to the point of pain. A consuming, self-possessing, addictive kind of pain.

With Jesse already buried snuggly inside, every inch Roark added felt like a heavy, penetrating force, a burning pressure. But it felt *right*. I was in no danger. I could stop this whenever I wanted.

He shoved to the root and my nerve-endings screamed with biting pleasure, my body humming with a sense of belonging.

Jesse gripped the back of my neck and yanked my mouth to his, roughly tugging my lips between his teeth. Heat spread through my body, roaring toward that climatic peak. I needed more. I needed them to move.

It took them a few awkward thrusts to find their groove, but once they fell in sync, their cocks moved as one, pounding to the same diabolical beat.

Their hands and mouths were everywhere, their bodies gliding under and over me, muscles contracting, and breaths choking. The scent of sweat and sex chased my inhales, and the reverberating sounds of their groans aroused me beyond sanity.

Roark's chest covered my back, his hips pumping, his teeth biting my shoulders. I didn't know how Jesse bore the weight of both of us, but he didn't complain as his hands pulled my hair at the roots and his tongue vigorously thrust against mine.

"So fecking tight, love," Roark panted in my ear.

Could they feel each other through my inner wall? Imagining it made my hips move faster, my hands caressing every inch of hard, flexing muscle within reach.

Jesse let his head fall back against the mattress, his mouth hanging open to accommodate his heavy breaths.

A look passed between them, one that had Roark grinning and Jesse hardening his eyes. Their hips slowed, stopped, and the way they stared at one another turned me on more than anything else they'd done that night.

"Kiss him, Roark." I pulled in a ragged breath and shifted to the side, dropping my cheek on Jesse's shoulder. "You want to."

Roark gripped a handful of Jesse's hair and leaned down. Jesse didn't move to meet him, but he didn't fight him off either, his eyes frozen in an unblinking glare.

My pulse went wild, and my pussy squeezed around Jesse's cock. He groaned, and Roark swooped in, mashing his lips against Jesse's.

Jesse didn't kiss him back, his mouth slack and partly open, but a moment later, his hands shot to my waist, his fingers digging against my skin, and they began to move.

Their jaws stretched and rubbed together, their tongues tangling and teeth nipping. Then their thrusts quickened. Jesse's hips rotated and ground seductively against me as Roark slammed into my ass.

I cried out, trembling with intoxicating pleasure. The sight of their hungry mouths molded together and the friction of their hard bodies flexing around me, *in* me, ripped me open in a burning explosion of colored lights and choking screams. As I shot into ecstasy, their heads turned and their mouths covered my neck, my face, and my lips.

We were tongues and hands and skin, driving our hips as one entity. I came again, and as they released with me, I wrapped my arms around Jesse's neck. Roark gripped my hips tightly, their cocks pushing and pulsing until I thought I might pass out.

I lost track of how many times I orgasmed that night. We showered and hydrated and fucked until my free-falling world went black. Maybe they blacked out, too. All I knew was I slept heavily, peacefully, between two of the men I loved while dreaming about finding the third.

THIRTY-NINE

The desolation in Kentucky, Indiana, and Illinois was the same as all the other places I'd been since the plague scored its toxic claws across the earth. Vegetation rappelled the sides of buildings, human skeletons scattered the roadside, and tangling nets of dense shrubbery formed canopies around houses and alleyways. The deterioration offered countless hiding places for aphids, men, and hell only knew what other carnivorous creatures.

But passing through ecosystems of decaying bodies and flourishing ivy with Link behind the wheel was a far different experience. He didn't hide from the desperate eyes of survivors. No, he stopped the van, jumped out *without* his crossbow or other visible weapons, and approached them.

Like he was doing now, striding across the cracked urban street in some city in southern Illinois, headed directly toward an office building. He stopped at the gaping hole where the door used to be and shouted something indiscernible. He'd said there were men in there, but I didn't see movement.

The chilly November air lingered in the van long after Link slammed the driver side door. I knelt between the front seats, my hand on Jesse's thigh where he'd moved behind the wheel. He curled his fingers around mine, his eyes locked on Link through the windshield.

"He's insane," I mumbled.

Darwin's wolfy head pushed its way under my arm. I nudged him behind me, coaxing him with an ear scratch to keep him out of view.

"He's doing me bloody nut in, the mentaller." Roark climbed over me and lowered into the passenger seat, folding the edge of his dark red trench coat over his scabbard.

We'd plundered supplies from a number of desolated stores along the way, searching for warmer clothes and more food. Hunter did most of the gathering, but we'd chosen our own wardrobes. I found it mildly amusing that Jesse and I dressed alike, both decked out in black leather pants, motorcycle jackets, and boots.

The cargo areas of our six vehicles held our stash, as well as Shea and Darwin, me and my guardians, Link and the five men we left Charlottesville with, and eighteen others Link had enlisted along the way.

Twenty-nine people comprised our expedition, and we needed more.

We needed an army.

Traveling for two weeks now in a caravan of vans and trucks, the diesel engines ran surprisingly well on Paul's plastic containers of cooking oil. My house in Missouri was a thousand miles from Charlottesville, a drive I could've made in two days before the plague. But now, the highways buckled in a crumble of asphalt and rusting metal, and the search for restaurants with fat fryers was an endless effort of stop, security sweep, collect, and go.

Then of course, there were the delays that came with recruiting.

Which was why Link had left us parked on the side of the road as he set off toward the cluster of tall buildings, the glass fronts shattered and blanketed in green waves of kudzu vines. He used varying tactics to gauge a person's ethics, claiming the face of a moral man in the civilized world no longer existed, and while indicators of integrity in this world were difficult to detect, they were there if one knew what to look for.

Hard to argue that. Two years ago, I would've stopped to help a bleeding man on the side of the road. Now? I'd hit the fucking gas pedal and not look back. Did that make me a bad person? No, man, it was called survival.

Since I could only see out the windshield, I shifted around Jesse to steal a glimpse at the side mirror. It showed no movement or signs of life amid the abandoned cars and overgrown sidewalks.

Beads of sweat formed on my temples. "Where's the rest of our caravan?"

Jesse kept his eyes on the windshield. "They pulled off when we entered the town so that some could follow quietly on foot."

I took his word for it. He had a better view from the front passenger seat, where I saw nothing riding in the windowless rear with Roark and Darwin.

Every town had a few survivors and ten times as many aphids. Which was why I'd wanted Shea to ride with us. Keeping her in sight would've eased some of my anxiety. But she'd stubbornly refused, preferring to stay with Paul and Eddie in one of the trailing vehicles.

Link stood outside the broken glass door of the building. There was no cover to protect him from bullets. No shade to hide his expression. Only the glare of the sun, the blades I assumed he concealed beneath his denim jacket, and my stabby fingers, which were currently sliding to my arm sheathes where they fit snuggly beneath my sleeves. Not that I could do any damage at this distance.

"He's ballsy." Jesse gripped my hand and returned it to his thigh, his eyes on the back of Link's bald head. "But not insane. He has snipers with crossbows there." He glanced at the twisted shell of an overturned semi down the road. "And more surrounding our van."

I felt the occasional internal vibrations of aphids, but they quickly snuffed out, which meant Link's men were definitely in the area, keeping it clear of inhuman threats.

"Still den' like this plan." Roark narrowed his eyes on our self-proclaimed leader across the street.

My pulse sprinted. I didn't know about a plan. "What plan?"

Link held his hands up as three youngish men stepped out

of the crumbling building. Tension strained their filthy faces, their fingers tightly gripping knives and sledgehammers, their postures twitchy with distrust.

Facing the man in front—a lanky blond with a pistol aimed in two hands—Link kept his arms in the air as he talked, holding their attention.

I couldn't hear a damned word he said. "What's the plan?"

Jesse shushed me, his thumb stroking over my hand as he watched the confrontation.

Something wasn't right. The creases spreading from the corners of Jesse's eyes, the bob in his throat, and the way he caressed my fingers, it was all so…regretful. But why? We were relatively safe in the van. The keys dangled from the ignition. If Ballsy McBaldy's little meet-and-greet ended with a bullet in his head, we could get the fuck out of Dodge before those weapons turned on us.

Link continued to run his mouth, one hand rubbing his head, the other gesturing as he talked. Whatever he was telling them made them widen their eyes and shake their heads.

Nodding, Link turned and pointed to the van.

My breath caught. "Somebody better tell me what's going on."

Jesse reached back and grabbed Darwin's collar, his eyes on Roark. "That's your cue."

"Load of fecking rubbish," Roark grumbled.

"Cue for what?" I spun to face Roark. "What's he talking about?"

Roark slid around me and swung open the side door. Wordlessly, he grabbed me around the waist, threw me over his shoulder, exiting the van and striding toward the front bumper.

To do what? To carry me toward those men? What the hell?

"My bow!" I stretched for the van, but the door was already shutting on the worried eyes of Jesse and Darwin.

Roark restrained my thighs against his chest, circled the front of the vehicle, and crossed the street, whispering sternly in my ear. "Den' ye touch the blades under those sleeves."

Seriously? Whatever the *plan* was, it was too late to demand answers. Didn't stop me from giving him a solid toe kick in the thigh.

"Oomph." He lowered his grip on my legs and smacked my ass so hard I bit my tongue.

Bastard! I dug my nails into the back of his coat, frustrated I couldn't get to his skin. "You're going to pay for that, goddammit. Put me down."

I attempted to jerk myself free as he closed the distance and stopped beside Link.

"See?" Link gripped the back of my thigh. "Told you I found a woman. Tight fucking cunt, too. Like I said, we'll let each of you have ten minutes with her. We just need something to eat."

The blood drained from my face, even though I *knew* Jesse and Roark would never allow those men to touch me. This was the plan? Tempt them with an unwilling woman and see how they responded?

I tried to scan the street for snipers, but hanging upside down with my pulse in my throat, I couldn't see anything but broken asphalt and the back of Roark's coat.

"How?" asked one of the men in hushed disbelief. "Women didn't survive."

Roark dropped me to my feet, spinning me to face three pale faces. His hand gripped my jaw roughly, and his fingers went for the zipper of my jacket, dragging it down and pulling it open. Then he reached for the hem of my shirt.

"Don't do this." I clutched the muscles in his forearms, shoving with wasted effort.

He yanked my shirt up and over my breasts.

"No!" My wretched shout cracked in the cool air. "No, dammit. Let go!"

My nipples pebbled in the crisp breeze as I tried to pull the shirt back down, twisting and bucking in Roark's hold. One arm wrapped like a steel bar around my waist. The other hooked around my throat in a strangle hold.

I really needed to escape the arm beneath my chin, but it was a solid weight of iron and determination. He wasn't cutting my air, hardly using any strength at all, and here I was, engaging every muscle in my body and burning my way to exhaustion.

Where was Jesse? Why was he allowing this? He and Roark were supposed to be my protectors, yet I felt anything but protected right now.

Link captured my hands, shackling them between my back and the immovable wall of Roark's abs. My lungs wheezed, and my chest crushed beneath the shock of utter panic.

Roark kept his arm against my throat, his huge body stopping my backward retreat. As if manhandling me into submission and baring my scarred chest to Link and strangers wasn't enough, he shoved his fingers down the front of my pants.

I was humiliated. I'd never been modest about nudity. Hell, I'd exposed myself countless times while commanding aphids. But this was forced, my control taken from me. Last time this happened… Fuck, I couldn't think about that. I already looked weak, helpless, and I despised that feeling. It soured inside me like a cold, dead thing, bubbling with rotten acid, ready to explode in a stomach-emptying fit of rage.

I didn't care what purpose my humiliation served. They should've fucking *asked* me.

"Let go of me!" I fought against the unbending force that was Link and Roark, kicking and growling and spitting, my skin reddening beneath their grips. "Motherfuckers! You're going to regret this."

"Let her go." The blond man in front aimed his gun at Link's head, his hands and voice shaking. "Let her go now!"

The two men behind him balked with frozen expressions, the whites of their eyes stark in sunlight as they took a step back, their weapons forgotten in their hands.

In a blur of movement, Link released me, disarmed the blond man, and turned the gun on him, pointing it directly between his eyes.

Before the other two men could react, Link laughed, lowering the gun and patting the guy's face. "You'll do, kid. All I needed was a flinch, like your buddies there, and it would've been enough. But you went hog wild and stood up for her. I respect that." He flipped the pistol and handed it back, grip first. "But if you ever lose your weapon like that again, I'll kill you myself."

Roark tugged my shirt back in place and let me go. Adrenaline crashed through my veins, and my heart banged heavily in my chest. I couldn't look at him. Didn't want to be anywhere near him.

As I ran back to the van, a stream of Link's men slipped out of nowhere. Crossbows at the ready, they jogged in the direction I'd come from.

The door of the van opened for me and slammed shut as I crawled in.

I scooted to the far side of the cargo area and hugged my knees to my chest, waiting for my breathing to normalize and my energy stores to replenish.

Darwin licked my face, his weight leaning against me as I stroked his fur. I just needed a few minutes to pull my thoughts together, but Jesse wasn't having it.

He gripped my arm and yanked me toward the front, planting my ass in the passenger seat and kneeling beside me. "Tell me why I stayed here instead of taking Roark's place."

I gnashed my teeth. Jesse knew I'd be fuming mad about this plan. Better for him if Roark played the bad guy, right?

"Because you're a fucking coward."

"Evie," he growled, his voice hard and impatient. "Think past your anger."

I looked away, my gaze locking on the back of Roark's head. He stood halfway between the van and the building where Link and his crew calmly talked with the new men. Roark anchored his hands on his hips, his head down, his thick boxer's shoulders lifting and tightening around his ears.

This was why Jesse sat me here, so I could see the regret clinging to Roark's posture. Or maybe it was so I'd notice the driver's side window rolled down and the seat adjusted to lean toward the steering wheel.

I dragged in a deep breath, cooling some of the heat in my blood. "You stayed in the van so you could hide behind the driver's seat and train your arrow out the window."

Roark could gut an army of men with his sword, but not from thirty yards away, which meant he had to be the one to drag me out there.

Jesse reached up and stroked the backs of his fingers over my jaw. "I never took my eyes off the blond guy's trigger finger. Link's snipers were ready, but I will *never* leave your protection in the hands of a man who isn't one of your guardians."

"Why didn't you just tell me the plan?"

He dropped his arm, resting it across my thigh. "Those prospects needed to see fear on your face. The kind you can't fake. You knew Roark wouldn't hurt you, but you don't like to appear weak. That's what drove you to fight with every breath you had."

I hated that he knew all my pathetic shortcomings. I curled my hands in my lap, my head tilting away.

As far as recruiting went, offering those men a woman to rape was an effective way to test their integrity. They might've given in to their carnal urges eventually, but those first few seconds were telling. A rotten man wouldn't have flinched. Especially not in this sadistic world.

Link's previous recruiting methods had taken much longer, involving hours of conversations while he attempted to flesh out strengths and weaknesses. In the last town, he pretended he was stabbed and pleaded for help. He hadn't expected the approaching men to help him. He'd been looking for a glimmer of sympathy in their eyes. Instead, those fuckers raised their guns to finish him off. Needless to say, he'd left a few dead bodies castrated in the street.

Jesse gripped my chin and turned my face toward his. "I never would've agreed to this if I didn't think you were strong enough to handle it." He kissed my lips. "You're over it."

That sounded a whole lot like a demand, but yeah, I was over it.

"Now you're going to help *him* get over it." He angled my face toward Roark, the hardness in his tone at odds with the tender way his fingers released my chin to glide down my neck. "He fought this plan since we left Charlottesville. The alternative was to use Shea, but we decided you'd be less forgiving if we involved her."

My nostrils flared. He was damned right about that.

"He's upset, Evie. When he gets back in here, you're going to do whatever you need to do to make him un-upset."

My lungs released a sharp breath. I'd give it a go, but Roark was a master at brooding in self-depreciation. Maybe I should return his rosary beads.

The men across the street began to scatter, leading the new recruits back to our vehicles. The newbies carried their backpacks and weapons, probably the only things they owned. Most of the men we'd met over the past two weeks were like us. Vagabonds, looking for something, with no place left to call home. Link didn't promise them a roof over their heads. He offered something better: a brotherhood of soldiers, an honorable cause to fight for, and maybe someday, a woman and children to love.

Of all the men who'd passed his tests, not one had declined his offer to join us.

Link followed Roark back to the van and slid in behind the wheel, starting the engine.

I opened the side door for Roark. He stared a hole through me as he stepped in and sat on the floor behind the driver's seat. Darwin came over and sniffed him from boots to neck then curled up beside him.

"Want to know something crazy?" Link turned in the seat, wearing a maniacal grin.

"Not really." I sat on the floor in front of Roark, meeting those tension-filled jade eyes.

"Those guys had heard of us," Link said.

That drew my attention. "Us?"

Link glanced at the side mirror, probably checking to see if the caravan had caught up, and turned back to me. "They said some men passing through were talking about a guy with black eyes"—he widened his for effect—"and the blonde beauty I was gathering an army for."

Holy fucking shit. I shared a look with Roark then Jesse, their shock as gaping as mine. "How is gossip spreading that fast? The men we've met either joined us or died…very fucking gory deaths, I might add."

"Yeah, about that…" Link put the van in gear and pulled onto the road. "Apparently, I have a feared reputation of castrating."

"Have you left any balls intact?"

"Nope."

"There's your legacy. You'll be right up there with Billy the Kid, Jack the Ripper, and Dahmer the Milwaukee Cannibal. What will they call you? Link the Emasculator?"

He slammed his hand against the dash, hooting with laughter. "I like that."

"You would."

Returning his hand to the wheel, he tapped his thumb. "For every survivor we encounter, there are ten more you don't see, watching from the safety of their hidey-holes, paying attention, and spreading the gossip."

I pinched the bridge of my nose. I hadn't thought of that. "So those three men already knew who you are, already knew all about your little gelding fetish? They were on their best behavior."

"They knew my reputation as a brutal motherfucker and still stood up to me. That says a lot, Evie."

Whatever. I could argue semantics all day, and frankly, Link's mental stability really worried me sometimes. But I had a more urgent matter to address.

Roark sat with his back against the wall of the van, one knee bent, his hand moving over Darwin's pelt as he watched me with the wary look a husband might've given his wife when she turned into a nymph. Like I was going to suck the blood from his soul, but he loved me too much to stop me.

I crawled over to him, made myself at home in his lap, and hugged his neck.

A relieved breath stumbled past his lips, and he cautiously moved his arms around my hips. "After everything you've been through…"

"Shhh." I ran my hands through his hair and nuzzled his neck, showing him without words I was fine. *We* were fine.

He kissed my temple, his accent nursing the words. "I didn't want to do it."

"I know."

He leaned his head back until our foreheads touched, my hair falling in a curtain around us as he whispered, "I'll make it up to ye tonight."

Wouldn't be any different from any other night for the past two weeks. Whether we were sleeping in the van, an abandoned building, or beneath the moon, he, Jesse, and I managed to find an hour or two of privacy. Just one of the many security advantages of traveling with a band of soldiers.

My lips meandered across his cheek, bringing my mouth to his ear. "What position are we going to try tonight?"

His breathing picked up. "I'm going to ride ye from behind while you're licking Jesse's balls."

The huskiness in his whisper reverberated between my legs.

He kissed my lips, and all the air seemed to circulate toward him. "Then Jesse's going to flatten ye while I watch."

Any lingering anger I might've harbored vanished with those words. Yeah, maybe I was an easy lay, but I'd never been a casual lover. When I gave my body, my heart went with it. Jesse and Roark were part of me. They'd become my sanctuary, and now that I had them, I wanted to spend as much time as I could in the refuge of their arms.

That night, Roark made good on his promise. In the secured wing of a dilapidated hotel, I writhed beneath Jesse's weight as Roark lay spent beside us, catching his breath.

The mattress groaned with the force of Jesse's thrusts, the fire in his gaze burning me everywhere it touched. I reached for Roark's cock, knowing how hungrily his arousal fed on the sight and movement of our bodies. Once he recharged, he would join us again. But I couldn't wait. Jesse had hit the right spot, the perfect tempo, and my orgasm was seconds from reach.

Just as I was about to fall over the edge, the tingling low in my belly took on the ugliest form. Dozens of aphid vibrations broke through my concentration.

Darwin's head popped up from the floor. He sprung toward the closed door, whining and pacing in front of it. Muffled footsteps pounded on the other side and faded down the hallway, followed by shouting.

"Fuck." Jesse slowed the roll of his hips then stopped, his jaw clenching.

I knew the aphids could sense my arousal, something to do with the pheromones I sent out, but it had been so long since they'd disrupted me in a moment like this.

Staring up at Jesse, at his just-fucked hair, at the frustration replacing the heavy-lidded look in his eyes, I didn't want this to end. I always hated those green bastards, but dammit, I *really* hated them right now.

Just die already!

The vibrations in my belly vanished. Just like that, every single one of them blinked out at the same time. Poof. Gone. I gripped my stomach, as if I could somehow find the sensations with my hands.

"Evie?" Jesse pulled out of me and glanced around the room.

"Wha' is it?" Roark joined Jesse's side, his gaze sliding to the door.

It crashed open, and Link stormed in, his clothes covered in black blood and hunks of fleshy pieces.

I yanked the sheet over my body, but his eyes were distracted, staring at—I glanced over my shoulder—nothing?

"An army of aphids got past our perimeter." His dark gaze leveled on me. "Then their bodies simultaneously exploded from the inside out."

FORTY

Dressed and armed with my blades and bow, I stood in the lobby of the three-story hotel, taking in the scene piece by piece, and there was a lot of foul, unrecognizable pieces. I covered my nose with my hand, but the signature stench of rancid aphid bowels seeped in with my inhales and made me gag.

Across the dimly lit room, a man bent at the waist and retched on the floor. The dozen or so guys standing around holding flashlights and kerosene lamps looked just as green around the gills.

I didn't blame them. Bits of organs, bone fragments, and ripped flesh clung to the walls and broken furniture. Double-jointed legs scattered here and there, still identifiable yet no longer attached to a body.

I gagged again, repulsed and baffled. Surely *I* didn't cause the aphids to self-destruct? I willed them dead all the time, but I didn't have the power to make it happen. Maybe the Drone was behind this? Or the aphids did it to themselves? But that didn't make sense.

Darwin traipsed through the guts, nose to the floor, rooting through the entrails. I cringed, thinking about all the crap he would track into bed. Not sure why I cared about something as insignificant as dirty paws. We would all need a good scrubbing after this.

Link strode by, shining a flashlight at the gore and shouting at the men. "Start digging through the shit. Look for anything that might tell me what happened here."

"Like what?" one of the men asked.

"I don't know, a beating heart or a footprint or the goddamned magic ring of invisibility." He aimed the beam at a row of men, their pale, nauseated faces stark in the glare of the light.

Most of the men were half-dressed, wearing boxers and holding axes, as if they had woken when the security was breached and grabbed the nearest weapon.

"Hurry up!" Link shouted. "I don't want to see anything but assholes and elbows until this place is picked clean."

A few feet away, Shea's posture mirrored mine, her hand over her nose, her tall frame bracketed by Paul and Eddie. In the front of the lobby, the boards that had covered the doors lay broken and splintered on the carpet. The aphids had been in a hellfire hurry to barge in. Only to blow up?

"Wha' are ye thinking, love?" Roark scanned the carnage, his shoulder brushing against mine as he sheathed his sword at his hip.

"We've seen aphids explode numerous times, right? But only when my blood enters their systems. Obviously, that's not what happened here."

Jesse stood beside Roark, arms crossed with his fist pressed against his mouth, lost in thought.

Then his eyes sliced toward me. "I know you felt them arrive."

Um, yeah, he was buried eight-inches inside me at the time. He'd probably felt them, too.

He studied my face with that calculating gaze of his. "What were you thinking about right before you felt them die?"

I raised my eyebrows and lowered my voice. "Coming on your cock?"

Roark made an amused noise in his throat.

Jesse rubbed his knuckles over his jaw, his expression marked with discomfort. Or grouchiness. Probably both. "What else?"

"I was just as irritated as you were, Jesse. I wanted the fuckers to die so we could…fin…ish…"

It wasn't possible, was it? I'd never been able to kill them with my mind. The notion was crazy.

Tell that to my accelerating pulse.

Jesse and Roark looked around the room, their eyes sharpening, no doubt following my train of thought. Roark's lips parted, and Jesse stood taller, his arms dropping to his sides, fingers twitching.

I gestured at the slaughter. "I just mentally wished this into existence?"

Jesse arched a brown brow. "Didn't you?"

I didn't know, but later that night, I had the opportunity to find out.

Squatting outside the front of the hotel, I dipped Darwin's paws in a bucket of water and washed off the bug guts while Jesse and Roark helped Link and few other guys re-barricade the front doors.

My head snapped up at the sudden encroachment of aphid transmissions. Four pulsing threads wove through my insides, drawing invisible lines down the road.

"Hey, guys." I rose, my attention on the dark stretch of asphalt. "Four inbound aphids." I grabbed Darwin's collar and hurriedly ushered him behind the boarded door and safely inside. "Before you kill them, I want to try something."

Link scratched his bald head, passed me a look that said *You're a freak*, then glanced at his men, giving them a single nod.

Jesse moved to my side and anchored an arrow, training it at the road. Roark shifted behind me, his arms sliding beneath my shirt, ready to support me.

But I didn't just want to try the new command. I wanted to try it without help. If there had been some kind of genetic restructuring of my abilities, I needed to retest my limits.

Stepping out of Roark's embrace, I glanced at him over my shoulder. "I'm going to attempt this without your energy. There's only four aphids, so if I pass out—"

His eyes narrowed into emerald slashes.

"—catch me?" I grinned, met the same unhappy glare from

Jesse, and turned toward the street.

The sound of Roark's sword unsheathing echoed across the parking lot. Boots scuffed around me, and my hair lifted around my face in the chilly breeze.

Stretching east and west, the jagged tops of crumbling buildings rimmed the moonlit skyline, and there, between the rubble of foundations, emerged four glowing outlines.

Their bulbous bodies skittered toward us on soundless feet, blurring through the shadows as if trying to remain out of sight.

The guys wouldn't be able to see them, not the way I could with my evolved night vision. Their neon forms filed into the street, their pupil-less eyes locking on our group with the barren parking lot stretched out between us.

Pulling in a sturdy breath, I concentrated my mind on one simple thought. I willed them dead.

The wet sound of bursting flesh splattered the silence, their innards spraying the pavement like glow-in-the-dark paint balls. The vibrations inside me evaporated, and in their place rose an invigorating energy, like a full-body shot of oxygen and caffeine, hopping beneath the surface of my skin and fortifying my muscles. I gasped, as if I'd just awoken from a deep sleep, and all the toxins in my body had washed away, my tissues repaired and renewed.

Jesse's bow lowered, and Link let out a loud bray of laughter.

My heart thudded in my chest, my head swimming through the implications. I did that without skin-on-skin contact. Without blacking out or shivering with loss of energy.

I swiped at my nose and glanced at my hand. No blood.

How was this possible? I just killed aphids with the will of my mind and felt fucking amazing.

Jesse's concerned expression filled my view, his hand resting on my cheek. "Your eyes are black. No whites at all."

The spots on my back had probably morphed as well.

He angled my face into the moonlight. "Your pupils

stretch so wide they swallow the rest of your eyes. They're reverting back now. Did your vision change?"

"No." I blinked a few times, peeking over his shoulder to watch Link's men run across the parking lot and investigate the splatter.

Whatever was left of the aphids was now completely void of the fluorescent glow.

If I could do this every time, it didn't matter if the aphids grew smarter, faster, and more organized, right? So why did the prophecy warn against evolving creatures? And how did a special world-saving child fit into the equation?

Shifting my gaze back to Jesse, I stared into the infinite copper wells he called eyes and wished for another superpower, one that would grant me access to his raw, unfiltered thoughts. "Are you thinking about the prophecy?"

He released his hold on my face. "I can't put my finger on it, but I'm…I don't know. I'm missing something. Something crucial." He laced his hands behind his neck, rubbing them over the back of his head, his biceps stretching the leather sleeves. "Or maybe I misinterpreted the predictions."

Roark stepped beside me and touched my lower back, adding pressure to guide me toward the entrance of the hotel.

"Until we figure it out, we have a brutal aphid weapon." He glanced at Jesse as he held the door open for us. "I den' know about ye, but watching her dominate, I was seriously chubbed up."

Jesse winked at me over his shoulder, the corner of his mouth ticking up. Grabbing my hand, he hurried me past the godawful aroma in the lobby. Darwin bounded ahead, leading us back to our room on the second floor.

The plumbing didn't work, but we had a bathtub, containers of water, and mini shampoo bottles we found in the bathroom. Standing in the tub, I gave Jesse and Roark sponge baths, then they returned the favor. Few things in this world rivaled the sensuality of four lathered hands stroking over my skin in the glow of a flickering candle.

My arousal returned quickly and desperately, fueled by an

endless energy deep in my core. Whatever this newfound power was, it made me ravenous. For food. For sex. For *them.*

They fucked me late into the night, stopping only to feed me dried rabbit meat and crackers, then fucked me again. Eventually, they crashed with exhaustion, and I lay wide-awake between them, marveling at the sexual need and alertness that still buzzed through me.

We hadn't put clothes back on, and just thinking about their nude forms ran an electric pulse up and down the length of my body. Careful not to wake them, I slid toward the headboard to sit against the pillows, propped up between their heads, my gaze hungrily devouring the musculature of their shoulders, asses, thighs, every perfect inch of them.

They lay on their sides, turned toward me, the sheet tangled around their lower legs. The candlelight gently swayed the shadows and illuminated Jesse's deep bronze skin and Roark's paler yet sun-soaked golden hues.

Asleep, they were unguarded and completely relaxed. No pretense of bravery and strength, and still they looked so powerful, dangerous, and ready to fight. Their bodies were stacked muscles on top of more muscles, each brick and bulge knitting together in a stunning arrangement of masculinity.

Roark was taller and broader while Jesse was harder, rougher around the edges. With Jesse's legs slightly parted and the bottom one bent toward me, his cock lay long and flaccid against his thigh, no doubt chafed from hours of use, but no less beautiful.

Roark's cock was concealed by the position of his leg, but I knew its shape and size by memory. He was proportioned, flawless, and every time I laid eyes on his girth, tasted it, and felt it moving inside me, I was lost in a tingling, heat-surging-through-my-blood haze of desire.

I reached toward his leg, my fingers softly tracing the line around his pelvis, between the edge of his abs and bend of his hip.

The deep rumble of a groan reverberated in the back of his

throat. Without opening his eyes, he curled an arm around my waist and dragged me down until I lay pressed against his chest. "Need sleep, love."

I kissed his gorgeous mouth, trailing my tongue along his bottom lip. "I could go for a few more hours. Maybe Jesse—"

"Is worn-out." Jesse's groggy voice drifted over my shoulder.

But a moment later, he inched against my back until I was smashed between slabs of hot, hard, *fatigued* muscle.

His lips trailed a path of kisses over my shoulder, and his cock hardened against my ass. Oh God, my inner walls burned and throbbed in anticipation. What the hell was wrong with me? I wasn't usually *this* horny. Why now?

Why not?

Because Jesse was tired and had already given me hours of orgasms.

"Hey." I reached back and stroked the rock-hard flex of his ass. "Go back to sleep."

His teeth sank into my shoulder, and his hand shoved between us, gripping his cock. He swept the warm, steely length across my butt cheek, slid it between my pussy lips, and paused to tease the tip against my opening.

My nipples hardened against Roark's chest, and a ripple of pleasure wobbled through me, heating between my legs. Roark grew hard against my thigh, but his eyes remained closed, his breathing even.

Jesse gripped my hips, pulling me back against him, and buried his shaft in the slick heat of my cunt. I was primed for him, wet and wanton, my channel clenching around him as I rolled my hips back and forth in gentle grinding movements, gliding along his length.

He thrust slowly, lazily, in a drugging rhythm, his pelvis lightly rotating, stilling, and nudging again. I wondered if he was falling in and out of sleep and loved the thought of that, wanting him to sleep inside me every night.

His jaw rested against the back of my head, his breaths soft and consistent against my hair. Just when I was certain he'd passed out, his fingers moved over my hip, across my belly, and sank between my legs. He left them there, curling against my folds, even as my movements rubbed the back of his hand against Roark's cock.

I rocked between them, snapping my pelvis gently, reaching for that blissful spot that would send me over. The friction of Jesse inside me, the peaceful expression on Roark's sleeping face, the scent of their male musk surrounding me, all of it kindled into an aching precipice of pleasure.

My climax came in a low, quiet tide of quivering rapture, flaring every cell in my body with intoxicating warmth. On the cusp of the orgasm, Jesse's hand between my legs clenched, and he grunted, his muscles hardening then loosening as he sighed his release.

"I'll never get enough of you," he mumbled into my hair.

A moment later, I knew he was asleep, his cock soft inside me, his fingers slack against my mound.

My hunger for them hadn't relented, my mind and body restless. Why? I suspected it had everything to do with my new ability.

Had I held the telepathic power to kill all along without knowing how to tap into it? Or had some external trigger switched it on? What changed? Intimacy with Jesse and Roark? Were they fueling me through sex? If so, why didn't sex with Michio have the same effect?

Or maybe it was something I ate? I grinned at the childhood memory of my favorite cartoon sailor gobbling spinach. Wouldn't it be badass if I could defeat the Drone with a can of spinach and a thought?

Good grief. I must've been high on arousal and pheromones or something. A clear-headed, wide-awake, happy high. One that teased a million thoughts through my head.

I thought about the reason I'd left the mountains all those months ago. The hunt for nymphs. The spread of the cure. I wondered if Elaine was alive, and if any nymphs were following Shea and me now. I hadn't sensed any since we left

Virginia. Maybe because we were traveling on wheels, moving at a higher rate of speed, and never lingered in one place longer than a night.

Weighed down with those thoughts, I finally slept, but for the next three days, my energy levels rose to spectacular heights. We stopped frequently for fryer oil and more recruits, but the drive was no longer delayed by aphids. Each time I felt them, the impulse to mentally zap them became automatic. Vibration. *Die.* Repeat.

As Link led the caravan off the highway and down the main drag of my home town, my effusive high tapered. The chirrup of locusts, the perfume of lilac blooms, the narrow, macadam roads, the old railroad tracks, all of it hit me with an aching swell of nostalgia as my recollection of Grain Valley clashed with the abandoned ruins it had become.

I hadn't been home in two years and four months, and a deep trembling panic sank into my bones, spreading out through my muscles and shivering my skin. I didn't want to be here, couldn't face the memories waiting in that house.

It was on the tip of my tongue to tell Link to turn around. My teeth chattered, my lips numbing with the need to demand he drive away.

But how would I find Michio?

How did I even know Michio would be there?

I just know.

Horseshit. I couldn't sense him, hadn't seen him in the dream. I was operating on the precarious whim of hope.

Darwin panted beside me as I leaned against the wall in the rear of the van. I ran my fingers through his coat, over and over, seeking comfort, until Roark grabbed my arms and pulled me across the van and into his lap.

He held my cheek against the beat of his heart, his steady breaths pacing mine. He didn't have to ask me what was wrong, didn't tell me we could turn around and leave. He simply held me, waiting for me to talk or not talk.

"Is this the neighborhood?" Link's voice broke through my thoughts.

Roark gripped my face and pressed his lips softly against mine, whispering into the kiss, "I'm here, love."

Nodding, I kissed him back and rose to my knees to crawl between Link and Jesse in the front seats.

Link stared out the windshield. "You said there was a Pump 'N Go with a red roof?"

I followed his gaze, and across a crumbling parking lot stood the gas station at the front of my neighborhood. A brutish woman, Jan, used to work there, always glaring and grunting when I bought cigarettes from her. I'd hated her attitude but missed it now, my stomach twisting with the loss of my old life.

"We're here." I glanced at the side mirrors, taking in the line of eight trucks and vans behind us.

Forty-two people made up our crew. If the Drone had taken up residency in my house with an army of aphids, I should be able to kill them with a thought while our soldiers fired hundreds of arrows into the Drone's melted face. Only, he'd always overpowered my abilities, his control over the aphids stronger than mine.

I blew out a breath and reminded Link of my concerns.

"I came for a fight, Little Ladybird." He unbuckled his seatbelt and reached for the gear shifter. "Which way?"

"It's the eighth street on the right. Top of the hill on the left." I gave him the house number.

He started to put the van into drive.

Jesse's arm shot out and gripped his wrist. "Evie stays here until the property is cleared."

It was a softly spoken statement, but there was nothing soft about Jesse. His eyes hardened, his fingers tightened around Link's arm, and his stubble bristled with the clench of his jaw.

"Not this again." Link glanced at the hand on his arm and narrowed his glare at Jesse. "She can kill the aphids and prevent casualties. She's going."

Too bad I couldn't telepathically reach my house from here. I needed to be a lot closer. "I can wait at the bottom of my street. That would be close enough but still out of sight."

The sharp angles on Jesse's face darkened, his profile etched in displeasure. "If you can sense the Drone's army, he can sense *you.*" He glared at Link. "This is as close as she goes until the area's been swept."

Silence coiled through the van as Link and Jesse exchanged murderous looks, the fermata of tension stretching and straining so long I struggled to breathe.

Link cracked first, yanking his arm away. "I'm in charge, and I'm telling you right fucking now, we're taking her with us." He grabbed the gear shifter.

Jesse's pupils dilated. Oh shit. I reached out to touch him, an attempt to calm him, but Roark's arm hooked around my mid-section and yanked me backward just as Jesse launched from his seat.

He slammed Link against the door, his palm flat on the glass, his other hand holding a compact machete against Link's throat. I didn't know he carried a knife, didn't even see where he'd pulled it from, but there it was, its lethally curved blade producing a trickle of blood down Link's neck.

"I let you *think* you're in charge." Jesse's tone was calm, deadly calm.

His hard-edged features and powerful body bowed over the other man. Primed packs of muscle, wild hair, intense eyes, the severe lines of his jaw, every threatening inch of him demanded compliance and promised a painful death if Link so much as breathed wrong.

"Never turn your back on the quiet ones," Link mumbled to himself, his fingers wrapped around Jesse's wrist, his eyes tightening into slivers. "Knew you'd cut my throat eventually."

Jesse cocked his head, his face slacking into a bored expression. "Do as I say, and you might keep your neck."

Behind me, Darwin growled deep and low. I reached back and smoothed my palm along his muzzle.

Link shifted his hips in the seat, his head pressed against the window. "Are you getting blood on my shirt?"

A narrow dribble painted a crimson path from the blade,

down his throat, and dotted the collar of his white t-shirt.

Link met my eyes over Jesse's shoulder and must've read the confirmation in my expression. "Fuck, man. This was a clean fucking shirt."

A muscle jumped in Jesse's cheek. "You're going to jump in one of the trailing vehicles, check out the house, and report back to me."

Link's lips rolled together. "Unless I'm killed when I get there."

"You wanted a fight." Jesse arched a brow in challenge. "I expect you back in ten minutes with my report."

I leaned forward, pushing against Roark's arm. "The van that Shea's in stays here, too."

Too bad Shea couldn't sense aphids. I might've considered sending her ahead to see if she could feel them.

"Fuck." Link's nostrils flared. "Fine. Get off me, asshole."

Jesse slid back to the passenger seat and sheathed the blade inside his leather jacket. Link remained pressed against the door with his hand around his throat, and only when Jesse gave him a curt chin lift did he grab his crossbow and exit the van.

He waved his arms at the waiting vehicles, directing them where to go. Seven of the eight trucks whipped by. The van that held Shea pulled behind us and parked, and the last truck picked up Link along the way.

I blew out a heavy breath. All the men had been given a description of Michio. They knew what the mission was and most importantly, they knew not to kill him unless he'd been compromised. I chose not to acknowledge that possibility.

Roark shifted around me and slid behind the wheel, turning the key and shutting off the ignition.

I knelt on the floor between them and met Jesse's eyes. Darkness edged his expression, but when I blinked, it was gone.

There was a quiet kind of brutality in this man, a ruthlessness concealed beneath the leather, like his knife. He wasn't pompous or mouthy or reckless, so it was easy to underestimate him. Until it was too late. He was a man who feared nothing. *Except my death.*

I wished I could unburden him of that worry, but the most predictable, certain thing about this life was death. No one could escape it. "A machete? You're full of surprises."

"Says the woman who can blow up aphids with her mind." His lips twitched, and he grabbed me beneath the arms and hauled me into his lap. "It's a khukuri not a machete, darlin'."

Sitting sideways across his thighs, I pulled open his jacket. The curved blade tucked securely in a leather sheath, beneath his arm. "What other weapons are you hiding?"

Roark rubbed his jaw, his eyes roaming my body. "Wha' has gotten into ye?"

"Nothing at the moment, but we have ten minutes to fix that."

Jesse pinched my chin, angling my head toward him. "Seriously, Evie. Something's up. We're not complaining—"

"Definitely no complaints." Roark grinned.

"—but you're insatiable. You've always been a sexual creature, and Christ, I love that about you." Jesse lifted his hips and nudged himself against my ass. "But this is a whole other level. Do you feel different? Have you noticed any other changes?"

I gripped his hand and held it between mine in my lap. "I don't know. I'm hungrier. Hornier." I peeked up at his hooded expression and looked down at our hands. "I have so much energy I feel like I'm bursting with it."

Roark draped his arm over the steering wheel, his expression thoughtful as he gazed out the windshield. He opened his mouth to say something, then squinted, his posture snapping straight as one of our delivery trucks came speeding down the street toward us.

He rolled down the window, and the black truck skidded to a stop beside us.

Link leaned over the door, deep grooves lining his forehead. "It's gone."

My heart raced. "What's gone?"

"Your house. It's burnt to the ground."

FORTY-ONE

I stared at the black hole that had once been my house, my gaze stumbling over singed wood beams and melted glass windows and twisted metal railings. Grief, fury, and harrowing pain scorched through my veins and burned my lungs, laboring my breaths, made worse with the inhalation of black dust.

It was just a house. A house that had been designed by Joel and me, the foundation poured with our dreams, the walls strengthened with the laughter of our children, and the roof buttressed with our love. Before the plague, I'd never envisioned leaving it. But when I was chased away, forced to abandon it, I'd carried with me a seed of comfort that the house was here, sheltering the archives of my past life like an impenetrable vault.

With no one around to put out the fire, there was no roof, not a single wall left standing, the foundation crushed beneath the destruction. Annie's closet of ruffled dresses…*Gone.* Aaron's collection of Star Wars action figures…*Gone.*

I didn't need to ask *how* or *who.* My house hadn't just burned to the ground. It was swallowed by thick layers of spider webs.

Scalding hatred burned the back of my throat. What a vile son of a bitch, leaving his webby funk on everything he destroyed, on everything I loved.

I stepped through the rubble of charred wood and soot, my boots tangling in nets of silk strings. The dappling shadows beneath the fallen walls no longer smoldered, the embers long gone. I couldn't sense the dead aura of the Drone or the pulse of aphids. Couldn't feel the warm hum of Michio's presence.

Nothing lived here, nothing remained but the lingering aroma of smoke and burnt memories.

I'd left Darwin in Shea's van with her, but Jesse and Roark hovered like shadows at my elbows. It would've been unnerving and downright fucked up to take my lovers on a tour of the home I'd shared with my family, but I would've preferred that to *this*.

Every incinerated flake that stirred beneath my steps made me shudder. Each groan of settling timber penetrated my chest and tightened my insides into an agonizing knot of hell. My shoulders hunched around my ears, my arms crossed defensively, and my entire body trembled in pain.

I wanted to be stronger, or at the very least, *appear* stronger. Forty men stood around watching me, and every one of them had lost something or someone meaningful. But the reminder didn't help me stand taller or braver.

I looked out across the backyard, a view I'd once cherished from my deck. Blackened debris filled the in-ground pool. The maple trees rustled, covering the ground with dead, brown leaves. The valley of rolling hills and lavish homes now lay in ruins of cement and weeds. But they weren't burned. No, that calamity only fell upon *my* house.

Jesse's hand slid into mine, pulling my arm away from my torso. "Annie and Aaron…" He cleared his voice, softening it. "Their spirits used to talk about this place. The pool. The lightning bugs. The little lizards they would catch near the rock wall."

Swallowing past a thick throat, I stared at the corner of the yard where the rock wall once stood and willed their ghosts to appear, if only for a moment, so I could trace their sweet faces with my gaze while I told them I loved them and missed them so, so much.

"Joel cremated them here." My voice cracked in the crisp air. "He spread their ashes over the property."

I was so thankful he hadn't buried them, that their tiny

bodies weren't stuck in the ground beneath the sad waste of their home.

A terrible noise rose up in my throat, the sound shocking me. I covered my mouth, blinking burning eyes and wondering if I'd finally cry.

But the tears didn't come, not even when Roark's arms came around me, squeezing my chest to his.

I held onto his strength, my thoughts spinning into a mess of shattered images. I saw the day I'd brought Annie home from the hospital, carrying her into the house for the first time, her little body wrapped in pink blankets. I heard the patter of Aaron's footsteps when he sneaked into bed with Joel and me at night. I smelled the rich aroma of Cavendish tobacco that clung to Joel's skin when he made love to me.

Then I felt the pain, digging, clawing, and biting through my mind until all I knew was pain. Memories held power, the power to shut everything off and hurt so deeply and viciously that nothing else existed. So much fucking pain.

"We're still here." Roark's brogue rumbled over me, his embrace squeezing my ribs. "Ye still have us."

Jesse moved against my back and touched his forehead to my shoulder.

Roark's words and Jesse's silent support struck a chord, plucking me from the paralyzing depths of memory and yanking me to the surface.

My home had been destroyed long ago and not by a fire. It stopped existing when my family died. But Jesse and Roark were still here. My new family. I wasn't alone.

Closing my eyes, I let the ache of my loss fall away like tears. Then I pulled in a shredded breath, blinked rapidly, and cleared my eyes of dust.

"Yeah." I stood taller, breathed a little bit easier, and strengthened my stance. Smoothing my palms over the breast of Roark's coat, I stretched on tiptoes and kissed the soft hairs that had grown on his chin. "Thank you."

I reached back, found Jesse's hand, and gave it a squeeze.

"Now what?" Link strode toward us, his crossbow slung

over his back.

"You have trackers, right? Put them on the Drone's trail." I stepped out from between Jesse and Roark, ready to get the hell away from this dead place. "If people are talking about us, let's drag them out of their hidey-holes and find out what they've heard about a man with a cape and wings."

Link's head turned slowly, ever-so slowly in my direction, as if he were deliberately trying to intimidate me with…what? A slowly turning head? Whatever.

His black eyes took their time, too, finally resting on mine. "That's your plan?"

"Got a better one?" Jesse asked, his eyes scanning our surroundings.

"Nope." Link grinned.

Apparently, he wasn't holding any grudges against Jesse. Smart man.

I moved to walk back to the van, refusing to give the charred remains of my house a soul-sucking good-bye, but as I took a step, I felt…twitchy. Another step, and a warm, glowing sensation settled over me, like someone had turned on a bulb and held it close to my skin.

Then, as if a door had been opened to a deep unseen world that buzzed with electricity, a wave of static energy released into the air and trickled through my body in steady, humming pulses.

I spun, lungs pumping and eyes frantically searching the street while my mind narrowed on nothing but that hum. "Michio?"

The cool breeze whispered back, breathing icy tendrils beneath my hair and down my nape. But the hum remained, stronger now, searing through my blood.

"Ye feel Michio?" Roark turned in a circle, visually probing the houses and overgrown yards. "Where?"

As the hum quaked through my body, I tried to trace the source. It didn't draw outward in threads like the aphids. It spread like a beam of light. I should've been able to pinpoint where it concentrated, but it felt like it was coming from every direction.

"Everywhere?" I panted hopeful gusts of air and scrambled over the rubble toward the street, looking in both directions. "I don't know."

Jesse paced around me on the street, his bow in one hand, the other raking through his hair as his sunlit glare burned over the landscape. "I don't like this. What do you mean *everywhere*?"

The humming sensation felt like Michio, but it didn't. The night Michio left, I could sense his general direction. Granted, it had only been seconds before he blinked away. But now?

"There's no clear direction." I curled my hands into fists. He *had to be* out there, and my heart thundered with every second that passed. Every second that I might've been losing him. "Let's spread out."

The moment the words left my mouth, a blur of movement spread over the horizon. I whirled, turning completely around, my gaze darting in every direction. I couldn't see that far to make out what they were, but the blur of countless tall, dark shapes seemed to emerge from everywhere. In a few seconds, they would be surrounding us.

My muscles stiffened and heated as I reached for the bow on my back and nocked an arrow. The hurried mass of movement propelled toward us with lightning speeds. Seemingly man-sized. Or aphid-sized? I didn't feel aphids, but holy fucking shit, they didn't move like humans.

They moved like Michio.

The flash of Roark's sword glinted in my periphery. Jesse planted himself at my side.

"They're not aphids or nymphs," I shouted, loud enough for forty soldiers to hear.

Footfalls pounded around me. Men shouted. Knives and other weaponry sounded as they slid from their leather holsters. And one clear, baritone voice boomed, "Fuck yeah. Let's fight!"

FORTY-TWO

The sun shone in my eyes, harsh and glaring, but the thunder of fast-moving footsteps was clear as day. The approaching stampede reached my ears before I could identify exactly what was coming. The tremors in my hands shook the bow and the humming in my veins strengthened as the noise grew closer, and the blurring shapes took form.

Men. Hundreds of hard-eyed, snarling men leapt over broken fences and bounded across the roofs of cars, hurdling everything in their way to cover the distance between us.

Why did they make my insides hum? It had only been seconds since I first felt them, not enough time to evacuate to our vehicles. What did they want? They were charging too aggressively and urgently to have come with anything but the intent to kill.

Could we defend ourselves against their numbers? Some of the approaching men carried assault rifles and handguns, but most were armed with weapons like ours.

I stared down the shaft of an arrow as forty soldiers spread out around me with knives, axes, and crossbows at the ready. Jesse and Roark stood at the edges of my vision, flanking me.

"Don't leave my sight." Jesse stepped closer, his arm bent with the pull of the bow string, his elbow grazing my head.

My ears rang with the thump of my heart, my fingers trembling to release the arrow. But they weren't close enough, and I needed to make all twenty of my arrows count.

Our circle of men widened, stretching outward, and suddenly, several broke away. They ran down the street, clutching hunting knives and hacking at the approaching men in their paths.

A rifle went off, then another, and just like that, arrows thickened the air.

It was easy to differentiate between the two sides. Our men shouted, made expressions, and gestured to one another. The others were strangely stoic, aside from their snarling, and didn't make eye-contact.

I sighted a man with blond plaits of hair forty yards away, his jeans and shirt tattered and smeared with dirt. He trained his crossbow on me, no surprise on his face at the sight of a woman. But he hesitated then angled away and shot someone else.

A pained grunt hit my ears. I closed off my emotions to it, couldn't think about the people dying or the bullets whistling past or the arrows skipping across the ground around my feet.

I focused on the target, took note of the wind direction, and released the arrow.

It punctured the blond man's chest, and he stumbled back. As I reloaded, his lips drew back in a cruel snarl, revealing over-sized canines.

My pulse rocketed through my body. "Fangs!" I screamed hoarsely, and found Jesse's eyes beside me. "I saw fangs. They might be able to heal themselves."

Goddamned fucking Drone. He'd bitten others? Was this *his* assembled army? Oh God. An army of superhuman bloodsuckers.

"They're not dying," someone called out.

Jesse released another of his black and red feathered arrows then thrust his chin over his shoulder, shouting, "Hit them in the head!"

Where was Michio? Was he involved? My blood buzzed with the hum of his presence. But it wasn't *his* hum, was it? It was the hum of hundreds like him.

Die, die, die, I chanted soundlessly, but the blond fucker I'd hit climbed to his feet, ignoring the arrow in his chest, as he raised his crossbow.

Fuck. I waited for the breeze to still and fired again. The arrow sliced into his head, and he dropped to the ground. I reached for the quiver, anchored the next shot, and aimed at a horde of approaching men, firing at the fanged faces.

Darwin's barking muffled from the van across the street. The coppery scent of blood tickled my nose, and the cries of wounded men pierced my ears.

My teeth sawed the inside of my cheek as I sighted a black man. He snarled with a mouthful of sharp teeth and swung an ax at a slower, fangless man.

Inhale. Exhale. Shoot.

My shot burrowed directly in the fanged man's ear, and he collapsed to the ground. I grabbed another arrow.

Roark's sword flashed beside me, and a decapitated head bounced off my boot. Blood drenched the matted hair, and fangs pressed against dead lips.

They all had fangs. *They'd all been bitten.*

The sword whistled out of sight as Roark's footfalls scuffed behind me, his grunts alerting me that he was hewing down anyone who approached my back.

I fired arrow after arrow, keeping at least one of my senses locked on Jesse and Roark. They glided around me, remaining out of my firing path yet close enough that I could track the rasps of their breaths.

Everywhere I looked, men fought in a wild fury of bows, guns, and knives. And so many fell. Our men. The other men.

I released the next shot and killed a young, pale guy with black hair. How far away had he traveled? What had led him here? Had he been truly evil and deserving of death, or was there something more manipulative at play here?

I still couldn't sense the Drone or any of his aphids. Around me, the asphalt, broken curbs, and overgrown grass glistened in red. The sight of so much death magnified the ruination of the sagging, neglected houses I'd once called my neighborhood.

The skin on my fingers abraded with each arrow I launched. Adrenaline soaked through my body. My muscles trembled. My breaths tightened, and my lungs strained and burned.

"Evie, you're almost out," Roark shouted behind me.

I reached for the quiver, and sure enough, I pulled the last arrow.

How many men did we have left on our side? Not nearly enough to take down the hundred or so fangy ones blurring around us.

I wouldn't die here, not if the prophecy was accurate. But Jesse and Roark? The thought of them lying on the ground and staring back at me with sightless eyes was enough to re-energize my mind and muscles with determination.

Anchoring my final shot, I inched toward a heap of nearby bodies. I could collect five arrows there and a few more beside the car in the driveway next door. And I still had my arm sheathes.

"Evie?" Jesse fired one after another, his neck craning between shots to look for me.

"I'm at your seven o'clock." About thirty feet from him and Roark, I bent down and plucked the feathered shafts, planting my boot on the skulls to pry them free.

"I'll get her," Roark shouted, but as he turned, five men charged him.

I trained the arrow on the closest one and let it fly. The man's head kicked back in a spray of blood. I snatched another arrow from the skull beneath my boot as Roark swung the sword, lopping the head off the next one, then another—

"Evie." A steady, achingly-familiar voice whispered over my shoulder.

I stopped breathing and whirled, stumbling over the bodies.

No one was there. A few yards off, a man I recognized from our crew fired his crossbow in the opposite direction. But no Michio.

A low, glowing hum trembled through me, the warm sensation stronger, more powerful than I'd ever felt. It lit up every cell in my body and slithered around my bones from head to toe.

I scanned the vicinity, my gaze darting in every direction. "Michio?"

Strong arms wrapped around me from behind, pulling my back against a hard chest. I glanced down at those arms, the musculature wrapped in olive skin and dusted with dark hair.

The warmth of his embrace, the beat of his heart against my back, the hum in my blood, all of it promising that I'd finally found him. He was here. The guardian I'd been chasing.

My heart soared, and I tried to turn in his arms, but they tightened, allowing me no leeway to move. "Michio? Let me see you."

"Shhh." He breathed against my ear and yanked the bow from my hand, tossing it away.

"Wait!" I jerked against him, unable to wriggle an inch. "What the fuck?"

He hauled me higher up his body, and my feet lost purchase. He flipped me over his shoulder, knocking the wind from my lungs and wrenching the quiver from my back. I got a glimpse of his cropped black hair, then the ground was spinning. We were moving, racing away.

My first thought was that he was carrying me to safety like some chauvinistic barbarian, but when I lifted my head and found Jesse and Roark, dread sank deep into my core.

They sprinted after us, their devastated eyes locked on mine and their mouths moving, shouting... They were too far away, the distance between us stretching, the street blurring into the horizon.

They vanished from view in the span of a heartbeat, but I was already shoving, twisting my body, and screaming. "Put me down! I can't leave them. They're going to die back there!"

The neighborhood spiraled around me, morphing into commercial buildings, the main drag of Grain Valley streaking by. Fucking hell, he'd taken me too far from them.

"Put me the fuck down, goddammit!" I smashed my fists against the bare skin on his back, bucking against his clutch on my legs.

He was too strong, moving too damned fast.

I stretched for the sleeve of my jacket to yank it up and release a blade. "Stop. Stop right now!"

Before I reached my arm sheath, he stopped, and my neck whiplashed as he dumped me on my ass. Raising my head, I glimpsed nothing but corn fields, which meant we were miles from the battle.

My eyes traveled over his crisp, black fatigues, the ridges of muscle of his broad torso, and landed on his unreadable expression. He didn't appear to be further evolved or mutated. No wings. His fangs were hidden behind the flat line of his mouth.

Wasn't he happy to see me? Why was he just standing there, staring? Staring but not really *seeing*?

He was the master of blank faces, but this…this wasn't the man I remembered. I wanted to hug him, kiss him, and tell him how much I missed him, but his eyes held nothing. No thought. No emotion. They were clear and brown and *hollow*.

My heart ached for agonizing seconds before I shoved it away with thoughts of Jesse and Roark fighting for their lives.

I climbed to my feet and gripped his hands where they dangled at his sides. "Michio? We have to go back."

Nothing. Not even a blink.

"Are you okay? How did you find me? Who are those men attacking us? Have you seen the Drone?" When he didn't respond, a tremor rippled through me, and my throat sealed up. "You need to take me back. Our guys are getting slaughtered. We have to help Jesse and Roark!"

Frustration burned up my cheeks. I yanked my hands away, fisting them at my sides. "Say something, goddammit!"

Slowly, he lifted his arms and cupped my shoulders. I searched his face for a glimmer of something. A twitch of humanity. A trace of love.

One of his hands lifted so fast I didn't see it until it struck against the side of my neck. Shock gripped my body. There were nerves in the neck…lots of nerves…and pressure…

Stars blotted my vision, swallowing Michio's heartless expression until there was only darkness.

FORTY-THREE

I woke with a throbbing ache behind my eyes, lying on my side and curled in a ball. Chilly wind blasted my hair into my face. The rumble of an engine vibrated my bones, and the steel floor clattered with movement.

I was moving.

With a jolt, I sat up, dizzy and *alone*. Icy gusts slammed against the back of my head. I reached out to brace myself. My hands bumped into wire walls, and I blinked, groggy and confused.

Terror clawed through my insides as I looked around. I was trapped. Caged in a chain-linked box in the back of a pickup truck and speeding through the night.

Chains tethered the cage securely to the truck bed, and a padlock hung from the sturdy door. My heart raced, magnifying the ache in my head. No water, no blankets, nothing occupied the 3x5 foot space but me.

Grasping at the sleeves of my leather jacket, I yanked them up. My arm sheathes were gone. Tremors surged through my hands. Unarmed. *Confined.*

Michio had done this? Caged me in the back of a truck like a goddamned animal? No, Michio wouldn't have done this. The man who had snatched me from the battle was like an unknown enemy, not one of my guardians. Panic rose, hot and angry, burning through my lungs.

Where were Jesse and Roark? Did they survive the battle? My chest tightened, and my breaths grew harsh and painful. They had to be alive. I refused to believe otherwise. Maybe they would catch up with me somehow? They could be out there right now, watching me like always.

The pavement blurred behind the truck, illuminated by the dim glow of the taillights and bleeding into thick blackness. No headlights trailing behind. No tracks for them to follow.

The hope of them finding me and watching over me was disintegrating, ideas left behind in a fleeting dream or on a hemorrhaging battlefield.

I clenched my hands. How did I end up here? Michio must've drugged me to keep me asleep until he reached the truck? I didn't remember anything since the strike to my neck earlier today. Or yesterday? How much time had passed?

Rage surged through my veins, pumping to the clipped beat of my heart. What happened to Michio to make him do this? Where the fuck was he? I could sense him, could feel the hum all around me.

I spun and found the rear window of the cab open. Inside, the wide shoulders of two men filled the single bench seat. The driver wore a baseball cap, his blond hair frizzing around his nape. And the passenger… Despite the shadows in the cab, I could make out the perfect symmetry of his profile, the sculpted angles of his hairless jaw, and the seductive almond-shape of his eyes.

Gripping the support bars of the cage, I pulled myself to my knees and scooted to the side so that I could see his profile. The cold metal bit into my fingers as I yelled through the open window, "Did you drug me, Michio? Why the fuck am I caged?"

He stared toward the center of the front dash, maybe so he could watch me out of the corner of his eye, but there wasn't a flinch in his expressionless features.

"Where are we?" I raised my voice, shouting over the wind. "Did you hear me? Where are you taking me?"

He didn't twitch an eyelash. Didn't acknowledge me at all. What was wrong with him? He would never put me in danger. Even under his imprisonment in Malta, he protected me, took care of me. This man was not Michio.

The Drone must've done this to him. But what? How? What had he been through to reduce him to this…this empty thing? My chest ached for him, my body tightening with worry.

Up ahead, a red trail of taillights snaked into the dark. At least a dozen vehicles traveled in some kind of caravan. Who were they?

I swatted the hair out of my face and scanned the surrounding darkness. Every few breaths, I felt the distant buzz of aphids, the sensations flickering as we sped in and out of range.

The terrain appeared flat and barren beyond the occasional abandoned car. I couldn't see buildings or road signs. Were those fields? Kansas? Were we heading west?

Hazy clouds hovered over the moon, crisscrossed by the wire ceiling of my enclosure. I didn't know how to navigate using moon phases or constellations, and the landscape was so dark I couldn't see a damned thing.

I turned back to the cab. "Where have you been for the past four months? Did you find the Drone? Who's in all those cars?"

Could Jesse and Roark be with them? Certainly not willingly. Not with me back here in a fucking cage.

Michio didn't blink, didn't give me so much as a sideways glance.

"Why aren't you talking to me?" Frustration and hurt edged my voice, straining my words. At this point, I knew I wouldn't be getting any answers, but I had to keep trying. "What happened to you, Michio? Please look at me."

When he didn't, I slammed a hand against the cage wall, rattling it, and shifted my attention to the driver. "Who the fuck are you? Did Michio bite you? Were you part of the group that attacked us in Missouri?"

I paused between each question. When he didn't respond or blink, I continued with more, hoping something I said would finally break their torpid silence. "Where's the Drone? Can you feel my presence the way I can feel yours? You know, the hum under your skin? I bet you can. I bet you can feel how fucking pissed I am right now!"

Nothing. They were stiff, unresponsive entities, like robots, driving the truck, following the snake of taillights, staring straight ahead. They didn't communicate with each other, didn't exchange a single look.

Were they mentally controlled? How deep did that control reach? Could the Drone hear me talking to them? Was he actively broadcasting commands or did he give them orders and send them off?

Thinking back to the battle, none of our attackers interacted with one another. While our guys gestured and shouted and worked together, the fanged men simply drove ahead, single-mindedly focused on killing.

What the fuck was going on?

The darkness of the cab seemed to cling to Michio's apathetic demeanor. Shadows accentuated the slack outline of his profile. His strong hands lay palms down on his thighs, his athletic body calm and indifferent. What if he'd been harmed so badly his mind had been altered? What if he couldn't come back from it? God, I wanted to wrap my arms around him.

Up and down, my gaze roamed every inch of him I could see, lingering on the most memorable attributes. His flawless skin had once felt like velvet beneath my hands. The cords in his thick neck used to stretch when he orgasmed. His full lips had tasted like the most exotic spice beneath my tongue. And his fangs, both imposing and erotic, were presently sheathed.

"Did you bite them, Michio? Is the Drone controlling you?"

No response.

I refused to believe he'd killed the Lakota, but maybe he'd seen Elaine? Did he know where she was? Did he know if Jesse and Roark were alive? Not that I'd trust his word on this topic.

The man sitting before me reminded me so much of the stoic Dr. Nealy from a year ago. When I'd met him, he'd been my captor, the doctor who'd held me prisoner in Malta while leading me to believe Roark had died.

But back then, I'd glimpsed traces of emotion beneath the blank mask he tried so hard to maintain. A mask he wore for my protection. And now? I didn't sense a disguise or pretense.

No one could fake this kind of cruel callousness. He was simply *not there*.

The Drone was behind this. It was the only explanation. He could command the aphids better than I could, which lent itself to the idea that he could control the men who'd contracted his spider pathogen. Men like Michio.

Wherever we were headed, I was certain the Drone would be waiting, and I wouldn't be able to defeat him unarmed and caged. Michio was my only chance. I wouldn't give up on him.

"Remember the first time we made love? We were soaking in the bathtub and you were upset because you thought you'd been too rough with me. You said you were supposed to take care of me, not injure me. Do you remember?" The memories barreled through me, crushing my chest and thickening my voice. "It was the night before we broke out of Fort Manoel. The night before we escaped the Drone."

His lack of expression only deepened my hurt.

I tightened my grip against the cage wall. "We've made love so many times since that night. Do you think about it? Did you miss me at all? Dammit, Michio, I miss *you*. Please talk to me."

Woodenly, he reached toward the space between us, and my pulse went nuts. *Finally, a reaction!*

Gripping the window lever, he slid it shut and pressed the lock. The cold *click* punched me in the gut. But instead of succumbing to the burn behind my eyes, I lashed back in a fit of fury.

My fingers curled around the metal wires, and I shook the cage with all my might, banging it against the glass, trying to free it from its heavy chains. I jerked and screamed, willing the damned walls to break and pleading for him to open the window, all while glaring murderous daggers at the back of his head.

Eventually, I stopped banging and screeching and closed my eyes. Hands aching and voice raw, I slumped against the wall of the cage and surrendered my body to insufferable mourning. I trembled from head to toe, frozen in the frigid gusts of wind, scared out of my mind, and suffocating under the harrowing pain of betrayal.

I hugged my knees to my chest, and for just a few moments, I allowed myself to wallow. I let all the *why me* questions unfurl through my head, feeling sorry for my pathetic existence and blaming everyone for every miserable thing that had happened to me. I didn't try to contain my breathing as it worked its way into a wheezing series of wet hacks. And I cursed Michio. I cursed him even though I knew *this* man wasn't him. Mostly I cursed him for sitting in the warm cab while I froze my tits off in the back.

When I finished wading through my wretched neuroticism, I evened my breaths, flexed my fingers, and squared my shoulders. I hadn't lost my fight.

A comforting realization settled over me. Michio didn't know I could blow up bugs with my mind, or that I didn't need skin-on-skin contact, or that my body contained an endless flow of energy that made me feel like I could run all the way back to Missouri.

I sat still as stone, hiding the power I'd yet to understand. A secret I would keep in my pocket until I needed it.

For now, I needed to regroup, watch and learn, and figure out how to find the doctor who'd once taken care of me, the lover who'd seduced me, the man who—I *knew* deep in my heart—still loved me.

I slept for a couple hours, maybe more, and woke as the golden glow of dawn flushed the horizon beyond the tailgate. The sun was behind us, so we were headed west. Moments later, we passed two weathered road signs.

Leaving Kansas Come Again and *Welcome to Colorful Colorado*

A few miles into Colorado, the band of twenty-some

vehicles pulled off to the side of the interstate. As our truck crept alongside the caravan and headed toward the front of the line, I climbed to my knees and frantically searched for Roark or Jesse or a familiar face.

The chain of parked vehicles consisted of small trucks and cars of the fuel-efficient variety. I didn't see a fanged mouth—were they retracted?—or recognize a single face as fifty or so men checked engines, refueled from containers they hauled, and urinated on the side of the road. No one talked or shared a glance, yet they worked like synchronized machines alongside one another. The sight made the hairs on my nape stand on end.

Something wasn't right about them, beyond the whole kidnapping thing. Not only could I feel their auras humming beneath my skin, but their presence seemed to repel nearby aphids. The insectile vibrations were there, a dull buzz in my gut, but the aphids didn't come within a visual distance. If anything, they fled.

Though I had been unsuccessful in commanding these blank-faced men to die on the battlefield, I tried again. Focusing on two men standing beside one of the cars, I silently breathed, *Die.*

Nothing.

Shit.

We reached the front of the line and circled back to return to the tail. Not one vehicle held a cage. No familiar faces.

I was the only woman.

The only prisoner.

No Roark or Jesse.

Grief slammed into me with the force of a tidal wave. I slid to my butt, wrapped my arms around my waist, and tried to reign in my raging breaths.

My imprisonment on Malta had almost destroyed me, but I wasn't the same person I was then. I'd dragged my ass out of a dungeon, survived the bowels of a volcano, watched the bodies of my Lakota companions burn to ash, and faced the charred remains of my beloved home.

Those events had hardened me, but what fortified my every breath was the bond that had evolved amid the hardship. I'd formed a profound, impenetrable stronghold with Jesse and Roark, one I would fight for, bleed for, and kill to protect. *That* made me stronger than every one of my muscled, empty-eyed captors.

I would stay strong and keep my head clear and my eyes open. No more wallowing. No more hopelessness. I *would* see Jesse and Roark again.

With these thoughts, so began my second imprisonment under Michio.

FORTY-FOUR

The next two weeks were much like my captivity on Malta. But instead of a guarded tower on an island, I was caged like a mangy dog in the bed of a truck.

Three times a day, Michio offered me food and water. Instead of bribing me to eat, he wordlessly took it away when I didn't touch it. Instead of humoring my questions with mind games, he gifted me with blank silence. Instead of giving me baths and carrying me to the toilet, he tossed me two buckets. One he filled with water to wash with, a wasted effort since I refused to remove my pants and jacket. The other bucket was to shit in. I really hated him for that bit of degradation and told him as much.

But everything else had been the same. The caged restlessness. The dread of the unknown future. The endless ache for Jesse and Roark. And my insatiable libido.

Michio might've lost his soul, but his body was here, healthy and well cared for, taunting me with the confident glide of his strides, the sculpted planes of his beautiful face, and the movement of his muscles beneath flawless skin. Sensuality was an idiosyncrasy of his physical structure, whether he was looking at me with desire or not. And there were no looks from him, neither with interest nor *dis*interest.

The other men didn't leer at me either. They stared at nothing with hollow eyes and expressionless faces like Michio. They did what was needed to keep me alive, but I was never allowed out of my tiny prison.

I tried to escape. Holy hell did I try every time Michio

opened the gate to the cage. But each attempt earned me a blurring punch in the ribs. He hit me hard and often, his strikes too fast to counter, his strength unstoppable, and his vacant expression firmly in place. I might've been able to move like him, but I couldn't outmaneuver or overpower him, and the bruises on my torso added up. Eventually, I stopped trying.

It was a sign the civilized world had well and truly ended when men could haul a caged woman in the back of a pickup across several states without getting stopped. We passed lone wanderers, gangs of men, and several gun fights already in progress, yet no one tried to wave down or approach our caravan. They probably assumed I was a nymph.

A screaming, begging, coherent nymph. Whatever. I never stopped calling for help.

Atrophy set into my muscles. I couldn't stand, couldn't fully stretch out. So my arms and legs weakened and shrunk, and my pants began to sag off my hips. And the smell… The leather blocked the wind but sweet Jesus, my clothes reeked of body odor and stubbornness.

Still, I refused to undress, especially when we hit the snow and ice in the Colorado Mountains. There were a couple days I was certain I'd lose a few fingers and toes to frostbite, but it was the cliffs that sent my blood pressure into the danger zone.

Cliffs.

Every road we took hugged the very edge of a steep drop. How would I die? Would the truck lose traction, sail down the side of the mountain, and explode into a fiery inferno? Or would Michio yank me out of the cage at the highest point and shove me over himself?

I suffered through some minor panic attacks as the caravan made its way west through Utah then south along the edge of a nearly continuous range of mountainous cliffs. The drastic changes in elevation and climate made my stomach turn and my body shudder between sweating and freezing.

The cage grew smaller and smaller with every mile. I ached

to stand, to stretch, to *run.* I needed out, needed out, needed out! I tried screaming, kicking and punching the cage walls, and spitting in their faces. Nothing moved my captors.

In Arizona, the interstate carved its way through narrow walls of gorges. Instead of cascades of evergreens, there were reddish-brown cliffs. My demise stretched out around me, the *Thelma and Louise* ending playing a continuous loop in my head. It made my desperation even more desperate.

During one of our rest stops in barren butt-fuck nowhere, I shouted for Michio's attention, as I often did, while he dug through a supply pack beside the truck. "You remember the prophecy? The cliff, Michio? You took me to fucking cliff country! Is this your plan? You really want me to die?"

How were Jesse and Roark going to find me? I was so far away. *Too fucking far.* It would take a miracle.

As expected, Michio gave no indication that he heard me. But I didn't relent. I shouted and pleaded through the Nevada desert while glaring at the towering, rocky peaks of never-ending cliffs.

It wasn't until we reached Las Vegas that I finally calmed down enough to eat the scraps of meat Michio tossed in my cage. "Where are we going? Do you even have a destination?"

I was met with an exaggerated expression of nothingness. As he turned and climbed into the cab, I gave his back a middle finger and screamed, "Fuck you, you limp infertile dick!"

It was a moment of weakness. I really hadn't given up on him. Besides, passion was better than indifference, right? Even if my passion was uncouth, immature, and really fucking angry. At the very least, it kept my blood pumping and my skin warm.

We drove through Las Vegas without stopping. The over-the-top, buzzing city of indulgence lay in a pile of rubble. Torched skyscrapers looked down upon overturned cars, shattered signs, and gutted slot machines. I could almost smell the singe of useless, burnt money.

Soon, the crumble of concrete and glass gave way to a brown landscape. The dirt, the dusty wind, the leaf-less vegetation, everywhere I looked was brown. It was late in the day, and the sun dipped *behind* us. Why were we heading east again?

All signs pointed to Hoover Dam. Literally. The road signs counted down the miles to the famous tourist attraction. If I recalled correctly, it was also the largest hydroelectricity facility in the world.

A fortress in a canyon, powered by water, with miles of underground tunnels, Hoover Dam was exactly the kind of practical, pretentious domain the Drone would choose to rule from.

I shivered despite the sun-warmed breeze.

Less than an hour passed before the massive cliffs closed in around us. I knew we were close when electrical substations began to crop up, the steel lattice, heavy-duty wires, and transformers jutting out of steep surfaces of rock.

That was when I saw them.

The truck swerved, dodging a nymph in the road. It was the first in a long line of hobbling nymphs. One, then two, then dozens of them. They walked in the direction of the dam, heads down and stringy hair hanging in their faces.

I couldn't feel them, not a single icy prickle, and this puzzled me far more than the fact that they didn't seem to sense *me*.

From my perch in the bed of the truck, I stared beyond the slanting electrical towers, craning my neck to see around the twisty bends in the road, searching each sickly creature for some kind of reaction.

The nymphs didn't lift their heads, didn't shift their pupil-less eyes, and didn't falter in their determination to plow ahead. Some wore shreds of tattered clothes. Others were completely nude, their skin baked by the sun. My chest ached as I watched them trudge along, their cadaverous frames jerking with each step, their backs bowed under the affliction of the virus. I couldn't feel their pain now, but I remembered it clearly. They were as trapped as I was.

When was the last time I felt one of their chilly whispers through my gut? Virginia? Right before I'd lost consciousness for two weeks? Had something changed in me then? Or did I lose the ability to sense them when I came into my new power?

Whatever the catalyst was, it was a blessing. Crippled to a state of seizures and vomiting was not how I wanted to arrive at our destination.

A hairpin turn spit us out alongside the Colorado River, and up ahead, some kind of checkpoint halted our caravan. Bracketed by the river and a steep rocky wall, there was nowhere to go but forward or backward. We motored slowly, stopping and starting toward the dam and presumably the Drone who now presided over it.

Barbed wire gates barricaded the passageway, guarded by twenty armed men. The road continued beyond the gates and across the dam, the monolithic wall curving inward against the pressure of the river. On top of the dam's entrance sat a tall, plain concrete structure. I assumed it housed one of the elevators that went to the tunnels in the canyon below.

I struggled to see around all the vehicles as the guards checked each one, pushing aside the gates, and stepping back to allow entry to the dam. They wore the same blank expressions. No talking. No gestures. Mindless fucking robots.

As we inched forward, the nymphs on the road moved past us, stooping, shuffling quickly, keeping close in line, and intently following some unseen path. Why?

The reason waited just outside the gates.

My heart crashed into my ribs as I took in the row of ten women—*cured women*—chained to concrete posts. Their postures sagged, faces pale, bodies nude, their hair sticking to their heads in matted clumps. A few women weakly jerked their arms against the shackles. The rest simply hung in defeat, their blinking eyes the only indication of life.

My chest heaved and my breathing ratcheted, the struggle to suck air made worse when I saw the lumps of bodies at their feet. Skeletal frames. Thin skin. Long, jagged nails. *Comatose nymphs.* None were crawling out of the bottom of the pile, which meant someone was dragging them off before they woke. To take them where? To do what with them?

The sharp, sickening talons of fear and shock flayed the lining of my stomach. Why would the Drone create nymphs only to cure them now? Why do it by cruelly hanging women to posts outside the dam? My blood boiled, and my jaw clenched with pain. I gripped the cage wall, shaking it with horrified anger. Where had these women even come from?

The answer darted out the door of the concrete structure, smiling and running straight for our truck, her belly round with pregnancy and her eyes locked on Michio.

Elaine.

FORTY-FIVE

Elaine approached with hurried steps, clutching the bulge of her belly, her upturned face alight with excitement. The sight of her, alive *and* pregnant, seized me by the throat and stole my breath. There were so many opposing reactions whipping through me, but the strongest feeling settled in my gut. *Don't trust her.*

Her wide, smiling eyes were fixed on the cab of the truck, her entire visage radiating with health and actual fucking emotion. But why wasn't she in a cage like me? Why wasn't she expressionless like everyone else here? And why was she so over-fucking-joyed to see Michio?

My hands clenched against the wire walls of my prison. I needed to give her the benefit of the doubt and hear her out, even as every muscle in my body burned to attack her. A jealous tantrum would not get me out of this.

Our truck parked against the guardrail atop the dam, and she stopped beside the passenger door.

"Elaine!" I rattled the cage. "What happened to you?"

Her throat bobbed with a swallow, but she didn't look at me. Slowly, her smile widened, aimed at Michio.

If he smiled back at her after depriving me of emotional interaction for two weeks, so help me God, I would slice his cheeks from mouth to ears and stretch his smile so wide his jaw would open like a bear trap.

His profile shifted toward her, but the line of his mouth remained flat.

I loosened my grip on the cage. "Elaine? Why won't you

look at me? Did they fuck with your head?"

She turned her neck slightly, her eyes flicking over my battered appearance. My lips were cracked from the wind and sun. My hair stuck to my face in a ratty ball of grease. Sore, oozing blisters covered my swollen knuckles from superficial frostbite. No doubt I looked like shit hit the door twice, yet neither shock nor sympathy touched her bowed lips.

Her lack of concern slipped beneath my bravado, wrapping cold fingers around my heart. I had cured this woman, freed her from her agonizing sickness, and had never asked for gratitude or support in return. We didn't have that kind of relationship, but I needed her now. I spent two weeks emotionally alone and craving human touch, and dammit, I just really needed a hug. But there wasn't a chance in hell it would come from her.

"I'm great." Her smile seemed genuine, especially as she looked back at Michio, further twisting the pang in my chest.

A length of blue cotton wrapped around her slim frame and head, leaving only her doll-like features exposed. I cringed, recalling how the Drone made me wear something similar on Malta. He preferred women covered the way Elaine was now, which suggested he was here, even though I couldn't sense his oily presence.

The thin fabric flowed around the hillock of her abdomen, her hand smoothing over the bump. The gesture crushed me with memories of my own pregnancies, but amid the sorrow was a bright spark of happiness.

Cured women could become pregnant.

How large had the population of cured nymphs in Arkendale grown? How many women were spreading across the country right now, curing and recovering and making babies? Hundreds? Thousands? Certainly more than I'd ever thought possible, which made everything I'd been through so fucking worth it.

No matter what happened to me, whether I escaped this cage or rotted in a grave at the bottom of the canyon, the future of humanity had a fighting chance.

But on the heels of my excitement came the worry of so many unanswered questions. What about the prophecy? Were evolving mutations still a threat? Was the nymph virus still in the air? Would babies inhale it with their first breaths and die?

Before I could stop myself, my thoughts spiraled into memory, until all I could see was Annie and Aaron lying together in bed. Their bodies frail and fighting for life. The light draining from their eyes. Their hearts slowing. Stopping.

The terrible pain in my chest scorched through my body. I braced against it, forcing the burn to harden into frigid steel.

Maybe the virus was long gone. But what if the babies were born as something other than human? Like an evolved species? Something more dangerous than the creatures already prowling the planet?

Michio opened the door and unfolded his tall frame from the truck. Elaine's hands twitched at her sides, as if trying to decide whether she should touch him or not.

My own hands flexed against the cage. She'd always showed interest in him. Clearly, that hadn't changed. Her exuberance in running out here hadn't been one of surprise. She'd been expecting him. Missing him.

My heart thumped heavily. How long had they been together? Had he left me that night in Georgia and run straight to her? *Who was the father of her child?*

I hadn't seen her in what? Four…five months? Michio had been gone at least four months. Given the size of her belly, she was well into her second trimester. The father could've been Tallis, one of the Lakota brothers, or someone she'd fucked on the way here. Or Michio.

Except Michio was infertile. Or a liar. Didn't matter. Maybe he was shooting blanks, maybe his emotions were broken, but none of that meant his dick didn't work. And he'd been painfully clear about wanting a child. Even if that child wasn't biologically his.

The driver stepped out of the truck and strode toward the rear. Michio joined him, and together they began to remove the chains. They weren't unlocking my cage. They were freeing it from the truck.

My stomach hardened as I narrowed my eyes at Elaine. "Why are you running around freely? Where the fuck is the Drone?"

"Evie," she said in a scolding tone. "Don't be rude."

"Rude?" I slammed a hand against the wire wall. "I've been locked in a crate for two fucking weeks, Elaine. We're way past rude. Who's the father?"

Her eyes tracked Michio, clinging to him with way too much desperation. When he didn't return her stare, she lowered it to her sandaled feet. "Tallis or Naalnish. I'm not sure."

Both gone. Their tender smiles and protective demeanors flashed through my head. My hands fell at my sides, and my lungs struggled to fill. Both men would've made incredible fathers.

My thoughts hurdled to my own protectors. "Michio took me from Jesse and Roark. Why would he do that?"

Michio didn't twitch at the sound of his name, his hands moving fluidly as he unlocked the chains.

I dropped my forehead against the side of the cage, promised myself Jesse and Roark were alive and coming for me, and gave Elaine firm eye-contact. "What happened to Michio?"

She lifted her chin, fire flaring in her brown eyes. "It's for his own good."

"*What* is for his own good?"

She rested her hand on her belly. "Us."

"What does that even mean?" I gnashed my teeth, seething the words. "What happened to his mind, Elaine?"

Michio shifted toward the last tether, his movements emotionless, his body a wooden shell. She stepped into his path, halting him with her palms on his bare chest.

I tried to wrangle back my anger, but it powered through, trembling my body and poisoning my blood. "Get the fuck away from him."

The western horizon cast shafts of orange hues across her

complexion, her eyes glowing in the dim light. Tendrils of shiny, black hair fell from her headscarf and framed her face as she stared up at him with doe eyes.

She was all soft curves and slim lines, feminine and well-groomed, so much prettier and healthier than I was. She knew it, too, sliding her body closer to his as she swayed those goddamned hips.

Stretching on tiptoes, she cupped the back of his head, raked her fingers through his hair, and kissed him, long and hard. His mouth remained slack yet pliable as her tongue flicked over his lips, her belly rocking against his unmoving frame.

Rolling heat slammed through my gut, my neck and jaw stiffening with rage.

She was lucky I was caged, because I wanted to kill her. Right fucking now. And maybe him, too, even as I knew he wasn't himself and wouldn't have chosen this. But I was so insanely angry I couldn't think clearly. Why wasn't he fighting whatever was harnessing his mind?

He might not have kissed her back, but he didn't turn away either. He didn't punch her in the ribs. Didn't shove her in a cage. He just stood there, hands at his sides, and let her slobber all over his mouth. What else had he let her do for the past four months?

I felt sick, abandoned, *replaced.* As irrational as those feelings were, they were very, very real. Jealousy surged from the dark, blood-thirsty corner of my soul. I tried to shove it back by reminding myself I'd shared my heart *and* my body with two other men.

But that was different. I hadn't left Michio for Jesse and Roark. He left *me*. I didn't rip him away from his protectors, lock him in a cage, beat the shit out of him, ignore his pleas, and force him to watch an ungrateful asshole lick and suck on my lips.

She stepped back, hand on her belly, rubbing it with a contented sigh.

I lowered to my butt, refusing to give her the screaming,

jealous fit she was likely anticipating. "You're fucked up. You know that, right? Pawing a man like that who clearly doesn't have control of his own mind? Are you raping him, too?"

A muscle jumped in her jaw, her eyes flicking to Michio. "You don't know what you're talking about."

Michio grabbed the back of my cage, and with screech of metal on metal, he dragged it to the tailgate. The steel tray beneath me ground against my aching joints, and I adjusted my weight, balancing on both knees.

Elaine turned, sashaying back to the concrete structure and the elevator waiting within.

On the opposite side of the road, the calm water of the Colorado River stretched along the bluffs of the canyon and pressed against the dam. I didn't know how the intake towers pumped the water and carried it to the other side, but the churn of the turbines rumbled somewhere beneath the elevator, generating hydroelectric power at the bottom of the canyon.

Michio and the blond driver lifted my cage, hefting it up their chests, and carried me toward the elevator shaft. The structure sat at the precipice of the dam, and from my lifted position, I could see around it and down the backside of the dam wall. We must've been a hundred stories in the air.

Vertigo hit me with a wave of light-headed, stomach-dropping dizziness, souring my insides and shivering my skin, and it was in that moment that I knew. *This* was the harbinger. The fated cliff.

Dread swelled in the back of my throat. My hands slicked with sweat.

I contemplated the long fall to termination, or freedom, depending on how I looked at it, and wondered when the omen would shove me over. I could see it coming, felt it thrashing through my veins. "I'm going to die here."

"Don't be so dramatic," Elaine said from the threshold of the elevator.

She stepped to the rear of the lift as Michio and Blondie carried me in. The tray beneath me tilted with the cage, knocking me to my hip and punishing the bruises already there. I gripped the sides to steady myself, but when they dropped me on the floor, my face slammed against the wire wall.

Elaine smirked, her gaze glued to Michio. What a delusional bitch. Michio was clearly not himself, yet she looked at him as if the world's most sought-out bachelor had consciously chosen her to be his queen.

The doors closed with a shuddering sigh, and the elevator descended. The space was large enough to hold twenty people, windowless, and illuminated with electric lights in the ceiling. Humidity clung to my face, and my ears popped as we sank into the canyon.

Elaine tucked her hair beneath the scarf, vanishing the black locks from view. "You'll love it here."

I wasn't going to hold my breath for that.

She drummed her fingers on the ledge of her belly. "The dam is self-sustained. The water generates enough power to serve over a million people. It can run for like ever. Did you know that?"

Did she seriously think I cared?

She chattered on like I wasn't sitting on the floor in a cage and reeking of unwashed misery. "We have plumbing and electricity. Plenty of food and supplies. It's safe and—"

"Are there other women roaming around here like you? Or are they all in cages and chained to posts outside the dam?"

She paled, and her mouth pinched in a line, her eyes darting to Michio.

He stood in front of the other guy in the corner of the lift, staring blankly at the wall. God, it hurt to see him like that. I missed him. Missed him so damned much. How was I going to free him? Words hadn't worked, and considering he didn't trust me enough to carry me into the elevator without the cage, I doubted I'd get a chance to punch some sense into him.

I looked up at Elaine. "Where's the Drone? I assume he's our next stop?"

Her hand twitched against her stomach, her lips rolling between her teeth.

I stiffened. Despite her unkindness, she was still a person, an invaluable woman, who had also once been the sad girl I'd saved in the mountains. What had happened to her? Most often mean people were victims of abuse themselves, right? What if the Drone had harmed her? Broken her?

I climbed to my knees. "Are you afraid of him? Has he hurt you?"

She glanced at Michio, gave a slight shake of her head, and looked away.

The elevator dinged.

I was carried out into a dark, cave-like opening. From there it was a series of metal stairways cut through rock, more elevators, and seemingly miles of inspection tunnels. Interesting how they kept me in the cage. Either they weren't taking chances with me escaping or they thought I was too weak to walk.

Walking would've been a challenge, given the sores on my feet, but my legs were strong enough. I was certain of that.

I continued to badger Elaine with questions, but evidently, she'd left her tongue in the elevator. She trudged along behind us, irritatingly tight-lipped, her gaze glued to the back of Michio's head.

Dim lights illuminated the archway ceilings, the natural rock walls barely wide-enough to accommodate the width of my cage, and the ground slanted at a steep grade. It felt like I was in a maze, crisscrossing the interior of the dam. But my captors didn't falter, turning each corner like synchronized puppets, gliding from tunnel to tunnel with Elaine trailing wordlessly behind.

It was cooler down here, with a slight cavernous breeze. The deeper we went, the staler the air became, tinged with an earthy, musty aroma, like limestone and old cement.

The sound of machines clanged in the distance, growing closer and reverberating through my body like aphid threads. A moment later, the final tunnel dropped us into a wide, brightly lit room.

My ears rang against the loud vibration of generators. Eight of them sat in a line, each the size of a yacht, cylindrical in shape, wrapped in metal sheets, and topped with massive steel rotors.

The room stood four-stories high, the concrete walls stretching to steel rafters. Grated overhangs offered walkways along each level, connected by metal stairs, all of which led to countless doors—presumably rooms—and more tunnels.

And aphids.

I'd thought those vibrations in my stomach had been caused by the whir of the turbine blades, but I saw them now, their spiny bodies creeping behind the generators and prowling along the walkways, their clawed hands gripping the railings.

Pupil-less eyes tracked our approach, their hunger pulsing through me in waves, but they remained at the edges of the room and out of our way. The Drone's pets were always so well-behaved when he was around. Little did he know, I could blow them up with a thought.

"Where is he?" I shouted over the mechanical noise.

Michio and Blondie carried my cage through the open space, and Elaine scurried up beside Michio, her eyes following the nearest aphid about thirty feet away.

I felt him before we reached the next turn, his presence a dark beacon amid the aphid vibrations, chilling and malignant, thrumming with power.

They carried me out of the generator room, through narrow walkways lined with breaker panels, down more tunnels, and stepped into an open doorway.

Elaine held back as they dropped my cage on the concrete floor of an unfurnished room the size of a large office. The blond man slipped out and closed the door. Michio remained beside my metal prison, and Elaine never stepped in. Maybe she couldn't stomach whatever was about to happen to me. Or perhaps she went to ready her bed for Michio. Neither of those thoughts helped my burgeoning dread.

A mattress lay on the floor, the only furnishing, unless I counted the metal shackles drilled into the concrete wall above it. Fucking great. I wasn't sure which was worse, the metal box or the waiting chains.

Seven unarmed men stood in a line, six of them wearing the empty expressions I'd come to expect. The seventh man in the center smiled at me, all fangs and onyx eyes.

The Drone's swarthy face drooped with melted skin, his flamboyant cape wrapping around his shoulders and concealing his wings. "Eveline. How was your trip?"

I had so many questions my throat convulsed with the urgency to spit them all out. But the Drone was all about respect and authority. I'd play along, because eventually he would fill me in on his big plans. He was vainglorious like that.

I leaned against the chain-linked wall and stretched out my legs. "Accommodations were top-notch." I patted the side of the cage. "You really out did yourself this time."

He touched his cheek, fingers slithering over the wax-like flesh. "Only the best for the woman who melted my face."

"How did you survive?"

He unbuttoned the cape at his neck and let it drop to the floor. Dark, twin peaks rose above his head and stretched like webbed arms behind the line of men. Finger bones framed the top of each wing, bending at a joint, similar to the elbow or shoulder. The tip of the joint hooked up and out, shaped like a lethal-looking claw.

The webbed sections were obscure, leathery, and lined with veins, but toward the tops, they hardened, shell-like and smooth. They were a hybrid between a bat and a beetle, which might've been strange on a winged animal. But on a human, wings of any variety were enough to make my breath stick in my throat, which of course was the purpose of his little display. Oh, how he loved to intimidate.

The ghastly things folded back in, and the nearest man grabbed the cape from the floor, spreading the black fabric over the wings and hiding them from view.

The Drone's head tilted. "There was a passageway beneath the overhang. I flew to it, but as you can see, my face skimmed the surface of the lava."

That close to the lava, there shouldn't have been anything left. Apparently, he was able to heal, like Michio, but not completely given the disfigurement. Next time I killed him, I needed to remember to rip off his wings first.

He stepped toward the cage and leaned over it. A slippery toxicity oozed from him, infecting the air, burrowing into my skin, and making a shivery home in my pores.

His eyes took me in from head to toe, his expression unreadable beneath the hideous sag of flesh. "I expected you to return to me in much worse shape, Eveline. You suffered harsh conditions, unable to stand for two weeks, yet here you sit, without any assistance. You're pale but not sick. Weak but still alert. Blistered but not broken. It's as if you've tapped into a hidden, superhuman energy source."

I molded my expression into one of disbelief despite the wild beat of my pulse. He was right. I should've been half-dead. I mean, I was healing like a normal person, slowly and painfully. Blisters covered my knuckles, my muscles and bones ached, and spasms hammered along my spine from slouching for so long. But beneath the bruises and sores, my body hummed with vitality, pushing my mind past the pain and keeping me awake and focused.

What would he do if he knew I was evolving? Hell, what was he going to do regardless? I assumed everyone here had been bitten, and through that venomous bite, brainwashed. Except Elaine. She was just as nasty and ignorant as ever.

I glanced up at Michio and searched his face, finding his gorgeous eyes cold and flat. My heart broke every time I looked at him, my fingernails curling into my palms. "What did you do to him?"

The Drone slid his gaze to Michio, who then stepped around the cage and unlocked the padlock. The door swung open.

That was weird. He'd looked at Michio, and Michio

opened the cage. I was certain something had passed between them. Something I couldn't sense beyond the persistent hum. Whatever it was confirmed my suspicion. The Drone was commanding Michio and all the fanged men the way he silently controlled the aphids.

My stomach turned with worry for Michio. But I held onto hope. If the Drone really was using some kind of coercive persuasion, that meant Michio's mind was still in there, trapped somewhere behind those dead eyes. If I managed to kill the Drone, Michio would be free. Right?

But in a room of fanged men, outnumbered and unarmed, it was difficult to believe the monster, who had survived all my attacks before, would easily fall now. Then again, I stopped subscribing to *easy* a long time ago.

"Go ahead." The Drone made a shooing motion. "Come on out."

Was it a test to see how much strength I had? I could crawl, but could I walk? I shouldn't be able to, yet I felt hyped-up, bursting with energy. I bet I could run.

I took my time crawling out, deliberately dragging my legs behind me and contorting my face in pain. Some of it was real as joints I hadn't used in two weeks protested against the effort to support my weight. The rest I drew out, rising to my knees, falling on my ass, and whimpering before trying again.

Had I emerged without an audience, I would've staggered to my wobbly feet by now. Instead, I climbed up the outside of the cage and moved to drop again.

Michio's arm swung out, and the back of his hand crashed against my face.

I slammed against the floor on my back, biting my lip against the impact, my hands flying up to clutch my aching cheekbone. A backhanded hit to the face stung like a son of a bitch, but a hit from Michio struck deep, far beneath the surface of tissue and bone. I felt it like a blade through the heart.

I glared through blurred vision at the Drone. "Why?"

But I knew why. He was displeased with my performance

and what better way to hurt me than through the fist of the man I loved?

Crawling to Michio's boots, I gripped his legs and lifted my gaze. "I know you're in there, trapped and fighting. You're not alone, Michio. I won't give up on you."

He stared at the wall across the room, still as a statue, his nonresponse constricting my chest.

The Drone circled the cage, hand in the pocket of his black slacks, and stopped beside Michio. "You've gone soft, Eveline. And so has Dr. Nealy." He reached over and palmed Michio's groin, vile fingers stroking and squeezing. "But Elaine's been working on his softness. She's quite smitten."

He was baiting me, but I couldn't control the burning sensation in my stomach or the rash decision to jolt to my feet. I shot to my full height, swaying on jelly legs, and smacked the Drone's hand away from Michio's cock. He let me, grinning as he stepped back, evidently thrilled I'd proved his theory that I held some sort of inhuman energy.

I stood on shaky yet dependable legs. "Why am I here? What do you want?"

"I want you showered and dressed to my specifications."

I set my jaw and planted my feet in a wide stance. "I won't fight you if you release Michio from whatever spell you've put him under."

He tsked. "No, Eveline. You'll cooperate because you want to know what happened to your Lakota friends in the mountains. You want to know what I'm doing with the women outside of the gates, and what will become of Elaine's child now that Michio's bitten her."

My skin tightened, and my stomach heaved, burning a fiery trail of acid through my throat.

He studied his razor-sharp nails, his tone callously conversational. "You're going to do as I say, because if you don't, Dr. Nealy will kill your lovers, *after* I've sucked every drop of power from your veins."

FORTY-SIX

I rubbed my upper arms, my mouth dry and throat tight. Dammit, the Drone was right about my thirst for answers. By threatening Jesse and Roark, he'd confirmed they were alive and knew where they were or how to find them.

And if Michio had bitten Elaine, where were her fangs? Maybe they were retracted, but why weren't her eyes glazed over like the others?

Had he given her a seductive bite? I clenched my fists. Did he fuck her while he sank his fangs into her?

At my side, Michio stared off into the distance, his eyes as unmoving and stiff as his posture. For all I knew, he was thrashing and screaming inside his head, perpetually isolated, unable to communicate in any way.

Maybe he'd left me in Georgia *because* of the bite, because he hadn't been able to resist the pull of the Drone. But there had to be a limit to the Drone's persuasion, a boundary he couldn't force Michio to cross. And Michio was stronger than most people. Even under the influence of the Drone, would he actually try to kill Jesse and Roark?

Michio knew I would survive the physical beatings, but if he retained any memories or feelings at all, he also knew my guardians' deaths would destroy me. He would fight that with every ounce of strength he had, and I intended to fight right alongside him. Not with muscle and weaponry. Neither of those worked against the Drone in the past. Instead, I needed to understand and outsmart the monster who'd taken Michio's mind.

I stood beneath the press of his black gaze, my skin itching to draw away from the thick, malicious aura that slithered from him. The bottomless holes of his eyes, the gruesome hang of flesh that comprised his expression, the arrogant way he looked down his bubbled nose at me, all of it effective in making me feel smaller, weaker. But I refused to cringe.

Fuck, I had so many questions I trembled with the need to puke them all over his polished shoes. But I didn't want to hear his litany of carefully filtered answers. I needed to see beneath the caviler facade. To do that, I needed to surprise him.

"Are you happy?" I gestured around the room, indicating the audience of vacant men. "With them, with whatever your plan is, does all this make you genuinely happy?"

His gaze reached deep into mine, prying and scouring, before turning inward, thoughtful, his hand lifting to touch the hanging flab of his cheek. "True happiness is a destination, is it not? I still have more to accomplish. Missteps to correct. But that's where you come in."

I wasn't sure what to make of that response, but I reminded myself that his pretentiousness served to hide his weaknesses.

"The shower. Come." The Drone strode out.

Michio and the six other men in the room turned as one toward the doorway and formed a horseshoe at my back, prepared to usher me using whatever force necessary.

Their auras hummed beneath my skin, Michio's included, but I couldn't discern him from the others, which terrified me. How different was he from these mindless droids? How much of him remained, locked up inside that head of his?

I followed the Drone into the hall and looked left and right. I could run. Could count exactly how many steps would take me to the next turn and the turn after that. I could blow up every aphid in the dam and momentarily distract the Drone. I could find a loose pipe, a hammer, something hard and lethal to swing at the men who tried to catch me. I knew how much force it would take to smash the skull and terminate the brain. I knew it would take me about thirty minutes to climb the tunnels and sprint away from the dam. And I knew if I escaped, if I ran away like a scared little girl, I would be leaving Michio behind and sentencing Jesse and Roark to death.

With a deep breath, I jogged after the Drone and caught up to his side, the muscles in my legs and back complaining with each step. "You said you could suck my power. How? With a fang in my vein? Or some sort of psychic mind tap?"

If he could truly drain my abilities, why hadn't he done it already?

The Drone strode beside me, hands in his pockets, watching me out of the corner of his droopy eye. A slow smile scrunched the folds of skin, and his tongue curled around one fang, answering my question on *how*.

My stomach twisted and tumbled.

Three of the men from the room slipped ahead of us. The other three remained at my back, while Michio stepped to my side, caging me between him and the Drone. Together, the nine of us marched beneath the yellow glow of the overhead bulbs, three rows of three, me in the center.

Subway tiles covered the floors, walls, and ceilings, and more tiled passageways veered off at every turn. We passed open doors that gave way to concrete rooms filled with cots and bunk beds. No other furniture. No personal belongings, memorabilia, or framed photographs. No women. No people.

I stared at Michio's hand, where it hung at his side so close to mine. If I reached for it and laced our fingers together, would that make me as desperate as Elaine? What if he jerked his hand away? I wasn't sure I could take much more rejection.

Whoever was walking beside me, this zombie-like creature wearing Michio's skin, wasn't the man who had revolted against the Drone in Malta, who rejected Elaine's affections in the mountains, and who loved me so much he couldn't be near me without touching me in some way.

Positioning me between himself and the enemy, not linking our hands, not kissing me, refusing to even look at me, all of it went against every instinct he had.

I gripped his hand, his skin cold, and his bones unresponsive between my fingers. When he didn't pull away, I squeezed tighter, my voice cracking as I glanced up at the Drone. "You're controlling his mind, aren't you? And the others, too? But not Elaine?"

The three men ahead of us turned into a doorway, and the Drone paused at the entrance, gesturing me to follow inside.

How many men could the Drone command? How immense was his power to be able to control the minuscule actions of so many?

Still holding Michio's hand, I shuffled into a large tiled bathroom and hoped the Drone would follow, only because he was the only one here who seemed capable of talking.

Four toilets lined the back wall, the privacy stalls removed, leaving behind broken bolts and faded marks on the floor. Small sinks hung beneath mirrors on the left, and a shower head dangled from one of the pipes in the center of the ceiling. The chrome finish was shinier than the other fixtures, suggesting it had been recently attached.

Michio pulled away from my hand to reach up and twist two small wheel valves on the overhead pipe. The steel joints and fastenings groaned, and with a sputter, water burst from the fixture and sprayed the drain in the floor.

The sound of running water triggered a forceful pressure in my bladder. I pointed at the toilet and raised a brow at the Drone.

When he nodded, I plodded across the room, unzipping my jacket and dropping the smelly thing on the floor. The white tank top beneath was now stained yellowish-brown with sweat and dust. Ugh. I dragged the leather pants down my sore hips and sat on the nearest toilet.

While seated, I unlaced my boots and removed the rest of my clothes. The absence of talking in the crowded room made the stream of my pee sound louder than it should've been.

Three of the men stood in the hallway, barricading the

door. The other three took posts around the bathroom, and Michio remained at the center, staring at exactly nothing and seemingly oblivious to the fall of water drenching his boots and black fatigues.

I used toilet paper, flushed, and in five steps, stood nude beneath the warm cascade of the shower. Holy shit, that felt incredible. I was hyper-aware of every drop that hit my matted hair, each trickle across my scalp, and every tingling river that coursed between the valley of my breasts, zigzagging down my torso and sluicing around my legs.

The only man in the room capable of expression was difficult to read thanks to the disfigurement of his face. But as he scrutinized my nudity, it wasn't with lust. I needed a dick and a branch on his family tree, like his brother, to earn a look like that from him.

Instead, he pressed a hand against his stomach and stared at me with…*pity*? "You look unwell."

I glanced down the length of my body. Yellow and purple bruises blotted my torso from Michio's fists. My hipbones protruded disgustingly against my pallid skin, and blisters covered my feet from two weeks in damp boots. The Drone had already said he expected me to arrive in bad shape, so what was with the comment? Did he actually feel bad?

Oh, the irony in that was so painfully ridiculous I actually smiled, albeit sadly. I held onto the edges of that smile as I let the water smother my face. It felt euphoric, purifying, like an emotional shedding of torment. I could actually feel two weeks of grime sloughing off my body and swirling down the drain.

I wanted to get lost beneath the cathartic sensations, but I had a mouthful of questions and the Drone's attention. "What happened to Michio? Are you controlling his mind?"

"No, not his *mind*." The Drone stepped behind Michio and placed a hand on his shoulder. "I control his body, or technically speaking, I command the motor cortex of his brain and all the peripheral nerves attached to it."

Adrenaline charged through my blood, ramping my pulse. I

jerked my head out of the spray and faced him. "The motor cortex? What does that mean? That you control his actions? But he can still think and feel on his own?"

My gaze traveled over Michio's frozen stance and locked on his dull eyes. Was he trapped inside his body, silently screaming for me to help him? If the Drone could do that, could the motherfucker stop the beat of his heart with a thought? Or simply make his lungs quit working? A heavy, horrified feeling sank into my stomach.

The Drone caressed a hand over the cropped hair on Michio's head. "The motor area only controls the *voluntary* muscles. I haven't been able to overpower the brainstem and other lobes of Dr. Nealy's brain."

My heart hammered so fast I struggled to focus on what that implied. "The other lobes? The parts that regulate breathing, heart rate, consciousness, language…reflexes?"

Reflexes were involuntary. If that was the case, Michio would be able to control the functions that kept him alive, right?

I reached up and cupped Michio's face with both hands. "Can you hear me? See me? Michio, please look at me."

"He perceives everything, Eveline, but he can't look at you unless I allow it. He blinks on his own. His lungs work because they have to. His heart will flex and contract until it no longer can. But I control the voluntary muscles, the actions that require conscious thought."

Beneath my hands, Michio's face contorted into a vicious scowl. His lips drew back, his fangs jutted out, and his breath hissed against my face.

I yanked my hands away and stumbled back. I couldn't help it, even though I knew the Drone mentally molded Michio's expression. I'd never seen him look so terrifying. "This is how you control them? You bite them, and it gives you access to their brains?"

"Yes and no." The Drone stepped away, kicking drops off his shiny black shoes and shunning the water like an aphid. "Wash your hair."

What would happen if I splashed him? His hands and face were the only parts of him exposed. Maybe his skin would bubble and boil, but was it worth his wrath and the certain end of this conversation?

My head swam as I looked around for soap, willing to do anything to keep him talking.

Michio's expression returned to vacancy, his hand reaching down to grab a bottle from a bucket against the wall. Mechanically, he squeezed a dollop of shampoo on my head. I rubbed it in with shaking fingers, knowing the Drone had commanded every movement Michio just made—*every movement he'd made since he'd snatched me in Missouri.*

None of the beatings had been initiated by Michio. If he was consciously aware… Oh God, he would've watched with horror every time his fist reared back, would've felt each time my body gave and buckled beneath his strikes. It would destroy him.

I looked at the Drone with disbelief. "Your control must be limited by distance. And how many men can you realistically direct at one time?"

"There is no limit." He licked his shriveled lips. "When a man is bitten, it doesn't matter if he's on the other side of the planet. The venom hits his brain, and it instantly and permanently belongs to me."

I struggled to digest that. "There's no way you can coordinate all of the movements of that many men."

There would've been long periods where most of them just stood around, as if in sleep mode.

"I give them a series of basic commands, like a computer programming language, if you will. They can do what they want as long as they don't deviate from the orders I set in their brains."

Shit. These men were like robotic extensions of his body. He didn't have to ever leave here. Didn't even have to wipe his own ass, if he didn't want to. I felt sick.

"If anything happens to me, the programming lives on." The Drone paced around me, avoiding the spray of water, his hands folded beneath the cape on his back. "I've programmed the *entire* brain of every man who's contracted my venom through a bite. That is, every man but Dr. Nealy."

A dark-haired man with a snake tattooed on his neck stepped away from the wall. Without warning, he began to choke, his mouth gaping as if the air had been vacuumed from his lungs.

I wrapped my arms around my waist, my breaths escaping in spurts. "You're strangling him?"

The man's body held completely still, hands at his sides, as his face turned purple and blood vessels popped in his eyes.

"I stopped his lungs." The Drone cocked his head, calmly studying the stages of suffocation.

Oh God. Did I want this stranger to die? Was he a good man who had been brainwashed? Or an inherently evil man who willingly signed up to kill for the Drone?

A moment later, the man gasped and stepped back to the wall like nothing had happened.

I breathed a sigh of relief. "How do you recruit them?"

The Drone resumed his circuit around me, the cloying scent of his insanity burning my nose. "I have hundreds of spiders across the country—"

"Spiders? That's what you call the men who are bitten?" I scanned Michio's face, stark in its blankness, but still gorgeous in his fearlessness. He was *not* a fucking spider.

"Yes. My spiders are out there right now, offering superhuman abilities—speed, healing, strength—in exchange for servitude. Dr. Nealy aside, no man is forced to join me."

"They join out of greed."

His eyes darkened. "I call it ambition."

"Do they understand the level of fanaticism they're signing up for?"

The air writhed around him, sparking with his anger. "They agree to *support* my efforts in Allah's name."

"Okaaaay." I realized I was poking an unhinged monster, but I doubted anyone had ever sat down with him and made him question his delusions. "You're taking away their freewill.

That kind of defeats the power of faith."

"I'm removing their clumsy reasoning and replacing it with *true knowledge*." He met my eyes. "I don't know why the venom acts as a tether to mental processing or how I've gained access to reprogram their frontal lobes. I'm a biochemist not a neuroscientist. But the ability works in my favor." His fanged smile was smug and sharp. "When I die, they will continue to carry out Allah's will."

Holy shit, that was way more fucked-up than I'd imagined.

I absently rinsed out the shampoo, my voice quiet, reedy. "What is Allah's will?"

"It's really very simple, Eveline. I'm creating a planet free of susceptibility, temptation, and weakness, one that will bring mankind into contact with Allah and fulfill His commandment in making *La illaha ilallah* the only law of the world."

Whatever that meant. It didn't matter whether or not I understood his religion. In his mind, he was the champion of his faith, striving for his version of a better world, just like everyone else. But unlike my guardians, who aspired to protect and free mankind, the Drone embraced violence and repression as a means to improve humanity. However deeply skewed that was, he believed his species of altered brains would bring him closer to feeling complete.

"But you said Michio was exempt?" My gaze roamed over Michio's face. "You haven't altered *his* frontal lobe?"

"I can't." The Drone's eyes hardened amid the soft droop of his facial features. "Just like I can't access the brain of a bitten woman. Why do you think that is?"

I massaged my temples, my head pounding. He could only control the motor area of Michio's brain and none of a woman's? What did they have in common?

Me?

Michio had never technically bitten me, never injected me with venom. His fangs had grazed my skin, but he hadn't *drank* my blood. No, wait, that wasn't true. He'd told me in Georgia he'd been consuming the blood leftover in my transfusion vials. So, yeah, my blood *had* entered his body.

And every cured woman carried my plasma in her veins.

I gripped my throat. "My blood."

"That's right. Your blood. The potency of the venom is the same whether the bite comes from me or my spiders. I rarely sink my fangs into a vein anymore. I don't get much pleasure from it. But for you, I will make an exception. Now ask me why I haven't bitten you yet."

My voice quivered. "Why haven't you bitten me?"

He stopped behind me and dragged his despicable talons along my hips. The spray of water peppered his fingers, his skin sizzling beneath the droplets. Bubbled sores formed and disappeared just as quickly. He was allergic to water and able to heal the reaction.

The stale scent of his breath trickled over my shoulder, his nails on my hips pulling me away from the stream. "The venom from the bite makes both men and women *infertile,* my dear. If I bit you now..."

"I wouldn't be able to conceive," I said, numbly.

"Very good."

The words he'd said when he visited me in a dark dream brushed the back of my mind. *You shall become my queen. Together we will populate the world with Allah's chosen.*

I wrestled with my lungs, begging them to sound quieter. "Why are you sinking your fangs into the world, knowing they won't be able to reproduce?"

He dragged his sharp teeth across my shoulder, instigating a belligerent shudder through my body. "I have a supply of unbitten men who impregnate the women. After the women conceive, they're bitten."

My breath burst in and out as I pulled away from his clutches, my voice shrill. "What does the venom do to the pregnant women? The babies?"

Did he intend to impregnate me by one of his non-spider men? Then bite me?

Suddenly, I felt unnervingly vulnerable. I needed clothes, protection, something. A towel and a pile of blue cotton sat on one of the sinks, so I darted for them, drying quickly.

Then I wrapped the full-body-length semicircle of cotton—similar to Elaine's coverings—around my body and neck. Behind me, the water shut off.

The Drone watched me with pleasure as I covered my body. "Every woman alive today carries traces of your blood, which acts as a vaccine against the venom. Women don't acquire the superhuman benefits of the bite. They can't bite others because they don't have fangs. And unfortunately, they are able to block my attempts to alter their minds."

Women like Elaine. So the only effect the venom had on women was infertility. But these were pregnant women.

I covered my mouth. "You get them pregnant. Then you inject them with the venom. And the babies…" I dropped my hand. "What happens to the babies?"

"When the women are bitten, their fetuses become hybrids. The venom in the mother gives me access to the entire unborn brain as it develops in the womb. This allows me to mold their minds before they're born, whether they are male or female. And unlike other animal hybrids, they will be fertile."

His plans for propagating a new race seemed ill-devised if every cured woman could only conceive one child.

"How do you know? Have any been born yet?"

"No." He rubbed the scarred flesh on his chin. "Did you know I can read Dr. Nealy's thoughts?"

The random change of topic had my head kicking back. "How can you read his thoughts? What thoughts?"

He lifted a shoulder, his gnarled mouth crooking up in a sinister smile. "I know everything he knows."

My breath caught. "That's how you found my house." Through countless conversations with Michio, I'd explained every detail of my home to him. The location, the pool, the Japanese Maple out front. "And the Lakota… That's how you knew where they were." My heart squeezed painfully. "Why did you kill them?"

He sighed. "You won't appreciate my methods unless I start at the beginning." He strode to the door, waving at me to follow.

I drew a deep breath and shuffled after him, my legs kicking at the wrap of fabric. His six *spiders* and Michio formed their three rows of three around me, and we headed back the direction we'd come, presumably to the room with the shackles.

The Drone's gaze traced the tiles of the corridor as he set the pace, his long-legged strides eating up the floor beside me. "When I visited you in Georgia, I could've taken you then. I'd planned to, in fact, but I learned a number of startling things that night. Things that altered my entire campaign."

I dug through my memories, trying to figure out what he was talking about, and came up blank.

He slid a hand into his pocket. "I discovered I could read Dr. Nealy's thoughts that night. You see, I hadn't bitten anyone who had lived long enough to demonstrate the effects. I saw him move and heal like me, and through his thoughts, I learned about Elaine in the mountains and the woman you'd cured right there in Georgia. But the most enlightening bit of knowledge I gleaned that night pertained to the prophecy."

The march of boots around me punctuated the heavy beat of my heart. Why the hell did he care about the prophecy?

"It's just a hokey premonition. Doesn't mean anything." The lie rolled smoothly off my tongue, but I couldn't stop the trembling in my hands.

Beside me, Michio showed no outward signs of listening, but the Drone had said he could perceive everything. Was he moaning and screaming and mentally clawing inside his skin? My chest collapsed, aching for him.

Our group turned and entered the room with the shackles and mattress. The cage had been removed, and a stool sat in its place. The last man in shut the door behind us.

I did *not* want to be confined again, but if I fought my way out, I knew I would be fighting Michio's possessed body.

I placed a hand on his forearm, seeking solace in the sinewy muscle and familiar olive skin. Maybe it comforted him, too, and for a fleeting moment, I imagined he was fully aware and in control, poised to stand by me, ready to protect me.

"I'll give you two options." The Drone lowered to the stool and braced his elbows on his thighs. "You can willingly lie on that mattress and lock yourself in. Or I can use Michio's body to force you into the restraints. His fists will connect with your face. His boots will bruise your ribs. His grip will tear your skin. It will hurt you, but I assure you, it will hurt *him* far worse."

Anger surged through me, shredding my throat and rushing out in unfiltered, furious words. "You've talked a lot of shit, goddammit! But as far as I can see, Michio is gone. Gone! Where the fuck is he? Because when I look in his eyes and—" I choked, reaching up to cup Michio's face then dropping my hands and turning away, my chest heaving. "I can't see him. Not a flicker or a glimpse of the man he was. He's not fucking in there!"

Silence stuffed the room, pressing against my chest. It was a hopeless situation, one that ended with me in chains and whatever the Drone had planned next. Rape? Pregnancy? A baby with fangs? I didn't know because we hadn't finished the conversation.

"I'm here, Nannakola."

The voice floated over my shoulder, lifting the hairs on my arms. *Michio's* voice.

I spun toward him, and his expression…oh my God, his expression was anguish creased with fury, deep and open, grooved with heartache and glowing red with murder.

"Michio?" My heart banged wildly as I reached for him, my hand hovering beside his cheek, so close I felt the heat radiating from his skin.

His arms hung at his sides, his body relaxed. His stoic posture was such a contradiction to the thunderstorm contorting his face my brain struggled to comprehend the paradox.

"I've given him control over his facial muscles." The Drone said, matter-of-factly. "And now his voice."

"I'm so sorry." Michio's face twisted in horror, his deep

timbre cracking with agony. "Oh Evie, I'm so fucking sorry. Sosorrysosorry. I can't…I can't— Fuck! I'm going to kill—"

His mouth slackened, and his expression emptied.

FORTY-SEVEN

"Noooo!" My heart pumped frantically as I launched at Michio and hugged his torso. "Bring him back. Let me see him again!"

Michio's body didn't respond, his arms dangling in my embrace.

A few feet away, the Drone remained perched on the stool, watching us with his head slightly tilted, his eyes unfocused, and a smirk on his melted mouth. Fuck him.

I reached up, pulled Michio's face to mine, and stared into his flat eyes. "God, Michio, I missed you so much." I peppered desperate kisses across his blank face and wrapped my arms around his neck, touching our foreheads together. "I love you. I'm here. Right here. We're together, okay? This isn't your fault. None of it. Dammit, I know you can hear me. Just…just don't give up."

He didn't move beneath my touch, didn't meet my eyes. But he was in there, locked behind that terrible shell of an expression. Sweet fucking hell, he was still here.

A surge of raw anger made its way along my limbs, curling my fingers against his shoulders. We would get past this, starting with severing the Drone's head. Or wrenching off his arm and stabbing him in the eye with it. If his death didn't release the minds of his spiders, we would kill them, too, then save the women outside the gate. Then side by side, we would find Jesse and Roark.

I replayed the violent fantasy of our escape over and over until all I saw was a red haze of vengeance. My hands shook as

I slid down Michio's chest and turned toward the Drone, my gaze hitting my target like a sharp, flinging blade.

Operating purely on instinct and rage, I didn't think as I flung toward him, fingernails aimed for his shriveled face with every intention of clawing out his eyes and tearing the flesh from his skull.

An arm caught me around the waist, halting my momentum mid-air, and wrenched me backward before I made contact with that vile face. I choked, losing the wind in my lungs as strong hands blurrily spun me around. Everything happened so fast, my fists swinging and dodging, my heart pumping rapidly, and the room whipping around me.

All of it came to a stop as Michio's knuckles slammed into my jaw. Fiery pain jarred across my face, and star bursts dotted my vision as I landed on my back on the mattress.

Pinning me with a knee on my chest, Michio reared back to hit me again.

"Wait!" I panted, my face throbbing as my gaze locked on the Drone. "I'll cooperate. Don't make him hit me again."

Michio rose in a blink of fluid motion and stood at the foot of the mattress. It killed me to think about the torment he must've felt watching his own fist connect with my face.

I stared up at the glassy eyes that couldn't meet mine and said, softly, "I'm so sorry, Michio. I won't make you do that again."

With numb movements, I adjusted the wrap of fabric to cover my legs and torso. Then I collected the restraints near the wall and snapped the steel shackles around my wrists, each one locking with the sound of defeat.

The four-foot long chains gave me enough room to lie down or stand. Or to strangle the Drone if he came close enough.

But he wasn't stupid. His guards didn't carry weapons near me for the same reason he remained on the stool and out of reach.

"I'm restrained now. Can't go anywhere." Lying on my back and braced on my elbows, I jerked each arm against the chains to punctuate my point. "Let Michio talk. Give him control of his face or his voice again. Give him *something.*"

The Drone studied Michio, tapping his fingers together between his knees. "I can't do that. He's very…unhappy at the moment."

Michio was probably detonating inside, which was painful to accept, and so fucking confusing, given the bland look on his model-perfect face.

Even as I despised the Drone for breaching Michio's privacy, I had to know. "What is he thinking?"

A gruesome smirk rose amid the melted skin of the Drone's visage. "He's imagining all the ways he's going to kill me. It's sadly barbaric." Lines formed across his mutilated brow. "And of course, I can hear his pathetic lamentations to hold you, to give you comfort. I'm afraid you've ruined him."

"Let him hold me." My voice was urgent, pleading. "What would happen? If anything, it'll calm both of us down."

Slowly, the Drone straightened on the stool and propped an ankle over a knee. "Very well."

Michio crumpled to his knees and toppled over me. His expression didn't change, but the muscles in his biceps flexed as he woodenly caught his weight, hooked his arms around me, and pulled me into the cage of his body.

His hand cupped the back of my head, and it was with that specific gesture that I finally felt him. *His* touch. Our bond. God, I hadn't realized how much we needed that. It was such a small mercy that grip on my head, yet it meant everything.

I pressed a kiss to his sternum and found myself hurdling through an unexpected stream of visions. I imagined massaging his back after he'd spent a long day of providing medical care for a civilized world. In the next image, I made dinner—lasagna and bread sticks—of which Roark appreciated the most. Then I washed Jesse's hair while we soaked in a tub. So fucking domesticated, yet there it was, filling my chest with longing.

I tried to hold on to it, to keep my guardians with me, but as Michio rolled us to our sides, chest to chest, I felt the essence that made him who he was vanish from his touch.

His arms locked into place around me like insentient steel bars, his breathing tempered into inhuman steadiness, and his fingers lay lifeless against my back. His muscles held me, but *he* no longer animated the movements.

The chains clanked as I trailed a finger down his arm, and goosebumps cropped up along his skin. Goosebumps! Oh God, Michio could feel me.

I settled against his chest, melting against the familiar lines and ridges of his body, and reached deep with my mind, seeking the man that hummed beneath my skin.

My fingers lingered on the crook of his elbow then traced the bulge of his bicep. With each caress, I showed him how much I missed him, that I'd been incomplete without him, and that I knew he was with me, even if he couldn't show me.

For too long, I'd carried a deep empty space in my heart. He was the part that had been missing, and now that I'd found him, the other two-thirds of my heart were missing.

I glared at the man responsible. "Where are Jesse and Roark?"

The Drone shrugged. "Where you left them. I pulled the army out of Missouri after Dr. Nealy secured you."

My pulse raced with hope. He'd already said he would have them killed if I didn't cooperate, which was why he'd kept them alive.

"They won't find you." He rubbed at a water spot on his patent leather shoe then lowered his foot to the floor. "You were transported in a vehicle. There are no tracks. Nothing to lead them here. But if I need to motivate you, I have spiders and aphids covering every mile of the continent. I can find your guardians within hours. Would you like that?"

I didn't bother responding. I suspected he'd burned my house so that I wouldn't have anything to cling to, but it was just a house. My guardians were my home.

Jesse and Roark must've been out of their minds with worry. No doubt they were trying to find me this very minute, but how? Would they look for witnesses? Men we'd passed on the way here?

The nymphs. My heart skipped. The nymphs would travel in from every direction, attracted to the women outside the dam. If Jesse and Roark followed them, they would find me. It was scary to hope, but it fluttered through every cell of my body, lifting me, giving me confidence. I just needed to delay the Drone's plans for me, whatever those plans were, until Jesse and Roark arrived.

I met his eyes, the visual contact so unnerving I ached to look away, but I held firm. "You said I wouldn't appreciate your methods unless you explained it from the beginning."

"Yes." He leaned forward and rested an arm on his knee. "The prophecy, the evolving species, the powerful child, all of it changed the course of my plans."

The evolving species troubled me the most because I couldn't make sense of its meaning. I tried to recall the conversation I'd had with Jesse the night he told me about the prophecy. *The creatures would evolve…you won't be able to save future generations from them…but our daughter can…without her, there will be no human race.*

My fingers moved restlessly over Michio's arm. "Surely you already knew the aphids were evolving?"

"The aphids have nothing to do with the prophecy. Dr. Nealy believes…" The Drone passed a glance at Michio. "Yes, he still believes the prediction refers to the evolution of my newest creation."

"The spiders?"

"The hybrid spiders currently being conceived."

My stomach roiled with lava and acid. "You still haven't explained why you're so certain your hybrids will be fertile."

He grinned. "Why would the world need a powerful child to save it from a species that couldn't reproduce?"

Shit, he was right. Jesse assumed the predicted threat was aphids because they didn't age or starve. But that was before he knew I could kill them with a thought. And a single generation of spider hybrids wasn't enough to threaten the future of mankind. But if they could reproduce, would they take over the planet and devour what was left of the human race?

I swallowed. "Why do you have so much faith in this prophecy?"

"Because Dr. Nealy does. As much as he continually disappoints me, his conclusions are never wrong."

I tightened my arms around Michio, knowing he could hear this conversation and hating that he couldn't participate. "I don't understand what you're trying to achieve. You created nymphs. Now you're curing them to create a new species? Was the nymph virus one of the missteps you referred to?"

He touched his face, something he did often. I supposed his fall into the lava river would be considered a misstep.

"As you witnessed on Malta, the nymphs cannot successfully reproduce. But the prophecy assures me the hybrids will flourish. You see, missteps and flaws are necessary to learning."

Ugh. Was I wasting my time trying to reason with him? "Sometimes our flaws are the very things holding us back from true happiness. They can warp our views and limit our understanding. They make us stubborn and scared. You must know that? And you're smart enough to know that the prophecy is against *you*."

The Drone stared at the floor, such an uncharacteristic mannerism. Was I getting through to him?

He shifted his pensive gaze to me. "What are your flaws and warped views, Eveline?"

Since he had access to Michio's thoughts, he already knew every damned one of my insecurities and weaknesses, the most detrimental being my failure to fulfill the prophecy.

If I'd slept with Jesse two years ago, if I'd been more convincing about my feelings for him and removed the IUD, the prophesied child would've already been born. I wouldn't be here, probably wouldn't have met Roark and Michio, and wouldn't have cured the nymphs. But Jesse would've been raising our child right now as a weapon against the Drone. A child that could've cured as well as saved humanity.

It was a heaping pile of what-ifs, and none of them felt *right,* but they were a helluva lot more optimistic than what Michio and I faced in this room.

My chest squeezed, aching to talk about it. What kind of desperate loser voiced her concerns to a genocidal nut-job? Well, I wasn't that desperate.

"You don't have to tell me, Eveline. Dr. Nealy just answered it in his head." He smiled, sickeningly. "Let's see…you believe your biggest flaw is your refusal to get pregnant. You can't stomach the thought of bringing a child into this world. And you've been hiding behind that excuse as a way to ignore an impossible decision. The prophecy predicts your death, which means this child dooms your guardians to a life without you. But by not having the child, you've doomed the human race to extinction." He leaned back, folded his hands on his lap. "How'd I do?"

Michio knew me better than I knew myself. And now the Drone did, too. I expected exactly zero sympathy from him. He initiated the extinction of humanity and didn't give two shits about my guardians.

He stared at Michio's slack face. "Dr. Nealy is conflicted about this, as well. But I have a solution for both of you."

Oh, fuck. I was just bursting with high hopes.

He brushed the fabric on his thigh, watching his hand straighten invisible wrinkles. "I find no pleasure in the death of anyone."

Seriously? He wanted to offer a solution and began with *that*?

He lifted his gaze to mine. "You know as well as I do, nonviolence doesn't stand a chance against its adversaries. Pain and death will always sit at the heart of peace. And I want peace, Eveline, which is something that would've never been achieved among humans. A new species was necessary in removing man's imperfections."

"You're creating a *mindless* species. That in itself is an

imperfection. You're trying to play God, except God gave his creations freewill."

He compressed his lips then rubbed them with a talon-tipped finger. "I'm not *playing* anything. I'm simply choosing not to turn my cheek. It would've been a morally grave action to allow humanity to continue as it was. You said it yourself. Human flaws are the very things holding mankind back from happiness."

Oh, good grief. "A sane person would try to teach, convert, heal, or reform flaws *not* wipe the entire flawed species off the planet. Why did you kill the Lakota? They were as close to peaceful and flawless as humanly possible."

"I needed a cured woman. After scraping Dr. Nealy's mind, I chose Elaine over the one you found in Georgia because she was healthier. When I collected her, your friends fought to keep her. I did not wish to kill them, but they were in the way."

My throat tightened painfully. "You're a monster."

"I accepted the path Allah chose for me and am fully prepared to bear the responsibility of it."

I pulled Michio closer to me, knowing my next question would trouble him. "Why didn't you just take me the night you found me, instead of Elaine?"

Then the Lakota would still be alive.

"I wasn't ready for you, Eveline. I didn't have an army, didn't have a place to secure you, and I'd only just learned about the venom's effect on the brain. And Elaine...well, she's much easier to manipulate than you."

"Is that why she roams freely around here?" I stroked my thumb in slow circles against Michio's arm. "What did you do? Promise her Michio in exchange for her obedience?"

He nodded, smiling his lava-licked smile.

"You made Michio follow you that night, didn't you?"

"Yes. I controlled him through the power of suggestion. He didn't know it was happening until he found me in the mountains with your dead friends."

I glared at him with *Fuck you* eyes. *Fuck you* for killing the Lakota. *Fuck you* for forcing Michio and me to come here. *Fuck you* for putting a thousand miles between us and Jesse and Roark. And *fuck you* for curing nymphs by hanging women on posts.

"I suppose I should thank you for not killing my dog."

The skin where his eyebrows should've been dug together. "Dog?"

Weird. Darwin must've left the mountains for no other reason than because he missed me. My stomach sank as I pictured him with Jesse and Roark. Where were they? How long would it take for them to arrive?

I buried those questions before they consumed me. "Where are all the women you've cured? Are they caged beneath the dam in a dirty dungeon? Please tell me you've outgrown that nasty habit."

He laughed, a hellish sound of nightmares. "You and Elaine are the only women behind the gates of the dam. I have breeding facilities all over the country. The women up top were only here long enough to see you arrive. They've since been moved back to their nests."

I stopped breathing. Breeding facilities? Nests? The women weren't here? Oh my God, they weren't here. That meant the nymphs would stop coming. Jesse and Roark *wouldn't be coming.*

It felt like he'd just broken apart my chest, ripped out my hope, and replaced it with wretched devastation. How would I free Michio? How would I get his mind back? Locked in his paralyzed arms, I struggled to breathe, to hold myself together, as the Drone rambled on.

"Women are the blood of your blood, Eveline. With the exception of a few like Elaine, the majority have your…strong-willed traits. It makes it difficult to manage them. So I pulled a representative from each hive to witness their *queen* arrive in a cage. To provide a little discouragement for bad behavior."

I clenched my fists around Michio. "You keep them in cages?"

"I keep them in shackles in rooms like this one. In nondescript buildings in various cities. It's temporary. Which brings me to my permanent solution. The solution that solves both our problems."

The door to the hallway swung open, and a black-haired man of Middle-Eastern descent strode in carrying a large black bag. His eyes darted around the room and locked on mine, his lips twitching at the corner as if he were trying to stifle a smirk.

He wasn't controlled through a bite, but he was here, seemingly voluntarily.

The Drone straightened on the stool. "This is Dr. Jaffer. He's going to remove your IUD. Then he will have intercourse with you until you conceive."

My chest heaved as panic gripped my body. "That's not a solution. It's fucking rape."

"I'm giving you a child, Eveline. A child that won't seek to destroy everything I've created. I would inseminate you with *my* seed, but as you know, infertility is a side-effect of the venom."

My stomach clenched, and heat swelled through my muscles as my anger exploded. "You can't do this, you sick fuck. The prophecy said my child would save mankind. You're fucking yourself if you get me pregnant."

Technically, a lie. The prophecy stated only Jesse could father a world-saving child.

The Drone cut sharp eyes at Michio, and his melted lips drew back in a vicious snarl. Was he reacting to Michio's thoughts?

Michio was listening to this shit, living this hell alone in his head, unable to outwardly express himself. But he wasn't alone, and neither was I.

The chains rattled as I molded my body around him, his frame fitting perfectly against mine. Holding him, comforting him, wanting to protect and save him, I felt all of it reciprocated, not in the physical sense but through the bond we'd shared for so long. If given a choice, I wouldn't want him anywhere near this place, but fuck, if he hadn't been here, I would've been uselessly tearing my wrists up trying to get out of these chains.

The Drone folded his arms, studying us. "The prophesied child will not come into existence. Once you conceive, I will bite you. The venom will give me access to the fetus' brain, and it will become *my* child. Then, together, my child and I, will drain your power."

The ache in my chest was unbearable. My body shook violently, and bile rose to the back of my throat. "Why can't you just let Michio and I go and leave us the fuck alone? Michio was your best friend, Aiman. You have a deep and defining history together. Like *family*. Have you forgotten that?"

For a flickering moment, his eyes softened and the cruelty slipped away. Then he blinked, and the hard, razor-sharp eyes returned. "I need an heir. I can't control the women because of your blood. I can't silence Dr. Nealy's vexing thoughts because of your blood. There's power there. The child you birth, *my* child, will be the ultimate hybrid between your power and mine. You will give me a child that can't be defeated, one I will groom to follow in my footsteps."

Everything inside me choked. I couldn't breathe, couldn't speak, couldn't move a fucking finger. My outrage was so visceral and painful it took over my body. I'd never felt so helpless.

My torment reached rock bottom when Michio sprung away from me. As if yanked by strings, his body jerked mechanically, shuffling backward, and slammed against the wall by the door.

The Drone turned toward Dr. Jaffer. "Remove the IUD."

FORTY-EIGHT

My muscles shook, a full-body spasm that clattered the chains. I lay on the mattress, legs squeezed together, arms folded around my torso, as sweat gathered beneath the layers of wrapped cotton.

The heavy thump of Dr. Jaffer's bag dropping on the cement floor echoed my heartbeat. As he opened it, the sound of the zipper scraped down my spine. The lingering look he gave my chest, his kneeling position at my feet, his hands resting on my ankles, every movement promised certain hell.

The removal of the IUD alone would be painful. Worse would be the rape that followed. To go through that again, while the man I loved watched helplessly, would be like reliving the hell in my father's basement all over again.

With my feet unrestrained, I could land a hard-hitting kick to his temple and knock him out. Maybe he would be less inclined to touch me when he woke. But I couldn't. Michio had been kept in the room for a reason, and I'd promised him I wouldn't make the Drone use him as an enforcer again. I was going to have to find another way out of this.

I looked around the room, taking in the blank-faced men along the wall. Six more obstacles.

"This is rape." I glared at Dr. Jaffer, my voice strained. "There's no going back from it. Once a rapist, always a rapist."

Digging through his bag, he paused to flash me an *oh-it-won't-be-so-bad* smile. My foot twitched to break his pearly-white human teeth.

The overhead light cast a pukey glow across his mahogany-brown complexion and round facial features. In his thirties, he was lean and average-looking with dark eyelids, thick eyebrows, and a shadow of stubble above his lips. If he grew out his black hair, he could've been the Drone's twin.

I angled my neck to see around him, trying to find the Drone's gaze. "Are you two related?"

"No." The Drone leaned sideways until those sinister eyes filled my view. "But the resemblance is deliberate. The child will be of my venom not of my blood, but our likeness in heritage and features will serve as a visual reminder that I am the father."

My insides writhed with hatred. I squeezed my eyes shut, blocking out the monster. But I couldn't escape my surroundings, couldn't slip away from the restraints, the stale air, and the hopelessness. All of it reminded me I was going to die in this dam, that Michio would be given to Elaine, that I would never see Jesse and Roark again, and that my child would be raised by a madman.

It took Dr. Jaffer forever to collect his tools from his bag, but forever wasn't long enough. When his cold fingers dragged the cotton skirt up my legs, my eyes snapped open. He forcibly ruched the material around my hips, and I squeezed my knees tighter, my breaths wheezing out of control.

My soon-to-be rapist shoved a wedge beneath my hips and gripped my thighs. "Open your legs, Ms. Delina."

I didn't. *I couldn't.* My ribs compressed, restricting my lungs.

Michio stepped away from the wall, arms hanging at his sides, but they wouldn't remain there for long if I fought this.

I wanted to die, yet I couldn't even do that. I couldn't do anything but lay here while Dr. Rapey shoved his hand inside me.

"Aiman!" I strained my neck to see the Drone. "Let Michio sit by me. The least you can do is let me hold his hand."

Being separated would make this worse. Even if Michio couldn't control the grip of his fingers, the linking of our hands might soothe both of us. And maybe, just maybe, I could free him through that connection. I held onto that idea because, dammit, I desperately needed to hold onto something.

When Michio knelt robotically at my side, I grabbed his fingers and laced them with mine, the four-foot chains allowing me to hold our hands against my stomach.

His ever-present hum caressed the underside of my skin, and slowly, my breaths evened out. I focused every thought on Michio as the doctor spread my legs and flicked on a penlight. I soundlessly spoke to Michio as the cold metal of the speculum stretched my entrance. *You can fight this, Michio. Break his hold. Dig deep.* I clenched the hell out of Michio's hand as the doctor's fingers invaded where I was open and vulnerable.

Each pinch and scrape along my inner walls ratcheted my pulse. Every second that passed felt like it would never end. By the time the doctor removed the speculum and leaned back, I'd squeezed Michio's fingers so hard our knuckles were white.

"Her cervix is blue." Dr. Jaffer looked over his shoulder at the Drone. "The uterus is swollen, and there's no IUD."

Shea said the string could hide during a vaginal exam. But what was wrong with my cervix and uterus? Was this guy even a doctor?

The Drone leapt from the stool and slammed against Michio, wrapping fingers around his throat, choking him.

I grabbed at the Drone's hands, but they were iron claws around Michio's neck, and all Michio could do was lay limply beneath the strangulation.

"Shut up!" He shouted at Michio, his sagging face livid red, his lips curling back to expose the razored points of his rage. "If you don't calm down, I will put you back in Elaine's bed and leave you there for the rest of your miserable life."

"You're choking him." I pried at the Drone's fingers as

panic flooded me. "Let him go!"

Why the fuck was the Drone attacking him? And these threats about Elaine were tearing my insides apart. The Drone wouldn't even have to chain him to her bed. The motherfucker could control his body, make him touch her, pleasure her.

The Drone pulled back and rose to his feet, adjusting his cape as he glared at Michio. "That's *my* decision, Dr. Nealy. Not yours." After a pause, his eyes hardened. "Of course, he is. You've been thinking of nothing else for the past four months."

My head swam as I listened to the one-sided conversation. Dr. Jaffer kept his eyes on his lap. The six spiders along the wall stared at jack shit like silent statues, empty men without opinions, because the Drone had reprogrammed their frontal lobes. The same thing he intended to do to my child.

My child.

"What is Michio saying?" I gathered his dead weight into my arms and settled his face on my chest, my fingers stroking through his hair. "Let him talk."

The Drone ignored me, turning his attention to Dr. Jaffer. "I want an ultrasound." His eyes flicked to Michio and returned to Dr. Jaffer. "Transvaginal."

My breathing accelerated. The IUD was there. It would show up on the ultrasound, just like last time. Wouldn't it?

Uncertainty hardened in a pit in my stomach. What if I was already pregnant?

My thoughts tangled, and my body shook maliciously. I was so fucking scared, but I felt something else, too. Something stronger, buzzing with energy and life and purpose. I couldn't explain it, but all I could think was, *This isn't the end. It's the beginning.*

As Dr. Jaffer pulled the machine from the bag and plugged it in, the Drone paced beside us, arms crossed, tapping his lips with a long finger.

"It would be more efficient if you asked her those questions directly." He glared down at Michio's face, where he lay on my chest. "Just remember, I'm only keeping you alive for your knowledge. I can just as easily pull your thoughts while Elaine is bouncing on your dick." He bent down and flashed his fangs. "The first whimpering, off-topic comment that leaves your mouth, you're done."

My arms banded tighter around Michio, my heart aching for him. How many times had the Drone threatened him with Elaine? How often had she raped him?

Blood overran my vision. I was going to kill her, slowly with my hands while they empurpled her flesh and snapped her bones, then brutally with my blades, bleeding her until her vicious poison drained from her eyes.

Michio's jaw moved against my chest. "When did you first have sex with Jesse?"

My hackles went up. Not because of the question. I knew it would be the chief thought on his mind. It was his flat voice. The lack of inflection didn't belong in this delicate conversation. He would be upset, seething with jealousy, and he couldn't express himself. It wasn't fair to him.

I tipped his face toward mine and kissed his forehead as I said to the Drone, "Give him control of his face. Or let me hear the pitch in his voice. He sounds like a fucking computer."

"No," the Drone snapped. "Answer the question."

Goddammit. I would, only if Michio had asked it. "Is it his question or yours?"

"His. I'm allowing it because I want the answers."

I held Michio's strong jaw in my hand as I thought back to my first time with Jesse. Two weeks in the cage. Another two weeks traveling from Charlottesville. "Four weeks ago, give or take a few days."

The Drone hissed, his grotesque features distorting around his fangs.

I pulled in a ragged breath, my gaze on Michio. "We used an ultrasound before we had sex, and the IUD was still in position." I kissed the smooth skin between his brows, lingering there. "I'm so sorry you can't show me how you feel. This is not how I wanted to tell you."

His eyes stared off somewhere behind me. "Have you fucked anyone else?"

There it was. His voice sounded electronic, his demeanor benign, but the way he'd phrased the question conveyed his anger. He was showing me how he felt the only way he could.

"I've been with Roark." My voice cracked, not with regret but with longing. "Only my guardians, Michio." God, I missed them.

The Drone returned to the stool and perched on the edge. "The priest is sterile." His eyes simmered with shadows. "If she's pregnant, this is the prophesied child."

The energy inside me swelled, spreading out and igniting my body.

Michio's monotone droned against my chest. "Have you experienced any changes in your body?"

Could he feel the strange power rushing through me? Did he know about my ability to kill aphids with a thought?

No way would I mention these things in front of the Drone. "No."

I wanted to covertly pinch Michio or give him some sign I was lying, but if he knew it was a lie, so would the Drone.

The Drone regarded me for an unnerving moment. "You walked out of a cage after two weeks of immobility."

Wait till I blow up your pets, asshole. Not sure how that little trick would help me, but right now, it was the only ace I had.

Dr. Jaffer held up a skinny probe that attached to the ultrasound machine by a cord. "It's ready."

He pulled my legs open. I didn't fight him and instead wrapped my shaky arms around Michio's shoulders, my chest hitching beneath his head.

I felt a slight pressure between my legs. The machine chirped and beeped. The doctor studied the screen, and my breath stuck in my throat as I waited for him to speak.

"There's definitely no IUD."

"How?" My stomach buckled. "Where would it go?"

The Drone stood and strode over to the machine, crouching for a closer look, his expression as indecipherable as the screen.

Dr. Jaffer kept his eyes on the monitor, shifting the wand inside me. "They can fall out. It's rare, but I've heard it could happen during urination. If you peed outside in the dark, you wouldn't have noticed it." He glanced at the Drone, back at the screen. "It's difficult to tell at this stage, but given the size of the gestational sac, I estimate her at around four weeks pregnant."

The world slammed to a crashing halt. A sharp burn lit behind my eyes, trailing fire down my throat, and swelling hard and powerful in my chest.

I was pregnant.

Jesse's child.

My daughter.

The prophecy.

The doctor removed the probe, and I rolled against Michio's body, shoving the skirt over my legs. I enveloped him in my arms, holding him as tightly as I could, imagining his agony, his fears, and his regrets, all of it centered on my prophesied death.

"Michio, it's going to be okay." I choked, aching to hear his voice. "It's going to work out."

This was supposed to happen, decided ahead of time. A fate that couldn't be altered. I'd known about it, and deep down, I'd even believed this moment would come, but the shock of it and all the implications it brought curled my body into a trembling, conflicted mess.

The Drone spun toward us, the fire in his eyes aimed at Michio. "You do not have an opinion!" he roared. "That was your final warning."

Michio twisted out of my arms. I tried to hold on, but he was an unstoppable machine, the sharp movements of his legs wrenching him to his feet, jerking him toward the door, into the hall, and out of view.

I crawled after him, straining against the shackles and digging my knees into the mattress. "What are you doing with him? Bring him back!"

The Drone stormed toward the door, pausing to watch Dr. Jaffer collect his bag and hurry out. Then the six spiders followed suit.

Standing in the doorway, the Drone turned his glare on me. "Michio will be in Elaine's bed…indefinitely. I may not have control over his reflexes, but the body has a way of giving in to persistent stimulus. And Elaine is very persistent."

I launched forward, my arms snapping behind me, as the shackles yanked me back. "That's rape, you son of a bitch! Don't do this! He doesn't deserve this!"

"Rape." The Drone licked his lips as if savoring the word. "Do you think you've dodged your own *rape,* Eveline?"

What? Would he send Dr. Jaffer back in for the man's own enjoyment? He wasn't that charitable with his employees. Every action served *his* purpose.

He leaned against the door frame and crossed his arms. "I could bite you now and make that fetus my own. Or I could dispose of it in any number of ways and resume where we left off with Dr. Jaffer."

I sank back into the mattress, my arms winding protectively around my belly, around the energy surging through me. What would happen to him if he bit me? Would the child hurt him? Or would he gain her power? I didn't know, and by the look on his face, he didn't either.

"I need to think." He swept out and slammed the door.

My heart hammered away the minutes as I waited. Minutes pulsed into hours, and hours became days. Eventually I lost track of time, locked within four walls, isolated inside myself, like Michio.

Every day, the Drone's spiders fed me rice and unrecognizable meat and swapped out the shit bucket. No more toilets. No more showers. No change of clothes. The shackles never came off my wrists. I wasn't allowed out of the room.

And Michio never returned.

I spent days stumbling through my thoughts, staring at my flat belly, and agonizing over people. People I wanted to kill. People I wanted to meet. People I missed with the entirety of my being.

Jesse and Roark. I was desperate to tell them I was pregnant, and my stomach ached and festered at the possibility they might never find out.

Michio. I trembled and raged, thinking about what Elaine was doing to him. I didn't know how to reach him, didn't know what I could do to take his pain away.

Annie and Aaron. Sometimes I dreamed of them holding their new baby sister, and it filled me with the sweetest, most harrowing ache. I couldn't bear how much I missed them and wasn't sure I would survive those lonely moments of longing. I just wanted to hold them so tightly, but they weren't here…they weren't here…

Joel. He'd told me to listen to the song. To love again. I was so grateful I had, but I hoped, wherever he was, that he knew I would never stop loving him.

The Drone. His presence was a constant pulse in my gut. I could feel him moving around the dam, his oily aura rioting my nerves and swelling my throat with dread. Would he bite me? Would he find some horrible method of abortion? How long would it take him to decide?

Me. A mother again. I was overwhelmed beyond all reason. Stunned, terrified, and so fucking overjoyed. The longer I lay there, imagining what she would look like, laugh like, fight like, the more attached to her I became. Even as I knew I wouldn't live long enough to experience any of those things.

My daughter. She was the power buzzing inside me. Her existence changed everything. For my guardians. For the Drone. For the world.

My ribcage felt too weak to contain everything I felt. There were moments when I thought it would burst open, and all of my darkest thoughts and most hopeful dreams would explode in a terrible, beautiful wail of tears.

But that didn't happen. So I thought about blowing up the aphids. It would cause a frenzy in the dam and the Drone would come. I was tempted. Fucking hell, I was tempted to end this godawful waiting, this not knowing, this mind-fucking game the Drone had forced upon me.

If I killed all the aphids now, though, how would that help me? The Drone could not only block my ability to control his pets, he could sense whenever I tried. He and I and the aphids, we were all connected by invisible threads. If I plucked those threads and signaled the aphids while the Drone was nearby, it would alert him as well.

I needed him distracted when I attempted it. I needed to do it as a way to magnify that distraction. But how and when would that happen?

It was in one of those moments of deliberation, when the door to the hall opened. I expected the spiders, a clean bucket, and a bowl of rice.

But it was Michio. A thinner Michio, with dark circles beneath his eyes and a bundle of rope dangling from his hand.

FORTY-NINE

I scrambled to my knees and jerked against the shackles. "Michio?"

Deep longing throbbed in my chest at the sight of him standing in the doorway of my prison, *alone*. No visual or telepathic trace of the Drone. No other guards. Had he come to free me? Had he somehow escaped the Drone's harness on his mind? His expression was unreadable, which it often was when he was tempering his emotions.

The rope in his hand restricted some of my hope.

He strode through the room, his long gait making a direct path to me. Black fatigues hung loose and low on his narrow hips, his chest bare, the cage of his ribs visible along the sides of his abs. Were they not feeding him? Or was he somehow refusing to eat?

The steep ridges of his torso jutted against his stretched skin, as if dehydration had severely cut away his honed physique. He was still beautifully built, but his body was harder, sharper, like his muscles had been replaced with razor-edged steel parts.

My thoughts leapt to Elaine, torturing me with images of her fingers tracing those lethal edges, her hands and body violating him while he lay in her bed, unable to fight her off.

I balled my hands into fists and willed him to meet my eyes, to say something, to frown or smile, to give me some sign he was here on his own and not under the command of the Drone.

When he reached the mattress, his sunken cheeks, his too-narrow face, and the remoteness in his bruised eyes forced me to face the cruel reality. Michio was still as enchained as I was.

He knelt at my feet and unraveled the rope, staring over my shoulder. "Don't make me hurt you."

God, I hated that terrible, insentient tone in his voice. I knew the Drone had moved his mouth to taunt me with those words. And in the next few minutes, the Drone would make him do something worse with those ropes.

Michio looked past me like I didn't exist, making it hard to believe he was still in there and still loved me. But I felt him, the vitality of his life force caressing beneath my skin. I had to believe his dreams and fears and the heart of who he was hadn't been starved and raped out of him.

The chains clanked as I sat back, closed my eyes, and drew a determined breath. I wouldn't give up. I owed it to my guardians and my unborn child to survive this. The energy in my blood charged at the thought, my womb pulsing and stretching to contain the power growing inside.

"We have an unbreakable bond, Michio." I knew the Drone could hear me through Michio's thoughts, but I refused to filter my words. "A bond that doesn't require touch or voice. Even when I can't see or hear you, I feel our connection in the electricity humming between our souls. We are one in our suffering, our resistance, and our love. You know what that means to me?" I opened my eyes and hardened my expression with conviction as I stared up at his distant gaze. "It means I will never abandon my heart. I will never forsake you. No matter what happens, I will protect our bond and this child."

In a blur of superhuman speed, he coiled the heavy nylon around my ankles and wound it up my legs, locking my thighs together in a net of elaborate knots. Stunned at the swiftness of his movements, I tried to jerk away, but in that single breath, he'd bound me from feet to hips and removed my ability to walk. Even if I could've physically fought him off, I wouldn't have. I wouldn't allow the Drone to use Michio's body to hurt us.

He rolled me, his hands flying through the knots as he transformed the bindings between my legs into some sort of rope seat. The harness looped around my upper thighs, cupped my ass, and cinched beneath my stomach. What the hell was he doing?

I didn't see him pull out a key, but the shackles suddenly fell from my wrists. Before I could snap my arms up, he'd replaced the cuffs with a row of zip snare knots from my wrists to my biceps. The rope laced my arms together in a straight line and fastened them to the harness at my pelvis, preventing me from lifting my hands.

He leapt to his feet, and his grip on the rope around my arms jerked me with him. With my ankles locked together, I wobbled as he tied off the ends at my back and wrapped the remaining length around his forearm.

My God, he'd finished the binding before I'd even had time to panic. I stared down at my trussed-up body, unable to move a limb, barely able to breathe. If I tried to move, I was certain I'd topple over. How the hell would I go to the bathroom?

The blue cotton wrap I'd worn for days—*weeks?*—bunched beneath the maze of ropes, the cotton soiled with sweat and frayed along the edges. Evidently, I wouldn't be changing clothes. Not that it mattered. It was the only thing I owned. No, even these tattered rags belonged to the Drone.

Michio had tossed my bow and quiver in Missouri, and my arm sheathes were probably discarded when he'd locked me in the cage. The sheathes Joel had given me were all I'd possessed from my life with him. My chest ached.

I owned nothing.

Except control of my mind. Thank fuck I still had that.

Michio gripped my hips and slung me over his shoulder. The bent position strained my insides and trapped my arms beneath me, my legs uselessly hanging against his chest. Every inhale squeezed the ropes tighter, constricting and pinching.

It would've been a waste of breath to ask where he was taking me, so I let my forehead rest on the hard expanse of his back and pressed my lips against his skin. My kiss expressed all the emotion surging through me, every pang of worry and ounce of love I felt for this man, who was confined by restraints that were tighter, harsher, and more damaging than mine.

He strode into the hall, and six men peeled away from the walls, surrounding us. I craned my neck as the hollow-eyed spiders moved into two rows of three, staring without seeing. Michio stared straight ahead. I stared at the floor. Christ, we all stared at fuck-all, moving in silence, as if desensitized to one another, numb and dumb. Was this what the future would look like? A planet of fissured brains, where individualities were ripped away and the husks of bodies mindlessly marched to the beat of a whack job? I shuddered.

We drifted along the tiled passageways, through the generator room, then veered into the cavernous tunnels of natural rock, up metal stairs, ascending elevators, and more tunnels. The clomp of boots filled every crack and cranny of the damp spaces with an ominous, synchronized march of dread.

Pinpricks tingled my bound hands beneath the weight of my body, and blood rushed to my head, pulsing behind my eyes. Hanging upside down, my view was hindered, but I didn't glimpse a single man, spider, or aphid wandering the passageways. I sensed insectile vibrations, though, the threads strumming from above. From the surface of the canyon.

Not knowing where Michio was taking me or what would happen when I arrived made this long, miserable trip even longer and more miserable. Had the Drone made a decision? Would he bite me and drain the power growing inside me? Or would my child enervate *his* power and destroy him? Would he chance the bite? Or would he kill her in my womb? Or was there another option I hadn't considered? All I knew was every tunnel, staircase, and elevator took us *up*. We were headed out of the dam. Why? Was he taking me to one of the breeding facilities?

My blood chilled, and tremors gripped my body, the edges

of my mind fraying with every step Michio made toward ground zero. I wanted to scream and kick and freak the fuck out, but I held onto my wits as best I could, seeking comfort in the flex of his strength beneath me and in the knowledge that he wasn't detached like the spiders surrounding us.

Even though this child wasn't biologically his, he would fight for her as if she were his own. He maintained conscious thought, which meant he could reason, form ideas, and analyze. The Drone could read his mind and therefore learn any plan he might've constructed, but Michio was the most intelligent man I'd ever met. His brilliant mind was always ten steps ahead. If anyone could think his way out of this, it was him.

As the final elevator ascended, the aphid vibrations in my gut grew stronger. I raised my head, angling to see around Michio as the doors slid open.

Sunlight greeted me, the burst of warmth blinding my cave-dwelling eyes. I squinted, blinking, taking in the street, the daunting precipice of the dam, and the hundreds of waiting aphids.

A sea of green bodies crowded the street that traveled across the curved ridge of the wall. The thundering buzz rippling over their spines revealed their hunger, but they didn't concern me. One thought, a wish I wouldn't make until I needed to, and they would be nothing but bloody smears on the asphalt.

Unless the Drone's power could block me.

My pulse accelerated then spiked into a frenzy as I gazed upon the enormity of the dam stretching to the gorge below. Hanging over Michio's shoulder at the center of its peak, I was surrounded by endless, open blue sky. The only way off was down. And waiting for me at the destined edge was the man who would likely push me.

The Drone stood on a small concrete overhang that extended over the back of the dam. As Michio carried me toward the observation deck, the spider guards encircled us, ushering us along the half-wall of the ledge and away from the aphids.

The dam's massive girth and the red rock of the canyon on either side plunged into a platform of cement below. The vast, steep distance to the bottom pulled on my insides with a whirling sense of unsteadiness.

No one could survive a fall from this dam, not even Michio with his healing abilities. The impact would splatter a body into pieces.

Michio set me on the narrow ledge of the overhang beside the Drone, and panic fired through my nerves. I couldn't move my hands, couldn't hold on to the edge. My equilibrium was already fucked up from the spinning effect of vertigo, made worse without the stability of my legs.

I jerked forward, leaning away from the sharp slope and pushing my weight against Michio. I wanted to beg him to protect me, to sweep me away from the ledge and wrap his strength around me, but my pleas would only torture him. No doubt he was as terrified as I was.

The six spider guards formed a barrier at the mouth of the overhang. If I could somehow hop away from Michio's firm grip on my ropes, I'd also have to hop through them. And though I couldn't see beyond the swarm of aphids on the street, I suspected there were more spiders patrolling both ends of the dam.

The sun peered over the eastern horizon, winking at me all bright and shiny, completely unconcerned that my daughter's future literally hung in the balance. Its fiery glow did little to warm the cool breeze that chilled the sweat on my face.

I reached deep, digging up my courage, and met the Drone's eyes. "Why are we here, a hundred stories in the air?" *Tempting my fucking fate?*

"Sixty-seven stories." The Drone leaned against the three-foot wall of the overhang, hands in his pockets, his cape rustling around his boots. "It's Christmas morning."

As if that explained everything. He was Muslim, for fuck's sake. But he'd chosen Christmas morning to bring me to this ledge for a reason. My stomach sank with dread.

"Seventy percent of this country believed their savior was born on this day." He shifted to stare out over the landscape of rocky cliffs. "Where was their savior when I released the virus? If I'm the pestilence in their bible, why didn't their god save them from me?"

Roark would say the final days were God's plan, but waging a religious debate with a lunatic while precariously perched on the ledge of the Hoover Dam sounded like a terrible idea.

"I'm not a believer." I leaned closer toward Michio, trying to slide my feet to the ground, but his grip on my hips kept my butt on the edge.

The Drone rubbed the folds of his cheek. "But you believe the fetus in your womb will save mankind?"

It wasn't a question of religious faith, spirituality, or scientific study. The prophecy was unexplainable. A phenomenon that defied human concepts. Every prediction Annie made had come to pass, and those of us affected by it couldn't discount its legitimacy. Not me. Not my guardians. And not the Drone. That must've been eating at his rotten, deranged heart. But I didn't want to give him a reason to shove me off the ledge, so I kept my mouth shut.

In the span of a heartbeat, he was on me, his claws digging into my face, and his chest bowing me backward. My upper half hung backward over the edge, my breath lodged in my throat. At least I wasn't face down and staring at my death.

Michio stood to the side, arms dangling, eyes glazed. He wouldn't be able to lift a finger to catch me, and as sure as this fall would kill me, it would kill him, too.

I mentally reached for the aphid threads and strummed a silent command. *Attack the Drone. Kill the Drone.*

The Drone laughed. "You can't control my army, Eveline." His lower body pinned my legs to the wall, the only thing keeping me from plummeting. "We've reached a causality dilemma. Do you know what that is?"

I couldn't speak, couldn't fill my lungs. My hands twisted against the rope, grappling for the fabric of his shirt and unable to find purchase.

"Which came first? Me or the prediction?" His septic breath slithered over my face. "Was your death on a cliff prophesied because I drop you? Or do I drop you because of the prediction?"

Don't drop me. Sweet fucking hell, don't let go. I couldn't tell if he was fucking with me or if he had every intention of throwing me over. Probably both. My stomach bucked, pushing bile to my throat.

I flexed my arms against the bindings, my body suffocatingly wrapped like a roll of carpet. Where was the extra length of rope that attached to my back? My heart skipped. It had been wound around Michio's arm. If I fell, could he catch me? Or did he fall with me? Oh God, I couldn't see the rope, couldn't see him at all. Fuck, all I could see was his body splattered beside mine sixty-seven stories below.

Desperation poured from my throat. "Michio! Don't…don't let him do this. Fight him. You're strong…dammit, you're stronger than him!"

The Drone's smile oozed with calm confidence. "Dr. Nealy believes he can outsmart me by *not* thinking about rescue attempts. But how does one make plans without thoughts?" He studied Michio's impassive expression and looked back at me. "I'm afraid he has nothing to offer you."

The Drone hadn't broken him. Not Michio. Maybe he'd found a way around the mind-reading? My head spun, my breaths wheezing. The only thing I could count on was death if the Drone let go.

I closed my eyes to fight down the urge to puke, certain he would drop me if I spewed on his cape.

After a few heavy breaths, I glared up at him, my skin tearing in the grip of his claws. "We wouldn't be here, on the brink of this cliff, if you didn't know about the prophecy."

"Are you certain? I determined this location long before I discovered the predictions. Whether or not I would've killed you *here* is a matter of assumption. But think about it,

Eveline. If the cliff or the child are necessary causes of your death, then your death necessarily implies the presence of one or the other. I can't ignore the fact that both the cliff and the child happen to exist, right here, beneath my fingertips."

My insides revolted, shooting acid up my chest and into my throat. I gagged and lost the battle with my stomach as vomit trickled over my cheek and fell into oblivion.

He released his claws from my face and stepped away. The world moved in slow motion as I suspended there, my legs clenched around the edge and gravity pressing me backward. My muscles strained and my stomach contracted against the gorge's determined pull.

Michio grabbed the rope on my arms and swung me up, stabilizing my body on the ledge. Dizzy and terrified, I gasped, panting for air. *I didn't fall. I didn't fall.* For a hopeful moment, I thought Michio had snapped his invisible chains to save me, but one look at his empty face told me otherwise.

The Drone curled his disfigured lips, letting me know I was still alive because *he* willed it. "The prophecy is either something or nothing. Which leaves me with the conundrum of Plato's Beard that argues nothing *is* something."

Fuck, was this why he'd left me in that room for so long? Had he spent all that time talking himself into tangled circles?

Saliva collected in my mouth, my stomach threatening to heave again. I spit on the ledge, breathing past my lips, and glared at him out of the corner of my eye as I wiped my cheek on my shoulder.

His smile flattened, and his pupils dilated. "The fetus in your womb will not be born."

My heart stopped.

He glanced at my neck and returned to my face. "But before I destroy it, I will drain it of its power. And yours."

"She's a *her*, you sick son of a bitch." Horror trembled through my body and quivered my voice. "She's stronger than you. She'll kill you. Stick your fucking fangs in me, and we'll see who's left with the power."

It was all conjecture. I didn't know shit, and my fucking

panic was seeping through the cracks of my composure.

"Once I bite you and pull the power from your body, you'll become infertile, weak. You'll no longer be of any use to me." He stretched out his arms and looked around the canyon. "So here we are, fulfilling the prophecy. No matter what becomes of the bite, Dr. Nealy has been ordered to push you over the moment I release your vein."

I shook my head in denial, even as I knew I'd reached the end with no way out. It didn't matter if the bite backfired and I imbibed his power. I would already be on my way to the bottom of the cliff. He probably would've flown me over the gorge and bitten me high in the air if he was certain he wouldn't lose his power. But he didn't know.

Which was why he'd chosen this location to do it. *Bite me and push me.*

My fear was sudden and manic. Ferocious energy pummeled through my limbs as I thrashed forward, bucking against Michio's hands on my hips. I needed down, needed off this fucking ledge. "Let me down. Let me the fuck down!"

I had no defense. No mobility. No weapons. I was out of time and out of options. Feverish breaths pumped my chest as desperation seared my nose and closed up my throat.

The Drone stepped toward me, his fangs pushing past his lips and his jaw stretching open. Fucking hell, he was leaning toward my neck. I tucked my chin and jerked away, swaying on the narrow peak, my hips pinned down by Michio's unforgiving strength.

The Drone grabbed my hair and wrenched my head back, exposing my throat. I couldn't escape him. His breath hit my neck, and my chest caught fire. The moment his fangs tried to touch my skin, I would kill the aphids. But I knew it wouldn't be enough.

A distraction would only delay him briefly. He was going to kill my baby. Jesse's daughter. Mankind's future. The backs of my eyes burned, and tears engulfed my eyelids, staining my vision in red. I tried to fight it, tried to be strong, but the painful sob pushed past my throat and tore from my lips.

Warm rivers drenched my cheeks, and my throat spasmed with keening noises. Holy hell, I was crying. A tear hadn't breached my eyes since…never. Never had been a long damned time without this release, and now that it was happening, it fucking poured out of me in gasping, choking, nose-clogging hysterics.

The Drone grabbed my jaw, his claws digging against my cheek. "What's wrong with your eyes?"

I slammed my teeth together, my face stinging where his grip punished my skin. "I'm crying, you asshole."

He let go of my face like I'd infected him. "Dr. Nealy. Check her eyes."

Michio's unfocused gaze moved in, his vacant face blurred by a cloud of red. He touched the inner corner of my eye and held his finger up, the tip wet with blood.

My *eyes* were bleeding? More tears fell, streaking hot trails down my cheeks. His nostrils flared.

His nostrils flared.

The Drone would've commanded his finger to move, but his nostrils? No, that was a reflex. Had the smell of my blood triggered a reaction in him?

What if Michio bit me? I sucked in a wet breath. That would be better than the Drone's bite. My pulse picked up. Why would that be better? Shit, I didn't know, but my heart clung to the idea, desperate for it.

I closed my eyes. How the fuck could I get him to bite me?

When I glanced up, he was staring at me. I blinked, trying to clear away the red film. Was he actually looking at me? His eyes were glassy, but they seemed to be locked directly on mine. I panted, and his lips parted. Oh my God, his lips fucking moved! It was a reaction. It had to be. *Don't think, Michio. Clear your mind and respond to me.*

The Drone gripped the back of Michio's neck. "Why are her eyes bleeding?"

A frenzied buzz waved over the surrounding aphids. Did they smell my blood or were they picking up on the Drone's emotions?

I stretched toward Michio as far as the ropes allowed, until my blood-soaked face was an inch below his nose, our lips a kiss away.

His eyes emptied, and his voice droned callously. "A subconjunctival hemorrhage can be caused by high blood pressure, vomiting, or bleeding disorders, however, the blood should not exit the eye."

My heart sank, and for an eternal moment, I thought I'd lost him.

Then his head lowered. The shift was minuscule, maybe involuntary, but it was enough to graze his fangs against my jaw.

The Drone slammed into us, knocking us closer to the edge as he bellowed, "No!"

His talons slashed at my face and tore across Michio's arms and back. He shoved his hands between our chests, screaming as he tried to wrench us apart.

The wrestling teetered us backward. Somehow, Michio leaned with me, keeping his mouth near my neck. But I'd been scooted too close to the slope, hanging on by the hook of my legs on the edge.

My stomach hurdled to my throat. Another forceful jerk, and the Drone would successfully push me over the wall.

Michio's lips brushed my skin, but the pushing and jostling prevented him from sinking his fangs in. He was so stiff and frozen, locked in his body. I tried to bend toward him, hoping…fuck, I hoped the bite would give him the power to free himself.

Three of the six spiders bolted toward us, joining in the Drone's efforts to hit and claw us apart. The size of Michio's body deflected most of the strikes against me, but his flesh wasn't made of Kevlar. The scent of his bloody wounds tinged my laboring inhales.

"Stop it! Get away from him! Fucking stop!" My helpless screams didn't distract them from hurting him, from making him bleed.

The Drone's commands must've been pounding in his

head, ordering him to back away. Which meant he was fighting it. But it wasn't enough. Without control of his hands, he wouldn't be able to hold on much longer.

With my neck straining to reach Michio's frozen mouth, I balanced on the edge of the wall by my bound legs, rolled my gaze to the aphids, and whispered, "Die."

Hundreds of bodies exploded across the tarmac. Tiny particles of blood projected upward in a black mist, and the aroma of rot hit the air.

The Drone stumbled back, eyes wide and pawing at his chest. Then he doubled-over and let out an almighty howl. "What have you done?"

The spiders wobbled, spinning around and snarling with feral expressions. Were they mindless? Disorientated?

It was that flickering moment, that beautiful distraction of time, that allowed Michio to launch. His arms hooked around my back, and his fangs slammed into my neck.

The sting of twin pricks bloomed into a blistering heat and crashed through every cell in my body. The energy in my core flared to life, throbbing and humming as it sought to bring him closer.

I felt it the instant the power inside me latched onto him. The strength in his sculpted body hardened around me, and his fangs dug deeper as he released the venom. No, my unborn child *pulled* his venom into my system, drawing it deep inside me, and *her*.

The Drone lifted his head and growled with a low, deadly reverberation that conjured images of bleeding dungeons and horned beasts. "Release her."

Michio crowded around me, suspending us way too close to the perilous edge as he greedily sucked, his jaw locked against my throat. The drugging sensation of each pull on my vein, the feel of his strong arms folded around my body, and the hardening of his cock against my hip curled waves of pleasure between my legs.

But the distraction with the Drone had only given Michio a moment of freedom. The spiders snapped into a rigid formation, and Michio's movements began to jerk and stiffen as he fought the Drone for full control of his body. The longer he drank, however, the stronger he seemed to become.

He dragged me off the ledge and tore his mouth from my neck. The caverns of his black eyes stirred to life, sharpening and glinting with the promise of vengeance. The sinews in his neck stretched, and a series of twitches raced across his arms and chest, his strength flexing and tightening.

Slumped against the wall and unable to move in my restraints, all I could do was watch, mesmerized, as he regained control of his body.

His teeth clamped together, and his lips retracted, exposing red-stained fangs. He threw his head back, and his cheeks puffed with the violent escape of a roar. The guttural resonance penetrated my chest in a silken explosion, his rage thrumming through my bones and pebbling goosebumps along my skin.

He was magnificent and terrifying, and holy shit, I was so glad that anger wasn't aimed at me.

Michio spun, but his target was already charging. The Drone's cape fell to the ground, and his wings snapped out. He blurred around Michio, his vicious eyes locked on me.

My heart raced as I tried to hobble away from the ledge, but I hadn't managed a single inch before he collided with my body and flipped me head first off the side.

The ground disappeared, replaced by air and the dizzily whirl of the canyon walls. I was sinking. Oh God, I was falling, and there was nothing to catch me but…fate.

Michio's pained roar followed me over as I left my stomach, my breath, and my heart on the ledge.

FIFTY

My pulse hurdled past my ears as I fell head first into the Black Canyon. Indescribable fear exploded in my chest and spilled out in an anguished cry. The torment was unbearable, knowing I wasn't the only one dying. I would've sacrificed my life for the future of humanity, but *she* was plummeting with me, bound to my womb and my fate.

Michio's roar thundered through the gorge, and my insides tore apart at the sound. Bloody tears streaked from my eyes, carried away by the whipping wind. I'd only fallen a few yards, yet it had lasted an eternity.

Before I could contemplate the remaining seven-hundred feet, the ropes snapped against me, pinching my skin and wrenching the air from my lungs. My feet continued to plunge for a half-second as my torso jerked upright and slammed against the concrete wall.

I came to a sudden halt, suspended sixty-some stories in the air. I gasped at the jarring pain in my bones, my head spinning with disorientation, and jerked my chin skyward.

The nylon around me cinched and pulled toward a knotted point at my back. From there, the extra length of rope reached ten…twenty feet up and disappeared over the concrete ledge.

The fibers creaked as I twisted and swayed. Holy fuck, I was caught. *For now.* Had Michio grabbed the rope or did it snag on something? Oh God, how long would it hold?

All that training Jesse had put me through wouldn't help me now, not without the use of my limbs. The bindings from my ankles to my biceps had been tied in a way that distributed my weight, the loops around my upper thighs and pelvis providing a makeshift seat that didn't put pressure on my womb. Michio had planned this, or at the very least, prepared for it. But how did he do it while the Drone was infiltrating his thoughts?

The vibrant hum of his aura stroked through my skin. I mentally traced the invisible trail, following his warmth up the wall and over the ledge. He was still up there, still alive. What happened to the Drone? He'd been right behind me when he pushed me over. Had Michio hauled him back? Were they tearing each other limb from limb?

I couldn't help him. My pulse sprinted. Fuck, I couldn't protect him.

The rope jerked, and I bumped against the wall, squinting against the blinding sun, refusing to remove my eyes from my lifeline. Who or what was holding the other end?

A black wing blurred over the wall then snapped out of view. The rope pulled, hitching me up then sliding free, plunging me downward and collapsing my stomach, as it dragged sideways along the edge.

The cord snapped taut again, stopping my downward spiral and whooshing the air from my lungs. Was Michio holding it? While he was fighting the Drone and the spiders?

My heart hammered as I strained my hearing, listening for pained grunts or scuffing boots.

Silence closed in around me. I expected to see the Drone's sinister eyes emerge over the ledge at any moment, followed by the stretch of his wings and the swipe of his talons as he severed the rope. I waited, my throat constricting and my breath slipping.

Something jerked the cord, bouncing me up and down and side to side like a swinging yo-yo. It yanked and slacked and yanked again, the nylon rubbing along the ledge and back, fraying the threads from the friction. Whatever secured the other end wasn't stationary.

My funny bone slammed against the cement, shooting

pinpricks through my arm. The disorientation was nauseating as I spun again. None of my limbs were free to buffer the constant collisions against wall, but I tried to keep my head angled as my spine and shoulders took the brunt of the abuse.

A black shoe appeared on the ledge, joined by its twin. The Drone rose up, towering above me as he stood on the wall. Crimson rivulets dripped from the gouges in his melted face, his black shirt and pants shredded, exposing bloody gashes beneath. He turned, and his furious eyes locked on the rope.

No, no, no! My chest heaved, and my mouth stretched to scream when something whistled above my head.

The Drone staggered, his gruesome visage contorting with outrage as he stared down at the black and red feathered arrow harpooned in his chest.

"Jesse." My whisper came out shaky, breathless, and full of stunned disbelief as I tried to whip around, frantically tracing the path the arrow had flown.

The Drone ripped the shaft free from his chest, tossed it, and launched for the rope.

But my lifeline was moving, yanking sideways, away from the Drone, and sliding downward…oh shit, it was loose, plummeting me into the gorge and shoving my guts to my throat.

I fell several heart-gripping feet before I crashed to a stop. I raised my head and found Michio, the source of my salvation, as he tackled the Drone's back. The end of the rope coiled around his arm, cutting off his circulation and turning his skin red and blue. Blood smeared his face, his eyes and fangs feral, as his hands curled around the base of the Drone's wing.

In the distance, shots rang out, followed by men shouting and cursing. Somewhere near the entrance of the dam? I didn't know how Jesse and Roark had found me, but I was certain that it was them wreaking havoc on the Drone's guards.

A guttural howl snapped my attention back to the Drone. Instead of standing on the ledge, he was now bent over it. He clawed at the wall, his cheek smashed against the concrete, and his eyes wide with... Panic? Fear?

Above his blood-soaked face, Michio leaned over and raised the skeletal arm of a torn-off wing. Hunks of flesh hung from the joint where it had been ripped from the Drone's body.

Michio's slivered eyes cut straight to me, piercing through my soul as if sharpened on the lethal edge of a blade. His expression was chillingly beautiful, like an ice storm, paralyzing and enchanting, the harsh lines of his bone structure hardening with brutality. No longer was his bearing frozen with indifference. He was malice and fangs and vicious strength, a blood-thirsty guardian angel.

With the end of my rope wrapped around one arm and chords of muscle flexing in his other, he flipped the wing in his hand and reared it back like a spear.

"Eveline." The Drone's fanged smile dripped with venom, his madness peering out of the darkness of his eyes. "Fate cannot be changed."

His words shivered across my skin as Michio stabbed the clawed joint of the wing into the back of the Drone's head.

The sound of crushing bone echoed through the canyon. The corner of the Drone's frozen smile tented outward into a bubbled point, stretching the melted flesh of his face until the clawed tip burst through his cheek with a pop of blood and bone fragments. I saw the moment his life evaporated from his eyes and felt his insanity flicker out, releasing my insides from the black stain of his aura.

Michio stared down at me as he thrust the bone of the wing again and again, ripping through brain tissue and splitting the skull. He held my gaze as he pushed harder, shoving the clawed tip out through the Drone's gaping mouth. A landslide of red lumps dribbled over the Drone's distended jaw.

Without looking away, Michio removed the gruesome weapon, shoved his hand into the back of the skull, and pulled out what was left of the Drone's brain.

If he intended on eating that, there was a good chance I'd

throw up and never kiss him again. Eating brains certainly wasn't Michio's style, but sweet mother, the terrifying look etched across his splattered face made me question the extent at which he was willing to go to ensure the Drone would never come back from the dead.

It wasn't until he hurled the mangled brain into the gorge that he shifted his eyes away from mine and to the rope coiled around his other arm. I released a sigh of relief, so fucking ready to plant my feet on solid ground.

He left the Drone's corpse hanging over the ledge, and sidled a few feet away from it to hoist me up. His blood-slicked hands flew over the nylon and closed the distance between us. I ascended as quickly as I'd fallen, and in the next breath, his arms were around me, suffocating me in the intensity of his embrace.

The bodies of the spider guards scattered the pavement behind him, sightless and unmoving. The report of gunfire ricocheted every few seconds from the dam's entrance, but the hum of the surviving spiders was dwindling. Our guys were winning. God, I had so many questions, but as Michio's arms grew tighter around me, I decided all of it could wait. He needed this. I needed this.

My body instantly melted in his arms as I listened to the labored rasps of his breaths, captivated by the trembling in his muscles and the tornado of emotions storming across his face. He'd single-handedly given my daughter a future. In turn, he'd given the world a gift. There would never be enough words to tell him how thankful I was, but I would spend the rest of my life, however short that was, pursuing his happiness.

He carried me away from the ledge and toward the street, his boots squishing through the remains of aphids and stepping over the bodies of the six spiders. Some were missing eyes. Most of the heads were caved in as if a vengeful fist had crushed their faces and destroyed their brains.

"You killed all of them with your bare hands," I said in numb awe, staring up at his blood-stained face. "While holding onto the rope."

He settled me on the sidewalk and attacked the knots on my arms, freeing them with superhuman speed. "There's thirty or forty more spiders at the gates." He moved to the rope around my pelvis and legs, his breaths growing faster, louder, his voice throaty and clipped. "They have to die."

Shit. Were they thinking on their own now? With the Drone no longer controlling them, what happened to their minds?

The commotion of gun shots and shouting at either end of the dam grew quieter by the second. A moment later, all I could hear was the sound of Michio's heavy breathing.

The final knot fell away from my arms, and I snapped them up, reaching for him. But he jerked away, moving down my legs to fumble with the remaining rope. A tremor bunched through his shoulders, and a seething hiss pushed past the clench of his fangs. He was still so very angry, his skin stretching to contain the torment churning inside him.

I couldn't take his pain away, but I could relieve at least one of his worries. "I felt the spiders humming under my skin. You know, like the aphids, but different. But right now, the only hum left is yours. The spiders are dead, Michio. Are you able to feel that, too?"

He raised bloodshot eyes to my face, his hands shaking against the rope on my legs. "I've only ever been able to feel *you.* I'm the only one who can." He scrubbed a hand over his jaw, his fingers smearing through the blood as he looked away. "I'm the only one who could track you."

"How? Because of the venom?" I thought of the breeding facilities and the spiders that would likely be guarding those locations. "Can you track the spiders the way you track me? Or do you already know where the women are?"

"No." His jaw set. "My ability to sense you has nothing to do with the venom. I don't know where the women are, and the spiders can't telepathically sense one another or me." He pulled the last of the rope from my body and jumped to his feet, his fingers dragging over his scalp, his voice scathing with anger. "I can feel you because I consumed your blood."

Oh. It made a convenient tracking device, which explained why the Drone had sent him to retrieve me from Missouri and why Michio was so bitter about being able to sense me.

I rose on shaky legs and stepped toward him, aching to wrap my arms around his rigid frame. But his brown eyes drilled into me, warning me to stay back. He glared as if the mere sight of me caused him deep pain.

My heart clenched with yearning, to comfort him. To protect him. I needed to reconnect with him on both a soulful and carnal level, but to do that, to *reach* him, we needed to scrape away all the regrets and heartache.

"Michio—"

A voice boomed in the distance, the familiar baritone echoing from somewhere near the entrance of the dam. "Whaaaaaaa-hoooo, motherfuckers!"

Link was here. Maybe Shea, too? A sense of peace settled over me. Despite Michio's turmoil, the flutter in my chest told me everything was going to be okay.

"The Drone has hundreds, if not thousands of spiders across the country." Michio turned away from me, facing the ledge, his hand gripping the back of his neck. "All of them are programmed to bite and breed until there are no humans left. The babies already conceived are programmed to do the same." The guttural quake in his voice punched all the way to my core. "As you already know, these creatures are harder to kill than the aphids. And they can *reproduce*."

I touched my belly and the future I held there, my mind spinning with questions about the women and the breeding. But the pain in Michio's voice ran much deeper than the Drone's plans.

"Michio, look at me." I stepped closer, reaching for his back.

"Evie, I—" His shoulders hitched with the start of a sob, but he cut it off and spun away before my hand made contact with him.

Deep, nasty gashes covered his arms, neck, and bare chest. Most were already healing, but his physique was too thin, his skin too pale, and there was so much blood clinging to his body, he looked like he'd crawled out of the bowels of an exploding aphid.

His muscles twitched as he paced before me, his eyes flickering with fire and refusing to look at me. "I can't—"

He pulled at his hair, crumpling over, and made a bone-rattling, keening noise in the back of his throat. Then he straightened, and his feet pounded the pavement as he resumed his furious pacing. Sinews stretched in his neck, his biceps contracting as he removed the remaining rope from his arm.

My eyes burned, and my hands trembled. He was working through something in his head, and I wasn't sure whether to stop him with a hug or stand out of his way.

Another sob crawled from his throat, but he growled over it. "I can't face this. I can't…I can't live with what I've done to you."

I stepped in front him and placed my palms on his heaving chest. "You can't face *this*? Me, standing right here, breathing and desperate to hold you? You can't live with *you* being the reason I'm not splattered at the bottom of this cliff?"

Dark, haunting pain shadowed his face as he touched the gouges in my cheek. "I can't face *this*." His hand lowered to the puncture marks on my neck. "Or *this*." He crouched, lowering until he was eye-level with my stomach, his hands separating the shredded strips of cotton to reveal the yellowish bruises on my torso.

"Michio—"

"I can't live with *this*." He reached out to touch the marks then yanked his hands away to gingerly hold my wrists, his dark eyes glaring at the raw skin from the shackles. "Or *this*," he choked, his fingers moving to my belly and the life that grew there. "This…" His sob broke free, and his shoulders curled forward with an abusive shudder as his forehead rested on my stomach. "This child…she's going to…" He stared up at me, his tears streaking white lines through the blood on his face, his palms framing my flat belly. "She will be the end of us."

"You're wrong." I squatted before him and cupped his stubborn jaw, my heart hurting and soaring at the same time. "She will be your beginning." I pulled him against me, curling up in the power of his embrace. "This...this new world was never about me, Michio. *She* is your future."

He tensed against me, the storm inside him vibrating and shaking, until finally, it exploded with a roar. "I drugged you, beat you, and locked you in a cage. All while you were pregnant!"

"Aiman did those things, dammit. And from what I can tell, it hurt you more than it hurt me or the baby." I drew in a calming breath and narrowed my eyes. "Where's Elaine?"

His teeth snapped together, the grief on his face buried beneath a fog of fury. "He sent her to one of the facilities this morning." His eyes came back to mine. "He was going to let me follow you over the cliff. The only mercy he was willing to grant me."

"Let you? Oh God, Michio." I hugged him tightly, pushing my hand through his hair.

We had a long way to go to repair the damage, but as our bodies molded together, we eased into a synchronized, rhythmic sway of breaths. I had faith we'd eventually come out the other side whole.

I had at least eight months to heal him.

Eight months until she drew her first breath.

Eight months with my guardians.

"Evie!"

I leaned back, my gaze flicking in the direction of the familiar accent, my chest hitching with excitement.

Beyond the carnage of hundreds of aphids and backlit by the sun, a dozen silhouettes jogged up the road, headed toward us. Among the group, I could make out Roark's broad shoulders and the arch of Jesse's bow on his back.

Michio pressed his lips to my temple. "Go, Nannakola. I'll be right here."

I turned back to him and kissed his blood-stained mouth.

"Come with me."

"I took you away from them, remember? If I were in their position—"

"You didn't—"

"They don't know what happened." He stroked his thumb over my jaw. "Let them have a minute with you before we dig into the last four weeks."

Four weeks. Fuck, it had been that long? In some ways, it felt longer.

"You're a better man than me, Michio Nealy."

That earned me barely a twitch of a smile, but it was something. With his hands on my hips, he lifted me up to my feet, rising with me.

He kissed the top of my head. "I love you." He nudged me toward the approaching men.

"Love you, too." I squeezed his hand and took off.

Thirty feet away, Jesse and Roark picked up their speed, leaving the group of men behind as they sprinted toward me. Neither of my guardians smiled, their faces creased with worry, but their happiness was evident in the gleam of their eyes and the way they glanced at each other as they closed the distance to me.

I slowed my jog so I could look at them for a moment. I just needed to *look,* because fuck, I thought I'd never be able to rest my eyes on them again.

Jesse still had his stubble, the reddish hues glowing in the sunlight. Roark's blond curls were shiny and twisting at the ends as though they were dreading again. His strong jaw was covered in a month's worth of whiskers. Jesse's leather pants and jacket and Roark's trench coat were ragged and blood-splattered, but my guys looked healthy, uninjured, and as arresting as ever.

Jesse ran quicker and reached me first. I thought my heart might leap from my chest when his arms enfolded me and swung me around in a circle. As he hauled my body up his chest, the noises rumbling from his throat conveyed a bevy of emotions, part-laughter, part-groaning, and there was definitely a deep growl in there.

When he stopped moving, I looked up at his face and found his eyes glaring daggers at the overhang and the man I'd left there.

"Hey." I wrestled an arm free from his tight hold and gripped his scruffy jaw, pulling him back to me. "You should be kissing him, not glaring at him. He saved my life."

"I know. I was there." He nodded his chin at the canyon wall on the far side of the dam then lowered his brow, touching it to mine. "You took my heart with you when you fell from that cliff. I didn't think it would beat again."

I pulled in a deep breath, inhaling his woodsy scent, our lips an inch apart. "If you hadn't distracted the Drone with the arrow—"

Huge hands wrapped around my chest and yanked me back. Jesse's arms fell away as Roark spun me and cupped my face. I got a glimpse of his jade eyes right before his lips landed on mine.

I turned my head, cringing at the condition of my hygiene. "I haven't brushed my teeth in over a month, Roark, and I need—"

"Shut up." His hands on my face forced my mouth back to his. What little argument I'd put into stopping him was driven away by the dive of his tongue. He didn't wait for me to open my mouth, and instead barged right in with forceful, hungry licks. The stretch of his jaw coaxed mine, and in the next heartbeat, we were sucking and tasting and eating each other up.

"You left us," he rasped between kisses.

I slid my tongue along his bottom lip and grinned. "You found me."

Jesse crowded behind me, his hands on my back, sliding over the tattered rags and curving around my hips. He followed the lines of my body, perhaps checking for wounds or maybe reacquainting himself. Whatever the reason, I didn't want him to stop.

As Roark covered my mouth with his, plunging his tongue

and heating my core, Jesse moved his lips to my ear. "We missed you, Evie."

It wasn't a sensual declaration. There was too much heartache straining the words.

I slid my mouth away from Roark's and kissed the breast of his trench coat. "I missed you, too. We have so much to talk about. I…" I looked up and fell into Roark's glimmering eyes. "How did you find me?"

Jesse stepped to my side and stuck two fingers in his mouth, releasing a high-pitched whistle.

I heard him before I saw him. The scrabble of toenails. The low whine. My pulse raced as I spun.

Link stood some thirty feet back and let go of Darwin's collar. In a blur of black and tan fur, Darwin tore away from the group of men and raced toward me, his tail straight out and his tongue swinging from his panting mouth.

I met him half-way and fell to my knees as he leapt against me with his paws on my shoulders. I fell back, laughing at the feel of his slobbery tongue on my face, his thick coat between my fingers, and the whip of his tail as he drove his big head against my neck.

Gripping his furry cheeks, I pressed my nose to his muzzle. "*You* found me, huh?"

"He rode with his nose out of the window." Jesse ran his hand lovingly down Darwin's back. "He went crazy whenever we missed an exit or turned the wrong way."

I kissed the space between Darwin's huge brown eyes, smiling at the mystery of this amazing animal.

My smile grew bigger when a curvy pair of long dark legs stepped beside me.

Shea gripped my arm and yanked me to my feet. "You look like shit." She pulled me into a hug and said, softly, "But I'll take this over the alternative. Oh honey, your boys…" She sighed. "They've been out of their minds."

I closed my eyes, my heart sinking with the news I'd yet to share with them. I should just blurt it out. Rip off the Band-Aid.

When I opened my eyes, Jesse and Roark were watching me, each wearing his own private smile. They felt what I felt, that overwhelming joy of completeness. The Drone was dead. We stood on a fortress that would protect us indefinitely. And we were all alive, breathing, *together.*

With two words, I was going to decimate their peacefulness.

I'm pregnant.

Say it, Evie.

With a quick scan, I glimpsed a number of familiar faces. Link, Paul, Eddie, and Hunter, they were all here. Dozens of men lingered in the distance. Link's legendary army. I shook my head with a small grin, then leaned around Shea, seeking out Michio.

He stood across the street that traveled over the dam, enveloped in Roark's hug. Fuck, my chest swelled at the sight of that. But when Michio raised his head, his eyes were still hardened with torment. He was waiting for the bomb to drop, knowing that Jesse and Roark were moments from feeling the anguish he felt now. I swallowed around the ache in my throat.

"I need a shower," I announced, stalling. "And a toothbrush." Such a coward. "And a bed." Large enough for four people. Good God, how would that work?

I reached down and ran my fingers through Darwin's hair, seeking his strength. It was going to be a long night.

PART 3

FIFTY-ONE

I stood in a large public restroom beneath the surface of the dam and stared down at the filthy rags that hung from my body. After the near-death events of the day, a cocktail of hormones and adrenal fatigue tingled through my system and numbed my limbs.

The Drone was dead. The cure for nymphs had been dispersed. My guardians were here, with me, all of us together. And I was pregnant. Now that my life was no longer in immediate danger, my focus had radically shifted. I needed a place to safely have my baby. And I needed my guardians to be her home.

Walking through the bowels of the dam without restraints or guards had allowed me to look at its monolithic, protective wall with new eyes. Elaine had said I would love it here. Maybe the rapist bitch was right. I ached to tell her so while I cut out her tongue and stuffed it up her foul ass.

On the way down here, Shea and Darwin had run off to investigate the dozens of rooms and miles of tunnels. I wanted to explore with them, but my guardians and I had more pressing matters. Like washing all the death from our bodies. And talking. We all had questions.

The door to the hall was propped open, and there were no barriers blocking my view of the three of them. The rumbling of their voices floated over me as they ironed out security details with Link. The barricades needed to be rebuilt. The guards needed rotation schedules. And the breeding facilities needed to be found.

I'd kept the cotton wrap secured around my neck and torso to ward off questions about the bite mark and bruises until we were alone. God, I both longed and dreaded to be alone with my guys. If only we could skip the *how's* and *why's* of what had separated us and jump straight to the part where we made up for lost time.

As they discussed the layout of the dam with Link, the enthusiastic buzz in their inflections loosened some of my nerves. It sounded like one question was getting answered. They wanted to stay here.

I'd traveled enough for ten lifetimes and was more than ready to plant my ass on the couch of complacency. The dam offered electricity, plumbing, and fortification. A haven for a pregnant woman.

Shea squeezed past the men and strode through the bathroom, turning the faucets on and off, her huge brown eyes crinkling with awe. "This is the third bathroom I've passed on this level alone. They all have hot water. Can you believe it? And there's a huge storeroom stocked with food near the kitchen."

"There's a kitchen?"

"Looks like it's been recently added." She lowered her voice. "Dude, did you see the Drone's bedroom?"

A chill crawled over my scalp. "No. Thank fuck."

"He'd brought in all kinds of ornate furniture and artwork. The only thing missing was a gold toilet. Seriously, it looked like a museum, except every inch was smothered in spider webs." A shiver bunched her shoulders.

"Jesus. We need to gut it. Burn everything."

"Already on it. Paul and Eddie are hauling everything to the surface and looking for anything that might lead us to those other women." She touched my arm. "Do you mind if Paul, Eddie, and I take that room? I mean, it's huge and has an attached bathroom, so if you want it—"

"God, no. It's all yours." I'd have nightmares sleeping in the Drone's space.

"I need to tell you something."

Her serious tone snapped my eyes to hers. "What's wrong?"

She shook her head, and a smile stretched across her pretty features. "I'm pregnant."

My breath caught, and my muscles locked in shock. A good shock. "Holy shit, Shea. I'm so happy for you."

Her eyes lowered down my body, and her smile fell. I followed her gaze and realized my hand was pressed against my stomach. I dropped my arm. Shit.

"Oh my God," she whispered and covered her mouth. "Evie? How? The IUD? I saw it myself. Oh God, Evie, is it—"

I pressed my hand over hers against her lips, my eyes darting to the door.

My guardians were still immersed in conversation. It sounded like Link was updating Michio on Arkendale.

"It's Jesse's." I kept my eyes on them as I spoke quietly. "I don't know what happened to the IUD." I looked back at her. "Jesse and Roark don't know yet."

Tears brimmed her dark eyes, threatening to spill over my hand. I pulled our arms down and held onto her shaking fingers.

"Don't you fucking cry," I said, under my breath, glancing at the door. "They'll come in here, demanding answers."

"You have to tell them," she whispered, harshly, and a tear rolled down her cheek. "Shit, girl. It's going to destroy them."

"Shhh. I know." I held her face in my hands, touching our foreheads together. "I'll tell them tonight."

She gripped my wrists, her head nodding against mine. "We have the ultrasound machine and we can get more equipment. We can find doctors and specialists, whatever we can do to prevent…" Her voice cracked, and her face crumpled.

What warmed me the most was what she *didn't* suggest. When a mother's life was at risk because of pregnancy, abortion was usually the solution. It was a testament to how well she knew me to not bring it up.

I kissed her brow and leaned back. "It's going to be okay. This is a good thing."

She stared at me as if I were already lying on my death bed.

"What can I do?" She looked around the bathroom, eying the bucket of shampoo and soap, the three toilets, and the stack of towels on the nearby shelf. "Is there anything you need?"

A pair of comfy pajamas and fuzzy slippers? *Good luck finding that.* A case of cold Guinness? Oh wait, I couldn't drink. Oh, ice cream would be good. Right. How about a long night's sleep wrapped in three pairs of strong arms? *Fingers crossed.*

I glanced at the hall and back to her. "Can you find the room Elaine was in and gut it, too? Michio can tell you where it is."

Her brows furrowed. "Elaine? The chick from the mountains?"

"Yeah. She did some really awful things," I whispered, hardening my expression to let her know I wouldn't elaborate. "Can you also set up a room for me as far away from that one as possible? One large enough to sleep the four of us?"

"You got it." She wiped her face and put on her best smile, a gesture I knew she was making for my benefit. "Eddie's cooking dinner. I'll have food brought to your new room, okay?"

I squeezed her hand, my chest swelling at the sight of her glowing with health and pregnancy. "Thank you for coming here."

Her lips compressed, rolling between her teeth as if holding back a cry.

I gave her a smile that I hoped portrayed everything I felt for her. "You could've stayed in Arkendale. You could've gone anywhere. But you didn't. You stuck by me when I was sick in Virginia. And you came here to find me. I just wanted…" I lifted my shoulders, my hand hanging awkwardly in hers. "Thank you."

Her chin trembled. "You saved me, Evie. Gave me the chance to love again. To start a family. You gave me *life*. A life made so much fuller with you in it."

The backs of my eyes pricked. Fuck, now *I* was going to cry.

She drew a deep breath and patted my cheek. "No crying, remember?"

Then she gathered her composure and made a beeline for Michio. They'd only just met as we walked the tunnels down here, but when he learned she was the woman we'd cured in Georgia, a spark had momentarily returned to his eyes.

He leaned down as she whispered in his ear. His jaw hardened, and his gaze sliced to me. He turned and pointed down the hall, jogging his finger as he gave directions to the room where Elaine had done God knew what to him.

Shea vanished from view, and a moment later, the commotion of footsteps and voices crammed the hall. A group of battle-weary men gathered around Link and my guardians. I only recognized one face.

Hunter's long black hair hung in his eyes, his arms wrapped around a huge duffel bag and my bow and quiver. "Link, where do I put this stuff?"

Link slipped into the bathroom and gestured for him to follow. "Leave it here."

Hunter set the bag and bow on the floor and looked up at me, smiling. "Hey, Evie."

I gave him a small wave, but Link was already ushering him out with a hand on the back of his neck. "Thanks, kid."

Link waited for him to leave then turned back to me. "So." He tipped his bald head, studying me. "You're alive."

"So are you."

"*I* didn't fall from a cliff." He grinned, rubbing his jaw. "That prophecy is a real bitch, huh?"

He had no idea. I forced my hands to my sides, resisting the impulse to touch my belly. "Were the guts and glory of battle everything you hoped for?"

His black eyes sparkled under the glow of the ceiling lights as he sniffed the air with a dramatic stretch of his nostrils. "Smells like history in the making, Little Ladybird." He nodded at the bag on the floor. "All your clothes and other belongings should be there."

Wow, that was thoughtful and unexpected. There was something off about Link that would always make me uncomfortable, but beneath his disturbing demeanor, I wondered if his intentions weren't completely vain. Link the Emasculator could very well be Link the Bighearted in disguise.

I bit my lip, hiding my smile. "Thank you."

He headed toward the crowded hallway and paused at the door, passing me a glance over his shoulder. "I'm sending a couple men to Arkendale tonight. It'll take them a month or longer to return, but I thought you'd want news of the peninsula's progress."

Another *thank you* tumbled from my lips, but he was already gone, striding down the corridor and barking orders.

I knelt beside the bag and opened the zipper. Jeans and t-shirts made up most of the bulk, but nestled on top were three things I thought I'd never see again. Roark's rosary, Jesse's turquoise stone, and the arm sheathes and blades Joel had given me. I stroked each with trembling fingers, the remembered textures and curves sending a warmth of love through my chest for the men who'd given them to me.

A pair of scuffed-up boots stepped beside me, followed by two more pairs and the thunk of another bag on the floor next to mine. The door shut, and the lock clicked.

Michio towered over me, his brown eyes dark with regret as he stared at the sheathes. "I'm so sor—"

"Don't. The only thing you have to be sorry about is your guilt." I climbed to my feet and shifted into his space, staring up at him. "No more apologies."

Irritation drew lines across his gorgeous features. He speared his fingers through his hair, walked to the sink, and gripped the edge, bracing the rigid bend of his upper body on stick-straight arms.

I wanted to wrap him in a hug, shake him, and tell him to move on. But he wasn't ready to let go of his feelings. He was probably still trying to wrap his head around exactly what he was feeling. He mourned hurting me even as he knew it hadn't been him delivering the punches. I suspected he was also working through his acceptance of the child that would both end my life and save mankind.

Peace didn't come without tragedy, and love didn't bloom without pain. Irony and ambivalence were the layers of life. He would come to terms with this just like every other struggle we'd endured over the past two years. I just needed to be patient.

Jesse leaned against the locked door, watching me in his usual silent way. Roark drummed fingers on the scabbard at his hip, wearing a brooding expression that slitted his usually smiling eyes. And Michio, braced over the sink on stiff arms, looked as though he were seconds from ripping the porcelain from the wall. The large bathroom felt too small for all the unspoken things bouncing between the four of us.

I shattered the silence with an easy question. "How did you find the arm sheathes?"

Roark shot a weary glance at Michio's back. "Darwin found them on the side of the road in Missouri. His nose scented them out the window of the truck."

"That dog will never cease to amaze me." I shook my head, smiling. "Thank you for bringing them back to me."

"We have a rake of questions, love." Roark shrugged out of his trench coat and dropped it with his scabbard on the floor. Then he reached over his head and gripped the back of his t-shirt, yanking it off. "I know you're tired, so we'll talk while we clean up. Just give us the highlights, starting with why the feck Doc took ye from us."

Anger clipped the edges of his brogue. Evidently, the hug he'd given Michio an hour ago wasn't one of forgiveness. And the second I removed the scraps of cotton from my body, his temper would explode, likely in fists raining down on

Michio's face.

I fingered the scarf around my neck, stalling. "Aiman knew Michio had the ability to track me. He used mind control to send him to my house— Wait." I stared at Michio's back. "I saw Aiman in a dream. In my home. If he was trying to lure me there, why did he need you to track me?"

Michio looked up and met my eyes in the mirror, his hands tightening around the sink. "I don't think he knew about the dream. I didn't know about it. We passed through Missouri on our way here from the mountains, stopping only so he could destroy the home you might want to return to."

That was fucked up. Worse was imagining Michio watching Aiman burn my house while locked in his body, unable to stop it from happening.

"Hold on, for feck's sake." Roark's accent thickened with impatience. "I'm still stuck on *mind control.*"

I opened my mouth to explain, but Michio cut me off.

"I'll tell them." He pivoted to face me, his body straight and stiff. "Take off your clothes, Evie."

The hardness in his voice and the bore of his gaze brooked no room for argument. He could explain the mechanics of Aiman's control better than I could, but I refused to remove a stitch of clothing without some promises.

Glancing at each man, I folded my arms over my chest. "No fighting. No weapons. No violence of any kind until everyone has heard everything. Promise me."

I got three terse nods, but the tension in the room condensed, pressing against my skin. Their breaths lengthened, and their bodies flexed as they guardedly watched each other and me.

Two long steps carried Michio past me. He reached toward the ceiling and turned the valves to activate the shower head. It was the same modified set up as the other bathroom, just an attachment added to an overhead pipe in the middle of the large space and a drain in the tiled floor beneath it.

He moved away from the spray of the water and stared at me with an unwavering expression, waiting for me to expose the bite and bruises.

As I slowly unwrapped the rags, Roark removed his boots and pants. My insides clenched at the sight of his imposing nudity, my focus momentarily distracted by his cock, so full and heavy, hanging against his thigh and reminding me I hadn't had an orgasm in over a month.

I caught him gazing at my body, not directly, but from beneath his blond lashes as he kicked his clothes away from the water.

Jesse stepped away from the wall, his stark glare locked on my yellow-spotted ribs. "The fuck?"

"I did that." Michio glared at the bruises, his eyes like blood-stained doors into the dark dungeon of his thoughts. "I drugged her. Locked her in a cage for two weeks in the back of a truck. Made her defecate in a bucket. Froze her through the Colorado Mountains without so much as a blanket to keep her warm."

The collected hike in breaths eroded away any calm that was left in the room. It felt as though someone had sprayed a can of bloodthirsty testosterone in the air.

"What's he talking about, Evie?" Jesse's voice was stone grinding on stone, his stance deadly still.

Roark paced behind Jesse, hands clenching at his sides, glaring at Michio.

Frustration bit at my insides. "Michio, don't—"

"They need to know!" His voice was hoarse and thick with guilt, his eyes drilling into Jesse and Roark as if begging them to hurt him. "I punched her every time she tried to escape."

Jesse flew at Michio, his face burning with rage, his khukuri suddenly appearing beneath Michio's jaw.

"Jesse, no!" I didn't know where the knife had come from. Under his invisible jacket? Beneath his tight leather pants? Out of his ass? Telekinesis? Nothing surprised me anymore.

Roark was right behind him, his fist rearing back to swing. Fuck! I grabbed his waist, my stomach spinning as I twisted around him.

"You promised." I glared at the back of Jesse's head and

pushed against the hard press of Roark's heaving chest, shouting at both of them, "He wants you to punish him because he's hurting, but none of this was his fault."

Michio lifted his chin, moisture sheening his eyes as he leaned into the lethal edge of the knife.

I pushed harder against the corded muscles of Roark's torso. "Tell them, Michio!"

FIFTY-TWO

With my hands pressed against Roark's naked body, I struggled to hold him back. I leaned harder, with my shoulder then all of my weight. I wished I hadn't removed my clothes and revealed the bruises. I should've explained the marks first instead of relying on Michio to defend himself.

A few feet away, Jesse and Michio were still dressed, locked in a lethal embrace with Jesse's knife against Michio's throat. Jesse glared at Michio, his eyes burning, while Michio stared back, silently begging him to sink the blade.

"Jesse, I know you won't hurt him. You saw him save my life up there." I knew he was reacting without thinking, and Michio was giving him an easy target. "Michio, tell them what actually happened or I will."

Jesse jerked the dagger away but didn't back up.

After a heavy swallow, Michio unraveled Aiman's plans, the mind control used on him and the spiders, and how my blood in the women worked as a vaccine against the venom. He spoke in anguished tones, each word more hollow than the last.

Jesse and Roark backed up, staring in horrified disbelief.

"You understand now?" I waved a hand over my bruises. "Aiman used Michio's body to hurt both of us."

Jesse and Michio remained outside of the spray of the shower head, and Roark pulled me beneath it.

As the warm water enveloped us, he wrapped me in his arms. "Shh. It's over. It's all over. He can't hurt you anymore." He lifted his eyes to Michio. "Or you."

"Fuck." Jesse dropped the khukuri on the duffel bag, his eyes staying with Michio as his anger slipped behind the furrowed grooves in his face. "That's fucking…I don't know what it is. How did you break your mind free to kill him?"

Roark's fingers traced the mark on my neck. I suspected he wanted to ask about it. Maybe he was already figuring it out, but he remained quiet as he shifted his attention to Michio.

"Aiman controlled my voluntary movements and knew all of my thoughts." Resentment seeped through Michio's voice. "So I shut off my mind."

"What do you mean you shut it off?" I held my head out of the water as Roark rubbed shampoo into my hair. "Are you talking about meditation?"

I recalled all the times I'd seen Michio sitting cross-legged on the floor in Malta, with the backs of his hands on bent knees, ankles on opposing thighs, eyes closed. A pose used in Buddhist meditation.

"Yes. I quieted my thoughts and focused on my breaths in self-forgetful concentration. In doing so, I surrendered my body to physiological response."

Jesse tread a path through the room, his leather pants straining against the flex of his thighs. Anxiety was better than anger in this case, but it didn't make his pacing any calmer. "That's fight-or-flight reaction, right?"

Michio nodded, staring down at his empty hands. "I didn't know if it would work, but I trusted my unconscious reflexes when it came to Evie."

I rinsed the shampoo from my hair, my mind spinning with questions. "The rope…I don't understand. How did you tie it so diligently without thinking about how I would fall with it?"

His slack expression and sad eyes tightened my throat as he said, "I'd been in a state of meditation for two weeks. When Aiman commanded me to restrain you and bring you to the surface, I let my instincts guide the intricacies of the knots."

God, he'd been through so much, and my heart thumped with the need to protect him from the emotional aftermath.

The wounds on his arms and upper body were closed up and healing beneath all the blood. But his ribs jutted sharply around the stacks of muscles in his chest.

I left the warmth of the falling water and gripped his wrist, pulling him toward the shower head. Before he moved into the water, I reached down to remove his pants. It was such a familiar thing to do, yet I hesitated. *Fucking bitch Elaine.*

I looked up and asked with my eyes. *Do I have permission to strip you? Is it okay to touch you here?*

He glanced at my hand hovering over his groin, his dark brows furrowing. Then he nodded.

My fingers fumbled to loosen the belt and slide it from the loops of his pants, my voice soft. "Why are you so thin?"

"My stomach wouldn't keep food down." He stared at my body, his eyes roaming over my curves, but his gaze seemed to be lost to whatever nightmare Elaine had branded on his soul. "Another reflexive response Aiman couldn't control."

I left his pants hanging on his hips to circle my arms around his waist. The tight muscles of his back bunched beneath my palms as my fingers slid over his skin, holding him to me. He stood there like a steel beam in my arms yet he seemed so unsteady, leaning against me.

Finally, his hands lifted and eased up my spine, slowly, way too cautiously to satisfy my impatient need for the kind of touches he used to give me, but patience was exactly what he needed. I owed him that and so much more.

The scent of deodorant soap mixed with masculine musk reached my nose. I stood just at the edge of the water with Roark fully immersed behind me. He quickly scrubbed down his body then moved his lathered hands to my ass, taking extra time to massage and re-massage the bubbles into my skin.

When Roark's breathing grew heavier, I knew he'd moved far past patient, his every stroke promising he'd fuck me into oblivion before the night was over.

With agonizing tenderness, Michio traced the edge of the marks on my neck as he told Jesse and Roark about Aiman's intention to drain my power and kill me, skipping over how the prophecy had led to that decision.

He explained how the bite and consummation of my blood had ultimately broke the Drone's hold on his mind. "I didn't consciously try to bite you, Evie. I was operating on pure reflex, guided by my physiological response to fight."

He assumed it was fight, but I suspected his body knew my blood was what it needed to overpower Aiman.

"I wanted you to bite me, and your body knew that. Thank fuck your instincts were stronger than Aiman's control of your actions."

We shared a look, a connection forged in hardship and love. Had he felt what I felt during that bite? The veracity in it? The way we'd conformed to our need to come together despite the odds against us? Had he felt my child reaching for him during the bite, drawing on his venom and absorbing his essence? I couldn't ask without jumping into the prolific conversation of my pregnancy.

Jesse removed his shirt and toed off his boots. "You're telling us the spiders don't have control over their reflexes like you did? They're programmed to mindlessly bite others? Then what?"

As Michio talked through the effects of the spider bite, Roark crouched behind me, his hands sliding the soap down my legs. My senses were heightened to his every touch, my skin shivering beneath the stroke of his fingers. He seemed single-mindedly committed to his task, his breaths attuned to mine, but I knew he was clinging to every word Michio said.

I looked for the shampoo to wash Michio's hair, and the bottle appeared beside me, clutched in Jesse's outstretched hand. He stood outside the splash of water, still wearing his pants. I reached past the bottle and cupped his jaw, relishing the scratch of his whiskers against my palm. I wanted to draw him to my mouth and suck the plump flesh of his bottom lip. I wanted to kiss along the line of his neck and lick the hollow of his throat. I wanted him twitching and groaning as I teased my mouth down his abs.

When I accepted the shampoo from him, he freed the

button on his waistband. His pupils dilated as his gaze swept down my body and returned to my face.

Sweet pissing hell, he just removed his pants.

Michio watched us, not with jealousy but with something more…hesitant. Respect? Whatever it was softened his eyes and evened his breaths as he kicked off his boots. His pants and briefs followed.

It was torture-laced pleasure, standing there surrounded by three fiercely beautiful, naked men with all their sharp angles, warm skin, and visible strength. My fingers itched to touch. My mouth watered to lick as memories of their bodies moving around and in me sent a current of need through my core, gathering heat between my legs.

I reached toward Michio's head and worked the shampoo into his hair. "You guys are killing me."

Roark dragged soapy hands over my hips. "Goes both ways, love."

Jesse's eyes hooded and his hands clenched at his side. I glanced over my shoulder and found Roark's cock thickening where it hung between his legs. But neither man moved to take it further, perhaps sensing that something was off about Michio.

The spray of a single shower head wasn't big enough for the four of us. Jesse stood on the edge, completely unabashed with his nudity as he waited to rinse off.

He regarded me intently. "Are you still feeling overly-aroused?"

My clit throbbed at the gruffness in his voice. "Given the circumstances over the past month, I haven't been. But now? I'm nursing a pretty big ache."

Michio studied the other men for a long moment before looking down at me. No doubt he was thinking about pregnancy hormones and how Jesse and Roark had been on the receiving end of my libido.

I threaded soapy fingers through Michio's hair, reacquainting myself with the thick texture. I tried not to stare at his hips, ridged with sharp edges and deep indentions, or the thin trail of dark hair that led from his abs to the black curls below, or his thick cock… I tried not to think about all the ways Elaine had violated him and hoped he would eventually let me replace bad memories with loving ones, one kiss at a time.

He gripped my waist, bringing our bodies closer, his thumbs stroking across my hips. "Are we done talking about the spiders?"

Jesse scratched the scruff of his jaw. "Just so I'm clear… When they bite, the venom programs the victim to bite and program other men and so on?"

"Until there's no one left to bite," I mumbled.

Behind me, Roark rose to his full height and tossed the bar of soap to Jesse, switching places with him. "Sounds like a race of mindless vampires with humans on the menu."

"Not completely mindless." Michio tilted his head back and rinsed. "They're programmed to worship Allah, but with Aiman dead, they're able to make decisions, think, and fight on their own, as long as the outcome serves Aiman's purpose. They'll pass on that programming to every man they bite. Women will be forced to breed with fertile men, then the spiders will bite those men, too, all in an effort to create Aiman's chosen race. The present generation of women are immune to the programming, but their offspring are not."

I met Michio's eyes through the spray of the water. "Maybe the women will revolt?"

"Maybe. But they're pregnant, which will restrict the risks they might be willing to take." His eyes flicked to my stomach, a subtle glance, before returning to my face. "The babies in utero have already undergone Aiman's programming. As new generations are conceived, the spiders will continue to bite the mothers, rendering them infertile while infecting the babies. Which means the newborns will be programmed like the others."

The fucks were flying now, slipping under breaths as Jesse and Roark looked at one another.

Michio painted a future that put a hollowed-out species at

the top of the food chain, one that worshiped a god without questioning their beliefs. A species void of freewill and inquisitiveness and everything that made humans *human*.

Since Michio had bitten me, would his venom program my baby? I didn't think so since he was immune to the programming. But how would my daughter stop this from happening to others? Could she reverse the effects of the venom? Could she kill the creatures with a thought? Would her life be burdened with great suffering and difficulty as she fought to free mankind?

Jesse's jaw hardened into stone. "When the prophecy referred to evolving creatures, it wasn't talking about the aphids."

"No." Already knowing this didn't stop the dread from festering in my gut.

Roark strode away, yanked a towel from the shelf, and wrapped it around his waist. "How do we find the women?"

"Follow the nymphs?" I trailed after him and grabbed a towel for myself, watching their expressions as I dried off.

"It's a start." Roark removed athletic shorts from the second bag and stepped into them, mumbling, "Fecking actual dirtball knoblicker doesn't just die and leave us well alone. Oh no, he has to leave a mingin' mess behind him." He yanked the shorts to his waist and looked up. "When do we leave?"

Michio paused in his cleaning, and his eyes shot to mine, his thoughts as transparent as the water sluicing over his skin. As soon as Jesse and Roark learned I was pregnant, we wouldn't be going anywhere. For safety reasons. And because the child in my womb held more answers than we'd find on the road.

I pulled on a pair of cotton shorts and a t-shirt. "If my blood is a vaccine, maybe we could start passing out vials, or clone it somehow?"

"Evie," Michio growled. "You can't."

Because I couldn't drain myself of the nourishment needed by my baby. Fuck.

Jesse strode to the bag and pulled out two pairs of

sweatpants, tossing one to Michio. "It's not a bad idea. We could draw her blood in small doses. We have electricity here to refrigerate it. Though I don't know how we'd disperse it."

Michio dressed, pinning me with a stern look. "Tell them."

My chest crushed beneath the weight of his command.

"Tell us what?" Jesse's head snapped up.

His lower half was covered in sweatpants, the smooth skin of his chest glistening with water and his cheekbones sharpening with the intensity of his scowl.

Michio stepped behind me. I waited for him to lash out at Jesse and Roark for fucking me. Waited for him to blame Jesse for knocking me up.

Instead, he folded his arms around my waist and touched a warm kiss to my temple. "Do you want me to tell them?"

I shook my head and dug deep, searching for the right words.

Roark watched me struggle, his mouth turned down and his jade eyes several shades darker than usual.

I feared their reactions. What if they suggested an abortion? No, they would never want that. What if Roark turned on Jesse and beat the shit out of him? Or what if they weren't upset? If they reacted with relief because humanity's future was more important than my own? I mean, it was, but… Fuck, I was tangling myself up in *what-ifs*.

I pulled in a deep breath and pushed it out. "I just…I want you guys to be happy. I'm…God, I'm so happy, and I want you to feel this way, too."

My eyes teared up. Fucking hormones.

Roark crossed his arms and gave me a *What the hell?* look while Jesse cocked his head and stared hard into my eyes.

Shit, I was dragging this out, making it worse. "I've experienced some weird changes. The extra energy. I can blow up bugs. The…uh, high-octane sex drive."

Jesse's eyes snapped wide, and his gaze dropped to my stomach.

"No." Roark shook his head, his arms falling at his sides.

I clenched my fingers around Michio's hands at my waist.

"I'm pregnant."

FIFTY-THREE

As the words left my mouth, Roark spun away and smacked his palms on the wall. His head dropped between the support of his arms, and the muscled line of his spine pinched as he sucked in a heavy breath.

My ribs constricted so tightly it felt as though everything was suffocating inside.

Beside him, Jesse paled. His shock quickly tightened into denial then darkened into anger.

"There must be a mistake," he growled. "The child can't be mine."

The steam-filled bathroom closed in around me, the rush of my breaths adding to the stifling humidity. Had I been where Jesse and Roark stood now, listening to one of them tell me, in not so many words, he would be dying, I would've been in denial, too. Then I would've lost my fucking shit.

But instead I stood on the other side, enveloped in Michio's arms, my heart breaking and my legs locking, braced for the ground to shake beneath the quake of their outrage.

Jesse's eyes narrowed on Michio behind me. "She had an IUD." The landslide of his voice grew louder with each word. "I saw it on the screen!"

He wrestled to temper his fury, his features distorting then smoothing as he reined himself in.

His tone lowered as he glared at Michio. "The child has to be yours."

God, it hurt to see him grasping for irrational straws. Even more painful was watching his desperation wet the corners of his eyes.

Michio shook his head, his tone gentle. "You know she's not mine, but she will be. I intend to raise her with or without you."

His declaration was a calming whisper in my veins, filling me with weightless relief.

"This can't be happening." Jesse's gaze swung around the bathroom and locked on Roark. "I want proof of his infertility." His hands fisted at his sides, his feet braced apart, his neck blotching with the rise of blood. "This is not the prophesied child. It's not!"

Roark lowered his arms and leaned a shoulder against the wall, his eyes pink and glassy, and his brogue cracking. "How far along?"

"Four weeks." I watched with a tight throat as Jesse and Roark slumped beneath the gravity of my response.

Jesse pressed a fist against his forehead, and his mouth parted, fighting for air. Then he straightened and glanced around again, as if looking for an answer that disproved the one he refused to accept.

When his gaze returned to me, it was wider, harsher, and unblinking. "This is my fault. I knew better." His jaw flexed, and his voice thundered through the room. "I fucking knew about the prophecy and did it anyway!"

I pulled out of Michio's embrace and took a cautious step forward, my hands up, placating. "There's no blame here, Jesse." I touched my stomach. "This was supposed to happen."

"No." His teeth clenched, his lips drawn back as he glared at my hand on my belly. "Not this." He stabbed a finger in the direction of my womb so forcibly his entire body launched with the thrust of his arm. "Anything but this!"

He pivoted and gave me his back, his hands curling around his nape, yanking his head down.

Here was a man who could hold conversations with ghost children, take down hordes of aphids, and fire an arrow into the eye-socket of a human without a hitch in his breath. Yet he struggled to deal with this.

"Two years." He turned back to me, his long strides engulfing the space between us. "Two years I stayed away, kept my fucking dick to myself." He bent at the waist with the force of his shouting, his shoulders curling forward. "Why did I even bother waiting? What the fuck was the point of an ultrasound, huh?"

I backed up, my heart hammering. "Calm down."

He stepped with me, his expression a fuming-red canvas of misery. "I might as well have just fucked you with a goddamned pistol and pulled the trigger"—he shoved his face in mine and pointed his hand at my temple like a gun—"because the outcome is the fucking same!"

When he stormed across the room, my breath released in a staggering hiccup, my eyes burning, welling with tears. I moved to follow, but Michio hooked an arm around my shoulders and pulled my back against his chest.

Jesse kicked the bucket of soap and sent it careening into the wall. I flinched, and hot tears raced down my cheeks, trickling over the seam of my lips.

Near the door, Roark's expression was a steel plate of armor, hiding his thoughts, his body poised like a sword, ready to tackle Jesse if this went too far.

Jesse crouched at the far end of the room, a hand on his brow, rocking with labored breaths. He seemed to force down his grief momentarily as he glanced at me. Then his breathing sped up again, his gaze snapping back to the floor as he moaned with wet, angry sounds and gripped his head with both hands.

More tears rained down my cheeks, and I tasted copper, my vision blurring in red.

I shoved against Michio's arm. "I need to go to him."

"Evie?" Roark pushed away from the wall and erased the distance between us in three hurried strides.

His hands cupped my face, tipping it upward, staring at me with horror. "Your eyes…" He looked up at Michio. "What's happening to her?"

"If you're asking for a medical answer, I don't have one. I just saw this for the first time today and would need to do some scans." Michio kissed the top of my head, his free arm locking around my waist. "Though I assume a Catholic priest would have his own theories to explain the enigmatic language of her tears."

Roark's chest hitched, his mind likely trawling for biblical explanations.

I blinked, swiped at my cheeks, and stared at my bloody fingers, my voice thick. "It's about as fucked up as the spots on my back."

Footsteps approached, and Jesse moved in. His hands closed around Roark's on my face, tilting my head toward him.

A lone tear wandered over Jesse's cheekbone and vanished into his whiskers. "Oh, God, Evie." His trembling fingers moved over my face, wiping at the bloody tears. "I'm sorry. I'm so fucking sorry."

He gathered me in his arms, seemingly oblivious of Roark and Michio holding onto me. Eventually, the other arms fell away, leaving Jesse and me in a shaky bubble, our bodies molding together so tightly I couldn't tell where my heartache ended and his began.

Tight muscles surrounded me, our swaying movements setting a rhythmic pace with our breaths. I held his stubborn jaw in my hands, my fingers lost in his hair. Would our daughter inherit his auburn highlights? Or the depths of his faceted copper eyes? Or the tiny, off-centered cowlick that whorled at the peak of his hairline? I hoped she had all of his endearing features.

I hoped she acquired Roark's passion, too. And Michio's analytical mind. If she embodied even a fraction of my guardians' qualities, she would be an influential force of nature.

Roark and Michio sat shoulder to shoulder against the wall, watching me. Michio's legs were bent, his chest leaning forward and his arms braced on his knees. Roark's head rested against the tiles, chin up, and his hand on Michio's back.

I'd once thought emotions were a sign of weakness, but my guardians were a powerful display of torment. Eventually, the shadows on their faces would flee, and their slumped shoulders would fortify. Even now, they were absorbing the shock, not cowering beneath it. They plowed over obstacles rather than sidestepping around them, because adversity was the foundation of their strength. I might not have had conviction in a god, but my faith in the men I loved was unwavering.

Jesse lowered to a squat before me, his hands gliding over my breasts, testing their weight and perhaps checking for tenderness as he studied my face. They felt the same, but I was still so early in my pregnancy.

He lifted my t-shirt, tucking the hem beneath my boobs, and smoothed his palms over the vertical plane of my stomach.

"We're having a baby," he said, his voice hushed.

The sound of his wonderment took hold of my mouth, stretching my smile so widely it lifted my whole body. "Yeah. We are."

His eyebrows dug together, his fingers sweeping over my hip bones and returning to the valley of my belly. "You've survived five prophesied deaths. You'll survive this one." He looked up at me, his eyes tapered into steely determination. "We'll beat this."

Fate cannot be changed.

Aiman's words didn't have the same shivery effect on me now that he was dead. The pregnancy was the last of my predicted deaths. No others followed it, because this one couldn't be evaded. I wouldn't voice that, though. Not when Jesse was finally starting to see past his grief.

"Let's beat the prediction." I pushed my fingers through his hair. "But can I brush my teeth first?"

"Yeah." He pressed his lips to my belly button, adjusted my shirt, and straightened until our eyes were level. "I'm freaking out, Evie, but it's no excuse for making you cry. God, I'm such a dick."

"Fear is a dick, and you, Jesse Beckett, are fearless."

"But not dickless?"

I laughed, and fuck, that felt good.

He dragged a thumb over my cheek and raised it between us, staring at the smear of blood. "Never seen you cry. It's like your soul is bleeding."

With a gentle finger, I traced the downward bow of his mouth. "If my soul is bleeding, it's with love and happiness. Don't you get it? This was never about me. Our daughter is the reason I survived the virus, the reason I fell in love with three unbreakable protectors. *She* needs you."

"And I need *you.*" He ran his hand through my wet hair, staring intently into my eyes. "I need you so much."

I breathed deeply, filling every crevice inside me with need, his and mine.

Roark's accent floated over my shoulder. "Are ye familiar with Our Lady of Akita?"

I turned in Jesse's arms and shook my head.

"I am." Michio leaned back against the wall. "It was a weeping Madonna statue in Japan. I heard about it when I lived there. It cured illness, right?"

"Yeah." Roark pulled a toothbrush and paste from his bag, rose to his feet, and strode to the sink. "The statue's ectoplasmic tears were actually filmed by a television crew and shown during news broadcasts throughout the world. What made it unique was its apparition of the Virgin Mary and the messages she delivered."

A shiver coursed through me. "You think it was the real deal then?"

"It was the only one of its kind to be sanctioned by the Vatican." He held up the toothbrush and hiked a brow at me.

Jesse followed me to one of the sinks and perched on the edge of another as I accepted the brush and cleaned my teeth.

"The apparition delivered messages? What were they?" I asked around the minty bubbles.

"Warnings of the end times." Roark swiped a thumb at the corner of my mouth. "The Virgin's apparition spoke of the terrible punishment that would be placed on all of humanity, stating, 'The survivors will find themselves so desolate that they will envy the dead.'"

When the plague hit, I had envied the dead. Now that I wanted to live, I was forced to stare death in the face. Talk about the irony of life.

I spit, rinsed off the toothbrush, and handed it to Roark.

He reloaded it with more toothpaste. "Genesis 3:15 says the serpent's head will be crushed by the seed of a woman."

My head kicked back. "Are you implying my daughter is that biblical seed?"

"I'm not finished. The apparition at Our Lady of Akita referenced that verse in one of her messages when she said, 'Sin came into the world by a woman and it is also by a woman that salvation came to the world.' In the Church, we called that Co-Redemptrix."

The fact that I shared the name of the woman with sin sent a prickle down my back, but that didn't mean *I* was the woman with salvation. "I don't have any designs on redeeming mankind, Roark."

"Ye weep blood and cured humanity."

"So? I'm not a statue or a Virgin apparition."

"No, but someday, your image will be carved in wood, sewn onto cloth, and cast in metal." His tone was both sad and reverent. "Your face will become an object of worship and adoration. You'll be the iconic memorial of the healing of women, and the mother of the new world's messiah."

I bristled to refute every damned thing he said. "Suggesting that anyone would carve my face into anything is awfully optimistic, considering the programmed minds taking over the human race."

Roark glanced at Jesse beside me then looked away and popped the toothbrush in his mouth.

"He's right, Evie." Michio joined my side and tucked my hair behind my ear. "I don't think any of us are ready to discuss the credibility of the prophecy and the child's role in the future. But no matter what happens, you will be remembered."

Ugh. "I don't want that."

"Humble and fierce," Jesse said quietly against his fist where it rested on his mouth.

"I'm being serious," I grumbled. "This is a pointless conversation."

Michio regarded me with a thoughtful gaze. "You don't see what everyone else sees, Evie. You have a subtle luminousness surrounding you. It's not just one thing, but the whole of everything inside you. It's like a tactile glow that shimmers from you and inspires others to be better. You can lift a man from his lowest point without even trying."

"You're biased." I rubbed my arm, my eyes pricking. "That's your love talking."

Roark cleaned off the toothbrush and passed it to Jesse. Then he turned to me and pressed a kiss to my lips.

"You're doing what ye feared ye couldn't do." He stroked a hand over my belly, his *r*'s rolling from the front of his mouth. "That alone inspires us to stand tall in the overwhelmingly large and momentous future. Do ye understand?"

I nodded as his words settled around my heart. They admired me for bringing a child into this brutal world, knowing how much the idea had terrified me. It still scared me. The Oh-Jesus-what-the-fuck-am-I-doing? kind of terror. But I wasn't doing it alone.

Roark dipped his head and kissed my lips. Sweetly, tenderly, his mouth caressed mine. The sound of Jesse brushing his teeth faded as I sought Roark's minty tongue, melded against his lips, and fell into his kiss.

He tasted every inch of my mouth, and I opened for him, breathing him in, licking him with devotion and yearning. His oaky scent was my elixir, embedding itself in my skin and bringing my arousal to life.

His hardening length began to rise against my belly, and I whimpered. His fingers curled around my lower back, dipping beneath the waistband of my shorts and teasing the top of my butt crack. I shuddered as a wave of need clenched between my legs. I wanted his hot mouth there. And his cock. Fuck, I'd missed him so much.

When we came up for air, Michio was rinsing our communal toothbrush, his eyes watching us intensely in the mirror. He'd seen me kiss Roark countless times, but this time was different. He knew my intimacy with Roark had moved far past foreplay.

Jesse waited by the door with our bags. A moment later, Roark and Michio joined him.

Flushed and hungry, I met three pairs of eyes. I needed food. Wanted sex. I stood there, not speaking, just staring, unsure how to breach the topic Michio might not be ready for. He'd never shared me with another man, and we still hadn't discussed what happened with Elaine.

With a tug at the hem of my shorts, I licked my lips. "I asked Shea to set up a room for us. With one bed." I waited for a reaction and was met with steady stares. "The four of us sharing a bed."

Jesse and Roark glanced at Michio, who stared at me with an unreadable expression. Was his temper burning behind that hardened mask? Was he dreading sharing me with two other men? Or was he nursing the aches he couldn't outrun? My caged captivity? Elaine's violation? His venom in my blood and its repercussions on me and the baby?

Whatever it was hovered like a thick cloud between us, begging to be shouted.

"I don't need skin-on-skin contact anymore, but I still need you. All three of you." I blew out a breath, frustrated that I was the only one willing to voice what we were all thinking. "You're going to make me spell this out, aren't you?"

Roark crossed his arms over his chest. "I rather enjoy watching ye struggle to ask for it, love."

The corner of Jesse's mouth twitched, his gaze on the floor.

Michio rubbed the back of his head and shifted his weight from one foot to the other. "She's tiptoeing because she's worried about *me*." He looked directly in my eyes. "For the four months I was separated from you, I thought of nothing but them taking care of you in *every* way. Trust me when I say it took most of those long months to replace my resentment and jealousy with contentment. I've found peace in the knowledge that they were protecting you and loving you when I couldn't."

He looked at Jesse and Roark, and they nodded, their eyes communicating mutual respect and understanding.

I walked toward Michio and reached up to tug his face down to mine. "What happened with Elaine?"

Out of the corner of my vision, I could see the questioning looks from Jesse and Roark.

Michio gripped my hands and pulled them down. "It's in the past. That's where we're leaving it."

"Ye told Link she was compromised." Roark narrowed his eyes at Michio. "She's still alive, out there somewhere. Is she a threat? Wha's her involvement with ye?"

"She's not a threat. It's done." Michio glared at the door, like he was a twitch away from running through it. "I'm moving on."

Jesse and Roark shared a look.

Ruthless venom simmered through my blood. "She raped you."

"Evie, dammit." Michio turned toward the door and flipped the deadbolt.

"You don't move on from that without talking through it." I touched his arm. "Every time I think about it, my stomach knots up. I'm fucking vibrating with the need to kill her."

He swung back toward me, aggression rippling through his voice. "When I see her again, *I* will kill her." He pulled in a breath and schooled his expression. "Right now, I want you to eat and rest. I'm going to do a full exam on you tomorrow. Run some tests. Your health is my *only* concern. Are we clear?"

"Yeah." I felt like I might choke on the air, but at least the starting points of future conversations were out in the open now.

With a cursory glance at Jesse and Roark, he led us out of

the bathroom.

FIFTY-FOUR

Somberness rode on the curls of steam that followed us out of the bathroom. But the air became easier to breathe the moment I saw Shea and Paul waiting in the corridor.

They sat against the wall, heads bowed together in quiet conversation, with Darwin sprawled between their outstretched legs.

Darwin's single ear perked up. Then he came running, jumping around my feet and rubbing his wet nose against my palm. I gave him the head scratches he wanted, and he scrambled away to pester Jesse for more of the same.

Paul rose and pulled Shea to her feet, as they smiled at one another affectionately. When she scanned my guardians' faces, her expression faltered. Given their pale complexions, dark circles under their eyes, and arms hanging at their sides, she didn't have to ask if we'd discussed my pregnancy.

"Your room is ready." Sympathy creased her eyes as she searched my face. "Are you okay?"

I nodded. "We will be."

A few minutes and a couple tunnels later, we stood in a large utilitarian room. Empty shelves lined the concrete walls. Two queen mattresses and box springs had been shoved together to make a massive bed in the center. Mounds of blankets and pillows lay on top, round and accommodating like the curvy form of a pregnant woman.

Beside the bed stood a folding table, covered with bowls of steaming food. Darwin circled it, his muzzle huffing at the scents of roasted meat, seasoned noodles, and mixed vegetables.

"It's not a fancy dinner." Shea strode to the boxes that sat by the door. "But Eddie can do wonders with canned food and his concoction of spices."

My mouth watered. "We're grateful. Please pass along our thanks."

"I will." She dug through the first box and removed a bottle of whiskey, offering it to Roark. "Merry Christmas."

Her reminder of the day staggered me. The last time I'd celebrated Christmas, I was sitting in Joel's lap in our Missouri home, watching Annie and Aaron open their presents.

I no longer had wrapping paper and ornaments and homemade desserts, but I'd been given the priceless gift of togetherness with my guardians and the new life blooming in my womb.

"Bushmills?" Roark placed his hands on Shea's face and smacked a kiss on her lips. "On de ball, young lady."

He accepted the amber bottle and set it on the table.

"It's the only Bushmills I found in Hunter's stash, so enjoy it." She tilted her head. "Though, I have to ask. Why Bushmills? I mean, isn't it Protestant? I thought Jameson was the Catholic whiskey?"

I grinned. I'd asked him this once, too, and had been thoroughly schooled on Irish whiskeys.

"Ach. That was an American myth." He gripped my hips and steered me toward the table as he answered Shea's question. "The master distiller at Bushmills was Catholic, even though it was located in predominately Protestant Northern Ireland. And John Jameson himself was Protestant…and *Scottish.*"

He said the last word as if it left a bad taste in his mouth. Oh, my very proud Irishman. But I knew the real reason he clung to that particular brand was because it reminded him of his life before the plague. It was a drink he loved during a time he missed. It was his way of coping with this new life.

Shea laughed, softly. "Well, consider me educated." She reached into another box and removed a cell phone and attached charger. "These things don't have much use unless you can find one with music storage."

She turned toward Jesse, who stood nearest to her, and dropped it in his hands.

Excitement fluttered through my veins. "It works?"

She nodded, her smile beaming. "Hunter's been collecting them. This one had the most variety of music. No Christmas songs though." She shrugged. "Merry Christmas, you guys."

Paul's mocha skin softened around his eyes as he stared down at her, his love evident in the way his whole body seemed to gravitate toward her. She had that effect on people, her goodness and selfless energy a pillar of infectious strength. She was going to be a wonderful mother.

After we said our *thank you's* and *good-night's*, she patted her leg. "Come on, Darwin. Eddie made you dinner, too."

With his tail swishing behind him, Darwin followed Shea and Paul into the hall.

Jesse shut the door and plugged the phone into the wall outlet near the table. As he swiped at the screen, Roark, Michio, and I dug into the hearty meal. There were no extra dishes, so we ate directly from the bowls with a mismatched collection of utensils.

A moment later, a familiar low-key riff of guitar chords strummed through the phone's speaker. Wordlessly, the four of us sat on the bed, passing the bowls between us and listening to *Nirvana's* "Come As You Are."

How long had it been since I'd heard music? Five…six months? I'd left my music player and solar charger with the Lakota in the mountains, but it had been before that, long before the plague even, since I'd heard this song.

The grungy instrumentals vibrated through me, conjuring memories of my rebellious youth, when my biggest fear in life was my dad catching the scent of weed on my clothes.

My guardians appeared to be lost in their own memories. The dim glow of the overhead light illuminated their naked chests. Jesse and Michio wore sweatpants, their abdominal muscles rippling with the rise and fall of their breaths. Roark's powerful calves were exposed beneath his athletic shorts, his legs stretched out beside me. As he reached for a forkful of meat from the bowl next to Jesse, his narrow waistline creased, accentuating the ridges of his eight-pack.

I swallowed down my arousal with a flavorful bite of lemon-peppered noodles. "This song makes me think of high school."

Roark lay on his back and tucked a hand beneath his head, staring at the ceiling. "Same here."

Made sense. He was thirty-five, like me.

I looked at Jesse, the youngest of my guardians at age thirty-one. "You were in elementary school when this song came out, right?"

"Yeah." Jesse sat on the far end of the bed with his back against the wall, his leg bent, and an arm draped over his raised knee. "I was still on the Lakota reservation. My parents didn't divorce until I was in high school."

Which was when he left the reservation to move to Texas with his dad.

And now, there were no more Native American reservations. No more cultural prejudices for that matter. Some religions might have perpetuated, but there were so few people left, most faiths would likely be gone within a generation or two. Especially if Aiman's programming succeeded in exterminating free will.

Sitting cross-legged beside me, Michio set his fork down, his gaze inwardly focused. Youthfulness etched his profile, from his wrinkle-free olive complexion and thick black hair to the symmetrical bone structure of his face and the hairless skin around his full lips. I wasn't sure he could grow facial hair, which made him appear even younger. He could easily pass as twenty-something, yet he was the oldest of us at age thirty-nine.

I nudged his shoulder with mine. "A kiss for your thoughts?"

The corner of his mouth twitched, despite the pink rimming his soft brown eyes.

He leaned down and pressed a chaste kiss to my lips. "I was thinking of Isabella. She loved this band."

I gave him a gentle smile. Isabella had been his girlfriend through med school and years after...until the plague hit. He'd told me one night in the mountains that he'd been too focused on his work to marry her.

Reaching for his hand, I interlaced our fingers. "You look sad."

He traced the skin between my knuckles. "I should've set her free to marry another before... It doesn't matter now."

I wished I would've told Joel I loved him more often. I wished I would've spent less time in the office and more time with Annie and Aaron. We all had regrets. It was easy to second guess every action with the clarity of hindsight.

Roark reached around Jesse and snatched the phone. He flipped through the screens, his thumb pausing and his eyebrows crawling up his forehead. "*Dropkick Murphys*? Now that's the shot."

As we finished eating and moved the empty bowls and water bottles to the table, the cacophony of upbeat drums, guitar, and bagpipes pounded through the room. Roark sang along, his gruff vocal melody a blend of punk, old Irish lilt, and sexy swagger.

I loved his accented voice and how his jade eyes glimmered when he sang. I loved the way his shorts stretched over his groin, the thin material highlighting the line of his long cock. I loved how hard his muscular thighs were, remembering the flex and press of them as they spread me open. A spasm clenched in my pussy, intensifying an endless ache.

Jesse and Michio moved the table near the door, and I sprawled on the bed beside Roark. He opened the Bushmills, drinking directly from the bottle as I scrolled through the music selection.

Social Distortion, My Chemical Romance, Pixies, The Cure... Wow, my finger hovered excitedly, unsure what to choose next. I paused on a cover song by *Guns N' Roses.*

"Live and Let Die" was poignant, classic, and man oh man,

I could sing my heart out to it. But would the lyrics be too much reality so soon after our discussions of fate and prophecy?

Screw it. I tapped *play.*

The sonic trill of the vocals warbled through the speaker, and a shudder shimmied over me. Ahhh, I really loved this song.

Roark jerked his head toward me. "You're fecking morbid." He set the bottle of whiskey on the floor and reached for the phone. "Give me that."

I rolled to my stomach and buried it beneath me, unintentionally muffling the music in the blankets. "It's a great song. I'll sing it for you."

A hand closed around my ankle, and I glanced over my shoulder as Jesse yanked me down the bed. I tightened my grip on the phone and belted the chorus, laughing.

"You're acting the maggot, ye dirty cow." Roark rolled me over and tried to pry the device from my hands. "And ye sing worse than Axl Rose."

"Hey! I love Axl's voice." I sang louder and fought off his grabby hands, grinning defiantly.

Jesse crawled up my body and buried his face between my legs, his hot exhale soaking through the cotton of my shorts.

"Ohhh fuck." My inner muscles clamped down and spread a burst of pleasure outward, quivering down my legs and shivering across my skin.

Out of the corner of my eye, Michio leaned against the wall, watching us from beneath hooded brows.

Roark plucked the phone from my hands, and the song switched back to *Dropkick Murphys.*

Jesse propped his chin on my mound, his expression full of satisfaction. "You're too easy."

I blew a lock of hair out of my face. "You play dirty." Holding his gaze, I rolled my hips. "But since you're down there…"

The phone landed somewhere above my head, and Roark's mouth crashed down over mine. The plunge of his tongue sparked a pulsing fire between my legs. I bit at his lips, meeting his lashing kiss with the same urgency, my arms twining around his shoulders.

Jesse yanked my shorts off and pressed my knees to my shoulders, spreading my thighs and exposing me to his gaze. The cool air chilled the wetness of my arousal, but in the next pounding heartbeat, his hot mouth replaced the chill, his tongue laving at me hungrily.

The combined sensations of Roark's tongue in my mouth and Jesse's tongue in my pussy surged through me, consuming me. I slid my mouth away from Roark and reached my arm out, searching for Michio. But he was already there, his warm breaths coating my neck as his palm slid beneath my t-shirt.

My nipples hardened, and my hands wandered frantically, stroking heated muscle and grabbing hold of soft hair. I closed my eyes, marveling at how well I could differentiate them. Some of the variances were bold, like the whiskey taste of Roark's mouth and the velvety-soft feel of Michio's hairless face. But I could also identify the coarser texture of Jesse's hair, the callouses on Roark's fingers from the sword, and the exotic fragrance of Michio's skin.

With my knees held against my shoulders by Roark and Michio, Roark caressed his mouth down my body, shoving my shirt to my neck as he went. Michio's lips moved in, his kiss gentler, more cautious, one hand holding my knee near my face, the other framing my cheek.

I licked at his lips and sucked on his tongue, encouraging him. But he seemed to be holding back, suggesting his uncertainty about our foursome and all the shit from the past month lingered too close to his mind. I tried to keep his focus right here with us, moving my hands to the angular lines of his face and kissing him with every shred of love and desire I felt for him.

The path of Roark's mouth momentarily distracted me as he bit at my breasts, nibbled down my belly, and joined Jesse at my opening.

My body sank into the mattress as need roughened my

kisses and weighed down my limbs like a heady drug.

Michio pulled back and stared down my body, his heavy-lidded eyes taking in the view of Jesse and Roark fucking me with their mouths, their tongues sliding together and tangling inside me.

They dipped in and out, dragging soft, warm lips through my folds, their stubble abrading my inner thighs. I cried out, grinding against their mouths, my whole body reaching for them and my pussy constricting around their tongues, overstimulated and seeping with desire. It was unlike anything I'd ever felt.

I clutched at Michio's strong neck and guided his lips back to mine. I needed to come. Fuck, I was dying to release on their tongues. I rocked my hips while inhaling Michio's breaths, tasting his mouth. Roark's grunts and Jesse's nibbling teeth made me hotter, wetter, more needful, and I whimpered against Michio's mouth. Dammit, if one of them didn't sink into me soon, I'd go crazy.

Michio pulled away. His rigid length tented his sweatpants, but the arousal I used to see so clearly in his eyes struggled to peek through the mounting clouds on his face.

Jesse licked and nuzzled, following my seam downward, toward my ass.

I held back the urge to bow my back, my attention on Michio. "What's wrong?"

Roark pressed kisses over my mound and glanced up at Michio though his lashes. "Too much, lad? Too soon?"

I reached down and stroked Roark's whiskered jaw, silently thanking him for his compassion.

Jesse moved his mouth to the back of my spread thigh, pressing a kiss there as he waited for Michio's response.

Michio regarded them intently for a long moment. "Are you two…?" The sharp slash of his cheekbones were stark with discomfort. "I don't care what you do. I'm just trying to understand your relationship."

I didn't fully understand it either, but I was hopeful. With my fate hovering over me, I wanted my guardians to love one another so much they would satisfy each other in every way. Because a bond between them was more likely to pull them through my death than one they might find in a fragilely new relationship with another woman.

Eventually, I would start planting seeds about the future, assuring them of my acceptance of them moving on with another woman or *women* or with each other in the same way Joel had done for me in the letter he'd left me. But right now, it was too early, the news of my pregnancy too raw. Right now, I simply wanted to show them how much I loved them.

Lifting up on an elbow, Jesse met Michio's gaze with a challenging one. "We're still trying to figure it out."

I wasn't so sure Michio's hesitancy had to do with what was happening in *this* bed. I lowered my legs to the mattress and sat up, bending my neck to put my face within an inch of Michio's. "This is about Elaine, isn't it?"

Michio looked away. "Evie, I'm fine."

The darkness shadowing his eyes and the straining tension in his shoulders were anything but *fine*.

I touched his cheek, turning his face back to mine. "If you're not ready, we can take this slower. We can wait—"

"Like hell." Roark rose to his knees and rubbed a rough hand over his eyes. "Jaysus, Doc. She's all laid out, primed and ready for ye. I can see you're as chubbed up as we are, so wha'ever this is, it's in your head. Let's hear it."

"Roark." I glared at him.

"Wha'? He needs to talk about it."

Michio slid off the bed, adjusted his pants, and strode toward the door. "I just…" He turned the knob, facing away and hiding his expression as he stepped into the hall. "I need to walk."

The door clicked shut behind him.

"Bloody hell." Roark climbed off the bed. "Feck!"

"I'm going after him." I dug through the bedding, searching for my shorts.

Jesse located them and hurled them across the room, where

they landed in one of the boxes by the door.

"Dammit, Jesse." I moved to go after them.

He rolled on top of me and pinned me to the mattress, craning his neck to glare at Roark over his shoulder.

"I'm going." Roark braced an arm on the wall by the door and stared down at the hard bulge pressed against his shorts, his tone frustrated and resigned. "Just give me a bloody minute."

I'd seen the look on Michio's face before he retreated and recognized the vulnerability, confusing anger, and aching loneliness, having suffered in the grip of those emotions after I was raped in my father's basement.

I pushed against Jesse. "I've been through what he's feeling. I can relate to him. It should be me who talks to him."

Jesse grabbed my wrists and held them above my head, the hard weight of his body distributed over the length of mine. "Roark would be better for this conversation. Doc is your guardian, your protector, the kind of man who doesn't get raped by a woman—"

"But—"

"He's not thinking about the circumstances, only that he failed to stop it." Jesse closed his eyes, opened them. "He'll choose sulking and hiding over vocalizing his weakness to the woman he's supposed to protect."

"Damn male egos," I mumbled. "They're like fragile, hormonal teenage girls."

"That's right, and the wrong word, the wrong silent non-word, will make him feel like he's not the man you need him to be." He brushed the hair from my face. "Let the priest handle it."

A sharp pang twisted in my gut. I hadn't considered that Michio would be worried about my opinion of him.

"Okay. Just..." I met Roark's eyes across the room. "Tell him I love him?"

Roark nodded. After another glance at his softening erection, his gaze traveled over our bodies and fastened on Jesse's eyes. "Try not to finish before I get back." A grin spread across his handsome face. "Ye should tell her how horned up ye get when I watch ye stroke your flute."

With that, he stepped into the hall and shut the door behind him.

Jesse rubbed his forehead and reached for the phone. "Don't listen to him."

"Too late." I poked his ribs. "Tell me."

He messed with the screen, and a moment later, set the phone above my head.

A shimmering percussion of xylophone scales tapped through the speaker, followed by the soft groove of falsetto vocals. The electronic beats dripped with sensuality, as if flowing aimlessly through a sexual trance.

I arched a brow. "Sex music?"

"Glass Animals." His pelvis rolled against mine. "Gooey." He whispered the song title on a warm breath, deeply and seductively against my ear.

With a fluid sweep of motion, he yanked my t-shirt over my head, leaving me nude and trembling for his touch. His eyes heated into molten copper, and his tongue darted out to wet his bottom lip.

When he settled on top of me, I wrapped my legs around his ass and stretched my neck to capture his mouth. Our tongues rolled lazily, the rock of his hips matching the tempo of our kiss and the melody drifting around us.

My body liquefied beneath the grind of his cock, my mind wandering back to the month Jesse and Roark spent together. "You let him watch you jerk off?"

The heat of his body enveloped mine, his lips distracting as they slid across my jaw and wrapped around my ear lobe.

I dragged my palms down the hard expanse of his back and dipped my fingers beneath the waistband of his sweatpants, gripping handfuls of his muscular ass. "Tell me about Roark watching you."

He inched back, shifting his weight to his knees, his gaze falling on my nipples. He licked each taut peak, blew lightly against them, and watched them shrivel and tighten. Then he did it again, every stroke of his wet tongue and fanning chill of breath making my cunt pulse and heat.

"Are you embarrassed about it?"

His magnetic eyes slid upward, locking on mine, and he blinked. "No."

I touched a finger to his mouth, slid it inside, and trailed the moisture over his lush lips. "Do you have any idea how much it turns me on imagining you two together? Please tell me."

He grunted a short sigh. It could've been the hypnotic bassline throbbing through the speaker, but his expression seemed so soft and relaxed, almost dreamy, as he regarded me.

Lowering his chest to mine, he braced on his forearms and legs and molded his perfectly-honed body over and around me. "The first time, we were asleep in the van."

The first time… I clenched my thighs around him. "Did you always sleep together?"

"Yes." He smirked. "He's clingy."

"He's adorable." With my hands on his ass, I pulled his lower body against mine, shuddering against the drive of his hard length along my folds. "What happened?"

"I woke, thinking about you." He buried his face in my neck, licking and nuzzling, his fingers twisting in my hair. "There wasn't a second that passed when I wasn't thinking about you, but that night, I was plagued with images of you naked, wet, and needy. I was so fucking horny, and Roark was the only other person in the van."

He ground his cock against me, shooting electric pulses through my body.

"So you touched yourself?"

He nodded against my neck, his whiskers scratching my throat, as he shoved a hand between our bodies. Leaning back just enough to look into my eyes, he dragged a finger along my slit, teased me open, and stroked through my dampness.

The voluptuous cadence of the background music morphed into a new seductive rhythm, and our bodies pulsed and rocked to the sultry beat.

I held his gaze, panting with uneven breaths as his fingers slipped through my folds, soaked with my arousal, and lifted to rub tight circles around my clit. His touch grew heavier, rougher, fingering my opening, the heel of his hand grinding against my mound.

"Keep talking." I clawed at the steel brawn of his backside, my body trembling with the need for more. More of his touches. More of his drugging twang.

He dragged two fingers through my slick flesh and sank them deep inside me, wrenching a moan from my throat. "I was fucking my hand, imagining the tight clasp of your pussy, when Roark woke beside me. I was too far gone to stop him."

He watched me with hooded eyes as I flexed into each thrust of his hand, grinding my clit against his palm. Driven, seeking, reaching for that intoxicating release of pleasure, I fucked his fingers with abandon.

"You didn't stop while he watched you?" Just imagining it arched my back.

He caught a nipple in his mouth, his fingers thrusting harder, faster. Then he released my sensitive bud, his tongue curling around it. "I didn't stop him when he wrapped his hand around me."

Ohmygod. I tangled my hand in his hair and pulled his head up so I could see his face. "He jerked you off?"

"Yeah." His affirmation and the flex of his fingers inside me drove my pleasure toward the brink of free fall, rising, tipping, losing my balance.

My body seized around the pressure, exploding in a thousand chaotic sensations, firing my nerve-endings and shooting stars across my vision. I sighed blissfully, my chest heaving and my skin flushed and tingling as I floated in his arms.

He removed his fingers, shoved down his pants, and kicked them off. Then he wedged his hips between my legs, spreading me open. With a hand wrapped around the base of his cock and his forehead pressed against mine, he sank into me with a stuttering exhale.

I gasped at the fullness of him, my hands clinging to the strength in his shoulders. For a suspended moment, he held himself still, buried and stretching, his thick girth pulsing against my inner walls.

He lowered his mouth and tasted my lips. His tongue, so soft and wet, drew mine out, teasing, flicking, and rubbing together.

Then he moved, flexing his hips and slipping from my pussy, only to plunge again, deeper, rougher. I moaned into his mouth, my fingers sweeping over the bunch and play of his muscled back. His thrusts sped up, his arms hooking beneath me and pulling me tightly against him.

We were as close as physically possible, slick with sweat and arousal, our bodies melded, fingers and tongues curling, legs intertwined, his cock deep inside the most intimate part of me. Fuck, I loved this, this carnal connection, this gooey throbbing bond melting us together.

Grunting, he dug fingers against my back and drove his hips, gliding his length along my sheath and fighting with labored breaths to reach deeper with each thrust. I rose to meet him, absorbing the force of his pounding, his balls slapping against my ass and his tongue whipping wildly against mine.

Another orgasm swelled inside me, accelerating my breaths and coaxing moans of need from my lips.

He broke the kiss, leaning back to watch me come, always watching, always intensely focused on my pleasure. His lips parted, and his pupils dilated, the pace of his breaths in sync with the hammering of his hips.

What would he sound like if Roark were kneeling behind him, fucking him as he fucked me? Would he groan louder? Thrust harder? I mentally rearranged the image, inserting Michio between them. Much better. They would find unimaginable pleasure if they opened their minds to it. God, I longed for them to want that, to love one another, to find comfort in each other's arms. Now, while I could enjoy the experience of seeing them together. And later, so they could turn to each other after I was gone.

I embraced the fantasy as I fell over, my cunt gripping Jesse's cock as I came, whimpering and panting and scratching his back.

He followed me over with a guttural shout, his head kicking back and the cords in his neck straining against his throat.

I loved watching him come. It was like releasing all over again, witnessing my pleasure echo in the movements of his body, his parted lips, and heated eyes.

As he caught his breath, he held me close to his chest, held my gaze with unblinking intensity, and held my fingers against his lips. He filled my heart, my thoughts, and my womb. The guardian of my mind. The father of my child. I would love him for as long as love existed. A lifetime. An eternity. I would love him longer than that.

We twined together, a sweaty tangle of limbs and breaths, his cock still twitching inside me, as I thought about the conversation that had carried us to this sated moment.

"Did you come with Roark's fist around your cock?"

He half-groaned, half-laughed, and looked over his shoulder.

"Not exactly." Roark leaned against the wall beside the closed door, his arousal stretching the crotch of his shorts.

When the hell did he return? I hadn't even heard the door.

Jesse looked back at me, not a hint of surprise in his expression at Roark's presence.

He brought his lips to my ear, his voice a deep whisper. "I came in his mouth."

FIFTY-FIVE

Velvety and evocative, Jesse's whisper was like a caress of lips along my neck, as if he'd said those delicious words just to watch me shudder and melt beneath him.

We lay chest to chest, fully nude and wrapped tightly together, his heavy muscles blanketing my much smaller frame as his softening cock slipped from my body.

I pressed deeper into the mattress to better see his face. "You're fucking with me."

"Keep your mouth open like that, and I'll shove my dick in it."

I shivered, and my lips curled into a filthy grin. "Is that what happened with Roark?"

His chiseled jaw, strong cheekbones, and hard eyes constituted a visage of seriousness. He didn't smile back, didn't acknowledge or refute my question. He simply stared at my mouth, like he was content to do nothing else for as long as I'd let him.

Unfortunately, we would have to finish this conversation later. I met Roark's eyes over Jesse's shoulder. "Where's Michio?"

"He headed to the surface to find Link. He doesn't trust the crazy wanker like we do, so he's double-checking the security." Roark crossed the room in long strides, angling toward the side of the bed, where his bottle of whiskey waited. "He's nursing a dose of tender wounds, love."

His brogue resonated off the cement walls and echoed painfully inside my ribcage.

Jesse slid off me and shifted us to sit against a pile of pillows at the head of the bed, bracketing my hips with his thighs. He tapped the screen on the phone, muting the music, and pulled a blanket over us to chase away the chill.

I reclined against his chest and searched Roark's face. "Did Michio confide in you? Did he talk about Elaine?"

After a long pull on the whiskey, Roark lowered to the bed beside us. With one foot on the floor, he bent his other leg on the mattress and leaned on his knee, balancing the bottle on the bedding.

"He told me everything." His voice was as hard as his eyes. "Elaine is a dickhead. A dirty, lousy-dick-sucking dickhead."

My brain latched onto *dick sucking.* Anger ignited the air in my lungs, burning through my voice. "What did she do to him?"

"She molested him for two weeks. Never succeeded in getting him fully hard, but it didn't stop the manky cocktrough from riding him, creaming all over him, and fucking with his head."

My quickening breaths wavered the air, my hands tightening into fists.

Jesse hooked his arms around me and uncurled my fingers, twining our hands together in my lap. "Did you help him? Counsel him?"

Roark lowered his head, his eyes peering up to level on Jesse. "I told him the same things I told *ye* after the Lakota died."

Jesse nodded, the movement rocking his chest against my back. "Okay."

"Okay what?" I angled my neck to see Jesse's eyes. "What did he tell you and Michio?"

"That you are the cure." His thumb stroked over my fingers. "Not just for the nymphs, but for the deepest, hardest-to-reach aches. That your love has the power to soothe a tormented mind and mend a broken heart. He told me I only needed to let you in." He dropped his head back against the wall. "Of course, it wasn't until you knocked me on my ass in a river that I heeded his advice."

My chest hitched, and I lowered my gaze to the blanket, overcome by Roark's impression of me and the reverent tone in Jesse's voice. I wasn't as strong as they thought. Not nearly as selfless in my purpose. Not like Shea, who would devote her life to helping strangers. This brutal world had corroded any benevolence I might've had once, and now, I could count on one hand the number of people I'd allowed in my heart.

I lifted my eyes and found Roark watching me. "It goes both ways, you know. I wouldn't be whole without the three of you."

"We know that, love."

"How did you leave things with Michio? He'll return to our room after he checks on the security, right?" I would go to him and drag him back if I needed to.

"His mind is all twisted up, but he's working through it." Roark's eyes softened. "He'll come to ye when he's ready."

"That'll be tonight though, right?"

My heartbeat was slow and heavy as Roark swigged the whiskey and swirled the bottle, watching the amber liquor slosh against the sides.

"He won't spend another night away from you," Jesse murmured at my ear.

Roark capped the bottle and set it on the floor. "I prayed for him on the walk back to the room."

"Uh huh." I rested my head on Jesse's shoulder. "You prayed for me, too, and look what that got you."

Roark grabbed the bedding near my feet and yanked, stripping the covers from my body as his eyes feasted on the apex of my thighs.

"Yeah," he said, gruffly. "Look wha' it got me."

My breathing sped up, and my pussy clenched beneath his gaze, soaking with arousal. Holy fuck, his expression was mesmerizing. The cleft of his whiskered chin, the way his lips separated and his eyes smoldered. I ached for him to put his mouth on me, to taste Jesse's essence coating my swollen flesh.

Shifting on the bed, Roark crawled toward me, the

mattress sloping beneath his weight. He shoved his knees between my legs and put his face in mine.

Emerald glints of light and desire ringed his irises, his breaths rushing past his lips, as if he'd just run miles to reach me. "I love the way ye look at me, those gorgeous eyes begging me to give it to ye, balls and all."

I angled toward him, seeking the feel of his lips on mine. He swooped down, ducking past my mouth, and clamped his teeth around my nipple, jolting a sting of pleasure through my chest.

Jesse swept the hair from my neck and licked the skin along my throat, his chest rising and falling against my back.

Need sizzled through me, awaking every pleasure zone in my body as Roark lifted his head and took my mouth, his kneeling position between my thighs spreading my legs further open. He sucked on my lips, and I suckled his in turn, writhing on top of Jesse.

Roark thrust his tongue, panting, nipping, his chest pressing my back against Jesse, and their bodies wrapping me in a cocoon of warm sliding flesh.

"Spread your legs," Roark breathed against my lips.

I stretched my thighs over Jesse's and relaxed against his chest, thrilling in the feel of his erection swelling against my back.

Roark stripped off his shorts and knelt between my legs, his hard cock rising from the *V* of his muscular thighs. A pearl of precum clung to the plump head, his veined length slightly curved and jutting toward me, heavy and ready.

I squirmed in the cradle of Jesse's strength, my body molten, aching for the feel of Roark's fat cock stretching and stroking my pussy.

Roark reached down, teased his fingers along my folds, then dug them ruthlessly inside me, working his hand as his tongue tangled and rolled with mine. Groaning, I flexed my hips, the flesh between my legs so sore and wet, my inner walls gripping and sucking his driving fingers.

I needed them inside, needed them pounding and sliding

and groaning together. "Fuck me. Both of you at the same time."

Roark shared a look with Jesse over my shoulder. I didn't know what that meant and couldn't see Jesse's face. Before I could ask, Roark took hold of my hips and dragged me away from the other man.

Holding me to his chest, he dropped to his back and with his hands clutching my thighs, he slammed me down on his cock.

I clung to his shoulders, my head falling against his neck, as I moaned and ground against him, bucking to meet his desperate thrusts. His hands explored the curves of my breasts, the bend of my waist, palming and squeezing the flesh of my ass.

The mattress dipped with Jesse's movements, and the warmth of his fingers swept down my back. Roark fucked me harder, his grip tightening, as he hammered wildly between my slippery thighs.

Jesse touched and kissed every inch of my body, his fingers and lips heating my ankles, my inner thighs, my nipples, my neck, and everywhere in between. When his caresses moved to my pussy, I clenched around Roark's thick invasion, my breaths stumbling with anticipation.

Roark slowed to a stop, his chest heaving, and his heavy-lidded eyes watching me from inches away.

Jesse leaned over my back, slid a finger in my cunt, and dragged it alongside Roark's shaft, as he brought his lips to my ear. "You think you can fit us both in this tight cunt?" He stroked my opening, stretching my flesh around the steely length buried there. "I'm not so sure."

I lifted my hips, sliding up and down on Roark. "Stop teasing and fuck me."

Behind me, Jesse nipped at my shoulder and pressed the broad crown of his dick to my entrance, rubbing it against the base of Roark's length.

Roark kissed me, his fingers digging into my ass, and his body trembling as if struggling to keep still as Jesse worked himself inside. My sheath soaked Jesse's entry, stretching and pulsing around his added girth. But inch by determined inch, I swallowed him, both of them, my body throbbing as it adjusted to the overwhelming invasion.

"Fuck." Jesse clutched my hips, his forehead dropping to my back. "Goddamn, that's tight."

The stretching sensation raced through me like fire. Heart pounding, I held myself utterly still. Jesse's grip was firm on my hip, and the soft stroke of his thumb made me shiver.

Roark held me against his chest, staring up at me hungrily, his mouth open to accommodate his ragged breaths.

"Ready?" he asked, hoarsely.

I nodded and braced my hands on his shoulders.

He pumped, and Jesse followed his lead, thrusting in time with the flex of Roark's hips, their cocks gliding as one, moving faster, deeper, the slap of our bodies growing louder and more frenzied. Jesse kept his weight off my back and touched a hand to my belly, as if to tell me he was mindful of the precious life in my womb, that he would take care of me and not push me past an unhealthy limit.

Roark regarded Jesse's hand on my stomach, his eyes softening and shifting to mine. Then they crinkled with mischievousness. Holding onto my ass with one hand, he grasped my neck with the other, tightening his fingers to control my movements, to leverage against the ramming force of his need. But he didn't constrict my breathing. He quickened it, owning my pleasure and giving it back tenfold with the clench of his fingers and the stab of his cock.

With both of them filling me, panting, fucking, grunting, Roark's tongue in my mouth, and Jesse's teeth on my shoulder, I plummeted into a sublime state of intoxication. My nipples tightened painfully, my muscles quivered, and my body melted into hot butter in their hands.

The snug clamp of my cunt gripped them side-by-side, but as they plunged over and over, sinking deeper, driving harder, they fell out of sync. Urgency replaced focus, finesse morphed into savage fucking, and Jesse slipped out. He wedged himself back in and after a few vicious thrusts, fell out again.

"Shit." He shifted against me, his knees adjusting on the bed. "Slow the fuck down."

Roark groaned against my mouth. "For feck's sake, lad. I'm almost at the vinegar strokes."

With a brutal lunge, Jesse sank into me. A guttural, satisfied growl rumbled in his chest, and he kicked his hips, slamming deep, pushing, pulling, sinking, groaning and—

I yelped as the hard drive of his cock hit the skin just behind my opening.

"Fuck!" He shifted around me, the mattress bouncing, as he crawled along my side.

I turned my head, tracking the sound of his heavy breaths. "What are you—?"

He shoved his cock past my lips. With his hand in my hair and his knees beside Roark's head, he fucked my mouth with aggressive strokes, spreading the tang of my pussy across my tongue.

As Roark's thrusts picked up, I planted my palms on his chest and greedily sucked, lapping at Jesse's shaft, the slurping suction of my mouth merging with the sticky, wet sounds of Roark's plunging cock. I squeezed my inner muscles, and Roark groaned, punching his hips and quickening his pace.

With my face turned to the side and Jesse buried in the back of my throat, I couldn't see Roark, but he could see me. He watched my cheeks hollow with the force of my sucking. Traced a finger around my mouth as Jesse's girth parted my lips. Fucked me with Jesse's balls inches from his face. And tenderly touched my chin, jerking his hips, as Jesse's cock popped free, dripping with my saliva.

I flattened my tongue along the veins that textured Jesse's length, dipping to nuzzle the sensitive underside, as I peered up at him through my lashes. "Did you really come in Roark's mouth?"

Roark stilled, his hooded eyes narrowing on Jesse.

Jesse tightened his fist in my hair and circled his hips, brushing the inflamed head of his erection across my lips. "I wanted to fuck *your* mouth."

I teased his delicate slit with the tip of my tongue, savoring his salty fluid. "Answer the question."

"I already told you I did," he said, his voice low and husky.

"How many times?"

"Every time he put his obnoxious mouth on me."

A rush of sinful heat gathered between my legs. My God, I would've loved to have seen that.

Jesse tenderly stroked my cheek with his thumb as he glared down at Roark. "He doesn't understand the meaning of *no*."

Roark reached up and curled his fingers around Jesse's cock. "Tell me *no* now."

With one hand in my hair, Jesse seized Roark's jaw with the other. "No."

"No, ye won't tell me *no*?"

"No." A croaked whisper, as if gasped from a battlefield, where primal need fought and conquered reluctance.

Roark's rigid length jerked inside me. "Good."

"What?" I looked between them. "What are you guys doing?"

"We're communicating, darlin'." Jesse pressed himself into my mouth, pushing against Roark's grip and shutting me up as he glared at the other man. "I will always say *no*."

"I trust *no* will always mean *yes*." Roark pulled Jesse from my mouth and stroked a tight fist along the swollen length. "Say it again."

Jesse's eyes fired with challenge, his jaw rock hard and twitching. "No."

Roark slid his mouth around the head of Jesse's cock. I watched, aroused out of my mind, as his tongue flicked out to lick and suck the long shaft. Then, swallowing Jesse whole, he propelled his hips, fucking me and working his mouth, his eyes closed, and his hands holding me in a bruising grip.

Groaning, Jesse rocked forward, his thighs trembling as he twisted fingers through my hair and shoved my face toward Roark's lips.

I hungrily joined him, my mouth fusing with his, kissing him, sucking Jesse, my hands digging into Roark's shoulders as I circled my hips and rode his cock.

The sounds of our growling and panting vibrated through the room. Roark clutched my slick thighs, filling me with hard, powerful strokes. Jesse dug fingers in my hair, working his length in and out my mouth. Roark moved in, taking over with rougher licks and unsheathed teeth, sucking harder, far more aggressively than any blowjob I was capable of giving. He sucked a cock like a man, and holy hell, I'd never witnessed a hotter sight, nor had I ever heard the deep, animalistic noises he was able to wrench from Jesse's throat.

When Jesse slipped free of Roark's jaws, he returned to my mouth, plunging hard and fast. Roark stayed with me, licking at my lips as I sucked Jesse's cock. I ground my pelvis against his, inhaled his breaths, and lapped at Jesse's salty taste, keening, grabbing, and rolling with Roark's sadistic thrusts.

I loved Jesse's hand in my hair and Roark's mouth open beneath my kiss. I loved the way they watched me with intensity and devotion. Loved their bare skin against mine and the need tumbling from their lips in throaty grunts. And I loved their trust in me and their trust in each other.

The inconceivable bliss they gave me swelled in my belly and expanded through my chest, spreading outward. My insides heated and my limbs tingled with full-body stimulation. They climbed the tide of pleasure with me, muscles trembling, breaths staggering, and cocks digging with focused strokes.

As I came, millions of tiny pleasure-seeking sparks cracked and broke open, surging through me in rippling waves. I convulsed uncontrollably, my pussy clenching against Roark and my lips locking around Jesse. Their fingers tightened on my ass, my hips, and in my hair, as they spilled, pouring into me, the hot spurts of their orgasms leaking down my thighs and soaking my throat.

We collapsed in a pile of sweat-slick flesh, watching each other as our breaths evened out, our muscles twitching with gentle echoes. Slowly, our expressions, our bodies, the silence, everything ebbed into lazy contentment.

Side by side, Jesse and Roark lay on their backs, my thigh sprawled across Roark's, and my cheek pressed against Jesse's chest.

Jesse twirled my hair around his finger. "I love you."

I grinned. "And Roark."

"He's part of you."

I sighed, happily. "And Michio?"

Roark rubbed a hand over my thigh. "Every look from your guardians, every word, every breath, the very energy in our bodies, everything we are is a part of ye. And we love every part."

They weren't just a part of me. They consumed me. I knew their deep voices, their tastes, and their drugging scents. I knew the lines of their bodies, the brutal beauty of their expressions, and the thoughts behind their steady eyes. I knew them as well, if not better, than I knew myself. My mind, my body, and my soul. Three parts made whole. We were one.

My eyes drifted closed. "And my child?"

"Is our child." Jesse's timbre whispered through me, warming me.

"Three overprotective fathers."

Roark's hand moved to my belly, lightly stroking. "Three fathers to love her."

Deep, profound happiness soaked my weary muscles. I basked in it, sinking against their warm bodies, while imagining a tiny infant in Roark's huge arms, a rambunctious toddler pulling on Jesse's whiskers, and a hormonal teen challenging Michio's ungodly patience.

I longed to be there, to walk her through every precious stage of her life, but if I couldn't, if fate took me, I would be leaving her my heart. A very full heart, embodied by three strong and loving men.

The peaceful silence whispered by with the minutes, slipping into hours. Jesse and Roark hadn't moved beneath me, their soft breaths coaxing me to join them in sleep. But I waited, unable to close my eyes without resting them on Michio.

His distance was palpable in the hum beneath my skin. He was near, but not near enough. For hours, I convinced myself to be patient.

He'll come to ye when he's ready.

What if he was never ready? Maybe he needed me to knock him on his ass in a river. My Jiu Jitsu skills paled in comparison to his, but I could find another way to knock some sense into him.

Quietly, carefully, I slipped away from Jesse and Roark and crept across the room. I found my t-shirt and shorts and dressed as I tiptoed toward the door and turned the knob.

"Do ye want me to go with ye?" Roark asked, steeping the silence in his groggy, accented tones.

He didn't have to ask where I was going.

"No." I smiled at him over my shoulder. "Go back to sleep."

"Don't leave this level of the dam." Jesse rolled to his side, watching me with sleepy eyes.

"Should I be worried about the security?" I held his gaze. "I'll sense if there are spiders or aphids nearby."

"No. I just don't want you farther than a shout away." Jesse's protectiveness hardened his voice. "Promise me."

"I promise."

With that, I slipped into the hall, leaving the door open, and followed the pulse of Michio's humming aura. Down the corridor, passing two tunnels, I arrived at the cracked door of the restroom we'd showered in.

He would've felt my approach the same way I could sense him, his nearness brushing beneath my skin like a dark whisper. As I stepped through the doorway, I could see three toilets and the shower head at the center of the ceiling. No Michio. My nose twitched. Did I smell—?

Oh God. My lungs labored, drawing in the coppery scent of blood.

I darted around the corner and slammed to a stop.

Michio leaned over one of the sinks, and his stony eyes locked on mine in the mirror. No surprise on his face at my presence. Instead, his mouth was lined in pain and regret and…blood.

It trickled down his neck, smeared his bare chest, and splattered fat red dots on the sink. In his fist was a rusted pair of pliers, the steel-tipped jaw clamped around a pulled tooth.

A fang.

My throat constricted, and heart-wrenching horror cracked my voice. "Michio, what have you done?"

FIFTY-SIX

"Have you forgotten I *bit* you?" Venomous anger punched through Michio's voice, his eyes hard and pinned on mine in the mirror. "My bite made you infertile!"

"It saved me." My heart raced, and what wasn't trembling with worry was twisting with the need to console him. "*You* saved me."

Since I probably wouldn't live long enough to have more children, my infertility didn't matter. My concern lay only with my child. Would *she* be sterile? Aiman had been confident in the viability of future reproduction, though he didn't have proof.

Shaken but determined, I crossed the bathroom. Michio kept his back to me, the ridges of his shoulders tightening with each soft clap of my bare feet.

He dropped the fang and the pliers in the sink and gripped the basin with both hands.

God, how could he pull his teeth out like that? I met his eyes in the mirror.

Guilt. Bloody rivers of it ran from his clamped lips and dripped over his chin.

"If you hadn't bitten me, you wouldn't have broken Aiman's control and grabbed that rope." Three feet away, two feet, one…I touched his lower back, causing his skin to ripple over his spine. "If you hadn't given me that piercing kiss, you and I and *our child* would be splattered at the bottom of the dam."

He hung his head and spat a glob of blood in the sink. I

grabbed a towel off a nearby shelf, my attention fastening on the number of fangs on the drain. How were there three?

I wedged in front of his stiff frame, forcing his hands to release the edge of the sink. With gentle fingers, I tilted his chin up. My touch seemed to chase away some of the shadows in his eyes, and a glimmer of the man I knew appeared, staring down at me with a thoughtful, analytical mien.

His gaze swept my face, his expression tightening. "You smell like them."

Yeah, I could feel their come trickling down my inner thighs.

"I love them, Michio. And they love you." I wiped the towel over the crimson edging his mouth. "*I* love you."

He closed his eyes. "I'm trying…" His eyes opened, deep, exotically shaped, and fringed black lashes. "I'm trying to be a better man. A man worthy of love."

By pulling out his teeth? I flipped the towel, using a clean section to clear away the remaining blood from his chin and chest. "Can I make a suggestion?"

His eyes stayed with me while his hands remained stubbornly at his sides.

"Stop trying and just be yourself." I dropped the towel and lifted a finger to his lips, coaxing them apart to expose a full row of teeth, two of which protruded longer and sharper than the rest. "Where did…how…I thought you removed these?"

His soft lips moved against my touch. "I did. They keep growing back."

I knew he had inhuman healing, but to regrow his teeth that fast? I couldn't believe it. Hell, I couldn't fathom him pulling them out in the first place.

"You were afraid you'd bite me again?"

"I *will* bite you again." He leaned around me and rinsed his mouth out with water from the tap. "I won't be able to stop myself."

I shivered against that promise. Delighted in it. "When you bit me on the cliff, I wanted you to do it."

Chewing on the edge of my lip, I recalled the moment

he'd sunk his teeth in me. He'd been aroused as much as I had been, and any damage the bite might've caused was already done. What was the risk in doing it again?

He dried his face and returned to his imposing stance, looming over me and watching me from beneath dark brows.

"It didn't hurt." I dragged a fingertip over his needle-tipped fang and lowered my palm to his chest. "There was a sting then an incredible amount of pleasure. I'd love to feel that again, while we're not hanging from a cliff."

His fingers followed the curve of my neck, tracing the puncture marks. He leaned closer, his sweat pants rubbing against the hem of my shorts. I felt his desire as sharp as my own. In the swell of his cock. In the heat of his exhales warming my face.

His eyes, like dark brown caverns, stared down at me. Calmer now, but still filled with remorse. "When a nymph bites a cured woman, a healing agent is released and the wound quickly closes. When a spider bites, the damage festers, bruises, and can become infected. Why do you think the nymph heals while the spider harms?"

I had a bad feeling about where he was going with this. "Nymphs are driven to be healed, so I guess it makes sense for them to safeguard the source of the cure and preserve the continuation of human women. But the spiders…they're not seeking a cure."

"They're designed to wipe it out, to erase humanity. There is nothing good or beneficial that comes from this." He drew back his lips and flashed his fangs.

"You're not one of them."

He shut his eyes, not to shut me out, but to lock me in, to savor my words. I knew this because his eyelids lay gently closed, his lips softened, and his breaths eased.

When he looked at me again, his gaze was raw and vulnerable. "I loved biting you. Loved your thick, rich flavor spilling down my throat. Your taste, that feeling of consuming you, of being consumed by you, I want more, Evie. Your blood, your tears, your body, your heart… I want *all* of you."

His tall frame flexed around me, and he hissed menacingly past his fangs. "*That* makes me one of them."

If he wanted to scare me, he'd have to try harder.

"How many people have you bitten?"

"Two." A growl.

Elaine and me. My breath snagged on a bloodthirsty lump in my throat. I wanted to hunt her down and rip out her slimy spine. I balled my fists and scanned the room, searching for something to smash.

"Evie. Look at me."

I forced my rising temper to cool and lifted my eyes. God, he was stunning, with his eyebrows drawn together and his muscles all pumped up, as if prepared to chase me if I fled.

I wasn't planning on going anywhere without him.

His hands found my waist, holding me against him, and he lowered his forehead to mine. "Aiman made me bite her." His face twisted with disgust. "It was sickening."

I remembered him telling me in Georgia that Elaine was weak, that he'd sampled her blood from a syringe and found it ineffective in satisfying his cravings. Maybe she was just too tainted with evil.

His thumbs absently caressed the skin above my hips. "My venom was useless in enabling Aiman to take control of the child in Elaine's womb. So he bit her himself, only to discover my bite had inadvertently made the child immune to his programming."

My gaze flew to his, wide with surprise. "That means both her child and mine will be normal?"

"If by normal you mean they'll be in control of their minds, then yes."

"That's why he didn't make you bite others? Because you carry a vaccine?"

He nodded.

My mind raced through the implications. "You could extract your venom and distribute it to pregnant women. They could inoculate themselves with it to protect their children. How can you not see that as a good thing?"

"I can't extract the venom." He glanced behind me, where three of his fangs lay in the sink. "I've tried."

Oh. "But you can bite them."

"You want me to travel around the world, biting pregnant women?"

"Fuck no." I didn't want him to leave my side ever again.

He gathered me in his arms. "I won't bite strangers, Evie. It's too intimate."

I shivered and snuggled against his chest, soaking in his warmth. Slowly, unassumingly, I trailed a finger along a raised vein in his bicep, studying his face as I dipped downward, across the crease of his elbow and through the dusting of dark hair on his sinewy forearm. Every inch of him was gorgeous and oh-so very lethal.

Aiman and Elaine had tried to break him, but here he was, an indestructible stone wall standing like a divider in time, putting the past behind us and bracing against the future.

He watched me intently as I explored his narrow waist, tracing the ridge of the *V* that indented his hip and outlined his abs. I skimmed along the top of his waistband. Lingered on the thin path of hair that disappeared beneath the elastic.

It would be too easy to stay right there forever, wrapped in his protection and lost in the sensuality of his powerfully-built form. But we were in a public restroom with a sink full of fangs and unanswered questions.

I shifted my thoughts back to the conversation. "Your venom is altered because you consumed my blood. We could donate my blood to volunteers—to men since women don't grow fangs—and you could bite those men after they drink my blood and send them off to spread their bites to pregnant women."

But there was a downside. I met his patient eyes and realized he'd already considered this and found the holes in it.

I sighed. "Your bite would make those men infertile, and their bites would do the same to the women. All of which works against the proliferation of mankind. Fuck. What would happen if you bit Jesse and Roark? At the very least, it would vaccinate them against spiders. I don't know if they'd be down with you biting them. Well, Roark would probably get off on it, and he's already infertile. Your bite would protect them and—"

"Evie."

"Hmm?"

"We don't have to solve the world's problems tonight."

"I know. But there's an answer there somewhere, with your venom, my blood, our child—"

"Stop talking."

"But—"

He captured my mouth, kissing me like he had the first time during my captivity in Malta. Tender nips. A tongue touch. His lips tightly pulled over his teeth. Too much constraint.

I moved my mouth against his. "Let me feel your fangs."

His groan vibrated against my lips, and with it came the biting scrape of teeth. He ate at my mouth, delicately, expertly, guiding my tongue around his fangs, letting me feel their sharpness without drawing blood. Every lick and taste we exchanged stoked the blaze in my belly, fanning it downward, heating and throbbing between my legs.

He rolled his hips and nudged his hardness against my clit, and soon, his soft and steady kiss morphed into urgent and bruising. I gripped his shoulders, the cords beneath my hands bunching and his strength holding me up, as his kisses strengthened.

Fueled with urgency, his lips moved faster, his jaw pressed harder, fangs dragging and scratching, and his tongue…fuck, his tongue fought and wrestled and conquered. I couldn't match his aggressive strokes, didn't want to. I wanted to fall apart in his arms and let his hunger devour me.

He broke the kiss. "You've already been sated by two men tonight. You don't need—"

"I won't be sated until you are."

Perhaps it was a biological survival mechanism, like maybe my overcharged sex drive was meant to draw my protectors to my side and keep them so thoroughly satisfied they'd never leave? Whatever it was drove me to push this, to connect with him in the most primitive way.

I nibbled at his lips. "Blowing up aphids isn't the only weird thing I've acquired with this pregnancy. I have this supercharged energy and my libido… Trust me when I say you can't keep up with me."

Oh, I'd dangled a challenge there, knowing he would exhaust himself to prove me wrong. Honestly, of my three guardians, he was the one most likely to wear *me* out.

He arched a disbelieving brow and slipped a hand between our bodies. Fingers trailed over my stomach, and I knew he was thinking of our child as he lingered there, tenderly caressing, his expression thoughtful. Then he continued downward, beneath the waistband of my shorts, lower, deeper. He slid a finger around my clit, through my folds, and ahhh, I gasped as he dipped inside.

I adjusted my stance, parting my legs to ease the thrust of his fingers. His mouth fused with mine, plunging us into a furious melding of tongues and wet breaths. His fangs grazed my lips, and our need collided, hot and panting, deep and defining. I'd missed this, his exotic musk and overbearing possession. God, I'd missed him.

Lowering a hand from his shoulder, I brushed my fingertips along the outline of his long, hard cock, where it strained against its sheath of tight fabric. I waited for him to pull back, to give me a sign that he wasn't ready. But he deepened the kiss and ground his length against my hand, assuring me, *encouraging* me.

I wrapped my fingers around him through the cotton, stroking, reveling in the feel of his abs twitching against my arm. He groaned and jerked his hips, fighting to thrust harder in my grip. He fucked my fist urgently, dragging his hard length back and forth, limited by the strain of his pants.

He tore his mouth away and spun me toward the mirror. The reflection of his eyes captured mine as his fingers glided down my hips, sinking beneath my shorts and shoving them down my legs.

I watched him watching me in the mirror, my body singing beneath a surge of tremors and my pulse humming with his aura.

His gaze fixated on my swollen lips and lifted to my eyes. "You're devastatingly beautiful."

My chest hitched, and my nipples hardened beneath the suddenly itchy shirt. I shifted to remove it, but he was faster, yanking it up and over my head. Then he was on me, his chest blanketing my back, his fangs scraping my neck, and his hands moving everywhere, squeezing my breasts, tracing the scar on my chest, palming my belly, my ass, my inner thighs, his fingers seeking, sliding through my arousal, and fucking me until I lost the fight with my laboring lungs.

With his fingers still inside me, his other hand fumbled with his waistband, freeing his cock. His pants dropped to the floor as he lined himself at the apex of my legs.

He moved his mouth to my ear, studying my face in the mirror, his body trembling against me. "I haven't had an orgasm in five months."

The confession scraped from a lonely place deep inside him, roughening his voice and clawing my skin, like an echo from hell.

I reached back and caressed his jaw beside mine. "Not since the roof in Georgia?"

He pressed a kiss to my wrist and slid his finger in and out of my pussy. "No, and for five months, I couldn't even think about that night, couldn't relive the memory. Not once. Not with Aiman and Elaine…"

The crack in his voice shredded my insides. If he'd thought about us together, Aiman would've snatched the memory and tormented him with it. If he would've become aroused thinking about us, Elaine would've used it to her vile advantage.

Five months without sexual fantasies or self-pleasure to keep him company.

Those thoughts were a cruel torture, hardening his features

and sinking my heart. But he was here now, solid and breathing, *breathing heavily*, his body seemingly ready to demand repayment for all his forced self-denial.

"I'm barely holding it together, Evie. I'm so damned hard it hurts." He pressed himself against me, pushing against my opening. "Once I let go, it's going to be brutal. Frantic. Unforgiving. I have months to make up for. Months you spent with them."

My hackles went up. "Michio—"

"I'm not jealous, but I'm still a man. A man who is madly in love with a woman who shares her heart and her body with two others." His fingers curled inside me. "I can feel them inside you. Can feel where you've milked their pleasure, where they've satisfied you in ways I haven't in a long time. It makes me want to fill you with so much come all you'll feel is the pleasure *I* give you. I want to spill so deeply inside you it won't matter how many times they fuck you tonight, tomorrow, or next month, because you'll still feel *me*."

Maybe he'd mastered his jealousy, but he was competitive and possessive by nature. He would probably always vie for the strongest, fiercest position among my guardians, pounding his chest and staking his claim. It was part of who he was, and I would never try to change him.

He dragged his fangs across my neck, watching me in the mirror. "Have you had any cramps? Spotting? Any concerns with the pregnancy?"

His question didn't surprise me. He'd told me just a few hours earlier that my health was his only concern.

I clamped down around the wicked twist of his fingers and lifted on my toes, rocking against him. "Everything's great, Dr. Nealy. I feel healthier and stronger than ever."

Hunger glinted in the depths of his brown eyes, and his restraint shook through his muscles in waves, crashing against me. I trembled under the fierceness of it.

He slid his fingers out of me and pressed his thumb against my clit. "Put your hands on the sink."

My heart skipped, and the instant I obeyed, he entered me

with a hard, unapologetic thrust.

Holy shit. I adjusted my grip on the sink and hung on tightly. He didn't pause, didn't give me time to get used to his size, pounding his hips viciously, deeply, as his strangled groan echoed through the room.

The impact was jarring, battering the back of my pussy. He kicked my feet farther apart and threw his full weight and strength into the force of his fucking, as if attempting to chase away his demons and permanently brand my insides at the same time. It was shocking, insanely animalistic, and such a fucking turn on.

His hot, leaden weight bore down on my back, making me feel both fragile and protected. If the strength of his unharnessed passion didn't shatter me, the burst of pleasure splintering through my body would.

But he was attuned to my every reaction, his gaze roaming my body in the mirror, searching for discomfort. He knew me so well, knew how far he could push me, knew every secret spot that would hurl me over the edge.

The pressure of his thumb on my clit built in varying degrees. I writhed against it, throbbing around the steel rod of his pistoning cock. Fuck, he was so hard and swollen I felt every turbulent inch of him stretching me, ravishing me.

But it was the predatory look in his eyes in the mirror that sent me spiraling toward ecstasy. There was a feral glint there, prowling in the shadows. A warning. I braced for it a half-second before his fangs elongated and slammed into my neck.

The stinging prick quickly transformed into a full-body spasm of pleasure. Each sucking pull of his lips felt as though it were connected to my clit, pulsing with drugging intensity. I came instantly and violently, my mouth falling open in shock as I convulsed around the unfaltering drive of his shaft.

I slumped against the support of his arms, hovering in a blissful haze, as he drew on my vein, greedily, hurriedly, sucking and gulping and moaning, his fingers digging into my flesh as if expecting me to chase him off before he was quenched.

He could suck and slurp away, but if he expected me to come again, I would need a moment. Several of them. I couldn't even drag my eyes open.

As he found his release, he refused to leave me behind, his thumb rubbing my clit at the perfect angle, tempo, and diabolical pressure. He roared and shuddered against me, his fangs retracting and his head falling to my back. Sweet fucking hell, my body locked up as the onslaught of another orgasm took hold, jolting me through a rampant cascade of shivery tingles.

Spent and quivering, I collapsed over the sink, but he didn't stop his thrusting, didn't soften, and didn't pause to catch his breath. He released his hold on my sensitive clit, the only reprieve he gave me for the next minutes, hours…God, I didn't know. The room faded away, taking all sense of time with it, as he fucked me through an endless dream of hungry, needful orgasms.

Finally, he pulled out, only to whirl me around, clutch the backs of my thighs, and pound me against the wall. His insatiable tongue stroked my mouth, and I devoured him, his scent, his grunts, his orgasms, and every starving kiss he gave and received.

He slammed against my inner walls, digging deeper, driving harder. "I can't stop. Can't get enough. I'm losing my fucking mind."

I hooked my legs around his waist and held onto his shoulders. "Then don't stop. Don't let me go. Not now. Not ever."

Eventually, he did stop. When my limbs hung limply in his grip and every ounce of energy had been fucked from my body, he quickly found his final release and lowered my feet to the floor.

I floated through a heady fog of happiness as he held me beneath the shower and rinsed the sweat and come from our bodies. I lay my head on his shoulder as he carried me through the bathroom, collecting our clothes and drying us off.

When he reached for the fangs in the sink and turned to

drop them in the trashcan, I stopped him.

"I want those."

His eyebrows dug together as he wrapped me in a towel and knotted another one around his waist. "Why?"

For all the hours he'd just spent with me, touching every inch of my body, kissing my lips, sipping my blood, and making me climax over and over, how could he not understand?

"They're a part of you, and I want every last part."

Cradling my exhausted body in his arms, he regarded me for a long moment before wrapping the fangs in the bundle of our clothes and carrying me out of the bathroom with slow and relaxed strides. I felt sluggish and heavy, as though I weighed a thousand pounds, yet his muscles didn't strain, not a twitch, as he held me against his chest.

We didn't pass anyone in the dimly lit tunnels, though I might've nodded off, clinging to the view of his hooded eyes and swollen lips. "You had…um, a lot of orgasms."

The corner of his mouth twitched. "So did you."

"But guys have limitations. Recovery periods. Does your fast healing negate that?"

He nodded.

I chewed on my lip. "When the spiders bite humans, do they experience arousal?"

"No. The programming turned off that part of their brains. Their bites are neither intimate nor climax-inducing."

Since Michio wasn't programmed, the sink of his fangs was as sexual as the thrust of his cock.

His eyes glimmered. "Still think I can't keep up?"

Oh, he was definitely proud of himself. It made my heart flutter.

It fluttered faster as the door to our room appeared down the hall.

I kissed his neck, inhaling his masculine scent. "Is it going to be weird sharing a bed with them?"

"We've done it before."

When he was the only man I was intimate with. How

would he react if he woke to Jesse or Roark fucking me beside him?

I kissed him again. "It's different now."

"I know." His voice was gravely, and I couldn't decide if that was good or bad.

"Roark snores and invades personal spaces."

"I know," he repeated.

"And Jesse's grouchy when he first wakes up."

"I know."

"We're going to be okay. The four of us."

I waited for another *I know,* but it didn't come. Instead, he held me tighter, his chest hitching with a deep inhale, as he stepped into our room.

FIFTY-SEVEN

The door to our room was open, exactly how I'd left it, but the lights were off, the space dark and calm like the man who carried me in.

Michio shut the door and dropped our clothes, leaving the towels wrapped around us. As he strode toward the bed, my eyes slowly adjusted to the shadows. Jesse and Roark lay on top of the blankets, sprawled on their backs with enough space between them for me, as if waiting for me to fill that gap.

Where would Michio sleep? Squeezed in that narrow space with me? Or on either side of the guys? The way he tightly held me against his chest suggested he wouldn't be releasing me anytime soon.

Roark's sleepy brogue slurred through the silence. "Was beginning to think ye kidnapped her again, Doc."

I tensed. He sounded drunk. Even so, it was too soon to joke about what happened.

Michio reversed his steps, moving backward toward the door, and lifted his elbow along the wall. "I can see you were real concerned about it."

Amusement sifted through his voice as he bumped the light switch and flooded the room in a soft glow.

"Right." Roark squinted at the ceiling light. "I was going to come after ye, but this big hairy fella"—his arm fell over Jesse's chest—"got me shitfaced and tried to root the hole off me. Lovely it was."

Jesse made an exasperated noise and shoved Roark's arm away as he sat up. He wore a black pair of briefs, while Roark lay stark nude, stretched out and taking up half of the pushed-together queen-sized beds, as if he'd fallen there and hadn't moved.

The sound of his snores filled the room. He went from speaking to snoring? Jesus, how much had he drank?

As Michio carried me back to the bed, I raised a brow at Jesse.

"Don't look at me like that." Jesse stabbed a hand through his hair and glanced at Roark. "I couldn't get him to put pants on let alone separate him from his whiskey."

Roark's loud breaths suddenly stilled. "I'm *Oirish,* ye fecking skanger."

"Well, that explains everything." Jesse's tone couldn't have been drier, but affection warmed his gaze as he regarded Roark's closed-eyed, slacked face.

Roark responded with a soft snore, perhaps dreaming of shamrocks, blarney stones, and drinking Bushmills with leprechauns.

I tightened my arms around Michio's shoulders, my chest lifting with a surreal sense of peace. Last year, I was certain they'd never get along. This morning, I was convinced I'd never see them again. Would they always prove me wrong?

Michio scooted us into the bed, settling me between him and Jesse, with his long body clinging to the edge.

He looked at Roark's sprawled position on the other side of Jesse. "He's taking up half the bed, and we should roll him to his side in case he pukes."

The towel around Michio's waist threatened to slip off as he leaned across me, gripped Roark's shoulder, and shoved.

Jesse turned to help, his hands hesitating above Roark's nude lower half, while Michio shifted and twisted Roark's torso. With a heavy exhale, Jesse gripped Roark's muscular thigh and pushed it across the bed.

I could've helped. I really should have. But I was having too much fun watching them push and arrange Roark's dead weight into a fetal-like position. Roark continued to snore softly, and how I could find that sexy was anyone's guess, but there it was, his drunken snore inspiring me to take advantage of him.

Jesse sat back, glaring at Roark's ass, and shifted that glare to me. "You're enjoying this, aren't you?"

I shrugged, grinning. "You should spank him. You know, because he's drunk, not because I'd enjoy watching or anything."

He looked back at Roark, like he was considering it. Then he crawled into the space between us and collapsed on his chest.

Michio left the bed to turn off the light, but as he stood by the door in his towel, he stared across the space between us, his gaze losing clarity. Whatever he was thinking about, a part of him seemed to have suddenly left the room. It could've been anything from Aiman and Elaine to the spiders and my pregnancy.

When his eyes finally refocused, they weren't on me. He was staring at Jesse. "We're going to be okay."

Same words I'd said to him on our way back to the room, though it felt as if he were excluding me in this context.

Jesse rolled to his side, facing me, and hauled my chest against his. "Okay, Doc." He pressed a kiss to my head. "Okay," he repeated, his voice soft and sad, yet resolved. "Come to bed."

Were they talking about my impending death? It was hard to know for sure and too late at night to ask, the topic too heavy for my weary brain.

Michio hit the light switch and approached silently in the dark. He tugged off my towel, swapping it for one of the blankets on the bed, and slid in behind me. "Did you make him drink water?"

"Yeah," Jesse said. "A couple bottles before he passed out the first time."

I wrapped my arm around Jesse's narrow hips, bringing him closer and pressing back against Michio's chest to give them the warmth of my body. "Has he been drinking a lot over the past month?"

"No." Jesse's exhale brushed my face. "But after you left the room tonight, he decided to get *gee-eyed and celebrate.* His words."

"Celebrate what? Christmas?"

"Finding you," Michio said at my ear.

"And fatherhood," Jesse added.

Fatherhood. I turned that over in my head, loving the sound of it. I smiled in the dark, my muscles lovingly worn-out and our bodies curving together. There, cradled in strength and warmth, I fell deeply and blissfully into sleep.

I woke the next morning, groggy, still smiling, and deliciously aroused, thanks to the finger working inside me. In and out, it slid and curled, joined by another finger, then a tongue, winding me up and heating my core. I arched my back, my muscles tightening and relaxing, as I looked down my body and found Michio's dark eyes hungrily watching me from between my legs.

Turning my head, I was greeted by another pair of eyes, lighter in color, but no less inviting.

Jesse lay on his side, his head pillowed by his bent arm, and his sexy hair spiking in every direction. "Morning, darlin'."

I shivered at the sound of his deep timbre and clenched against Michio's seeking tongue. "Morning."

Roark's groan rumbled behind Jesse.

Michio lifted his head, kissing my inner thigh, as his gaze clinically examined Roark. "How do you feel?"

Roark sat up and brushed his tousled blond locks from his face as his eyes roamed my body. "After a shit, shower, and some of wha' you're having, Doc, I'll feel totally boxed off."

Oh, that man had no shame. I shared a smile with Jesse.

Michio climbed up my body and hovered over me on hands and knees. We were both naked. Him, hard as steel. Me, soaked and trembling. He didn't say *good morning,* didn't ask me how I was feeling. We simply stared at each other, communicating everything in that single look.

Roark lumbered out of the room, unabashedly nude. "I won't be long. Den' go anywhere, love."

Not a chance. Michio lowered his body and entered me, slowly, teasingly. He took me with gentle thrusts, kissing my lips, building, picking up his pace, and bringing me to orgasm, once, twice, before finding his own.

I left Michio spent and trembling and went to Jesse, riding him hard, licking his lips, and gripping his sexy hair. Michio watched with heavy-lidded eyes as Jesse groaned and kicked his hips beneath me, driving his cock with long, needful thrusts, his fingers twisting my nipples, and his heated eyes lingering on my mouth. When he came, I followed him over that welcome cliff, my grip sliding away from the edge, but I didn't plunge, because he was there to catch me, and together we soared.

The moment I caught my breath, Michio dragged me back, arranging my legs to straddle him, and fucked me again. Maybe one climax would never be enough for him. Or maybe this was his way of cementing his position in our bed as he kissed me, tasted my mouth and my body, and sank in and out of my heat, feeding me his hunger, his pleasure, and his cock. It felt as though he was giving me everything, with no intention of stopping.

Beside us, Jesse lay sated and still, watching us with a thoughtful expression, his fingers stroking my arm, my breasts, and my lips.

Eventually, Roark returned and nuzzled his way in, enveloping my senses with the aroma of soap and toothpaste, his wet hair dripping down his sculpted face, and his shaved jaw stroking like silk across my shoulder. He wasn't handsy with Michio like he was with Jesse, but he wasn't patient or passive either. His chest pressed against my back and his arm hooked around my waist, lifting me up and down on Michio's cock and hurrying the other man along.

Flexing beneath me, Michio gripped my thighs and raised a black brow at Roark. "Is this how it's going to be?"

"It can be however ye want, Doc." Roark relaxed against my back, his weight bearing down on me and pressing my chest against Michio's. "But she's gagging for both of us to give it to her up the rasher."

Oh my God. I hit his rib with my elbow. "Your mouth…I swear."

"Ye love me mouth." He reached behind me and positioned his engorged length at my entrance, sliding his plump crown against Michio. "Tell me *no*, Doc."

Jesse watched us, wordlessly, his lips a flat line, but there was a smile glimmering in his eyes.

"You talk too much." Michio widened his legs beneath me, spreading my thighs, as he held me against his chest, waiting.

Roark braced a hand beside Michio's torso and pushed, sliding through my slickness and filling my pussy alongside Michio. He thrust deeper, and a hiss streamed past Michio's elongated fangs. My walls clamped down, and my tissues stretched, tender and overworked, but the overwhelming pleasure powered through the discomfort.

Their grunting and panting magnified my need, their desire taking me with them, spurring me to satisfy them, to please them and hold them for as long as I could. Even more arousing was the eye-contact I shared with Jesse as they fucked me.

When Roark and Michio climaxed, they gathered me in their arms, panting, trembling, content. A moment later, Jesse crawled over the knot of limbs and rested his cheek on my inner thigh, his finger swirling through my folds where each of them had stretched and filled and spilled.

We lay in a mound of beating hearts and warm flesh and acceptance, fingers stroking, bodies twitching. Tangled together, expressions open, and gazes tracing and locking, our bond was palpable. Not just in the physical sense. I felt our chemistry in the air, vibrating between us, pulling us toward one another without shifting a muscle. It was bigger than me, stronger than them. It was immeasurable and profound and dependable, connecting our union in ways that couldn't be explained in words. But if I had to give it a name, I would simply call it *Us*.

Roark propped himself up on an elbow and leaned over Michio's chest, staring down at the other man. "Ye worked things out in your head? Ye seem...lighter this morning."

I agreed. Not just in the easy set of his shoulders, but in the way his face glowed. His eyes were *brighter*.

Michio curled a lock of my hair around his fingers, his gaze on Roark. "Yeah. You were right...what you told me last night, and I do feel better."

They must've been referring to Roark's advice about me somehow healing deep wounds? I wanted to argue against it, to set them straight, but thought better of it. They could think what they wanted, especially if those thoughts made them happy.

"Be careful, Doc." Jesse slipped from the bed and dragged on a pair of sweat pants. "Next thing you know, Roark will have us painting each other's fingernails and listening to boy bands."

Roark rolled to his back, grinning at the ceiling. "Ye cunts can lick me balls."

I leaned over and kissed the indention in his hip. "I don't think they're ready for that."

"His balls are all yours, darlin'." Jesse strode to the door. "I'm hitting the shower. What's the plan today?"

Michio snagged his own pants from the floor. "Evie needs a full check-up with an ultrasound. I want to run some tests, but I need equipment and a sterile environment. I also need vitamins, medications, and people." His voice deepened, heavy with grimness. "Nurses, doctors, specialists, preferably those who have experience in obstetric complications and at risk pregnancies that might require surgical interventions."

Silence blanketed the room, and I glimpsed the sudden bleakness in their eyes. I sat up and lowered my hand to my stomach, sliding it around my middle. I wasn't scared. Well, maybe a little. Not about my pregnancy, but I was scared for them. Adding to that was my fear that they would leave the dam to search for the things Michio needed and get bitten or hurt. Or killed.

Fuck, this was going to sound needy, but I said it anyway. "Don't leave me."

I'd make them take me with them if it came to that.

Roark curled his big body around my hips. "Den' leave *us.*"

My heart pinched. I would try my damnedest not to.

"Link can send Hunter and some of the others to collect what Doc needs." Jesse leaned against the door frame, studying me with his usual intensity.

"Do you trust this guy?" Michio looked between Jesse and Roark.

"He's a mentaller." Roark absently traced the line of my thigh. "But he's obsessively committed to leading any and all brigades attached to Evie."

"Alright." Michio strode toward the door. "Then I'll give him a list that'll keep him busy for a while." He paused, looking back at me. "Last night, he said there weren't any aphids outside of the perimeter. He sent patrols out, twenty miles in every direction, and they found remnants of exploded bodies. And not a single living bug."

Twenty miles? My pulse picked up. "I've never had that kind of reach. I wonder how far it extends? I haven't felt an aphid since I killed the ones on the dam." A horrifying thought slammed into my gut. "The nymphs…I don't know how to isolate them from my aphid commands." I gripped my stomach, clenching against the brutal ache there. "Oh God, what if I killed nymphs, too?"

"Evie, love, shh." Roark pulled me into his lap and pressed kisses to my temple. "You didn't kill them."

He didn't know this. He was just trying to make me feel better.

Michio appeared at my side, his hand in my hair, guiding my face to his. "You're borrowing that power from our daughter. Do you agree?"

My chest hitched, and I nodded.

"And our daughter is meant to save mankind, not destroy it." His voice was a deep growl, menacing in its conviction.

"Which means she won't kill the vessels meant to carry future generations."

I nodded again, my breaths calming. "Okay."

"Okay." He observed me closely, probably making sure I was truly okay, then he strode toward the door. "Jesse and I are taking a shower." He glanced at me over his shoulder. "Are you coming?"

FIFTY-EIGHT

Three hours later, we had showered and eaten oatmeal and a surprisingly tender meat from some kind of wild bird. After that, Michio had put me through an overly-thorough exam, using the supplies he'd carried with him from Georgia. He'd drawn my blood, prodded my cervix—or whatever he was doing with his hand inside me—noted my weight and measurements, checked my teeth and blood pressure, gave me a breast exam, and annoyed the piss out of me. No part of my body had been left untouched by his clinical fingers. When I told him I was done with this nonsense, he gave me a withering look that turned my insides to ash.

Now, with the ultrasound machine set up, he positioned the transvaginal probe and made adjustments to the numbers on the screen.

I lay in our bed, bracketed by Jesse and Roark, watching them take in the blip on the monitor. My skin tingled with excitement and my heart raced, my entire being waiting in anticipation of their reactions, as Michio explained the small white circle on the screen.

Roark gripped my hand, lacing our fingers together. "That's her?" His brogue was filled with wonderment.

I nodded, shakily. "Yeah."

Jesse's gaze flew from the screen to my flat belly. He touched my naval, splaying his fingers, his hand so large it covered my entire stomach from hip to hip.

His teeth worried the corner of his mouth, his eyes soft and glassy. "Is the baby healthy? Does everything look okay?"

Michio dragged his attention from the screen. “She’s healthy. They both are, as far as I can tell. But she’s only six weeks along. I need to run tests, and I can’t do that—”

“I know.” Jesse’s expression tightened. “We’ll get whatever and whoever you need.” Fear pushed through his determination, shattering in his eyes, as he looked down at me. “We’re not going to lose you.”

The sharp edge of his voice ripped and tore inside me. I moved to grasp his hand, but Roark beat me to it, pulling our laced fingers over Jesse’s on my belly.

Michio removed the probe and covered our hands with his. “The baby drew my venom when I bit Evie.” His eyebrows pulled together. “I don’t know what it means or how it will affect them.”

Jesse’s gaze lowered to my neck. “Both times?”

I wasn’t surprised he hadn’t missed the second set of bite marks. He didn’t appear upset, only eager to understand, which was a testament to how much he trusted Michio not to harm me.

“Just the first time.” Michio studied my face. “Can you think of anything else that’s changed or evolved in the past four weeks?”

I thought back and remembered the drive between Las Vegas and the dam. “I don’t sense nymphs anymore.” I looked at Jesse and Roark. “Not since Virginia. I passed numerous nymphs on the way here and didn’t pass out, didn’t feel their pain, didn’t feel anything. Do you think…?”

“She’s protecting you.” Michio sat back on his heels. “And protecting herself. It’s just a guess but not completely implausible, considering she’s given you the power to mentally wipe out aphids.” He climbed off the bed and packed his equipment away. “You need daily exposure to sunlight.”

“But you won’t go to the surface without one of us,” Jesse said, firmly.

I sighed. “I have all this energy. Unless you want to spend all day, every day, fucking it out of me, I need to run or something."

"There are miles of tunnels down here." Michio narrowed his eyes at me. "But pay attention to your heart rate. And I want you eating a full-balanced diet, including vegetables."

"Lots of canned mush, then." Roark rubbed his jaw. "Though that fella with the ronnie said he was going to start a hydroponic vegetable garden at the bottom of the dam."

I scrunched my nose. "What *fella*? And what the hell is a *ronnie*?"

"Link brought that farmer with him, love. Ye know, the lad with the hairy mouth mirken that looks like someone shat on his lip?"

I vaguely remembered a man with a mustache. "Does this farmer have a name?"

He lifted a shoulder. "I call him Ronnie."

Of course, he did. I gave him a scolding look, made ineffective by my wide grin, and reached for my clothes. "Are you done with all the poking, Doc?"

"Until tomorrow. Don't roll your eyes, Evie. These exams will be daily. Get used to it."

Michio hadn't been lying. For the next six weeks, not a day sneaked by without him prodding and sticking. I always received a clean bill of health, but he was diligent in his quest to not overlook anything, and not only during exam time. If I so much as sneezed, the medical bag came out.

Over the weeks, Link chased down the people and supplies Michio requested, and slowly, the equipment, medications, and doctors trickled in. Like Michio, the new physicians and nurses—all of them men—had yet to find anything worrying in my exams. Shea's pregnancy was deemed healthy as well, the ultrasound readings placing her one week further along than me. As the inches grew around our waistlines, she tired easier and slept more, while I felt stronger, hornier, and more energetic than ever.

I jogged the tunnels every morning. Darwin always joined me, as well as one or all of my guardians. It was one of my favorite parts of the day, stretching my legs, flexing my lungs, and tracing my gaze over the bunch and pull of their muscular, half-dressed physiques. Stopping myself from tackling them to the ground was more arduous than trying to keep pace with their long-legged strides.

The sinews tightening and straining in Jesse's powerful legs, the sweat clinging to Roark's boxer's shoulders, the sensual flow of Michio's effortless gait, all of their movements recalled every touch of their fingers, the heat of their skin, and the press of their thighs against mine. Just looking at them made me insane with need.

It was during one of these daily jogs, at the end of our sixth week of residency in the dam, when Link stopped the four of us at the bend in a tunnel.

He leaned against the natural rock wall, arms crossed over his barrel chest. "My boys are back from Arkendale."

My lungs heaved, more from my anticipation than from the three miles I'd just run.

Glistening in sweat, Jesse matched Link's posture on the opposite wall, while Michio stepped beside me, not winded in the least, and pressed two fingers over my neck to check my pulse.

Roark bent at the waist, hands braced on knees, and panted noisily. "Spit it out, fuckhole."

Laughing, Link ran his fingers through Darwin's fur as my dog circled around his legs. "The peninsula is overrun with women, as is the state of Virginia, and from what I understand, the entire Northeast coast."

I covered my mouth with my hands, my eyes pricking, and my heart leaping. All those women had been infected, trapped in their bodies with harrowing pain, and now they were free. To fall in love. To have children. To find happiness.

"Pregnancies?" Michio gripped my arm, lowering it to hold my hand.

"Over half are pregnant." Link passed me an amused look. "It's no secret the women are horny as hell."

"Aiman mentioned the same thing." Michio rubbed his thumb over my hand. "His doctors studied the cured women and reported hormone and testosterone levels had been altered."

Altered by my blood. I supposed passing on my sex drive was a benefit to repopulation.

Link glanced at Jesse. "I know what you're thinking. Security could be better. But this is no longer just a single town. These communities span multiple states with Arkendale at its center. There's been some growing pains, but I'm confident in the leadership I left behind to guide them."

Jesse nodded, his thoughts probably taking the same path as mine. We couldn't run a town or a state or a country. We were just meant to heal them and trust in their abilities to govern and take care of themselves.

Link met my eyes. "Arkendale hasn't seen an aphid in six weeks. And my boys didn't see any on their journey there or back."

"That's on the other side of the country." My pulse spiked. "They're all dead? Jesus, what about the nymphs? Did they see—?"

"There are nymphs." Link softened his voice. "A lot of them are still headed toward the east coast."

I blew out a heavy sigh of relief and squeezed Michio's hand.

"One last thing…" Link grinned widely, his black eyes glinting beneath the overhead light. "There's a pretty reliable rumor that some of the women boarded an oceanic cruise ship, and they're crossing the Atlantic right now to cure nymphs on other continents."

He left that news floating around us as he strolled away, his off-tune whistle following the tap of his footsteps.

"Ye did it." Roark's whisper sifted through me right before he swept me in his arms and twirled me around.

"*We* did it." I laughed as my eyes filled with tears.

We'd set out to cure the world, and it was happening. Just imagining the widespread repopulation felt like an explosion in my chest, shaking through my body, and gripping my soul. My guardians felt it, too, their eyes shining as they exchanged smiles.

Roark set me down. "Race ye back to the room?"

"What do I get if I win?"

He scratched pensively at his jaw. "Me."

Michio leaned around me. "And if I win?"

There was no *if*, considering his rate of speed was, oh, a few hundred miles per hour.

Roark grinned and pointed at Jesse. "Ye win him."

Leaning against the opposite wall, Jesse held his head down, his eyes peering up, watching us with a bored expression. But I didn't miss the twitch in his shoulders from his suppressed laughter.

We raced back, with Darwin on our heels, and when we reached the room, we all seemed to forget who'd won in our race to strip off our clothes and slake the hunger that had built on the sprint back.

We did a lot of that in the weeks that followed, sprinting and flirting, fucking and laughing, and the few hours we weren't together each day, we more than made up for at night.

Jesse spent the daylight hours with Link's army of fifty soldiers, improving the security and training them on weaponry. Any new recruits were sent to a work site Link had set up in Las Vegas. The women and nymphs who stumbled upon our doorstep were sent there as well. We kept our commune small and intimate, limited by supplies, food storage, and sleeping space. We were working on creating a community, but we weren't ready to support a village.

After I made my daily jogs through the dam, I always joined Shea on the rooftop of the generator room, the very spot I would've splattered had Michio not caught my rope. It was there that the farmer, Ronnie—he actually answered to Roark's nickname—set up the garden. Under his tutelage, Shea and I learned the mechanics of hydroponics, helped him channel the water and nutrients, and modified the system as the vegetables grew. And they grew fast. Fifty percent faster than soil plants. Eddie would have vegetables on the menu in a few short weeks.

When Roark wasn't with us in the garden, I often found him kneeling beside our bed or holing up in an empty tunnel with his head bowed. The larger the bump in my belly grew, the more he prayed. I always left him alone with his prayers, as his faith in God seemed to cushion the weight of the prophecy.

My fate. The big ugly thing my guardians didn't talk about. Yet when I peered deep into their eyes, I could see it there, the shadowy threat of my death like an impression looming in their thoughts. My healthy exams consoled them, but fate would come, most likely in the form of a tiny baby girl. Some days, my pregnancy felt like an endless fight against time.

Michio set up his lab in an old office near the generator room. After he took me outside for my daily dose of vitamin D, he would dart off to his research, bending over microscopes and studying my biology—or rather that of our daughter's. He never vocalized his assumptions, but I knew he suspected the same thing I did. She was the reason for my surplus of energy. When the time came to push her from my body, there was a good chance she would take all my superhuman quirks with her. Would she take my metabolic energy, too? My blood? And my final breath?

Day after day, we watched her grow and develop on the screen and listened to the physicians repeatedly confirm she was a girl. But every night, we left the medical exams, praying, gardening, and security worries behind us to satisfy other needs. Sometimes my guardians were patient and steady, content just to look at me, as if waiting for me to offer whatever I was willing to give. They already had all of me, so I would assure them, coaxing them with my eyes, reaching out with a husky whisper, opening my legs, and fingering my cunt as they watched with feral intensity.

But most often, by the time we reached our room at night, they were restless and worked-up, assertive and needful, climbing between my thighs, pressing me against the wall, bending me over the bed, and taking their pleasure. Michio always took me first then fucked me again after Jesse and Roark were spent. I never glimpsed jealousy in their heavy-lidded eyes. I saw ambition, maybe a little healthy rivalry, and always love and respect, for each other as much as for me.

It went on like that, week after week, month after month. Winter melted into spring. Spring bloomed into summer, and our baby grew, pressing outward and stretching my skin. Much like my deep attachment to her fathers. I didn't think I could love those men any more than I did yesterday. Then today came and proved me wrong. I couldn't fathom losing one of them, couldn't imagine wondering every second of every hour if that was the moment I would watch one of them die.

It was June when I reached the beginning of my third trimester, and I was stir-crazy, wired, and anxious to breach the conversation I'd put off for so long. I needed them to start thinking about what life would look like caring for an infant, seeking love and happiness, and slaking baser needs, without me.

Every day, I jogged the tunnels, my mountainous belly bouncing with the restless strides of my legs, using that time to frame my thoughts and plan for my family's future.

Shea had sorrowfully agreed to nurse my baby, but in the event she couldn't produce milk, I'd been gathering baby formula, with Hunter's help. If my guardians were privy to that effort, they'd never commented on it.

By the time we'd reached our seventh month, Shea had all but hibernated in her room with Paul and Eddie. I remembered my own endless exhaustion during my pregnancies with Annie and Aaron, but this baby was different. I couldn't sit still, my body a boisterous mass of surging blood and fire, nerves and power. A normal woman might've accredited the boundless energy to Ronnie's nutritious vegetables, but I hadn't been a normal woman in a very long time.

Link kept me updated on his attempts to locate the facilities where Aiman had sent all the bitten women. He'd captured dozens of spiders, but no amount of torture convinced Aiman's servants to release the locations. Link explained that they weren't exactly mindless, but their minds had been altered to unerringly and devotedly follow Aiman's requisite without concern for themselves or their own interests. With the spiders' speed and strength and growing numbers, only a fraction of Link's men returned from each mission.

Every time Link delivered one of these updates to me, he left me shivering in a blanket of ice-cold terror. I couldn't telepathically control the spiders and wondered how my daughter was meant to stop them.

I was alone in the bathroom, showering after a sweaty run and lost in all of these thoughts, when Michio slipped in and shut the door.

"When was the last time you went outside?" He reclined against the wall and gave me a narrowed look.

Evidently, this was a service call by Dr. Nealy. I would've preferred a booty call.

I rinsed out my hair and reached for a towel. "I was thinking about heading to the surface today."

No I wasn't. To be honest, I hadn't been outside in a week or longer. Michio had extended his hours in the lab, his mission in figuring out my genetic oddities growing more desperate every day. Without his nagging and with the June temperatures sweltering into the triple digits, I'd eschewed my need for Vitamin D. The last time I went outside, I thought my skin was going to melt off.

He pushed away from the wall and grabbed my clothes from the sink. "Have you considered the possibility that we've been deliberately keeping you inside?"

My head kicked back. "What?" That hadn't even crossed my mind. "Why? What's going on?"

"There's a lot of commotion out there." He positioned my shorts in front of me, holding them open so I could step into them. "We finally have it contained." He straightened, pulling my shorts in place and tenderly gliding his fingers over my big bump. "It's time."

"Time for what?" Suspicion rushed in around me, bristling my nerves. I pulled on the t-shirt, trying and failing to stretch it over my belly. "*What* is contained? Tell me!"

"I prefer to show you."

FIFTY-NINE

In a blur of winding tunnels and metal stairs, Michio carried me to the surface of the dam at superhuman speeds. At least he didn't leave me in suspense long. Within minutes, he stepped off the final elevator and onto the road that traveled the top of the wall. The desert heat zapped the moisture from my mouth, and sunlight blinded my eyes. But what crowded around the canyon stole my breath.

People.

Men and women as far as I could see. They lined the shores of the Colorado River. Gathered behind the barricades on both sides of the dam. Peered down from the surrounding cliffs. The density of their numbers strummed the air with a thunderous buzz. There must've been thousands congregated beneath the full glare of the sun.

The din of voices and the electricity radiating from so many lives evoked memories of going to baseball games with Joel and the kids, memories of the infectious emotional high that always hovered in a packed stadium. I hadn't witnessed this many humans accumulated in one place since before the plague. Such a profound contrast to the barren desolation I'd grown accustomed to.

I couldn't breathe in those first few moments as I eagerly scanned the crowds. They were too far away to derive expressions, but I could make out general details, such as the wide spectrum of ethnicities and the similarities in ages. Most were in their late twenties to early thirties. Some younger.

Men outnumbered women. Maybe ten to one? Many of

the women were visibly pregnant. Perhaps all of them were with children.

Were they seeking sanctuary? Food? Medicine? I didn't sense the threatening hum of spiders, but maybe they'd come for protection?

"Holy shit, Michio." I gave him a questioning look. "What do they want?"

He set me down and laced our hands. The asphalt heated the soles of my feet as he wordlessly guided me to the guardrail where Jesse and Roark waited. Darwin, Link, Shea, our whole crew was there, standing along the railing and staring out over the river and the surrounding mob.

When I reached the half-wall, a sudden hush settled through the canyon, reminding me of how an entire stadium could fall completely quiet while a single person sang the National Anthem. I shivered despite the Nevada heat.

"Not too close." Jesse barred an arm across my chest, forcing me away from the edge.

I stepped back, my breaths accelerating beneath the weight of countless eyes. The silence was so heavy my skin prickled with unease.

After a useless attempt to tug my shirt over my belly, I gave up. "Why are they here?"

Roark sidled behind me, his hands sliding around my waist and resting on my belly, as he brought his mouth to my ear. "They're here for ye, love."

"Why?" I couldn't tell if they were angry, hurt, excited...

"We'll let *her* tell you." Michio nodded at the main gate, thirty yards away.

Her? I craned my neck, searching the female faces that stared through the vertical rungs of the barricade.

Armed men slid the twelve-foot tall gate to the side, opening it wide enough for a lanky pregnant woman to slip through. The crush of people from the outside tried to follow, but the guards pushed them back with firm shouting and raised crossbows. Dozens of our men stood inside and outside of the gate, bows and axes gripped tightly in their hands.

Razor barbed wire and electric fencing reinforced the barricade on the other side of the dam, which required all of our foot and vehicle traffic to use the main gate. But that didn't stop the mobs from gathering outside both walls to get a glimpse through the metal bars.

The woman strode toward us, a hand on her pregnant belly and her long legs eating up the distance. None of the soldiers accompanied her, and the look of determination etching her pixie-like features compelled me to step forward. But Roark stopped me, his arms holding my back to his chest.

"Let her come to us." He glanced over his shoulder at the elevators. "The crowd is contained, but we want to keep ye close."

"Contained how? What if spiders come? All those people—"

"We have patrols around the perimeter." Jesse leaned a hip against the ledge beside me, arms crossed, and his bow on his back. "Hundreds of troops are spread out within a two mile radius of the dam."

They must've brought in Link's army from Vegas, and they'd kept me in the dark about what was going on.

I studied Jesse's relaxed posture for concealed signs of tension and found none. "Why didn't you tell me?"

Before he could answer, the woman closed the final distance and stopped within arm's reach.

She stood a head taller than me, her body firm and toned despite the roundness of her stomach. A very large stomach. Probably due any day. Sweat sheened her scalp, and her cropped blonde hair stuck to her hairline. She watched me with shrewd gray eyes, but I didn't miss the slight tremble in her hands as she rested them over her belly. Why was she nervous?

She licked her bottom lip and lowered her head, peering up at me through her lashes. "You're Eve?"

"Evie."

"Evie," she breathed, and it sounded like a plea. *Or a prayer.* "You're..." Her gaze roamed my face. "You're as beautiful as they say."

"Uh…thank you?" Embarrassed and completely off guard, I rubbed the back of my neck, sweating like a hog with my gut hanging out. "Who's they?"

She glanced behind her at the armed men and returned to me. "Whoever has seen you, I guess. Your name is whispered on every breath from here to the coast."

Questions lumped in my throat, but I managed to remember my manners. "What's your name?"

Her shoulders squared, even as her chin remained tucked to her chest. "Selene."

"Where did you come from?"

She looked around at my guardians. "They didn't tell you?"

I clenched my teeth. They hadn't told me shit. Jesse and Michio watched our interaction with soft smiles and even softer eyes. And Roark, still curved around my back, brushed my wet hair from my face and kissed my shoulder.

I returned my attention to Selene. "You're from the coast? Which one?"

Her trousers and tank top were clean, bearing a few haphazard stitches over holes and tears. No blood, dirt, or injuries. She didn't appear to have fought her way here, but her athletic physique and strong eye-contact suggested she could hold her own.

"I'm from Minnesota originally, but I came here from Oregon." Her eyes clouded, and she blinked it away. "I escaped one of the Drone's breeding facilities."

My insides flipped and tumbled, and my questions poured out, each one more rushed than the one before. "How? How many women? Where is it? Do you know where the other facilities are? Oh my God, are there still women at—"

"Evie." Michio gave me a stern look. "Let her speak."

When I gave her a nod, she explained how she and three hundred other pregnant women used chains, forks, and whatever makeshift weapons they could find to fight their way out of a tunnel system beneath Oregon State Hospital. They managed to kill the thirty spiders and human men imprisoning them, but only seventy women made it out alive. She knew nothing about the other facilities or how to find them, and she had never seen an aphid—only heard about them. She said there hadn't been any known aphid sightings since the day the Drone died.

My breaths scattered beneath the gravity of her news, and my fingers trembled against my lips.

She straightened her spine. "When we were cured, some of the human men…the men who…" She glanced ruefully at her belly and cleared her throat. "They explained a few things, such as how the world died with the Drone's virus and was rebuilt with the blood of one woman. *His queen.*"

Fierce resentment growled through my voice. "I was never his queen."

"I know. But it wasn't until we escaped and asked questions of every man and woman we passed that we learned who you really were and the salvation you would bring."

There was that word from Roark's discourse on Our Lady of Akita. *Salvation.* I couldn't see his face behind me, but I bet those jade eyes were glowing like the Virgin's mandorla.

What on earth were people saying about me? How did anyone even know I existed? I supposed word had traveled from Arkendale about the source of the cure, and perhaps Link's men circulated stories, but that information had likely twisted into wild fairytales as it passed from person to person. It made sense now why this strong woman kept her chin lowered. She was standing before me in misguided reverence.

I didn't want to disappoint her or shatter her fantasy, but I wouldn't delude her either. "What are the rumors?"

Blinking rapidly, her gaze fell on my stomach, and her hand shakily reached out. "May I?"

I nodded, my body stiffening against Roark as her fingers grazed the swell of my belly.

Making the situation even more awkward, she lowered to her knees and touched her forehead to my naval. "They say you fought the Drone in Iceland. That you killed all the bugs with a single thought. That you weep blood and move as fast as the spiders."

Oh. Well, most of that was true. I touched her cheek. "I'm not as fast as the spiders." I sighed. "Please stand up. The pavement must be burning your knees."

She remained kneeling with her head bent. "They say if a golden strand of your hair is used to sew a wound, the injury will heal within minutes."

"Wow." I laughed and shook my head. "News to me."

She looked up with a knowing smile. "They also talk about how you fly through the Black Canyon with blood-red wings, and the spots on your back represent all the creatures you've slain."

I turned in Roark's arms, lifted the hem of my shirt, and showed her my back. "See? No wings. And the spots are just pigment changes in my skin."

Pigment that changed whenever I controlled the aphids.

When she gasped, my insides constricted. I didn't want her to place false hope in me just because I had some biological anomalies.

I pressed my fingers into Roark's shoulders, his warmth burning my hands through his shirt, and met his eyes. "Tell her to stand up."

He kissed me with smiling lips and twisted me back to stare down at her kneeling pose.

She rested her palm over my belly, her head returning to its bowed position. "The prophecy says your daughter will destroy the spiders the way you eliminated the aphids." She looked up, and her eyes were filled with so much hope it staggered me. "She will reverse the programming and save our babies."

A hollow ache lodged in my chest, clenching tighter with each desperate word.

I didn't know how my child would save them, but I was willing to do whatever was needed to aid the effort, including dying while delivering her. "I hope so."

"She will." Selene rose and set her shoulders. "I can see it in your face. You know what's at stake, and you'll sacrifice yourself for it, just like the prophecy said."

Roark's breath cut off, and Jesse and Michio looked away, their jaws hardening and postures stiffening.

"The people know this, as well." She stretched out an arm, making a wide gesture to the surrounding crowd.

With nerveless fingers, I rubbed the ledge of my belly. "That's why they're here? For my child?"

"They came for you." Her gaze lingered on the women at the gate. "For a glimpse, an encouraging word, or a touch of your hand. For your blessing, a token of your strength, so that it might carry them through the years ahead."

My throat dried as I struggled to parse my conflicting emotions. I was shocked by what people thought of me. Hopeful for the future. Sad to not be a part of it.

Hundreds of faces peered through the gate, staring back at me like a waking dream. Thousands more watched from the river's shores and surrounding bluffs.

I swallowed. "How many of the pregnant women have been bitten?"

"Most of them." She absently touched her neck, the marks no longer there, but the venomous consequence shadowed her eyes. "The few who haven't been bitten know it's only a matter of time."

They faced an unthinkable future. If we couldn't reverse the programming, the spider babies would have to be killed. If they were born with fangs, who would be able to hold them? When they walked and became mobile, grew faster and stronger, who would be able to stop them? Killing them young, perhaps as soon as they were born, was the safest option.

Selene held her pregnant belly, probably only days from giving birth, and stared at me grimly, fully aware of what she would have to do.

Maybe my daughter would save them, but not without their help. I gazed out over the masses of surrounding people. I'd arrived here on the ruthless wings of confusion and adversity, fighting, killing, and surviving, just like them. Yet here we stood, together as a whole, undivided. Was it a sign that peace would return? That a harmonious world waited beyond the horizon? My daughter would need their continuing persistence and faith in humanity, and right now, they needed mine.

I pulled out of Roark's embrace and angled toward the gate. The silence lifted, and dense murmurs roared into excitement.

Roark grabbed my hand, halting me. "This is why we didn't tell ye they were here."

Because they thought I'd find my way into the crowd before it was contained? I wasn't *that* reckless. Jesse and Michio blocked my path with their arms crossed.

I tugged against Roark's grip. "If it's contained, let me go to them." I lowered my voice. "If I remain behind an iron wall, it'll foster distrust. They need my hope, not my fear."

Michio's nostrils flared. "We knew you'd say that."

Selene stood to the side, her head down, watching us out of the corner of her eye.

I stopped pulling against Roark, and instead stepped toward him and wrapped my arms around his waist, cradling our child between us. "I'm not going to die out there." Assuming the cliff was no longer a threat, I would at least live long enough to give birth. "I'll stay near the gate and away from the ledge."

The blazing heat was brutal, drenching us in sweat, but Roark smelled like soap and musk. He was strong and steady and…testing the hell out of my patience as he shared a look with Jesse and Michio behind me.

My aching need to soothe those people far outweighed whatever risks he was conjuring in his stubborn head. "Come with me."

Jesse made an amused noise. "Oh, we'll be with you."

And so they were. With Jesse and Roark pressed to my sides and Michio at my back, I walked through the gate. Selene disappeared into the crush of bodies, and the guards circled my guardians and me, weapons raised and ready. But they didn't need to interfere. The crowd didn't push, didn't attack. They lowered their heads. Then they lowered to their knees.

"No, don't kneel." My heart thumped slow and heavy, my hands finding and gripping Jesse's and Roark's. "Please, just…everyone stand up."

Bodies continued to sink to the ground, rippling from the front row and spreading out, until all I saw was a wave of kneeling people in every direction. Those who peered up from lowered heads, looked at me with awe and respect.

It was too much. My nerves ran wild, shaking my legs and numbing my tongue. My throat caught fire, and a moment later, my eyes joined in, burning and aching and flooding with moisture. Shit, my tears. I raised a hand to quickly wipe the blood away.

Roark caught my arm. "Let them see."

But it wasn't me they revered. I mean, they didn't know me. They knelt before the promise of a miracle, an iconic image of a woman who carried a prophesied child, a baby who might give them a reason to not have to kill their own.

I sniffed, wiped my nose, and sniffed again. Then I drew in a deep breath and shouted through the canyon. "Hi. I'm—" Crap, I didn't need to state my name. "You don't need to kneel. Please stand up."

No one moved.

I turned to Roark, silently begging him to do something.

His emerald eyes lingered on my face a little too long, his smile a little too mischievous. He leaned in, brushed his lips against mine, and lowered to his knees.

My face flushed, and I grabbed his shoulder, tugging. I might as well have been trying to lift a mountain.

I turned and watched, horrified, as Jesse and Michio joined him on their knees. Behind me, Shea, Link, all of my friends—*my equals!*—were kneeling with their heads bowed. The only ones standing were the armed guards. Oh, and my happy-go-lucky dog, who stood on the inside of the gate with his tongue lolling between the bars.

Ducking my face against my shoulder, I whispered at Jesse out of the corner of my mouth. "Get your ass up."

His hand encircled my ankle, his thumb stroking.

Fine. If I couldn't beat them…

I dropped to my knees. But I didn't make it to the ground. Michio caught my hips mid-drop and hoisted me back to my feet.

Twisting at the waist, I looked around for an escape. I didn't want to run, but I'd come out here to offer comfort and encouragement, not to tower over them as if they were second class citizens.

I took in all the faces nearest to me and paused on a young, pregnant girl who couldn't have been older than eighteen. The fresh bite mark on her pale neck was a knife in my stomach. Had she been raped? Or was she carrying a child she'd created with a husband or boyfriend?

She brushed her tangled brown hair from her face and met my eyes. A shaky smile lifted her lips. Her chest rose with a deep breath, and her expression glowed with expectation. Hope in the face of the tragic future she carried in her womb.

Her faith bolstered me. Jesse's hand on my ankle helped me find my voice.

Stretching my lungs, I spoke as loud as I could. "Thank you for coming. I…uh…"

What should I say? Even if I'd had months to prepare a speech, I wouldn't have been able to produce a message that would vanish their problems. And I wouldn't give promises I couldn't keep.

So I spoke from my heart. I told them about my family before the plague, about my journey here, leaving out the gruesome details and focusing on the heroic people I'd met along the way. I talked about the Lakota and their respect for all living things. Ian, the young man who'd helped me cross the Atlantic. The brutish Icelandic men, who didn't speak my language but sacrificed their lives to lead me to the volcano. My guardians, who dedicated every breath to protect me. I unfolded stories about Georges and Tallis, Shea and Link, and the proliferation of Arkendale, and how the peninsula began with the determination of Link's men and women.

As my words echoed through the canyon, I knew only a fraction of the congregation could hear me. But my stories would ripple, like their kneeling postures. The details might change, but the meaning would carry: Women wouldn't be here without the extraordinary acts of ordinary people. People just like them.

When my voice grew too hoarse to shout, I thanked them again. Then I spent the next three hours greeting the continuous rotation of men and women. Many of them had dogs with them, which filled me with warmth. The world needed more loving companions like Darwin.

I touched pregnant bellies, rested my hand on countless bowed heads, and whispered words of encouragement. At first, I wasn't sure what to say, but as I looked into each set of eyes, it was easy to simply say what I felt. When a woman smiled, I told her she was beautiful. If a man had a soldier's bearing, I told him he was strong. *You're brave, remarkable, thoughtful, gentle, earnest…* I gave them my honesty and approval like a chant.

The crowd of thousands queued without an end in sight. I could've gone another three hours, but the sun was waning, and exhaustion drew circles under my guardians' eyes. Michio, less so, but the three of them never left my side, their vigilance straining their shoulders and tightening their necks. At the very least, they needed to eat.

I gripped Jesse's hand. "It's time."

There would be a tomorrow and a tomorrow after that. I couldn't offer food and shelter to thousands, but I would return to the surface in a gesture of hope.

I lay in bed that night, perpendicular to Roark's body, curled on my side with my head on his chest, as Jesse and Michio molded around my lower half. My limbs felt lighter, my heart fuller, my entire being immersed in the essentials of life. I had love with three men, hope with my child, and purpose for my existence.

My guardians had been unusually quiet through dinner, and now, with their eyes closed and breaths even, they were either asleep or deep in thought like me.

Our daughter was due at the end of August. Two months. Was that all the time I had left? I needed to reach more people outside. Needed to collect more baby supplies. Needed a name for our child. Needed to talk about the future with her fathers.

I needed more time.

SIXTY

The next morning, I woke with a tiny foot pressing against my bladder. She stretched and twisted in my womb, each movement surging a shock of pulsations through me. I'd felt her aura strengthening over the past month, but her life force was substantial today. It felt like Michio's humming vibrations, only more pronounced, as if I were inside *her* instead of the other way around. She felt like a warm conductor of emotional and living energy. The kind of energy that could expand beyond all boundaries.

And prevent me from sleeping in.

The lamp in the corner remained on to light my nightly trips to the bathroom. Beneath the dim glow, Darwin lifted his head from the floor, watching me as I sat up, careful not to wake the guys. I needed to burn off some of this restlessness in the tunnels, and they needed their rest before we headed back to the crowd outside.

Their sprawled positions formed a triangle of hard muscle and naked skin around me. They lay on their sides, facing me, where I slept in the center. But I mostly slept *on* them, arms and legs entangled, using some part of them as a pillow.

Slowly, quietly, I climbed over Michio's legs, slipped off the bed, and glanced back at their relaxed faces. All eyes were closed.

I pulled on a pair of shorts and gathered my hair in a ponytail.

"Such a shame," Michio's husky voice whispered from the bed behind me.

I turned to face him. "What?"

"It's a sin to cover those perfect curves." His sleepy gaze wandered over me. Along my bare legs. The huge hillock of my belly. My bared, swollen breasts. My parted lips. For a long, unhurried moment, he just stared. "Turn around."

The chill in the air tightened my nipples as I gave him my back. Or maybe it was the heat of his eyes roaming my body.

"Damn, Evie. I love the round *O*-shape of your ass, and the way it sits high when I look at you from the side. Must be all the jogging, because the firmness of your cheeks and your tiny, little waist…you don't even look pregnant from behind. It's all—"

"Right here?" I pivoted back, palming my stomach. I'd carried each of my pregnancies this way, front and center, all in the belly.

His pupils dilated. "Come here."

A blanket covered his lower half, but his nude torso was enough to visually feast on. All those deep cuts and sharp ridges made my fingers tingle. He'd gained his weight back over the past six months, and his olive skin positively glowed with health. He claimed my blood had brought him back to life, which he took in sips several times a week. I often wondered what would happen to his cravings when he no longer had me to quench them.

I strode toward the bed, stopping in front of him, a quick glance confirming Jesse and Roark hadn't woken.

Michio propped up on an elbow and cupped a hand around my stomach. "You've never looked more beautiful."

His compliment sifted through me like a caress, stirring up my overloaded energy.

"I've never felt so hyperactive." I stared down into his brown eyes. "I can really feel her this morning, the way I sense you, but it's crazy rambunctious."

"I hope I'll be able to sense her like that someday," he said thoughtfully. Leaning closer, he trailed the tip of his nose around my belly button. "She's going to keep us busy."

"And test your patience."

"And make us proud."

A feeling of fullness expanded my ribs. There was so much energy and emotion and life inside me, I didn't think I could contain it all. "I love you."

He kissed my naval. "Love you." Another kiss, and his eyes lifted, the warmth there emulating his words. "Do you want me to jog with you?"

"I have Darwin. Go back to sleep."

He watched me as I pulled on a t-shirt and headed to the door, but a deeply accented voice stopped me.

"Ye forgot something."

I grinned and returned to the bed, where Roark grabbed the back of my neck and pulled me toward him. He kissed the spot beneath my ear, the juncture of my shoulder and neck, a light peck on my lips, and released me to kiss my belly button.

Then he dropped on his back and closed his eyes. "Carry on."

With a shake of my head, I slid around the bed to Jesse. He lay face up, his head near the edge of the mattress, eyes closed. I angled over his lips, staring at him upside down, inches away.

His mouth twitched into a smile a second before he cracked his eyelids. "Morning, darlin'."

Oh, I would never grow tired of that deep, groggy rasp. "Morning."

I kissed him upside down, the scruff on his chin tickling my nose. His lips were full and warm, his tongue a delicious invasion as he rubbed it lazily against mine. It was an unassuming kiss, his lips gliding along mine for no reason other than to show me affection. It made me feel loved, cherished, wanted.

When I leaned back, he trailed his knuckles across my cheek and jaw. "We'll take you to the surface after lunch. We have some things to do this morning."

I straightened and ruffled his sexy hair. "What kind of things?"

"Man things." Roark rolled away, fluffing a pillow beneath

his head. "Now be off with ye. I'm sleeping."

Darwin and I left them to it, our feet echoing through the tunnels as we worked off our energy. After several sweaty miles, I ate tomatoes, spinach, and grits with Eddie and Shea in the kitchen. Leaving Darwin to finish his chow of meat, I showered, jotted down a list of supplies on a notepad, then wandered the corridors in search of Hunter.

I caught him at the elevator that led to the surface. "Here's the rest of my list."

He accepted the paper, his eyes moving over my scrawl, his hand repeatedly pushing his long hair from his face.

"If you ever want a haircut, I know a couple guys."

Jesse and Roark still cut each other's hair, and now Michio's as well.

The corner of Hunter's mouth tipped up. "Roark offered last week. Said I don't need to keep my ears warm in this heat." He looked up from the paper. "There's a girl…"

Oh, boy. Three words that began and ended with heartache.

I cocked my head. "She likes your hair?"

"Wrapped around her thighs." He waggled his eyebrows. "She's at our Vegas refuge. I'm on my way there now." He looked back at the list. "What's a onesie?"

"It's a jumpsuit thing. Whatever. I just need warm-weather baby clothes, and if you have time to be selective, avoid pink."

Shea was having a boy, and it would be easier if everything was shared.

"Got it." He squinted at the paper. "*More* diapers?"

"Different sizes. I wrote it all down."

"Yeah, okay." He tucked the list in his back pocket. "There's a baby store outside Vegas. I'll take a few guys, a few trucks. We'll just clean out the place. I'll be back in a couple weeks."

"You're the best." I gave him a hug. "Good luck with the girl."

He hit the button for the elevator and winked at me.

"Don't need luck."

"Then you might want to pick up some things at the baby store for your…don't-need-luck future?"

He turned white, his eyes widening, as he stumbled backward into the elevator.

"Repopulation is a hard job, Hunter." I jogged away, grinning. "But we've all gotta do it."

My next stop was Dr. Belhap's makeshift office on the east side of the dam. He and three other physicians checked me over, monitored the baby on the ultrasound, and drew my blood. The latter was at my behest. I'd made them draw one pint every day and store it in a *just-in-case* refrigerator. To study, to cure nymphs, to satisfy certain cravings, whatever might be needed after I was gone.

My guardians had fought me on this. An average person could only donate one pint every fifty-six days, but I had a beyond-average ability to replenish my blood overnight.

After the exam, I had a couple hours to spare until lunch, so I ran the halls, thinking about girl names. I wanted something deep and symbolic, but every idea I came up with sounded clichéd. If the guys already had their own picks, they'd been tight-lipped about it.

A ten minute jog carried me to the generator room. As I passed through it, I sensed Michio's aura growing stronger. The lab was on the other side of the dam. Why was he over here? I followed the hypnotic pulses, my skin humming and warming when I approached the door of a room the men used for marital arts training. I pushed it open.

Jesse lay on his back on the concrete floor in the center of the large space. Roark sprawled atop him in the opposite direction, face shoved against Jesse's groin. In our bed, it would've been a sixty-nine position. But here, with Michio squatting beside them and barking instructions, it was a Jiu-Jitsu north-south pinning hold. Either way, it was an intimate embrace and sexy-as-fuck.

Michio looked up, unsurprised to see me. He could sense me across the country. Of course he'd tracked my approach.

"Everything okay?"

"Always, Doc." I slipped in, shut the door, and perched on a threadbare couch near the adjacent wall. "Don't let me interrupt your *man things*."

Jesse shoved an arm between Roark's legs and craned his neck, seemingly working harder to get a glimpse of me than trying to dismount Roark.

Michio scolded Jesse for incorrect positioning, which made Roark laugh and tighten his arms around Jesse's waist.

"Fuck, you're a heavy bastard." Jesse grunted, turned his head, and bit the inside of Roark's thigh.

"Bloody fecking hell!" Roark jerked away and fell on his back.

Jesse flipped over and scrambled after him, grabbing his legs, then his hips, and assumed a mount position, laughing at Roark's mistake.

Michio grinned as he watched them. When he met my eyes and his smile softened, it hit me that the three of them had reached the kind of connection that could bolster them through my death. They trusted and depended on one another, fought and fucked together. And they made each other laugh.

They would likely fall in and out of despair in the dark days ahead, but as long as one of them was always standing, he would be able to support the weight of the other two. With that conviction, I would die with a calm spirit, an inner peace, carrying with me a lifetime of smiles.

Of course, there was a piece of me that was absolutely terrified to die. To no longer be part of their relationship. To not be around to watch my daughter grow up. But I tried to keep that fear locked away so it wouldn't consume the time I had left.

Michio walked them through various techniques, readjusting Jesse's leg and swatting Roark's ass when he plowed down on Jesse with brute force instead of practiced technique. I'd taught Roark Jiu-Jitsu when we were holed up in his bunker in England, but he was rusty. And unusually aggressive.

I suspected some of it was due to our gentling sex life. The frequency hadn't ebbed, but I'd sensed them holding back with shallower thrusts and softer grips, tempering their need to dominate me roughly and vigorously. And with my belly in the way, our positions had become limited and monotonous.

They'd stripped down to their briefs, their skin glistening with sweat and stretching tight over packs of muscle. Their powerful bodies rolled together in a panting, shoving, pulling clench of strength and skill. The sight made my internal muscles convulse. Another minute of this, and my shorts would be soaked.

Jesse climbed between Roark's legs, barring an arm across his throat, grunting, hips grinding, seeking Roark's submission. They might as well have been fucking, because they moved just like that during sex. If only they would pull their cocks out and mash their mouths together.

Fuck if those images didn't make my pussy spasm. Slick fluid seeped through my folds, preparing my body for them to slide in and soothe the ache. I wanted to lick Roark's sculpted pecs, dig my nails into Jesse's perfect biceps, and bury my teeth in Michio's thick neck, while they fucked me with the same savage aggression they were using on one another now.

Carved abs dipped into waistbands. Cotton cupped and strained half-hard bulges. Maybe they were aroused because I was watching. Though Roark could get hard from the brush of a stiff wind, and given the number of times his hand grazed Jesse's cock, perhaps their arousal had nothing to do with me.

Michio's crouched position hid his groin from view, but he seemed to look at them differently. More closely? Not just with the analytical eye of an expert martial artist. His gaze roamed their grappling physiques with curiosity, affection, and something akin to desire as he lingered on the swells between their legs. He'd bonded with them on a platonic level over the past six months, and the intimacy the four of us shared in our bed crossed the boundaries of most heterosexual men. But he'd never shown sexual desire for them. Until now.

I was beginning to think this sparring session was less about learning new skills and more about pent-up testosterone and assuaging their need to rut and fight and blow off steam.

The thought was excruciatingly pleasurable. I could've sat there all day, watching them strain, wrestle, and grind against each other. I didn't move for the next hour, my attention clinging to the flex of Roark's ass as he dragged his groin over Jesse's chest, and the way Jesse stared at Michio right before he mounted Roark's hips, and how Michio swept in and dominated both of them in a blur of technique and speed.

Individually, they were viciously strong. Together, they were gloriously deadly. In the training room. On the battlefield. And in our bed.

I ached to be in the wrestling pile with them, lying beneath them with my legs spread, feeling Jesse's muscles trembling as he sucked Michio's shaft, the jerk of Roark's fat cock between his thighs as he watched. The way that cock would feel, fucking me with deep, heavy-hitting thrusts. I needed their tongues, their fingers, and their swollen hardness. The ache to connect with every inch of them was as sharp as Michio's fangs.

As if they could smell my arousal, all three heads turned in my direction.

Michio rolled away first, rising fluidly to his feet and striding toward me. "How wet are you?"

I whimpered, and a quiver raced up my legs, sending another gush of heat through my pussy. "See for yourself."

Jesse and Roark followed, Jesse veering off toward the door, while Roark dropped on the couch beside me.

Roark's hot hand gripped the hem of my shorts. "Lift your hips." Three words, thickly accented and given with a stern glare.

I raised my ass, belly heaving heavenward, as Roark stripped the fabric down my legs and off my feet. Michio knelt beside my thighs, his eyes locked on mine as he pulled my shirt over my head, leaving me nude and trembling.

Jesse slid the deadbolt, locking the door, and the click

echoed through me with a tightening clench.

"Open your legs." Roark breathed beneath my ear.

It was just a whisper, but it roared through my body like fire. I obeyed instantly.

The pad of Michio's finger slid through my folds, collecting my wetness. "We were going to do this in our room but had prepared for the possibility of you coming here."

"Do what?" I gave him a confused look and glanced at Jesse and Roark.

Jesse grabbed a duffel bag from the floor by the door and joined us, kneeling between my legs, with Roark on the couch beside me and Michio on my other side.

Something passed between the three of them in an exchange of glances. It was subtle, but they seemed to be leaning closer together, eyes focused and direct, shoulders pushing back, and lips pressed together, as if they were mirroring each other's decisive resolve.

I was the odd man out. "What the hell is going on?"

Michio captured my clit in a merciless pinch, and everything inside me liquefied.

He released me, his hand resting on my leg. "When Aiman held you captive, he could've found Jesse and Roark and changed them into spiders. Do you know why he didn't?"

I knew why Aiman hadn't killed them, but I hadn't considered the possibility of turning them into spiders. Jesse and Roark regarded me with steady eyes. They must've already discussed this. I shook my head.

Michio brushed his fingertips across my inner thigh. "Because he didn't know if they had been consuming your blood like I had. I didn't know either. They could've nicked you with their teeth during a kiss. Could've accidentally ingested a splattered particle of your blood during any one of your injuries. His attempt to turn them into spiders might have instead turned them into walking vaccines. It was too risky, and he was arrogant enough to believe they weren't a threat to his plan."

Jesus. I didn't know if they'd consumed my blood either. It

was possible, but it would've been such an imperceptible amount. "Why are you telling me this?"

Roark kissed my shoulder. "Jesse and I have been ingesting your blood, love. The vials ye fill every day? He and I and the fifty other men who reside in this dam have been taking sips every week for the past couple months."

A flood of emotions surged through me, increasing the energetic pressure beneath my rib cage. If any of the men were bitten, *if Jesse or Roark were bitten*, they would be immune to the programming.

I smiled, shakily, my throat aching. "Thank you. That is... God, that makes me feel so much better about your safety."

About whatever happened *after my death.* I couldn't say it aloud, not while I was nude with my legs spread. But I would die knowing my daughter's fathers wouldn't be turned into mindless spiders.

Jesse gripped my knee, sliding his hand upward until his fingers met Michio's at the crease of my thigh and hip. "Doc is going to bite us."

My eyes widened as images of Michio's fangs sinking into their necks flashed through my head. Would they come the way I always did? Instantly and violently? It was exhilarating, overwhelming, the way my body responded to the idea.

I looked at Roark. "You're okay with this?"

He shrugged, and the corner of his mouth lifted. "Doc's superior agility annoys the bloody hell out of me."

I shifted my attention to Jesse. "You'll lose your fertility."

He touched my belly. "I'll have my hands full with this one." His eyes hardened. "We need Doc's strength and speed, Evie. Every day we put this off is a risk we take with our lives." He lowered his gaze to my stomach. "With her life."

Made sense. If the dam fell under attack by spiders, it would be easier to protect our daughter with equivalent power.

I met Michio's eyes. "You said you were going to do something in our room. You were referring to this? You're going to bite them now?"

"Yes."

With that one word, Michio's entire demeanor changed from analytical doctor to dominating lover. Moving faster than my eyes could track, he blurred behind Jesse between my legs, his hand closing around Jesse's and guiding their fingers to my pussy.

Jesse went still, staring determinedly into my eyes. He wasn't scared or nervous. This man feared nothing. They'd obviously already discussed how this would go, but I was still whirling over the news.

"Will you bite the other men in the dam as well?"

Jesse and Michio slid their fingers inside me, stroking my arousal along a rising wave, as Roark answered. "We've seen what Doc's bite does to ye."

It turned me into a quivering, explosive blob, detonating with so much euphoric pressure it felt like an out-of-body experience.

I grinned, my inner walls clamping around their invading fingers. "You don't want to be responsible for giving our soldiers the best orgasms of their lives?"

"It would be awkward." Michio lowered his head and scraped his fangs along Jesse's shoulder.

Fuck, I was so absorbed in that promising gesture, it took me a moment to register that Roark's hand had joined Jesse's and Michio's. Together, the three of them traced my opening, slipped through my wetness, and thrust inside me, shooting a spiral of pleasure through my body.

Roark leaned over my chest and swirled his tongue around my nipple. "We want to give ye something, love."

Their fingers stroked my sensitive flesh, turning my cunt into an achy throb of heat. In about two seconds, I would give it right back in a gripping explosion around their hands.

Michio removed his fingers and bent toward the bag on the floor. When he set a bottle of lube on the couch, my ass clenched in anticipation.

"That's not for you." Michio slid his hands around Jesse's ribs, his fingers lowering over twitching abs and lingering on the waistband of Jesse's briefs.

He never touched them like that. Never in such a sensual or suggestive way.

My gaze flew to Michio's eyes, hoping, pleading, and he stared right back with unwavering intention.

Jesse kept himself relaxed, not a single flinch against Michio's wandering touch, as he worked his fingers alongside Roark's inside me. "That look right there on your face… Fuck, Evie. You've never asked us for this, but we know how badly you want it."

It. They didn't spell it out, but I desperately needed them to. I needed to know I wasn't imagining it. "Say it. Tell me so I understand."

Roark shifted to face me, his free hand sifting through my ponytail, lightly pulling. "We're going to give you our virginities."

SIXTY-ONE

My whole body ignited beneath a turbulence of uncertainty and hunger as I scanned the depths of Jesse's and Roark's eyes. I expected taut expressions and edgy gazes, but their faces were composed, confident, and accepting. They fully intended to let Michio fuck them. *For me.*

Roark released my ponytail, removed his fingers from between my legs, and reclined beside me on the couch. "We've been discussing this for months, love."

So they weren't rushing into it. They'd had time to talk through it, perhaps fight about it, and come to terms with it. But why?

Jesse's kneeling position between my legs put him right in my view, with Michio on knees behind him, both of them watching me closely.

I leaned back on the couch, nude, struggling to breathe, and drenched in shock. "Don't do this for *me*. You've already given me everything. I can't… I mean, it would be a significant and wonderful moment to experience with you. No woman in her right mind would talk you out of this. But I know you guys." I looked each man in the eyes as I addressed him. "Roark, you already gave me your virginity. And Jesse, you fiercely told me once you weren't into dudes." I turned to Michio. "When the four of us are in bed, your focus is always on me. You've never shown desire for them."

Michio didn't verbally object. No, he simply brushed his lips across Jesse's shoulder.

It felt like my insides were splintering and exploding at the same time. I didn't want them to do this as a means to console me in my final days. On the other hand, if they took their relationship to this level, it could solidify their future together.

Or wedge a mountain of shame between them.

I glanced away. "As much as I want you to be together in this way…" I squeezed my eyes shut. Was I really saying this? I blew out a breath and gave them a firm look. "I won't enjoy it knowing you're doing it solely for me. I'll be wondering if you're hating every minute of it, or if it will make things uncomfortable between you. What if it tore you apart?"

Michio's hand remained on the waistband of Jesse's briefs, his mouth hovering over Jesse's shoulder, as he held my gaze. "I'm going to bite them, Evie. It serves a practical purpose, but you know as well as I do, it's a deeply intimate act. Perhaps more intimate than sex. Since I trust Jesse and Roark with my life, biting them will bind us in a way that will expand all of our comfort zones."

Because he expected to have an orgasmic reaction with them. My God, I loved the promise of that.

When he bit Elaine, he'd said he was too disgusted and enraged to become aroused. But that wouldn't be the case with Jesse and Roark. He would likely respond to them the way he always did with me. With the exception of the time on the cliff, he'd never bitten me without viciously burying himself inside me, as if the bite was connected to the animalistic part of his nature and drawing blood instinctively turned him into a fucking, rutting beast.

I suspected this was why the conversation about anal sex was initiated. I could imagine Michio laying it all out matter-of-factly. *If I bite you, there's a ninety-six percent probability I will mount you and fuck you.*

Jesse slowly thrust his fingers in and out of me, his gaze like liquid fire as he examined my face, my heaving chest, and my swollen flesh wrapped around his curling touch. Bowing over the roundness of my belly, he put his free hand on my shoulder, the position of his fingers deliberate, pressed against the bend of my shoulder and neck, his thumb stroking the pulse in my throat. A dominating grip, one that commanded me to submit to whatever they decided.

The nerves between my legs charged, and my lungs raggedly filled with air, my doubts vanishing with each spiking jump of my heart.

He leaned in. "Every time you watch us together, your breath picks up, your little nipples harden, and your pussy—"

I tightened the muscles around his fingers.

"Fuck, darlin'." He stroked the soaking rim of my opening. "Your pussy knows how desperately we want you. And while you're watching us together, all this wet heat will only get wetter and hotter."

The slurping sounds of his driving fingers filled the room. Already my orgasm was building, from his words, his touch, and my filthy imagination as my mind composed a naughty choreography of calloused hands, tight asses, and hard cocks, all slipping and grinding together.

He slid his fingers from my pussy and raised them to Roark's mouth as he intensely watched me. Roark gripped his wrist and greedily licked, sucking each digit between full lips, eyes locked on mine.

Desire mounted, and I felt trapped beneath it, unable to move, imprisoned by anticipation to find out what they would do next.

Michio leaned against Jesse's back, his hand wrapping around Jesse's length, which strained hard and thick against its cotton cage.

"Turning you on turns us on, Evie." Michio palmed Jesse's bulge, fingers tightening. "Does he look like he's hating this?"

No, Jesse appeared to be struggling to calm himself, his hips rocking forward to grind against Michio's grip.

The next few seconds passed in a haze of heavy breaths, shared glances, and soft caresses as they stripped off their briefs and spun me around, positioning my body where they wanted me. I ended up lying lengthwise on the couch, angled more on my side than my back, and legs spread with Jesse's cock at my entrance. Michio knelt behind Jesse, and Roark bent over my head, hand on my chin as he tilted my mouth toward his shaft.

Jesse held still as Michio's arms came around his waist. Fangs dragged languidly across Jesse's shoulder and neck, eliciting a ripple of twitches along his abs. When Michio's fingers found the patch of hair at the base of his hard cock, my lungs burned for air and my bones turned to lava. There was something so fucking tantalizing about watching Michio's hand drag through those short hairs, as if the hairline served as a forbidden border. With each scrape of Michio's fingers past that trimmed line, I could feel the last of our boundaries falling down around us.

With the length of my leg upward along Jesse's chest, he trailed fingers up and down my inner thigh, his pectorals trembling against me. The room filled with the sounds of anxious breaths as Michio worked the lube over himself. Roark rubbed his length along my lips. Then he met Jesse's eyes.

They thrust at the same time, Roark filling my mouth and Jesse hard and deep between my legs. My hands flew toward them, seeking to deepen the connection, my fingers lacing with Jesse's on my belly and finding Roark's grip twisting in my hair. Their bodies rocked in sync as I licked and sucked Roark's girth and lifted my hips, meeting Jesse's thrusts.

Every jolt of pleasure through my body, each sound I moaned around Roark's cock, reflected in their eyes. I felt as though I was at the apex of their world, and heaven and hell knew they were the center of mine.

I knew the moment Michio was ready. Jesse stopped moving, buried to the hilt inside me, his hands resting on my belly. Roark pulled out of my mouth and shifted away, as if to not block my view of Jesse and Michio. Roark braced a knee on the edge of the couch beside my breasts, the jut of his swollen shaft bobbing from between his sculpted thighs. Then he leaned toward Jesse and captured the other man's mouth.

Jesse's tongue rolled with Roark's, the underside of their jaws stretching and flexing as they deepened the kiss.

Michio angled away from Roark and brought his lips to the other side of Jesse's neck, gripped Jesse's hips, and breathed, "Ready?"

Jesse slipped half-way out of me, his knees adjusting on the cushion against the back of my thighs. "No." His voice was thick, but a nervous smile twitched his lips.

Michio sank into him, a primal thrust of fangs and cock. With a shout, Jesse drove into my cunt, pounding rapidly, ruthlessly, his neck straining against Michio's bite, his muscles tensing, and his hands flying over my body, gripping and caressing my breasts. As hard as Michio was moving, entering Jesse in a place no one had gone before, there had to be some pain. The bite must've been mitigating that.

Jesse's muscles shook, his eyes locked shut. He held off his climax for a few more seconds then roared against Roark's mouth. "Fuck, fuck, holy fucking shit!"

Watching him get off with Michio buried inside him, in his vein, in his ass, while he kissed Roark and thrust between my legs was enough to send me over. The shock wave of my release rolled through me, and I rode the orgasm for long glorious seconds, jerking my hips.

Michio continued to pump, his lips locked on Jesse's neck, and his smoldering gaze fixed on me. A moment later, he tore his mouth away, dropped his head back with fangs tinged in blood, and groaned. His hard-packed muscles shook with his climax. Then he pulled out, and his heated gaze turned to Roark.

"Hold the feck on, Doc." Roark pointed at him. "I told ye I wanted to be inside her when we did this."

Michio gave a stiff nod as Jesse slipped from my pussy and sat back on his heels, visibly shaken.

I leaned toward him, as much as my belly would allow, and touched his whiskered jaw. "Are you okay?"

He gave me a dark look, the only warning I got, and attacked my mouth. His tongue coiled with mine frantically and passionately, answering me in the best way imaginable. Too soon, he broke the kiss and lifted me into his lap with my back to his chest. His hands slid around my stomach, caressing in soft, wide circles, covering the entire expanse of my bump as he reclined back against the arm of the couch.

Michio stepped back, cleaned himself with a towel, and reapplied the lube. Roark passed him a curious glance then moved in toward Jesse and me, burrowing between our legs. First his mouth and that sinful tongue, licking and sucking my swollen flesh. Then his hips, spreading my thighs and taking Jesse's legs with them.

Given the size of my belly, it would've been easier to turn around and let him take me from behind. That had become our go-to position. But they were doing this for me, so that I could enjoy the pleasure of watching them.

Roark bent over us, careful not to put weight on the baby, and looked at Jesse behind me. "Did it hurt?"

The vulnerable question made my heart pang. "You don't have to do this."

"I'm talking about the teeth, love." He leaned in and nipped at my breast then raised a brow at Jesse.

"You want me to admit I liked it," Jesse said in a bored tone.

Michio tossed the lube and stepped behind Roark. "He liked it. I felt his shudder from his neck all the way to his toes."

Jesse didn't respond, but his cock was already swelling against my back.

I groaned. "God, none of you will need recovery time now. With your greedy bodies in a constant state of hardness, I'm probably going to start walking funny."

Roark grinned and palmed my belly. "Ye mean, waddle funny?"

"Fuck off." I grinned back.

Michio reached behind Roark and did something with his hand that made Roark lower his head and moan. "The effects of the bite will be gradual. At least it was for me. Small changes over the first month." He shifted, lining his cock to Roark's backside, and wrapped his hands around Roark's hips.

"Roark?"

Anchoring his arms beneath my knees, Roark raised my lower body to meet his hips and entered me, inch by teasing inch. He quickly found his pace, stroking my inner walls, grunting, and staring into my eyes. Each long glide of his shaft shot sparks of sensations down my legs, teetering me on the edge of orgasm. Jesse's lips on my neck and hands wandering my body only heightened my arousal.

Michio took him the same way he'd taken Jesse, fangs in his neck and one hard thrust, fucking him furiously, which only seemed to make Roark hungrier, needier, and more aggressive. I would never tire of watching them together, their powerful bodies and husky groans, working harder, reaching deeper, and seeking their pleasure.

But what captivated me the most were the affectionate touches. Jesse's hand gliding over Roark's where he pinched my nipple. And Michio's thumb lightly stroking Roark's jaw as he held Roark's neck against his mouth.

As Roark and Michio trembled through their orgasms, I moaned with them, and let the sights and sounds of all three of them take me over. Their panting breaths, impassioned groans, every flex and bunch of their gorgeous bodies overwhelmed me with happiness.

We didn't stop after that, those initial releases only taking the edge off. We moved to the shower near our room, where they took turns fucking me under the fall of water. I'd never seen them so wound up and insatiable. They touched each other without hesitancy, tongues sliding together, and eyes connecting without embarrassment or regret. It was as if something had unlocked between them, the power to openly express companionship and love, the permission to freely act on desires, whatever it was seemed to lift a veil from around us, one I hadn't even known was there.

Eventually, obligations pulled us away from one another. For the rest of the afternoon, we ate, visited with the never-ending queue of people outside, and ate again.

But by nightfall, we returned to our room, where they

explored one another, openly, hungrily, and always with me at the center of their focus. When they weren't stretching and filling every hole in my body, they were fucking each other, watching me, feeding off the desire in my eyes. Michio never bottomed, but Jesse and Roark swapped positions with each other in a whirlwind of deep thrusts, bruising hands, rasping growls, driven and vicious.

I hadn't understood the real strength in their passion until I witnessed them unleashing it on each other. They didn't have to be gentle or kind. They took and conquered like men in war, all while holding my gaze, fully aware that the sight of their flexing bodies gliding together set me on fire. Their eyes clung to me, lured me in, and held me with them. I knew they cared for one another, but they didn't abandon their proud, competitive natures. Each man was here for me, fighting the others for my attention and love. If I hadn't been watching or participating, they wouldn't have been together on this level, fulfilling my every fantasy. I hoped someday they might love one another as much as I loved them.

It was late that night when we finally crashed in bed, muscles sore and tired, and desires thoroughly quenched. Jesse was curled around my side, and Roark's head rested on my chest, his body at a right angle to mine, with the bedding twisted over our nude skin.

I traced a finger over the bite mark on Roark's neck. "Have you thought of names?"

Michio had left our sweaty pile to grab something from his bag by the door. He straightened, cupping a piece of metal in his hand, and looked back at me. "How about Moria?"

Roark made a face. "Where are we, in Middle-earth?"

"Moria." Jesse tried it out, his voice hacking. "It makes my throat hurt."

"Fine." Michio strode back and climbed in beside Roark, his head next to mine and his gaze on Jesse. "What would you name her?"

Jesse drew a circle around my belly button with his finger. "Prudence. Because she's going to be prudish, modest, innocent, and…prudish. Very prudish."

Michio snorted. "Makes me think of plums."

"And ancient old aunts." I sighed. "I've had a few ideas."

Michio propped his elbow on the pillow above my head, his chin resting on his fist. "Let's hear them."

"Faith, Hope, Harmony, Grace, Destiny… They all fit, but they feel…I don't know. Names like that set expectations. She'll have enough of that as it is, so yeah, I'm not in love with any of them." I turned my head and eyed his hand, where he held whatever he'd removed from his bag. "What is that?"

He lifted it above my head. A medallion fell from his grip and caught on a length of silver chain, dangling over my face. I grabbed it, cradling it in my palm for a closer look. My breath caught.

The medallion was about two inches in diameter and cast out of silver. Embedded in the metal was the turquoise stone Jesse had given me, a black bead from Roark's rosary, and one of Michio's fangs.

My ribs tightened, and my hands shook. I licked my lips, working my throat to find my voice. "You made this?"

"I had one of Link's guys make it. Lift your head."

Michio fastened it around my neck and leaned back, watching me with boundless devotion etching his face.

I held it against my chest, the length of the chain placing it directly over my heart. "I love it. I…" The backs of my eyes pricked, and I cursed my damned pregnancy hormones for turning me into such a whimpering mess. "You guys have given me so much."

Jesse kissed my neck beneath my ear. "We feel the same way about you, darlin'."

A sweet, comfortable silence fell, broken when Roark sat up and grinned. "We should call her Betty."

Jesse scrubbed a hand over his face. "You call every woman you see a betty."

"Then it'll be easy for me to remember."

There was a good chance we wouldn't be agreeing on a

name, but I got a kick out of listening to them joke about it.

"How about Bertha?" Jesse asked.

He sounded so serious, but I knew he was fucking with us.

Michio frowned. "You want Evie to give *birth* to a *Bertha*? I suppose it's kinder than just cutting through the crap and naming her Placenta or Vagina."

Roark closed his eyes. "Anyone who names their child that should be punished with terrible torture in unquenchable fire." He rolled to his chest, staring at my belly. "Let's just call her Schartzmugel and be done with it."

Jesse tucked an arm beneath his head, his eyes smiling. "Hi, my name is Schartzmugel, and I'm here to save the world."

I rubbed my temples. "I'm not sure whether to laugh or cry."

Roark lowered his head and kissed my hip bone. "We want ye to choose the name. We'll love anything ye pick."

"Okay."

I ran my fingers through his hair, the strands soft and gentle, so unlike the tangled dreads from our life on the road. It was symbolic, really, of how easy and orderly our routine had become. Living in the dam, with electricity and haircuts and a bed, it felt...normal. Like pre-plague, feel-good normal. I wanted to grab onto this moment in time, hold it for them, and leave it with them after I was gone. But I couldn't stop the future or the pain it would bring them. All I could do was give them my approval to take whatever path they needed to find this feel-good normal again.

"Promise me something." I waited for them to look at me. "I've spent a lot of time in my head, trying to figure out what to say to you, how to make it better after—"

"Evie." Jesse growled, his expression stony.

Beside me, Roark and Michio stiffened.

"Just listen. When I die, promise me that when other women—"

"We're not talking about this." Roark slid off the bed, stark nude, and strode toward the door.

"We have to talk about it." I crawled to my knees, facing

him. "For my peace of mind. Please!"

Roark stopped and shoved his hand through his hair, seemingly trying to rein in his emotions. "You're going to live. That's all there is to it."

My chest tightened.

Warm hands slid around my hips and pulled me back. When I turned, Michio stroked a finger down my cheek, the desolate look in his brown eyes squeezing my lungs.

His lips compressed, as if holding back something, then parted with a shuddering breath. "I'm trying to fix this. I'm *trying*…I just…I don't know what's broken."

He'd spent months in the lab, studying my blood work and DNA. So many tests, and they all came back healthy. *I* was healthy.

My eyes burned as I cupped his face and rested my forehead against his. "There's nothing to fix. This is supposed to happen."

"Bullshit." Jesse rose to his knees on the mattress, hands clenched at his sides. "We're going to defeat this."

"How? You can't fight it with an arrow or a sword. You can't tie a rope around me and pull me away from it." My voice rose, shaky and thick with sudden tears. "It's coming, this…this…whatever this is that decides what will happen. It's conspicuous and ugly and inescapable, and dammit, I don't want it to take you with me."

I couldn't leave knowing they would become so lost in grief that they couldn't find their way back.

Silence blanketed the room. The sound of misery.

A hot trail of tears dripped down my cheek, and I swiped at it, staining my fingers in red. Ugh. I couldn't even cry like normal people. I went a lifetime without crying, and now this? Blubbering all the time and making a damned mess.

No more tears. I refused to let a single drop of negative energy steal what time I had left.

"I just want you to be happy." I drew in a calming breath. "Maybe I should leave a letter like Joel did. His words strengthened me through some dark and lonely times."

"We won't be alone." Roark returned to the bed and wrapped his body around my back. "And we den' want a letter."

"We want you." Michio pulled his gaze from me, shared a look with the others, and returned to my face. "We have you here and would rather hear it now…" His jaw tightened, and he looked away.

Jesse gripped the back of Michio's neck with a firm squeeze. His earlier tension loosened from his muscles, his eyes lidded with a wretched kind of resolve. "We'll listen. What do you want us to promise?"

I slid out of Roark's embrace so that I could see all of their faces. We sat in a tight circle on the bed, leaning toward the center, toward each other, our breaths mingling and our bond coursing like a current of energy around us.

As I moved my hands to my belly, they followed suit, their fingers curling around mine as I spoke. "Promise me you won't struggle alone. Whether you find another woman or several women, remain as open to love as you are in this moment. But don't let her or them rip apart the bond you've created between you. Schartzmugel needs her fathers together and united."

"Bloody hell, love." Roark hooked his arm around my back and pulled me against his side. "Before we met ye, we were resigned to be single and lonely."

Michio gripped my hand, head down and gaze on the bedding. "But we didn't just find you." He lifted his eyes and looked at Jesse and Roark.

They'd found each other. Closeness and trust that could only be shared between brothers, best friends, lovers. My heart beat slow and steady through my veins, comforted, content.

"We promise we won't be alone." Jesse's eyes were hard with conviction, his voice rough with emotion. "These guys are hard to get rid of."

"Yeah, they are." I smiled with trembling lips. "I have one more request."

Every moment I'd spent with them over the years had been

a gift. Jesse's angry glares when I first met him in the mountains, Roark's flirting and frustrating celibacy in the bunker, my captivity on Malta under Michio's constant care, all of those interactions were gifts. No matter what we were doing, I cherished every second of their company. And now those seconds were slipping free from my grip. It made me greedy, desperate, for more of their time.

"No more parting ways in the morning to spend long hours in the lab or gardening or training soldiers. Spend the next two months with me. The four of us. In bed or running the tunnels. Eating, talking, laughing, touching, I don't care what we do, I just want to do it together."

Their somber, thoughtful gazes caressed my face, and my fingers trembled, aching to strangle my fate. Each beat of my heart felt like a leap toward the final one, when I would no longer stare into their eyes or feel their breaths on my neck.

Fingers entwined, Michio carried my hand to his lips. "You didn't need to ask."

For the next two months, they gave me the most valuable gift of all. We spent every second together, and time flowed in a river of smiling, bickering, fucking, kissing inseparable intimacy. Not a moment was wasted.

It was the best two months of my life. And probably theirs as well. Jesse and Roark strengthened in speed, and when their fangs came in, so did their cravings. Sips of my blood quenched them, but they also drew from each other. Their blood would sustain them, and maybe the vials I'd been saving could be used to create a vaccine or cure. I hoped.

At the end of August, Shea gave birth to her baby. When he inhaled his first breath, the air didn't kill him. Either the nymph virus was gone or recovered nymphs were able to pass along their immunity. He had ten fingers and toes and perfect, healthy *human* organs. With his thick black hair and huge eyes, he looked just like Paul. She named him Eddie.

My guardians didn't hold him, their demeanors guarded, hesitant, and their eyes full of dread, as if his arrival was a harbinger of the darkness that was to come. That night, they fucked me gently yet with so much trembling desperation it scared me. *They* were scared. It was like they knew.

The next morning, I woke with an overwhelming urge to watch the sunrise, so on our way to breakfast, we stopped in the garden at the bottom of the dam.

Crowds still gathered in the thousands around the canyon, a revolving congregation of people coming and going, searching for a glimpse of me and my massive belly when I made my daily trips to the surface. The sheet-metal walls around the garden provided privacy from all the eyes peering through the barricades around the dam, but the open rafters allowed sunlight to nourish the vibrancy of greenery within.

The gardener, Ronnie, worked on the pipe system in the far corner. Darwin darted over to him with enthusiastic sniffs and licks, while the four of us walked through the rows of plants. Rich, shimmering hues of green exploded beneath the golden breath of dawn. Beyond the garden's metal supports, the sun peered over a red-rock bluff, casting the sky in a fiery glow and warming my skin. It felt like the beginning of life.

As the shimmering rays chased away the shadows, my guardians stood strong and glorious under the strengthening twilight. Mother Nature's most beautiful creations. Just looking at them made me lightheaded. The deep jade pools of Roark's eyes. The reddish hues of Jesse's strong, whiskered jaw. The symmetrical angles of Michio's sculpted face. But none of that was as beautiful as the souls beneath their perfect forms. How lucky I was to have loved them.

We reached the center of the garden when a fist of pain clamped my stomach. I shouted out, stumbling forward, shocked by the violence of it. My cervix had been dilating normally, and I wasn't due for another week. Fuck, why did this hurt so badly? My previous births had been gradual, small cramping, before building into active labor. This…this was too sudden. Too violent. Something was wrong.

Jesse and Roark grabbed my arms, their eyes wide with terror.

Michio put his worried face in mine. "Breathe, Evie. Slow

and deep."

But the next contraction was already bearing down on me, cutting my breath and robbing the strength from my body. The pressure between my legs hurt worse than anything I remembered, and the need to push overpowered all thought.

I couldn't resist it, could feel her stretching, breaching, trying to wrench her way out of me. "I need to push!"

SIXTY-TWO

The contractions hit me one right after another, each stronger, longer, and closer together than the last. My legs cramped, and nausea gripped my body. I needed to sit. Fuck, I needed to push. But Jesse and Roark held me up, attempting to shuffle out of the garden and into the dam.

"Wait." Michio grabbed my shorts and yanked them down, crouching as he touched between my legs. He looked up, his shock clear in his wide eyes. "Send for the obstetricians."

"We need to take her *to* them." The fear straining Jesse's voice punched a different kind of pain through my insides. "She needs to be in the room with all the equipment."

Another contraction slammed into me, rocking me against Jesse, and a gush of wet warmth ran down my legs.

"She's already crowning." The urgency in Michio's voice sent chills down my spine. "I…I could pick her up and speed there, but I'm afraid the velocity—"

"Fuck no!" I screamed.

I would not give birth while being carried through a tunnel at a hundred miles per hour.

"Put her on the ground," Michio said, his eyes stony and focused.

"Ronnie!" Roark shouted for the gardener, his hands digging into my arm as he crouched with Jesse and eased me onto my back.

The moment the cold concrete touched my spine, I started pushing. I couldn't help it. The increasing pressure in my back, the unbearable pain in my abdomen, the suddenness of the contractions, it was all too much. Too much fear, too much confusion, too much pain. And not enough time. I was already at the bottom of the cliff. There was nowhere left to fall. No escape. This was happening. I grasped Roark's arm. Oh God, I wasn't ready.

I would never be ready.

But I had no choice. My body was already contracting and pressing, driving her out.

Roark's head swung around and jerked to a stop. "Ronnie, get the doctors. Go!" Then he roared, "Run like your arse is on fire!"

Ronnie's speeding footsteps echoed through the garden and faded into the dam. A second later, Darwin approached in a flurry of clicking toenails, his wet nose sliding across my neck and his tongue lapping at my face.

Jesse guided him back and grabbed my fingers. "We're right here, darlin'. Squeeze my hand as hard as you need to."

I tried not to hold the tension in my face as I bore down and focused on pushing where it mattered. I screamed and grunted, clutching Jesse's hand and scraping my nails across Roark's leg. Shit, it hurt like a motherfucker. My shrieking protests were delirious, and every frenzied thump of my heart flooded me with adrenaline and uncertainty.

Michio knelt between my legs, yanked off his shirt, and wiped what must've been the top of her head. Without removing his eyes from my spread legs, he thrust an impatient hand toward Jesse and Roark. "Your shirts."

He tossed the one in his hand, the fabric soaked in blood, as he grabbed the others from Jesse and Roark.

Panic rose, shaking my limbs. "Why am I bleeding?"

Was the baby's life in danger? Was she stuck in the birth canal? What if she died with me? I tried to claw my way out of my mounting fears, but the tension in my guardians postures escalated my blood pressure and sealed up my throat.

"What's wrong?" Jesse leaned toward Michio, his eyes wild with terror as he stared between my legs. "Oh God. Jesus, fuck." His voice rasped with horror. "Why is there so much blood?"

Michio lowered his face between my legs, his fingers moving around the baby's head inside me. "Sudden and rapid contractions, vaginal bleeding, abdominal pain, all indicators of placental abruption." Panic clipped the edge of his rushed voice. "Keep pushing, Evie. We need her out."

I crunched my body and pushed with all my might, howling and shaking, stopping only when I needed to breathe through the unbearable pain.

Roark raised my hand to his mouth, his lips moving silently against my fingers as he prayed.

Another surge of contractions powered through me, ripping a scream from my throat. My muscles locked up, and frantic desperation thundered against my ribs. As my fingers spasmed in the strong hands that held me, I sought their eyes, needing their strength. But I only saw more pain, their expressions contorted in a heartbreaking visage of anguish.

My chest tightened, aching to take away their torment. "I'm fine. It's just labor pains." I huffed between pushes. "Almost over."

Jesse brought his face to mine, squeezing my hand to his chest and smoothing down my hair with his other. "I love you." His voice cracked. "God, I love you so much. You'll get through this."

Roark glanced over his shoulder, his hand falling to my face, his thumb stroking my jaw. "Where the feck are they?" He turned back to me, agony rutting deep grooves around his eyes. "You're brilliant, love. Strong and beautiful. I'm so fecking proud of ye."

I gave him a grateful smile and looked at Michio. "Is she…" A wave of dizziness and chills shuddered through me, weakening my body. "Is she going to be okay?"

Michio kept his attention on his hands, his arms flexing between my legs. "I need her out now! You're losing too much blood." His tone sharpened, spiked with imperative. "Push, Evie. Push!"

The unmistakable stench of dread sweltered the air. Jesse's

grip on my hand clenched harder. Michio's expression grew tighter. And Roark's chest heaved as he caressed my face.

With each push, I felt my blood, my energy, and my life flowing from my body. She was taking it with her, leaving a burst of yellow and orange across my vision. The sky overhead glowed with the arrival of dawn, swirling around us and chasing away the chill. I was floating, up, up, up into the sky, carried on the translucent rays of light. Every sunrise was different, but this one was far brighter, stronger, and more luminous than all its predecessors.

This was the first light of the future.

An urgent voice echoed on the surface of my awareness. I reached for it, tried to feel it, embrace it, and crashed back to the concrete floor in the garden.

My body was a block of ice, freezing my nerve-endings and weighing down my limbs. No energy. No strength. The garden was losing its vibrancy, the edges swallowed by thickening shadows.

"Evie." Jesse's agonized face filled my view, tears sheening his eyes, and his voice so strained his words garbled. "Keep your eyes open. Look at me."

"The baby?" I whispered, or at least I thought I did. I tried to see around him, couldn't lift my head.

"Her airway is cleared." A weighted moment clung to Michio's words, then…

A high-pitched wail hit my ears. My breath hitched, and my chest swelled. The sound of her beautiful voice filled my entire being, and I heard myself crying, my vision flooding in red.

I blinked, clearing my eyes, as Michio leaned over me and placed her tiny body on my chest. Oh my God, she was real. She was here, breathing, warm, mine. *Theirs.*

I tried uselessly to raise my arms, desperate to hold her. A second later, my arms lifted, guided by Jesse and Roark, their hands adjusting mine into an embrace around her body. Their arms wrapped around me as I peered down at her for the first time.

Pink skin, eyes closed, a tuft of coppery hair, her little fist nuzzled against her mouth. She took my breath away.

"Perfect," I choked and smiled at her fathers.

They didn't return my smile. Michio had already moved back my legs, his face a sheet of white and taut with distress. I couldn't feel pain or pressure anymore, and it became harder to fill my lungs with air. He knew… My heart shattered into thousands of jagged shards. He knew I was fading. Oh God, I was dying, and I needed more time with him.

"Michio, stop. Come here."

"No, goddammit!" His shout scraped over my skin, his face sculpted in stone. "I can fix this."

He bent between my legs, blood up to his elbows, his hand inside me, his other pressed on my belly, compressing my uterus between his palms. Jesse's hard glare fixed on Michio, his arm wrapped around me and the baby. Roark, a gorgeous mirage with tears dripping off his cheeks like water, stroked a finger across my brow and pulled me closer, as if trying to draw me into his despair.

I didn't have to see their faces to know what was happening. I smelled the blood, tasted Roark's tears as they fell upon my lips, and heard Michio's frantic breaths. My life was seeping from my body in shivering waves, and an approaching hush rang in my ears. Pitch-black smothered me, and my muscles twitched to escape it.

Evie, don't listen to them. Don't follow them. A weak plea, calling from a distance. The voice grew louder, more demanding.

"You're not leaving us, Evie!" Jesse shouted. Hands gripped my face. "Evie! Open your fucking eyes!"

Light bled in and with it came the buzz of wings. Red wings. Black spots. They danced like dust motes in the sparkle of the sun, hovering around Michio's tear-streaked face, climbing through the blond halo of Roark's hair, and fluttering past Jesse, following the path of his stricken gaze.

Their flight took them to the far side of the garden, and there, hovering at the edge of my vision, was Annie and

Aaron. Preserved forever at the sweet ages of seven and six, they held hands between their transparent forms, watching us.

I whimpered, both longing to hold them and fighting to stay.

"No!" Jesse screamed at them, his arms pulling me against him. "You're not taking her!"

The swarm of ladybirds circled around them, pulling on my breaths, waiting.

"I can't get her uterus to tighten." Michio was sobbing now, his shoulders jerking through each violent shudder. "Her blood's not clotting."

"Please, come here." I wheezed, my skin trembling. So cold. Numb. I couldn't move. Every breath was a tremendous effort.

He climbed up my body and straddled my hips, bracing over me and the baby. Defeat twisted his face. "The doctors are coming. They'll be able to help."

But I knew they couldn't. Machines and surgeries and blood transfusions wouldn't stop this. Fate was inevitable, and this baby needed my energy, my power. I wouldn't take it back.

Jesse and Roark wrapped around my sides, enveloping me in the heat of their bodies, their hands soothing, their breaths fast and wet.

"Evie." Jesse cupped my face. "Stay with us. Listen to my voice."

I forced my heavy eyelids open and concentrated, not on the apparitions and ladybirds that beckoned me, but on the familiarity of his timbre, on Michio's eyes begging me to fight, and on the love radiating from Roark's soft touches.

A tear skipped down Jesse's cheek. "We're going to find a boat. A really big, fancy yacht. Even bigger than the one in Italy. You remember it?"

I nodded weakly, my heart clenching.

"It's where we're all going to live as soon as you recover. The five of us and Darwin." His voice broke, his fingers tightening on my face. "It'll be our own private sanctuary in the ocean. When you see it, you won't ever want to leave. We'll have the sun on our faces and the water to protect us from aphids."

"I think I killed all the aphids."

A sob scratched from his throat, but he cut it off and attempted a smile. "So you did."

Roark leaned in, one hand on my head, and the other molding over the baby's back as she slept. "We'll skinny dip in the water every morning. None of us will wear clothes. Ever." His brogue rolled thickly, heavy with tears. "Ye won't be able to keep your eyes off me."

He successfully molded his lips into a full grin, but it didn't touch his liquid emerald eyes. He squeezed them shut and pressed his face against the side of mine as he struggled to muffle the keening in his throat.

Michio stared at me with what could only be shock as tears silently rained from his frozen brown eyes. I hoped he was ignoring the wet feel of my blood on his hands and instead was thinking about the yacht and the joy they would find together. As he inched closer, he adjusted the baby to snuggle against my neck, which allowed me to turn my face and kiss her soft, warm cheek.

His face drew nearer to mine, his tone sharp. "Don't give up, Evie. Don't you leave us."

My breaths shallowed, and darkness closed in around me, but I fought it. Fought to keep my eyes open. Fought for another precious moment with my family.

"I'm not afraid," I whispered, making every breath count. "I'll always be with you, right here." I stroked my finger against our daughter's tiny shoulder. "I'll always love you."

We had all lost people we loved. Death had become so ingrained in us it was easy to let it overshadow what was right in front of us. But they held the tiny embodiment of life in their arms. They had never had children so they couldn't fully understand the magnitude of happiness and love she would bring them. They would discover it soon, and they would wonder how they ever lived without her.

I couldn't feel her weight on my chest, and my lungs lost their grip on the last of my air. My breath streamed away, acceptance of my fate stealing my fight.

"No." Jesse said, sternly. "Don't you dare let go. You'll fight this. Fucking fight it, Evie!"

The sounds of Roark's sobbing trembled the air, and Michio's body rocked against mine, wracked with his misery. With shredded breaths, they demanded I stay awake, pleaded for me to keep my eyes open, their shouts gentling into desperate kisses on my hands and face. When each of their mouths found mine, I tasted the salt of their anguish, and I knew they tasted my *good-bye.*

I'd given them my mind, my heart, and my body. Staring up at them, with their beautifully strong faces backlit by the rising sun, I sank into darkness.

I was their sunset.

And she was their glorious sunrise.

"Dawn." I managed one more breath. "Her name is Dawn."

When Evening fell from the sky,
the ground shook with the sobs of her people.
She left us in darkness.
But from her rivers of blood rose a great star.
She'd given us the sun.

~ Father Roark Molony

SIXTY-THREE

Roark

Evie was gone, and the garden sank into a deep terrible silence, except for the shreds of air ripping from the fissure inside me, the empty hole where her soul used to be. I tried to reach for God, my lips numb and straining to find words of prayer, but the only sounds I could form were those of unbearable anguish.

Jesse jumped to his feet and raced to the far side of the garden. "Nooooo! No, Evie, please!"

He swung his arms through the swarm of ladybirds, his bloodshot eyes tracing their path as they flew toward the sky. It was as though they were carrying away her spirit. And ours with it.

"No no no no no." Jesse dropped to his knees, holding his head in his hands, his body shaking with great, hiccupping sobs. "She's gone, she's gone. Oh God, she's fucking gone."

The torment inside me hardened into a knot of indescribable hell, sinking like a fiery brick. The agonizing sounds of Jesse's vocal chords shoved it deeper, twisting and burning in my stomach.

With shaking hands, Michio gathered our baby into his arms and pressed her against my chest. The moment I secured the little bundle in my clumsy hands, he grabbed Evie's body and dragged her into his lap, his head falling back with the sudden force of his roar. Darwin was right there with him, whining and licking Evie's pale face, as Michio sobbed and screamed her name until his screams became my own.

I ached to comfort him, both him and Jesse, but grief was pouring from my throat, violently, uncontrollably. It made the baby cry, her tiny wails tearing away my breaths, as my body shook against the brutality of inescapable pain.

"Shhh." I cupped her scrunched up face in my hand, my vision blurring. "Dawn." So beautiful and precious, just like her mother.

The stomp of feet surrounded us, voices rose, followed by the sudden wrench of Shea's crying. But nothing was as loud as the agony thundering in my chest. Holding Dawn carefully against me, I crawled through the pool of blood and wrapped an arm around Michio's rocking body, hoping to console him, needing to lean on him.

He didn't give me his eyes, but his hand flew up, searching for mine. I caught his fingers, and he squeezed tightly, pulling me closer with Evie's body cradled between us. Closing my eyes, I dug deep inside me, and after several struggling moments, I found the strength to administer the sacrament of Extreme Unction.

"In nomine Patris, et Filii, et Spiritus Sancti." A torrent of tears and misery fell out with the words, splattering the chest of the woman I loved. Once I was able to fill my lungs again, I whispered the prayer I'd dreaded for eight months. "Let there be extinguished in you all power of the devil by the imposition of our hands, and by the invocation of the glorious and holy Mother of God, the Virgin Mary..."

A pair of familiar hands pulled Evie's shorts on, dragging them up her bloody legs and working them into place. I looked up and collided with Jesse's red eyes.

He reached for Dawn. "The doctors need to check her over." He didn't sound like himself, his drawling accent scratching hoarsely, torturing every syllable.

I released Michio's hand and lifted the baby, watching as Jesse walked stiffly toward the waiting doctors, his eyes locked on the child in his arms.

Michio's sobs had ebbed into wheezing breaths, his face

buried against Evie's neck, and his grip on her body showing no signs of letting her go.

With my arms now free, I pried him away from her and held him against me as I finished the sacrament. "By this holy unction and his own most gracious mercy, may the Lord cherish every perfect action you committed through sight, hearing, smell, taste and speech, touch, ability to walk." As I said the words, I touched her eyelids, ears, nostrils, lips, hands, and feet.

Michio rubbed his eyes then narrowed them at me. "You changed the verbiage."

I nodded. "The Lord doesn't need to pardon her sins."

"She was perfect." He caressed her face, staring at her with infinite longing.

I knew what that felt like. I ached to hear her voice, to feel her touch, to see her stunning smile just one more time.

Jesse returned and bent over Evie. He gathered her hands in his, pressed his mouth against her fingers, and leaned down to kiss her lips. "I'll miss you." His stomach buckled, as if giving beneath a punch. He breathed through it, eyes closed. Then he opened them and kissed her again. "I love you."

Squeezing my shoulder as he stood, he strode out of the garden and into the dam's tunnel system.

I lifted Evie's hand and traced the bumps of her knuckles. Michio combed his fingers through her hair, staring vacantly at her face, both of us delaying our good-byes. Darwin hadn't left her side either, his furry body pacing back and forth, panting, and letting out whines of distress.

Shea squatted between us, her dark skin glossy with tears, and gripped our hands. "We'll clean up the baby and prepare…" She stared at Evie, chin trembling before she hardened her jaw and continued. "She told me what she wanted. We'll take care of it. Go find your boy."

As she slipped away, I crawled over Evie's body and touched our foreheads together. "Thank you for loving me. I promise we won't be alone. I will always love you and worship you."

I trailed my nose along hers and kissed her lips for the last time. I let myself cry, let my love wet her beautiful face. Then I pulled myself away and found Michio's eyes. "I'll wait for you at the door."

From the edge of the garden, I watched him hold her, whisper to her, and kiss his good-byes. When he finally wrenched himself away, he tried to pull Darwin with him. Together they fought, dragged their feet, and eventually joined me at the door.

He raised his bloody hands and stared at the medallion he'd removed from her neck. "She said she wanted our daughter to have this."

"I know." I closed my fingers over it, wrapping around his, and squeezed.

We walked through the dam to find Jesse. It was easy enough, since we could sense one another the way we'd only recently been able to sense Evie. The absence of the bright hum of her aura was yet another emptiness to pile on top of the emptiness.

We found Jesse in one of the passageways, crouched against the wall, head in his hands. He stood when we approached. We didn't speak, didn't have to. Together we ran the tunnels. We didn't sprint at the superhuman speed our bodies were now built for. We jogged at Evie's pace, with Darwin at our heels. We jogged every mile within the dam. Then we did again and again. Our muscles flexed, our legs moved in sync, and I imagined Evie running alongside us, watching us, her huge golden eyes heating with love and desire. I kept an eye on Jesse and Michio beside me, their expressions etched with shock and sadness, and their gazes lost in thought. Lost with Evie.

That night, we stood along the railing on the surface of the dam, facing the Colorado River and the pyre that floated between the shores. Moonlight illuminated the wood planks and the lifeless body of my soul lying atop it.

The hushed din of the surrounding crowds echoed between the canyon walls. Everyone was here. Shea and her baby, her sobbing frame supported by Paul and Eddie. Link, Hunter, Ronnie, the soldiers, the physicians, all were accounted for, united in their grief.

Darwin paced the length of the half-wall, restless and searching. He broke my heart.

I patted my hip. "Darwin, *hier*."

He came, leaning against my leg as I scratched his head.

Beside me, Michio snuggled Dawn to his chest, holding her as tightly as he'd held Evie only hours earlier.

Jesse leaned around Michio, a flaming arrow anchored in his bow, and met my eyes. When I gave him a nod, he turned back toward the river, aimed, and released. The ball of fire arced through the black sky, and the pyre roared into flames.

I smelled the smoke, tasted her death, and felt the inferno of reality. It left me cold.

Evie had made a lot of preparations before she died, but with regard to her funeral, her instructions to Shea had been simple. *Do whatever would give the people hope.*

When the intake towers pumped the river water, along with her ashes, and carried it to the other side, they believed the turbines would pull her essence from the water and generate enough energy to resurrect her. That was their hope.

It was a fool's dream, but I'd learned that with Evie anything was possible.

Jesse and Michio watched the blaze climb toward the sky. Dawn sucked on her finger, asleep against Michio's chest.

I closed my eyes and prayed, but in my most harrowing moment, the prayers offered no comfort.

As the fire died down and the pyre sank into the river, Michio spoke into the night sky. "You told us she was the cure for the deepest pain." His voice strained. "We lost our cure."

I touched the sleeping baby in his arms. "Now we have her."

Jesse stared at the river. "When Evie's husband died, she did this alone."

We weren't alone.

Side-by-side, we braced for the eternal hour of darkness ahead.

But she'd left us with a bright light to help us find our way out.

She'd given us Dawn.

The distance between hypothesis and conclusion is
measured in scientific steps.
But how do you measure love?
The steps begin with a leap of faith
And end with a very hard fall.

~ Dr. Michio Nealy

SIXTY-FOUR

Michio
Six years later…

Before Evie, I'd arranged my life around my pursuit of scientific knowledge, a disciple dedicated to raising questions and chasing possibilities. When the plague wiped out ninety percent of the human race, my focus narrowed and clung to one significant answer. The only possibility. The sole surviving woman.

She wasn't just the answer to our extinction. She was *my* answer. To everything.

I gave her my heart, freely, and she wrapped hers around it, making it bigger, stronger, and mighty enough to share with her Lakota, her priest, and her daughter. Three people, who loved me as much as Evie had.

Most of the time.

Right now, they were staring at me like I didn't have a heart at all.

"Daddy, be nice." Dawn wrapped her arms around Darwin's graying neck and gave me a pouty look, one that reminded me when I was being a cold-hearted dick.

Jesse lay on the blood-soaked tiles in the living room of our houseboat, bowing his back in agony and seething through his fangs. "What the fuck is wrong with you?"

For a tough guy, he could whine like a little girl. Though I probably should've given him a warning before I'd yanked the arrow from his chest. It wasn't a fatal injury. The spiders would have had to hit his brain to make me worry.

But I did worry. Every time he and Roark raced into battle without me, my insides hemorrhaged. It had been my turn to stay behind with Dawn, and I hated that. We were meant to fight together and die together. I'd barely survived Evie's death. I didn't have the strength to bear theirs.

I set the arrow aside and rubbed a hand over my face. Jesse was in pain, and all I'd offered him was a clinical glance and a harsh grip on his neck while I ripped out the metal shaft.

Of the four of us, Evie had always been the softer one. Without her mitigation, we tended to deal with our problems shoving and growling like a pack of wolves. Any gentleness that remained in us was reserved for Dawn.

If Evie were here, she would've molded her body around Jesse, kissed his lips, and told him she loved him.

I only did those things when I was hard and hungry. With my fangs in his neck.

Maybe he needed a hug? I opened my arms and tried to stifle my grin.

"Fuck off, Doc." His annoyance sharpened his glare. "Just stop the bleeding. I've got shit to do."

Roark sat beside him, blood dripping from multiple bite marks, his face a grimace of pain. "Dawn, do your da a favor and grab the whiskey in the galley."

She jumped up from her squat beside Darwin, determination shining in her golden-green eyes. Evie's eyes.

I grasped her tiny wrist, stopping her retreat. "His drink can wait. Put your hand here." Guiding her fingers over the hole in Jesse's chest, I pressed firmly. "Can you hold it?"

"Of course, I can." Her jaw set, and she stared up at me with the gaze of an old soul, but her youth was unmistakable in her musical voice, the dusting of freckles on her nose, and the way her free hand twirled the coppery lock of her hair.

At the age of six, she'd seen more blood and death than I had as a thirty-year-old doctor before the plague. But she was fearless, ambitious, and stubborn. Just like her mother. Her gentle laugh, enthusiasm in learning, the confident way she carried herself, so many things about her reminded me of Evie. The similarities anchored me. She was like an extension of Evie's soul, and I needed that connection.

I moved to the mess that was Jesse's leg and carefully picked out the artillery shell fragments from his skin and muscle. "How many spiders this time?"

Our luxury four-bedroom yacht resided on Lake Mead, a speedboat's ride along the Colorado River to the dam. We moved out of the dam two months after Evie's death, fixed up the largest boat on the one-hundred-mile lake, and made it our home. We'd sunk all other watercraft and prevented trespassers from breaching the towering jagged bluffs surrounding our waters.

When we needed reinforcements, our men at the dam came within seconds of our blaring siren. And vice versa, like this morning.

I lifted Dawn's hand from Jesse's chest. The bleeding had stopped, the hole sealing with new skin.

"Several hundred spiders." Jesse laced his fingers through Dawn's on his chest. "They broke through the dam's barricades again."

Which explained the multitude of wounds and bite marks.

Dawn's eyes widened. "Is Eddie okay?"

Roark unraveled her fingers from her hair, her tiny hand disappearing in his grip as he guided her onto his lap. "Eddie's fine, lass."

While I worked in the lab at the dam every day, she spent those hours with Eddie, the oldest of Shea's three children. Shea provided them with a strict curriculum. Jesse and Roark taught them weaponry. But in the evenings, Dawn learned hand-to-hand combat under my tutelage.

I pried the last of the shrapnel from Jesse's leg and sat back on my heels. "Fatalities?"

"We lost eight men and three women." Jesse rose stiffly and gestured toward Dawn. "Let's go clean you up."

As I watched them retreat, hand in hand, through the kitchen and down the hall, I agonized over his words.

Eleven people was a huge hit. Seventy-five men and women resided at the dam. Only a handful had volunteered to receive the vaccine I'd spent the past six years developing. The serum worked the same way my bite did, but without the intimacy of orgasm. It prevented the infection of the spider programming and could easily be reproduced and distributed across the continents. But like the spider's bite, the side-effect was infertility.

The nymphs were cured, and the aphids had been exterminated. Worldwide, there hadn't been a reported sighting of either in years. But every day, spider babies were delivered into the world, growing fangs within hours after birth and biting their parents. The vicious infection was overrunning the planet with mindless, vampiric creatures, outnumbering us three to one. Their numbers were growing. Those who still had freewill were desperate to keep it. The horror stories I'd heard about mothers performing abortions on themselves kept me awake most nights.

But I couldn't disperse a vaccine that would create an infertile species. Not after Evie gave her life for the future of humanity.

Roark hadn't moved, his green eyes roaming my face. "Den' give up, Doc." He shifted, kneeling before me, gripped the back of my neck, and brought his forehead to mine. "Den' give up on us. Jesse and I…we're right here."

I closed my eyes and grasped his shoulder. "I know."

"Den' give up on our girl either."

Fierce conviction snapped through my voice. "Never."

The problem was, our beautiful daughter, who had endured six years of my poking, swabbing, plasma-drawing examinations, was as normal and human as her best friend, Eddie. I'd ingested her blood from vials and still couldn't sense her aura like I could with Jesse and Roark. Her blood didn't cure programmed spiders. She was immune to the programming but didn't have fangs or spots or superhuman speed. She had the power to make my heart swell, but did she have the power to save mankind?

I could analyze physical things, such as inherited conditions derived from DNA, molecular function, and interactions among genes. But I couldn't use the scientific method to prove she was the solution we were waiting for.

Prophecy was a concept that correlated to faith, which was something that couldn't be studied under a microscope or grown in a petri dish. I just had to believe. As a man of science, that was something I struggled with on a daily basis.

Maybe she would eventually grow into her power. Or maybe something significant would trigger it the way the virus had set off Evie's biological changes.

Dawn was defined as the moment after which the sky was no longer completely dark. Until that moment, when she was ready to rise, my job was to protect her, train and prepare her, and love her.

That night, I sat on the edge of her bed beside Jesse. Roark stretched out on the other side, with Dawn tucked into the blankets between us. Darwin curled up at her feet, but he would move to her side the moment we left the room.

The soft slapping sound of water against the hull floated in through her window. A candle's flame swayed lazily on her bedside table. Darwin's steady snores vibrated the mattress. All was peaceful, warm, real. This was my favorite part of every day.

Jesse adjusted the blankets around her sweet little chin. "I love you."

Roark and I echoed him.

"Love you, too." Her eyes drifted closed, her auburn lashes fanning over her cheeks. Then she popped them open. "Will I see Eddie tomorrow?"

Roark pressed his lips to her forehead. "You'll be kissing him again by sunrise."

"Yuck." She scrunched her nose then leveled us with a curious look. "Who did Mommy kiss the mostest?"

"The most." I leaned over her, bracing an arm on the other side of her legs. "What do you mean?"

Her brows stitched together. "Which of you did she love

the best?"

I rubbed the back of my head and looked at Jesse. "I'm not touching that."

Jesse stared at Roark, who was grinning like an asshole.

She shifted her sleepy gaze to me. "I bet she kissed you the mostes— The most because you're the prettiest."

"Be the love of the lamp lighting Jaysus, that's a load of bollix." Roark rolled to his back and said to the ceiling, "She's craictose intolerant, that one."

She giggled and poked a finger against his mouth. "Did Mommy talk funny like you?"

"No, baby." Jesse leaned against the headboard. "Your mother could actually form words and make sense." He closed his eyes. "And she was by far the prettiest."

I could still see her in my mind, every perfect inch of her. One of my biggest fears was losing that image. We didn't have photographs to trace or recordings to listen to. What if my memories faded? What if I couldn't picture her anymore?

A heavy silence fell around us, and I knew Jesse and Roark were thinking about her, too.

We had good days and bad days. For years, I blamed myself for her death, anguished over all the things I could've done differently that morning in the garden. Guilt eventually morphed into acceptance and settled on purpose. I strived to be a good father, to be an emotional and physical support for Jesse and Roark, and to help the people. *Her people.*

Evie hadn't left me as a hollow shell. She'd made me a better man.

I bent toward Dawn's face and kissed her nose. "Whose turn is it to tell a story?"

She turned toward Roark and pulled on his beard. "It's yours, Da. Tell me another one about England."

"Let's see…" Roark settled in, pulling her back against his chest, his finger stroking the medallion around her neck. "One time, your ma and I sought safety in a bank vault. 'Twas barely big enough to hold the two of us. Aphids surrounded us, prying at the door, trying to claw their way in."

Thirty minutes later, she was asleep. We kissed her *good-night*, slipped from her room, and wordlessly went our separate ways. We all had our own bedrooms with king-sized beds, where we each attempted to retire alone every night. But eventually, always, they showed up in my room.

We hadn't slept apart since before Evie died.

In my room, I lit the waiting candles. We had a generator but used the power sparingly. Besides, the flickering flames soothed me. I'd spent most of my nights with Evie beneath the soft glow of a flame. I was glad for its light now.

I stripped down to my briefs and reached for my lab notes, but as I stared at my scrawl, the words blurred. All I saw was her. I pictured her with a rifle raised in her small hands, her beautiful blonde hair whipping around her face. I pictured her surrounded by nymphs, her arms out in supplication, letting them sip the cure from her veins. I pictured her standing among thousands of people at the dam, giving them hope through her selfless words.

I saw her naked, and once the image of her full breasts and round ass formed in my mind, I couldn't summon the memories of her wearing clothes. She was nude aiming her bow. Nude running the tunnels. Nude rocking against my body.

Blinking, I tried to push those thoughts from my mind. I couldn't go down that heartbreaking path. But I'd already shoved my briefs down my thighs, my cock in my hand, engorged, aching. I buckled over, stroking, twisting my grip, remembering her graceful neck, rosy nipples, quickening breaths, and full lips. She licked those lips, the soft wet flesh made for my kiss, my cock. Like her cunt. Tight, warm, drenched, gripping my fingers, sucking my shaft inside. I was in her, fucking her, kicking my hips and grunting like an animal.

My lungs strained for air, my arm jerking, shaking. I came and stared blankly at the wet streams of my need dripping over my thigh. Emptiness swept through me. It was always the same. I fucked my hand, thinking about her, but the hole remained vacant. I couldn't fill it. Not without them.

The warm hum of their approach vibrated beneath my skin. I looked at the door, watched it open, waited as Jesse and Roark joined me on the bed.

No one said a word. I couldn't read their thoughts, but I didn't need to. Their emotions, desires, and fantasies were mirrors of mine.

I crawled toward them, made them groan, tremble, and muffle their relief into the pillows, as I poured my love into their bodies. They filled everything left barren by the loss of Evie, quenched the veins that no longer pumped with her blood, and squeezed my heart with something different, but no less intense. I always thought of her when I jerked off. But when I was with them, my thoughts were as well. Like now, lying between them with my arms around Roark and my legs entwined with Jesse's.

They were my warmth when the chill of grief enveloped me. They were my voice when I couldn't find the words. They were my legs when I struggled to stand back up. And I endeavored to be the same for them.

Jesse never saw Evie's spirit again after that morning in the garden, but he still looked for her. Roark never put his cassock back on, but he still prayed. And I hadn't scientifically proved Dawn would save the future of mankind. But I believed.

I believed in her.

The Trilogy of Eve concludes with Evie's legacy.

DAWN OF EVE #3

OTHER BOOKS BY PAM GODWIN

LOVE TRIANGLE ROMANCE

TANGLED LIES

One is a Promise

Two is a Lie

Three is a War

DARK ROMANCE

DELIVER SERIES

Deliver #1

Vanquish #2

Disclaim #3

Devastate #4

Take #5

Manipulate #6

Unshackle #7

Dominate #8

Complicate #9

DARK ALASKAN ROMANCE

FROZEN FATE

Hills of Shivers and Shadows #1

Cage of Ice and Echoes #2

Heart of Frost and Scars #3

DARK COWBOY ROMANCE

TRAILS OF SIN

Knotted #1

Buckled #2

Booted #3

STUDENT-TEACHER / PRIEST

Lessons In Sin

STUDENT-TEACHER ROMANCE

Dark Notes

ROCK-STAR DARK ROMANCE

Beneath the Burn

BILLIONAIRE REVENGE

Dirty Ties

OLDER WOMAN / YOUNGER MAN

Incentive

DARK HISTORICAL PIRATE ROMANCE

King of Libertines

Sea of Ruin

ABOUT PAM GODWIN

New York Times, Wall Street Journal, and *USA Today* bestselling author, Pam Godwin, lives in the Midwest with her husband, cats, retired greyhounds, and an old, foul-mouthed parrot. She traveled the world for seven years, attended three universities, married the vocalist of her favorite rock band, and retired from her quantitative analyst career in 2014 to write full-time.

Her interests veer toward the unconventional: bourbon, full-body tattoos, and tragic villains. Equally peculiar are her aversions to sleeping, eating meat, and dolls with blinking eyes.

EMAIL: pamgodwinauthor@gmail.com

www.ingramcontent.com/pod-product-compliance
Lightning Source LLC
Chambersburg PA
CBHW020348310726
48979CB00015B/2551/J

* 9 7 8 1 9 6 6 5 3 7 1 2 0 *